Assassins of Alamut

A Novel of Persia and Palestine
in the Time of the Crusades

Assassins of Alamut:

A Novel of Persia and Palestine in the Time of the Crusades

by

James Boschert

www.penmorepress.com

ISBN-13: 978-1 942756 125 (Paperback)
ISBN-13: 978-1 942756 132 (Ebook)

BISAC Subject Headings:
FIC014000FICTION / Historical
FIC002000FICTION / Action & Adventure
FIC031000FICTION / Thrillers

Cover by Christine Horner

Address all correspondence to:
mjames@penmorepress.com
M James
920 N Javalina Pl
Tucson,AZ 85748
USA

1.0

Contents

To Danielle

My Soul Mate

Who shares my love of faraway places.

T.M. Grundner

Talon's Journey

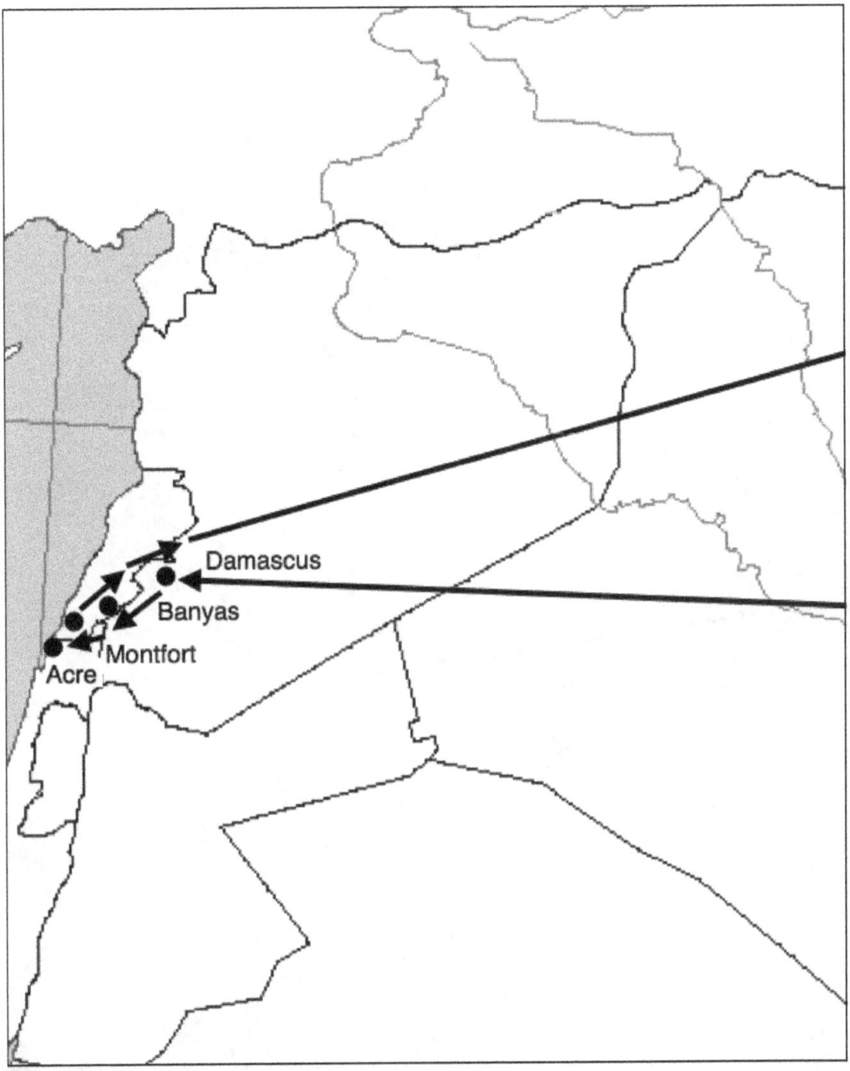
Damascus
Banyas
Montfort
Acre

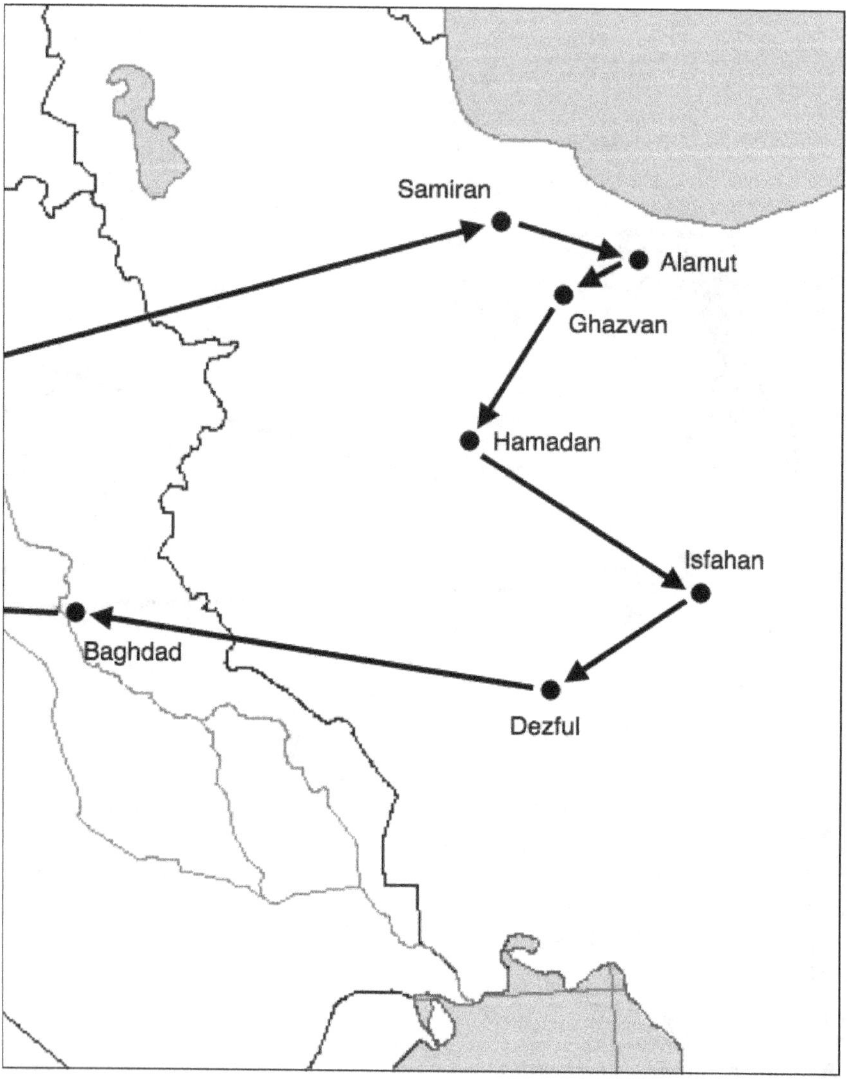
Samiran
Alamut
Ghazvan
Hamadan
Isfahan
Baghdad
Dezful

A GLOSSARY OF PERSIAN WORDS

Atabeg - Military SelJuk chief or governor
Barbari - Long, flat, corrugated bread
Bātinīs - Assassins
Bazaari - Men from the bazaar
Chai Khane - Tea House
Chash - Subservient "Yes"
Doogh - A drink made of yogurt
Ferengi - Foreigner
F*ida'i* - Assassin
Genab - *"Sir"*
Ghilim - A mat woven of goat hair or wool
Gorban - Lord
Gorban e Shoma - "Worship to you"
Hakim - Physician
In Shah'Allah - "If Allah wills it"
Khanom - Madame
Kharagi - Foreigner, Outsider
Khoda Hafez - "God protect"
Lasiq - Novice
Maast - Yogurt
Madrassa - College, school
Maidan - Public square in a town or village
Masjid - Mosque
Nan - Flat bread
Nizirite - Member of the Niziri Ismaili people
Rafiq - Senior member of assassins
Rais - Headman
Salaamed - To bow and call for *salaam*: "Peace"

Samiran - Rud Samiran river valley
Sarvan - Captain
Shah Rud - Valley of the king
Syce - Groom
Tar - Earliest twelve-stringed guitar
Taroff - Debt of gratitude
Timsar - Military rank of general
Zor Khane - Working house, or gymnasium

Fate is an ill that no one can avert.
It wields its sway alike o'er Kings and Viziers;
The King who yesterday, by his rule devoured Kerman,
Becomes today himself the meat of worms.
— Baba Tahir —

Chapter 1
Ambush and Capture

Talon whirled around to stare toward the source of the shouts of alarm from the men of the baggage train, which had just come under attack. He saw the looks of fear on the ashen faces of the women with whom he had been riding as they, too, turned to stare at those shouting.

The knights on their large horses wheeled to face a group of mounted, armed men charging down the slope from the east. The men-at-arms guarding the train, some with bows and others with long pikes, ran back to group themselves around the women and baggage train.

Talon reined his young mare in as she jerked her head and skittered at their approach. His eyes were wide and unsure, and he wanted to be told what to do, but everyone was busy dealing with their immediate concern—which was to stay alive.

A pikeman ran up to him and seized his reins. "You have to stay with us, young master," he shouted, his voice hoarse. "The knights will deal with the savages." Talon nodded, wrenched the reins back, and followed him at a canter to the tight knot of women and other men-at-arms grouped around the wagons.

The knights had run headlong into the charging Saracens, and a mêlée had developed. It was hard to see anything amid the dust and turmoil of hacking and slashing men, screaming into each other's faces as they tried to dismember each other with axes and swords. Riders collided and fell with shrieks of pain coming from both horse and man as they tangled on the ground. The men were desperately aware of the urgency of getting up to face an enemy on their feet, rather than risk being pinned to the ground and getting trampled or stabbed where they lay.

Talon felt a trickle of fear, but thinking of his father, he forced himself to control it and look calm. All the same, his mouth was dry and there was a lump in his stomach, but he concentrated on what was going on, trying to make some sense of it.

Then there was a shout from behind, and everyone turned to face the rear of the baggage train. There were shrieks of alarm from the women in the wagons, and yells and shouts as the soldiers tried to form a defense. Panic set in as a second group of horsemen came out of nowhere and hit the column from this unexpected direction.

The first attack had been a feint to draw the knights on their heavy horses away from the real target. Now they were being attacked in earnest, and it was everyone for himself. Talon's guard abandoned him and ran toward the new conflict, leaving Talon near a wagon that contained two women who cringed together in wailing terror among the baskets and baggage. He held his mare in check, still unsure as to what he should do. His uncle, fighting with the knights, could not come and give directions either to him or the soldiers.

The battle soon became a chaotic, undirected fight with no one in charge. The foot soldiers, with no leaders, battled for the wagons with the enemy horsemen, and others on foot darted in and out of the battle, stabbing and slashing at unwary soldiers and horses alike. Talon had his new sword drawn, but had a hard time controlling his mare, unsettled as she was by the clash of arms and the fighting men's yells.

A fog of dust and noise descended on him as the battle rolled past. Two horsemen, not of the knights, dressed in long flowing robes and flashing chain-mail shirts, drove a knot of foot soldiers back, hacking savagely at them while they retreated. The cursing, swearing group barged backward into Talon's mare, crowding her hard against one of the wagons. They were soon gone into the swirling dust before Talon could worry about being attacked. He was trying to calm the terrified mare when the foot soldier that had talked to him earlier came reeling past, blood flowing down his face from a jagged head wound. Others followed, many limping away in panic, their eyes white with fear and shock on faces gray with dust.

Then out of the crowd of struggling men and horses darted a thin figure in loose brown pantaloons and shirt, wearing a dirty turban wrapped around his head. He ran up to Talon's mare and seized the reins, tugging on them, shouting at him in some foreign tongue.

Without thinking, Talon leaned over the mare's shoulder and slashed down at his would-be captor's head. He saw the blow make contact and felt a strangely satisfying feeling radiate up his arm. The figure screamed and disappeared underfoot.

Adrenaline was now taking control. He had killed his first enemy and wanted to scream his victory to the world. His fears evaporated at this first taste of fighting, and he instinctively understood how warriors felt at the onset of battle. He now wanted to charge anything and everything, to cut and slash until he had carried all before him.

Another figure, dressed in a similar manner as the first, rushed at him out of the writhing mass of men, horses, and clouds of dust, carrying a long, curved sword. Talon saw the movement and was about to hurl himself at the approaching enemy when his mare stumbled and fell, and he toppled over her head to land at the feet of the oncoming figure. He heard his mare scream and narrowly missed being hit by her flailing hooves. Someone had stabbed her in her chest as she went past, ripping out her insides. She lashed out with her hooves in her death throes, screaming her agony to the world.

Winded by the fall, he lay there in the dust, choking. Then, as he tried to get back on his feet, a hard hand smacked him across his face, knocking him flat on his back. Before he could do anything, someone flipped him onto his face and a knee crushed into his back, while his arms were seized and tied behind him. He was hauled to his feet and bundled away from the surrounding battle.

His captors shouted at each other with voices rapid and guttural and shoved him ahead of them. They seemed to be in a hurry to get away from the scene of the battle. In his dazed state, he could make no sense of what was happening to him, although he vaguely wondered why they had not killed him.

They ran over the rise of the slope, and he was forced to run with them. It was very difficult to do with his arms bound painfully behind him, but his captors gave him no respite and drove him on.

Whenever he fell in the dust they hauled him to his feet with curses and blows, half dragging him forward toward a group of horses held by people dressed in similar garb.

There was shouting as they came together, and then he was hauled unceremoniously onto the back of a horse, his feet tied under him, and they set off to the northeast at a wild gallop. His dazed mind registered the screams of the wounded and the shouts and clamor of battle that were rapidly fading behind him as they rode.

The group of horsemen galloped for many miles. Talon had a splitting headache and was desperately thirsty. The people he was with were all good riders, so the chance to escape never presented itself. He could not guess where they were going, but they continued northeast for the rest of the day.

The sun was setting when they came over a rise and Talon saw a castle ahead of them. The men, who until now had been very tense, relaxed and seemed glad to get here. He heard the word *Banyas* used several times as they pointed to the fortress.

The gates of the fort had opened, and the group entered a small courtyard. Talon was dragged off the horse and thrown to the ground, where he lay staring at the feet and legs of the strange people who had captured him. There was a lot of talk, and he was prodded a couple of times; but he stayed where he was, exhausted and frightened, wondering what was to become of him.

His captors did not enlighten him. Instead, he was chained to a wall by a manacle locked onto his wrist, then left alone. His thirst was now overwhelming. He tried to indicate that he needed water but received a kick for his pains. He cowered against the wall and waited in the dark and cold. Late that night, someone brought some soup and a piece of hard, flat bread, which he wolfed down, his hunger and thirst overcoming any pride he might have felt.

He awakened in the small hours of the morning to hear shouts in the distance, and then more shouting as the occupants of the fort called back. They opened the gates to the arrival of another party. He could see in the torchlight that this group was larger, and escorted several additional exhausted prisoners. They were tied to each other by ropes around their necks, their hands bound, their faces masks of fear and exhaustion. They fell into an untidy heap not far from where Talon lay. In the flickering light of the smoky torches, carried high by the fort's occupants, he recognized the priest, Jean de Loche, and a couple of the foot soldiers from the baggage train.

He called to Jean, his voice more a croak than a shout, but he was heard, for Jean swung round his shaggy, tonsured head, and gasped, "My Lord Talon! Oh God, how could this have happened? Are you wounded? Dear Lord, have mercy on us, but at least you're alive."

He got no further. One of their captors strode out from the crowd with his sword drawn, shouting at the priest and kicking him into silence, then beating him with the flat of his sword.

Talon lay back. It was better to be silent than to incur the wrath of this bad-tempered man, who seemed to be one of the leaders.

The next morning they were awakened with kicks and shouts, then the whole party continued their journey north, riding all day. There was no stopping, except to water the horses and eat a sparse meal of dry, flat bread and figs along the way. He noticed, in spite of his fatigue and hunger, that they were moving into a fertile land where cultivated fields and irrigation ditches occupied the flatter areas of the valley.

Groves of palms and huts huddled around wells, and he noticed man-made ditches carrying water to fields. There were people, tending small herds of sheep and goats, who stared curiously as they went by. He glimpsed small guard towers on the low hills in the distance, where sentinels watched for enemy incursions.

His guards were no longer tense and talked rapidly back and forth. He knew he was being watched all the time so he made no effort to break away, his instinct for survival coming to his aid where his pride might have harmed him. He, at least, was riding a horse, whereas the priest and the other prisoners were stumbling along in a wretched state. One of the foot soldiers, who had been wounded in the side, was in particularly bad shape. He had difficulty walking, and this forced the others to support him and half carry him. Their captors thrashed at them cruelly with leather thongs any time they tried to stop and rest.

Late that night they arrived at the walls of a large city and hustled through a small side gate, along dark, narrow streets, and under darkened arches until they came to a large, well-fortified house, guarded by men in similar garb to their original captors.

Talon and the other prisoners were forced down stone steps into the bowels of the building and through long, dark tunnels to a big wooden door with huge metal studs. This crashed against the wall as one of the guards wrenched it open, and they were all driven inside. The door clanged shut as their captors left them in the dark. Their pleas for water were ignored.

Talon and Jean found one another in the dark and sat together against the wall. It was cold in the room, and it wasn't long before Talon was shivering. Jean must have felt it; he reached over and held Talon's shaking frame, trying to keep the boy warm even as he got colder.

Later, when the whimpering and frightened talk had quieted, the door banged open and a pail of some sloppy-looking stew and disks of flat bread were dropped in the entrance. The door slammed shut with another reverberating clunk. The prisoners rushed to seize what they could find of the food in the dark, but Jean waded in among them and, using his large fists, laid about him, shouting at them to stop being animals and to help themselves with care or they would spill the soup and get nothing. It was hard for him to keep an eye on the others, but they heard him, and apart from a few curses, they complied. He came back to Talon, forced some soggy bread into his hands, and told him to eat.

*****

While the prisoners contemplated their uncertain future, two stories up in the palace, the men who had brought them in had prostrated themselves, praising a large man seated on a raised platform. He endured the praise patiently then, with an impatient motion of his hand, he spoke.

"You brought prisoners but not much booty. What happened? Was the caravan too well protected?"

The leader of the group sat up and responded. "*Timsar* Esphandiary, we were taking advantage of the fact that there were a group of Seljuks from Damascus, the men of Nur-Ed-Din, waiting in ambush. We watched and waited until they had committed to the trap, which, Your Highness, they executed well. Then, while they were fighting the armored Franks, we went in among the *ferengi* and, in the confusion, attempted to take what we could."

The general shifted his position on the platform. "Well, what did you find?"

"Your Honor, we think that we have a boy for ransom. He was well mounted and well dressed. He looks like a noble boy. There is a priest as well."

The general looked at them, reflecting on what they had achieved. The fact that these *fida'i* of his had been able to come away with captives while in the midst of the Seljuks was not a bad effort, a credit to their skill at stealth and speed. Still, they'd brought back a boy and a priest; meager booty. He pondered the possibilities. The boy could be held for ransom, and the priest might be useful.

The General and his men were in the most hostile of cities. This was the domain of Nur-Ed-Din, the Sultan of Damascus, who hated his kind, the Ismaili. Nur-Ed-Din would stop at nothing to destroy them all, if he could find them. The Seljuks hated all Ismaili, deeming them heretics and deviants from the Sunni way.

Now the general had a noble boy as a prisoner. He rubbed his shaven chin and pulled at his mustache while he contemplated his eager followers, who waited on his every word. "We'll leave tomorrow and take the boy, the priest, and a few of the others with us. Bring them with you and make sure they live. Put the remainder to death when we have gone. I shall be going on ahead to talk to the Master in Samiran. I don't want any of the other Ismaili here in Damascus to know we've left until we're well on our way."

"*Chash, Gorban,*" they all murmured as they bowed again and hurried away.

General Mahmud Esphandiary sat sipping tea, thinking about the boy. He had an idea that might appeal to the Agha Khan. It would take seed and grow in his mind while he was on the long road to Persia.

So it was that the boy Talon, son of Sir Hughes de Gilles, went into captivity, and commenced his long journey into the heartland of Persia, accompanied by a priest and three soldiers.

Lord, Who am I, and of what company?
How long shall tears of blood thus blind mine eyes?
When other refuge fails I'll turn to Thee,
And if Thou failest me, whither shall I go?
– Baba Tahir –

Chapter 2
Sir Hughes and the Templars

Sir Hughes de Gilles sat quietly on his huge horse; his normally erect figure slumped over. He watched the activities of the men-at-arms as they poked through the wreckage of the caravan. He ignored the flies as they buzzed around himself and the horse, his features glum as he contemplated his men's gruesome work. The foremost thought in his mind was, what could have happened to his son?

His men-at-arms were turning over the dead. Most of them were men, but there were a few women, and all had been left where they lay for two days. All around was the stench of death mingled with the acrid smell of burnt wagons. The stink from the bloated bodies in the glare of the hot sun was barely tolerable. Those scavengers of the dead, the crows and vultures, had taken refuge in the trees, where they cawed and squawked their anger at being disturbed. Huge bloated flies were everywhere, and their buzzing was a constant background noise to the subdued voices of the humans as they toiled. No stranger to death himself, Sir Hughes nonetheless regarded the scene with a mounting disgust.

"What have they done with my son?" he raged, even as he gave orders to the men to keep searching.

He was a large, stocky man of Frankish heritage. His mop of light brown hair contrasted sharply with his sunburned face. His sharp, hazel eyes now stared morosely at the scene from under bushy brows. He was sweating under his chain mail tunic, which the outer skirt did nothing to protect from the blazing sun. The links of the mail on his shoulders were hot to the touch. He dismissed the discomfort; his whole being was focused on the events that had transpired.

The wreckage of the caravan extended back a hundred yards. It ran along the base of the stony embankment that sloped gradually up to the northwest side. On the south and east, there were the twisted, sparse trees of the small wood from which the main attack had materialized. His military eye saw clearly how the first attack had taken place on the bank, drawing off the knights in a ruse that could have been avoided. Curse his brother for being such a hothead and so gullible. Not for the first time, Sir Hughes' fist clenched on the reins as he fought to bring his anger under control.

His brother was a good fighter, but no tactician, and as a result, his son was gone. His brother was there among the horsemen moving slowly around looking for signs of his son. Phillip was staying out of Sir Hughes' way. His concern for the boy notwithstanding, he did not want any more of his brother's wrath upon his head this day.

A light breeze came in from the west and stirred the dust off the road, lifting rags and fluttering cloth streamers draped over the remains of one of the wagons nearby. The low calls of the soldiers to each other intruded upon his thoughts and woke Sir Hughes to the business at hand. They must bury the dead and recover what they could. That would not be very much, as the corpses and the wagons had been picked clean of anything useful, or even of personal value, for the relatives to claim.

He took off his hot iron helmet, wiped his brow, and then shouted at his Sergeant-at-arms to have all the bodies pulled together and to detail a burial party. A priest, borrowed from a nearby hospice, stood watching the proceedings, waiting to perform the rites over the dead. His ragged garments were tugging in the light wind, his tonsure gleaming in the bright light of the day.

Replacing his helmet Sir Hughes nudged his horse forward and rode the length of the caravan in the vain hope that he might find some clue as to where his son had gone. He saw the remains of the mare his son had been riding, its head thrown back, its teeth bared in a dreadful grin of death. The carrion feeders had dispersed what remained of its entrails. There was neither saddle nor bridle on the corpse of the horse. Sir Hughes stopped and looked around. He was becoming convinced that his son had been taken; but he was still in dread they might find him dead nearby.

His exhausted and chagrined brother, Phillip, had been sure that the boy had been whisked away before anyone noticed and could make chase. Indeed, there would have been no way to follow Talon and save the remains of the caravan at the same time—not that there had been much left to save, Sir Hughes seethed.

He recalled the sorry group of knights and refugees who had made it back to the castle two days ago. The shout from the gate tower had brought Sir Hughes running to the battlements along with many from the castle population to watch, horrified, as the ragged group of survivors approached the castle. His eyes had searched frantically but in vain for his son riding near his brother. By the time Phillip had dismounted in the castle yard Sir Hughes' anguish had almost overwhelmed him. Striding up to his brother, he had demanded to know what had happened.

"Where's my son? Where is my son!" he'd almost shouted.

"He is taken, Sir Hughes. We were attacked by the Turks and many were killed, but I think he was taken!" Phillip had croaked. He was covered in dust, his tunic torn, with bloodstains still splashed over his chain mail. He had stared back at his brother with haunted eyes. He was clearly very weary, but his eyes betrayed his grief as well.

Sir Hughes had staggered back as though struck. "Why? Why could you not stop them?"

"They came upon us with a frontal attack that drew the knights away, and then struck from behind and destroyed the caravan. By the time we had fought off their frontal attack the damage had been done... and... and Talon was gone." Phillip had lowered his eyes and stared at the ground. His shame at losing his nephew clearly weighed upon him heavily.

It had taken Sir Hughes a long time to summon the courage to meet with his wife. He had trudged up the wooden stairs on leaden feet to the tower chamber where Marguerite was waiting and told her the tragic news. Marguerite had gone as white as a linen sheet. She had given a low cry and would have fallen had be not rushed to her side to help lower her into a seat by the window.

He stayed near her on his knees holding her icy hands as she tried to come to an understanding of the horror that had befallen them. After some moments of utter silence she had forced herself to sit up and, with a shaking hand, accepted the leather cup of water he found for her. Her face was set tight with shock as she visibly gathered her shattered senses in the face of the devastating news. He held her arm while she sipped a tiny amount of water.

"Do we have nothing to tell us what happened, other than his disappearance?" She'd enquired in a whisper after some moments of utter silence.

Sir Hughes would have answered her but at that moment Phillip had stamped into the chamber and she'd directed her question again at him.

Phillip looked at his brother as though for permission to talk and, when he received a nod, proceeded to relate what he knew.

They'd listened to him in silence, their eyes boring into him as he talked. When Phillip finally stammered to the conclusion of his story, they continued to look at him with an accusing silence. Phillip stared back with a helpless expression on his face, shuffling his dirty leather boots. He shifted the weight of the sword on his belt and scratched his side through the mail shift he still wore. He was unwounded, but bruised and ragged.

As the story unfolded, Sir Hughes quickly realized what had happened. He knew that, no matter what, Phillip would have been in the thick of the fighting, even as he forgot his main responsibility to the caravan. It took a mighty effort not to stride across the flagged stone floor and strike his brother across the side of his head.

Phillip, a large and very strong man himself, had sensed the anger and seen the rage in his brother's eyes. He worshipped Hughes and was in an agony of guilt at the failure to protect his son. So he stood there and waited while the silence settled into the room, disturbed only by the sounds coming through the window from the courtyard below.

After a few minutes of silence, Sir Hughes, in a low voice, more a growl, had dismissed him. Without looking at Phillip further, he turned to his wife.

Phillip stood there for a couple of seconds, coughed nervously, and in his rasping voice, said, "Brother, I can get men and ride out at once to search. Let me do this."

Sir Hughes turned on him, his face white with fury, and spoke louder than he meant. "No! We can't afford to lose more people today. Besides, what can we find in the dark but more ambushes and foolish fights? We shall call on my lord Reynolds for more men, and then send out an expedition to find out what we can tomorrow or the day after. If my son is dead, then he's dead. If he's alive, then he's a prisoner, and we don't know where in this God-forsaken country he might be. Did you at least try to search? Did you look for him?"

"As the enemy disengaged, we called and searched as we could, my brother. There were few men left, and we had to protect the remaining women, but we did all we could. I swear it."

Sir Hughes motioned with his hand, and Phillip turned and left. He knew the tone and knew, too, that to argue at this point would be futile and even dangerous.

Sir Hughes turned back to his wife and, leaning over her, took her hand in his large one. Her hand was cold, even though the evening still contained a lingering heat.

"My lady, we will do all we can to find Talon and bring him back. Damn Phillip and his stupidity! I wish to God that I had not given him this mission. He lacks all responsibility, even if he is as brave—and as stupid—as a lion."

Even in her distress, Lady Marguerite was beautiful. Through bloodless lips, she whispered.

"What if he is a prisoner? Then perhaps it's only a ransom we must pay? Oh God, Hugh, tell me that this might be so?"

Sir Hughes answered carefully, "Phillip is sure that he was taken, and one of the men-at-arms said that the Saracen have been taking a lot of prisoners lately. Did you hear him say that they also took the priest? We must pray and, somehow, wait. I'll call upon Sir Reynolds and his Templars to find out if, indeed, he might be held for ransom. Those knights are strange, but they have intelligence of this land and the people that we do not. Can you be strong, my Love?"

"Yes... yes, I shall be..." but the word would not come out. As she tried to finish her sentence, the full impact of what had happened finally hit her. She coughed, a small choking sound, and leaned forward. Her face seemed to go slack with pain, then, suddenly, her body doubled over. Tears streamed down her cheeks and she clutched his hand to her breast. He knelt again, placed his other arm around her shoulders, and held her in silence while she shook and sobbed with grief.

After some long minutes, she ceased crying and lifted her head. Her face was red and streaked with tears and his hand was wet. She looked up at him with an utterly lost expression in her eyes.

"I am sorry Hugh. It's just... I am just so filled with fear for him," she whispered in her despair.

Sir Hughes took a corner of her wimple and wiped her face gently, then stood up. His heart was breaking with grief for the loss of his son, but to see his wife this way so wounded him that he felt unmanned.

He called for a maid and commanded her, "You will stay with my Lady and care for her every need." Then he addressed Marguerite. "I must go and find out as much as I can, my love. Forgive me." He stamped out of the chamber and down the stairs to the outside courtyard.

Sir Hughes regained some of his composure while he questioned the remnants of the survivors of the battle to try to piece together the details for himself. He was aware that Phillip was getting blind drunk in the main hall at the base of the keep. He kept away, as it profited no one to have a family brawl at this time.

He sensed the sympathy from the people as they gathered to hear the story repeated many times that evening. As the shadows grew long and fires were lit in the yard for the men-at-arms and their families to cook by, people came to him and added tidbits of information to what he already had.

Late that evening Sir Hughes stood for a long time on the parapet looking east. As usual in this land, at this time of year, the sky was cloudless. The stars were a blaze of light in the night sky, and he could have made out the constellations without effort; but he was not even remotely interested in them.

He ground his teeth as he thought of his boy as a prisoner of the Saracen. The hate, ever there, grew as he stood alongside the battlements, fueled by the impotence he felt at the way the kidnapping had been accomplished.

* * * * *

Early the following day Sir Hughes reached the ambush site. A group of mounted men, about a hundred yards away, were watching without expression. These were the Templars from the castle of Lord Reynolds—hardened men for whom death was a way of life. This event was of small importance to them, other than the fact that they respected Sir Hughes and would help him if they could.

He rode to them, conscious that they were watching him carefully as he came. There were five Knights Templar; big men in full armor, mounted on large horses. Their bearded faces were impassive under the iron helmets they all wore. The red cross of their order was stitched onto the left breast of the light cotton tunics they wore over full chain mail hauberks. These men were hard-bitten veterans of a hundred engagements with the Saracen. Although they seemed relaxed on their heavy mounts, they were alert. It could be seen in their eyes, cold and impersonal, searching the horizon constantly, even as they observed his approach.

"My lords, Knights," he said as he reined up near them, not too close, for they stank. "Would you be able to obtain some intelligence of this event from the Saracen?"

There was a pause.

"We might, Sir Hughes." This came from a big, burly knight with a huge, bushy red beard that straggled from his helmet and all over his steel chain mail. "We'll enquire of our sources as to what may have happened to the prisoners. My lord, I think this was a small expedition, not a large band."

"Large enough to keep my men busy," Sir Hughes rasped, bitterness in his voice. "Was there some other purpose than loot and rape?"

"There was looting, my lord, as you can see, but for the most part the women were spared. Although some died, none were taken prisoner that we can tell. Your men could tell you more, I think."

"Whom else did you lose as a prisoner, my lord?" This came from another of the knights who was well armed, although less heavily built than his companion. He, too, had a beard, but it was well groomed, and he seemed better dressed and mounted than his companions.

"They took the priest, sir, among others of the common service," Sir Hughes answered, with some surprise in his voice. "Why the priest? To have some sport? They are a cruel people, by God; but I doubt they would burn a priest for sport."

"It would be unusual, my lord. They respect the men of the cloth in all faiths, sometimes even more than we Christians." The man turned to his companions and spoke in a low voice, questioning them.

There was a murmur of voices too low for Sir Hughes to catch, and then the slim knight who had spoken to him last lifted his head and said to Sir Hughes, "There's another possibility, my lord."

"Pray, what, sir? Is it to be ransom?"

"That's possible, my lord. We hope this to be the case, for then we shall hear quite soon as to the terms. However..." He paused, choosing his words carefully before giving an opinion. "My companions and I think there may be another reason, but we have no surety. There is a sect of the Saracen in the mountains to the north and east, some way north of Damascus, called the Assassins. They have fortresses just to the north of here, as well. Have you heard of the Old Man of the Mountain?"

"Yes," Sir Hughes said, "but how could he or they be part of this?" His tone was sharp.

"We can't tell as yet, my lord, but there's something here that smells of the Assassins' work."

"How will we know?" Sir Hughes asked. "All I know of them is that they're to be feared above all men in this land, but no one knows much about them at all."

"We know of them and their ways. They even pay us tribute. If they have the boy and others, we can demand them back. If, that is, they have the prisoners."

Sir Hughes stared at the five men. "How can it be that you have the Saracen so firmly in your sway?" he asked in an incredulous voice.

"They fear us more than we do them, my lord," was the laconic answer. "If you're finished here, we'd like to return to our castle and start making enquiries as to the whereabouts of your son."

Sir Hughes glanced around quickly to check on his men to ensure he was not vulnerable, and then nodded. With a jingle of harness and stamping of hooves, the five grim knights turned as one and moved off to the north to Lord Reynolds' castle, half a day's ride away.

Sir Hughes watched them leave. He was in a pensive mood. These men were a peculiar order, and he always dealt with them with care, as they seemed to fear nothing. Their story of the Assassins was startling and intriguing, although he was sure he wouldn't learn much more from these men. They kept their secrets. He turned back to his own men-at-arms, hurrying them on with the burial and collection of remnants from the caravan.

Later in the afternoon, the armed party made its way back to his castle. The scouts were well dispersed forward of the main body, so Sir Hughes was confident that if they ran into trouble, he would be given ample time to respond. This left him with time to reflect upon what he might tell his wife and to ponder the Templars and their extraordinary relationship with the Assassins.

Of the Old Man of the Mountain he knew nothing, but resolved that if his son were harmed in the keeping of one such as this, then he would find a way to avenge himself upon these mystical people, whatever their powers.

The sun was sinking into the horizon as they came within hailing distance of the shadowed walls. The guards opened the gates to the armed party and let them in, exchanging greetings and questions as the tired and dusty party filed by.

Sir Hughes dismounted and made his way, with Phillip in tow, up to the second level of the keep to where his wife waited.

As the two brothers stamped into the room, she turned from the window and gave her lord a wan smile. "Is there news, my lord? I beg you, what news?"

She looked exhausted from grief and lack of sleep, her otherwise attractive features gaunt and drawn with lines etched alongside her mouth that had not been there a few days before.

His heart went out to her, but his reply was gruff. "No, my lady, there was nothing to find or to tell as to where he might be. He is not dead at that place. We examined every blade of grass and turned each stone for sign of him. We had some Templars with us; they thought it might be that he is a prisoner and that indeed a ransom could be demanded by the captors once they know who Talon is."

She gave a sigh and a restrained smile and composed herself with a visible effort, but said nothing.

Phillip strode to the large, heavy table at the corner of the room and poured himself some wine. It never occurred to him to offer any to the others. He'd poured half the contents down his throat before he became aware that Hughes was looking at him. As he caught his brother's eye, Hughes gave him a tilt of the head and eyes to indicate he was to leave. Phillip nodded again and left without a word. The big wooden door slammed shut on his way out.

Sir Hughes shook his head. "My brother," he said. "I know he's anguished at what has happened, but I am not yet ready to forgive his stupidity."

Marguerite smiled again, this time with all the warmth she felt for her husband. "He is a brave bear with a good heart, Hughes; and he is not forgiving of himself. My lord, he loves Talon as much as you or I."

"This I know, my love. But there is another possibility, and you should prepare yourself for this eventuality."

She gave him a sharp, fearful look.

"I mean that there is another possibility that's more uncertain than just a ransom. The Templars think this was the work of the Assassins. If that's the case, the story becomes more complicated, and I know not where it leads."

She looked shaken. "I know of the Assassins... we all have heard of them. But what do they have to do with our son?"

"I don't know; but the Templars told me this 'smelled' of them. My God, but the Templars themselves smell of carrion. Do they never bathe? I cannot stand downwind of them. Who are they to talk of smell?"

In spite of herself, his wife gave a short laugh. "Can the Templars help?"

"I found it very surprising that the Assassins pay tribute to the Templars! If I had not heard it from one of these knights himself, I would never have believed it."

"Oh, Hughes, how I wish we had not sent him on that expedition to Jerusalem!" Marguerite exclaimed, her voice breaking.

Sir Hughes strode over to her and took her hands in his.

"Don't give up hope, my lady," he said as gently as he could. "I think the Templars will help. If the Assassins have him, they'll force them to return him unharmed, if indeed they really hold such power over these accursed people. We must pray for God's help that He will deliver Talon to us."

He walked back over to the table and poured two goblets of wine. He took them over to her side, gave her one, and raised his to hers.

"I am so hungry I could eat one of those juicy wenches I keep seeing in the yard," he said with a lame attempt to raise their spirits.

"Ah, my lord, I neglect my duties," exclaimed his wife with a tearful smile. "If you can contain yourself I shall see to it forthwith. Dinner, that is—not the wench."

* * * * *

Several days later the sentries on the walls called down to the busy courtyard that a group of knights was arriving. There was immediate bustle as space was cleared to receive the visitors, and a messenger was sent up the stairs of the keep to warn the lord and lady of the impending arrival of the newcomers.

Sir Hughes just had time to don a jerkin and his sword. The gates were flung open, and a cavalcade of Templars came trotting in under the tower bridge and halted their horses in the yard. Grooms ran out to take the horses while the knights dismounted. The people in the castle yard stopped what they were doing to observe the newcomers with that silent respect granted to an elite company of warriors.

Sir Hughes walked over to greet them. Lord Reynolds was the leader, while the other seven were composed of the former five knights Sir Hughes had met on the previous occasion and two unfamiliar faces.

"My lord Sir Reynolds, welcome to my home," Sir Hughes called out and bowed to the tall, lean man in full chain mail.

Lord Reynolds stopped in front of Sir Hughes and took his helmet off, shaking his dark brown hair free before extending his right hand to clasp Sir Hughes'. "Well met, Sir Hughes. I trust you are well in spite of the events of late."

"Well enough, my lord, although it's painful to have no news. Do you bring some to me?"

"Of a sort, Sir Hughes. Of a sort." He seemed uncomfortable.

"Pray tell me, sir... I cannot bear to wait another minute. If you know anything, put me out of my pain."

Lord Reynolds smiled. "Will you not extend us some of your hospitality first, sir, or must we burn up in the sun?"

Sir Hughes was brought up short. "My lord, forgive me, I forget my manners. Please accompany me to the keep with whomever of your men you choose, where we can see to your needs. The remainder of your men will be well looked after by my kitchen staff." He gave orders to the captain of his guard and then turned back to his guests. "Sirs, please come with me." Lord Reynolds gestured to one of his knights to follow, and the three men walked to the keep and the stairs.

Lord Reynolds glanced back and, nodding to the knight mounting the stairs behind them, said, "Sir Hughes, this is my trusted knight secretary, Sir Guy de Veres. He is a man of many skills, not least a soldier, but he also gathers intelligence for me, as he speaks the Arabic tongue very well."

Sir Hughes stopped and extended his hand. "Then, Sir Guy, I presume that you will inform me as to the whereabouts of my son. Let us take some refreshment while you do so."

They stamped up to the main chambers and there encountered Marguerite seated by the east window. "My lords," she greeted them. "My lord, Sir Reynolds, welcome to our humble house. May I offer you wine?"

"My lady," Lord Reynolds murmured as he strode across the room and took her hand. "I hope that you are well... under the circumstances."

Lord Reynolds accepted wine, but Sir Guy, eyes down, not looking at Marguerite, declined and satisfied himself with water. They took seats, but Sir Hughes could not contain himself.

"My lord, torture me no longer. You're here to inform me of my son, of that I am sure. You must not keep us in suspense any longer, I beg of you."

Lord Reynolds smiled and raised his left hand as though to halt him. "You're right, Sir Hughes, but it is Sir Guy who will have to tell you what we know. Please tell them all that you have told me, Sir Guy."

The young knight put down his beaker of water and leaned forward on his seat. "M'lady, Sir Hughes, what information we have gathered is not yet verifiable but it is at least news, and for the most part I trust my informants."

Sir Hughes swatted at a fly. "Tell me, man, what of my son?"

Sir Guy glanced at Lord Reynolds and gave a brief smile. "Very well, Sir Hughes, I know this much. Your son is alive; that news is confirmed."

There was a suppressed sob from Marguerite, and Sir Hughes slapped his thigh with a broad hand. Before either could speak, however, Sir Guy continued.

"Your son was taken by the Assassins, but not those with whom we have agreements. That he is alive is verified not just by the messenger but by my own sources in Banyas Castle, who have actually seen him. The prisoners came through there on the night after the ambush, and he was among them, as well as the priest." He looked at Sir Hughes.

"The sense is that these people are from Persia and not from this region. Why they've come all this way to capture prisoners we can't say. My informants are as puzzled as we are. It's possible that the people who command the Assassins in this region are being untruthful, that's often their way, and are working with those of Persia under the command of one known as the Master. One fact is clear: they do not have him in this country. He's gone, they think, to Persia."

He stopped at this point. There was a long silence in the room as Sir Hughes and his wife digested the information. Marguerite was as pale as a ghost, while Sir Hughes looked stunned.

As the silence grew, the sounds from the courtyard intruded, unnoticed by the people in the room. Lord Reynolds sipped at his wine, watching the couple across from him. Sir Guy still leaned forward, as though waiting for some reaction.

When it came, it was measured. Sir Hughes asked, "What does this mean for us here, Sir Guy? Can we rescue him? Is there hope of his escape? Or will there be a ransom?"

Sir Guy looked at him from under his black brows, his expression sympathetic.

"Sir Hughes, the lands to which we think he is taken are vast, with wild mountains that could swallow an army without a trace. Any who survived would end their lives as slaves to these people, something I have heard about many times since I came to this land." He saw their consternation. "I have questioned my informants, and they cannot explain this, either. We considered torturing the messenger who brought the news, but he insisted he knew nothing more and that death was welcome. We would not gain anything new from him, as they do not fear death, so I let him go."

"I would have butchered him," Sir Hughes growled savagely. "Who is this master, anyway? I'd like to get my hands around his throat and shake him to death."

Sir Guy sat back on his chair. He glanced at Lord Reynolds, who nodded. "M'lady, Sir Hughes, what is known of these people is mostly legend. However, they do exist, and they are perhaps the most dangerous people in this land and beyond, into far Persia from where they come. There are many of them, and they are very hard to detect, as they wear no uniform. They are not part of the

Saracen armies, yet all hold them in fearful respect. They come and go, in the night or day, without being seen."

Sir Hughes asked, "Are they then magicians that they are invisible?"

"No, sir, but they are skilled in the art of being inconspicuous, and in this manner they can move at will, without detection, through cities and towns that belong to Saracen and Christian alike. They are feared by all, in particular by the Saracen, who wish they did not exist even more than we Christians do.

"What we find interesting is that they wage war upon their own kind as much as they do upon our people. In fact, they spend more effort in that regard than upon us Christians. They are masters of murder and fear no man, being glad to go to their Paradise once they have killed their victim.

"We of the Templars do not fear them, and they know this. This is because they know that if they kill one of our leaders, it would not affect us in the same way that it would if they killed a sheik or sultan, so they leave us alone for the most part.

"They are led by one known as the Agha Khan, from distant Persia, but their local leader is called Rashid Al Din and by another name: The Old Man of the Mountains." Sir Guy did a fair impression of the correct way to pronounce this name. "We have an uneasy truce with this man. It is his followers who have told us of the boy's abduction and that he might be well on his way to Persia. Not even these people would dare to disobey the Agha Khan. There is no hope of ever catching them or of forcing them to give the boy back. The best we can do, Sir Hughes, is to keep our intelligence awake and listen for any news when chance should present it to us. I am very sorry, my lady."

Sir Guy stopped, and once again there was a long silence. A fly buzzed frantically in the water jug. After a few minutes, Lord Reynolds shifted and then rose to his feet. Sir Hughes and Sir Guy hastened to follow. Marguerite remained where she was, rigid in her chair, hands folded in her lap, knuckles white as she tried to contain her grief.

The men shuffled their feet in an embarrassed silence. Making a brief bow, Lord Reynolds turned and left the room. The other two men left in single file, stamping down the stairs in silence. There was almost relief at coming out into the bright sunlight to the bustle of the yard with its smells and activity.

Lord Reynolds turned to Sir Hughes and, clasping his hand in a firm grip, said, “Be of good faith, Sir Hughes. Sir Guy here has very good intelligence of the Saracen, and we will let you know as soon as we know something more.”

Sir Hughes returned the handshake in silence and nodded, not trusting himself to speak. With somber faces, the two knights strode over to their companions, who were standing with the horses. A brief command was spoken, and the whole group mounted and turned their horses to the gate. There was another low command, and they moved forward. The captain of the guard shouted to the gatekeepers, and the great doors swung wide. The silent group of men followed their leader out onto the dusty southern road. At any other time, Sir Hughes would have been impressed at their discipline, but today he had other things on his mind.

As the gates crashed shut, Sir Hughes walked with a deliberate pace over to the wooden stairs that led to the walls facing east and climbed them with legs made of lead. The entire community in the castle who could see him paused to watch. He reached the top of the stairs and then stood against the parapet, watching the receding Templars and the cloud of dust lingering behind them.

The castle came back to life, while in the keep Sir Hughes’ wife wept as though her heart would break.

Ah, make the most of what we yet may spend
Before we too into the Dust descend;
Dust into Dust, and under Dust, to lie,
Sans Wine, sans Song, sans Singer, and— sans End,

— Omar Khayyam —

Chapter 3
Arrival and Execution

With the scent of dawn in the air, the sentry stirred and yawned. He disliked guard duty. It made a mess of his sleeping hours and took him away from the warmth of his wife and bed. However, the dawn here on the high rim of the huge gorge was a reward for the long night without relief.

He tugged at the leather belt he wore, adjusting it for comfort. It was a fine belt, made in Ghazvin of well-dressed cowhide, dyed red and woven with leather thongs along its rim. It creaked with the weight of his sword and pouch. The sentry was very proud of the buckle. The brass glowed a deep gold when he polished it. This belt allowed him to feel good and to swagger in the company of others. He was constantly fingering it, even here with no one to look and envy him. It had cost him almost a week's wages, and his wife had not talked to him for three days.

His features were typical of the people from this region, dark and lean to the point of being almost emaciated. His almost black eyes, deep in their sockets, were alert and fierce. His nose, as thin as the beak of a hawk, jutted out above a sensual but cruel mouth. His well-kept mustache trailed down on either side of the mouth to waxed tips. To an onlooker, he would present a dangerous aspect and command respect, even though he was not above the rank of common soldier here. He was a young man by the day's standards but already a seasoned soldier who had two pitched skirmishes in his past and several dead to his credit. Thus, although he was tired, he was alert.

Moving out of the cover of the shadows along the wall, he leaned over the edge of the parapet, hawked and spat, then blew his nose with his fingers in the time-honored manner, wiping his fingers on the back of his pants. He propped his spear against the battlements, lifted one foot onto the archery recess, and leaned his elbows on the ledge. Leaning forward, he could see for miles in either direction, up or down the gorge. There was little he could not see from this vantage point on the castle walls, and once again he thought this must be the way an eagle sees the world.

The sky in the east paled as the dawn heralded its arrival.

The light of the day's beginning was approaching at terrific speed. It flared up from behind the mountains to the east, from behind the great mountains of the Alborz, where the sacred peak, Damavand, stood head and shoulders above them all. The tips of the summits turned pink, then red, and then the colors blended to ochre and soon after, light browns and tan.

It swept over the hills in a silent rush, bathing the sides of the mountains on either side of the valley in a sharp glow. Every feature was thrown into sharp, clear relief, leaving great gashes of black shadow where the ravines refused it and the overhangs turned it away. It would try for every recess in a while when the sun followed its advance guard. Over the razor-sharp eastern peaks it came, a great fiery ball in the sky, driving the shadows and phantoms of the night far up the western reaches of the gorge to make them disappear altogether over the rims of the farthest peaks to the west. It would be another hot day in this summer of 1168.

The man stood still, watching it with a wonder that had never died since the first time he had beheld it as a young boy.

Behind him, the castle began to stir. The chickens were awake, and the roosters challenged each other. He heard the creak of the winch as the leather buckets were lowered into the cisterns down in the yard of the inner keep. Then came the slip-slap of sandals as the maids and womenfolk headed for the gates located at the north wall entrance. The murmur of their voices carried up to him in the quiet, calm air. They were going up to the low huts on the hillsides, where the goats and sheep were herded at night, to do the milking.

Somehow, this castle seemed to force its presence upon mortal souls. The wall that he was leaning on ran the entire perimeter of a ledge that ran round the mountainside, overlooking the ravine.

There was a sheer drop from the walls on the south side cliff of some three hundred feet before the slope of the mountain spread away and down to the river. The sole access from below was up a long and winding path that tested the wind of fit men, taking an hour to climb.

An inner keep located to the western end of the outer ring of defenses towered over the whole. Two parallel walls, leaving a courtyard in the middle, joined two great towers. These walls were very wide and composed of many chambers and rooms. On the ground floor was the accommodation of the servants, kitchens, and storerooms, while the upper levels served as halls and chambers for the members of the Agha Khan's family, their retainers, and the dormitories.

Along the top of these walls were the battlements that faced north and south, respectively, while the two towers covered the east and western sides of the rocky spur. Long, narrow arrow slits opened to the north side, thus limiting the amount of light to those chambers on that side. More allowance had been made for light on the south side. There were several rows of larger, shuttered windows that, when opened, allowed the rooms to remain cool in summer. This also provided access to the sun to warm them in winter while providing a spectacular view over the gorge. As ever in this dry land, water was of paramount importance if a castle was to withstand a siege. Thus, in the center of the inner courtyard, there were cisterns, dug deep and well lined, that could keep the inmates with water for several months, if need be.

The inner courtyard had an area of garden in startling contrast to the grimness of the castle as a whole. This was colorful and green with a profusion of flowers, shrubs, and low trees. Narrow paths wound in and out of the shrubs. In its center, there was a small fountain that could be set to flow when the mood suited, although it was not being run now. Water in the summer was always conserved with care, and even small luxuries of this kind were limited in their use.

An open passage with light columns ran away from this corner, placed to allow shade and a cool passage to run on either side of the garden. This area was walled off by a light lattice, to keep servants and soldiers at a distance from the family of the Khan as they took their ease.

With the exception of the horses, which were always stabled in the outer courtyard, the livestock were brought in when there was danger of attack. But no attack had come about since the Assassins themselves had taken the castle in the time of Hassan-e-Sabah. This was Samiran, one of the castles of the Assassins, as they were known by the Franks in Palestine, and the Ismaili or *Hashishini* by all who knew of them in Persia and the eastern world of Islam.

Ruled by the Agha Khans for several generations now, these people had instilled fear and respect as far west as Palestine and farther still to the east into Afghanistan. It was a brave man indeed who came against them, although there were many who had tried and failed—and died in the attempt to control the power of the Agha Khans.

This castle, from which came so the men most to be feared in the world of that day, was itself one of the most imposing sights in the land.

A traveler coming along the long shallow valley that bordered the gorge would not see the castle at first, although he might well know of its location. Its color, much the same as its surroundings of brown and sandy stone, would hide it until he was almost beneath it. But then, as he gazed in awe at the mountains rising steep and almost sheer from the river on the south side, he would turn his gaze to the north and there would be the place for which he searched. Its high battlements would seem to tower menacingly over him out of the mountainside, even though it was well over several miles away, and he would know without any doubt that this was Samiran.

It had not been taken by force; instead, it had fallen through trickery, and then to the legendary and infamous Hassan-e-Sabah, the first Grand Master or Agha Khan, as he had become known.

By this time, the population of the castle was awake.

The sentries were impatient; they wanted to be relieved, and the guard commander had not yet shown up. When he did arrive, the replacement guards assembled in the *maidan* shuffled to attention and shouted a ritual greeting. Lean and tough as his men, the guard commander's presence brought them upright and alert.

The sentry waited for his relief to come to where he stood on the battlements. He dared not leave before his replacement came. The last man who had done this no longer lived. He had died screaming from his infected wounds after his lashing, days after the punishment had been inflicted. The man had failed to notice visitors coming up the mountain to the castle. No one wanted to repeat the mistake.

Just as his relief was about to come onto the battlements, a slight motion caught the sentry's eye. Yes, there it was again. His sharp eyes had picked up some motion on the winding track leading out of the gorge far below. A small line of people was coming up the path to the castle. They were moving very slowly and would take at least an hour to reach the gates, but nonetheless he knew his duty. He thanked Allah that he had noticed the movement in time.

He turned and called in a high clear voice down to the guard commander, "*Sarvan*, I see people coming up from the river. They come up the road and are ours with horses."

His officer tilted his head up to the sentry. "How many?" he shouted back.

"Fifteen, *Sarvan*."

The officer nodded his head, just deigning to have heard the news. But he would report it to his commander, Mahmud, *Timsar* Esphandiary as fast as possible. He detailed off one of the newer sentries, who ran off to the inner keep to pass the news.

* * * * *

A crowd gathered later in a large circle around the perimeter of the *maidan*. They knew there was to be entertainment and didn't want to miss anything. They pushed and shoved to get a better view of the prisoners huddled in the middle of the castle courtyard or *maidan*, as it was known. There was much chatter and yelling as people called out to each other and pushed to get a better view. The guards held them back to form a space with the shafts of their spears, good-humored but firm. This event was to be a controlled one, and the guard commander wanted space.

The prisoners were grouped together in an apathetic huddle. They were exhausted from the journey, and the final climb to the castle itself had stolen whatever reserves they might have had left. No one had offered them water or sustenance since breakfast that morning and little enough then. All they wanted was to lie down and sleep, but they sensed this was not to be.

The people of Samiran saw that there were three men, one of them a Christian priest, all of them bearded and unkempt, filthy in their rags, with sores on wrists and ankles. A boy along with the men stood out, not just because of his age but because of his bearing. Of all the prisoners, the boy stood the proudest, although he was clad in rags and weariness was etched into his gaunt young face. He was afraid, but he tried with desperate effort to hide it with clenched jaws and defiance in the stance of his body. However, his eyes gave him away to those who could read them. The others were muttering prayers in a gasping gabble, with fearful looks at the crowd.

There was a movement on the battlements on the east tower, and a figure appeared. He placed his hands on the parapet and regarded the prisoners. His sharp, piercing visage gave menace to his appearance, and his dark brown clothing added to that impression. He stood looking down on the party of prisoners and the crowd gathered round them. Slowly, the noise died down as more and more people in the crowd noticed him. They became quiet, although he said not a word.

He motioned with his left hand at the priest and the boy as though to move them out of the way. The commander shouted an order, and two of the guards seized the priest and the boy, half dragging them out of the center. They forced them to one side where others grabbed them and made them turn and face the center. The silence continued, but it was alive with expectation and excitement.

The two prisoners in the center became aware of the silence about them. Both of them turned and noticed the man on the parapet. They squinted up at him, knowing their fate was bound to his commands, and their fear grew. He gave no further orders, standing above them all, remote, menacing.

The prisoners' eyes were wild with fear now, and they were both moaning. One of them started to wet his already stained pants, which elicited a low jeer from the crowd, the first sound since the arrival of the figure on the battlements. The two men were bewildered and terrified, almost back-to-back, facing the crowd, isolated. The guards withdrew to the perimeter, joining the wall of spears, preventing all hope of escape.

There was a light whoosh and then a clatter as a sword flew out of the crowd and fell at the feet of one of the men. They both started, the sweat flying off their faces as they whirled at the noise and beheld the sword in the dust. There was, again, no sound from the crowd, just the buzzing of the flies that settled on dung and flew around their heads. The two men looked at the sword as though it were a snake, ready to strike. They dared not move, refusing to believe that this was happening. Nonetheless, they were very aware of their impending doom.

Finally, with a hopeless cry, one of the men dashed forward and seized the sword. He snatched it out of the dust and fell back with the other man, the sword now held on guard. A low murmur came from the crowd, and a sense of heightened expectancy filled the air. The heat of the day, hunger, and thirst, combined with the tangible fear that came off the men, made the boy Talon feel nauseated; it was overpowering. The priest, Jean, at his side, kept his head down, muttering frantically the long list of Ave prayers. His rosary having been taken from him long ago, he was twisting and turning his empty fingers in the filthy robe he wore.

A young man appeared in the ring with the two prisoners. He appeared without warning, and again the two men started, both facing around, desperate to see whence more danger would come. The one without the sword hung behind the other as though he could save them from what was to come. Their breath came in hoarse gasps.

The young man, more a teenage youth, was dressed in white with a white turban that had a red band through it, worn tight on his head. He was barefoot and wore wide, loose pantaloons and a loose shirt tied at the wrists and waist with fine cords. He appeared to be unarmed, showing both his hands spread wide, his expression blank. He beckoned the man with the sword without words, encouraging him to come and take him. His stance was ready and well-balanced, calm and waiting, a chilling smile on his handsome, dark face.

It seemed to unnerve the prisoner with the sword. His eyes were popping with fear as he looked at this apparition who, with calm expression, invited him to attack. His mouth now open and his breath rasping in the hot air, his gapped teeth gave him the appearance of a cornered rat. His companion was no better, peering over his shoulder at the object of this fellow's fright, his head swiveling to and fro as he tried to watch in both directions at once. The man with the sword knew he was staring a smiling death in the face. At last, deep within him, he found the last vestiges of courage that his wretched soul could muster and threw all he had into one, last, desperate gamble. He ran straight at the youth in a crab-like motion, slashing the air in front of him.

The youth did nothing; he just stood and watched. The slim, curved blade came ever closer as the whimpering man rushed at him. Then, just as it seemed that the blade should slash his hands off, the youth was no longer where he had been. There was a white blur as he sidestepped the swordsman, and then he was alongside him. Few saw the knife come out of its hiding place and how the youth moved it down and back up again in one long pulling motion. There was an audible gasp from the crowd. The youth was once again on guard, but this time behind the man with the sword, who had stopped in his tracks as though he had run into a wall.

The prisoner looked down at himself, his knees buckled, and he fell forward into a kneeling position, his back to the youth. The sword fell from his fingers into the dust. His hands went to his abdomen as he tried to stop his lifeblood and insides from falling out. His head came up then as he shrieked in agony. His cries of horror and terror pierced the watching prisoner boy like arrows and turned his insides to water.

As though this were a signal, the youth stepped forward and, seizing the upturned jaw of his victim with one hand to force it farther back, he plunged his knife deep into the man's throat, choking off the rest of the scream. Stepping out of the way of the stream of blood that arced upward, he allowed the body to fall over onto its side, where it thrashed out its death rattle.

The second man was on his hands and knees, blubbering with fear. The crowd, now having smelled the scent of blood, bayed for more. The air became filled with the eerie sound of a high-pitched singing as the women in the crowd trilled a high pitched continuous "Li li li li," more of them taking up the sound until the air was filled with the sound that froze Jean and Talon's blood.

The young man looked to the tower as though for instructions and approval. The menacing figure made a dismissive sign with his hand and turned away, pointing at the boy and the priest as he went. The youth moved into action very fast. He reached down for the sword and glided over to the man in the dust still crying and moaning, his head down, not daring to look up. The sword flashed up and down, and the man's head leaped from his shoulders, followed by a long stream of blood. The body flopped over, and the heels beat their death tattoo into the dust.

The crowd cheered and chanted in praise of the youth who turned to wave to them, the dripping sword in his right hand, the head of the prisoner in his left hand still dripping with gore. The foul smell of death was everywhere.

Talon felt like vomiting. The bile came right into his throat and stifled him, leaving him wanting to choke. He made a desperate effort not to vomit out his heart. His knees were shaking, and his bowels were ready to void. He could not take his eyes off the victims and the beautiful, deadly youth who had put on such a murderous display of skill. Talon was fascinated, as though hypnotized by a snake.

His ears were full of the eerie singing and the chants of the crowd, his nostrils full of the smell of death. He forced himself to turn and look at the priest. What he saw was not reassuring. Jean, the priest, was on his knees. His muttering now had an insane note to it, and there was drool coming out of the corner of his mouth. His eyes were shut and his whole being quivered with terror.

The sight of the abject state of the priest gave the boy Talon that tiny amount of courage he needed and allowed him to regain some of the composure he sought.

His back straightened and his head came up, and although he could not see, as his eyes were full of tears and his mouth trembled, he felt he could throw his pride in the face of his captors. No one could hear the frantic beating of his heart nor know how close he was to being sick. If he could just control the wobble in his disobedient knees, he could at least retain his pride.

Unbeknown to him, he was being observed with a keen eye by one of the onlookers, who gave an approving nod to himself, followed by the faintest of smiles, as he observed the struggle that was going on inside the boy.

At some signal, the guards hauled the priest upright and then half dragged them both away from the courtyard. The crowd began to disperse, leaving the two bodies in the dust, where already a cloud of flies was gathering over them. The guards hustled the two bedraggled figures through the inner gate and then down some stairs into a long, dark passage. They opened a door on the right and almost threw the priest into the black hole beyond. The door slammed and bolts rasped into place. They half carried Talon to another, and again a door opened into a black hole. He found himself pushed hard, stumbling into the blackness.

Talon fell on hands and knees as the door slammed into place and the bolts were rammed home. He lay in absolute silence, only the sound of his labored breathing in his ears.

There was no light of any kind, and he felt utterly alone. Bit by bit his defenses started to crumble, and the fear that he had for so long held at bay came rushing in like a crowd of dark demons to overwhelm him. All that he knew and understood, loved and held sacred, had been taken from him. There seemed no future and perhaps a death similar to that which he had just witnessed.

He began to cry softly, a low moan coming from deep inside him that he failed to stifle, and then the tears came in a wash. Great wracking sobs came out and shook his skinny frame as he sat with his knees drawn up to his chin on the floor of his prison.

My horse said yesterday to me: "There is no doubt
But that your stable is a coign of Heaven;
Here is not grass nor water, straw nor grain,
'Tis fit for Angels, not for beast like me."
– Baba Tahir –

Chapter 4
Planning a Future

Mahmud, *Timsar* Esphandiary, general of all the troops for Mohammed Khan, stepped into the passage and looked up the stairs that curled into the gloom above.

To an observer who knew him, it would seem that every time he was summoned he became a tiny bit apprehensive. It always came when he was about to mount the stairway to the first floor.

By the time he got there it would be over, and he would have himself back under the iron control he lived by. His sandals slapped on the cold stone of the worn stairs as he mounted. He knew well enough what this summons was about, and his mind was working out the permutations of what would transpire when he got to the master's chamber. He knew that a lot would depend upon his words. The boy might live or die; he himself might be taken to task for bad judgment and find himself on the defensive.

By the General's observations, the boy was a plucky lad. Mahmud would have bet that he was ready to vomit at the execution he had been witness to, but the lad had braced his legs and stared straight out at the rest of the world as though nothing could reach him. These Christians of the noble families were tough people.

The *timsar*, from habit, wondered if Arash, the Khan's uncle, would be there. It was no secret that they disliked one another. Arash Khan could not let a time like this pass and not play his devious intrigues. One of these days... but that could wait.

There was a shuffle of feet and a challenge above him as the guard, hearing him approach, went through the ceremony of, first, letting him know that they were awake, and second, alerting whoever was in the room that someone approached.

Esphandiary called out his name moments before he rounded the stair pillar, and a spear was hastily pulled back from its "on guard" position in front of him. His guards saluted him, and he gave back a curt nod before he rapped on the heavy wood door and spoke his name through the grille set into the door at eye level. The door was opened from within, and he stepped into a large well-appointed chamber.

The decor of the room had been kept to a minimum. The elegance and presence of the room lent a powerful backdrop to the personage who was seated on a large cushion in front of a low, ornate table near the window. Near him, seated on a carpet, was a magnificent hound that watched him. Regal and poised, she squatted on the carpet with her front paws crossed, looking for all the world as though she had been conducting an interview with the master. The hound was a saluki from the southern deserts of Oman, a gift from one of the hunting sheiks who had met the master during his travels. The master found the dog's aloofness amusing, as it was directed not only at his retainers and family, but at him, too. She was the only creature he knew who did not bow her head to him. But her color, light browns and tans with feathering at her ankles, her beautiful head, and deep, soulful eyes would have beguiled a colder man than the master. Besides, she was an extraordinary hunting hound and thrilled to the chase. The light-footed gazelle of the mountains were no match for this swift animal.

Sitting back from the Master in the sunlight thrown by the open window was the brother of the saluki. He, too, was a magnificent hound. Mahmud knew that both were devoted to the master and would have been at his throat at any indication of menace to their lord.

Scrolls and books made of sheets of expensive paper from Baghdad were placed in careless profusion on shelves and against the walls. This was the library and study, the master being a man of many languages and interests. Mahmud knew that here he was safe from a tongue-lashing, as the master reserved that for another room, the one in the tower.

He moved with three quick strides across the room and saluted in silence with his hand across his breast, bowing low, his eyes never leaving the master all the while. He knew better than to speak.

Mahmud waited. The figure seated on the cushion was a slim, wiry man of almost thirty. The aquiline features, sharp nose, and thin, strong mouth were thrown into sharp relief by the light from the window. He was well groomed, with a neat, full mustache. Deep-set eyes that were piercing and intelligent gazed out at the world above high cheekbones. His long, well-formed nose added to the impression of a hawk at rest.

The master was dressed in long, flowing robes, clothes that denoted a man at ease in his house, not meant for the outdoors. He wore a light robe of brown cotton that reached to feet clad in elegant slippers. Over this he wore a filmy over-cloak of dark brown, lined in gold thread with huge sleeves. His head was covered with the usual turban of loose turned cotton with a long strand hanging back over his shoulder. There were small rings in his ears. But for these, and a single large ring on the middle finger of his left hand, he was without adornment.

To Mahmud, he emanated power. This was confirmed every time he turned his fierce, hawk-like eyes upon a person. His eyes were almost yellow. Mahmud thought them the eyes of a lion, a predator, utterly without mercy. He knew this to be so for the master's enemies, but knew also that this Grand Master was more intelligent than most men and to be feared for that, as he relied upon logic more than any passion.

The master turned from his contemplation of a letter. Laying one elegant hand upon the page to keep it down from the light breeze coming in from the window, he smiled at Mahmud, showing even white teeth. He waved Mahmud to another cushion placed in front of him. Mahmud moved to the cushion, and sweeping his sword forward, he sat cross-legged, placing it with care across his thighs.

"Mahmud Esphandiary, my old friend, you are well?"

"*Gorban e Shoma*, Agha Khan. I am well. I hope you are well." Mahmud kept the pleasantries to a minimum as the master preferred, having no patience for the elaborate greetings that accompanied even the briefest encounter among his countrymen.

The master nodded, and just as he was about to make a comment, there was the same commotion outside as before, followed by a knock on the door.

"Arash, at your service, Agha Khan."

Again, the door was opened, and another man appeared out of the gloom of the corridor. He was elegantly dressed in long robes, rather like his master, but more ornate and decorated with bright colors and images of birds. The material of his cloth was very fine. His fingers were covered in rings. Although he possessed the same sharpness of feature as his nephew, there was a difference that was unmistakable. Somehow, he lacked the aura of sheer power that bespoke the leader of this clan. He had a weaker chin, hidden under a well-kept beard, and eyes that did not quite meet those of another. The presence of this man held menace of a different form. He was not as lithe as his nephew, and there was clear evidence of a life of indulgence, but there was, however, no mistaking his eyes. Of a similar color to his nephew, they resembled more those of a cobra.

He made a grand entrance, seeming to glide over to the two men by the window. Mahmud heaved himself to his feet but did not salute. He bowed low, however, as he did not want to offend the Agha Khan. The act did not pass unnoticed by Arash, annoyance showing just by the merest flicker of his eyes.

The master greeted him according to his high rank of uncle. With equal formality, Arash returned the greeting as though neither had set eyes upon the other for days rather than hours. The master motioned him to be seated. It would not escape Arash either that he had the cushion to his nephew's right, Mahmud thought, but he gave no indication that it bothered him. Instead, he seated himself with a flourish and arranged an attentive look upon his face. His fingers strayed to his graying beard and stroked it, a gesture Mahmud always found irritating.

The master lifted his right hand. A hitherto invisible servant brought over three small silver goblets filled with wine on a silver tray. He served the master first, then the master's uncle, Arash, and last Mahmud. The servant, once he had performed this duty, retired. The two visitors waited until the Master lifted his goblet, then they lifted theirs, giving a silent toast and a small sip.

The master reserved his best imported wines for visiting dignitaries and royalty. He enjoyed observing their shock when it was presented to people unused to drinking wines because of their faith. The Ismaili did not suffer this constraint and could drink wine if they desired. The Master and his father before him had ordered it to be so. However, at times like this, he also enjoyed a good wine with his most faithful general and his uncle.

The master opened the discussion. “I thought Darius did well today, Mahmud. See that he is rewarded, but not too much. He is to be sent on to Alamut to complete his initiation.”

“Yes, Master, I shall see to it,” Mahmud replied.

“We have news of events in Palestine.” The Agha Khan tapped the letter with an elegant forefinger.

Both men stirred. He had their full attention. News of the great battles going on in Palestine was awaited with keen anticipation, even though it was sparse when it did arrive, and not often accurate.

“It would seem that the Christians are doing better than they should. They are now trying to attack Cairo and Egypt.”

“I have heard, Master, that they have been increasing the numbers of their Knights Templar. Is that so?” Mahmud asked, who always wanted to know of the military dispositions of the enemy before all else.

The master humored him. “This is true, Mahmud. Indeed, these men are formidable and have become familiar with our ways, so they become harder and harder to surprise. However, they are still the Christians you and I remember. Hardheaded, stubborn, and I daresay that their strength is their very weakness. It will not bend to any situation; thus we can almost always outwit them in the end.”

Mahmud nodded. He remembered well, and the scars on his neck and face were there to remind him whenever he forgot. He smiled with the feeling that all fighting men know when they are with a comrade-in-arms and they have survived. Young though he might be, Mohammed, the master, was a veteran of the wars in Palestine, and the general considered this a singular quality.

Arash interjected. While he was no stranger to the ways of war itself, he preferred to use guile whenever he could to win his way. “Is it the Templars who are causing the trouble this time, Master, or are they doing the bidding of some Christian King at present in Palestine? King Baldwin of the Franks, perhaps?”

“We have lost ground. In fact, Ascalon has fallen, which is more of a disaster for the Egyptians than anything else. We may have lost a few cities, but not the war, and the Christians do not have an inexhaustible supply of knights able to fight in the heat of

Palestine." There was a pause.

"However," Mahmud said, "they are fearsome fighters. Think of what they could do if well led. They would be at our own gates. As it is, they have outfought vast armies of Egyptians and Kurds, Turks, Persians, and many others with small, fearless armies of their own."

"What is of most concern to me is the consolidation by Nur-Ed-Din over the region of Syria," the master replied. "He hates our kind, and he is beginning to put his faith in a nephew called Sal a-ed-Din."

Arash nodded his head as though in agreement. "We should pay attention to Nur-Ed-Din, Master. He has a serious grudge against the Ismaili."

"Your intelligence indicates that from all angles, my uncle. The Seljuk Turks are a menace withal; they too are *kharagi*; you are to be commended for your diligence," the master said without looking at him. "I am charged to attempt to find out more of the Christians, however, and you will have to help me think of a means."

Mahmud shifted his weight. He had been waiting for this moment, but now he hesitated, deferring to Arash. He need not have worried. Arash came in hard.

"You do not mean, I hope, Master, to include the boy in your plans? I had hoped to have him for sport," he said this with a barely concealed leer.

The master, who had become still, turned his head and eyes upon Mahmud. "What do you think, Mahmud?"

Mahmud hedged. "I am not sure why you would go to all the trouble to agree to have me bring him here unless you had some plan for him, Master. As to what we can do about the Franks and Germans, that will take longer to think through."

The Master smiled one of his rare, amused smiles. "Mahmud, if we remember what it is that we do best, we might consider that Palestine this boy, when a man, would be invisible in the courts of any infidel king."

"We might also be harboring a viper to our bosom, Master," Arash interjected. "If we train this boy in our ways, ways no one in their world can even contemplate, and he gets away from us, then we have not served ourselves well." Arash's hand tightened on his lap. "Let me have him, and then I can perhaps obtain ransom for him, or perhaps kill him."

"The time for ransom is past, Uncle, and besides, I doubt if he would survive your kindness," came the dry response.

Arash barked a short laugh and shrugged, but there was something else in his eyes when he looked down at the floor. The master continued. "How would we go about preparing this boy? My wish is that he commences training, and if he passes the first tests, he can continue; if he fails..." His voice trailed off. He looked at Mahmud.

"You will take him over for the training. I wish to know if, indeed, there is any intelligence inside that dirty creature. When he is ready for initiation, Uncle, you may have him to work your magic upon. We will discuss how best we can apply that means."

"There is courage, Master, that I know," Mahmud said. "Many a grown man would have lost all control at what he witnessed. This one was ready to vomit but didn't. He has good blood."

The master grunted. "I know that now. Our reports tell us that his parents are close to the throne in the Frankish army." He turned to his letter, saying, "We shall have to see. It is just the seed of an idea now; we shall have to watch to see if it grows into more than just a weed. One thing we can depend upon, time is on our side. This can take years, if necessary, to resolve. It might help with our plan to get people closer to the thrones of these barbarians."

"The boy is a Christian, Master," Arash snapped. "What do we do about that?"

"Circumcise him and teach him the ways of the Ismaili." The master's voice had turned cold. Not even his uncle wanted to take it any further.

Mahmud cautiously raised his hand. "Master, there is also the priest."

"Ah yes, the priest. We will use him for his Latin. Do you know if indeed he is educated?"

Both men shook their heads. Why did the Master want the priest for his Latin? Their questions went unanswered for the moment, for neither cared to speak.

The master turned his head to look out of the window into the courtyard. The other two took this as a dismissal and stood. Mahmud saluted as before and clattered down the stairs. He cared little for Arash. He was sure the boy would never be safe from him, whatever the master had planned.

"*In Shah' Allah*. So be it," His mind was already planning what to do about the training, and also considering the implications this would have for the other acolytes.

* * * * *

When the two men had left, the master turned back to the letter on the table. There was little warmth between him and his uncle. He had inherited the title of Agha Khan by right of direct inheritance from his father, but Arash still felt that he should have a greater share in the power as a whole. While this had never come to a head, fear being the main constraint, he knew that if he showed any weakness, Arash would pounce and deal a killing blow... if he thought he could get away with it.

Not for the first time, he wondered why he had never dealt with this in the time-honored fashion: the garrote, the knife, the quick silent death, and disappearance. No one would have said or done anything to stop him, and more than one would have been glad to oblige the Agha Khan. Arash Khan was hated and feared everywhere. However, Arash had made himself a master at the game of intelligence-gathering and was now almost indispensable. Therefore, it seemed not to matter that he also had some questionable habits and made free with them whenever he went to the cities, dangerous as it was to do so. The Agha Khan forced himself to concentrate on the letter.

The news was confusing; the infidels were gaining ground in all directions and some wanted his help again. Where force of arms failed, the Caliphs and minor sultans and viziers would remember him, the enormous power he held, and his ability to use guile and cunning where they failed with force of arms. Even though, he reminded himself with a sardonic smile to himself, they detested and feared the Ismaili, calling them *Bātinīs,* believing them to be atheists and deviants, in particular the Ismaili from the region of northern Persia who lived in the soaring mountains of the Alborz.

There were no great leaders on the side of the Islamic armies at present and no indication that there might be, other than perhaps Nur Ed Din. The Arabs and Persians hated the Seljuk Turks, who in turn distrusted them. This was one of the reasons for the infidels' great success. Although he knew well how the jealousies and intrigues tore at their leadership, they could fight as one when the time came. Whereas the Islamic forces could not, it seemed. In fact, his own quarrel was more with the Seljuks and their Sunni faith than with the Christians. While they were indeed the enemy of Islam, the real enemy of the Ismaili was the Sunni faith. For the time being, he would wait out events and see if there would evolve a stalemate from which he could profit.

Mohammed Khan settled back in his cushion and reflected on the times and his position on the chessboard of the present. Little motes of dust floated in the warm air stirred by the light breeze coming from the courtyard. The low chatter of the women below failed to disturb his thoughts, and the drowsy afternoon seemed to have quieted the whole castle. Even his hounds had placed their majestic heads upon their paws and appeared to be sleeping.

He thought back to his grandfather, Hassan-e-Sabbah, the founder of the sect. Hassan had come to this wild, high remoteness and bound the fierce people, the mountain men of the Alborz, to him with a mixture of fear and superstition that held to this day. They called him the Agha Khan, and he had taken these people and gone on to instill fear in all of Persia with his cult of followers, known in this region by some as the *Hashishini*, more often as the Ismaili, and by the infidels as the Assassins.

Their influence extended now into Syria, almost two months' ride away, their power was a match for that of almost any caliph or vizier in the old region of Persia. However, it was tenuous at present and needed more substance. The man, Rashid al Din, who had been put in place to control the sect in Syria was becoming too independent, and that was worrying.

Now the Christians were here. They came from out of their cold, forested countries to fight for a God that seemed even more bloodthirsty than his own. At least Islam had tolerated the Jews and Zoroastrians, and indeed the many other Christians from the Holy Land, giving them freedom to worship as long as they paid the special taxes and acknowledged the overrule of Islam and the One True God. The Turks had ended this tolerance, and now the Crusaders, as they called themselves, cared for none of this, it seemed. They sacked every city they came to, whether it surrendered to them or not.

His respect for their fighting abilities did not extend to their faith or to their sense of unity. His spies had told him too much of the in-fighting and jealousies that prevailed in their various courts. He pondered how best he could exploit this weakness of theirs.

A soft knock on the door announced another visitor. His sister entered the room, with a shy step. As he contemplated her features and form, he was struck, not for the first time, by the poise and beauty of this sibling of his. She shared the determined chin and the wiry ease of movement that characterized him, but her eyes always reminded him of their mother's.

They were great pools of darkness surrounded by gray irises, the gray of the mountain stone in winter, except that they had a warmth to them that no stone could have possessed. On occasion, he had seen them flare with anger and knew she had inherited a ruthless strength from their father that few would want to clash with. Then they became ice, and the inner soul was hidden as the perfect eyes came together in a single focus, and woe betide the offender. This girl was of true Persian stock. She would be tall when a grown woman, and light of skin, with raven-black hair, indeed a beauty, just as her mother had been.

But now she came to him, a leggy, self-conscious, adolescent girl. His thirteen-year-old sister was her usual self, diffident and respectful to her brother but warm and lively, too. He smiled one of his rare smiles, one reserved for his sister sibling, and lifted his arms to greet her. She came over to him, but found her way barred by two ecstatic hounds, their tails wagging furiously, their almond eyes smiling. They snaked their bodies low on the floor and pushed their noses at her, their delight at seeing her matched by her pleasure at being accosted by them. She looked over to the master and, her eyes wide with fun, gave a delighted laugh, all pretense at decorum lost.

"There you are, brother. You see, while you may command their obedience, it is I who own their souls."

He laughed back, a low, quiet laugh. "I can see, I can see, but then, I suspect you will command more than *their* hearts in time, my sister."

Extricating herself from the two salukis, she came over and, her composure back in place, with a polite tone greeted him. "How are you, brother? I come to ask if you wish to eat here or with me."

He pretended to give the matter much thought. "My Rav'an, I am well, and I will eat with you this evening." His response was just as formal, but there was a light gleam in his eyes that did not escape her. He received her kiss and returned it, then waved her to a cushion.

"How have the studies been today?" he asked.

"Well, my brother, well, but I am a little bored. I wish that I might ride out and perhaps hunt, if you would permit it?"

He gave a low snort of laughter. "Women are not supposed to gallop about the countryside, showing themselves off to the entire world."

It didn't, in fact, bother him at all that his sister preferred to hunt and ride than to attend to women things. He knew full well that if she had been in any other place but this mountain fastness, she would have disappeared by now into the depths of a palace to emerge when the time came as a wife to some lucky prince or other. He was very proud of his sister, and although her destiny was going to be tied to one of his alliances in time, he did not want to begrudge her life until then, as he had no brothers now and the two had become very close. It was a shame he had not been able to spend more time with her since their father's ill-timed death.

He pretended to consider this as a weighty problem, watching her attempt to control her impatience. At last, when it seemed she could bear it no longer, he gave in. "Yes, you may, but... you must have a guard. Either Mahmud or his guards must accompany you."

"Oh, my brother," she said with fond exasperation. "I am well able to take care of myself; you know that."

"Indeed, I do, Rav'an, but humor me, light of my day. You are growing up, and while this is my domain, these are not the times for a young lady to ride out on her own. There are lions, too. I heard reports of a lion seen but the other day over in the other valley. They have still not tracked her to her lair."

"Very well, Master, I shall ask for assistance from the General." She tried to hide her disappointment. Then she asked, "I heard a boy came in with the caravan. Do you intend to kill him?"

The master told himself he would have to get used to her direct manner. Just like their mother, he thought, a rueful smile twitching his lips.

"Yes, indeed, a boy did come. How you came to know about it, I probably should not ask. But no, I have not decided his fate yet, and you should not be so inquisitive, young lady."

Undeterred, she asked, "Will he be trained like the others?"

"That, too, is a question you should not be asking. All in good time, my sister. Now, go to Mahmud and ask him for his company, and if he is too busy with my affairs, then ask him for an escort. You may take the hounds with you, because if you do not I shall have no peace. In God's good name, I implore you to bring them back as well as yourself. Now go."

He pretended to sound stern, but she was not fooled. She kissed him on the cheek and led the way out of the chambers, the two happy salukis weaving about her on feathered, springy legs.

Mohammed went back to his contemplation. The boy again! His mind worked at that puzzle for a while, and then he had it. The boy had to grow up to be a young man before he would be useful, so there were at least three years to go. During this time he would be trained in the arts of the dagger and other tools of assassination, so that when the time came he could be effective. Arash Khan was a master at the black arts. When the time came to lay the seed of his victim's destruction, he would be able to reach the boy's mind. That victim could even be a king,

The priest was of less value but could nonetheless instruct the students in Latin and the Frankish tongue. One never knew when this kind of knowledge would open gates and allow entrance to protected areas. He turned his attention back to a long missive, delivered that day by one of his shadowy messengers. It gave intelligence of the situation in Syria and the sect of Ismaili he had established there. He, Mohammed, would have to go there one of these days and bolster the organization, perhaps persuade Rashid Al Din to work more in tune with him. It was time he established his influence in the heart of the Christian kingdom.

Black is my lot, my fortune's overturned,
Ruined are my fortunes, for my luck is brought low;
A Thorn, a Thistle I, on the Mountain of Love,
For my heart's sake. Drown it in blood, O Lord.
— Baba Tahir —

Chapter 5
Samiran

Talon had lost track of time when the door to his cell opened, he was dragged to his feet and then hustled to the entrance to the tunnel. Evening light spilled into the dark corridor. He blinked and shielded his eyes from the unaccustomed glare. A huge figure stood at the entrance and barked a command. Bemused and bewildered, he stared up at the dark, menacing figure and then hastened to stand straight. The man came forward and grasped him by the arm, speaking to him in Farsi. He had learned the rudiments of the language along the painful road to Samiran, but in his present state he could not comprehend what was said. The man shook him again and made the same demand.

Talon shook his head, and cried out in French that he could not understand. The man seemed to relent.

"You will obey all commands from this day forward," he said in loud passable French. Talon gaped at him and then nodded. With instinctive pride, he fought against the unyielding grip. In spite of his weakness, he rebelled against such treatment, so he fought, a futile and feeble effort, until in the end he gave up and sagged in the man's grip.

"Do not fight. Do not try to escape. Do as you are told and you will live," the man said, his tone harsh. "If you do not obey, you will be punished and you will die."

Talon nodded mute reply.

"My name is *Timsar* Esphandiary. I command all in this castle. I am the general of all the forces of the Agha Khan. Your life is in my hands to do with as I will. You are as nothing in this land. Do you understand?" This last was delivered with a shake and was spoken in a much louder voice.

By now he had Talon's full attention, so the boy nodded again. He was exhausted, and this bluster was just more torment. The General continued for a few minutes and then left the tunnel entrance, leaving the door open. Immediately, a younger man strode in and, seizing Talon by the arm, proceeded to march him out into the open air.

Talon allowed himself to be dragged into the large building, up some stairs, and along corridors until he was very confused and had no idea where he was, other than they were higher up in the castle. They went down a narrow passage until they stopped in front of a wooden door.

The young man threw the door open, and they entered a dormitory. There were twelve pallets in two rows on either side of the room with a walking space from the door to the narrow window left clear. There was almost no light, as the window was shuttered and it was growing dark.

The noise that had been coming from the room before they arrived stopped abruptly when the door opened to reveal the surprised faces of eleven boys in various stages of undress among the pallets. The young man gave some loud commands, and the boys responded in unison.

Talon was pushed into the room and was pointed to one of the pallets. He moved toward it, watched by the other boys in the room. The guide issued orders to the oldest boy in the room and then left, slamming the door shut.

Talon was deposited in the room, wondering what would happen next. Two of the boys came over and, taking Talon by the arms, showed him to his pallet, where he almost fell backward from weakness. He felt bruised all over and ready to cry. Nevertheless, his pride was still intact, in spite of all that had happened, and he held onto his self-control as hard as he was able. He would cry later, he decided, when he was quite alone, whenever that might be.

The older boy in the dormitory shouted some orders to the others, and they retreated to their own beds. They began talking to him, some of them with loud voices, as though that would help him understand better. But he was still at a loss with the language, and their chatter was far too rapid for him to be able to follow their words. They tried sign language, pointing to various things and naming them. There was a lot of laughter at this and some boyish clowning as they pushed and shoved each other to get near him and stare.

He nodded with a polite smile, thinking that this might be better than the scowl he had reserved earlier for them all. It provoked some smiles back and then a pat on the shoulder as one of them muttered something to the others. They nodded with seeming approval. Then, the excitement over, they started to prepare for bed. The boy on Talon's right was a dark, slight lad with black, deep-set eyes, lanky and bony but with a wide smile that showed good, even teeth.

He seemed to want to get to know Talon better, for as he made ready for bed, he talked to Talon, showing him where to place his clothes. They were all quite uninhibited as to their nakedness and pranced about with silent mirth when it looked like they were on the edge of provoking another visit from authority.

Talon began to realize that there had not been very much animosity. There was just one boy in the room who kept his distance. He slept on the other side of the room near the door and seemed to be one of the seniors. In spite of being unable to grasp the language, Talon was quick to sense the pecking order in the room. That boy did not like what he saw of him and spoke to the others, pointing at him and making derisive motions with his hands. Talon decided that if he were to survive whatever was to come, he had to understand what was going on as fast as possible.

His immediate problem was to get undressed and into bed without attracting too much attention. He was exhausted from the rigors of the days just gone and the preceding months on the road. At the same time he was keyed to the point of trembling with the tension left from the recent introduction. Pretending he was semi-conscious, he made an apologetic grimace to his pallet neighbor and rolled over onto his side, facing away. His exhaustion dragged him down into a black sleep close to unconsciousness.

The other boys talked about him late into the night, wondering why he was among them and what was to become of him. Would he be one of them, or was there something else in store for him? No one had told them anything other than to leave him alone when he came in, which they had done readily enough. They did as they were told in everything. However, they were more than curious about him. There had never been a *ferengi* allowed to live long in this castle, and never one who was placed among the boys, as far as they knew.

One thing they decided he did need was a good bath. He stank the whole room out, and that could not be allowed beyond this night, Also, he hadn't even undressed to sleep. What sort of barbarian was this? He looked almost white where his clothes covered him, although his face and hands were nut brown from the sun.

"Hey, did you see the color of his eyes? Green. No, blue. Hard to tell in this light. If he gets that old he will slay the women."

"Well, that's not going to happen, so don't worry. There will still be one left for you to dip it into, even if you are the ugliest monster in the place." There were muffled hoots of laughter.

Where had he come from and what was he doing there? The speculations were endless. Rostam, the boy by the door, had already made up his mind. The masters were going to use the boy as part of their training. This one would be dead soon enough.

Mehmet, the other senior boy, and a more thoughtful one in all respects compared to his peers, felt there was something else going on. He knew with certainty that if the masters had no time for a person, then that person died. They were not given a bed to sleep on. They had their throats cut and were thrown off the walls to lie on the mountainside for the wolves, foxes, and other carrion-eaters.

"No," he said out loud. "There is a reason for this one. We will have to wait and see. Get some rest, you scabby lot of honking donkeys. We have to get up at dawn." He turned over and went to sleep without effort.

One after the other, the remaining boys dropped off to sleep. Soon, silence descended. But, there were dreams and nightmares to be found in sleep, too. Few of them were free of these as they wrestled with their youthful fears, seeing the demons that they could put aside during the day when they were kept too busy to think, but which welled up from the subconscious to haunt them in the dark hours of the night.

*****

Talon was awakened by his new companions and made to run down the steep path to the river with the other boys in the morning. There he had the unpleasant experience of being made to wash in the freezing water of the river while they laughed and poked fun at him. They then ran off back the way they had come, leaving him standing bewildered and confused. He grabbed his loincloth with one hand and labored up the slope in pursuit of the chattering boys as they scampered up the dry, stony ground. He was out of breath and stood gasping in front of the senior when he got to the gate, his chest heaving. With an impatient rebuke for being slow, the senior waved him through the gate, where a dour-looking guard was standing, regarding the boys.

Then they went to breakfast, another new experience for Talon, one among so many that time blurred as he tried with desperate eagerness to regain his equilibrium in this utterly strange environment in which he now found himself. The food was basic, but good. Squatting on the ground or sitting cross-legged, they were served their food by women who came to their corner of the yard and put out the meal on woven wool mats.

They were given boiled eggs and *nan* with some yogurt or *maast*, as he was later to know it. He recoiled from his first sight of it, as it came in a small earthenware bowl covered with flies. He was holding the bowl, wondering what to do with it, when his grinning companion of the dormitory took it off him.

The other boy held the bowl with one hand, then scooped the white skin off the top and cast it aside onto the ground. There, inside the bowl, was a white cream, a small amount of which he scooped onto a torn-off piece of the flat bread. He offered the bread to Talon, who, although hungry, was nervous about eating it. The boy was quick to realize this and put it into his mouth instead and ate it with obvious relish. Then he scooped up some more and again offered it to Talon, grinning and talking at the same time. Talon took the piece and gingerly put it into his mouth. It tasted fresh and very sour, so much so that he screwed up his face, which prompted his new acquaintance to laugh out loud. However, he enjoyed the taste enough to indicate that he would like some more. The other boy gave him back the bowl and pointed to the bread on the mat in front of him.

They were all eating as fast as they could, stuffing bread and eggs into their mouths, talking at the same time, and making a mess all over the area where the food was laid out. Talon had just begun to get into his stride when he learned why they ate so fast. It seemed as though they had barely begun when there was a shout near the keep and a man came out, followed by several other youths.

They were heading in the boys' direction, who stopped what they were doing at once and leapt to attention, spilling food all over the place, wiping mouths with the back of hands and trying to look inconspicuous. Talon, by now a little better tuned to the tone of his existence, had also scrambled to his feet with a mouth full of egg, which he was still trying to swallow when the men came up to the group.

With sharp words they started separating the boys into groups, which were then herded off by the youths in various directions. Talon found himself alone with the fierce-looking man with as fine a set of mustaches as he had ever seen. To Talon's surprise, the man spoke to him in acceptable French.

"You are to stay with me. I will teach you Farsi and Arabic and you will learn as fast as you can. Do you understand?"

Talon first gaped and then said quickly, "Yes, sir, I shall."

"My name is Jemal. You are to call me *sarvan*, which means captain. I am a *rafiq* here. You will do everything that I tell you or you will be punished and it will be severe. Do you understand?"

Once again, Talon nodded mute acknowledgement of the man's authority.

"Follow me," Jemal commanded. He led the way. They crossed the large space between the keep and the outer walls to a place where Jemal could sit comfortably, and Talon was commanded to sit down and listen. This he did with fierce attention, trying to catch every word that Jemal spoke, and to hang onto it without letting it slip away. All the while, he was scratching at the sores covering his chest and under his arms. The fleas and lice were still with him.

Finally, Jemal had to stop and ask him in French why he scratched so much. "You are like a dog. You never stop scratching, and it is very rude," he stated in French.

"I am sorry, sir," Talon said. "I cannot help it; I have these sores all over me that I got when we were coming here."

Jemal looked at his new ward in disgust.

"*Sarvan*, you call me *sarvan*. You probably have fleas," he stated. "And lice, too, I would not be surprised. You *ferengi* never wash. Are all of you so disgusting?"

Talon hung his head. His long greasy hair all but covered his face. "I don't know, *Sarvan*, but I don't recall having fleas when I was in Palestine."

Jemal sighed. "Wait here. Don't go anywhere until I come back."

He ambled off to talk to one of the women in the yard. They were both looking at him as they spoke. She asked a couple of questions and then left with a comment flung over her shoulder, laughing as she went. Jemal came back to the boy.

"Come along, *ferengi*. What is you name anyway?"

"Talon, *Sarvan*."

"Hmm, Talon, you need a hot bath to get rid of the fleas. We will have to clean you up before we can continue with your lessons. I cannot have you scratching like a dog all the time when you are at lessons. You will come with me. The women will fix things and take care of you."

There followed a mortifying experience for Talon that he remembered with embarrassment long after. Jemal, brooking no argument, took him to the area where four or five women were congregated. After some discussion, they all went into one of the low mud huts nearby. The woman with whom Jemal had first talked was already pouring hot water into a large wooden half barrel that came up to Talon's waist. Jemal told him in French to take his loincloth off and get into the tub. He could barely restrain his amusement at the stark terror in the boy's eyes. He later told his companions that he thought the boy looked as though he were ready to jump off the edge of the cliff rather than do as he was told.

Jemal pushed the boy to the tub. "Get in."

Talon wished he had died on the road to Samiran. The women were watching in high amusement, their arms crossed under their ample breasts, smiling at each other but also feeling a little sorry for the skinny *ferengi* boy as he tried to hide his shame from their inquisitive eyes. He was the first they had ever seen, other than the two *ferengi* who had been executed earlier that month. Then the one who poured the water shouted at them to go about their business and bustled up.

She pulled his arm and made him get into the hot water, which came up to above his knees. He stepped in gingerly, and she made him face away. Taking up a coarse cloth and a piece of rough brown soap, she proceeded to scrub his hide with vigorous strokes from the top of his neck to the back of his knees. He stood still, enduring her rough attentions, wishing all the while that he were dead.

Then she made him sit while she started on his hair. She shouted for Jemal, who was gossiping with the women outside, who were asking him all about the boy. When he came in, she said something and pointed to Talon's lank, greasy hair.

Jemal nodded and said to Talon, "We will cut off your hair. It is full of fleas and lice. It will grow again."

Talon had thought that his torment ended here in the tub, but now they wanted to make him bald. His shame was so great that he wanted to drown in the tub and never be seen again.

The remorseless attack on his dignity continued as they proceeded to scrape the hair from his head, from ear to ear. They left it looking like a white, mottled egg with a wide-eyed, scared face painted on it. When the woman and Jemal had finished, he was, however, clean. His sores were salved with something that smelt horrible but was soothing. However, he felt more naked than he had ever been in his life.

He learned from Jemal that the woman was named Alaleh. Jemal respected her and made it clear to Talon that he was to go back to Alaleh if ever he was sick, as she was a witch with herbs.

*****

Before long, Talon became used to the hard training. The boys rose at dawn, regardless of the weather, and ran up the mountain to the ledge or down to the stream. Up on the ledge, they often had some form of instruction in self-defense. If the senior student felt in the mood, he would tell them of some of the legends their predecessors had created. Talon found he understood more and more of what was being said to him by his companions. After breakfast, either one of the rafiqi or a senior students trained them in one or other of the basic fighting skills.

This included archery, sword, and knife fighting. They were taught to use long or short sticks as weapons, having been informed that this would perhaps be the only weapon they might have at any time on the road, other than a concealed knife.

This was the kind of thing Talon had started to learn at his father's castle, so it was easy for him to adapt. He enjoyed the stab and parry when the instructor allowed them to pair off and practice on each other.

His partner was most often the boy who slept to his right in the dormitory, Reza, who was very fast and beat him every time. Reza had a cheerful disposition and seemed to like him enough to talk to him whenever the chance came.

At first it was hard to understand each other, and they spent a lot of time gesturing and grimacing, with a good deal of laughing on Reza's part, as they tried to explain what they meant. Reza showed him what to do on most occasions, and kept the teasing to a minimum. Talon applied himself during this form of training—although he often found it frustrating to receive a blow from the mercurial Reza, who always seemed not to be there when he aimed one at him—because it served to concentrate his mind away from his situation.

Barked knees and rapped knuckles forced him to pay attention; the instructors were not gentle people and often used him when demonstrating a point to the students. The blow would land and he would fall, to much laughter from his companions. He knew better than to protest, forcing back the tears of pain and humiliation. He resolved to get beyond the present and to one day be good enough to deal out some of his own punishment.

Reza would shuffle over to him after one of these episodes while they were eating and talk to him. He could not always understand what Reza said, but the meaning was often clear. Talon, keeping his head down to hide the tears welling in his eyes, would nod and indicate he understood, feeling better that he possibly had a friend here. There were many nights, when the rest were asleep, when he would remember his former life. Then a wave of hopelessness would wash over him, and he would cry himself to sleep.

Talon discovered that, of necessity, he could follow a conversation in a matter of days, but using the words for himself proved much harder, as he lacked a foundation. The teachers were not insensitive to this, and as their instructions regarding the boy had come from on high, they made sure that as much as possible was explained to him. Some of them spoke a little of the Frankish tongue, and this helped.

He was removed from the class in the middle hours of the afternoon and taken to the inner courtyard where one of the *rafiq*, usually Jemal, would explain the basic structure of the Persian language to him and write the words with chalk on a slate.

He was expected to pay close attention, but he found it very hard. They gave him no kindness, and often shouted at him as though he were stupid. He had learned his lesson, however, and never stood up to them, accepting meekly the verbal abuse while trying to will the knowledge into his head. His progress was slow but sure, and one day a visitor surprised him.

Jemal had just finished explaining the elegant Persian verb structure to Talon, who had just seen the light, and realized that it seemed not unlike his French language. He was feeling more confident, when there was a shout. Jemal called back a response.

He heard the slap of feet on the hard ground and the mutter of voices, and then, to his surprise and delight, Jean de Loche was coming toward him. He gasped and stared. The priest was cleaned and dressed in a way quite unlike Talon had seen him at any time before.

In fact, he had glimpsed the priest a couple of times since they had been brought to the castle, but then the priest had been filthy and haggard, as he was half dragged from one place to the other. Talon had imagined him suffering awful trials at the hands of his captors in the dungeons below.

Whenever he had seen Jean, Talon had followed him with his eyes but had soon lost sight of him. In any case, he usually had something he needed to concentrate on or the wrath of an instructor would descend upon his head. It often came in the form of a sharp, painful thwack across the shoulders from a stick.

Yet here Jean was, looking clean and tidy, his beard clipped and his hair cut short. Jean was dressed much like the other people around him. He had on a single shift of light, well-woven wool with the sleeves rolled back. He had lost a lot of weight, although he was still thickset. His features creased into a delighted smile as he approached Talon, but a quick glance in Jemal's direction told him to hold his peace. Talon stood up and they grinned at each other, wordless with pleasure.

Then Jemal moved off with the guards to ask what was going on, so the priest whispered to Talon. "It is wonderful to see that you are fine, my lord; you look well."

"I am well," Talon whispered back. "I have been so worried for you, Father. What happened to you?"

"I am to learn Farsi," Jean began, but he could not finish.

Jemal and the guards saluted each other and parted, and he moved back to them. "You"—he pointed to the priest—"you learn Farsi with the boy." He turned to Talon. "You teach all you can. Make him learn quickly."

Talon nodded, still grinning. Jemal shrugged in annoyance, but without further ado, he went back to the work they had been doing before the interruption. Talon and the priest sat cross-legged on the ground and listened as though their lives depended upon it.

Thereafter, Talon looked forward to the lessons. It gave him a chance to be with Jean and hear what had gone on from his perspective and to tell him of the new life he was leading. They slipped words to each other in whispers whenever Jemal left them for any reason or was talking to some other visitor. Talon learned that Jean had spent several weeks in the dungeon, unsure if he was to live or die, reliving the terrible executions they had witnessed again and again, until he thought he would go mad with fear and uncertainty.

At one point, he had not seen the light of day for more than a week and eventually lost all sense of time. His jailers came only to bring him food, but other than that, they left him alone. His cell had been carved out of the solid rock upon which the castle stood, so he felt entombed and terrified by the claustrophobia that gripped him. One day, the guards had come for him and dragged him out of the cell. His legs would not function properly. The guards dragged him in front of the same man they had met in Damascus.

"Mahmud Esphandiary," Talon said. "He is the general of all the Agha Khan's men."

Jean nodded. "You know what he is like, frightening and dangerous. I fear him. He said that I could live if I did his bidding. I don't have to tell you how I answered that one." He rolled his eyes. "He told me to learn Farsi well and to be prepared to use my Latin and Greek. What do you think he meant?"

"I have no idea. But I do know that you are alive and that there is some hope for us both."

"You are right, my lord. Praise God we are alive and that you are well."

"Jean, you must not call me that while we are here. I do not think it will help either of us if they hear it. Just call me Talon. Or if you have to, Your Excellency the Grand Vizier of Samiran," he finished with a grin.

Jean stifled a snort of laughter. "I understand. They watch everything we do and hear all that we say. Do you remember the Latin I taught you? We can converse in several languages and I doubt that they can follow all we say, but we should be spare with our words."

Talon nodded again, then Jemal came back and it was time for some history.

Jemal Shahigan was a retainer of the Agha Khan because he knew the country, its history and people better than most. In his former life, he had been one of the active members, a *rafiq*, or companion, and had carried out the duties required of him so well that his reward had been promotion. He no longer had to go on perilous missions.

Although he had been irked when given the task of teaching Farsi to the two barbaric *ferengi*, he bore it with stoic calm. It was a command from his lord and master whom he worshipped, so he resolved to teach them as well as he knew how.

Thus it was that he not only taught them the structure of this beautiful language and forced them to pay attention to its intricacies, he also insisted that they learn something of the country and its history, too.

Jean knew little of the Ancient Persian Empire; the Western world of that day was ill informed as to how empires east of the Holy Land had fared over the ages. He was fascinated by the knowledge Jemal imparted. If Jemal had a conceit at all, it was his knowledge of his own people's history. As he, like many of his kind, believed the world revolved around his country, he gave history from his point of view. The priest and Talon, although mostly Jean, as Talon found lessons other than martial arts boring, were given a good picture of how Persia had become great.

The invasion of the Arabs and the conversion of the land to Islam preoccupied Jemal, and he fell to discussing the many advantages Islam had brought to his people. Neither the priest nor Talon were in a position to argue, but it struck Jean that Jemal had a patchy knowledge of events and glossed over much that could have been of interest.

Nevertheless, they began to learn about Jamal's people and the origins of the Agha Khan and the Ismaili order of Islam. Jemal explained that the Ismaili were the third point of the triangle of the three denominations of Islam of that day.

The Ismaili, he told them, were a very powerful sect of Islam that did not accept the same tenets as the other two, that the mountain fastness they were living in was the great stronghold of the Ismaili, and that they looked to their Agha Khan for guidance in everything. He told them of the Sunnis, and that the hated Seljuk Turks were Sunni, and of the Shi'ites that lived cheek-by-jowl with the Ismaili, but that they, too, were mortal enemies. Each of them considered the other heretics.

However, the power of the master extended across the world, and this was how, when he had crooked a finger, Talon and the priest had become his prisoners even in far away Palestine. Talon and Jean were awed by this thought and talked about it often.

The priest had an active and inquiring mind. He delighted in hearing anything he could of the history. Many times, to Talon's chagrin, he would push the discussion along some line or other that went right over Talon's head. Talon would yawn and lean back, half listening to the drone, as the two men examined some detail of the Qur'an that Jemal had brought up, the priest, in his halting but ever-improving Farsi, and Jemal, delighted to have for once an attentive and enquiring student, even if he was an infidel.

One afternoon, the two men were so involved in some point of history that Talon, bored, tried to figure out how to escape. He came to when Jemal stood up. He jumped to his feet to make the usual bow to his teacher, along with Jean, as Jemal left them. The sun was low on the western mountain peaks by now. Night came swiftly in this mountain-locked valley, where the great castle of Samiran dominated the caravan route to the west and north to Tabriz. There was now time for the two of them to crouch again and talk before they went to supper in the kitchens.

"Father."

"Yes, Talon?"

"There was a girl over there just now; did you see her?"

"Was she exquisite and delicate as a wraith?" Jean asked, with a twinkle in his eyes. He was not above teasing Talon when the opportunity presented itself. Talon shoved him on his knee with a dirty paw.

"I did not see that much of her. I just know there was a girl over there, just now, watching us. I have seen women, but few children and fewer girls in this part of the castle before."

"Hmm, no, I do not know of any girl. But, wait. Yes, it could be. I have heard that the master has a young sister, but I have never seen her, and I do not know if she is here or not. Never mind that, though. How are you doing with all this fighting? I wish I understood what they were up to, training you like this. There's something sinister that I do not understand."

"Nor I, but it is better than being in a dungeon," Talon said with feeling.

This was always the riddle they came back to. It had also become clear that the priest was to be used for some purpose as well, and again they could not guess what.

A Falcon I,
And as I chased my prey,
An evil-eyed-one's arrow pierced my wing;
Take heed ye Heedless! Wander not the heights,
For him who heedless roams, Fate's arrow strikes.

– Baba Tahir –

Chapter 6
The Hunt

And so the months passed.

One day, when the group of boys and their instructor were high in the mountains overlooking the valley of Samiran, a runner came with a message for their senior teacher, Kamran, who had just finished talking about the various cities that lay to the south, this being a part of their education. The stories of the ancient and glorious cities on the high plateau called the Dasht-e-Hamidan fascinated Talon as much as the other boys. Cities such as Hamadan and Ghazvin, cities with palaces and *masjids*, were so beautiful they could beguile a traveler into staying far longer than he had intended, just to continue to view their beauty.

Kamran paused to listen to the messenger, and then he told the assembled group of boys that *Timsar* Mahmud Esphandiary wanted them to go back to the castle. They were to collect some clothes and small belongings and then travel some distance to the east where they were to stay for the week. Bedding and weapons would be provided at a watch post located there. It was one of the many posts that lined the upper reaches of the mountains, as a protection from surprise.

The boys were hungry for breakfast, but there was no complaint, as it was frowned upon and often punished with a thrashing on the spot. Shrugging off their hunger, they trekked back to the castle where they collected a few necessities and reassembled in a noisy group, carrying small bags of their personal belongings.

They were then ordered to follow the runner as he took a series of paths that led higher into the hills. For the next half-day, they traversed the ridges and high goat paths until they could see the small cluster of huts below them, which would be their home for some days. The huts were perched on an outcrop next to a low tower that commanded the best view up the valley.

The ground around them had little grass, and was strewn with boulders and scree, which gave way farther down to fir copses and stunted trees. Even farther down the mountain, the slopes were covered with a little grass or covered with long swathes of scree and boulders. Small valleys and gullies led off from the main valley of the Samiran Rud, most of them sporting a tumbling stream with dense patches of trees alongside the pools and waterfalls.

The boys were tired but excited. This was the start of one of the stages of the initiation, and they were all nervous as to whether they would do well. The time they spent here would be for hunting and practicing the art of evasion, attempting to get past the guards and make it to their intended victim without detection.

There were other diversions as well. They would be allowed to hunt the high upland gazelle, using bows and javelins and the speed of their own feet. The older *fida'i* and the *rafiqi* instructors, not the boys, might even go down to the village that nestled farther down the valley and play with the women.

They came down to the huts in a rush, kicking up dust with feet hardened by running on all kinds of ground, not feeling the rocks and sharp stones as they rushed to be fed. There they met the smell of cooking and all the hubbub of a kitchen in full swing. Ali, one of the cooks from the castle, was presiding over the cooking with two small boys in constant attendance, stirring soup in a great pot over a large fire.

There were large trays of *Nan*, the flat unleavened bread, for the boys to reach for and then dip into the wooden bowls they were provided with. They were told that they would also have rice, which was a privilege, as it came from the north and was scarce. The boys shouted, jostled, and shoved each other to get a place in the line, Talon and Reza among them. Ali yelled with a good-natured voice at them to stop making a noise and wait until he, Ali al Hovya, was ready to feed their worthless carcasses.

Eventually, they all received their food and were told by the gruff cook to waste none of it. There was plenty for all, including some figs and apples. Ali had even found some salted pistachios and left them in a small sack for people to come and grab a handful.

Talon, who was by now beginning to feel like one of the boys, was greeted with a grin from Ali. "Here, foreigner, take your soup."

There was no talking while they ate, the silence broken only by slurping and the rattle of wooden spoons in the bowls as the boys wolfed down the basic fare, stuffing the bread into their mouths as fast as it would go. They knew the next meal might be a day away or more, so they wasted no time in making sure of this one.

Talon and Reza sat off to one side, eating quickly and watching for the chance of more.

"I hope we can hunt," Talon remarked.

"We have to do well first, that is what I heard," Reza said between mouthfuls. "Did you hunt before?"

Talon swallowed the last of the soup straight from the bowl and then wiped it clean with a piece of *nan*. "My people hunt all the time," he said in a matter-of-fact way. "I was too young to know the art of falconry, but I had a hawk anyway, and would have learned. I was often with my father or his men on local hunts for gazelle and wild sheep. It's the best thing in the world." He yawned and stretched.

Reza looked at him. "I have never hunted," he said.

Talon turned to him, surprised. "Never? What then do your people do?"

"I never knew my parents," Reza said in a flat tone, "so I was never taught by my father to hunt. You will help me?"

Talon nodded. "I will try."

When they finished their meal, they went to join the others to practice the art of archery. Talon reveled in this kind of training and did well. His instructors noted that as he grew into puberty he was gaining in bulk in comparison to his peers, and this was proving to be an advantage in some instances.

The Persian bow was a light weapon, as compared to the longbows Talon was more familiar with. It was made of laminated wood, strips of wood bonded together for strength, compact and easy to carry. He'd been told it could be used on horseback as well as on foot. It required moderate strength to draw and shoot, and if there was strength in the forearm, that assisted with the accuracy.

Talon did as well as some of the older boys at target practice.

His arrows could find their mark at well over fifty yards. Reza kept up well with his peers, but acknowledged that Talon had the better bow arm.

They quickly fell into a routine of rising with the dawn and scrubbing the sleep out of their eyes in the freezing waters of the stream nearby, then going on the runs that carried them over hills and through the sparse woods. At this height, the dew was heavy and the mornings very cool. Their breath came in steamy clouds as they gasped their way up the steep paths.

They would return hours later, panting and hungry, to a stew or soup, plenty of *nan*, and sometimes meat that Ali and his urchins had prepared. The hot, fresh bread made their mouths water just thinking about it. On other occasions Ali would produce yogurt in big wooden bowls and toss onions at them, and they would feast on this, enjoying the sharp taste of both.

Close fighting with wooden knives was the most common form of their continual training, which took up most of the day. Often the knife-fights were carried out with a bit too much enthusiasm, and many a boy sported livid bruises and welts on his ribs, legs, and arms. Being boys, they accepted it as normal and joked away the tears of pain when an accident occurred.

Later in the day they went on a hunt or fished the streams for the delicious trout that could be found in the deep, cool pools of the mountain streams, if one knew where.

Ali rewarded the successful hunters with the best parts of the game or fish whenever it came in, to encourage more effort. Much yelling and joking went on over near misses and clever moves. The luckless ones became the butts of much jesting, whereas the exploits of the lucky became more and more exaggerated as an evening wore on.

Talon enjoyed the hunt most of all, as this was a test of the best of them. They went out on foot to seek the light-footed gazelle and mountain sheep. These glided like wraiths among the trees near the streams where the tender grass grew, or skipped along the points and edges of precipices along the high mountain slopes. The *rafiqi* and *fida'i* knew most of the best places to hunt and took small groups of them in different directions.

Talon had the bad luck to be in the same group as Far'az, one of the more senior boys, who had always had a bad feeling toward him and made sure he knew it. The earlier sly punches and tripping had been replaced with sneers and disparaging comments about his accent, calling attention to his status as *kharagi*.

Talon made it plain he wanted nothing to do with Far'az and would not be drawn into a very one-sided fight. This behavior drew approving looks from Kamran, past whom little went unnoticed. Forbearance and control was considered a virtue.

One afternoon they set off over the mountain into another valley behind their own. This was the first time Talon had been out of the Samiran Valley in all his time at the castle, so he was excited at the prospect.

They carried bows and short throwing spears for finishing off the wounded gazelle or sheep. Each of the boys carried a small leather bag with some dried meat, cashews, pistachios, and raisins. They all had a short, curved knife strapped to their waists. They wore tunics of loose cotton, gray from much washing, over an undershirt, tied at the sides, with loose, baggy trousers that came down to below the knees, and a long, loosely tied head cloth wrapped round their heads with the ends slung over the shoulders.

The *rafiqi*, on the other hand, wore colored tunics of expensive dyed cloth, yellow and red predominant, with intricate patterns on their coats, belts of dyed red leather, and ornate overcoats of fine camel wool. They and they alone wore turbans and boots as a mark of authority and seniority. Most carried a bow and a javelin for the hunt. The weather was not cold, although at these heights it could become very cold at night.

The small group climbed the mountain until the cluster of huts became mere dots in the distance down in the valley. As far as the eye could see, snow-covered mountain peaks jutted into the sky. Looking west and south, if he strained his eyes, Talon could make out the faint outcrop upon which was perched the castle with the gash of the gorge below.

They came to a narrow pass and went through to the other side so that they looked down into another steep valley more forested than the one they had left. The woods commenced a few hundred feet below their position and continued to the floor of the valley in clumps of densely packed firs mixed with aspens and oaks.

The group had maintained silence, as was the norm. They set off down the slopes at a hand signal from the *rafiq*, negotiating the slides of scree and the boulders that were in their path. They came to the tree line in a rush. As they approached the first trees, the *rafiq* gave a sharp hand signal for everyone to stop.

The group froze at once and started to check out their

surroundings with great care. The *rafiq* bent to examine something in the soft ground and then gestured the group to form round him. He pointed down with his left hand, the fingers grouped into a half circle. There, imprinted in the soil, was the unmistakable pugmark of a large predator—the footprint of a lion.

Everyone became very excited, whispering and gesturing to each other. Talon was as excited as the others; but the *rafiq* whispered them back into silence with a fierce gesture. The mark was just hours old, from what he could judge, so there was every chance that it would be very close. It was a dangerous animal and could wait in ambush. They had to exercise extreme caution from here on.

This was the first time Talon had ever seen a lion's paw mark, and he was impressed. It was large enough to encompass the whole of the *rafiq's* spread hand when he placed it over the mark.

The *rafiq's* eyes were blazing, but he held his excitement in check and issued his orders calmly to the others. They would track it as far as they could as a group. If they lost the spoor, they would split up and circle until they hit the trail again. They set off, this time in a half crouch, their eyes searching every rock and gully, listening and smelling with every nerve in their bodies. The *rafiq* led, his keen eyes picking out signs as they went; Talon was amazed at his unerring instinct for the right direction.

Although the floor of the forest was loamy, the twigs and low branches would make a lot of noise if trodden on by accident. However, the boys had enough training to make sure they did not compromise the group. After about half an hour, the *rafiq* stood to his normal height and gestured them all to gather round.

"Its trail has disappeared," he whispered.

He indicated that he and Reza would move to the left of the group and cast about in a downhill direction for the trail. A low birdcall imitating the jay would draw the others to them. Anything more, and the lion would bolt if it heard. He motioned Talon and Far'az to take the right hand direction.

Talon rolled his eyes at Reza to show how unhappy he was with the arrangement and received in return a sympathetic grin. Far'az told Talon in a sharp whisper to follow him and to keep his bow prepared, while he led the way with his throwing spear.

They went to the right of their former trail and covered almost a mile of track through alternating dense thickets and copses. Their progress took them down a steep, sparsely wooded slope into an area where the trees were denser.

After a half hour of careful walking, they came upon a stream. It gurgled and tumbled down from higher ground to settle into a fast-moving but smoother and shallower space of water that traversed their path. They were about to cross it when Far'az jerked his head up and stared at a jumble of boulders at the far end of a small, grassy space. He pointed to the other side of the fast moving water.

"There," he whispered in Talon's ear.

Talon stared across the stream at the boulders. They made perfect cover for a large animal. Bushes near the boulders were jumbled against a low cliff that blocked their way. Aside from the rippling song of the water as it washed over the stones, it was very quiet.

Almost too quiet. Talon's senses came alive and he strained to see into the recesses of the rocks, but they provided no information, so he turned to Far'az with a look of inquiry on his face.

"Where?"

It was late afternoon now, and slender shafts of light that penetrated the forest lent a ghostly feeling to the place. Light was fading and details were becoming indistinct.

Far'az touched his nose, then pointed. "The perfect place," he whispered. "We have to be very careful now." He moved his hand down to the edge of the water. "You'll have a perfect shot at about twenty-five yards. I will go forward and see if my nose is right. Shoot well."

Talon leaned close to him. "Should we not wait for the others, or go back to find them?" he asked in a hoarse whisper.

Far'az gave him a glare of contempt. "Is the *ferengi* afraid? Are there no men where you come from?"

Stung, Talon took up his position as instructed and glared back at Far'az. "Go," he whispered.

Far'az edged slowly down the shallow bank of the stream and began to wade across. The water came up to his calves, but he was painstaking about each placed foot. When he reached the other side, he paused and cast a brief look back to check on Talon, who stood braced at the stream edge with his bow taut for a quick pull and loose.

For what seemed like an eternity, Talon watched Far'az move

across the short, grassy area to the rocks.

Far'az had almost reached the rocks when there was a deafening roar that shattered the silence, and a large tawny shape hurled out of the crevice above the boy and crashed into him. Far'az had no time to move his spear into the lion's path. The roar had shaken him enough to disorient him, and now the lion was on him. They went down with a shriek and another roar.

Talon was stunned by the noise, and an enormous fear gripped his insides. He managed to draw the bow with shaky arms and look for an opening. It was an impossible shot. The two bodies were tangled in a struggling mass with dust concealing the details from him.

The lion was now right on top of Far'az and was holding him down, his teeth deep in his right shoulder, tearing at him with its claws. The shrieks and roars of both reverberated off the cliff walls. Talon had an overwhelming urge to run for his life.

Instead, he splashed across the stream on rubbery knees, pointing the bow at the writhing target, trying desperately to see if he could loose the arrow at the lion. He came right up to the entangled pair, who were quite oblivious of his presence. Giving a scream of his own, he braced his feet within a yard of the writhing, blood-covered pair, and loosed the arrow into the lion's back.

With a shrieking wail, it turned from its former victim and hurled itself on him. All Talon could do was to fall back and hold the bow in front of him as he stared into the gaping jaws of the maddened animal. The charging cat brushed the bow aside. For an instant, the slits of its eyes bored into his, and Talon knew he was staring into the eyes of death. He felt an enormous blow to his chest that bowled him over like a reed, then the lion was gone past him. With a yowling roar that seemed to shake the trees, it made for the stream, leapt it clumsily, landing heavily, then tore off into the clump of thick undergrowth fifty yards away, disappearing from view.

Talon was shaken and bleeding. His chest hurt where the lion had torn at him, but his concern was for Far'az, who was crying and moaning where the lion had left him. Talon clambered to his feet, watching the space where the lion had gone, then staggered over to the other boy.

His instinctive reaction was to make sure of his weapons, and he located the short spear that had been thrown aside when Far'az was down. His bow, however, was broken.

He knelt by his companion's side and gasped. The lion had bitten Far'az's right arm and shoulder with deep scours and had left deep claw marks on his neck and head, which were covered with blood.

The boy was aware of Talon, though, and roused himself enough to ask hesitantly through bleeding lips, "How is my arm? I can't feel it." His eyes showed their whites all around the irises. Dust and congealing blood made him look like a living corpse in the half-light.

"It is bleeding a lot," Talon gasped. "I have to stop the bleeding or you'll die."

Far'az nodded, he knew what Talon meant. "Take my head cloth and tie off the arm above the gash, use a rock under my arm to place pressure there," he croaked. "You have to do this quickly."

Talon looked round for the cloth, which had been torn off in the fray, and lifted up the boy's arm, tying it off high up against the shoulder with a small flat rock between the arm, and the cloth against the ribs. It stemmed the worst of the bleeding, but there were other wounds that needed to be addressed, and he knew it was just a matter of time before Far'az became unconscious from shock or the lion came back to finish them off.

With a speed born of desperation and fear, he dragged Far'az to the shelter of the cleft, praying that there would be no surprises to meet them when they got there. The effort exhausted Far'az, who groaned with agony at every move. Talon reasoned that it would give him a slight chance to prepare if the lion came back. He kept his weapons very close.

As they came panting and crying to the entrance, Talon made a cursory inspection of the recess and discovered it to be little more than an overhang with a rock in front of it, good protection from another attack. He pulled Far'az as far as he could under the overhang, making sure there was room for him to stand at the entrance if the need arose. It was very cramped in the confined space and stank of cat urine. By the time Talon had dragged Far'az in, he was panting and sweating profusely in the still air. There was a lot of blood over both of them from the move and their respective wounds.

Now Talon concentrated on the incisions the cat had left in Far'az's neck and head. Far'az would survive these if they could be cleaned, but he needed to be quick. However, some wounds were deep, especially in his arm. There was no question that Far'az would be unable to walk, but Talon could not leave him under any circumstances either. They were trapped.

He prayed that the others had heard the clamor and were running to see what it was all about. But as the evening wore on, he began to realize that they had gone too far. They were on their own until morning, as no one could track them in the dark. His own chest was beginning to stiffen and burn. The adrenaline was wearing off and exhaustion was creeping up on him. His mind exulted at their narrow escape, but he knew they were still in mortal danger and that his companion could die overnight.

He could still hear the muffled screams of the lion. It seemed to be moving away but he couldn't be sure. He wondered if it had been a mortal wound. In the panic and the struggle, he could not be sure what damage he might have inflicted. He hoped fervently it would go off somewhere and die. He broke out in a cold sweat as he contemplated their predicament.

They had to have water, so he hurriedly gathered their leather bags, and, emptying their contents onto the floor of the recess, he moved out with fearful caution to the stream. He carried the spear this time. There was nothing but the silence of the woods to greet him, not a bird sound of any kind, which set his hackles up.

He made the stream, however, and after filling the two pouches hastily, he scrambled back to the overhang. He knelt over his prone companion and poured some of the water from the pouches on him. Far'az gulped what he could, his parched, torn lips causing him to cry out. He began complaining of a lack of vision and the cold.

All the clothing they had was what they wore, so Talon took off his head cloth and wrapped Far'az around the neck and shoulders with that. Then he took off his over shirt and spread it over his companion. Shivering, he looked out at the dusk and wondered what would come first, the lion or help.

He gave a start when Far'az muttered.

"What did you say?" he asked.

"I was foolish to try on my own. Did you kill the lion?"

"No, but I did shoot it at very close range in the back. I did not kill it. I am sorry."

"A man with a bow cannot often kill a lion in one shot," Far'az grunted. "It usually takes many men with spears and bows. Are we protected here?"

Talon nodded in the gloom. "For the time being, but I pray that help comes before the lion returns, or another lion that has smelled the blood. There is much blood."

There was silence for a time.

"You did well... you saved my life... I am grateful. May Allah protect us both tonight," Far'az mumbled.

Talon said nothing. They still had to get out of this predicament before they could boast of anything.

As dusk came, it brought the cold. It settled into the glade and crept up to the two huddled forms in the cave. Talon tried unsuccessfully to get Far'az to eat some raisins, but Far'az was going into shock and could not be reached.

Knowing that a disaster was descending upon him with the silence of his companion, Talon lay alongside Far'az and tried to keep him warm. It helped a little, but they were soon shivering again as the cold crept into their bones.

The night was lit by a sliver of moon that left a faint light in the glade. Its cold light seemed to intensify the chill that he felt to be creeping into his very soul. His jaw ached with the chattering of his teeth.

As the night wore on, Talon was desperate to stay awake while his companion slept soundly from loss of blood and sheer exhaustion. He prayed to his former God and then to Allah with equal fervor, hoping one or the other would take time out for his sake. It comforted him not at all.

He started at every sound, imagining that the lion was at the entrance. His weary eyes were sore and gritty with fatigue and began to play tricks on him—seeing shadows where there were none, movement where there was none.

He heard sounds all around as the night life got under way and the little creatures went about their business, starting fearfully when a mouse scuttled over their legs, jerking round when he thought he heard the swish of motion in the dry grass outside their shelter. An owl hooted in the distance and later a small creature shrieked in its death struggle with its killer.

He kept shaking his head, tossing it from side to side and rubbing his eyes hard to wake himself up. He moved his limbs in the cramped space to ease them and wake them up, all the while feeling an overwhelming tiredness coming over him. His resistance finally left him, and he fell into a dream sleep full of monster lions and even larger Persian soldiers fighting together.

He woke with a start. How long had he been asleep? Hours, he knew, by the false dawn that was beginning to illuminate the glade. His panic mounted as he realized that he had betrayed them both by falling asleep. Turning to his companion, he found Far'az sleeping, his breath ragged, but otherwise safe.

It was almost dawn. Something had woken him. What? He didn't know. Far'az might have called out in his agonized dreams. Talon felt Far'az's brow. He felt hot, his forehead clammy with sweat.

Talon inspected the entrance to the cave, looking for warning signals. His nerves were jangling wildly as he considered what might be out there.

Far'az woke and gasped through parched lips, "Water, I must have water."

Talon checked the pouches. To his horror, there was no water left. It had all leaked away! He contemplated the awful task he was now faced with. He turned to Far'az to try to hush him and whispered, "There is no water; the pouches leaked. I will get water when there is more light."

"I am dying of thirst. You must get me some water," Far'az complained. He was becoming delirious and began to shout. Talon tried to quiet him, his fear of attracting the lion making him desperate, but he only partially succeeded when he whispered to Far'az that he thought the lion was still out there. In spite of the dawn chill, they were both sweating with apprehension or fever.

Light from the false dawn was gradually being replaced by the more substantial glow of dawn. Talon was desperate with worry and knew that the decision to go for water could not be put off much longer.

He began to gather his shredded courage and push aside his exhaustion. Taking up his spear and the two bags, he moved past Far'az to the entrance, the wound on his chest making movement painful. He wanted to make very sure that the coast was clear before venturing forth in this light.

He crawled with care through the entrance and stood up in its shadow. The light in the glade was faint but he could now make out the trunks of trees and the dark furrow of the stream, its gurgle the only sound he could detect. The rustling and chattering of the night animals had stopped. His mouth was dry as he moved over the dew-damp ground. Although he licked his lips, no moisture came to them.

He crept very cautiously toward the sound of the water. Feeling horribly exposed, he sidled across the grass, his eyes darting everywhere, every nerve screaming alarms. However, there was neither movement nor sound to drive him back into the cave in panic.

At last he came to the water's edge. His eyes swiveled to and fro to examine every shadow. He dipped the first bag into the water with his head up watching the far bank, then turned to watch the water pour into the bag.

There was a tiny sound, like a discreet cough. The terrible realization dawned on him even as he reacted—he was trapped. His head shot up and he twisted wildly toward the sound.

The creature exploded at him from across the stream. It flew over the intervening ground with a grunting roar, but its charge was ill coordinated, as though it were having trouble running. Talon spun around to face the attack with a scream of his own, his pouches forgotten, and the spear held at the ready.

He just had time to plant himself, feet apart, the spear up, before the animal hit him in the chest and drove him back into the stream. The two of them fell and landed in the water with a huge splash. Talon went under, fighting to get away from the huge cat that was clawing at him.

He came up choking and gasping for breath, water streaming from his eyes, expecting to be savaged by the teeth and claws of the great creature. He could not find his spear and began to babble with fright.

Then he became aware that nothing was attacking him, and as he regained his self-control, he looked around fearfully for the cat, to find that it had impaled itself on the spear and was quite dead, its weight on him lightened by the buoyancy of the water moving around them. It dawned on him that he was still alive but close to drowning, so he jerkily extricated himself from under the lion and crawled to the bank, where he vomited and retched until he was spent.

Gathering his wits, he looked back to the lion. It seemed enormous in the half-light. A hysterical laugh came welling up as he realized how lucky he had been. He felt like dancing and screaming with the wild emotion that erupted in his breast.

"I've killed it! I've killed it! I have killed a lion," he shrieked in the madness of his triumph and then kept repeating it as he gazed at his victim half floating in the stream.

He approached it with great care as though still expecting it to jump up and attack him. He reached down and seized a large paw, then used all his strength to haul the lion over onto its back. His spear jutted out of its chest; it had pierced the beast through the heart. He knew he had no idea where the spear had been pointed when the animal hit him during the attack, and again gave thanks. He pulled the spear out because he knew that until help arrived he must be armed.

In his weakened state, it was difficult to do so, but eventually the spear came out. He fell over backward into the freezing water again. This time it revived him, waking him up enough to realize that his leg hurt, as did a streak of pain along his jaw. He ignored them for the moment. He had duties to perform, and they were urgent.

He seized the pouches and filled them. Running now, he rushed to the cleft and called Far'az. "It's done. It's done! The lion is dead. Far'az, wake up. Wake up! The lion's dead," he babbled as he shook his companion awake.

Far'az opened his bloodshot eyes and looked up at him. "Water," he croaked, "water!"

Talon had to swallow his need to shout and control his impatience long enough to make sure Far'az had enough water, even returning to the stream to obtain more.

Far'az was much weaker. He had lost a lot of blood overnight. He was coherent, however, and listened while Talon rattled on about the lion and the last struggle in the stream.

He smiled weakly. "You are a warrior after all, Frank. Allah be praised he gave you strength. May he deliver us soon to our friends." He sighed wearily and sagged back.

Talon explained that he didn't think they could make it anywhere in the condition they were in, so he would try to leave a sign in the area to lead others to them. Far'az agreed that he was too weak to travel, but pressed Talon to go and find help. Talon pointed out that he could not leave him, as there was a real possibility that there could be other predators in the area. In the condition Far'az was in, a large rat could carry him off for dinner. Far'az gave a feeble grin at that.

Talon shared the last of the raisins and some nuts with Far'az, persuading him at last to eat. Then, having made sure his new friend was as comfortable as possible; he left to leave marks along their former trail.

He was not gone long, and when he came back, he concentrated on his own wounds. He had garnered a slash to the left cheek, and his chest wound was bleeding again. He felt stiff and sore, and his leg was seizing up from a new gash in his left thigh.

His weariness now came in waves. The excitement having worn off, he found it increasingly difficult to think with a clear head or move without pain. Finally, he staggered over to the cleft where Far'az was sleeping and fell to his knees, darkness coming in too fast to resist.

* * * * *

They found him there that noon, fallen across Far'az's feet in a deep sleep. The *rafiq* and Reza marveled at the sight that met them in the glade. The whole story was there for them to read.

Talon woke to Reza holding his head, trying to pour water into his mouth, but most of it seemed to be going into his nose. He came to, spluttering and choking, to see the *rafiq* and Reza stooped over them both, looking astonished and awed by what they had seen.

His first concern was Far'az. He struggled loose from Reza and turned to Far'az to find that he seemed comfortable, although very weak.

"He must be taken out and back to the castle, and we must hurry. Insha'Allah he will live if we are quick," the *rafiq* said. "We three are all there are to take him back. Can you manage to help?"

Talon sat up slowly. "Yes, Allah willing I can help," he said. "But we have to take the lion skin with us."

"We will skin it and leave it in a high tree," the *rafiq* said. His tone was stern but he was smiling. "It will be too heavy to bring with us as well as Far'az. He is in danger, and so are you. A lion claw wound is dangerous."

"You are right," Talon said. "We must get him back as soon as we can."

The *rafiq* gave Reza instructions to help him dress both the boys' wounds, using plenty of the icy water from the stream and cloth torn from their own attire. Talon tried to keep from yelling as the cold water was used to clean his wounds, gritting his teeth until his eyes watered, but try as he might, the pain still made him cry out. Far'az was too far gone to make much of a fuss over Reza's crude attentions.

Then they went over to the lion and looked at it. It lay in the undignified position that Talon had left it when he pulled the spear out. It was a female, and Talon was secretly glad it had not been a larger male. He regretted to see such a magnificent animal dead like this. It rested on its back, looking for all the world as though it were asleep and waiting to have its stomach scratched. Reza prodded it with his spear to test its deadness and then laid his spear aside and moved closer to feel and prod the dead animal with his hand. It was stiff with rigor mortis and soaked, but they managed to drag it to the bank and begin the task of stripping it of its skin and head. It was a gory task, and the work left them tired but satisfied, as this was a huge trophy that should not be left to the scavengers.

Reza climbed into a tall plane tree, and they passed the skin up to him, where he placed it high in a fork of the tree. Content that it was safe for later collection, he climbed down and joined the other two.

They left the glade with Far'az staggering between the *rafiq* and Reza while Talon took his turn to find the trail. Far'az was very weak from the loss of blood and half delirious by now. The *rafiq* was sure he had a fever, and this boded ill. Their sense of urgency was heightened by the knowledge that wounds of this kind could kill as surely as a sword thrust if not treated.

Talon lost count of time as they retraced their steps. He was unable to keep to the path in places. Where there was no path, he needed help from the already overworked Reza and the *rafiq*.

After what seemed to be many hours later, they emerged at the top of the woodland and were spotted by a rescue team that had come down from the pass to seek them.

The other boys and their *rafiq* covered the distance in a rush to find out what had happened. Their astonishment was evident in the awed looks they gave the members of the party, especially Talon. They were silent as they listened to the tale put forward by Reza, who embellished it shamelessly for the benefit of the audience. Talon, who was too exhausted to say anything, limped along in the group, nodding when prodded for confirmation.

Some rushed off back to the camp to obtain help and perhaps even transport. The rest of the group supported Talon and formed a cradle for Far'az as they struggled to make it up to the pass.

Before long they came over the hill, and there beneath them was the camp, and to Talon's joy he saw donkeys coming up the hill to greet them. He was sure he could not have made another step along the way.

Were it not folly, Spider like to spin
The thread of present Life away to win—
What? For ourselves, who know not if we shall
Breathe out the very Breath we now breathe in

— Omar Khayyam —

Chapter 7
Wounded

Talon knew very little of the nightlong journey back to the castle. They had passed a long afternoon at the camp waiting for the General to come with the men to take them back to Samiran. Talon had lapsed into a semi-conscious state. The litter he was carried on swayed and bumped all the way, but its rocking motion, combined with his utter exhaustion, helped to keep him in a deep sleep. Of the kind, Mahmud Esphandiary reflected as he watched the invalids, that only the very young can sleep.

The general drove the small party hard. They were all veterans of war, tough mountain men. They knew wounds and what could come of them if not treated quickly and well, so they understood the urgency—the boys had to be taken to a place where the wounds could be dressed. The group jogged most of the way, carrying their burdens along the sides of the mountain, down steep gullies and across racing streams, their sharp, thin features illuminated by the flickering torches carried by other runners. Their gasping breath left a thin mist behind them as they trotted along. The General rode alongside them, shouting encouragement whenever they stumbled or fell, driving them along with his will.

They came to the gates of the great castle of Samiran just as dawn was breaking. Its rays struck the dull-colored sides of the walls, sending each stone into sharp relief. The bearers were staggering with fatigue, wide-eyed and gasping for breath, their limbs cramped and bruised. The sentry had already alerted the guards, who rushed to the gates to open them.

Talon woke to the crash of the opening doors and the shouts of the men as they made their entry, but he felt feverish and dizzy. It was more comfortable to let the world go on without him. He hovered between sleep and waking as he was lifted up by someone with strong arms and carried along a passage, up some stairs, and then into a well-lighted room. As he was put down, he looked up and saw the General's rough-hewn features poised over him and realized the great man himself had carried him. He struggled to sit up, only to be pushed down by gentle hands into the soft coverings of the pallet he had been placed on.

"It is time to rest, young *shir*. You have no more lions to kill this day."

His rough voice was kind, quite unlike that which Talon had become accustomed to hearing. He stammered some confused words but relaxed, grateful not to have to do anything. He was feverish, and the room began to swim. He was dimly aware of the General's voice as he gave commands to the nurse Alaleh and another person as they bustled in with a jug of hot water and cloths to clean the wounds.

He was conscious enough to try to protest as he was undressed from his rags and bathed by the clucking servant. But as the sing-song words of praise and sympathy from the other person and Alaleh continued, along with the warmth of the cleaning cloths, he felt himself slipping, tumbling down into a long, dark tunnel that seemed to have no bottom.

The General had remained in the room long enough to take stock of the slashing wound across the boy's left breast and the rips along his leg. There was also the claw marks on the left side of his face as well. He knew that it would be touch and go whether the boy survived; the claws of a lion are full of carrion and carry infection that poisons the blood.

"You must care for him, Feza," he growled to the woman with Alaleh. "The boy must live."

"*Chash, Chash, Gorban*, we shall do our best," she clucked back. "But it may take the physician, if he is nearby, to be sure. The wounds are bad. They say he killed it all on his own... is it true, *Gorban*?"

"Yes, it is true."

"How brave. What a mighty warrior, and just a boy, a *ferengi* boy at that."

"He is a Frank," the General stated. "This young pup has courage." The general drew himself away from the window and headed for the door. "I shall instruct a messenger to bring the physician," he said as he made his way out to look at the other boy. Far'az was the least likely to make it through in time for the physician, but he would ensure that the boy got the best he could give him until then.

*****

Feza and Alaleh cleaned the wounds, and then Alaleh applied some ointments that smelled of herbs and sharp, clean grass. The boy, naked and asleep on the pallet, felt none of the pain that it would have inflicted had he been awake. Both Alaleh and Feza were glad for him.

After Alaleh left to attend to the other boy, Feza contemplated his form with sharp, dark eyes that peered out from under wrinkled brows. She observed a well-built young man in the making, his light skin obvious where his loincloth had covered him. Other than that, his lean, adolescent body was as brown as a nut, and but for the lighter, finer hair on his head, the sleeping boy could have been any mother's son from the Alborz mountains.

She had never been this close to him, but her sharp eyes had noted the long lashes and the startling green eyes. Those eyes! She nodded her wise old head as she laughed quietly to herself. They would beguile many a fair maiden if he lived long enough.

Talon dreamed that he was fighting two and then three lions, all of them snarling at him, trying to come into the cave where he and Far'az crouched. Far'az was telling him to go out and get water even while Talon was trying to keep the lions at bay. He tried to tell Far'az that the lions were in the way, but Far'az refused to help. This made Talon angry, so he turned on him only to find that there was a lion in his place, and it was coming straight at him. He felt a huge panic coming over him. With a scream of terror, he woke, thrashing and crying, struggling with the covers.

Hands held him down and spoke to him in a language he could not understand, and he was given a hot, brackish liquid to drink. He was bathed in sweat and trembling all over. His feverish brain told him he was not now in the cave but he still wanted water. His cracked lips sucked the cup dry and he mewled for more.

A woman's voice came to him as music. His body began to relax as she sang him a beautiful, rhythmic lullaby. He lapsed back into a restless sleep, his fingers picking at the end of the covers, before becoming unconscious again.

* * * * *

The physician who had come at the General's command had made the dangerous journey from Lamissar to Samiran in less than two days. The *ferengi* boy was delirious when he arrived. The poison had taken hold of him and the wounds stank. His leg, side, and face were all swollen and very red around the wounds. He was near death.

He and Feza cleaned the wounds again and again, forcing the boy to take medicine while they then applied more foul-smelling ointments to the open wounds. They would bandage the wounds again. Because the physician was a *hakim,* a physician who had taken his examinations from the *madrase* in Isfahan, he was skilled at sewing wide-open wounds, so he made sure that those were well sealed and then drained with a thin quill. After that, all they could do was to keep his body cool and pray that the poison had not gone too deep.

The physician had looked at the other boy and realized that he was too late, the mantle of death was on Far'az, and all he could do was to make the suffering less. The boy slipped away in the early hours of that first long night.

He had always found it curious that the young did not survive wounds of this nature and those of war as well as older men. How could it be that the young, with all the vigor of youth, could give up so easily? Perhaps they had not developed the stamina that it takes to recover from within. Or the meanness of nature, he decided. Perhaps that was what it was.

He gave the young Frank half a chance to pull out of this fever, although his wounds were nowhere near as serious as Far'az's had been. Nonetheless, a wound from a lion claw that ran deep was serious at any time.

The General, and even the Agha Khan, often asked after the boy, the General coming to stand over him and stare at the gasping, sweating boy as he raved in his fevers.

* * * * *

The physician was good at his profession. Farj'an Nazeri was from Cairo. He had fled to Persia because he, like the Ismaili, was a Nizirite, and times were unsafe for their kind in Egypt. Trained as a physician in Isfahan by the best in the Muslim world, he knew his craft well.

He knew how inadequate the tools of his trade were against infections of the blood, and so he worried. A learned man, he took his trade seriously and was innovative; he thanked his teachers in Isfahan for that. They had drummed into him that Allah helped if you used your skills to the maximum and that it did little good to just pray, though he knew that prayer was part of the treatment, so he encouraged Feza to put in a good word for the boy during her prayer times.

What is so important about this youngster? the physician wondered. He had heard that the boy had killed a lion on his own while attempting to save the life of the other. That was brave, but there seemed to be more. Well, all they could do was to hope that Allah was watching over this one, even if he was an infidel. He had heard that there was also a priest from the Christian faith here in Samiran. This made the whole thing even more intriguing. What was a priest doing here in the mountain fastness of Samiran? The wise and infinitely devious Agha Khan was up to something.

Farj'an Nazeri was a faithful follower of the Khan, but he was also intelligent, and now his curiosity was aroused. He resolved to stay, if he could, and meet the priest, if just to hear about the country from which he came. If the priest was a learned man, he might hear from him of some crumbs of Western philosophy.

It had been a long time since Farj'an had had this type of conversation, other than with the Khan himself. However, the Khan was forever taking care of his domains and was involved in the politics of the empire and the wars over in the Holy Lands, so he had little time for casual discussion with the physician.

The Physician distrusted the Khan's uncle enough to try to give him a wide berth when he was at Lamissar Castle, whence he had just come; Arash Khan was a devious and intriguing man who played everyone against one another at every opportunity. Farj'an hoped he would not run into him here at Samiran.

He came out of his reverie in time to help the indefatigable Feza calm the boy for the hundredth time and to assist with the drink. He gave her a tired smile. "*Khanom* Feza, you are a good nurse. Can you hold out for a few more hours? The fever will either break before daylight or we will lose him."

Feza peered back at him from under wizened brows. "Yes, yes, *Gorban Hakim.* I can stay. Would you send Alaleh to help me?"

He nodded his acknowledgment and left quietly, closing the door behind him. He made his way down the corridor and came to the head of the stairs but could not pass, as there was someone sitting on the top stair blocking his way. In the dim light coming from the guttering torch back down the passage, he could just make out the features of the thickset form.

He made to speak, but the form rose and turned to him. In the half-light, he made out the drawn, haunted features of a man in what appeared to be a ragged robe. The physician could make out the beard and once shaven tonsure. The man spoke quickly, in a low voice. "Sir, I think you are the physician. You have been with the boy. Please, I beg of you, tell me how he is."

It was the priest, Farj'an realized. The Farsi was good, but the accent gave him away, and the manner of addressing him was rude, but he made allowance for the man's concern.

"It is in Allah's hands now. I have done all I can for the boy," he said, his tone brusque, but not unkind. There was a sigh of resignation from the man and he clasped his hands together. The physician added, "He is strong and healthy. There is a good chance. You are the priest I have heard about. What do you do here so far from home?"

"You are right, *Gorban* Doctor. I am sorry I was so rude. But I am concerned for the boy. Yes, I am, was, a priest. Now I am a prisoner here. I grew up with the name Gerard, but it was changed to the name of one of the saints when I become part of the order. I am known as Jean de Loche, for that is where I come from, a town in France."

Jean realized he was babbling, so he quieted and waited respectfully for the physician to continue.

Instead, the physician reached out a long-fingered hand and turned him around, then pushed him down the stairs with his hand still on his shoulder. "I need some fresh air," he stated. "Come with me to the courtyard, and perhaps we can talk some more."

Later, Jean was to tell Talon of the encounter and the unexpected behavior of the physician.

They went down the stairs to the ground floor, then out of the building into the cool air. The physician breathed deeply. “Are you an educated man, Jean de Loche? Or are you another one of those cant-dribbling fools who set themselves up to lord it over even stupider people in order to gain some prestige?”

Jean turned to him in the gloom. “Sir, I would not say I was an educated man, because such a man is wise beyond most men, and that I am not. I do, however, enjoy to learn, and languages give me pleasure, not least because as each new language becomes familiar, so then too do the peoples who speak it. If you talk of mathematics, I do not possess great skills, rather admiring from afar those who use it effortlessly and understand its mysteries.” He stopped, feeling he might have said too much. He was afraid of being disrespectful.

But the physician’s hawk-like face broke into a tired smile and he said, “I will try to stay longer than I intended so that we might speak more of our people. You can tell me of yours and I will tell you of mine. Go now and rest. There is not much either of us can do for Talon at the moment. I will summon you if I need you or if there is a change in the boy.”

“Thank you, sir, thank you for coming to see the boy and for speaking to me. May God protect you, *Gorban Hakim.*”

Jean de Loch bowed and shuffled off to the other side of the compound, leaving the physician standing in the darkness.

“Well, I would not have come, but I was summoned,” he remarked to himself. “But this is becoming more and more interesting. I will stay to discover some answers.” He turned back to the building and made his way to the rooms that had been set-aside for him during his stay.

* * * * *

The fever broke at dawn the next day, and the exhausted boy slept a deep, healing sleep that meant his recovery was assured. Feza stayed with him, although she had not slept for three days except to catnap by his pallet. The physician departed to give the news to the Agha Khan and the General, and then to get some sleep himself, after he passed word to the priest that the boy was recovering.

It was during this time that there was a soft knock on the door of the chamber. Feza almost didn’t hear it. She struggled out of her sleep, rubbed her gritty eyes, and opened the door to a surprise visitor. Feza was wide-awake in an instant, her features a mixture of pleasure at seeing who it was and concern at the same time. There was Rav'an, still in her nightclothes, barefoot and carrying a jug of water, some *nan* and a small bowl of yogurt.

"My mistress, what in the name of all the spirits are you doing here?" she exclaimed in a heavy whisper.

"I thought you might be hungry, Feza, my dear old thing." Rav'an grinned and slipped into the room before Feza could stop her.

Feza was worried. "Rav'an, my love, my dove, you should not be here, you will catch your death of cold. Besides, if anyone finds out you are here, it will be my head. Then what?" She wrung her hands and grimaced, as she did when agitated. It had the effect of making her already wrinkled face more so. She looked like some ancient little gnome dancing on the end of some strings.

Rav'an was not above enjoying the agitation, but now she wanted to calm her, so she whispered back, "Don't worry, Feza. I only came for an instant. Perhaps I could see the young warrior before I go? Can I see him? How is he? Will he die?"

"I cannot answer all the questions at once," harrumphed the disconcerted Feza. "But yes, he is now out of danger and is sleeping. You must not disturb him. Oh, if someone comes it will be the end of me," she wailed in a husky whisper.

"Please, please, let me see him, I will leave immediately." Rav'an had already crossed the room and was standing over the pallet.

The boy lay on his back, the blanket half off, cast off in his sleep. Rav'an gazed down at him, noting the fine features and the hairless body of the boy. The bandages covering the wounds were tight round his chest. Her eyes traveled down to his stomach, and she gave a little gasp, as the blanket did not cover him well at all. His manhood was half exposed. She flushed as she looked, as it was the first time she had ever seen a naked man or boy. She continued to stare, absorbed by the sleeping figure.

Talon stirred; perhaps there was some kind of instinct that made him open his eyes. Without realizing it, he looked directly into Rav'an's eyes. She gasped and her hand flew to her mouth. His eyes were as green as the mountain grasses. They stared straight into her; but he closed them again and went back to sleep without making a sound.

She turned to Feza, to see that woman gazing back with a shrewd look of understanding and amusement in her dark, beady eyes. Abruptly, she laughed her croaking laugh.

"My mistress, this will not be the last time you see a naked man," she prophesied through her laughter. "Men call it all sorts of names, their spears, or their swords, but he didn't kill the lion with that one, I can tell you." She shook with laughter, tears of mirth coursing down her cheeks.

Rav'an glared at her, her face red with embarrassment, but she had to grin, as Feza in a laughing fit was comical. The tiny old nurse was holding her sides, her toothless mouth wide open as she laughed.

"Oh, Feza, stop it," she hissed. "You go too far." But she, too, was beginning to laugh, her hand in front of her mouth to stifle any sound. The snort she gave sent Feza off into another fit of giggles. They stood there shaking silently together until at last Feza recovered herself enough to wipe her eyes and to issue an order.

"Go... go. Now you must go, my dove. If he wakes or someone comes, I will be killed for letting you in. Go, my little sparrow. I will come to you later and tell you all."

Rav'an hugged her, then slipped out the door and sped down the passage.

Later came another knock on the door, far more peremptory. Once again, Feza woke, and grumbling under her breath she unlocked the door again. This time it was the General.

"Greetings, Feza, how is the patient?" he asked, his tone diffident. He was quite aware of how long she had been in the room and had sympathy for her dedication.

"The boy will live, *Gorban Timsar*," she said. "If we all leave him in peace to recover," she added.

The General said nothing. He was used to Feza and her liberties with her seniors, but respected her devotion to his master's young sister. He was sure the boy could not have had a better nurse.

He crossed the room and stared down at Talon. He was relieved that the young man would make it after all. They had recovered the lion skin and head. It was a magnificent animal, one that had gained a reputation among the shepherds of that region for killing their sheep and goats. By all accounts, it must have been a battle to see. The animal was heavier by far than the boy and must have been a daunting adversary.

He saw that the redness was still around the wounds but also noted that the smell was gone. He knew the dreadful stink that comes with the wounds that are going bad, spelling death to those who knew the signs. Talon's breathing was regular and even, the sleep deep, all good signs. He reached forward to move the blanket over the boy, then caught himself and turned to Feza.

"He is cold, you should cover him. It is still a dangerous period." He spoke more sharply than he intended, but Feza just nodded and moved to do so. The General left her to her duties. She watched him as he left, a curious look in her eyes. There was not very much that escaped her notice.

Talon woke to a bright day. The sun was high in the sky and its rays penetrated the room. Motes of dust danced in the rays of light that lanced across the room and illuminated the rich carpet on the polished wood floor. He could hear sounds coming up from the courtyard, women gossiping and the occasional tinkle of laughter as they went about their business. He could hear the clang of the blacksmith's hammer beating iron into shape on his anvil. The bleat of a goat and the crowing of a rooster all lent an air of normalcy to the waking. He listened to all the bustling sounds of the residents of a castle courtyard at their daily work.

He felt rested but very weak, and when he tried to sit up his chest and leg hurt so badly he groaned and sagged back onto the bed. Besides these injuries and the flame on his cheek, his head throbbed and his limbs ached. nevertheless, he had a desperate need to get up for another reason and felt that unless he did, there was going to be a disaster that would be too shameful to bear.

He prepared to try again, but as he looked up, he was startled to see, peering down at him, the wizened face of a tiny woman. Her dark, beady eyes peered out from under low brows amid a mass of wrinkles. He was convinced that he had fallen into the clutches of a witch. He shrank back into the pallet and stared back; his instinctive reaction was to perform the sign of the cross.

To his horror, she opened her mouth and displayed almost toothless gums in what seemed to be an attempt to smile at him. He gave back a tentative smile and was rewarded with a husky rattle as she said, "Welcome back, young warrior. Are you ready to kill more lions today?"

This evoked a nervous smile from him that turned quickly to a groan as his wounds reminded him of his condition. He looked down at himself to discover the reason for the pain. His whole chest was bandaged and felt very sore. His left leg was also bandaged.

"I am Feza. You have been in fever for many days."

His eyes widened, then he asked, "How is Far'az? Is... is he well? He was badly wounded."

Feza looked at him. "He has died, young warrior. Allah in his infinite mercy has taken him. His wounds were very bad and he did not come out of the fever. We did all we could for him. You had Allah's protection and were permitted to live." She patted his shoulder with her bird-like hand in a kindly manner. "You have been very brave. They will talk about your feat for many generations."

He was silent; she could see that he was disturbed by a mixture of emotions and was trying to master them even in his distress. His composure struck her kind nature.

Then he said politely, "*Khanom* Feza, I need to go, and if I do not I will make a mess."

She gave a cackle of laughter and the light came back into the room. "Of course, young man, I will get a pot. You are confined to the bed for now. Do not try to walk about."

She brought him a pot and then helped him sit up. She was surprisingly strong for such a little person. He was weak and went giddy as he came upright. She steadied him, and then, sensing his embarrassment, gave him the pot and went off to tidy things in the other part of the room. Talon had thought he was going to burst. The relief was enormous, and now he had time to take stock of the room.

It was not the same kind of room he shared with the other boys. This one, although spare, was far more richly laid out than the barracks. There was a single large window, wide open, through which came a light breeze and all the sounds of a bustling courtyard. He longed to go to the window and look out.

The pallet upon which he was lying was simple, but the carpets on the floor were fine, with rich colors. There were even drapes on the sides of the window, and a low, beautifully carved table nearby. The walls were for the most part bare, but the wall opposite his end of the room was decorated with elegant paintings of men in rich garments upon horses, hunting deer.

He noted with some surprise that there were hounds in the painting as well. This absorbed him while Feza bustled about the room. Finally, she said, "I will go and fetch you some food. I imagine you are hungry."

It was not a question, simply a statement. He nodded, then as though it had been waiting for him to think of it, his stomach began to clamor for attention. He was hungry beyond words and could barely restrain himself from begging her to hurry back. She left him thinking of all kinds of food and wondering if he would die of hunger before she came back.

It was while she was away that the physician came quietly into the room. Talon was lost in the hunting scene, memories of his father's hunts coming back to him while he gazed at the picture, so he did not register the entrance of that tall, elegantly dressed man wearing colorful clothes and an expensive turban until he was almost at the bed. Talon started with surprise and peered up at the newcomer. The man spoke slowly with a quiet but clear voice.

"You seem to be recovering, young man. I am the doctor." He took Talon's wrist firmly in a dry, cool hand and placed his thumb on the pulse.

Talon was mystified as to what he was doing, but was now used to waiting before he said or did anything rash. Instead, he murmured a polite greeting, then waited until the man released his wrist. The physician lifted the blanket off his chest and, raising the bandages, inspected the wound.

After this, he sat Talon up, placed his ear to Talon's back, and seemed to be listening carefully to his breathing. After a couple of minutes, he seemed satisfied and lifted his head. He then made an equally careful inspection of the wound on the boy's leg and looked closely at the slash on his face. He looked at the edges of the wounds, clucking to himself, and then sat back onto the edge of the pallet. The only sound in the room was his nasal breathing.

"You do not seem to be in so much danger now," he announced. "We have to keep the bandages on tight to close the wounds. You will stay here and rest for a few more days, and then we must find a quiet place for you to let the scars heal. The wounds can still get infected."

Talon nodded and lay back with relief; the medical inspection had tired him. Farj'an continued.

"One day you must tell me about the adventure. In the meantime, I shall come to see you as often as I am able to. There is a priest down in the courtyard who is asking about you as well. I shall send him up after the General has come to see you. You appear to have caused quite a stir here in Samiran."

Talon looked up at the sharp features and into the dark, intelligent, not unkind eyes of the man.

"May Allah bless you for helping me to recover, *Gorban*," he said hoarsely. He was very thirsty and his throat was dry.

"You can thank Allah yourself, but I would thank Feza in person when she comes back," said the physician dryly. "She, more than I, is responsible for your recovery.

"Now," he continued briskly, "you are to stay in bed until I allow you to get out of it. You are to eat well, drink a lot of tea, and, Allah willing, you will be out of this bed in about a week."

Talon nodded obediently.

"Yes, *Gorban* Doctor. As you command"

Farj'an glanced sharply at the boy. This was the kind of response that he heard from the students and trainees when he was addressing them. Was the boy being trained with them? He decided that it would be interesting to discover more, just to assuage his own curiosity. He got up and left the room with a swish of his long robes.

Talon lay back. So, the great Timsar was going to come and see him? He remembered having been filthy and ragged after his struggle with the lion, but someone had bathed him. Still, his long hair was matted. Since he had been in Samiran, he had learned the elements of hygiene from his instructors, all quite new to one from a castle in the Frankish world. Now he itched and yearned for a dip into a cold mountain stream!

He did not have long to wait in solitude. Feza came tramping in, followed by a maid who was agog to see him, and kept staring over at him as they prepared the food they had brought. Talon's mouth began to salivate at the delicious aroma coming from the two bowls. One was of mutton stew, and the other would be yogurt and cucumber. But first, Feza came over with a small cup of tea and helped him to drink it. He was desperately thirsty, so she gave him another, admonishing him to drink slowly.

Then the women propped him up with a cushion and gave him the small earthen bowl of stew and some *nan*. Feza supervised his eating. He was quite weak, so he had to take it one spoonful at a time with a little help. However, he managed to eat everything and then eased himself back onto the cushion, exhausted.

All the while the other maid had been goggling at him and asking Feza all sorts of questions in Farsi too rapid for him to follow. In the end, Feza lost patience with the young maid and drove her out of the room with several sharp commands.

She left without rancor, looking over her shoulder at the boy in the bed and smiling when he glanced up at her. Feza gave a grunt of impatience. The recovery of this young man was going to exhaust her more than his sickness, she thought to herself.

Even so, he was a beautiful boy, she reflected as he lay back, too tired to eat more *nan*. She forced another cup of tea into him and then pulled the covers back over his chest and let him sleep. He had dropped off almost immediately after the teacup had been withdrawn.

Talon slept for the rest of the day, unaware that the general had come back to see if he was capable of talking, or that the physician had made another appearance and checked his pulse again. Farj'an was more concerned now about any secondary sickness that might come about. He had known men who seemed to get over their direct wounds only to die from a chest complaint.

While little was known at the time as to why this was, he felt that it might have something to do with the weakness of the patient after the fight to survive the primary illness. He ordered Feza to ensure that while the windows were to be kept open during the day, the shutters should be closed at night and the boy kept warm at all times.

On the second day, the general visited Talon in the morning. The great man came in and seemed to fill the small room with his presence. Feza, who had been puttering about, made respectful obeisance to him and then left. Talon tried to get out of bed to pay his respects to the general, who waved him firmly back.

"Lie down, young man. You are not going to leave the bed until the physician says that you can," he growled.

The general sat cross-legged on a large cushion nearby and demanded a full accounting of the incident with the lion in Talon's own words. Talon, in his halting Farsi, told all he remembered from the time they had discovered the tracks, to the nightmare of the first fight, and then to the final struggle in the stream bed.

He omitted the details of the long night of terror and the crawling fear he had felt when he finally had to go out of the cave, but the general could read between the lines and kept his face impassive behind his large mustache. He was impressed with the matter-of-fact manner in which the young boy delivered the story. He would not have heard it told as simply by others, he decided. There would have been much in the way of elaborate addition had it come from one of the boy's companions.

When Talon came to the point where they were rescued, his words dried up and he sat there looking down at the bedclothes. There was a long silence as the general digested the story and looked keenly at the boy. Then, as though answering an unspoken question, he said, "You did well, young Frank. There is only so much a man can do for his comrades. After that, it's in Allah's hands." He was glad the boy responded with a nod. He looked up at the general and addressed him politely.

"We are all in the hands of Allah."

Mahmud got to his feet. He towered over the boy lying in the bed.

"It is time for me to leave. I shall discuss your condition with the physician, and we shall see about getting you better as quickly as possible." He tramped to the door and marched out past Feza, who was hovering in the corridor.

"I entrust his health to you, Feza," he growled as he left.

Feza went down to the kitchens and shouted for the maid to come and help her get the melon and fruit, as well as a little soup and bread together to take to the boy. Then, after she had ministered to him, she told him to go to sleep and not to make any noise. She, Feza, was going to sleep on the floor near to the door. The maid was banished with a glare from the formidable little woman, and peace settled over the room.

The night sounds began to come into the room with the shafts of moonlight through the panels of the shutters. Talon wondered how long he would be kept in this room. He didn't mind too much, but his restless body was not going to let him lie around for too long. He fell to speculating on his future but soon fell asleep, wondering where Jean might be.

The next day the physician summoned Jean away from his work, which at that time was menial, and told him to come with him to see the boy. They climbed the stairs together, then Farj'an went in ahead of Jean to carry out his usual thorough inspection of the boy's wounds and to ascertain that there was no temperature to worry about. Then he motioned Jean to enter.

The delight on Talon's face was a picture. He grinned hugely, wincing at the pain of the slash by his jaw. His pleasure at seeing Jean was warming to the priest, who, for his part, was hard-put not to rush over and hug the life out of him. Only the presence of the doctor inhibited the two from a more demonstrable reunion. Talon called over in French,

"Father, I see you. You have come at last!"

Jean responded in kind. "My son, you seem well. I have been granted permission by the kind doctor to come and see you!"

Then they collected themselves, and Jean, having apologized to the physician for their rudeness, asked permission to stay for a while. Farj'an told him that he could come each morning at this time and spend one hour with the boy for the time being, and maybe more later if things improved.

He left, with both of them voicing their thanks as elaborately as they could in their limited Farsi. Then Jean sat on the floor in front of Talon and said, "Now you have to tell me all about the battle with the lion. I've heard almost nothing; they all talk about it, but not to me!"

Talon sighed. "All right, Father, I will," he said, "but I've told the story so often that it's worn out!"

"No, my son, you cannot wear out a story like this. It can only get better with the telling! Now, start at the beginning."

* * * * *

"When he is up and out of bed, he should not join the others for at least a month. His wounds are deep and will take a long time to heal. That is a dangerous time, and he should be watched carefully."

The General observed the physician for a moment. He agreed with the doctor but did not know where he was going with this. "Go on," he said carefully.

"You have a garden here in Samiran where he can recuperate during this time until he can be sent back to the training, do you not, *Timsar*?"

"Yes, there is a garden. It is for my exclusive use and, of course, the Khan and his sister, should they wish to enjoy it while here in the castle." There was a slight pause. "Do you really think a garden would be beneficial?" he asked, skeptically.

"It would be better than the stables or the courtyard. He will forget the wounds if he is with his friends, and they will open and become infected. If we can force his rest when he is on his feet, it would be for the better."

"Very well, my friend, you have never advised me ill. If you feel it is important, it shall be so. Besides, I suppose he deserves some reward for his bravery. Did you see the size of that animal?" The General smiled at his friend. "Send him back to his instructors as soon as you can."

Farj'an decided to probe. "What exactly is he being trained for, general?"

The general looked back at him over the edge of his teacup. His answer was enigmatic. "The master has commanded it to be so."

The physician had to be content with that for the time being.

When you and I behind the Veil are past,
Oh but the long, long while the World will last
Which of our Coming and Departure heeds
As much as Ocean of a pebble-cast.

— Omar Khayyam —

Chapter 8
The Garden

Talon spent the first day in the garden feeling isolated and alone, then he began to enjoy the peaceful surroundings. He could still hear the activity of the large castle all around, but somehow this place provided an oasis of calm. Although he still felt some twinges of conscience at abandoning Jean de Loche, he knew that Jean could lose himself in the books and language studies without any trouble.

He found that being on his own in the relative quiet of the garden was restful, although a bit boring after all the activity he'd become used to in the course of a day with the *rafiqi*. After the intense training schedule, this was almost too quiet for a young and restless boy. He fidgeted, he felt restless, and because he was bored, his eyes often closed involuntarily as he struggled with the rules of grammar Jemal Shahigan had given him.

Jemal had also given him the works of Omar Khayyam to study. He had quite enjoyed that, as the verses talked a lot about wine and women, neither of which he knew much about.

The garden was very small but well designed to provide privacy. The paths wound around in elaborate curves and loops, with random niches where small shrubs and trees were placed strategically here and there. There were tall grasses growing around the roots of the trees, providing even more cover, although at this time of year they were dry and brown from the summer heat. Insects rasped and sang in the heat of the afternoon, while the occasional butterfly traveled from shrub to tree. There were few birds in this garden, some very shy sparrows, but otherwise not much life to disturb the heat-filled air.

It was on the third day that he noticed something. It was while he was sitting in a tiny recess enjoying the late afternoon sunlight. He had been watching it play on the dark, shiny leaves on the small lemon tree beside him, when he realized he was being observed.

He tensed while his eyes wandered carefully around the limited view permitted by the low trees and shrubs that surrounded the recess he was sitting in. Nothing stirred, and he almost missed it; then a hound's head moved. The rest of its lean body was almost hidden by the foliage. Its eyes were fixed on him, observing him in total silence and without fear. Indeed, he felt as though he were being challenged for being in the garden. Its gaze implied a certain self-possession that disturbed him.

He had not been this close to a hound since his capture, and he caught his breath as he watched the graceful animal. It was almost the color of the sunburnt grass, with flecks of copper in its coloring. This allowed it to blend with its surroundings, which was why he had not seen it at first. He knew that if it had not moved its head he would have missed it, the animal had been so quiet and still.

It must have heard some sound, for it turned its head away from him. The animal wagged its tail, but it still made no sound. There came a light voice from back along the path, which the hound greeted with a whine before turning back to watch Talon again.

On hearing the voice, Talon drew back into his recess. He had not expected company, least of all a female. He wished he was back with the other boys, away from this place. This was unexpected and unwelcome.

He was still wondering what to do, sitting awkwardly on the stone bench, when a young girl came into the tiny clearing. At first she did not see him, being preoccupied with the hound, speaking to it in soft tones as though it were a dear friend rather than a dog.

With a start, she noticed him and stepped back, her hand flying to her veil to pull it across her face. But then she stopped herself and regained her composure, stood still and regarded him with huge, gray eyes that showed no fear; rather, they regarded him with an aloof gaze and some arrogance that resembled that of the hound.

Talon was struck by her slim form but noticed that she was quite tall compared to other girls he had seen here at the castle. Her body was maturing; the swell of her budding breasts hard to hide under the light clothing she wore.

His gaze moved with a will of its own, from bewitching gray eyes set wide in an oval face with high cheekbones and a well-formed nose, down her exposed throat to the rise of her breasts. His eyes traveled on down to her tiny, delicate feet encased in ornate sandals, then back up past impossibly slim ankles. He took in the fine cloth of the skirt and the almost transparent veil, back up to the perfect oval of her face surrounded by a dense cloud of black hair that was so long it went down to her waist.

He flushed with embarrassment when he realized he was staring. He forced himself to look her in the eyes. He was rewarded with a cold, haughty look that indicated displeasure at being stared at thus and told him to keep his distance, but there was a curiosity there as well.

She spoke, or rather demanded, "What are you doing here? This is my garden." Her tone was sharp and peremptory.

"I-I was put here... to-to recover, by the General," he got out, his voice cracking. He coughed and started again, forcing his voice to come under control. "I was sent here by General Esphandiary, who said I should spend a few days here. The physician also said that I was to come here every day," he added.

There was silence while she digested this and observed him at the same time. "This is my brother's garden, and that has never been done before." Her voice, although sharp with evident annoyance at the intrusion in her favorite place, was clear and well modulated.

Talon scrambled to his feet and then as quickly began to bow to her. Looking up from his obeisance, he caught her regarding him with cool amusement. He flushed red under his tan.

"My lady?"

"Well? What is your name?"

"It is Talon de Gilles," he responded just as haughtily.

In spite of himself and the rigorous training he had received in obedience at the hands of the instructors, he was irked at the arrogance of this slip of a girl, no matter that she might be who he feared her to be, the sister of the master himself. He was acutely aware that he could say the wrong thing and get into very serious trouble if he did not take care. So he stood still, no longer meeting her eyes, awaiting developments.

The girl shrugged her slim shoulders, annoying him further. “Here you belong to my brother, so you are nothing anymore. You are a slave and this garden is mine. You are in my favorite place.”

“I am sorry, my lady, I did not know. I shall leave.” Talon was ready to do anything to get out of there. He turned to pick up his books.

“You will leave when I permit it. I wish to hear more of you.” She lifted her chin and glared down her pretty nose at him.

He was furious with humiliation at her tone, mortified that he was quite powerless to respond as he would have wished to such rudeness. To her, he was just another slave, but he could not bring himself to accept it that easily. It took a tremendous effort of will for him to turn round and present a polite face to her. All the same his feelings were easy to read, and they stood facing each other, separated by just a few feet, a silent clash of wills taking place. He was the first to put a stop to it, knowing he was risking too much by throwing his pride in her face.

“What would my lady wish to know about me?” he ground out, his voice cold, his eyes not wavering from hers.

Rav’an could see his closed expression and realized that she would get nothing out of him unless she modified her tone. She was struck by the boy’s demeanor. She saw the same boy she had seen on the pallet, feverish and exhausted, now standing in front of her, unfazed by her position and rank, or so it seemed.

She may have been young, but she owned some of her brother’s perception, which gave her the ability to read people well. She was struck by the battle she could see going on with his emotions, pride, and rage wrestling with obedience to her commands. He would not be easy to bully with words. She was unused to being met head on. It was new, but it didn’t anger her as it might have had it been anyone else.

Now that he was better and the gauntness of the illness almost gone, she could see the fine bones of his young frame. He was muscular under the loose, single robe he wore. The even cut of his features and the quiet way he stood gave her the feeling that there was an inner strength far beyond the years of this *ferengi* youth. She changed tack, her voice taking on a more enquiring tone.

“Were you once a lord?”

He shook his head, accepting the diversion. "I am... I was going to be a knight. My father was the lord of his castle, and I am his only son."

"You speak Farsi quite well for a *ferengi.* I also know why you're here. You killed the lion and were wounded."

"Yes. And it killed my companion."

"Was he your friend?"

"No. But I wanted to save him, and I did not."

There was a short silence.

"No one is blaming you except yourself for that. Allah the all powerful takes what he wishes when he wishes."

Silence ensued as the two of them reflected on her words and continued to inspect each other. By this time, neither was looking the other in the eye, but rather around each other. They were learning a language neither understood yet; their senses were doing the evaluation rather than the more direct method of looking and speaking, making both feel unbalanced and awkward.

Rav'an felt herself beginning to flush. She tried to divert herself with, "Tell me of your father's castle."

Talon released a breath he didn't realize he'd been holding. He was grateful for the invitation and responded in kind. "It is not as large as Samiran and is called Fort Sur Mont. It is not far from Lake Tiberius."

The long, difficult moment had passed. She looked at his books. "You can read? We have many books in my brother's library. They are in Arabic and Farsi, and many are written by our poets. Do you like poetry?"

Her questions were coming too fast for him to answer in time. He smiled at her then, and she liked what she saw.

"I cannot read Arabic yet, just some Farsi, but I do know of some of your poets from my teacher."

She returned a tentative smile of her own. Her hand strayed to the head of the ever present and still watching hound that had first discovered him. It nuzzled her hand, smiled with its almond eyes, and gave an affectionate groan. Then another came forward as though to say, "Me, too," and pushed at her robes. She laughed then, and stooping, took its head in both hands and shook it gently from side to side. It also made odd little groans of pleasure, its tail wagging. She looked up at Talon, who stood awkwardly, taking in the intimate exchange with wide-eyed interest.

Again she seemed to decide something, because after a tiny pause she asked, "Do you like salukis?"

"Please excuse me, my lady, what did you call them?"

"They are salukis. My brother was given them as a gift from one of the great sheiks of the deserts of Arabia, south of Baghdad. They are hunting hounds. They are the fleetest dogs in the world."

"They are beautiful," he said, and she could see he meant it.

On impulse, she bent over the smaller one, "Badura, this is Talon the Frank, who killed the lion." She indicated Talon with a wave of one elegant hand, while pushing the dog toward him with the other.

Badura seemed to understand, for she moved two paces closer to him, looking straight at him as though to say, "I see you."

Talon dropped to a respectful crouch, upon which the hound, with a quick look back at Rav'an, moved forward again to let him touch her. He knew hounds from his former life, so his respectful approach gained him approval with all three of his new acquaintances. The other, larger animal, also came forward to receive his homage.

"This is Djahi. He is the boy, and she is the girl."

Talon talked to them in French in a very low voice, to which they both responded with a cautious wagging of their tails and much sniffing with wet noses, but they did not lick him. He knew where to rub and where to stroke, so it was not long before they appeared to accept him. He was struck by their seeming lack of smell. Absent was the rank stink of the hounds he had been used to. In its place was a more pleasing scent. It seemed to be natural; but he thought it must be because she bathed them and spoiled them with scents. He deemed it wiser not to make his thoughts known about that.

"What is that language you are speaking to them? You seem to have a way with them. They are not at all easy to make friends with."

Looking up at her, he said, "It is French, my lady. I love hounds, and these are the finest I have ever seen."

She smiled shyly at the compliment. "You may call me Rav'an, at least when we are alone. You will come here tomorrow?"

He stood, hesitated, and then said, "If you permit it, my lady."

"Then we may meet again. Badoo, Djahi, come, it is time to go," she called. The two hounds left Talon to come over to her side once more. She turned to leave, glancing over her shoulder at him one last time. She seemed quite unconscious of her affect on him as she did so. Her look left him feeling stunned.

"May God protect you, my lady... er, Rav'an," he croaked.

Then she was gone, the hounds crowding along with her. The three of them disappeared from his view, like a mirage, leaving behind the memory and a tantalizing scent of fine perfume in the air.

He sat down hard on the bench, wincing as his leg wound twitched. His heart banged away in his rib cage; there was a bemused look on his face, and his mind roiled with turmoil trying to recall every detail of the exchange, of her face, her figure, and the words she spoke, all of it.

His felt light-headed. He could not understand his feelings; there was just confusion. He still smarted with humiliation at her earlier tone, but the warmth of her later attitude had eased that. Whichever way he looked at it, there was no doubt in his mind this girl had affected him.

He sat for a long time, motionless, heedless of the hot stone, reliving the moment. Then he shook his head. It could not be so. He was just a slave to the 'Assassin order and she had no place in his life, he less in hers. It would be reckless to allow another meeting.

She was not interested in him anyway; it was a humiliating lesson indeed to be on the receiving this kind of behavior. To his chagrin, he knew deep down that this was exactly how a lord or lady from his earlier life could behave to one of their minions, and they could and would dismiss that same minion without a second thought as soon as the interest faded.

It was impossible to concentrate on his work anymore; his restlessness drove him out of the tiny bower to find distraction by rejoining his companions. He decided he couldn't talk about the encounter to anyone, not even his now trusted friend, Reza. Word traveled in this castle faster than the pest and he knew it could be very dangerous for him if it got out that he was talking to the master's sister.

He also knew he couldn't hold the story inside for long and he'd have to confide in someone, which meant Jean de Loche. Wasn't he a priest, after all? If he allowed his thoughts to continue the way they were heading he would have to go to Jean for confession anyway. He resolved to find a way to talk about the incident and see what Jean would say.

Earlier in the day, he had heard the clang of hammer on iron at the forge in the outer keep. He resolved to put the chance meeting out of his mind for the moment and set off to find Kemal the blacksmith, whom he liked to watch as he worked his trade.

In spite of his remonstrations with himself, Talon looked forward to the next meeting. Rav'an represented an exotic variation from the hard routine of life he had become used to. Although there was, in fact, a lot of mental as well as physical stimulation for the boys, the thought of spending time with this elevated creature was exhilarating.

There was not a little danger. During his short time at Samiran, he had become aware of the taboos that surrounded the community. Women were not given the freedom he had come to take for granted at his father's castle, so there was an added excitement to being able to meet the princess.

The next time he prepared to visit the garden, he took more care with his manner of dress. Formerly, he had worn a single robe, as it was comfortable. Now he donned loose pantaloons and an over vest that came down to his knees. Furthermore, he decided he needed clean clothes for such a one as the princess. This tended to present problems, but he solved it by taking his clothes and limping over to find Alaleh, then begging her to help him clean them, as he suspected that they were gathering lice.

That worthy woman laughed at him, recollecting the time she had had to clean him herself. Now, looking at this young but growing boy who was, in her estimation, going to grow into a handsome young man, she nodded approvingly and agreed to make sure they were all washed. She had, of course, heard all about the lion story, but this presented her with a good excuse to hear it from him as a form of payment. So, he was forced to tell the story all over again, despite his weariness of reciting the tale.

He came to the garden early the next day, and then had a long wait, as Rav'an was otherwise engaged. When she did come, it was similar to the first time. First to arrive was Badura, who was less distant this time. He greeted the hound by kneeling on one knee and talking to her as she walked slowly up to him, her huge almond eyes regarding him with solemn interest, her tail wagging, her reserve apparent, but still willing to be friends. When her head was within reach he, in turn, reached forward and lightly stroked her under the lower jaw and then worked his fingers around to the back of her ears, murmuring endearments to her all the time. They were engaged in this tentative re-acquaintance when Djahi came bounding down the path, followed at a more sedate pace by Rav'an.

Talon glanced up and then stood to greet her. She was as lovely to his eyes as he remembered her. It was very hard not to just stare, but he forced his eyes to stay on her face and smiled into her eyes. "Badura came first, my lady, so I was paying my respects to her."

Rav'an smiled back. "She is a princess in her own right. It is perfectly correct for you to pay homage to her," she said, laughing. "Now you can say all the same things to me."

He smiled. "I would ask how you are today, my lady, and that it gives me great pleasure to see you."

She smiled coyly. "I am well. I hope that your wounds are better. I wish to hear about the lion hunt from you. I have heard it from many people, but I want to hear it from you. Will you tell me?" she almost pleaded.

Talon gave an inward sigh, but he wanted to please the girl who stood in front of him. More than that, he wanted to prolong their meeting as much as he could, so he nodded. "Yes, my lady, I shall tell you; will you be comfortable there?" He indicated the bench nearby under the fruit tree.

Rav'an said quickly, "Talon, please call me Rav'an when we are alone. That, too, pleases me." She smiled at him, and then sat on the bench near him.

His rolls of paper were between them, which represented as much decorum as he could manage for the moment. He told the story to her in his simple terms, not dwelling on his utter terror at the times when he thought all was lost. When he finished, he did not look at her but was conscious of her regarding him.

Then to his surprise and pleasure, a delicate hand came and rested upon his. The shock of her touch was electric. He looked up into her wide, gray eyes and saw not the gaze of a young and innocent girl, but a serious and concerned gaze.

"You must have been very afraid, Talon, but you did not flee. You stayed for your companion."

He gave a short laugh of deprecation for his actions. "Yes, Rav'an, but I was very frightened."

She still had her hand on his. "You *are* brave. My brother, the master, told me that if a man is afraid, but still does his duty, he is a brave man indeed. I would like to have you as my protector when I grow up."

He stared at her, too surprised to speak.

She gazed back at him her eyes solemn. "Will you be my protector, Talon?"

He hesitated, looked at her to be sure she was serious, and then went on one knee. "Forever, and forever, my lady," he stated, as earnestly as she had spoken.

Rav'an gave a light tinkle of a laugh that broke the spell but at the same time acknowledged his allegiance. She retrieved her hand and then turned and told the hounds that they had to respect Talon, as he was now bound to her.

From that moment forth, the two of them could talk to one another about most things without being awkward. That is to say, they steered away from any hint of intimacy between one another, but Rav'an had an inquiring mind and wanted to know all about his former life in Palestine. He enjoyed answering her questions and then would ask some of his own. He had studies to complete, and discovered in her an unexpected ally who was happy to assist him with the complexities of the language and its convoluted history.

He learned that at this time Persia was now part of the greater Seljuk Empire that stretched from the old Afghanistan to Palestine. She explained that the newcomers were Turks and in general were disliked, and feared in some quarters. Her people, the Ismaili, hated the Seljuks and on many occasions had struck devastating blows to their leadership by sending *fida'i* to slay one of their leaders when they least expected it. It was clear to Talon that she was proud of her people's ability to kill and firmly adhered to their doctrine.

She also had a good education with respect to the arts and poets. She challenged Talon to read the most current man of letters, Omar Khayyam, and to interpret his poetry rather than just reading it at face value.

They met often while he convalesced. Each time the bond grew a little stronger. Talon was sometimes, upon reflection, surprised that they were never disturbed in the garden, but he had not counted upon Rav'an's natural caution; she picked her moments, ensuring that they were never discovered alone together.

He knew he was accepted, as much by the way the hounds

greeted him as by the way she came to meet him. She now brought the occasional fruit for them to share, or nuts, raisins, and dates. Sitting under the plum tree, they would lick their sticky fingers, and then, while he'd wipe his on his pants, she'd take out a light linen cloth and wipe hers. He was enthralled by her clean scent and the hint of lavender—he now knew what it was—which accompanied her presence. The closest they ever came to intimacy was to sit head to head, reading.

Once or twice her hand would touch his, or her arm brush his; then he felt his face grow hot with the realization of how she affected his physical feelings. He was not to know that Rav'an, for her part, was in the same situation and would often spend an hour after their meeting sitting quietly in her rooms remembering every single word and touch.

Talon's wounds healed and he grew fit again, and he realized that he would have to go back to the classes and leave the wonder of the garden. The thought depressed him; he could not bear to look into the future. Rav'an noticed his preoccupation one day and asked him about it. After being evasive, he broke down and confessed that he hated the thought of having to go away, for once gone he could not come back.

Rav'an looked at him with those wide gray eyes. "No one knows you have been to see me all these days, Talon. Why should they know in the future?"

His jaw dropped. "Do you mean... do you mean that you want me to come here afterward?"

Rav'an smiled archly. "If you so desire to, my protector, we can meet from time to time. I shall send Feza to find you."

"Rav'an, I want to see you, the Lord knows I do, but it will be dangerous for both of us, much more than now," he responded, but his heart was beating hard as he said it.

She nodded. "I know, Talon. It will be dangerous, but I want to see you, too. I have no friends, for I am the princess. Will you continue to be my protector?" She smiled, but her eyes were suddenly full of tears.

He went to his knee and answered forcefully. "Forever, and forever, my lady."

Soon after that meeting, Talon was pronounced fit for duty and could not come to the garden again.

*****

The first day that Rav'an came to the garden and found him not there was a lonely one for her. She tarried at the seat under the fruit tree with the hounds, lost in her thoughts, oblivious of the birds and other small life that inhabited the garden. The beauty was lost upon the girl as she lamented her missing friend.

Indeed, Talon was the only friend she had ever had, so his absence from the garden was painful. Beyond that, she knew that there was something else of huge importance about their relationship. She now knew with a certainty that he'd affected her in a physical way too. His touch, those accidental contacts, and the timbre of his voice, all came back to haunt her now, and thus increase the pain.

She felt tears of self-pity rise in her eyes as she remembered their time spent together, a time she had come to look forward to very much. When would they be able to be together again? Dashing a tear away in irritation at her weakness and resolving to ensure that they could be together at least some times, she rose and went slowly back to her rooms and a sympathetic Feza. She was trailed by the hounds, who gave up lizard chasing to follow their forlorn mistress.

Not quite a Muslim is my creed
Nor quite a Giaour; my faith indeed
May startle some who hear me say,
I'd give my pilgrim staff away
And sell my turban for an hour
Of music in a fair one's bower.

— Omar Khayyam —

Chapter 9
Talon's Birthday

The ring of boys, all between fifteen and seventeen years of age, was spread in a wide circle. They were watching with avid interest the performance of two of their number in the center who circled each other warily.

Both were of about the same height, but one was dark and very slight, while the other, with lighter hair, was showing signs of becoming muscular. Both were around seventeen years of age. Both of them held a wooden dagger in his right hand and in his left a stick about three feet long.

They wore the usual cotton pants and wide, loose cotton shirts tied at the waist with a thin belt, and both were barefoot. They watched each other intently, ignoring the cries of encouragement from their respective fans on the rim of the circle.

Talon was relaxed, his eyes alert for the slightest sign of warning from his opponent. He saw a tiny flicker in Reza's eyes a split second before the other boy danced straight at him. Reza was so quick that, even with the warning, Talon had to twist very fast to counter the lunge of the wooden knife straight toward his midriff, followed by a blur of movement from the left hand as it slashed down at his head. There was a "click, click" as they parried their two sets of sticks, and then Reza went skipping away, foiled for the moment but not at all finished.

There was a buzz of appreciation from their companions at the duo's speed. The watchers grew silent as the fight intensified.

This time it was Talon's turn to lunge. Instead of going straight for Reza, he sidestepped and kicked out with his right foot at the other's leg. As Reza slid out of the way, Talon's dagger appeared at his side, and only with the most violent twist did Reza get away without being hit hard in the side. Talon followed up with his left-handed stick in a double slash to the shoulder. Reza had to jerk his arm up violently to protect his shoulder and neck. He again slipped out of reach before turning and coming back to face Talon.

The boys around them began to call encouragement again. Soon a small crowd had gathered, enthralled by the speed and counter-actions the two boys displayed. These two were among the very best at this game, and bets were made and taken—most of them on Reza; of all the boys, he was without doubt the fastest with the knife—whenever their instructors matched them.

There were many feints and thrusts, fast flurries of action from which neither seemed able to wrest the advantage and deliver the fatal blow. Reza decided to try to slip under Talon's guard. As fast as a striking snake, he did a double step and went into a crouch almost at Talon's feet. Then he began to uncoil in a manner that would have brought him up right under Talon's guard and his dagger into the boy's guts in the final blow of the match.

Talon, however, anticipated the move and did something Reza had not expected at all. He took a long step back with his left foot and, bending his right knee, dropped his whole torso down to a lower level that brought him almost face-to-face with the fast-moving Reza. Then he shot his arms forward with the dagger and the stick crossed in a thrust that concluded around the neck of the luckless Reza and pinned him, almost choking.

Before the surprised Reza could change direction in his defense, Talon bore forward and down, forcing him over backward. Talon followed Reza down to the ground, still holding the two sticks in an X across Reza's throat. Kneeling on Reza's chest, he very quickly drew the two sticks along the other's throat and in one lithe movement he stood up, leaving a surprised and bewildered boy in the dust.

The audience roared its approval, still not sure what they had witnessed, it had been so fast. Nonetheless, Reza was on the ground and Talon was standing. The match was over.

Reaching down, Talon grabbed his friend's arm and hauled

him to his feet. They were both breathing heavily, sweating and dusty, but grinning.

Talon put his arm round Reza's shoulders and laughed with him. "You do not often let me win, my friend," he exclaimed with a happy grin.

Reza laughed back at him. "You are too clever by half. Where did you learn that move?"

"I don't know, it just seemed to be the right move, rather than trying to get out of your way one more time."

"Well, we gave them something to watch anyway."

The two friends were surrounded by their colleagues in a noisy group as they all talked together, reminding each other of their favorite moves in the fight they had just witnessed.

Their instructor Jemal came over then, and the crowd of boys parted to let him through. He stood looking at Talon. "That was good, and very timely. Reza would have gotten through if you had continued much longer, I think."

Talon nodded and grinned. "I think so, too, *Genab Sarvan*. He is incredibly fast," He turned to his friend. "What's the score now? You have five to my four, I think."

Reza nodded. "It is true, Sarvan, but he"—Reza pointed at Talon—"is a thinker and does so on his feet. Have you ever seen a move like that before?"

Jemal shook his head. "No, you are both very good now, and should be teaching instead of being taught at this game. Now go and clean up. I have a class to hold soon." He smiled and dismissed the two students.

As he watched his two apprentices go, Jemal had a reflective look on his face. He might have been thinking of when the Frank had first come to Samiran.

"That one has changed; he is no longer a novice" he murmured to himself. "He is a match for almost anyone here now. What a difference." He shook his head again as his favorite student and subject of his pleasure walked off with his arm over the shoulders of his best friend, Reza.

Talon celebrated his seventeenth birthday with only Jean for company. He had been in Samiran for just over three years. He had filled out and lost the spindly appearance of his earlier years and was now growing into a strong young man standing at almost six feet, with wide shoulders and strong legs from all the running up and down the hills he and his companions did almost every day. Few of them could beat him at knife fighting, or with spears and swords, and he was the leader with the bow. The almost constant weapons work had calloused his hands and given him strong arms and wrists.

Jean contemplated his young ward on that day as the boy sat on his right.

"Your father would not recognize you today," he remarked, smiling. Talon turned to him with a grin. His teeth were good and flashed white. He said nothing but turned back to contemplating the castle below.

Talon was dressed in the local garb of loose cotton pantaloons tied at the ankle, and today he was barefoot, as it was late summer, and there was no need for protection from the cold. The soles of the lad's feet were like leather. He wore light boots sometimes, depending on the season. A loose cotton shirt was held closed around his slim waist with a narrow, red leather belt and an inexpensive brass buckle. He'd stuck a long, curved knife in a cheap but functional leather sheath, ready to his hand.

The boy wore a loose cotton turban that could act as a shawl if he were cold. His hair was long and well combed, pleated to the back. He sported the fine down of a youthful beard and mustache. The young man was very presentable, Jean decided.

He could pass for a Persian to any casual watcher, except when he turned and looked at a person. Then they noticed his eyes. They were deep set and green as the sea along the south coast of Brittany. Jean knew that with that physique and those eyes, there was palpable interest among the women of the castle as to how available the boy was, but Jean's keen ear for castle gossip had picked up no signs of indiscretion thus far. It wouldn't be long, he was sure.

The two of them had gone for a walk up the mountain trail and were sitting idly, watching the bustle down in the castle courtyard where a caravan, just arrived from the inland sea, was settling in for the night. The caravan had made camp both inside and outside the castle walls, as it was a large one. Tents and animals taking their rest surrounded the two great mausoleums that dominated the castle. Talon and Jean were discussing some rumors that had come in from Palestine, a place that seemed to be in everyone's thoughts these days.

There were huge forces at work. The whole of the Islamic

world, while not in a fever to rush out there and fight, was always interested in any news. Samiran was no exception, the young men constantly talked about when they would be released to perform their allotted task in its cause. It did not seem strange any more that Talon should be among them, a young man from the infidel world. What was more important was that he had been circumcised, was an Ismaili by faith for all intents and purposes, and was now considered one of them.

Talon sat on the ground, put his feet near the edge of the cliff, and gazed out over the valley. It was more of a gorge. The huge castle sat at the top of the north rim of the Qizil Uzan gorge, as it was known, tied to the side of the mountain that towered beyond and above this point.

The country around was wild and rugged, with a few small forests scattered about the plateau. It was excellent hunting country for hound and falcon, as he had witnessed, although he was not yet allowed to take part in this sport. That was for the Khan and his officers. He had often watched with envy as the parties of high-ranking officials accompanied the master or the General on hunting expeditions, taking their huge birds of prey with them.

The plain just to the south was known as the Dasht e Hamadan. The high plains of Hamadan stretched east by southeast for hundreds of miles, as far as the great salt desert of Dasht e Kavir. From Samiran, the huge, snow-clad peaks of the Alborz towered alongside the northern rim of this plateau to then break away north before the Desert of Salt and reach all the way into Afghanistan.

Positioned as it was at the gateway to the north and along the caravan route to the sea, Samiran was ideally positioned to exact toll and passage tax from from the caravans of the rich lowlands around the great inland sea. These caravans were laden with rice and dried fish, tea, and sometimes exotic pelts from the jungles near the coast, as well as the favored smoked or salted roe of the huge sturgeon that lived in the sea. They often brought great sacks of pistachio nuts and dried fruits, some of which they would sell to the people at the castle on their way through. These caravans had had to climb up the north side of this great range of mountains and go through the pass dominated by Samiran in order to proceed south to Hamadan and Isfahan or to turn northwest toward Tabriz.

The castle had been in the hands of the Ismaili for several

generations and was one of the most significant strongholds they possessed, not least because it exacted such a lucrative tax. This was one of the reasons the Agha Khan's most trusted man, *Timsar* Esphandiary, was the custodian of the castle.

Talon knew by now that the Ismaili lived in the depths of the Alborz, inhabiting its deep valleys, protected by the forbidding barrier of the mountain range that reached high into the roof of the sky. The famed castle, Alamut, was in one of the deepest of its narrow valleys. This fabled castle had more stories told of its sinister history than any other.

One of his favorite stories was about the original Agha Khan, Hassan-e-Sabah, who had come to the city of Ghazvin as a man without a home. He had had to live by his wits for some time.

He had been banished from the palace of the Sultan of Isfahan, because his enemies had trapped him into a rash promise to make accounting of the country's taxes. He had all but succeeded, but his enemies, which included the aging vizier, managed to make it look as though he had cheated the sultan. Only the passionate intervention by the great poet Omar Khayyam, his astrologer companion, had saved Hassan from the garrote or executioner's blade. Banished for life, he had come to Ghazvin, taken up his position in the maidan of that small city, and just sat there day after day.

Finally, the city elders, who were good *bazaari*, could stand it no longer. There was this well-appointed man in rich clothing that just sat there doing and saying nothing. It was clear that he was or had been a man of dignity and worth. However, no one knew who he was or why he was there.

So they went to him and begged him to tell them what they could do for him, as was their duty by the laws of hospitality in the Quoran.

Hassan roused himself from his reverie. "I want nothing, my lords, but to be left alone."

This state of affairs they could not stand for long, of course, so they came again and demanded that he ask for something, even if it were but a blanket, as they could not bear to see him there another day without being able to help him. Their faith would not permit it.

Jemal, who had told this story many times, often embellished it with his own version of things.

So this time, Jemal would explain, Hassan asked for a green

calfskin and all the land that it might encompass. The *bazaari* merchants thought this over and said among themselves: If this is all he needs, then we should give it to him, as then we would have discharged our obligations, and he can sit on his calfskin until he blows away with the leaves off the trees, as surely he will, come winter.

Feeling smug and satisfied that this had been a very cheap encounter with one of the upper class, they presented him with the flayed skin and sat back to watch what would come next.

"Hassan," Jemal always gloated, "reminded the gentlemen of their agreement, that he should possess all the land that could be encompassed by the calfskin. The *bazaari* nodded vigorously and, happy that they had fulfilled their duty to God and man, went back to the bazaar and their businesses.

"Hassan, in the meantime, took out his very sharp dagger and proceeded to cut the calf skin into a fine, fine thread. This he rolled into a ball, and then started to walk. He walked for weeks and weeks until he at last came back to the very spot he had left so long before. He had the end of the string in his hand, and this he tied to the end he had left behind.

"Then he called the Elders out of the bazaar, and reminded them once again of their promise. For the third time they all agreed, so he told them what he had done and laid claim to the whole of the region encompassed within the boundaries of the leather string, which included the castle of Alamut. This henceforth became his home and that of the generations of Agha Khans who would follow him."

Jemal explained that there were two morals to this story. The one said do not underestimate the cunning of the Agha Khans, ever. The other was not to trust your property to the Ghazvini, as they were so stupid they would give it away to strangers on a whim. Jemal then added that Hassan developed his cult and set about exacting revenge upon his enemies. This gave rise to the Assassins.

Talon came to enjoy listening to Jemal tell these fables and in doing so learned a lot about the country within which he was a prisoner.

Now Talon gave a fond look at Jean sitting nearby. Jean had aged since he'd been dragged to Samiran. There was a lot of white in his hair now, in particular along his temples, and his beard and mustache were almost white. He was nowhere near as fat as he had been, he himself reasoning that it was because he had eaten far less meat since their enforced stay at the castle. The Ismaili ate meat whenever it could be hunted, but wild game was no longer plentiful in the region. That which was hunted went first to the table of the General and the Khan, or his family when they visited.

The other meat was goat or lamb, but this was infrequent. Instead, they lived on the rich, sour yogurt, vegetables like onions and cucumbers, and, of course, rice and *nan*, the ever-present flat bread that came with every meal. They enjoyed radishes and eggplant fried in oil on occasion. Talon liked the fruit; there were apricots, pears, and apples to be had in the summer.

Sometimes oranges appeared, but not for long and not often. Nuts were often present in the kitchens. Like most of the other people of the castle, Talon could sit for hours talking with his new friends, clipping open pistachio nuts that had been sun-dried in salty water, which left great white streaks on the shells. Often as not the floor of the eating area would be carpeted with open shells that crackled and crunched under foot.

These were all new foods for him when he'd arrived here.

"Do you ever miss home?" Jean asked Talon abruptly, shaking him out of his contemplation of the castle.

Talon took his time to answer. "Yes, I suppose I do. I remember my mother and father and miss them. But my memories are fading; this has become home."

"I know," Jean said sadly. "But you do know, do you not, that this is just temporary, and that sooner or later they will make clear their plans for you, and this will end?"

Talon broke off a stalk of dried grass and put it between his lips. "Yes. One day I shall have to go to Alamut along with the other initiates and become a full companion, a *fida'i*. When that will be I do not know. What will follow after I do not know either." His tone suggested that he was not sure why they were asking themselves this everlasting question yet again.

Jean sighed. "I know you are comfortable here, but I worry and cannot but think that there is something ominous in our future."

Talon sat with his left side to Jean, who could see the scar left by the lion. It started from the side of his neck and ran along his jaw line—the only flaw in his otherwise handsome young face. Looking at the youth, Jean was struck by how mature the boy was in one sense, but how naïve and innocent he seemed as to his future at the hands of his captors.

ter what Talon thought of the Ismaili, and it was ever hat he was happy here, Jean never considered the two anything other than captives, even though everyone treated them civilly and without malice.

The castle folk had become used to the two of them being seen all over the area and gave them not a thought anymore. Nonetheless, Jean fretted and worried. He dreaded the future, especially a future he could not divine. He coughed, feeling a sharp pain in his upper chest.

Talon's sharp eyes picked out Reza on his way to join them. He jumped up and greeted his friend as he came bounding up the hill to meet him.

"Talon," Reza called as he arrived, panting. "The *Timsar* wants to see you and me. You should hurry. I think he is leaving."

Talon glanced down at Jean and gave him an enquiring look. Then he shrugged, as did Jean.

"Father, come down at your pace. I shall run down with Reza now, or the *Timsar* will be displeased with us," he called back as he sped off on springy legs.

Jean lumbered to his feet and, placing a friendly hand on Reza's shoulder, pushed the boy ahead of him. "Go you, too, Reza. I shall follow at a more dignified pace for a man of my age." He smiled. Reza grinned at him and raced down the hill after Talon, who was already almost at the gates.

Talon sped into the crowded courtyard, dodging a camel here and a pile of goods there. The whole area was cluttered with people, camels, donkeys, and baggage from the large caravan that had arrived earlier. He ran across the stable courtyard, then to the keep on the south side of the walled enclosure, past where the mews were located for the great birds of prey kept for hunting.

There he dived through the entrance past the guard at the door, who barely had time to turn and see a pair of strong legs disappearing up the stairs before the boy was gone. Bemused, the guard resumed the position he had held before the interruption, when another young man came charging toward him. This time he put the spear across the door and demanded the reason for Reza's wild approach.

"The *Timsar* wants to see me and Talon," Reza shouted. The guard was not one to dispute this kind of answer so he lifted the spear and told Reza to stop running and slow down.

Reza dashed up the stairs behind Talon, who was being admitted to the General's quarters. He paused there to wait for Reza. The two young men were admitted to the anteroom of the General's quarters, where they stood catching their breath. They gave each other a nervous grin, and waited.

It was very rare for a student to be called to the General's quarters. The two of them were burning with curiosity as to why. They both went hastily through their minds to check on anything they might have done that would make them eligible for punishment. Neither could think of anything, so they waited with growing apprehension for the servant to come back and take them into the General's quarters.

Not long after, they were admitted to the outer rooms of the General's suite. Both boys went down on their knees and made deep obeisance to the exalted man who stood before them.

Apart from some graying at the temples, the General was still the man Talon had first met when he came to the castle those four long years ago. He bade them rise in his quiet, commanding voice. They scrambled to their feet, to stand rigid at attention before him. He had the power to command them to jump out of the window to their deaths hundreds of feet below and neither would even hesitate should he do so. Their lives were his to do with as he pleased.

He surveyed the two young men in front of him for some minutes. What he saw was favorable. Talon, in particular, had grown well. The General recalled the excellent reports the instructors had grudgingly given of the boy's performance and the thoughtful report that Jemal had provided on his learning capabilities.

According to them, he was at the top of the class now and had learned absolute obedience, lacking nothing in courage, though that was general knowledge throughout the castle. The fight with the lion three years ago had established Talon's reputation.

His friend and companion of all the training and adventures stood next to him. Quite different, but nonetheless he, too, had done very well at all the exercises and was well recommended. Reza stood in stark contrast to his friend Talon. Where the one was tall, the other not of remarkable height. Whereas Talon would fill out to be strong in build, Reza would remain slight, yet very strong in his own right. He was as quick as an adder when it came to a fight, the General had heard from the instructors.

Both boys stood at attention, their eyes straight ahead, waiting for any command he might give them.

The general nodded approval. "I am to leave for Syria on the morrow." The boys stiffened. They were like hounds, he thought, watching them. If I told them to go and hunt something, they would begin to bay and charge off to do so. "I have a task for you."

Their eyes swiveled to stare straight at his, expectant. They shifted their feet and waited.

"I am to escort the Master to Syria, and we shall not be back before winter." As it was already late summer, this was reasonable to suppose. In four months, most of the passes would be closed and traffic would slow to a stop for three months in some places.

"I am informed that you are both ready for the initiation that takes place in Alamut for all the young men who are trained. It is time for you to go there and take part in the ceremonies that will make you full members of the brotherhood. Today you are *lasiq*; there you will become *fida'i*." He looked hard at Talon while he said this but gave no other clue as to his interest in the boy.

He continued. "The master has requested an escort for his sister to go with her to Alamut for the winter while he and I are away. He requested that I send one of my best captains and an escort, but also personal guards. He wants my people to ensure that she is protected night and day.

"You will fulfill this duty. You will protect her with your lives for the entire time you are on the road to Alamut. Your duties are not over when you get there, as you will have to take part in other ceremonies. The caravan here at the castle is going to Tabriz. We leave at dawn. You will leave within the week for Alamut. Make yourselves ready for that time."

He stood a moment longer, looking at the two eager young men, then turned on his heel and left. They fell to their knees and *salaamed* to his departing figure.

They could hardly contain themselves as they left the General's quarters. Reza and Talon rushed back along the corridors, jostling each other, laughing and chattering as they rushed down the stairs and into the bright evening sun. Reza did a cartwheel while Talon stood next to the sentry and watched, a huge grin on his face. Each in his way was enormously excited by the news. The thought of initiation was intimidating; but it was the culmination of all they had been taught, so they welcomed it. For Reza it was what he was all about.

In Talon's case there was more, much more. He was to escort the one person in the world whom he worshipped. He could hardly believe what he'd heard. As he watched Reza's antics, he realized that the General had not mentioned the priest. His heart sank; what was he going to do? He could not leave Jean here in Samiran. He felt protective of Jean and more: a deep affection.

They had buoyed each other up in the dark, hard times of their frightening early days here. During his long recovery from the wounds the lion had inflicted, Jean had kept his spirits up by being there with stories and jokes. He had to find a way to keep them together. He could not know for sure that when he was done in Alamut they would allow him to come back here to Samiran. Jean had hinted at this earlier, and Talon was now face to face with the unthinkable.

The one person who could help was the princess, but even there he might run into a refusal. She had no interest in the priest and might in fact not have enough influence with the acting castellan to get the priest released. One thing he was sure of, he could not go back up the stairs and ask the General, as that could bring serious wrath down on both their heads. He decided to wait until the General was gone and the castle had settled down before he went to see Rav'an.

Reza came bounding back to him and observed his long face. He beamed at his companion, then asked, "Why do you look so sad? You should be happy. We are going to fulfill our destiny, are we not? You should be very happy, Talon, my friend."

Talon nodded and punched him on the shoulder. "I am, Reza, forgive me. I just had a bad memory." He smiled. "It is past. Now let's go and make all our companions jealous that, not only are we going to Alamut, but are to escort the sister of the master there as well!" They went off arm in arm to the stables to greet an envious group of their companions, where they all sat and speculated for the rest of the afternoon.

Later that evening after supper, Talon went to look for the priest. He found him near the well, sitting on the low wall that bordered it, gazing up at the sky. Jean was absorbed in contemplating the heavens. He did not hear Talon come up to him. He jerked when Talon put a hand on his shoulder and said, "Father, we need to talk."

It was clear that his young ward was not in a happy mood. "There you are, Talon. I am all agog to hear what the news is, although I warrant I know," he added. There was a sad note in his voice.

Talon seated himself on the low wall of the well and faced Jean. "I am to go to Alamut some time very soon. They want me and Reza and soldiers to go with Princess Rav'an to Alamut, where she is to stay for the winter, and I am to be initiated into the order."

Jean shifted his bulk. "You do not sound very happy with the news," he remarked, trying to sound casual.

"Well, I am... I mean, well, it is an opportunity to see more and learn more, I suppose."

"Then why the long face?"

"You will not be coming with me," Talon blurted out. "It is not good to be separated while we are here in this country. You have said that yourself," he added almost angrily.

Jean stood and faced Talon. He placed a large hand on Talon's shoulder. "If it is God's will that we be separated, then so be it. It will be very hard to say goodbye for both of us. I know that, but you should not worry about me. They will not harm me for the present. You will always be in my heart, Talon, but for my part I want you to survive and one day make it back to our own people. This is not our home, and they are not our people. One of us should try to get home. That one should be you."

Talon shook his head. "I shall try to get permission for you to come with us. Do you want to come?"

"Of course I want to come, to see the Alamut and to perhaps see the gardens I have heard tell of, where the final initiations take place. The famous library, all of this I want to see, but most of all I want to stay near you and help where I can."

"Then it is decided. I shall approach the princess. I think she will hear me. But I have to wait until the Master and the General have left; then I can go to her."

Jean sighed and said, "So you have been with the Master's daughter before? Ah Talon be very careful. You know that if you're seen with her in her quarters it will be all over for you. There are those who would like to see you punished for an offense of this nature, and we both know what that means."

Talon grinned in the darkness. "Fear not for me—nothing dared, nothing won."

"That is exactly what I am talking about, my young friend!"

* * * * *

The master and his General led the caravan out of the gates of the castle to much ceremony, amid the clashing of cymbals and solemn beating of drums.

Pipes were played and flowers strewn in his path as the Agha Khan rode his beautiful Arab stallion out at the head of his men. The horse was dressed in fine cloths that fell almost to the ground. The Khan was dressed in his long, flowing riding clothes, an overcoat of silk and fine camelhair held in at the waist by a gold inlaid belt over his light riding attire. From a fine belt hung a jewel-encrusted scabbard containing a priceless curved sword of worked steel. His huge, white, red-banded, bejeweled turban denoted great rank. He carried himself with regal dignity, as indeed he should. He was the master of huge tracts of land and many castles. There were very few bold enough to test his power.

The General rode just behind him in the position of bodyguard, dressed in full armor, his mail shirt buffed, his colorful cotton tunic cinched by a worked leather belt that held his fighting sword in its battered scabbard to his side. A polished helm sat square on his head, its rim all but obscuring his watchful eyes. His horse, a large, well-proportioned Turcoman stallion, stepped high as though proud to be part of the ceremony. The horse's ancestry went back to the Parthian days when they were used to defeat the army of Crassus of Rome. It stood a full hand higher than the purebred Arab the master rode.

Behind the leaders came the standard bearers. Their banners were so long they had to hold the standard poles high to keep them out of the dust whenever the wind refused to carry them.

These were followed by high-ranking officers and a large number of acolytes, those who were now *rafiq*, or companions, and the lesser *fida'i*, all adepts and among the most feared in all the land. The escorting foot soldiers marched in a long column behind, chanting war songs.

The entire castle population had come to see them off. There was much excitement and rushing about, as the laggards of the caravan realized they weren't ready to leave and hastened to load their complaining camels and get going.

These great animals of the desert were used all over Persia and carried huge loads. They groaned and spat as their masters called to them and jerked their lead ropes to get them on their feet. No animal but the camel can complain as much, nor make as much fuss about getting to its feet.

The noise of people shouting, camels complaining, even a donkey braying, and the off-key music played all around was deafening to Talon's unaccustomed ears. He reveled in the festive atmosphere, though, as did his companions. This was holiday for them. They took up good vantage positions on the walls to watch the whole show.

The master and his escort had traversed the steep track to the base of the gorge before the last of the caravan made it out of the gates. It was almost mid-morning by that time; the sun was hot and dust was everywhere.

The castle seemed curiously empty after the master's departure. Talon and Jean turned away from watching the tail end of the caravan disappear, to observe the quieter activity down in the courtyard. They descended and walked through the dust to the stables where they usually went when they had things on their minds, and in this case, because it would be cooler than outside.

The strong smell of horses greeted them. Talon loved that smell and welcomed it every time he stepped into the stables. When he was near a horse his senses quickened and he felt more content with life. The two of them walked together down the middle of the long stables looking at the horses as they went.

Talon gave a critical inspection of each animal as they passed, as he fancied himself a good horseman. Indeed he was, but he also cared for the fine stock of animals the master and the General kept in Samiran. There were about thirty horses left from the former eighty that were kept in these stables, so there were many gaps in the lines.

As they sauntered down the lane, horses sometimes stopped eating to observe the two disparate figures. The one was tall and slim with a light step, the other short and stocky with a heavy tread. As they came to the stalls that held the princess' three personal horses, Talon stopped and fished in his baggy pants for a small lump of sugar called *Ghant*. It was rock hard, made of melted-down sugar extract. His companions called it the tooth-breaker. The horses loved it and he spoiled the three animals that belonged to the princess with it. Jabbar, his favorite, whose name meant Mighty or Brave, came over from his fidgeting and nudged him with his nose, expecting some gift.

"You are a pocket friend," Talon admonished as he rubbed the horse's head and ears. Nonetheless, he slipped some *ghant* into the beautiful Turcoman's probing muzzle. The horse was aged about eight years, stood at the withers a hand lower than Talon's shoulders, and was a rich, red-brown color all over. He had a long, silky black mane and a tail that almost reached to the ground. He was well groomed; Talon saw to that.

Laughing as the horse crunched the sugar and dribbled over his sleeve, Talon turned to the priest. "What more could a person want than a good horse, good weapons, and a lady to protect?"

Jean retorted that he preferred to sit in a comfortable place with a good book of Latin to read. "In fact, I yearn for the Bible, as I am losing my memory and lament the loss of some of those passages from which I derived comfort."

"If you can come with us to Alamut you might be able to read the books in that fabled library."

"God willing! Talon, do be careful when you go to see the princess," Jean all but whimpered. "It would be far and away worse if you were caught than for me to have to stay here without you."

Talon put his hand on the priest's broad shoulders. "I shall be," he said.

He sought out Feza. This was not easy, as she kept to the princess' quarters for the most part and seldom came down to the yard. It took almost two days to catch her on one of her forays to the kitchens, and then he almost had to ambush her.

As always, she greeted him warmly but with caution. She was very aware of the growing interest of her young princess in this handsome young *ferengi* and was unclear in her own mind as to how she felt about it, or indeed what to do about it.

His approached her with respect, as he always did, and disarmed her with a smile and with elaborate greetings. "Good day, *Khanom* Feza. May God's blessings be upon yourself and all your family. I hope this meeting finds you well."

Feza peered up at him from under her shawl, her black little eyes wary in her wrinkled face. "I am well," she replied. "Allah be praised and his blessing be upon you, young man." Her tone noncommittal, but she did not brush past him, as he had feared she might.

"*Khanom* Feza. May I ask a huge favor of you this day?"

No reply, just a look that said, "Perhaps, perhaps not."

He plunged on. "I have to talk to the princess before we leave for Alamut. It's very important to me. Just for a minute, and I shall not waste her time or yours. Please grant me this wish, *Khanom* Feza."

She looked hard at him. "I can ask, but be not surprised if she cannot see you. She is very busy preparing for the journey to Alamut."

He gave a deep bow to her. "May Allah bless all who live in your house, *Khanom*. I shall pray to him to protect you."

She cackled. "You had better, young man. I expect you to spend your nights on your knees for this favor."

He was left watching her as she shuffled off, shaking her head.

Talon passed the next day in a state of nerves, waiting for some sign that Feza had been successful, but nothing came. Consumed with worry and impatience, he had a bad day. His companions left him alone. It was easy to tell there was something on his mind and he had even snapped at one or two during the day. As this was very unusual behavior for Talon, they were curious but wary, so they left him alone.

It was late evening as he was walking alone through the gates, having passed an hour up on the mountain, when an urchin came up to him and slipped a small piece of parchment into his hand, then disappeared. His hand closed on the scrap and he walked on without stopping. As casually as he could, he went to the far south wall and found a torch hanging off the wall. In its spluttering light, he opened the scrap of paper and read, "*Nesfe Shab.*" Midnight. Nothing more. His heart leapt. He had been to the garden several times in the last year, with the hope of getting a glimpse of the princess and her beautiful hounds. Each time he had taken his life in his hands and had not even told Jean he'd gone.

Each time he came back without getting caught, he told himself that he would not go again; but he had, several times, having had each time a happy whispered meeting, even holding hands the once. That remembrance set his blood singing, and he could barely control his excitement.

This was danger and excitement of a kind that he had never experienced before, and he reveled in it. However, he knew that he had to be extremely careful. If they were ever caught together, the punishment would be severe. He has a vague idea that the rules for women were quite different from those for men, but no less harsh.

He had witnessed the stoning to death of a woman who was accused of consorting with other men outside her marriage. It was not a sight he wanted to see again; and he had even heard that the husband had falsely accused the poor woman. That had done her no good, as she could not defend herself against her husband's accusations. Talon could not imagine being the cause of any harm to Rav'an and resolved that he would not allow anyone else to be either.

Talon had difficulty sleeping that night. He lay on his pallet with the other youths in the same dormitory in which he had been placed four years ago. It seemed like yesterday that he had been thrust into the room, dirty and exhausted, to face the curious group of boys who were now his companions, among whom he was a respected member and many of whom he considered his friends.

Different they might be, as twelve young boys are going to be. However, the instructors had molded them all into tight group of youths, disciplined, tough, and obedient to every command, their youthful exuberance channeled into usefulness by the men who ruled them. Talon tossed and turned, trying not to draw attention to himself. He listened to the sounds of the others as they slept and tried to judge how deep was their sleep. He had decided that stealth, if discovered, would be harder to explain than simple restlessness. So, he decided on a trip to the midden to relieve himself as being the most plausible.

There was a waxing moon that sent shafts of dim light into the room through the closed shutters, causing deep shadows to form in the corners. The huddled forms of the sleeping youths under their blankets were just visible in the dim light. When he judged it to be near the middle of the night he quietly got out of bed and, wrapping his shirt around his shoulders, slipped his pantaloons on.

He headed for the door as though making for the midden without trying to use stealth. He even yawned in an exaggerated manner as he went, scratching his head and rubbing his eyes. No one stirred; his companions slept, dreaming the nervous dreams of the young, making small yelps and mutterings as he passed some of them. The door opened without a sound, and he was out into the corridor alone with the moonlight coming in through the casements in the walls.

Seconds later he was down the stairs and past the sentry at the door, giving him a graphic mime as to how he was going to flood the yard, he was so full.

Then it was a casual walk across the short distance to the stables and into the shadows next to the mews that held the great birds of prey. He stopped to check if anyone followed him. All was quiet in the castle grounds. Apart from the guards' muttering as they passed one another on the walls high above, and the distant howl of a wolf in the high mountains, the night was quiet.

Talon took a cautious route to the fence that enclosed the garden, hiding it from all but the most prying eyes. Here he slid into the shadows, once more checking his back trail before continuing to the junction of the high wooden palisade and the stone wall of the castle itself.

There he investigated the loose piling he had discovered many months before, to see if anyone had repaired it. It moved at his cautious push and he breathed a sigh of relief. Very quietly, he pushed the piling aside and eased himself into the dark. Once through, all he had to do was to pull it back into place and he was quite hidden from any searcher who did not know of the opening.

He squatted in the dark of the garden and listened to the sounds of the night. The garden had its own scents and little noises. He fancied he could even hear the sounds of a gecko as it scampered along the small stones nearby. But one thing was sure. There was no one else in the garden with him unless they were better than he was at keeping quiet.

Talon eased his way along the palisade and then, keeping to the shadows, moved like a cat to the rendezvous place, the old stone block that he and Rav'an had used as a seat under the plum tree. A shaft of moonlight rested on its surface, flooding the stone with a white light.

He stopped about five yards from the stone, and crouching down, waited. He prayed that she would come. He willed her to come because she wanted to see him as much as he wanted to see her. He had felt on the rare occasions that they had met over the last year that there was a deeper feeling than just interest from her. Rav'an had been careful not to give too much of her feelings away, which had always left him in a state of confusion. However, like a moth to a candle, he could not stay away for too long, so whenever the opportunity presented itself, he had come back.

Now he waited and wondered if he were doing the right thing. What if she did not come, or if she came but would not hear his pleas for Jean? He waited, consumed with impatience. Just as he began to think she would not come, he saw one of the salukis ambling along the path toward him. It was as though he were in full view of the hound.

Badura came straight to him and greeted him like a long-lost friend. She snaked her head and whined in a low whistle. Her tail threatened to topple her rear end, she wagged it so hard. He reached for her head and fondled her ears, murmuring endearments, and brought her head close to his, rubbing her lower jaw with gentle fingers. He was always surprised at the dog's clean scent.

He looked over Badura's shoulder and glimpsed Rav'an coming down the path like some beautiful wraith. His breath caught in his throat at the sight of her. Her garments were diaphanous in the moonlight, doing little to hide her form underneath. Her hair was loose and flowing over her shoulders, glowing with an ethereal light. Her face was a pale oval in the dark of her hair and indistinct, but nevertheless she seemed to show pleasure at the meeting. She came up to him and stopped with Badura between them.

"Talon, it has been long. Why have you not been to see me?" she scolded in a whisper.

Talon was wordless for a second, taking her in, his senses full of her. He breathed her clean scent and the trace of jasmine; his eyes could not stop drinking in her form. He felt stirrings in him that confused him. He collected himself. "M-My princess, I am s-sorry, b-but I could not come as often as I would have liked, either. It is dangerous for you as well as for me, and I could not risk your safety."

"Then why did you come this time with a strange message for me through Feza?"

"My lady, I came to see you for myself, but also for another reason that is urgent."

She liked that. "Did you really come back just to see me?"

He took her hand; she did not pull away. "First, my lady, we must get out of the moonlight."

He saw a gleam of teeth as she smiled at him. "Only if you promise not to compromise my honor," she whispered mischievously.

He almost let go of her hand he was so surprised. But their safety was paramount, and there was still a chance that one of the guards might catch a glimpse of this liaison from his vantage point high on the walls, in which case they were finished.

He drew her under the plum tree to get out of the light, and kneeled in front of her on one knee. She knelt on both knees as well, close to him but not too close. She did not try to release her hand, however, and he felt its cool touch in his hot, burning hand, feeling sure that she could feel his heat.

But she seemed unaware of his discomfort and instead gave him a look of enquiry. "Tell me of the other reason you needed to see me."

"My lady, you are aware that I am to accompany you to Alamut, are you not?"

She nodded. "I asked for a bodyguard just before the General suggested one. He was eager to agree, as he was ready to send some of you boys to Alamut for the initiation."

Talon bridled at the word "boy," but as he did not want to be rude, he let it go. "My lady Rav'an, the priest and I are very old friends, and I shall sorely miss him if we leave him here. Is there a way that can be found for him to come with us? He is a good man and, although an infidel, he is true of heart and would harm no one. Besides, he could be useful as a servant, as would I." He stopped, feeling lame.

Rav'an still knelt without words in front of him, considering his request. She said nothing for a while, just fondling the ever-present Badura with her free hand and looking at Talon. Then she squeezed his hand and slipped her own hand away. "I shall consider what I can do about this, Talon. I am not sure what excuse I can give to the castellan for this, but I shall think of something. I must go now. Will you guard me from all harm and be my protector?" she asked him a smile on her lips.

Talon placed both hands on his heart and swore his life away, to her delight; she enjoyed these solemn games immensely. She knew by now that, in truth, he would defend her, but they played this innocent game every time they met now. They smiled at one another, as would conspirators. She stood up. "Go, my protector," she whispered. "The roosters will be crowing soon, and we have to be in our beds for the entire world to see by morning."

"My princess, I thank you. May Allah protect you from all harm."

He disappeared from her sight, the only indication that he had been there was the eager stare that followed him from Badura the saluki.

Hugging herself with happiness, Rav'an sped along the garden paths with the saluki trotting on light, nimble toes alongside. She arrived breathless at the small door that led up the stairs to the General's and her own personal quarters. Feza met her at the door; as usual in a state of great agitation at the enormous risks her beautiful young ward was taking. Feza bustled her upstairs and into her chambers without further ado and then made sure Rav'an was in bed before going to her own bed, muttering all sorts of dire predictions to herself.

The girl lay for a long time, recalling the meeting. The very touch of the young Frank was electric, leaving her with many unusual feelings. Her whole being tingled at the memory, and there was a longing that she found unsettling but not at all unpleasant. It was almost dawn before sleep came.

We are no other than a moving row
Of visionary shapes that come and go
Round this Sun-illumin'd Lantern held
In midnight by the Master of the Show
— Omar Khayyam —

Chapter 10
The Passes to Shah Rud

Now that the general was gone with the master, the castle settled down to its usual routine, and the young students resumed their training. Talon and Reza were given little instruction from anyone now, as the preparations for the pending three-day trip got under way.

Talking to others, Talon discovered that they would have to pass the first night at one of the villages near the Shah Rud passes. This was the entrance to the series of deep valleys that, after many miles, led to the Alamut Rud, as the Valley of Alamut was known. The next day would take them to another castle called Lamissar, which was one of the oldest castles in the region, and from there another day to the great castle of Alamut. They would not be going to the famous Mayum Diz, one of the remotest of the Assassins' castles.

He wondered if he would be walking the entire way and didn't mind so much, but wondered how he was to protect the princess if he were on foot and she on a horse. He reasoned that the two bodyguards should be on horses, too, but as he had no one to whom he could explain this logic, he decided to wait and see.

The third day dawned bright and dry, but still without any news as to whether the princess had been successful. It was the end of summer and the rains had not yet commenced. The castle and the neighboring town were in the process of preparing for winter. The fields near the town and on the northern slopes of the mountain, upon which the castle was perched, yielded wheat and root crops, ready now in early autumn to be harvested. There were nuts, too, along with fruit from the many orchards in the area to be gathered and picked. These, along with root vegetables, would be brought into the castle and stored for the long winter to come.

The castellan had to decide how many animals would be slaughtered for the winter and how many he could keep, depending upon the harvest itself. Fodder had to be brought down from the high fields where the long grass grew. It was loaded on donkeys until they almost disappeared. All one could see from the side was a large bundle of hay or straw moving at a rapid pace down the paths on spindle-like legs.

The caravan that had just left would not be the last to go through this year, but there would be only a few more before the passes were closed. In winter, the deep snow and howling winds that swept down from the north stopped all traffic for months on end, which meant the castellan would have to ensure that the dried fish the caravans brought was stored with care so it would not rot, and that the grain silos were cleared of rats.

As this was not a time for ceremony, and the boys represented a cheap source of labor, they were often pressed into the work of clearing the silos and helping with hunting. The hunts were a source of great entertainment to these energetic young lads and they worked hard at it, often coming back with good kills.

Talon, Reza, and several companions often went out to the mountains on foot to hunt; they reveled in this sport and could cover large distances when they were in full cry after some small game.

They came back one midmorning through the main gates as a happy, dusty group of sweating young men, with rabbits and even a small deer on their shoulders. They were looking forward to a dip in one of the baths once they had delivered their game to the kitchens, if they could persuade one of the women to fill it with hot water.

Instead, one of the sentries who had been ordered to catch them when they returned shouted down from the walls to Talon and Reza to report to the guardhouse. They looked at one another with a question in their eyes, shrugged, and handed off their small burdens to their friends. They turned off to go to the small rooms set into the walls where the guards for the day took their ease in between spending time on the walls or the other places where they stood watch.

They came to the iron-studded door of the entrance and waited to see who might want to see them. The door was half open, so they could see inside where the captain of the guard was seated. He glanced up and motioned them in.

"Ah, there you are, my precious young fellows, come in."

"May Allah's blessings be upon you, *Genab Sarvan*," they chorused, once inside.

It was a dark room, none too clean, and smelled of sweat and unwashed men. The off-duty guards sat or slept in corners around the room's perimeter, while the captain had the place of honor at a table in the middle where he could watch the door and most of the courtyard outside.

Neither of them had seen this officer before, so he had to have come from one of the other castles, perhaps Alamut itself. Although Samiran was large, it was not so large that a regular captain of the guard would not know them, or they him, in the time they had been here.

"You are the ones that will be accompanying me and my men to Alamut," he stated as he picked his bad teeth with a splinter of wood.

They stared at him. He was a dark, solid man in half armor. His bare head was streaked with gray, pulled back into a ponytail. His pointed helmet was on the table. A battered, well-used sword was at hand nearby. He was a tough-looking character with a fierce, gray-flecked mustache and short beard, both well groomed. To the boys, he looked as old and weathered as any veteran of war could be. He had many years on them, and they could see that he had survived many battles or fights in his time. There were scars on his face and on his bare forearms. Calloused thumb pads and strong hands and wrists indicated a well-practiced swordsman.

He treated them as subordinates, not as inferiors. He knew his trade well and was aware of theirs, so he told them in blunt terms what he wanted.

They were to find the princess' three horses and get acquainted. These horses would accompany them to Alamut, although where they would be stabled he could not think, as Alamut could only hold about ten horses in total. Could they ride, he asked, his voice skeptical.

Talon bridled. "Your Excellency, Captain, sir, I have ridden since I was a baby."

There were grins from the loafing soldiers. Here was a good one; the captain might have some sport with this *ferengi*.

The captain turned to Reza. "And you, O Mighty One, did you too start when still sucking?" Reza looked back at him and in a polite voice replied, "I can ride, Captain. I looked after horses before I came here."

"You two are picked by the general, may Allah bless him, to protect the princess along the way to Alamut. You will stay with her at all times, and allow no one at all to come close to her. Are you clear about this?" The last sentence was delivered in a shout. They jumped.

"Yes, sir, your Excellency, Captain!" they shouted back together.

The soldiers grinned at one another at the entertainment.

"Be ready at dawn the day after tomorrow," the captain bellowed. "You had better be able to ride, or you will be tied to her stirrups to run all the way," he threatened in a good-natured manner. He waved them away with his hand. They both bowed very low and then ran out of the room.

Talon looked at Reza. "Well, that answered one question I had," he stated.

Reza shrugged. "I'm glad we are riding, far more fun. What was the other question?"

"Nothing. I was just thinking, that's all."

"Better be careful, Talon. Thinking is dangerous, especially in your case," Reza yelled as he ducked a wicked slap aimed at his head and ran off laughing.

Talon laughed, too, and ran after him, bent upon delivering a sound thwack to his friend's head. The two strapping young men ran across the yard, yelling abuse at one another, dodging people and donkeys with loads, churning up dust that disturbed others in the courtyard as they ran and slid during the chase.

Impatient servants and women folk yelled at them as they brushed past, but most of it was good-natured. Some of the women's glances lingered on the lithe young men as they passed, but they were too exuberant and involved in their game to notice.

The next day was full of preparations for the two young men. They had to pack their meager personal possessions and to ensure that they had warm clothes for the coming cold. Talon heard that during winter the deep snow locked in the whole of the Alamut Rud valley, sometimes for months. The cold could and did take a toll of lives every year, the frozen corpses of people and animals showing up in the late spring when the snows melted away at the start of the new season.

He heard stories of harrowing experiences from the soldiers who had spent time there, of wolves that attacked in packs when they found lone men on the road. But the stories were mainly about the dreadful cold of the mountains. Samiran was cold in winter as well, but this seemed to be a lot more extreme.

The boys went to the stable master and worked with him to put new shoes on the horses for the long journey. There were weapons to oil and sharpen, bows to be restrung, and spear shafts to be checked. There was clothing to be begged for over and above that which they each had, and neither of them had very much. Their friends among the soldiers and the instructors warned them that frostbite would take toes and fingers off if they did not protect them.

Feed for the horses was to be carried on panniers, and the boys were given the menial task of preparing donkeys to carry all the extra baggage. Then there was other work too, preparing the princess' baggage, which seemed to be an awful lot to the laboring boys. It was all baled and wrapped up tight in colorful rugs so they could not see what most of it was, which frustrated their curiosity. They would not take camels on this trip, as camels would slow them down. Talon didn't much like camels; he preferred horses above all animals, and then hounds. He wondered if the princess would be taking her two salukis with them. He guessed she would.

Then there came an order for another donkey to be prepared for another rider. They guessed that it had to be for Feza, the princess' servant. Talon decided that he would make sure the donkey was very comfortable for Feza, as she was getting on in years, and the journey, although a mere three days, was going to be a trial for the old lady. He stole and borrowed several well-padded rugs to put over the donkey's back for her to rest on.

There was still no permission to take the priest. Talon was getting worried that the princess had been unsuccessful. Ridiculous ideas occurred to him, such as hiding Jean in a bale or some such other desperate move. He had to discount them all and control his worry and impatience. He put his trust in Rav'an to find a way to take Jean with them.

There was not much talking that evening when a glum Talon and Jean sat in the eating hall, picking at their food. Not even the tasty nuts tempted them, which was unusual for Jean. Neither had the heart to talk about the impending separation that was now upon them. The following morning, just before dawn, the troop would leave with Talon, and they might never see each other again. Talon had a huge lump in his chest and sat slumped on the *ghilim*, hunched over his bowl, picking at the stew. Jean tried unsuccessfully to lighten the mood with a halfhearted attempt at humor, but after a few minutes he lapsed into a depressed silence.

The usual crowd of soldiers and their wives or concubines was seated on *Ghilims* and carpets around the hall or squatting in corners playing dice or bones. A noisy crowd had gathered near one of the smoky torches hung on a wall to watch two men playing Serratta, a game that involved moving small, smooth stones from one pocket to another on a carved wooden board. Whenever possible, a player confiscated his opponent's stones and placed them in a pocket at the end of the board. The one with the most in his pocket at the end of the game was the winner. The game was played on a beautiful carved board, well polished from much use.

Under normal conditions, this would draw Jean and Talon to watch, as this was one of the fastest, most exciting games either had witnessed. The game depended upon a good memory and the ability to count and deceive. Men would gamble everything they had on the count, including camels, horses, even their own wives sometimes, it was said.

However, none of this interested the two on the mat that night. The noise level was enough to almost drown out the call that came across the hall. Talon's sharp ears pricked up. He looked to the doorway and saw a guard at the door peering into the gloom. Jean's name was called again. This time he heard it clearly and nudged Jean.

"They are calling, Father. Someone wants you," he said in a loud voice.

Jean stood up and so did Talon. They pushed through the hall to the door where the impatient soldier was waiting. He jerked his arm and waved them over.

"The captain wants to see the *ferengi*," he said. "You come, too, Tal'on." They followed the sentry at a brisk walk back through the gloom of the evening to the guardroom where the captain was standing at its entrance.

"There you are," he bellowed. "You, *ferengi*"—he pointed at the priest—"pack your things. You are coming with us to Alamut."

He turned to Talon. "Why we would want to have a *ferengi* in the holy castle I do not know, but Allah works in wondrous ways, so it is not I who should question them, nor the orders I am given from the castellan," he remarked in a lower tone, as though Jean was not standing in front of him.

Talon nodded, speechless with happiness. "Allah does indeed work wonders, Captain, Your Excellency, sir," he croaked. "May He bless you forever."

The two of them bowed low to the captain and left. Walking back to the eating hall, Talon could hardly contain himself. "I want to dance and shout with joy," he whispered.

Jean, who was hugging himself with the same feelings, muttered back, "I shall embrace you later, you young rascal. How you did this I do not know, but you have done it." He gave a skip that Talon emulated, laughing, so that the two of them began to skip, and they performed a dance arm-in-arm along the path to the eating room.

As they came up to the darkened door, they sobered up and entered the warm, noisy room. The crowd at the Serratta game roared as one of the men playing made a coup that won him one of the rounds. Talon and Jean ignored the noise, went straight to the cook still ladling out food, and demanded more for their supper, as suddenly they were ravenous.

Talon and Reza said goodbye to their friends the next morning before dawn. They were sad to be leaving the happy group of youngsters who were to wait until the following year to be initiated. There were small presents and a lot of embracing, as they did not know when they would ever see one another again.

It was still dark when the boys, still rubbing sleep from their eyes, jogged over to the stables and went in to saddle up the horses and make ready for the journey. The party gathered in the grand courtyard, with some of their friends still hanging about. All the baggage was loaded, and all the men, including Jean and the two boys, assembled before the first lightening of the eastern sky. A donkey had been hastily found for Jean that he clambered upon in his clumsy manner. There was no talking.

The boys were dressed in their loose pantaloons tucked into long calf boots of soft leather that came up to just below their knees, as were the soldiers. Unlike the soldiers, however, they were not clad in chain-mail armor. They carried a quiver of arrows at their belts and had placed their bows in a short scabbard behind the left thigh, under the saddle flap. They both wore a loosely wrapped headpiece wound about and left hanging down their backs. Although not splendid, they did sport long over-tunics, well mended, to keep them warm on the journey while their meager belongings were in a rolled pack secured behind the saddles.

Both were allowed to carry a sword, neither of which was of the best, as they had had to beg for arms from the guardroom. In the end, and only by the intervention of the captain, they had been able to obtain this hardware to go along with their knives.

The troops and the captain were well armored in long chain vests, the sleeves of which came down to their elbows. Under this, each man wore a rough uniform of wool undershirt and thick over-shirt. Baggy woolen pants tucked into calf-length boots for riding completed their attire.

Talon envied them their armor. Each carried a long lance with a sharp, wicked looking spearhead. They held light, round shields on their left arms and a slim, curved sword hung by their sides. Some carried bows in scabbards behind their thighs with quivers full of arrows attached to their backs. The attire was finished off with a round, pointed helmet seated on their heads around the base of which was a tightly wound turban. All were well mounted on beautiful Turcoman horses that seemed to dance as they walked, their carriage was so light.

As the first streaks of sunlight came over the eastern peaks of the Alborz and drove the shadows flickering up the valley, the captain came to inspect the group. His men were standing at attention next to their well-groomed horses. This included the two boys holding three horses and two donkeys. He checked the harnesses with care, as a veteran of many journeys and battles will. His attention to detail impressed the boys, who resolved to respect him, even if he did make a lot of noise about it. Talon realized that there might even have been a reason for this noise, as the princess had not shown yet, and it was clear that the captain wanted to be on the road as soon as possible. The captain was almost done with them, having pulled and tugged at ropes and harness to see if they would hold, when there was a stir among the men.

First to come from the direction of the keep was Feza, small and bundled up against the chill of the morning. Talon and Reza turned to face her, and Talon came over with the donkey with the intention of helping her to mount. She stayed him with her hand and turned to look back. Rav'an came a few paces behind. In spite of the fact that she was also bundled against the cold and had a shawl over her head, there was no mistaking her bearing and who she was. The two salukis were on either side of her, and their own bearing, coupled with that of the princess, gave pause to the entire party, which stared in awe.

Rav'an was dressed as though for a hunt; her tunic was of the finest camelhair dyed bright red with complex patterns woven into the fabric. She, too, wore long, soft boots for riding, and a shawl that could be used as a veil should the need arise. She was not using it for that purpose during this ride; that was clear to all. The men reveled in the beauty of their ward.

Talon bowed low, as did Reza. The captain bowed, too, then watched from a distance. She nodded to Talon and walked over to her mare. Touching her mare, Kaleen, on the neck, she murmured something and then, without assistance, mounted astride. Then she looked down at Feza and Talon, as though to say, "Well, shall we get on with it?"

Talon tried to ignore the salukis' attention; they wanted to greet him in their usual manner. He was forced to avoid them, pretending that he wanted nothing to do with them. While doing so, he thought he saw a trace of a smile on Rav'an's lips. He assisted Feza in getting on the donkey's back and made sure she was comfortable, then he dodged over to Reza and grabbed Jabbar's reins, his chosen horse.

Everyone was mounted. This was a well-armed party of well-trained men escorting the master's sister to her hereditary home. Nothing would interfere with this mission as far as the captain, his men, and the boys were concerned. The roads along this area were full of the sultan's men, who would stop at nothing to capture such a prize, so everyone was alert from the moment they set forth from the protection of the castle.

The captain gave a shout to form up and get going. Everyone hastened to obey. The boys fell in behind the princess. She edged her mare forward to the captain.

He stood and watched her come and then bowed. "My lady," he growled, "whenever you are ready, if I might take the lead?"

She nodded. He bowed again, clasping his sword scabbard in his left hand, and turned his own Turcoman horse toward the gate. Having done so, he shouted the command to march forward, and at a slow pace the cavalcade followed. There was another shouted command, and the sentries ran to open the large, iron-studded gates and then to fall in along the wall to salute the party as it walked out.

The first part of their journey would take them across the two caravan routes that met near Castle Samiran. They descended into the gorge and then took the eastern route that would take them to a junction about ten miles along the gorge, where it opened out onto the great plateau.

Talon was excited. He reveled in the feeling of a strong horse between his legs and the fact that at last they were going on a protracted adventure. In his mind he was already defending the princess from her enemies and winning fame and glory. Reza riding next to him was just as excited, yet he too kept silent. They didn't want to draw the wrath of the captain down on their heads for chattering like a pair of magpies. Besides, being escort to the princess was a solemn business; they were both awed by their responsibility.

It was improbable that anyone would ambush them along this part of the journey. The most dangerous area was that which came before they could lose themselves in the mountain passes of the Alborz where the tribal Ismaili ruled supreme. Once there they could deem themselves out of danger. Thus, they had a gauntlet to run of perhaps twenty miles before they were out of danger.

The party proceeded with scouts ahead and a rear guard behind to ensure that there were no surprises. It would not do to be caught napping in the gorge, and the captain was an old hand at this. After a couple of hours of riding, they came out of the gorge onto the great plateau and could see for some distance. To the north, they could see the gigantic gap in the mountains that indicated the pass to the great sea, Daray-e-Mazandaran, as the locals called it, or the "Caspian," as Jean thought it was called. Talon had heard that there were dense forests where wild beasts roamed, even larger than lions, it was said, while in the sea were fish as long as a man.

The gap looked a like a missing tooth in the serried ranks of peaks that chased each other eastward. To the south were many low hills and small forests where they had hunted from time to time, beyond which lay the great lands of the sultans, bitter enemies of the Ismaili sect.

The road to the interior of Persia lay to the south and east. This was the road they were to take for a time before turning east into the valley passes of the Shah Rud. The party had to cross this open country before they could climb into the safety of the passes that lead to Alamut, deep in the high valleys.

There was no talking apart from a murmured comment from time to time from one of the soldiers or a growl from the captain. The two boys rode just behind Feza and the princess, with Jean behind them. Their eyes were alert as they scanned the surrounding country.

The captain, a cautious man, barked an order that sent his scouts even farther down the road to watch for trouble, then he positioned himself at the head of the cavalcade. He ignored the princess and her entourage in the middle of his escort.

In spite of the precautions, the whole group was tense. Talon wondered what would happen to Feza and Jean on their slower donkeys and the baggage train if they were attacked and had to flee.

Reza pointed out huge fissures in the surrounding plains and told him something of the earthquakes that could strike at any time and swallow up a whole town or village in a few minutes. Everything would just be gone, he told Talon, his voice low so as not to offend the captain out front. All that would be left would be a dust cloud hundreds of feet high and death everywhere. His parents had died this way in the northeast of the country near the Afghan border.

Eventually the party relaxed and the princess turned and motioned the boys to come alongside. She wanted to talk but could not do so just with Talon; it would seem innocuous if she was seen talking to both of them. The two salukis moved out as the boys came up. Both boys touched their hearts and then foreheads as they drew close, in respectful attention to her wishes.

She nodded politely to Reza then turned her head and gave a mischievous smile to Talon.

He frowned, trying not to smile back. In spite of himself, he felt himself go hot under the thick coat he wore. He almost wished they had not been asked to come forward. He was very uncomfortable.

Rav'an seemed not to notice his discomfort, though. In a low voice, she said, "The priest is with us, I see."

"Yes, my lady," Talon said, in an low tone to match hers. "I wish to thank you for your kindness, I did not know that you needed him at Alamut." This last was for Reza's benefit.

She flicked idly at a fly on her mare's neck. "Oh, Feza and I discussed it. We thought he should come and write for us, as he is a man of letters and now understands Persian well."

There was silence except for the clip-clopping of the horses' hooves while Talon contemplated an answer. Her reason for the priest being among them was plausible enough, given that he was indeed a man of letters and had a good writing hand.

Her next question unbalanced him. "You are to be initiated to become *fida'i* soon. I hear that the gardens are full of flowers, maidens for the taking, and there will be wine to drink. Will you tell me about this when you come back?" This last remark was delivered with seeming artless innocence.

Talon gulped. "My l-lady, I-I do not know anything of the initiation, but I am sure they will not allow us to talk about it after it is completed."

In fact, he and Reza had talked of almost nothing else during the short time they had remaining in Samiran, ever since they had been told they would become *fida'i*. They had speculated on precisely those things mentioned by Rav'an at great length. In the usual manner of boys in their early manhood, they were untried in the world of physical love. Although they knew others of the *rafiqi* and even *fida'i* who had boys as lovers, neither had the inclination to do so and had declined overtures of this nature.

However, they could not stop themselves from thinking of women at every opportunity. Often, as is the way of boys, they were crude in their conversations about it.

To have the princess confront him with this was a jolt to Talon, who had somehow placed her on a pedestal outside the carnal longings he had for mere mortal girls. He looked over to Reza to see if he had heard the question, and by the wooden expression he was greeted with, knew that he had.

The princess looked serious. "Well... no matter. You will become men at this time. Then we shall see," she gave him an enigmatic smile. Rav'an appeared to be amused at the comical expressions she saw on their faces.

Before any of them could think further on the subject there was a shout ahead, and the whole cavalcade halted abruptly. From far ahead the lead scouts galloped toward them at breakneck pace. It was not long before they were hauling their horses to a halt in front of the captain, shouting and gesturing behind them up the road. The captain listened attentively and then turned and shouted a command loud enough for all to hear.

"Get off the road and head for that small clump of trees in the foothills to the northeast of here. There is a large band of the sultan's men on the road coming this way."

He pushed through the throng of milling horsemen to the princess and her party. He glowered at the boys and said to the princess, "We have to keep out of sight, my lady. Please follow the men to the woods. If there is a fight, you and these two"—he indicated the boys—"must take to the foothills and to the pass. It is twenty miles northeast and should not be difficult if you are quick and stay out of sight. We shall all hope that Allah keeps us invisible to the heretics. But if not, I shall fight a rearguard action to allow you to escape. Now go!"

The whole troop of soldiers clustered round the princess' group and herded them at a fast trot to the trees, the tops of which could just be seen over the rim of the low hills to the north, less than two miles away. There was no sign of the oncoming enemy yet, but everyone was tense and worried by the scout's estimate of their numbers. There were many more than the escort could field.

They made the low hills without incident. The horsemen took the lead with the loaded donkeys trotting behind, urged along by blows from the drivers' sticks. Feza and Jean harried their animals to keep up. Everyone was nervous.

The captain kept to the rear with several of his men, casting an anxious eye at the dust cloud they were raising, hoping that the enemy was far enough back for it to have subsided before they arrived.

Everyone made the shelter of the trees and, still mounted, they clustered in the shade, looking around. Most were watching the captain and his senior soldiers clamber off their horses, throw the reins at others, then scramble back up the slope of the hill to lie watching the road across the dusty plain.

There was no talking. The only sounds were the buzzing of the inevitable flies that came out of nowhere to settle on everyone. Talon heard the distant bleating of a herd of goats from further up the dry stream bed they were in. He brushed the circle of flies off his mount's head. He could almost taste the collective smell of nervous people and horses. The clink of bridle bits and the stamp of horse's hooves served to distract as people listened with straining ears for the sounds of a large party of horsemen on the distant road.

The captain sighed and muttered a curse up on the crest of the hill. He told his men that he had hoped that they might be able to avoid this situation. He murmured some crude comment to his companions and one of them chuckled. They were calm enough, it seemed to the watching Talon, but he was not fooled into thinking that they were relaxed. He recalled the last time he had been in a similar kind of situation, and thought of how it would be this time if he were captured. He doubted if it would be better.

He turned to observe the princess and was relieved to note that she was calm and, in fact, was soothing Feza, who looked petrified. She was reassuring Feza that the captain knew what he was about and would not let anything happen to them. Then he glanced at Reza and received a grin from his friend. Reza would deal with whatever was sent his way in his usual manner, quick and deadly if confronted and calm enough in all other ways.

Talon saw the captain tense his shoulders.

The enemy party was coming from the southeast, from the city of Ghazvin. It was a large, armed party of cavalry escorting what seemed to be some kind of nobleman. It was without doubt a war party, but to the captain and his men it was difficult to decide where they might be heading, as the road took them to Samiran, and it was unlikely that they were bent upon trouble there. Perhaps they were heading for the coast? The large cavalry group was trotting along at a leisurely pace, and seemed to be unconcerned with anything.

The dust cloud raised by the captain's party was much diminished by this time, although there was still some indication that might give his party away. The captain wanted to sound confident, but he confided to his men that as an old veteran of many skirmishes, he knew that fate could play a poor hand as often as a good one. He and his men watched the party draw near to the point where his own had left the road, and then they observed several of the front riders come to a halt. They were curious about the disturbed ground, and then one of them turned his horse and rode off the road a couple of paces. They were talking and gesticulating at the same time, and then the one turned and threw his arm up to point in the direction of the captain's position. That was enough for the captain. He told his two men to stay where they were and then quickly shuffled back off the crest of the hill and ran the short distance to the standing group of riders.

"My lady, you must ride as I instructed, and you must leave now. Go up the stream bed and then, when close to the first steep hills, ride along them until you come to the first openings in the mountains. Go through these and find your way up into the passes. Once you are up there, you should be safe, but you must go now, and hurry."

He didn't even wait for her reply but turned to his men and ordered four of them to ride with the princess. The other fourteen he told to prepare to move into a fighting line at his command. He told the bowmen to prepare to take down enemy leaders as soon as they were in range. He wanted no heroics, and they were to stay near him. He was not going to get into a battle in the open with the other side if he could help it. Their purpose, he reminded his men, was to delay the enemy as long as possible. His worse fears were realized when his two soldiers called to him that a small party of the group on the road were coming to investigate.

"How many?" he demanded. "Five," was the response. "Then we shall ambush them," he growled, and set about the disposition of the men.

They dismounted and several men took the horses back up the dry stream bed in the same direction the princess and her group had gone, there to wait the outcome of the engagement with the enemy scouts. The bowmen were well hidden among the high rocks along the banks, while the spearmen crept into positions that would deny any escape once the first surprise was over. The captain sent a man back to the crest of the hill to watch for any other activity from the larger party on the road.

Then they waited. Again, an uneasy silence settled over the area, disturbed once more by the buzz of flies, the rasping of cicadas, and the ever-closer sound of the goats. They appeared to be coming down the mountain along the stream bed. He glanced in that direction but from his hiding place could not see anything.

There was the clip of a hoof on rocks as the first indication of visitors coming into the ambush area, a muttered curse as a rider was brushed by a thorn branch, and then suddenly the scouts were there, right under the noses of the captain and his men. With one quick movement, he stood up and hurled his spear straight at the leader. It was aimed true and struck the man in his midriff, jerking him back in the saddle. The man gasped with agony, then looked down at the protruding spear and saw that he was a dead man. Before he could even scream, a hail of arrows came out of the rocks and struck the party down. The remaining four did not even have time to draw their swords. The soldiers rushed out from their hiding places and hauled them off the panicked horses. They stabbed them to death, choking off all screams before they were loud enough to be heard.

The captain, as soon as he was sure that all the former riders were now bloodstained bundles on the ground, called softly to the men to seize the horses before they could escape. They headed upstream as fast as possible. Without a sound, the whole troop gathered up arrows and weapons and jogged in a noiseless pack upstream to their own mounts, dragging the victims' frightened horses with them. The captain figured that it would be several minutes yet before the alarm was sounded down on the road, at which time the whole party would come after him. He knew of at least three other defensive positions that he could reach in order to create further delay.

* * * * *

Rav'an and her group fled up the dry watercourse as soon as the captain gave his orders. Talon found that the donkeys managed to keep up a good pace over the inclined and rocky ground. Being sure-footed, they negotiated the difficult terrain somewhat better than the horses. They pressed on up, watching for the opening that would allow them to take a path parallel with the side of the mountain. Talon was fearful that they might miss it and get trapped in the high banks if they did so.

Coming around a corner, they ran head on into a large herd of goats. There was confusion as the riders tried to avoid them, and the goats, in blind panic, ran under the horse's legs. It was fortunate that they were all good riders, as a fall among these rocks could have been nasty. The donkeys, belabored by Jean and Feza, along with the pack animals, just waded through the throng of bleating animals and seemed impervious to the noise and chaos. Three young boys and an old man herding the goats ran away as soon as they saw the soldiers.

They got through after a while, in spite of the panicked goats bleating and running in all directions. The salukis thought the whole thing was immense fun and chased goats around until Rav'an called them back with a sharp edge to her voice. Then, suddenly, the princess laughed, the sweet tinkle of her laughter bouncing off the banks of the stream bed. The tension was broken and they all began to laugh; but they hastily caught themselves and urged the horses on. A sense of camaraderie had developed, so now they all felt closer because of the incident and the danger behind.

Soon they came to a wide break in the eastern bank of the stream bed and, pushing their horses up the steep slope, came out on the side of one of the hills overlooking the plains. From here, they could see a path that wound eastward, hugging the side of the mountain. They could not see where it ended, but Talon was sure that it led to the pass. The soldiers, while respectful, had their orders and urged the party on. They knew this country and were familiar with the route. They had indeed found the entrance to the Shah Rud Valley.

Glancing back as they left the top of the hill, Talon could see right down to the plain below. He looked to the southwest. While he could still see the road, he could not see the large party that should have been there. Instead, he saw a plume of dust leading to the base of the hills their own party had gone to for refuge. He realized, even though he could hear nothing, that the captain was engaged with the enemy.

They had to hurry. They were not out of danger yet. If, for some reason, the captain was overrun, and the enemy suspected that the princess had been with him, she would be pursued as far as the enemy dared, right up to the gates of the Ismaili country ahead. They raced on, trying to put as many miles as they could between themselves and the fighting that was surely taking place far below.

The sun was high in the sky by now; it was almost noon. The riders and the horses were soaked through with sweat and beginning to tire. The princess herself was disinclined to overrule the soldiers, but it was clear that Feza was very tired and needed a short rest. She told Reza in a low voice to call the soldiers back to them from their forward position, and then addressed them, but her tone was respectful.

The soldiers, being tough mountain men, were not tired at all, but could be persuaded that Feza was. She was one of their kind. They agreed to a short halt.

Watchful as always, the soldiers took turns keeping a lookout along the trail behind them. They had a clear view from the south side of the valley they were moving into, of the large mountain river that tumbled down the middle of the wide mouth of the valley in a series of rapids interspersed with long deep pools. From his vantage point, Talon wished he could cool off in the fast flowing waters.

The rest of the party dismounted. Feza was helped off her donkey. The old woman was tired but insisted that she could even make tea, if she had to. The princess laughed and told her that it could wait until they were out of danger. There was nothing to be done for the horses, but the riders dragged out cheese and yogurt for themselves. Some onions appeared along with some stale, flat, *barbari* bread, which Talon had come to like very much.

The food was quickly eaten, then washed down with water from some skins carried by the baggage animals. The view was spectacular from this vantage point and Talon could not get enough of the scene. The soaring mountains were familiar, but they seemed to climb even higher here than at Samiran. Reza's people were not of the mountains, either, so he, too, was impressed. Jean and the two boys sat on the dry ground with the reins of their horses and those of the princess' in their hands and looked out over the valley. Behind them Talon could hear Feza's high, strained voice, complaining that she was frightened, and Rav'an calmed her, reassuring her that they were well protected and there was no danger to worry about now.

There was a somnolence in the air after the meal, accentuated by the clamor of the crickets and the cicadas rasping in the heavy heat of noon. Talon felt relaxed and lazy and lay back, letting the sun warm his face.

He was almost asleep when there was a shout from the sentry posted behind. He rode over the hillside looking very concerned. They all stood up. The sentry called a warning and pointed down the wide valley. Far below and several miles back, there was a small party of horsemen, lances held high with pendants flying, galloping on an interception course to the route the party wanted to take.

The man was clearly worried, and then the others started to chatter in their local dialect. The princess with an impatient gesture stopped them with a sharp command.

The leader of the troop bowed low to her and said, "My lady, we do not know of the people we can see below. They will intercept us if we continue along this path. We have to descend to the valley bottom a couple of miles farther along. We think they are a patrol of the large party. We think they have bypassed the captain and are seeking to come in behind him. We have to leave now or we are trapped."

"Very well, we shall leave now," the princess agreed, and she replaced her food in the saddle bag. Feza and Jean were helped aboard their donkeys. The princess mounted in one lithe motion, disdaining assistance. The rest scrambled onto their mounts, and the party hastened along the path. They were some several hundred feet higher than the other party. They could see without being seen. However, it became clear to the agitated soldiers that not only was their own party less speedy than the unknown one, but they were on a collision course if they continued. As they hurried along the dusty path, avoiding rocks, scrub, and thorn bushes, Talon observed what he could of the oncoming party. He thought that they did not represent too much of a threat if they could be taken by surprise.

He rode up to the princess and told her what he was thinking. She glanced at him and saw some logic in his argument. She called forward to the lead soldier, who dropped back to listen to her explain the plan Talon had outlined.

He nodded and looked at Talon, appraising him. "Are you two good enough with the bows to keep them at a distance while we make the pass?" he asked, his tone dubious. "They will stick you with their spears like dogs on the run if you don't succeed," he added.

Rav'an controlled her voice when she replied for Talon. "He is very good and so is his companion. If you can get us to the passes, we can hope that help will be there, as it has been in the past. Can one of you ride hard to find out and bring help back for us?"

The grizzled lead soldier nodded the affirmative and gave an order to one of the younger men of his troop, who promptly galloped off as fast as his horse could go.

The leader of the soldiers told the men herding the baggage animals, five of them, to make themselves scarce in the rocky gullies of the mountain with their donkeys. Jean was told to stay with them and take his chances, which pleased neither him nor Talon, but they could not object. The soldier told Feza that she was to stay with the group of herders as well; but the princess interjected and told him, in a tone that brooked no dispute, that Feza would stay with her and ride behind her on her horse.

The soldier, whose name was Jamshid, nodded. He could not overrule the princess in this but said to her, "My lady, you must ride very hard indeed. Now it is up to the boys here to decide our fate. We surely need them to slow down the enemy."

Looking grim, she nodded and hauled Feza aboard the mare to clutch her from behind as though her life depended upon it.

Jean and the herders drove their charges into a deep cleft in the hillside, eroded by water flow long ago, and disappeared into the scrub and thorn bushes, leaving barely a trace.

When he was sure they were well out of sight, Jamshid gave the command. The remaining two troopers, the princess, and the two boys clapped their heels into their horse's sides and charged off along the narrow track. Talon and Reza had already strung their bows and clutched them in their left hands as they rode.

The party on the valley floor had not seen them up to this point, but their two paths were closing as the valley narrowed and grew steeper. It was inevitable that they should see the group of riders gallop down the hillside two hundred yards in front of them, then gallop at full tilt toward the passes a few miles farther away.

There was an excited shout from the enemy horsemen, and the chase was on.

The princess and her group at first gained ground, as they knew that every yard counted, but before long the pursuers began to gain on them. The two hundred yards became one hundred and fifty, then less still. Talon and Reza slowed their horses imperceptibly to give the illusion that the whole party was slowing, giving the princess and the soldiers a chance to pull ahead.

Talon, looking back, was sure that the others had no bows and called to Reza that he could see none.

Reza grinned and lifted his bow. "Say when we use them, Talon," he called back.

With the pounding horse beneath him, Talon knew the excitement of dealing out a deadly surprise. His adrenaline started to rise. He slowed Jabbar even more and Reza kept pace. Now there were just fifty yards separating them from the band behind. The pursuers were shouting as they came.

Talon gave a quick glance up the steep track ahead to ensure that Rav'an and Jamshid were well ahead and then shouted, "Now, Reza!"

They each hauled an arrow from the quivers on their belts, turned almost a full body turn toward the closing enemy, and loosed an arrow straight into their ranks.

The arrows struck home before any of the pursuers could react by lifting a shield. One of the arrows struck home, and a rider cried out and fell lifeless to the ground, an arrow embedded in his chest. Another clutched his arm and dropped back, cursing.

The whole party reined in at that and milled around, watching the two boys plunge up the steep slope away from them. There was a lot of fist waving as they shouted their rage after them. Then they came on again, having decided to take their chances.

Talon and Reza were waiting for them at the top of a rise. As the group charged up the hill, Reza and Talon rode their horses to the edge and looked straight down on them. There were howls of rage and fear as the boys let loose another couple of arrows. This time they aimed at the horses. One went down at once, while another went lame with an arrow in its shoulder. The boys loosed off another arrow each, taking advantage of the confusion. This time, two more men went down, one mortally wounded.

The screams of rage followed them as they galloped off again.

Looking back, Talon could see no pursuit and called to Reza. "I think we gave them a lot to think about."

Reza laughed. "Talon, that was a good plan. You are a leader. We are invincible!" he shouted, his black hair flying loose from his head cloth, back from his fine features, his eyes fierce with the high of adrenaline and battle. "We should go back and kill them all."

Talon shook his head. "We do not know if there are more, although I would like to. Remember our first duty, Reza."

Reza nodded and they slowed the horses to a canter to allow them to settle down. The path was getting steep.

Talon could not see the princess any more. He was just beginning to worry when he saw them ahead by almost half a mile. His heart stopped. Coming toward her was yet another party of armed men. He wanted to shout a warning, but it was too late. The newcomers soon surrounded her small party, but no one seemed to be fighting. He sat back in the saddle and breathed a sigh of relief.

Reza and Talon cantered up to the resting group surrounding the princess. There were almost twenty men sitting on horses. All were dressed much as the soldiers, and it was clear that some of them knew each other, since there was a lot of animated conversation.

The princess was off to one side, dismounted. A shaken Feza

sat on a large stone. Rav'an was talking to a tall man in fine clothes who stood before her in a pose that stated he was very much in charge, his hand on his sword handle.

The group turned and watched Talon and Reza approach. As they did so, Jamshid shouted to them.

"Allah be praised! Well done, you two, you saved the day. Did you kill any of them? Where are they now?"

Talon and Reza called that there were perhaps four still back there who could be dangerous, but they had killed or unhorsed several.

Jamshid wasted no time. Turning to the leader, he called, "*Gorban* Ahmad, can we go back and finish it?"

Barely turning to acknowledge the request, the man nodded and turned back to the princess. Jamshid gathered the larger party and hurled off down the mountain to finish the work the boys had begun.

"Well done again," he shouted as he went past at a gallop. The whole party disappeared, shouting and hallooing over the ridge to give chase to the survivors.

There was quiet after they had left. Talon and Reza sat their horses in respectful silence waiting for the princess. She wasted no time in putting a stop to her conversation with Ahmad, and walked over to her escort, who at once dismounted and knelt in front of her.

Ahmad strolled over behind her.

Rav'an gazed at the boys with a fond expression. "You are my protectors," she whispered quickly before turning to Ahmad and saying in a louder voice, "Prince Ahmad, these are the two students who are going with me to Alamut for their initiation to become *fida'i*. Talon had the plan to delay the enemy, who are everywhere, it seems. They have saved my life. I expect to reward them sometime soon."

Neither boy said anything in front of the prince. They held their tongues and waited.

He looked down on them with cold eyes and, staring at Talon, said, "I have heard about you. You are the *ferengi* boy, are you not?" Talon nodded. Ahmad said, his tone patronizing, "You do not have to worry about the princess from now on. She is in my care."

Rav'an was having none of this. "Their orders are to

accompany me all the way to Alamut, honored Prince. The orders of my brother, you understand?"

Ahmad shrugged. "Don't let them get under foot, then," he said as he turned away. "Come, Rav'an, we have much to talk about. I have not seen you in several years, cousin."

He took her arm and walked off with her. Talon, as he knelt, wondered if there wasn't some reluctance on Rav'an's part to be with the handsome, supercilious prince who called her cousin.

They did not have long to wait for Jamshid to bring his cheering, shouting, men back with him. They had a prisoner and several horses with them. They were jubilant as they came galloping back, waving spears and swords that had been bloodied in the skirmish.

Their prisoner, bound to one of the horses with his arms behind his back, was the one Talon and Reza had wounded in the arm. His face was gray with pain from his wound, which had not been dressed. He was shaken and scared. The guards kept slapping him as they rode by; it seemed almost good-natured, but there was an ominous note to their joking.

Jamshid reported to Ahmad and the princess that they had killed all the men in the enemy group except for one, who got away, and the prisoner whom they brought back for interrogation. He had also sent some of the men to pick up the baggage train.

Ahmad's eyes glittered. He would do the interrogation the next day, once they were at the village on the other side of the pass. He told Rav'an, "It was just as well that we came to your rescue, or you would have fallen into the hands of the sultan and his men."

Rav'an held her tongue at his patronizing tone. She had never liked Ahmad very much, finding him a spoiled brat as a child, and cruel as a youth. Now, as a young man with a lot of power, he would be as dangerous as a leopard, so she didn't want to contradict him.

Her own opinion was that she had the benefit of her two boys, both intelligent, brave "protectors," who would have kept her safe no matter what. What they had done this afternoon had impressed her, and they'd done it without the benefit of Ahmad and his band. She knelt on one knee by her hounds, who kept close to her with all the strangers about. They were nervous and their anxiety transmitted itself to her.

She calmed them by rubbing their ears and murmuring endearments. Before long they were dancing around her, expecting to be chased or thrown things to pick up, which they would run after but not fail to pick up—being salukis, they didn't feel the need. Talon kept his distance, although there was nothing more he would have liked to do than to play with the graceful animals.

The boys were made much of by Jamshid and his comrades. They recognized that the boys had done a brave thing, and done it well. They were unstinting in their praise, but there was still some reserve, as if the boys were a breed apart, and the soldiers didn't want to get too familiar. Talon thought to ask Jamshid what he thought of the chances for the captain and his men. They would probably be all right if they could keep moving, came the reply.

"That captain is a wily old fox," stated one of the other soldiers. "With Allah's help, and if they can hold the enemy off until dark, they can slip away and make it up to this pass without trouble. They all know the way along the mountain tracks *In shah'Allah*! "

Then there came a shout from down the pathway, and over the rim of the pass came the donkeys with Jean walking and puffing along with the drovers. There was a lot of joking and *salaams* as the two parties came together and people met up again. Jean ambled over to the boys and professed to be glad they had survived. It didn't take much for him to elicit their version of the engagement, which Reza began to embellish, much to Jean's amusement.

Having been dismissed by Ahmad in such a peremptory manner, they were eager for Jean's praise. He was generous with it, as had been the soldiers, although he tempered their good mood by mentioning that the poor wretch who had been captured was going to face a dreadful night at the hands of the soldiers. The boys grew serious at that.

Soon after, Ahmad gave the order to mount up. It was now late afternoon and getting quite cool. It was still about ten miles to the village where they would get food and lodging. The whole party mounted up, and the boys fell in behind the princess without being told. However, Ahmad decided that he wanted to ride with his cousin. He came up to her without deference and waved the boys back out of hearing range.

Rav'an glanced back at the discomfited boys and then looked forward. She said nothing. She put on as pleasant a face as she could and kept her veil in place.

It was not hard to notice as they rode that Ahmad was looking at her in frank appraisal. He had found, to his surprise, that the young, skinny girl he had known a couple of years ago was gone, replaced by a striking and poised young woman. Now he could hardly take his eyes off her.

He told her, "I was sent by my father from Alamut to meet the party and escort you, cousin. I thank my father for having insisted that I come to meet you."

Although the party was moving at a good pace, it didn't stop him from asking how her brother, the Agha Khan, had been, and other innocuous questions that Ahmad hoped would thaw her reserve. She responded politely, and although she did nothing to initiate conversation, she was not rude about it. They would be together for another two days, during which she hoped that he would not always be at her side. However, if he had to be, she might as well find out all she could about his and his father's—her uncle's—activities.

Ahmad, mistaking her reticence for shyness, set about trying to be gallant and to put her at her ease, so he turned on the charm as full as he could.

To the lads following behind, who rode without the benefit of being able to hear the conversation, it seemed as though the two of them were catching up and that the conversation was animated and very friendly. Talon seethed.

Feza on her donkey, also relegated to the rear, looked up at him and smiled. He looked quite glum. She sidled over to his larger horse. Using the distance between the two in the front and the boys to her own advantage, she proceeded to give them a brief résumé on Ahmad, and she warned them to stay out of his way as much as possible. He had a quick temper, and when aroused would lash out at whoever was in his way. He was a prince; he could not be touched, she warned the glowering Talon. She pulled away with a cackle and left them to think about it.

The party came over the last pass just as the sun was setting into the western peaks. They rode past the silent lookouts, and saw the village nestled below in a fold of the mountain. A protecting wall surrounded the scattered mud houses. Smoke billowed from the holes in the roofs of the buildings in which women were preparing evening meals.

The arrival of the large party created much excitement. The princess was expected. Word had gone around that the sultan's men had attacked her party and that there was still a battle raging down in the valley. People flocked to the gate to greet her and to *salaam* the prince, who clearly enjoyed the peasants' adulation.

The princess smiled and waved as she rode into the village. The women started "ululuing" and waved their arms from side to side, making a pleasant welcome. The whole party considered itself in Ismaili country, and short of an army coming up the pass, perfectly safe now.

They dismounted in the *maidan* where the *rais* for the village, an ancient old warrior of yesteryear, stepped forward to offer Rav'an and the prince his house, with refreshments for all and an evening meal to follow.

There was excited chatter on all sides as men greeted acquaintances and friends, and women chattered with Feza, demanding a full history on the spot, as she was well known to most of them. Children came up to stare and listen or just run around, getting under foot. The rank smell of goats and wood smoke pervaded the evening air, which was otherwise clear. It was becoming cold up in this highland fastness.

The boys decided to get their horses looked after with those of Jamshid and his comrades. Talon took the princess' reins once she was dismounted. He was surprised when she gave his fingers a light squeeze as she handed the mare over. Reza was treated like a common groom when he offered to take Ahmad's mount. Ahmad tossed the reins to him and walked off without a word.

The horses being their first care before all else, the boys hastened in search of water and feed. The animals had to be placed in a comfortable compound where they couldn't get out. A dozen barefoot, chattering boys came along with the two lads and their precious charges, offering advice and help as they went. It dawned on Talon and Reza that they were of acute interest to the boys because of their dress and their station.

Talon picked two of the tallest and seeming most competent to run after food for the animals. He and Reza rubbed the four animals down with straw kept in the covered sheds by the compound. The animals were tired and impatient to get free of their saddles and tack so that they could roll in the sandy area where they'd spend the night. Jabbar evoked a lot of laughter from the awed village boys, because he insisted upon having a thorough rub of his face with the saddle blanket before settling down.

After meticulously inspecting their feet and hides for any kind of injury, the boys let the horses go. All four danced off, Jabbar even bucking, then showing his teeth to the gelding belonging to Ahmad, before they settled down to a good roll, grunting with pleasure as they rubbed away the day's work. Talon and Reza watched, as did some of the older boys, who continued to ply them with questions about their training and status.

It was time to find out where the princess was housed; they felt their duty was not yet done until they knew she was safe. This was not hard; the village boys showed them the way to a modest mud-brick house, guarded by one of Ahmad's soldiers, who told them that the princess was in the house and that his master had instructed him to allow no one into the house except the princess and her nurse, Feza. Talon and Reza protested, but not too hard. They were hungry and thirsty and wanted nothing more than to be able to eat and find a place to sleep.

They were shown where to go for dinner. Jamshid was waiting impatiently for them with tea and food.

"Come along, boys," he called. "I have been waiting for the young heroes," he told his comrades. Jean was already there and gave the boys a tired smile of welcome. "We have to look after them; they belong to the princess," Jamshid said, without malice. Some of the soldiers chuckled, but it was good-natured.

The boys and Jean sat cross-legged on the hard ground and ate. They were ravenous. The hot, sweet tea revived tired limbs, and soon they relaxed into the mood of the evening. The soldiers were all mountain people who were fiercely devoted to the Ismaili cause and knew of no other leader than the Agha Khan. There was some curiosity about Talon and his background, but Reza deflected some of the interest, and Talon was able to deal with the rest.

Jamshid told them that Ahmad was taking care of the princess and that she was quite safe in his care. The boys and the *ferengi* should bed down with him and the soldiers. Talon wondered about how Ahmad planned to "take care" of the princess but didn't express his thoughts. He knew it would be foolish and dangerous to even joke about it.

They sat and listened to the desultory talk of tired men grumbling about this or that. Then it was back and forth as to the reason for the attack that day. There was a lot of speculation as to the fate of the captain and their comrades. No mention was made of the prisoner, who was nowhere to be seen. Talon thought it better not to enquire as to his fate. He was sure that he would know sooner or later.

By now it was quite dark, and the village was getting ready for sleep. The bleating of a single kid in the goat compound stilled, and there was silence in Jamshid's group.

Looking up, Jean nudged Talon and they both stared up at the night sky. There was not a cloud to be seen. The moonless ink-black sky was a blaze of light. Talon felt that if he reached up he could seize a handful of stars in his hand, they seemed so close.

There was awe in his voice when he said to Jean, "Did God make that entire sky, Father?"

He had not realized he had asked this in French, but Jean responded in kind. "Indeed he must have, my son, for I cannot conceive that it created itself."

They sat in companionable silence. Talon gave a huge yawn, and then was startled by a shout coming from the direction of the pass.

Instantly, the camp was transformed. The soldiers jumped up and began to run to the village gate. Men came to their doors to shout questions but got only garbled responses from excited but ignorant men milling about. Torches appeared and oil lamps were relit in the *rais'* house. The men on sentry duty opened the gate, and men on foot went pouring out. Everyone else waited, the boys with them.

Dark forms began to come into view. They were men on horses, and as they slowly came into view the crowd at the gate could see by the smoking, flaming torches that they were the remnants of the troop that had stayed with the captain far down the pass.

They were dirty, bloody, and exhausted, and there were not many of them. At their head, however, his head held high, his fierce mustache bristling and his back ramrod straight, came the captain. There was a brief silence. The shocked crowd saw how few there were, and then came a wave of shouting as men called questions at the ragged survivors. The captain said nothing. He rode slowly through the admiring, shouting crowd toward the *maidan* at the center of the village and there signaled his men to halt.

He barked a hoarse command to dismount. His men slid rather than dismounted from their worn-out horses and stood shaking with fatigue, waiting to be dismissed. The captain was hanging onto the pommel of his saddle. He was pale under his dark tanned features, but he managed to dismiss the men before he fell to his knees next to his horse. Immediately his faithful men rushed to help him. The soldiers and villagers crowded around, all of them eager to help and to hear the story of what must have been an epic battle.

Jamshid shouted in a loud voice for the crowd to give them room as, by Allah, no one could breathe and couldn't they see the great captain was wounded? "Give us room, let him breathe," he shouted.

The crowd parted. Ahmad walked into the space to stand over the half-prone captain, who, when he saw the prince come up, struggled to get on his feet.

Ahmad waved him down. "Get this man of men a place to rest, look after their horses, and make sure the men are fed and looked after at once," he said, his voice carrying to every corner of the maidan.

The crowd stood back as the men lifted the captain up and carried him to one of the houses at the side of the *maidan*.

As he left, the captain croaked to Jamshid, "Did the princess come through without harm?"

"Oh yes, my Captain. Allah was kind. Her two escorts made sure of that. We shall tell all when you are rested. Now you must eat and have that wound in your leg dressed as quickly as possible."

It took a long time for the men to settle down again. The tired men who had survived related the story of their brave resistance. Talon and Reza forgot all about sleep. They listened eagerly to the halting stories the men gave between slurps of new-made tea and bites of stew and bread.

After the group escorting the princess had gone ahead, they had ambushed the scouts that came to investigate, then they'd fled up the dry river bed. Just before the turn-off, they'd prepared another ambush on both banks of the stream bed.

Before that, however, they'd run into the goatherd, whereupon the captain told his men to round up the goats and drive them down the narrow riverbed in the direction of the enemy. It might slow their pursuit.

They knew the dead scouts must have been discovered by then, and surely the enemy would come looking for them, "angry as hornets and twice as dangerous," as one succinctly put it.

The example of the dead scouts should have made the enemy cautious. Instead, their anger made them reckless. They charged up the stream bed straight into the next trap prepared for them. The front ranks were massacred, but the numbers were great enough for the rushing enemy to jump over their dead comrades and charge up both banks to engage the captain's men.

The fighting was savage, as both sides gave no quarter and expected none. The din of battle raged all around. Men struggled to hack and stab their opponents to death in the choking dust of the battleground. They screamed into each other's faces with the madness of battle lust or shrieked in their agony as they died.

It became clear that the captain would have to retreat. He could guess that the enemy would soon find a way behind him, and then it would be all over. In fact they had, and it was just in time that the survivors of the small band managed to slip out of the fighting, taking advantage of one of the times when the enemy was regrouping.

They had ridden hard to another vantage point, with the enemy right on their heels. It was deemed fortuitous that there seemed to be no archers in the ranks of the enemy, whereas the captain had two remaining archers who did much damage during the retreat.

Thus it was they turned and fought wherever they felt they could hold ground and fled when the enemy came forward in larger numbers. As the day passed and evening came, the captain made plans to slip his men away. They were by now sadly depleted in strength, having suffered many wounds per man, and six dead. They were also without water now and had not eaten since morning. Exhaustion was setting in, and they could no longer hold a position with more than token resistance. Still, he held them together, this man of steel, even after he was wounded by a javelin. Men said that he merely tugged it free and killed the man who had thrown it with the same javelin. The men were in awe of their captain after such a fight.

As the sun set it became more and more clear that the enemy considered the fight not worth the cost. They became noticeably reluctant to get into another heavy engagement. Still, there were more losses. Darkness came. The captain called his men together and told them that they must ride for the pass as quickly as possible and meet up there. The wounded were to be taken with them; the dead were to be left behind.

They prayed that Allah had cast his protection over the princess, for whom they had sacrificed themselves, and that she had escaped.

Thus it was that the troop of seventeen men who had left the castle of Samiran that morning such a long time ago came to the village as a troop of seven. The men talked about their great feats of arms and about how this man or that had killed five men in one engagement, and six in another. It was obviously embellishment, but men who have survived will tell such tales of each other; such is the way of men who fight as warriors.

There were murmurs of admiration and praise from the others, hard, tough men themselves, who were envious that they had not been in that fight, which would be talked about for years to come. Someone stoked the fire and fed it with more dried dung. The flames grew and sent sparks high into the night sky. Water pipes came out and men smoked, passing them round from man to man, recalling other times when men had behaved as men should.

Some rolled into their blankets and went to sleep on the hard ground with the stars as their roof. It would not rain for at least another month, and although it was cold now, it was the best place to sleep.

But that is but a Tent wherein may rest
A Sultan to the realm of Death addrest;
The Sultan rises, and the dark Ferrásh
Strikes, and prepares it for another guest.
— Omar Khayyam —

Chapter 11
Lamissar

The next day the troops were assembled on the *maidan*, waiting with their horses. Ahmad came out of the house provided by the village *rais*. With him was the princess, looking fresh and ready to ride. Her two hounds were present, sniffing around the walls but keeping an eye on her as they did so. She was the trustworthy, safe human in their lives. Many of the soldiers would shun them, or even hurt them, if they were left alone without the protection of their mistress. Most Muslims shunned dogs and disliked having them around.

Ahmad gave orders to the troop leader to commence the escort of the princess to Lamissar, while he would follow with the remainder of the captain's men. It was impossible for the captain and some of the other wounded to ride just yet. The donkeys and their passengers would follow behind and get there later in the evening. Jean and Feza had struck up a friendship and spent time talking about their past lives. Jean was a lively companion for Feza, and she provided him with a fund of information that he would otherwise not have access to.

Assembling men and horses took some time, but at last, they were all ready to leave. So the party set off once again, but with Jamshid and another man in charge. A light mist at that early hour shrouded the tops of the hills and lent a ghostly atmosphere around the village.

They climbed a little higher for the remainder of that day, into the high valley that divided the vast Alborz Range. The mountains soared up on either side, into the sky like jagged teeth, their snow-capped peaks adding to the illusion.

There was more grazing in these highlands, although poor; the grass meadows were covered with coarse stubbed grass. Numerous small orchards of apple trees, cherry trees, and apricot trees were interspersed on the slopes near to the villages, along with scattered rows of ripe cereal crops waiting to be harvested. The party came up on several villages built on the high banks of the river that tumbled alongside their route. Some of the richer towns had planted groves of poplar trees, which gave them a softer aspect in this harsh land. There were occasional willows along the river banks, which were for the most part denuded of trees because the spring floods tore away most trees that tried to grow.

Talon listened with rapt attention to Rav'an. Not only did she have a musical voice, she had a very good understanding of the people and country she had grown up in.

This was all very new to him. From his earliest childhood, he had hitherto known the narrow strip of land known as Palestine that bordered the Mediterranean Sea. He had only heard of the rich string of oases farther inland that more or less followed the Jordan River. The Lake of Tiberius was dotted with palms where man had planted them, but there had also been much bare ground, such as the lands around Golan. He had been very surprised to see how rich in cultivated land Damascus was on his way through as a prisoner.

Here in these highlands, he saw people working hard to bring their harvest in. Small boys with flails beat the piles of wheat that men and women brought up on laden donkeys. Near each village, they saw herds of goats mixed with large, woolly sheep with huge fat tails, attended by old men or young boys. The animals were being brought down from the higher pastures to keep them alive during the cold of winter.

Most of the villages they passed through were not rich. The villagers would come out and greet the party, dressed in their coarse but colorful dyed clothes. Children screamed and ran around in excitement, the men and women hushed or clapped at them for silence and called out to the princess with offers of food and drink as she went by. She, in turn, would wave and call greetings.

Occasionally Talon saw a village nestled in a cleft of land, a protective cover of poplar trees shading the mud huts from the sharp sunlight. The poplar leaves were just beginning to turn golden and swayed in the light breeze, the gold shimmering against the light green of the other leaves as they caught the rays of the sun. Looking up at the mountains that contained this deep valley, he could see many of the gullies and ravines choked thick with stunted trees. Good hunting there, he assumed, and he was sure the trout in the streams would be fat and succulent.

Everyone was relaxed and comfortable within the safety of the valley. Danger was far off now.

* * * * *

At the start of the day's journey, the princess had been somewhat withdrawn, so the boys were, in turn, circumspect. They took their lead from Feza, who indicated that they should leave her alone for a while.

Rav'an had breathed a deep sigh of relief when Ahmad told her to go ahead that morning, as he had some unfinished business to attend to. She was sure she knew what that was, but had not asked him. Confirmation came as they were leaving the village: there came a shriek of agony and a lot of shouting and laughter from back among the houses; Ahmad and his men had commenced to send their prisoner to his maker as slowly and as painfully as they knew how.

It was an uneventful ride all day and soon they could see Castle Lamissar perched along the north side of one of the less accessible walls of the mountains.

* * * * *

Lamissar was a huge castle, located on the banks of a deep, fast flowing stream, which the locals called the Naina Rud. It had been built in a very bare area of land that did not provide much in the way of foliage. Surrounded by high, steep buttresses and pointed hills of bare rock, it looked very grim to Talon. The whole party had to climb along some narrow tracks to make the north gate, the single accessible entrance to the fortress. A natural precipice shielded the western side, while large, interlaced towers on the south side had no gates. The whole castle sloped up at a quite steep angle on the north side where huge towers were situated, guarding the main entrance. An arched entrance at the south gate was closed.

The fortress was, even to Talon's inexperienced eye, a very defensible place, as long as one could hold the north towers. If those fell, then everything within was at the mercy of the intruders, as the towers also dominated the castle grounds. He later learned that many very large water cisterns within the castle could allow it to withstand a long siege, if necessary. The interior of the walled enclosure was almost as large as that of Samiran, although the walls of this castle, with the exception of the mighty towers of the north side, were not of the same scale.

The many buildings within were spread around without much order to their layout, but more were close to the north gate. Rav'an was to stay in a huddled collection of buildings that were away from the main keep, closer to the south, where the stables were. Word had spread that she was coming, so the people of the castle assembled and gave a modest but enthusiastic reception, with much *salaam*ing and ululuing by the womenfolk, as they came under the massive gatehouse into the main courtyard.

The princess was greeted by the castellan on her arrival, with all the usual elaborate welcoming statements and counter-statements that accompanied meetings of this kind, then they walked to the accommodation he was providing her for the night.

The group of soldiers and Reza and Talon took the horses to the ample stables and spent some time rubbing their animals down, talking and joking among themselves. Jamshid didn't spare the boys; he ragged them about their skirmish with the enemy the day before, wondering why there were any left when he and his men went back. But it was kindly, and the rest of the men joined in, enjoying the banter.

It was clear the two youths had earned respect for their efforts. The conversation shifted to the captain's latest deeds and his great rear-guard action. Later, people began to drift off to find food and other acquaintances. There was even the possibility that there'd be women available for those adventurous enough, Jamshid said with a wink at the boys. He had correctly surmised that this aspect of their manhood had not been tested yet. They were abashed and found reasons to concentrate on their horses.

After the men had gone, the boys lingered over their grooming of the princess' horses and talked about this situation, not for the first time, and as they were friends they were free enough. Had either of them ever seen a naked woman? Reza ventured that he had seen his sister once with no clothes on as a small girl, but he had been unimpressed.

"What about you, Talon? Do the women walk about naked in the Frankish castles? I heard that they are wicked and loose and any man could take one whenever he wants."

Talon went on the defensive. "Reza, we Franks are not loose either. The priests are as bad as the mullahs for keeping people from sinning. To walk about naked is a sin. At least, I heard it was," he said, but it sounded uncertain. Then to shift the direction this was going in, "Remember when Nasim once had a whore in the town of Samiran? He went all sloppy, and driveled on about it being a wondrous thing to take one—although I am not sure if he knew what he meant by 'taking a woman.' Anyway, he got all poetic about it until he discovered that he had groin lice, and then he went about scratching all day, cursing all women."

They both laughed at the recollection of Nasim's discomfort at having to shave his crotch with a sharp dagger, while all the other senior boys clustered around, giving him useless advice and ribbing him. All the boys had been envious nonetheless. It was the overriding thought in their adolescent minds, and not one of them had any idea as to what to expect.

The two in the stables of Lamissar were off to speculating once again about what was in store for them at Alamut, where, they were told, they would get a glimpse of paradise and all the women therein. They boasted they would get to "do it" with a hundred or more, without quite knowing what that meant.

It became dark. They were forced to hurry and feed the animals for both themselves and the soldiers, who had gone off. Then it was out of the stables, looking for the kitchens and somewhere to sleep for the night.

They were at dinner when Ahmad and his small contingent of soldiers arrived at the castle. They had ridden hard and the horses were almost blown as they came in, steaming, sweating, heads down in the flickering light of the torches held by others in the yard.

Ahmad shouted for Talon and Reza, who had just finished their supper, and told them to take his horse and stable it for him. "Where is the princess?" he demanded.

They pointed out the jumble of buildings at the center of the large space between the walls, and Ahmad stamped off in that direction without even a word of thanks.

*****

Dawn came to the valley early, but the shadows took some time to leave Lamissar. The high pointed peak to the immediate east, which towered over the castle, shaded the fortress. The courtyard stirred at the call of a scrawny rooster.

The two boys had to dash some water into their faces for morning ablutions and then hasten to saddle not just their own animals, but also Ahmad's and that of the princess. The animals were not joyous at being interrupted at their morning feed but were cajoled into allowing the boys to groom and harness them up.

Jean came into the stable and greeted people with his usual morning cheerfulness. The troops accepted him. In spite of themselves, they quite liked the round, cheerful, infidel mullah, who could now speak their own language well.

The boys were able to bid him good morning, but because they were so busy he gave them assistance, as there was not much one had to do with the donkeys. He had become the minder of Feza's donkey and earned her gratitude each day as he assisted her to mount and dismount along the way.

Talon noticed that Jean coughed a lot. He searched for and found a patched old blanket to help warm him, thinking that he was cold. Jean, who looked pale, thanked him and told him not to fuss.

It was becoming colder these mid-autumn mornings. Everyone bundled into warm clothes before venturing off to get some of the sparse breakfast provided by the cooks. They could at least warm themselves on the bean stew that looked, as Talon told a snickering Reza, more like slimy horse snot than real food. However, it tasted very nice when eaten with the *nan*.

*****

There was somewhat more decorum in the main buildings as Rav'an and her servant made ready. She decided that she could not avoid Ahmad forever, so she quit the room soon after dressing, leaving Feza to pack up their things, and made her way down to the hall.

There she was met by Fatima, the castellan's wife, who

provided her with a simple but adequate breakfast of *barbari* and yogurt with goat's cheese, and something that was rare for these parts: olives from a barrel that had come from as far away as Shiraz. Tea came hot and steaming in one of the new bronze pots with a spout that had been brought from Baghdad, where the finest coppersmiths and brass smiths were to be found. A servant poured the tea into glazed pottery cups, which were hand-painted with depictions of horsemen and trees.

Ahmad walked in, looking rumpled and baggy-eyed. He greeted the seated people in a brusque manner, helping himself to a cup of tea and joining them with an abrupt nod to the hovering servant to bring him some soup. The nervous castellan was as civil to Ahmad as possible, inviting him to take some sweetmeat and talking about the furtherance of their journey to Alamut. Rav'an was not very interested in Ahmad this morning. S, and she was not looking forward to the remainder of her journey in his company. Breakfast was an uncomfortable affair.

* * * * *

Out in the yard it was all bustle. The soldiers and the boys hurriedly made ready. No one wanted to incur Ahmad's impatience that morning. The sun came over the top of the peak and flared down on the bustling castle yard, bathing it in the harsh light of day.

They were almost done when Ahmad stormed out, shouting for Jamshid; they were to leave at once. The princess came out within fifteen minutes, her two hounds alongside. Feza followed, with an assistant carrying the baggage.

Rav'an waited patiently for the donkeys to be loaded, coming over to Talon and Reza and taking her mare from them with a look and a word of thanks. There were no thanks from Ahmad as he snatched the reins from Talon. Talon shrugged and made off to take Jabbar from Reza. They looked at one another as he did so, but there was no time to talk. The party was on its way.

Ahmad wasted no time in positioning himself alongside the princess. They headed down the steep slope to the valley bottom where the trail wound alongside the river Shah Rud. They had many miles to go. The pace was snappy and the donkeys were running from the start. Looking back, Talon could see that the group with the baggage train and Jean and Feza would soon be left behind. It was clear that Ahmad was not going to wait for them, so he could do nothing but wave and concentrate on keeping Jabbar from getting too close to the two in front.

* * * * *

Ahmad was trying to get Rav'an to talk. Although she was not in the mood, she tried to put on a pleasant face and make the best of it. She discovered that her uncle, Arash Khan, was staying at Alamut for the time being, supervising the final training of the senior students so that they came away as full-fledged *fida'i*. He, Ahmad, was going to leave in the spring and go to Syria, where he hoped to be able to do some fighting against the Franks.

He bragged that he was keen to cross blades with one of the Franks and hack his head off as a trophy. Rav'an wasn't revolted at her cousin's crude language. She was quite used to men bragging like this, in graphic detail, usually for the benefit of a woman whom they wanted to impress. She was a product of her kind, having grown up with violence always nearby, and where, often as not, a mistake could be fatal. Men fought all the time. In fact, it was the honorable thing to do, to be a warrior, and serve a lord.

Instead, her responses were automatic while she adjusted her attention to their route. They would follow the difficult trail along the Shah Rud for many more miles, which took them some distance away from the river and then back again.

Neither Talon nor Reza had been allowed close to the princess since Ahmad had completely taken over as her escort. His stiff back and sharp gestures indicated that he was not getting the full responses that he had anticipated from the princess.

They were riding too far ahead for the boys to hear anything the two said, so Talon and Reza talked together about what they were to expect at Alamut. This would be their arrival at the very center of the Ismaili world—the high temple of the Ismaili sect. Their future existence would be dictated from this time on. Here they would be initiated for life and become a part of the most dangerous group of people in Persia and beyond.

After many hours, they came to the junctions of the Shah and Alamut Ruds. Just farther along the Shah Rud was the village of Shotor Khan. Here they would turn north and move up the steeper, higher valley for about five miles to the village called Gasor Khan, the village which supplied the castle with its essentials. This was more of a small town now, since the Ismaili had come to the area more than sixty years before. Rav'an had played with children in that village when younger, when she could persuade Feza to take her down the long steep path to the village.

From the village, one could look up into the heights of the mountain, which soared to more than 9000 feet above this high valley. Upon its flanks, they would see the mammoth rock that seemed to stick out of the mountain, as though some playful giant god of olden time had hurled it into the side of the mountain. There it had stuck fast, a large part of it sticking out over steep sides, making it impossible to scale from the south. Most of the castle was mounted on top of the rock, with some of the walls meandering up the steep sides of the mountain ridge. Jamshid explained to the boys that it was known as Alamut or Eagle's nest because of its location.

Rav'an had always been awed by her former home and was waiting to see what Talon's reaction might be when he saw it for the first time. In the meantime, Ahmad was talking and they had a long way to go.

The troop of travelers came to the Alamut Rud in late afternoon. They had made very good progress, but the horses were tired. The sparse midday meal had been eaten in a hurry, and then they had pushed on.

They splashed through a crude ford at the junction of the swiftly flowing rivers just upstream along the Alamut Rud, and then paused on the other side to water the horses. The sound of rushing water and the plentiful, tall poplar trees, now golden in color in anticipation of winter, gave Talon the thought that this was like a cathedral. He wondered how the fishing might be; the mountain trout must be wonderful. But even with that distraction, he had the uneasy feeling that there were eyes watching them. He had a sense of foreboding but could not think why.

The rushing of the water over the rocks as it ran into shallow rapids muted even the sound of the men talking. The depth of the river at this time of year was just knee high for the horses. Jamshid told Talon that in the late spring during the thaws the river rose almost four more feet and was a raging torrent. No man could pass then, and those who tried were often found the following summer, many miles down stream.

Talon enjoyed talking to Jamshid, who accorded him and Reza some respect and treated them as members of his troop. They derived comfort from this. They had not been able to talk to anyone else during the ride, as they were behind the princess, riding on their own.

The pause at the river was not long enough for the donkeys to catch up, but that did not deter Ahmad. He wanted to get to the castle in daylight, so he insisted that they continue. They would not stop at the village on their way. Rav'an cast a look of concern back along the trail, hoping that Feza was all right, and then joined the horsemen as they took the east trail along the Alamut Rud, heading north and upward to the castle.

They were in an even steeper valley now, and it seemed that they would have to go into the water as the banks of the wide stream closed in on them. Then they crossed the river via another low ford, and the trail left the river behind. The horses labored up steep slopes.

Then ahead of them was the castle.

The group paused, and Rav'an could not resist pointing for Talon's benefit, who stared in the direction she had indicated. He gasped; so did Reza, both stunned by the sight of that fortress perched on the monstrous rock so high above them. It was as though it floated, almost disconnected from the huge mountain of which it was a part.

The two boys gazed at what was to become their new home, wonder, eagerness, and a little fear mixed in their faces as they contemplated its impregnable position.

Ahmad shouted at the troop to continue. They labored up the last of the steep rises to the point where they were almost underneath the great rock. They passed some low huts and lean-to sheds, built into the cutaway of the huge surface that towered over them. On their way round the corner of the rock, Talon looked back down the long slope they had mounted. The river was a thin thread in the darkening valley below. Then they all dismounted and walked the horses the last few hundred yards past the castle walls, around to the north side, to the one gate.

There was a great deal of activity upon their arrival. The gates were opened, and curious people lined the walls to peer down at the party. A few voices called but no one waved. This was not the welcome that had become so familiar on the route here. People came out to stare and mutter, but there was not the usual cheerfulness Rav'an had come to take for granted elsewhere.

She stared up, hoping to recognize anyone she might have known a few years ago, but did not see anyone. A tiny prickle of apprehension came to her, as she began to remember how dark this castle was compared to Samiran's sunny environment. She hoped that Ali the stable master would remember her, and perhaps the servants, but as her brother was no longer in residence, most of the familiar faces would be with him.

They rode into the small yard, and people took their horses as they dismounted. Ahmad was acting the gentleman and offered to assist her to dismount. She politely declined, liking the fact that she was independent and could do things for herself. She was unaware that he didn't like it and took it out on Talon when he came to take the horses. She was sorely puzzled by the quiet, until she noticed that people were moving away and making space for someone to walk through.

Then she recognized her uncle. He was older and there were more gray hairs at his temples and in his mustache, but he appeared to be well. He greeted Ahmad in a perfunctory manner, and then he turned his attention to his niece.

"Welcome, my dear Rav'an," he said, coming up to her and reaching for her hands. He leaned forward and gave her a light kiss on the cheek.

She smelt his foul breath, and it was all she could do not to pull back from him. Instead, she gave him a bright smile and squeezed the dry hands that held hers. "Uncle, It is good to see you again. I have not seen you for four years, I believe," she said. He seemed to have aged about ten years since she had seen him last.

Her uncle, Arash Khan, released her hands and took a pace back, as though to see her better. "Those years have been kinder to you than to me, I think, Rav'an," he said smoothly, and smiled at her. "I swear that you have bloomed into the most beautiful of young women since I last saw you, my dear. If anything, more so than your very lovely mother, may Allah protect her soul," he said, his tone unctuous.

She smiled at him, and a light blush began to climb her throat at the frank scrutiny she was being subjected to.

He went on briskly. "But you must be tired, and so you should leave the horses to the servants, and go and inspect your quarters, my dear. I have had an army of servants preparing the rooms for you."

"Thank you, Uncle. I am thankful for your kindness. I am somewhat tired and would be glad to take some rest." She glanced over at the two boys who were standing with the horses a few paces away. "Uncle, these are two students who have come for their initiation. One of them is the Frank called Talon, do you remember? The one who killed the lion? They also saved me from the sultan's men as we were coming over the Shah Rud passes. I would like to recommend them to you as brave men who have been my protectors."

Her uncle said, "Ah, so he is here at last."

She looked at him, surprised at his tone, but he gave no clue as to what he meant.

He looked over to the boys, and then, with a flick of his hand, motioned them to come over.

They approached with the horses and both knelt before him. Talon looked up at him and saw a well-dressed, slight, dark man with salt-and-pepper hair and mustache, a face that showed dissipation, and sensuous lips. But it was the eyes that held him. They bored straight into him, and he felt a flicker of fear within as he stared into those obsidian, soulless eyes.

"The princess tells me that you two have performed well and have protected her from the sultan's men," he said in a low voice. "You shall be rewarded for this service."

Talon mustered enough courage to stammer. "Sir, we did only what we were charged—to protect my lady."

"Then it appears that you did your duty to her and to me."

Arash turned away and, taking the princess' arm, led her through the crowd, which began to disperse now that the Khan was going back into the castle.

Ahmad tossed his head and slapped his whip against his soft leather boots, then followed, angry, it seemed, that his father had not included him in the discussion.

Talon and Reza looked at one another, stood up, then led their charges in the direction that the other horses had been taken. They didn't say anything as they took care of the horses. They were too busy with their training. Some of the horses were led out of the castle and down the steep slope to where the huts and lean-tos were located, some way back down the mountain, there not being enough room in the castle for all the troop's horses. The castle could accommodate about twenty all together, which meant that only the horses belonging to the Khan, his family, and close retainers would be stabled there.

Rav'an's horses would be stabled in the castle, where they

would receive very good treatment, Jamshid assured Reza. The stable master, Ali, was very fond of horses and accorded them more respect than he did people. Jamshid said this last one loudly, to catch the attention of a plump man working with some boys at the end of the stable. He looked up, then came ambling over.

He smiled when he saw Jamshid. "Might have known you were here," he said amiably. "I hear that you can't ride good horses these days. Is that your camel?" He pretended to peer into the gloom at the horse Jamshid had ridden. It was an elegant Turcoman of a rich, dark chestnut color and didn't deserve the epithet of camel.

Jamshid pretended to be mortally offended. "Ali, you son of a dog, now I know for sure that you don't know the back end of a horse from the front," he growled, pulling a ferocious face.

Ali laughed. "It is good to see you, you whiff of hot camel fart, my friend." They laughed and clapped their hands on shoulders. Ali turned to Talon and Reza. "Who are these two grinning apes you have for company, Jamshid? I have not seen either of them before."

"New students from Samiran. They are good boys who did some protecting of the princess on the way when we ran into the sultan's men."

Ali looked at them as though appraising them. "If you protected the princess from our enemies then you are friends of mine; but, and this is just as important, if Jamshid says such of you, then you are indeed my friends."

The boys looked abashed at the praise, and then Ali and Jamshid left them to finish the horses while they went off to catch up on the latest news. Jamshid had to tell Ali all about the engagement with the Sultan's troop.

It was getting dark, and still there was no sign of the priest and Feza. They must have left the donkeys very far behind, Reza surmised. Talon nodded. It would be very late before the baggage train made it in, so they might as well get fed. They had noticed others of their age as they came into the castle yard, so they went to find out where they were to bed for the night and what they were expected to do in the morning.

Having not had instructions from either Ahmad or the princess, they felt a bit lost, but Jamshid, thoughtful as usual, had already talked to one of the more senior *rafiqi,* called Behzad, who came looking for them. He greeted them somewhat distantly, perhaps because he was so much senior to them, Talon thought, resentfully. He felt sometimes that he was going to be at the bottom of the pecking order for the rest of his life.

Behzad took them to the back of the castle to an area that seemed closed off from the rest. Reza asked about this. Behzad responded that it was not as large a castle as the others, so they had to be kept at a distance from the living quarters of the Khan and his family.

Their accommodation turned out to be better than what they had come to call home in Samiran. The two of them shared a single cell, which gave them much more privacy. It was sparse and cold, but they didn't mind. It was a luxury after the crowded accommodation they were used to.

Behzad informed them that they would spend a lot of time in the castle's library. There was much to learn. With winter coming there would not be much else to do, so studying was encouraged. Their training would commence on the morrow. They should get something to eat at the kitchens, which he pointed out to them, and get an early night. This came more as an order than a suggestion, so they complied, snatching a cold meal from the kitchens, where they ran into Jamshid and Ali enjoying a hot dinner. Jamshid waved, but the boys could not stay and eat. He let them go with a friendly goodnight.

All they had was their bedrolls. The bulk of the baggage was still on the road, so they unrolled them and settled in for the night. The conversation was brief. They were tired, and like all young people, they were instantly asleep. Neither woke when the baggage train, accompanied by Jean and Feza, arrived in the middle of the night.

And besides there shall be two gardens,
Green, green pastures,
Therein two fountains of gushing water,
Therein fruits, and palm trees and pomegranates.
Therein maidens good and comely...
Houris, cloistered in cool pavilions.

— *Sura* —
[Arberry's translation]

Chapter 12
Alamut

Talon and Reza woke to a new world, one that was to transform their lives. Their first taste of the future came with the rough awakening by their comrades, who made a lot of noise outside the blanket-draped doorway. They shouted at the two bleary-eyed boys to get dressed and come to breakfast as fast as they could, or they would go without. The two rolled out of their blankets and dressed in a hurry. They ran after the others, who were already halfway across the courtyard on their way to the kitchens.

The introductions were brief. The two knew, at least by sight, some of the twenty or so young men. These had also started their training at Samiran, several years ahead of them. Reza began telling anyone who would listen about their adventures against the sultan's men. Most of the young men were very interested, asking a lot of questions. A battle of the type the captain had fought was not something that happened every day.

The group lined up for bread and cheese, onions, *maast*, and *doogh*, a liquid form of yogurt that could be drunk out of a pottery beaker, then they all settled down as close to the central fires as they could to keep warm. It was a brisk, cold day. Autumn came to the mountains earlier than the plains.

The castle was a hive of activity. The harvests were being taken in at the villages of Gasor Khan and Shotor Khan. It was the task of the villages to supply the castle a percentage of their harvest. A constant stream of donkeys came and went with loads of grain, dried fruits, carcasses of sheep and goats and smoked meat, even sacks of stale *barbari* bread, which would keep all winter, if necessary. Any root crops that could be spared by the villagers found their way up to the castle, as did fodder for the horses, plus fuel for fires and many other goods that would be in short supply when winter finally arrived.

The fare in this castle was not exceptional and was indeed more basic than in Samiran, which, being astride the caravan routes, could take what it needed from them. The best of the dried fruit and what nuts and delicacies were available would be reserved for the Agha Khan or his family in residence.

People in the castle were tolerant of the youths. These were the future *fida'i*, and their role in the overall scheme of things Ismaili was very important, but they did not receive the kind of reverence accorded to the Agha Khan and his closest family. Neither did they get the respect that came with being one of the few *rafiqi* who had killed and escaped to live and tell the tale. These were respected by the *fida'i*, the current rank of most of the older youths at Alamut, more than anyone else, as this was what they aspired to become.

There was not much time to explore, nor were they encouraged to venture too far afield from the main castle. Talon and Reza lived in the central part, where most buildings, including the main keep, were situated. Several stories high, the keep was made of mud brick, mortared stone, and wood beams. The buildings petered out and became sparse toward an area where they could see trees, now shedding their leaves, and bushes—an area they were forbidden to enter. They surmised between themselves that this was where the gardens were located, part of the paradise that the boys longed to experience. Talon had learned from the princess long ago that gardens were very important to the people of Persia. They took great pains to design them and ensure that water flowed to their fountains by ingenious piping.

Here in Alamut's rarified atmosphere, life was very different from what Talon and Reza were used to at Samiran. Here was seriousness of purpose, with no joking and almost no horseplay. They were on the final phase of their journey to manhood in the service of the Khan and the Ismaili movement. The instructors drove them relentlessly and brooked no breeches of discipline.

They were instructed in the doctrines according to the Agha Khan Hassan II. Until recent times, Hassan's brother Muhammad, the son of Hassan the Great, had carried the faith of his brother with a strict adherence to the more conventional form of Islam. This had been along the lines of the Shi'ia faith, which observed Ramadan, the ritual month of fasting, and also included other rituals of the faith, such as the mourning of Hussein, called Ashura, when Shi'ites enter into a great show of public mourning.

Upon assuming power among the Ismaili, Hassan II had declared *Qiyama*, which implied that the Day of Judgment had already arrived. He had stated that all Ismaili were henceforth judged, and were indeed now in paradise. The trappings of religion were superfluous and no longer needed to be adhered to. He went so far as to persecute his own people when they tried to remain faithful to the old doctrines of the Islamic faith. However, the loyalty of these fierce mountain people was constant, and the Ismaili revered him as the next Imam. His followers felt that they were now in the exulted place.

His children had been exalted with him, which meant that his son, Rav'an's brother Muhammad, was also blessed with the status of Imam. Muhammad, the ruling Agha Khan, had inherited his father's position after Hassan II had been murdered. Muhammad had put to death the murderer and his entire family without delay. While his father had persecuted members of the Ismaili who were still true to the old faith, Muhammad was more tolerant and did not do so. They, in turn, gave him their unstinting loyalty.

The boys were now considered old enough to understand these things and why they were being trained and, indeed, what their fate was to be in the future. The *rafiqi* drummed into them over and over the mantra of faith to one person on this earth, the Agha Khan, and his bidding was law. To disobey would be to receive a death that would be ghastly, and to be denied paradise at the same time. Damned for all eternity.

What was paradise, they might well ask? The power of the Khan would give each one of them a glimpse of this final place, where anyone who had obeyed his master would go the moment he was slain upon the successful completion of his duty. The boys were the chosen ones. When at last they became *fida'i,* it would be their duty and honor to go on a mission, to slay one particular person of high or low rank on behalf of the Master. In doing so, there was every chance they would die in the process.

They would become martyrs and paradise would be theirs upon that instant. Very little was said of those who survived, but the question remained. There were stories of one boy whose own mother had disowned him for failing to become a martyr. Then there were others, like Jemal and Behzad, who had survived to attain high position.

Talon and Reza's impressionable young minds were ready for this kind of thing and believed every word, awestruck. They began to speculate as to what mission they would be commanded to undertake. In the manner of young men everywhere, they bounced from one subject to another without pause—from the prospect of what they would see in paradise, to which vizier or sultan they would have to kill in order to qualify for the privilege of going to the final, great paradise.

The duty that they felt as a mantle surrounding them did not stop their speculating as to what might be in store for them in paradise. Since both were without experience with regard to women, their speculation was exaggerated and wild. Their young, youthful bodies were screaming for release. The clever men of Alamut understood this, and worked them mercilessly at their trade, crafting them into the exact temper of killing steel that was required.

Gaining access to a defended room was one of the qualifications to be a *fida'i,* and it was much practiced. The instructors beat the ones they caught, so it was worth the effort not to be detected. Talon and Reza, both very fit and eager to prove they were as good as their peers, were in fact better at this than many others. One blustery night, Reza had no trouble slipping past two of his instructors when they thought he was miles away. Their consternation at his success was all the reward he asked for, and for days after he and Talon would laugh at it.

Talon fared almost as well, scaling the north wall of the castle one night with a rope which Reza had thoughtfully left hanging. As it was some distance from the area where the trainers were watching, he was able to avoid detection and gain entry. Neither he nor Reza saw anything wrong in cheating their instructors. It became a kind of "them or us" affair, since the two of them, being the newcomers, were accorded no help from the others of their class.

It was not long before Talon and Reza became known as the "Phantoms". It came to their notice when one of the more talkative students was complaining to his friends, without realizing that Reza was sitting in an alcove in the library.

The boy said that Talon had come right up behind him one

day, and he had not heard a thing. His frustration stemmed from the fact that he had thought that he was indeed one of the more alert students. Like all of his comrades, he had well-developed wide-angle vision. He was highly tuned to feeling anyone come close to him. He swore he had felt nothing, nothing at all of Talon's presence. "That *ferengi* and his friend Reza are like phantoms," he complained. "They are everywhere but nowhere. I do not know how they do this and they scare me."

The boy's friends had agreed with him. None of them liked the two newcomers much. No one seemed to be able to get close to them. In the hand-to-hand fighting with knives, which was the most common training, neither Reza nor Talon could be bested by any of the youths who had been in Alamut longer. This had started to cause resentment.

The talk had moved on to Ahmad and his father. Everyone was afraid of these two, especially of Arash Khan, the master's uncle. Tales of his depredations were legion, far and wide. He was said to have the best intelligence network in the world. His services were devoted to the Agha Khan, of course, but he himself was a legend in his own right.

No one had ever survived an interrogation, nor failed to give up his secrets to Arash Khan before he died. The name Mehdi came up at one point, and Reza smiled. Mehdi had been one of the instructors whom he had discomfited. Mehdi was also the one student in Samiran who had made life difficult for Talon. Now he was an instructor. Reza thought contemptuously that Talon could probably kill Mehdi without trying very hard. He himself could for sure, he told himself.

The small group of students continued with their low discussion of their leaders.

"Mehdi works for Ahmad," said one. "I see him spending a lot of time in his company. It is as though he is more for Ahmad than for the Khan."

No one said anything to this. The words were dangerous, and the thick walls of Alamut had ears everywhere.

The student hastened to add, "Everyone is dedicated to the service of the Agha Khan, aren't they?"

"Well, consider Behzad," asked another, to change the subject. "Isn't he one of the best of the instructors here? I like and trust him," he added. They all nodded their agreement. It was important to have someone to look up to at this time.

The conversation soon degenerated into gossip about women, which the boys had on their minds most of the time. As the bragging began, Reza slipped out of the library, undetected by his peers, and even had the satisfaction of moving out into the yard without disturbing the sentry at the door.

He wanted to talk to Talon. Without realizing it, the two were rapidly becoming inseparable. It was a comfortable relationship, where Talon took the lead most of the time but relied upon Reza to be there, which he invariably was.

He found Talon out in the yard talking to the blacksmith, Giv. Talon was absorbed in watching him fashion a short, wide blade that Talon had asked for. The two of them were discussing its potential. Giv liked what Talon had asked for and was busy flattening the haft of the knife when Reza came up. Giv smiled at Reza, who knuckled his forehead in deference to the master sword maker, and then grinned at Talon and asked him what they were doing.

"Giv is making me a special knife," Talon replied, returning the grin. "It is very wide but shorter than the normal ones. It will make a wide entry, and can be better concealed."

Reza looked at the knife, his eyes skeptical. It didn't look like much at this stage, but he decided not to deride it yet. There would be time enough to tease his friend about it later. Giv seemed to like what was being done, so he left it at that. He had to raise his voice over the hammering and roar of the fire. "Talon, I have to talk; let's go outside."

Giv waved them off and concentrated on his task, while the two youths went out into the weak afternoon sunlight.

"They are talking about us again, Talon," Reza said in a morose tone. "This time we are phantoms and they don't like that."

"I don't see why that should worry us. If they think like that, then we have them worried, not the other way around."

"I know, Talon, but we don't have any friends here in Alamut," Reza muttered, kicking a small stone with the toe of his boot. He looked crestfallen.

Talon put his arm round Reza's slight but strong and sinewy shoulders. "You are my friend, and I am yours. I don't know anyone else who I want as a friend, anyway. Don't forget we also have the princess. I am sure she is our friend, Reza. So don't worry, we can look out for each other."

Reza nodded. "You are right. In the business we are in there cannot be that many friends. And who knows, life might be very short. So who cares?" he said, brightening up.

"Do you know, we have been here for a month, and I have seen the princess but twice since we came here? I wonder what she does with herself, now that she is in her home."

* * * * *

As though his question had been heard, Feza came hurrying to find the boys at noon the next day with a request from the princess, who wanted them to ride out of the castle with her. They were to go hunting. Rav'an was the Princess; she had the authority to demand their attendance. Feza, as always, was somewhat panicked by the idea of her princess riding off alone with a pair of youths, even if they were Talon and Reza. She came cautiously down the steep wooden stairs of the keep to the ground floor, where she demanded to see the senior *rafiqi,* Behzad.

He came and asked her politely what he could do for her, upon which she issued her mistress' demands. He looked somewhat put out by the suddenness of the command, but didn't protest. He went off and called Talon and Reza over to him. They had been sitting cross-legged in a class, listening to, of all people, Jean. He had been talking to the students about the Christian faith, and the ceremonies used by the priests of his stature, information considered a necessary part of their training as Assassins.

Both boys' eyes were glazing over with boredom, so Behzad's shout was a welcome change to their routine. He told them what Rav'an wanted and also informed them that they had to have at least two men-at-arms with them to act as a guard for the princess. Behzad was nothing if not thorough, and his word was law to the youths.

Reza rushed off to find Jamshid and ask for two good riders. Indeed, if possible, could Jamshid himself come? Talon rushed off to get ready and then head for the stables to prepare the horses.

Making her way down the stairs, with the two excited hounds in tow, Rav'an passed people going up and down. All were respectful; a few were familiar, as she remembered. Nevertheless, there had been changes in the years she had been away. Still, Ali was there at the entrance to the stables, warming himself in the thin heat of the autumn sun. Although the sky was clear, the sun was not warm these days.

As she came across the yard with the hounds at her side, he stood straighter and greeted her as always. "*Khanom* Rav'an, God's blessings be upon you! I am happy to see you. You are the light of my day, and I hope you are well."

"Salaam, I am well, Ali, I hope you are well?" she responded with a smile. "I would like to ride the mare today. Will you prepare her for me, please?"

He bowed. "This instant, my lady. Are you riding alone?"

"No, I expect to have my escort here at any minute."

Ali smiled. "Might that include the *ferengi,* my lady? He is already in the stables."

Rav'an smiled a brilliant smile at Ali that warmed him better than the autumn sun, and, calling to her hounds, went into the stable. There she found Talon already done with the mare and now working on Jabbar and Reza's horse. The hounds were delighted to see him, and he them. First, however, he had to politely ask the princess how she was. They went through the usual elaborate greetings. They had begun to enjoy this ritual, started in Samiran.

Then, with an almost impatient toss of her head, Rav'an said, "I want to go hunting with the hounds, and of course I will need an escort, so you have been chosen."

Talon shook his head giving a rueful grin. "Not just I, my lady, but also Reza, and we were commanded to bring two troopers with us."

Rav'an was annoyed, but had to accept the fact with good grace. "Very well, Talon, but we shall have some time to talk, and you can tell me all about your training." Then, wickedly, "Has it progressed to the gates of paradise yet?"

He blushed, which she could see even in the gloom of the stables. "Er... not yet, my lady."

Rav'an wanted to laugh out loud, but thought better of it. Straight-faced, she said, "I am sure it is not far off now, and then you will be an accepted member of the *fida'i* brotherhood."

He nodded, hoping they would move onto safer ground. He changed the subject. "I am very happy to be going with you, my lady. The horses, too; they do not get enough exercise these days, and winter is not far off now."

There was a commotion at the door, and Reza burst in with the two men who would be the escort. One of them was Jamshid, grinning, happy because he had been detailed for guard duty. This was much more to his liking. They all came up to the princess, politely wished her good health, and then everyone was busy.

Talon just had time to pet the two hounds. They were very excited and wanted to get going. They knew full well what was in store for them. They uttered grunts and low, excited growls as they fell over themselves to get near him without being trampled by Jabbar. By now the horses themselves were sensing the excitement and becoming restless.

Soon they were all out in the yard, leading the horses out of the north gate and down the steep slope to the cluster of huts at the base of the rock. There it was safe to mount, and the party moved off slowly, picking its way down the pathway to the valley bottom. Almost an hour later, they were at the village of Shotor Khan, which the small party rode through without stopping.

Once they were down at the riverside, they turned north. The princess lead the way up the valley, with her hounds running off to the side, gaining pace as the ground became more suitable. Talon and Reza rode on either side of Rav'an, back a few horses' lengths to allow her space, while Jamshid and his companion trooper rode at the rear.

The horses wanted to run. Gradually, the riders let them move first into a canter, and then as they came to the longer meadows now holding just the stubs of rye, they let them gallop. Talon reveled in the sound of the horses' hooves thundering on the hard turf, and the jingle of metal as weaponry and chain mail rattled to the rhythm of the horses' pace.

The party came at a fast pace to the beginning of a long, wooded stretch that kept pace with the river. Without pausing, Rav'an drove her mare straight into the trees. She slowed her mare enough to ensure that they could negotiate the path and the low branches of the trees, but the pace was still fast. The riders behind had to work hard to keep her in sight as she darted in and around the well spread trees.

Then, suddenly, the two salukis sighted game. Rav'an was the first rider to notice, and changed direction sharply, angling to the right to point the two hounds. They were off without a sound. She followed with an excited shout back to the rest of them. Then it became a wild chase through the denser trees and up the ever-steeper hill. The small deer that had been disturbed first tried to head straight up the side of the mountain, but found itself being cut off from that tactic by Badura, who raced up the hill and forced it to turn back almost onto the old trail that wound up the valley. Djahi, in the meantime, had taken the more direct route for the deer and herded it back to the trail. The riders galloped at breakneck speed, all restraint gone as they hallooed and yelled at the hounds and their blowing horses.

The boys had strung bows with them and were trying to notch an arrow as they hurtled up the narrow path. The trees were short and had twisted, gnarled trunks. Their low branches presented a constant threat of severe injury to the careless. Rav'an was calling to Badura to get down and join the chase, but the hound was nowhere to be seen. A hundred yards ahead, Djahi was gaining on the racing animal.

Talon, still too far away for a good shot, knew that he could never shoot with the princess ahead of him, so he settled down to enjoy the chase and see what would happen. Reza swept alongside Talon. Both were shouting and laughing with the sheer pleasure of being on a fast horse, racing away from the gloomy, brooding castle.

Suddenly, the path opened wide into another of the long narrow meadows used by the farmers to grow their corn. The deer and Djahi were racing across the stubble out in the open. Without any warning, a flash of brown that was Badura came out from the right of the meadow and went straight for the racing deer, which saw the danger too late, almost managing to cut off to the left, but it could not evade the galloping hound that slammed into its side. It was knocked off its feet and they fell in a tangle of legs and bodies. Amazingly, it was almost back on its feet and near escape when Djahi charged straight into it from behind.

This time it went down, with a hound at its throat and one hanging onto its rear leg. The three animals seemed to be locked into a slow-motion dance that settled into a motionless display. The riders, who had now ridden up, were, for a couple of seconds, so enthralled by the deathly enactment that no one moved.

Then Talon was off his horse and had his knife out and in one swift motion took the deer by the nose, jerked it back, and stabbed it in the jugular, cutting its throat in one efficient stroke. The deer gave a violent jerk in its death struggle, then fell over onto its side, legs kicking as its life blood flowed onto the cold ground.

The hounds, sensing their work finished, scrambled up and stood watching, as did the rest of the horsemen. Within a few seconds, the life went out of the small brown shape at Talon's feet.

He turned to Rav'an and the others. "The hounds were magnificent, my lady. I have never seen anything like it before."

Rav'an was pleased. She called to Badura and Djahi and petted them as she dismounted, caressed their ears, stroked their long backs, and told them how wonderful they were.

Without more ado, the men gutted the small deer, then slung its body over the back of the horse belonging to the trooper who had come with Jamshid.

Talon had thought that Rav'an would want to go back to the castle after this, but he found he was mistaken. Instead she mounted, called to the hounds, and led the way farther north along the same track they had been following.

The others got on their horses and followed, curious as to what she was going to do next. Reza looked back at Jamshid, who just grinned and shrugged. He was just happy to be out of the castle and on a good horse. In the cool of the late afternoon, it was very pleasant for all of them to be out and about. Most of the trees were golden, in particular the poplars, which seemed to grow everywhere in the clefts of the steep valleys. Other, more stunted, gnarled oaks crowded the hillsides. Here and there was a fruit tree, often as not protected from the north winds by a low wall.

There were still signs of the last depredations of the Seljuk along the valley. A mere fifteen years ago, the sultan had brought an army right to the very walls of Alamut and laid siege to it. He had failed, but his men had ravaged the country for many miles. Since they came to Alamut, Talon and Reza had heard tales of the heroic defense put up by Hassan and his people against mighty odds.

The riders came over the crest of a low rise, to be greeted by a small caravan of farmers and herders coming back from the higher slopes. The valley quickly became full of goats and fat tailed sheep. Deferential men and boys bowed to the princess. She gracefully accepted their homage and even leaned down to talk to one old man who seemed to know her. The animals swirled around the horses for several clamorous minutes, then were past, heading down the valley to Shotor Khan. The princess reined up at this point and, dismounting, called Jamshid over and asked him to have the trooper hold the horses. She wanted to go down to the rushing stream nearby and admire the scenery. Talon had a flickering thought that she wanted him, and him alone, to come with her but suppressed the thought as being too presumptuous.

They followed Rav'an and the two inquisitive hounds down the slope to the stream. There were several poplars and even a willow along the bank, their fallen leaves forming a dense carpet on the ground. Rav'an seated herself carelessly and commanded the awkward young men to do the same. Jamshid declined politely, saying that he should keep an eye open for everyone. Talon and Reza squatted on their haunches at a respectful distance, but close enough to converse.

There was a momentary silence as they all took in the scene about them. The stream was shallow and not very wide. It could be crossed in two strides, but the water poured over the mossy rocks in places smooth and noiseless, like a deep, transparent skin. It rushed to the base of larger rocks and slapped its way past them rudely, as though its hurry brooked no discussion. The canopy of branches lent a cave-like atmosphere of seclusion to the place.

Rav'an said, "I don't like Alamut anymore."

At first Talon wondered if he had heard her at all, and then he wondered if he had heard her correctly. Rav'an cast a sideways look back to where Jamshid was squatting some paces away, just out of hearing.

"My brother sent me here for some reason, but I do not know why. The people at the castle are not the same. Everything is different. I wish we had not come to Alamut."

Talon wondered what to say. "My lady, were you not brought up here?"

"Yes, I was, and I remembered most of the good things, but I forgot the gloom that used to hang over the castle all the time—that does not seem to have changed. In fact, it seems more sinister than I have known it. There are many more secrets."

Talon gave a glance at Reza, who was looking pensive. "Why do you think the Agha Khan sent you here, my lady?"

"I am beginning to wonder, Talon. I am not sure, as he didn't tell me anything that I needed to pay attention to. I do know that he must have known that Arash, my uncle, would be here. I, on the other hand, did not."

Reza asked, "Do you fear something from Arash Khan, my lady?"

She glanced at him. "Everyone fears something from my uncle." Then she changed the subject. "How are my protectors doing at their classes? Do you find the training different from Samiran?"

They both grinned with relief at the change of subject and at the implied mockery as to their academic studies. Talon spoke first. "Reza says we are being called 'the phantoms,' my lady."

Rav'an laughed at that. "I can attest to hearing this said, too. You two are the envy of many for your stealth and skill with the small weapons. Do you not also like the studies that tell you of other peoples? I know that the priest talks to all of you about the Christians and their ways, so that as good *fida'i* you will be able to usurp their identities if the time comes to do so."

Reza shrugged. "It would be useful, my lady, if I could understand their peculiar ceremonies. They are very different from us."

Talon hit him on the arm with a bunched fist. "Hey, I am, or was a Christian once, Mister Reza," he said with a good-natured grin.

Rav'an smiled. "Is he so different from us, Reza?" she asked, her eyebrows arched.

Reza grinned. "Sometimes, my lady, when he thinks too hard, I worry that his head might explode."

They all laughed at that, and the conversation became more relaxed. The boys were glad of an audience. They lost their self-consciousness as they told her about their adventures and successes. They talked about their training and how they had been able to outwit their instructors from time to time. Their small victories against authority were important to them. As was her way, Rav'an listened and prompted, her tinkling laugh enchanting the two young men. It was not long before her magic had enslaved them both again.

Then Jamshid was standing and looking west toward the setting sun. His posture said that he thought that they should all be going back, and now. Quick to respond, Rav'an jumped to her feet, and called the two hounds back to her. The two came bouncing back from nosing around in the leaves and bushes nearby, their feet wet from wading in the water. Talon had time to call softly to them and get a nose in his hand as a reward.

The party, reluctant to leave this oasis of calm, mounted and began the long ride back to the castle. Arriving in the gloom of the early autumn evening, Rav'an parted from the others with smiles and respectful bows on their part. She skipped off to be scolded by

Feza for being out so late.

Later that evening, when Talon and Reza were eating supper with Jean, they had time to remember the afternoon with pleasure, and told Jean all about it. They both shared their interest in Rav'an's comments about her uncle. Jean shuddered at that, and told them that they should be very careful indeed, as to whom they talked to in the castle.

"Have you not noticed that Alamut is a place of secrets? People are not the same here as they are at Samiran. I have not felt comfortable since we arrived."

Talon thought about this. "I have not had time to think on this. Reza and I have been so busy that we can just make it to our beds at night, we are so tired. What is it that you feel about Alamut that frightens you?"

Jean replied quietly, "I cannot say just what, but it is as though there are terrible secrets here that are hidden in the very stones. I think everyone here is a bit mad, and everyone seems tense. Can't you feel it? It's as though they are all waiting for something to happen. The only thing I know is that I trust no one at all, other than you two." He coughed then, a long wheezing cough.

Reza nodded. "Talon, I feel something of what Master Jean is saying. This is indeed a very different place from Samiran. The people are very watchful and seem... yes, to be waiting for something to happen, just as Jean says."

Talon shrugged. "I have not felt very much of this, but I shall pay closer attention in the future. Perhaps the princess was sent here to spy?"

"She told us that the Agha Khan sent her here but she doesn't know why," pointed out Reza.

"You are right, Reza. Then we have to protect her somehow, and help her when she needs us." He yawned. "I am going to bed. It has been a good day, and I was glad to get out of here, especially to hunt. Those hounds were magnificent, weren't they, Reza? Father, I shall bring you a blanket. You have a cough, and up here in the mountains that cannot be good."

Jean stood up with them. "Goodnight, boys. God protect you. Stay out of trouble, won't you?"

"God protect you too Father, Goodnight," Talon said. "Yes, we will be careful." He winked at Reza. "Like phantoms."

Rav'an was making her way back to her quarters when she met Ahmad on the way out.

He looked irritated and stopped her as she made to go by. "Cousin, I heard that you went out of the castle for hunting today. Is that correct?" he asked in a truculent manner.

Rav'an nodded. "It was very pleasant, Cousin. Thank you for asking. I did enjoy the hunt, and, of course, the hounds did all the work. They were beautiful to watch."

"Why did you not ask me to go with you?" he demanded.

He was annoyed about something, but Rav'an could not believe that it could have been because she had not invited him along. Having discovered that Alamut was not the spacious castle that she remembered as a young girl, she now found it cramped, and the lack of privacy was irksome. Not only that, but every time she bumped into Ahmad, he adopted a proprietary attitude toward her that was disagreeable. She now felt a flush of temper.

"Ahmad, I went out on impulse and took an escort. I did not think of you, as I did the whole thing on impulse. I am sorry if I have offended you." She did not mean it, but also did not want a public quarrel over the issue.

His reply was condescending. "I and my father have charge of this castle, and you are part of that responsibility, Cousin Rav'an. You should always at least keep me informed as to when you are going out. There are still dangers there for a woman of your stature."

Rav'an was so annoyed she flushed, bit her lip, and then without another word left him standing looking after her as she stalked off. Storming into her quarters, she shouted for Feza to bring some tea.

The old lady came into the room from the bedchamber, where she had been cleaning the bedding, a surprised look on her face. One glance at her ward told her all she needed to know. "My dove, have you been talking to Ahmad again? How I hate that man. He is so rough," she said to make it clear that she was on her princess' side.

Rav'an laughed in spite of her annoyance. Feza was so perceptive at times, and her loyalty indisputable.

"Feza, my dear old thing, he just said something that annoyed me, is all. I will not be told what to do by him. He is not my brother, and that is that."

Feza cackled. “All right now, tell me all about the hunt. Did the boys try to seduce you? Did you behave yourself, my dove?”

Rav’an snorted a laugh. “Feza, you’re terrible. I did have the ‘two boys’ with me, as you call them, although they are both almost men now, but we had two soldiers as well, Jamshid, and another pimpled youth who calls himself a soldier. So even if they had known how to, they would not have been able to, so there.”

Feza cackled again. “You should be careful around the new *fida’i*. They think they are Allah’s gift to women after they have glimpsed paradise.”

Rav’an chuckled with her. “Hmm, I don’t think they have glimpsed anything yet, Feza. I teased Talon in the stables about it. He went so red the horses thought it was an early sunset.”

They laughed together. “But you know... he is such a handsome ‘boy,’ Feza. If I could, I would take him as my man. But it is certain that is not ordained for me. I know my brother will sell me off to some fat Seljuk sultan as *one* of his wives, so that they leave the Ismaili alone. I wonder why girls are not allowed to see what paradise looks like.”

“Because we are women and our lot is different,” Feza said, with some regret. “We women see paradise all too soon, and often as not in childbirth, although no one has ever told me what to expect. It all revolves around the men, and all they expect when they get there is naked women to do their bidding. I want a naked man to do my bidding when I get there.”

They both began to giggle at that. As usual, they could look at one another when this kind of thing was said and then dissolve into laughs that never seemed to stop. They soon fell into a discussion of other things, and very soon, the day was gone. Feza brought Rav’an her favorite stew of venison and wild mushrooms. The season for mushrooms was almost over. They ate some crushed barley pottage, and her favorite cheese with *nan*. Feza had found some radishes that were huge and sharp. There was even a small cup of wine to wash it down with. Rav’an wondered where Feza had found it.

Rav’an went to bed that night thinking of Talon and the lithe speed with which he had taken the initiative and killed the deer. He behaves differently from the others... neither like a slave nor a servant. But then, he’s the son of a lord in his own country. That must count for something, she thought as she fell asleep.

Heaven but the Vision of fulfill'd Desire,
And Hell the Shadow of a Soul on Fire,
Cast on the Darkness into which Ourselves,
So late emerg'd from, shall soon expire.

– Omar Khayyum –

Chapter 13
Fida'i

Arash Khan and Ahmad were discussing the princess.

They often ate late together, through no wish of Ahmad's, but his father insisted, as this was an opportunity to catch up on the local events of the day at the castle. Arash kept his eyes on almost every corner of the known world of Islam, from Egypt to Afghanistan, with his spies and intelligence agents, and did not neglect to keep an ear to the ground here in Alamut.

They had just finished eating and were enjoying a relaxing hookah pipe. Ahmad told his father of the hunting trip that Rav'an had taken without asking his permission

Arash nodded. "The next time you see her, inform her that she cannot just go out of the castle. She must have you as the escort, and be sure to get permission from me. I have a feeling that she is not here entirely for her own protection. I could even believe that my nephew sent her here to spy on us."

Ahmad was so surprised he nearly dropped the pipe he was holding. Smoke came out of his mouth, which was hanging open, and then he coughed for a couple of seconds. "What are you saying? Rav'an a spy? I have trouble believing this, even from you."

His father turned his black, cold eyes on his son. "I will let this impudence pass this time. You have not the sense of a goat sometimes, and I do wonder how long you will live with this keen intellect of yours. Think! Why should she not stay in Samiran or at some other castle? Why Alamut, and why at this time, just as we are preparing to make our move. Think, you dolt, why?" His words hissed out with the smoke he was exhaling.

His son stared at his father. "I-I don't know. I had not thought of it that way. But now you mention it, there is something there, perhaps."

His father's face twitched. "I knew you would see it my way. But my nephew has given me something else of value, too." He waited, playing the game he so often did with his son.

"What is that, father?" Ahmad asked, the predictable response.

Arash sighed. "The two boys who came with her, especially the Frank called Talon."

Ahmad looked interested, as though he knew what was coming.

Arash continued. "He is the one who will bring me my rightful place in the Ismaili. My nephew wants me to reach into his mind and leave a message with him. It is unfortunate for my nephew it will not be the message that he wants me to leave." Arash chuckled. "So, in fact, we have not just his sister as a hostage or a plaything for you, but I also have the means to take care of my nephew without there being the slightest suspicion laid at my door."

Ahmad looked across at his father. Like everyone at Alamut, he feared his father, but he also admired him to the point of worship. He knew he could not match his father's intelligence, but his loyalty was absolute. "Father, with you at the head of the Ismaili cause, we cannot fail to conquer all we meet, both on the battlefield and in the cities. When do you intend to reach into his mind?"

"Soon. They are ready to become full *fida'i,* so I should say within the week, when Behzad says they are ready. I hear they are doing well, those two."

Ahmad nodded. "No one likes them, but they are good, some say among the best we have had, both of them. The Frank is strong and very capable with weapons and stealth, while the other, Reza, can become almost invisible. The students have a name for them. It is 'the phantoms'."

His father chuckled. "Good. Then we have picked the right ones for the task at hand."

*****

The day came when Talon and Reza were told to leave the class and follow Behzad. He led them to the bathhouse that was close to the *Zor Khane*, where all the men worked out with large wooden weights that developed their shoulder and arm muscles. At the bathhouse, they were told to bathe themselves well and then meet him when finished.

The two knew without a doubt that they were going into the final initiation of their training. They looked at one another with wide eyes. In the bathhouse, where they obtained hot water and soap, they paid more attention to their ablutions than usual. They didn't look at one another, as they were afraid they might betray their thoughts. They dried off, casting nervous looks at one another, and then an attendant came in with two bundles of new clothes for them. The clothes were white cotton pants and white shirts that tied at the wrists and waist, wide and loose. They were given slippers of decorated kid leather that slipped comfortably onto their feet, although these too were very light.

Combing their long hair straight out behind and then, curling it into a bun, they wound on long, white cotton turbans that were lined with a red dye in the manner proscribed in their lessons. The last item they put on was a thin red belt of well-worked leather with a silver buckle.

When ready, they came to the door of the almost deserted bathhouse and presented themselves to a critical Behzad. He looked them over with eyes that missed nothing, then nodded his head, turned on his heel and led them off to the doorway of the keep.

They entered behind him, noticing that there was no sentry at the door for a change, nor did they run into any students charging down the stairway, as was usual.

The trio climbed the stairs to the third floor, and Behzad led them down a long, dark corridor. Nothing was said, and there was no other noise other than the slap, slap of their slippers on the wood floor. At the far end was a small, iron-studded door. Behzad stopped there and knocked once. A grill slid open and a pair of eyes looked them over, then bolts crashed and the door opened.

The boys were ushered into a plain room, with just a threadbare *ghilim* on the floor and a guttering oil lamp on a shelf recessed into the wall. There was a peculiar smell in the room that neither had encountered before. Behzad told them in a whisper to sit on the mat and wait. They complied nervously, all their instincts alive with apprehension, as they waited for the unknown to come to them.

They waited for what seemed an eternity, until a servant came in with a tray of tea and some small cakes. He offered these to the boys first and poured the tea. They looked to Behzad for direction. He indicated that they should partake of the offering, nodding to the servant. Talon took a small cake and held it until Reza had taken his. Behzad declined the cake but took the tea. They all sat in silence, drinking from the small cups, the boys munching on the small cakes. Talon noticed how delicate the cups were.

The attendant returned with a hookah and set it up in front of Behzad, who accepted the pipe and drew on the smoking end piece. He then passed it along to Talon and nodded for him to take a draw. Talon did as he was told, trying to imitate Behzad. But he pulled too hard and found himself spluttering with the unaccustomed smoke. Through the tears, he passed the pipe to Reza, who looked dazed, for some reason. Reza manfully pulled on the pipe and choked as well. He looked as though he was going to suffocate while trying to prevent himself from coughing.

Behzad smiled at them and demonstrated the technique of drawing slowly on the pipe and exhaling in a controlled manner. The boys copied his every move and soon were drawing on the pipe and beginning to relax. What they soon began to realize, however, was that they were feeling very drowsy. The first to fall over was Reza. Talon, although he fought the languor that was spreading through his limbs, could not fend off the enormous heaviness that came over him. The mat seemed a very comfortable place to rest. As the young men went to sleep, a secret panel in the wall opened, and two attendants came out. Behzad nodded at the sleeping youths and carried on smoking.

They were carried into other chambers and undressed, their bodies oiled and then left on silk covers.

The man watching the proceedings came out of his place near the doorway and stood over Talon.

He made himself comfortable on the edge of the richly made bed, and began to talk to the sleeping youth. His voice was insistent but sibilant and carried deep into the unconscious mind of the youth. He spoke a phrase several times and then sat back to observe the reaction. Talon murmured a response that came from deep inside him. Satisfied, Arash Khan stood up. He looked down on the sleeping form, and then motioned to the shadows.

A young woman, completely naked, moved out of the shadows. She looked to Arash for instructions but he indicated the boy and went back into the dark recesses of the room to observe. He enjoyed watching the youths' reaction when they came out of their stupor to find themselves with naked girls for the first time. He was interested to see how the Frank would behave.

The girl came to the sleeping Talon, laid a gentle hand on his chest, then began to stroke him. She looked long at his scars as she went into the practiced ways she had learned from others of her trade.

Talon woke up. He could not think where he could be, but it was not where he remembered being. He could not take in all the splendor. Here there was too much gold and silk around for him to be able to take inventory of his whereabouts. Besides, he could feel a stroking motion, and it was very intimate. He struggled to sit up and found himself looking into the dark, smiling eyes of a dusky young woman.

She smiled at him and pushed him gently on the chest to make him lie back. He sighed and did so, trembling with the newness of the sensations. The girl began to stroke him again. Her hands were soft and very sensitive; they discovered every inch of him. At first, he was embarrassed. He had never been touched like this before. He was beginning to enjoy the sensation, however, and it was not long before her ministrations were making him acutely aware of what was happening to him. There was nothing he could do, or indeed wanted to do, other than accept it, and wonder where it was going to end. She moved up onto his supine body, her hands busy all the time. She then offered herself to his touch and he could control himself no longer. He seized her and threw her on her back to rise above her and stare down at her. She smiled at him and then, without his even realizing it, she had guided him into her.

He gasped and arched his back to stare down at their junction. Then she placed her hands on his waist and began to move, slowly locking him into her, carrying him with her. Instinct took over and he began to move with her. His wonder at what was happening was soon overcome with the urge to rut, and he began to move harder and faster. It was over so fast that he was stunned. He felt his body coming to a rushing climax and came with a cry, his body momentarily, but completely, out of his control.

The girl didn't admonish him for his sudden precipitate rush. Instead, she lay with him as he collected his breath, all the while stroking him along his flanks and whispered to him.

He was giddy with the strangeness of it all and in a state of wonder at his situation. His senses seemed real, the touch and feel of the girl at his side seemed real. He had a real thirst for her that he could not and did not want to deny. He grew again under her skillful fingers and soon they were coupled again. This time she admonished him to be more patient and to take his time. He decided he liked her, and so he listened and learned that evening. She taught him what it was like to glimpse paradise, and to have new senses awakened by a sensual woman. She taught him to pleasure her and he found that his enjoyment increased as he saw how she responded to his ministrations.

Much later, he could do no more than lie there with her, half asleep, and to wonder at what chance had brought him here. She lay with him for a while and then clapped her hands. Another girl, younger than his companion, came into the room, bearing tea in tiny porcelain cups and small cakes that looked very appetizing. They whispered together, then his companion, without a trace of self-consciousness, got up from the bed and took the tray from the other. She dismissed her with a nod and served Talon some tea. He sipped the sweet brew from the delicate cup, and indicated that he needed more to slake his thirst. She smiled and took one of the cakes and fed it to him while they sat together on the silken bed.

He looked around, admiring the exquisite carpets, hanging on the walls and spread on the floor. The furniture was like nothing he had ever seen before. He could not believe the delicacy of the work on the wood. He ran his hand over the surface of the table near the bed and wondered at how smooth and polished it was. He turned back to the girl, smiled sleepily, leaned over to kiss her, and fell over onto his side, fast asleep.

The girl looked at him with some regret. She had enjoyed their brief liaison, but her work was done. She turned to the darker shadows and indicated with her hand the supine form of the sleeping Talon. Arash Khan stepped out of the shadows and waved her away. As she went, he tossed her a gold coin both for her services and her silence. She was one of the several women who came to Alamut for extended visits to provide this service.

It was a mutually agreeable arrangement, and none dared tell of what they did to anyone outside their group. Arash was clear about what he would do to them if he got wind of any one of them boasting. She skipped away, glad to be out of the same room as the man she most feared. Her fervent hope was that he would not summon her to his room for his own pleasure. She had heard he was very cruel to those he "loved." The Frank had been good, though. He listened and was attentive when she asked him to be gentle.

Arash watched the boy sleeping. He had enjoyed watching the young man advance into full manhood. In spite of himself, he had been impressed that Talon had made the woman cry out in her own ecstasy. Not many of these boys were capable of more than just rutting. He had derived sexual pleasure of his own in the watching and would enjoy the woman himself tonight. He stepped to the door, opened it, and gestured to the servants to come and collect the boy. The same two came into the room and dressed the inert Talon, then carried him out and into the foyer. They took him back to his own room, lay him down on his own bedding, and then left him. Reza was already there sleeping like one of the dead.

* * * * *

Talon woke in familiar surroundings. He sat up and looked over at his friend, who was still where he had been placed the night before. He looked down at himself and saw his new clothing. Then the events of the previous night came back in a rush.

He fell back onto his bed and tried to recapture every detail. He wondered how it had all happened, wondering if indeed it had. The ache in his loins told him that something had, and he consoled himself with the remembrance of the embrace and caresses of the wonderful young maiden who had known so much and taught him so much. It seemed as though he had dreamed it, even so.

He leaned over and nudged Reza, who woke as though he had been in a very deep sleep.

"Reza, what happened?" Talon demanded. "Did it really happen? Did you see paradise?"

Reza looked back at his friend, his eyes dull from the after-effects of the drug. "I think it was a dream too wonderful to have been real. What did you see?"

"I didn't just see, Reza. I felt and touched, and, oh, Allah, but she was beautiful! I think I did have a glimpse of paradise. What about you?"

Reza nodded. "I truly did meet with one of the *houris* of

paradise, and she gave me endless pleasure. I am still in wonder at what happened. How I long to be back in that place. I would die to be there!"

Talon nodded. "I wish it was of this world! But it was too wonderful! I have never seen nor touched such wonderful things. The woman was not of this world, nothing was."

"Are we now men?" Reza asked, wonder in his voice.

"Well, we have proven ourselves in war, and now in love," Talon said slowly. "I think we are now men, my friend. More important for us however, we are now *fida'i* in all but name, as we still have one more initiation to perform—to swear the terrible oath of allegiance to the master and commit our lives for all time to his service."

Reza nodded his eyes somber. "Yes, we do, but I wish to make a solemn oath to you and myself."

Talon looked at him sharply.

Reza continued. "You and I have been together now for many years, and always we have been through the same things together. I feel that God has ordained it thus. So, I say to you now that you are my brother and I am yours. I shall protect you with my life—always."

Talon felt tears come to his eyes. He stood up and embraced his friend. "Truly, Reza, you are my brother, and I am yours. I, too, swear in front of God that I, too, shall protect you at all times with my life, if it be so ordained."

They went out together into the watery morning. They saw Behzad on the *maidan* with the other students. They waved and went on to the kitchens without stopping. There they met with Jean, and the three of them went to a corner to eat their basic fare of bread and *maast* with tea and *Ghant* sugar.

Jean looked them over; he saw a change in both of them. There were subtle differences from the two boys he had been with the day before. Direct as always, he indicated their clothing. "You have both been initiated?"

Talon looked shifty. "Well, in a manner of speaking."

"What does that mean?"

"It means that we passed into the first garden, I think," Talon said. He sounded uncertain though.

"Tell me about it."

Talon was not sure he wanted to. It was all too recent, and he wanted to digest it for himself before sharing it with anyone.

Reza was not quite so inhibited. "We were shown paradise, and what it could mean for us when we serve the Master. We have always been told that we will go straight to paradise when we have done his bidding, and last night we saw what we have to look forward to. It was wonderful." He sighed and stared into the distance, a rapturous expression on his lean, smooth features.

"What was so wonderful?" Jean asked.

Reza looked at him. "The *houri*, the gorgeous woman who came to me, and showed me all the delights I can expect when I go to paradise. I wish I could die and go there now."

"I am sure that is what is expected," Jean said, laconically. "Talon, did you experience the same thing?"

Talon nodded. "Yes, it was heavenly... I do not know how to describe it, but I agree with Reza, if this is truly a window on heaven, I am in a hurry to go there, too,"

This whole conversation exasperated Jean. He felt that he was talking to two moonstruck youths who had been seduced. He had heard nothing of music, or the beauty of what he conceived to be heaven. But then, the Islamic heaven might be different, he surmised. He was not going to spoil their enjoyment of this dream they might have had. He did, however, think it prudent to mention that their duty to the princess might be better done without discussing this kind of thing with her. His instincts told him that she might not view it with much favor.

The boys nodded vigorously at that, and then, as they left the kitchens to go about their day, Behzad collected the young men. Without mentioning the events of the previous day, he made them swear that they would never discuss this with anyone. The Master would know if they did, as he knew everything. Both of them swore, without describing the conversation they had just had, and went about feeling guilty that they had even mentioned it to Jean.

Behzad went on to inform them that they would be presented to the Khan to swear their allegiance to him one day soon. They could now consider themselves real *fida'i* and could indeed be called upon to perform their duty at any time in the name of the master, regardless of the ceremony of the oath. They nodded mute acknowledgement of his command and went to change out of their new clothes back into their normal garb.

Alike for those who for Today prepare
And those that after some Tomorrow stare
A Muezzin from the Tower of Darkness cries,
"Fools, Your Reward is neither Here nor There,"
— Omar Khayyam —

Chapter 14
The Plot

Reza left the warmth of the library very quietly, slipped down the stairs, and hurried across the castle's courtyard. It was raining again. These days it never seemed to stop—a cold steady downpour that left everything damp and chilled. People went around in oiled skins, wool jackets, and furs, and looked for warm, dry places to hide. He found Talon as usual down in the stables with the horses.

Reza approached the subject carefully by asking Talon if he knew if the princess and Ahmad were betrothed.

Talon stared at him. "What was that, Reza?"

"Are they betrothed? Yknow, the princess and Ahmad."

"First I heard of it," Talon said, more sharply than he'd intended. Then he moderated his tone. "Why? What have you heard?"

"Well," Reza said in a puzzled tone. "I was in the library, keeping warm. I hate the cold and wet." Talon fidgeted. "Anyway, I heard Mehdi say something about the princess and her high ways. Also that when Ahmad had her in bed she would have to change, as for sure he would tame her. That is why I asked if they were betrothed. How else would she go to his bed?"

It was fortunate that the evening was nigh, or he would have seen how pale Talon had become. There was no hiding that he was disturbed, however.

"Reza, you must talk to no one about this," he said, lowering his voice. "I do not believe for a moment that the princess is going to bed with Ahmad. Not now or in the future, and words like that from Mehdi are very bad." He put his hand on Reza's shoulder. "Something is wrong, and I intend to find out what's going on."

Reza looked back at him and said, "Do you think they intend to harm her? I remember the promise we made to the General to protect her. We are still bound to that oath, you and I."

"Bless you, Reza, may Allah's blessings be on you for what you have just said. We have to be very careful. I do not know who else to trust in this place other than you and Jean, but we have to find out more."

Reza nodded. He looked thoughtful. "I could pretend to get close to Mehdi. We are now *fida'i,* and although not the same rank as Mehdi, he likes people to look up to him. You they will not trust, as you are still a *ferengi* to them."

Talon nodded. "Yes. I cannot get close to them, but I can talk to Feza and find out more that way. Let's meet here again tomorrow and see what we can put together. The stables or the mews are always places where we can be seen without attracting attention to ourselves."

Reza grinned, his white teeth flashing in the gloom. "I shall see what I can do to get close to Mehdi."

They went out from the dark stables after first making sure that none of the stable boys were around, then into the evening rain to go to the kitchens. Later, Talon sought out Jean. He found the priest huddled in the library near one of the braziers, reading one of the books of the great poets of Persia. He gave a wan smile when he saw Talon weaving his way around the pillars toward him.

"Hello, my boy. You know, these poets, Ferdousi, for instance, never talk about the cold winters of this country. I am cold most of the time these days. Still, the verse warms my spirit while the fire warms my old body." He looked at Talon. "What is the matter? You look very worried."

Talon responded in a whisper and in French. "I need to talk, and this is not the place to do so. Will you take a walk with me along the east wall where it is not so windy?"

Jean knew that Talon would not ask for his company on a walk in the rain unless something serious was up, so he nodded without speaking. He coughed and wiped his mouth surreptitiously with a rag he produced from his sleeve. Together they left the room. Going outside into the steady rain was not pleasant, but as there was not a lot of wind at this time, they could walk at a reasonable pace and converse at the same time.

Talon began slowly. "Father, you miss very little, I know, but there is something I have to tell you that perhaps you do not know about."

Jean nodded in the gloom, waiting for him to continue. After a pause, Talon resumed. "I have known the princess and we have been friends since I killed the lion," he said.

"Of this I am aware, but you have not... gone further, have you?"

"Oh, no, I could never do that. She is the princess," Talon said indignantly.

Jean smiled. "So perhaps you should just tell me what is going on?"

"Very well. We met in the garden at Samiran, and I think that I fell in love with her then, although as I had never done so before it was all very new. In any case, we met again several times. But just to talk and sit together, I could not stay away, and she always seemed pleased to see me."

"Hmm, I'm sure of that," said Jean, dryly. "Go on."

"Well, I got to know her quite well, and so when I heard something today, I could not believe it."

"What did you hear?"

"That she was betrothed to Ahmad."

"What?!" exclaimed Jean. "Betrothed? I did not know of this, Who told you, Talon?" He sounded very surprised. He started coughing, and their conversation ceased until he could regain his composure. Talon looked on with mounting concern. When Jean had stopped his violent hacking and wiped his lips, Talon related what Reza had told him.

He finished by saying, "We don't like the kind of talk that is going on about the Princess among the other men. Reza said that is sounds vulgar and disrespectful of her. Also he feels that they know something we do not and fears for her. We were ordered to protect her and now we are worried."

Jean listened, then said in a firm tone, "Talon, I know that you have feelings for the princess, but if they are betrothed you cannot interfere or you will die. You have to keep this quiet and not let your feelings surface under any circumstances." He took hold of Talon's sleeve. "But I do not know of any betrothal, and I shall go to Feza and ask for an interview with the princess. I am allowed to meet with her, as I am like a mullah. I do not need to be chaperoned, in any case. That has its advantages, one might say." He turned to face Talon, seeing the bewilderment in the boy's eyes. "Talon, heed me, be very careful now. We will find out for sure. Do not do something stupid that we will all regret. Promise me?"

Talon nodded. "Find out for me, Father, but I do not know what I shall do if it is true."

The next day it was still wet. Everyone was inside seeking warmth and a dry respite from the damp and cold of the autumn. Jean walked slowly to the princess' quarters and knocked on her outer door. With an effort, he suppressed a cough that threatened to surface.

Old Feza opened the door and peered out. When she saw the priest, she gave her toothless smile and greeted him. "What can I do for you, Priest?" she asked politely. She quite liked Jean, who had helped her on the journey from Samiran and meant no harm.

"Greetings, Feza. May a long life be yours and may your good health continue. I have come to ask a huge favor, and by God's grace you can assist me in this venture." He had to turn away as a bout of coughing wracked his frame. It went on for a couple of long moments. He was hunched over with the pain in his chest.

Feza watched this with increasing worry. She instinctively knew that this was not an ordinary cough. However, she waited for him to finish and then invited him to continue.

"I have come to beg an interview with her ladyship, the princess; just a very few minutes, but it is important," Jean wheezed.

She waved him into the room. Jean stepped through the doorway and then followed behind her across the room and to stand at the other opening. The princess stood there, in the middle of the other room, clad in a warm woolen dress and furs. She seemed pleased to see him, but there was a question on her face. Jean bowed very low and stood still, waiting to be addressed.

"We have not seen much of you since we came here a month ago, Priest," she said pleasantly. "How may I help you now?"

"*Khanom*, I hope I find you well."

Rav'an nodded. "Thank you, Priest, I am well. I trust you are, too."

"*Khanom,* I am aware that I might offend you when I ask you, but it is because of an overwhelming concern that I do ask."

"What do you ask?"

"*Khanom,* I shall try not to speak in riddles, but this is a very difficult thing I am about to ask you. *Khanom,* there is a rumor that... Talon and Reza heard that... that you are betrothed to the prince. Is this so? Should it be, I would be proud to offer my congratulations... if indeed that is true," he finished, feeling lame.

Rav'an's expression told him all he needed to know. Surprise, indignation, and then anger flitted across her face. "Who dares to suggest this?" she ground out between her teeth; she seemed to be barely able to control her outrage.

Jean had known that he'd be on very dangerous ground when he came to this interview, but now he knew that he should be very careful to say the right thing. "Talon and Reza have asked me to tell you this. They fear there is something going on, and you may be in danger. They wanted to make sure that you knew they were still faithful to the oath they made to Timsar Esphandiary. They, as I do, place themselves at your feet, to do as you bid them in all things."

Rav'an looked shaken. She nodded in an absent manner at then mention of Talon and Reza, then with a visible effort she collected herself.

"Priest, tell my two protectors that I am not betrothed, that whoever says so is a liar, and when I find out who it is I shall have them executed. I shall also be visiting Ahmad to tell him so. You may leave, Priest. I am indebted to you for coming to see me. Under the circumstances, it was brave." She smiled crookedly at him, but he could see tears in her eyes.

Jean bowed very low and left the room. When he got out of the apartments, he realized he was shaking. His cough, suppressed for too long, overwhelmed him and he hacked and choked for long minutes in the cold, dark corridor. He hurried off to talk to Talon.

* * * * *

Back in the room, Rav'an found somewhere to sit, and Feza fussed over her with some tea.

"Feza, what is happening?" Rav'an asked, confused. "Who

would start a rumor of this kind?"

Feza left her in no doubt as to that. "My lady, it can only have come from Ahmad himself, and I can guess at what he is planning. My lady, I do not think it would be a good idea to go to him with this. He would want to know how you found out, and then the boys and the priest would be in danger."

Rav'an nodded. "As usual you are right, Feza, my dear. I must talk to someone, though. This is terrible, and worse, a slur on me. They have no right to play games of this kind," she added angrily.

"Perhaps you should talk to Talon," Feza suggested.

"Oh, Feza, you know too much for your own good," Rav'an said, sounding a little embarrassed. "I shall talk to him later in the day. Can you see if he can come to the stables to examine my mare this afternoon?"

"There is something else going on, my dove," Feza said her tone thoughtful.

"What is that, Feza? What else can be going on?"

"It is the priest, my lady. I think he is very sick. I have heard a cough like that before when I was young. It brings blood with it and can kill."

Rav'an looked at her with horrified eyes. "Is he so sick, Feza? Is there nothing we can do for him?"

Feza considered. "I can find herbs and make medicine that will ease the cough and relieve the pain in his chest, but I cannot stop the progress of the illness, my lady. He will either defeat the sickness or he will not. That rests with Allah, the Almighty."

Rav'an said slowly. "He and Talon have been together for many years now. It will devastate Talon to hear this. Do everything you can for him, my dear Feza."

Feza nodded. "I shall, my dove."

Rav'an worried over the problem the priest had brought her. What were Ahmad and Arash up to? She suddenly felt very alone, and shivered. Her eyes filled with tears as she wondered what was happening to her world. Feza noticed and pulled her closer to the fireplace, clucking at her to stay there while she warmed up some spiced wine.

Then Rav'an's thoughts turned to Arash Khan. He was the most devious person in her small world and the one man whom she most feared to be near. His baleful presence affected the whole castle. He reminded her of one of those snakes with a hood she had heard of and had seen once with a traveling group of jugglers and peddlers. The snake had slithered out of the basket, its menace palpable to all the people who saw it. She had never forgotten that hooded creature or the absolute fear it had instilled in her. Arash was doing something that affected her, she reasoned. Even though Ahmad was headstrong and reckless, he would do exactly what his father ordered him to.

She sent Feza off with the message to Talon to meet her at the stables.

Rav'an saw no one around when she came to the stables later. There was still a light rain falling across the mountain, sweeping across the battlements of the castle. Water was trickling off the roofing onto the yard, making a dull dripping sound that seemed to accentuate the quiet when she pushed the door open. She stared around as she shook out her cloak and threw the hood back, looking for some sign of him. She could see no one in the gloom. She went in, shutting the door, then moved down the middle aisle between the horse stalls.

"Talon," she called softly. There was no reply. She moved cautiously toward Kaleen's stall, which was next to Jabbar's.

Then he was by her side, silent in the gloom. Rav'an stifled a scream. She had not heard even the slightest sound, yet there he was alongside her, so close she could have gone into his arms without effort. In fact, it took a huge effort not to. She stood there looking up at his face in the dim light and then took a pace back to compose herself.

"There you are, Talon. I did not hear you."

"My lady," he answered in a low tone. Then, taking her arm gently but firmly, he moved them both into the stall with Jabbar so that they could not be seen by a casual observer from the middle lane or near the door, yet they would not appear to be acting like conspirators should anyone come into the stables.

She was waiting for him to say something, but because he did not she opened the conversation. "You sent the priest to me, didn't you?" He collected himself and began to speak, but she interrupted him. "Why did you not come to me yourself?"

"*Khanom*," he whispered back, "we felt that for me or Reza to come to you would have been impertinent. Also we did not want to be seen near your apartments and have people associating us with you because we are afraid for you."

"You are?" she whispered, a look of open surprise on her face.

Inside, she greeted his words with a rush of relief. She felt that she was no longer quite so alone. "Tell me what it is that you fear for me, and I shall share my thoughts with you, Talon."

Talon told her what Mehdi had said, leaving out the crude references, but nonetheless implying that it was understood all over the castle that Ahmad had decided to take her for his own. "My lady," he whispered hoarsely, "are you betrothed to that man?" He needed to hear it straight from her. She gazed back at him, and her words told him what he needed to know. "Talon, I am betrothed to no one, and Ahmad is the last man I should wish to be betrothed to."

His breath came out in a rush. "Then you *are* in some kind of danger, my lady. Reza and I will try to find out more. We will let you know what we find out."

"I thank you, Talon. You are still my protectors both. My brother shall hear of this, I promise."

Talon shook his head. "First, we have to find out more. Reza is going to try to insert himself into the group from whom we heard the news. I, in turn, will attempt to find out more for myself."

She reached out and touched his sleeve. It was impulse, but she could not help herself. "Talon, these are dangerous men, skilled at the art of killing. You have to be more than just careful, or they will find out what you are doing, and they will kill you, I fear."

Talon closed his hand upon her cool fingers and squeezed them. "Have no fear, my lady; we must be careful, yes, but remember, they have trained us well. We have to find out for sure that this is not more than just idle gossip."

Rav'an reluctantly released her fingers. "I must go now or the possibility that we will be discovered grows. Please keep me informed through the priest and Feza. I thank you, Talon."

He suddenly pushed her to the entrance of the stall, as he went back to Jabbar, saying in a loud voice. "My lady, I think he has bruised his tendon."

She realized Talon had seen someone else in the building. "I do not know how he could have come to this condition," she said sharply, as though talking to a servant. She saw that one of the grooming boys had just come into the area and was about to start cleaning one of the horse stalls near the door. "I expect you to keep him warm, and to make sure this does not become worse." She turned abruptly on her heel to leave.

"Yes, my lady," came the subservient reply from the stall. "It shall be as you command."

She had to suppress a smile as she stalked out of the building, complaining aloud about the poor maintenance of her horses.

Talon heard her stalking across the courtyard, but then she paused. Talon moved to where he could see her unobserved. He saw that she had run into Ahmad.

"Rav'an," he said, as he strode up in muddied boots. "I trust you are not going for a ride on a day like this? You must ensure that I or my father is informed before you leave, especially in weather like this."

Rav'an seemed not to be able to help herself. "I was not aware, Cousin, that I needed your permission to go anywhere," she snapped.

He looked abashed. "I mean that there are still dangers out there for a lady on her own, and I would prefer to accompany you for protection." His swarthy features grew darker as he became embarrassed at her obvious annoyance.

"You forget that I grew up here as a child, and I am very familiar with the country here, cousin." She was still speaking sharply.

Ahmad showed his teeth. "My father has made it clear that you are to speak to him about going out of the castle. I recall mentioning this to you before. Perhaps you would like to discuss this with him?" This was said with some spite, his face suffused with anger at her attitude toward him.

"This I might well do, cousin. I shall not be held here as a prisoner when this is my brother's own house," she told him.

Ahmad worked hard to control his anger. "I understand, Rav'an, but you know my father. He gets these ideas into his head. It will do no good to go against his wishes. I am sure it is just his wish to protect you."

Rav'an was uninterested in his mollifying words. "I shall talk to him about this. Good evening, cousin." She turned and strode off, leaving him fuming.

Ahmad looked after her with a glare that told the hidden Talon much. Then Ahmad stamped off, leaving the courtyard empty.

* * * * *

That evening, Jean, Talon, and Reza sat together in a corner of the crowded kitchens, lingering over the evening meal, the remains spread around them. The boys cracked pistachio nuts while Jean ate a peach. There was rice scattered around, mixed with pieces of bread. The light was poor in this arched, ground-floor room, but there was enough to be able to see if there were listeners nearby.

"I talked to Mehdi this afternoon about doing some training with him. If this works, I shall be eating with him for a while." said Reza.

Talon and Jean nodded. "You should keep some distance between yourself and us then, for the time being anyway," Talon said. "I will keep track of Ahmad and see where and to whom he talks. We will have to use you as the messenger for us with the princess, Father. Is that is all right?"

"Of course. You and Reza should be careful, though. I like not the look of that Mehdi. He is very much Ahmad's man, and that makes me afraid." Jean suppressed a cough with visible effort.

Talon looked at his friend and mentor with concern. "Are you all right, Father? You do not look very well. Are you warm enough in that room of yours?"

Jean nodded impatiently. "I am fine. Don't worry about me. It is I who am worrying about you two. Please take every precaution."

"We have been well trained, Reza and I," Talon said with more confidence than he felt. "Reza, should we do something to show that we have had a falling out, to make your new friendship with Mehdi more convincing?"

Reza thought about it. "Yes, we do not have to fight in public, but we can talk against one another to set people thinking the right way." He grinned at his friend, who grinned back. "Perhaps we should display some dislike over some reason. We will have to think about it."

* * * * *

A full week was to pass before any notable incident was to occur. When it came, it was not in the manner that the boys had anticipated. By then, Reza was working well with Mehdi and his cronies and hanging out with them at every opportunity. The one time Mehdi came to a point of curiosity about Reza's avoidance of

Talon, as it had been clear at the onset that they were good friends, Reza told him that they had had an argument and that he was fed up with the foreigner.

Emboldened by this seeming rift that had developed between the two, Gaspar, one of the older students soon to become a *rafiq*, accosted Talon in the main yard one wet morning in front of his friends. There was some shoving, and Talon found that he had to knock a couple of heads before they would leave him alone. Behzad arrived on the scene and broke up the fight, then warned the group that he would not put up with this kind of thing.

After that, Talon was very much isolated, but he didn't mind.

Reza continued to work his way into Mehdi's good graces, who took it at face value; and it seemed to Reza, as he described it to Talon in private, that Mehdi was quite pleased about it.

Both Reza and Talon started meeting at odd times to compare notes, using a signaling system they had worked out. Reza had moved out of their room under the pretext that he preferred to be with his new friends.

A week later, Reza came to one of their meetings, looking worried. "We have been raised to love and fear the master all this time, is that not true?"

Talon nodded.

"Then I am confused. Mehdi has been talking to me a lot about the right Arash Khan has to hold the position of master."

"Does he mean that Arash Khan is to be the successor to the master if he dies?"

"Well, I suppose so, but the talk today was almost as though the Master *was* dead."

"Are you saying that news of the master has arrived and that he is dead?" Talon demanded to know, shocked.

Reza shook his head. "No, not quite like that, Talon, because I asked the same question, and they said no. It was more as though Mehdi knew something, and he meant the master was 'not yet' dead."

Talon thought about this. "I wonder if he has heard something, or if there is something else going on here in Alamut that we do not know about. Could the master be ill? I wish we knew more. This is not something I care to have Jean take to the princess. Besides, if the Master were dead, or dying, would we not have heard something by now? That is not something that can be kept quiet for long."

Reza nodded. "No, I agree, Talon. If that is the case, why has no one announced it officially? So what does it mean? I have to find out more, if there is more to find out. How is your watch on Ahmad going?"

Talon sighed. "He has spent a lot of time with his woman up in his quarters since the rains started. Perhaps now that it is drying out, he'll come out and do something else, I'd like to be able to get into his rooms for an hour to see if there is anything there that might tell us something as to his intentions towards Rav'an."

"I could suggest to Mehdi and the rest that we go hunting in the morning, if it is dry. Then it would be up to you to get into his rooms without detection. This would be a true test of your skills, my friend." Reza suggested. He grinned at Talon, who smiled back.

"Very well, Reza. You do your part and I shall do mine."

Reza was as good as his word. The next day dawned misty but with the promise of a sunny day ahead. Somehow, he had been able to plant the idea of going on a hunt. Ahmad led a large party of his personal men out on a deer-hunting foray that would take them down to the valley and then farther up into the highlands. Amid the shouts and boasting, Reza managed to give a wink to Talon that indicated it would be many hours before they returned.

Talon waited until the party was long gone before he began his perilous mission to gain entry into Ahmad's quarters. Were he to be caught, his death would be summary and very painful.

It was not uncommon for a student to be seen in the keep, as both Arash and Ahmad used some of them for their personal servants. Thus, Talon had no worry about walking into the large hall and mounting the stairs that would take him to the library where many of them studied. He peered inside the library to check to see if there was anyone in the low, many-pillared rooms, and assured himself that no one was there, not this early. Most of the students that had not gone on the hunt were finding places to hide and stay out of the way, he reasoned.

He knew which way to go once he had verified the library was empty. He had followed Ahmad on one occasion to see where his quarters were: on the next floor of the keep, which was the same floor as those of both the princess and Arash. He would have to be careful. The many servants still on that floor might find it odd if he were to be seen on that level. He decided to brazen it out and pretend that he was working for Ahmad on an errand and was meant to be there.

He bounded up the wooden stairs. Then, more confidently than he felt, he strode to the door of the prince's private quarters. He knocked on the door in a normal manner and listened for any sound that might come from the room. There was no sound. He had thought that perhaps the woman Ahmad had been keeping might still be there, but as he could hear no sound, it looked as though she might be gone for the time being.

His heart beating faster, he stooped and looked for any indication that the door was locked. It was typical of the doors in the castle, made of crude, unfinished wood, and it shut on a latch that could be barred from the inside. As there was no one about, he decided to see if it would open, and to his surprise, it did. In one smooth movement, he opened it and stepped into the room, shutting the door behind him.

The room was poorly lit, the light seeping in through closed shutters. He stood stock still, listening for the slightest sound that might give someone away if they were in the room with him. He heard a low snore. He flashed a look to the entrance of a room to his right, and then moved whisper-like to where he could look into the room. There on the bedding that lay strewn around, asleep in a tangle with the pillows and the quilt, lay a woman. It was Ahmad's concubine; sound asleep on her back with her mouth slightly open, snoring.

She was not fully covered; one arm was free, and one young breast was peeping out of the covers. Talon stood and stared. He could hardly breathe and his eyes were riveted on her. He had only once been this close to a naked woman before, and that was almost as though it had been a dream. There was nothing wrong with Ahmad's taste in women; Talon noted that she was pretty, and the sight of her was distracting. He shook his head and woke up to the reality of where he was.

She seemed sound asleep, but it would complicate things if she woke up. He was tempted to leave then and there, but he wanted to find something, anything, that might provide him with more information about what Ahmad intended to do to Rav'an. He made his way cautiously past the entrance. He came to the larger room that served as the living and workspace, where the scribe would work if Ahmad was in his rooms. Talon wondered if the servant would be returning soon. He had to hurry. The trouble was he didn't know what he was looking for

He slipped up to the low table near the fire and looked at the parchments on the table and the floor. There was an open box of gold coins and small bags of what he supposed to be coins, and there were several parchments in an untidy pile. He had not taken Ahmad for a scholar, but clearly, the man could read both Persian and Arabic. Now that he, too, could read, Talon cast his eyes over the letters, discarding what he considered irrelevant.

His eye settled upon one paper that had a very impressive seal attached to it. He picked it up and lifted it to the poor light coming through the shutters. He could make out the name "Nur Ed-Din" in high, flowing letters near the top with the greetings. The calligraphy was so beautiful and flowing that it became difficult for him to read it. But he felt that this had some importance, as Nur Ed-Din was no friend of the Ismaili, as far as he understood. This man was the leader of the Sunni forces in Damascus. Why would he write to Ahmad?

There was a stirring in the room where the girl lay. He realized that he had almost overstayed his welcome. He quickly tucked this letter into his loose shirtsleeve. It was all he had found in the short time he had been there that gave a clue of anything untoward. He seized one of the small bags of coins and slipped out of the room. He paused very briefly at the door to check that there was no one outside and then let himself out, making sure he did not wake the girl.

The corridor was empty, but he suddenly heard voices coming from the direction he had himself come from. He spun around to go in the opposite, unknown direction. He moved silently and fast down the corridor and turned left at a junction, slipping round the corner, moving as fast as he could. The voices of two men followed him all the way. He was getting desperate. He was a long way down the second corridor when one of the doors opened in front of him and Feza came out.

Talon moved very fast at this point. He took Feza by the arm and almost dragged her back into the room, shutting the door softly behind them as they stopped. She opened her mouth to squawk something, but he leaned down, put his finger to her lips, and whispered for her to hush, pointing behind him at the door. The two men who had been following walked past the door without pausing. He waited until their footsteps had receded before making his apologies.

Feza was indignant and wanted an explanation, but Talon just pointed to the other room and raised his eyebrows. Feza, realizing that something was amiss, nodded and motioned him to stay where he was and then spoke to someone in the other room. It was Rav'an. She came out and saw Talon standing there. Putting a hand to her mouth in surprise, she motioned him to come in. The two salukis came out to greet him with their tails wagging their rear ends back and forth, demanding attention from him even as he tried to make his way to Rav'an.

He joined the two curious women, dragging the parchment out of his shirt as he did so. Without ceremony he said, "My lady, we have to hurry. I stole this from Ahmad's quarters this minute, but I cannot read it well. Can you help?"

Although she looked shocked, Rav'an didn't question him. Instead, she took the paper to the window and started to read. Her lips moved as she read, and as she read, he watched her. She was dressed warmly in a wool skirt that came down to her ankles. Her feet were inside some loosely knitted woolen boots with felt soles. They appeared to be much too large, coming up to her calves. Her voluminous cotton shirt was tucked into her skirt and held in place with a narrow leather belt. She wore a woolen waistcoat decorated with embroidered patterns over the skirt. Her long, lustrous hair was braided into one long coil that fell to her waist. The light illuminated her profile, giving him the impression of an elfin princess in boots too large for her.

As she read, the frown on her face deepened, and then she began to gnaw at her lower lip. She was becoming agitated at what she was reading, but he did not interrupt. Finally, she stopped reading and dropped the hand holding the parchment to her side. Her other went to her forehead and pushed back against her hair. She was white.

A lost look came over her, at which point he had to ask, "My lady, is anything wrong? What is it? You look upset."

She turned a haunted look to him. "Talon, I do not understand all of the meaning of this letter, but I fear that my brother is in great danger. This is a letter from Nur Ed-Din, the Sultan of Damascus. Did you know that when you took the letter?"

"Yes, I knew that much, but I cannot read the calligraphy well. I was going to find Jean, but then I had to escape detection by coming into this room. Forgive me, Princess, I didn't mean to disturb you."

She gave him a fleeting smile. "I am glad that you did." She lifted the paper again to search for a sentence in the contents. "It sends Nur Ed-Din's greetings to Arash Khan. He is wishing him all good fortune in his endeavors. It goes on to say that should he be successful in his mission, then he, Nur Ed-Din, will be happy to welcome Arash Khan as an ally in all their future collaborations. And how can that be? My brother is still in Syria. He and he alone is the Master of the Ismaili.

What is Arash doing that excludes my brother? What do they intend to do, Talon? It is well known that Nur Ed-Din is a Sunni and hates our kind with a relentless passion. He would have us all massacred if he could. If anything, the Sunni hate us more than even the Shi'ites, and that is saying something! My brother is feared by all in Syria, and Nur Ed-Din hates him to the point of distraction."

Talon was mute. The stunning news left him wondering what they should do. Rav'an spoke again, this time in almost a whisper. "Talon, I am very afraid for my brother's life. What should I do?"

Talon tried to collect his wits. "The first thing I should do with this document is to return it, Princess, but then we would have no proof. However, if I do not, then they will miss it and turn the castle upside down looking for it. This is a very dangerous document to lose and to have fall into the wrong hands. They would not rest until it was found. I cannot understand how it came to be in Ahmad's hands to start with."

"My brother would believe me if I could tell him myself," said Rav'an absently. "The problem is that I cannot leave now to even go for a hunt without Ahmad riding with me. It would be impossible for me to go. I am a prisoner here."

"Whoever you do send must have some proof of this," Talon said. "How do we provide that?"

They stood in silence for a few long minutes thinking. Both had forgotten Feza, who had stood with them, watching the interplay with great interest and mounting concern.

"My lady," she said her cracked voice tentative. "Would part of the parchment be enough?"

Rav'an turned on her, eyes glowing. "Feza, you are wonderful. As always, you can find a solution. No, we cannot tear the parchment, but we can make it look as though Ahmad was careless and lost the seal." She turned to Talon. "Do you understand, Talon? The seal is that of Nur Ed-Din, and my brother knows that seal as well as any, because his men have intercepted many of his letters in the past. We should make it look as though the seal was cracked off by some careless action on Ahmad's part."

Talon looked at the large wax seal on the parchment. It was already cracked and split where the letter had first been opened. If he could cut under the remainder and include the elaborate ribbons that came with it, the plan might work.

Rav'an asked Feza for a small, sharp knife, and they worked to pry the larger part of the seal off the parchment.

They put the wax parts onto the small table with great care, and Rav'an, beginning to regain her normal self, said, "We must hide this and protect it with our lives. I shall keep it here with me, Talon. You have now to go back. Will you be safe?"

He smiled at her with more confidence than he felt. "My lady, I shall be all right. I must go now in case the servants come back."

She smiled at him in return, even as she showed her concern. "Do not get caught, my protector," she said, her voice husky. "May Allah protect you this day. I shall pray for you."

He turned and left the room. Feza went out into the corridor before waving him out. Before he went, he turned to catch a glimpse of the princess. She was standing at the entrance of her rooms with the two salukis at her side. She looked small and vulnerable in her ridiculous oversized woolen boots. They locked eyes for an instant.

"Go in safety, Talon," she whispered.

Then he was out into the corridor and walking softly but quickly back the way he had come.

Once again, he stopped at the door of Ahmad's quarters. It had been just a short time since he'd left, but it already seemed ages.

He slipped through the entrance and then paused, seeing the girl with her back to him, brushing her hair by the window. He moved as would a ghost behind her, replaced the parchment, then was gone.

Moments after he had gone, she turned to glance behind her, as she thought she heard something at the door. But she saw nothing, so she turned her attention back to the view and went back to combing her hair.

Talon hurried down in the corridor and moved swiftly back to the library, where he felt that at least he could sit down and pretend that he was occupied with a book. There were several students studying there now. He went to the stack of rolls near the window and sat down, becoming very engrossed in his reading.

Later in the afternoon, the hunting party came home. Tired and dirty, they tramped or rode in through the gates and shouted for their respective grooms or helpers. There was much banter and shouting as they described their adventures to others in the courtyard. They had killed well and there would be fresh venison on everyone's tables that night.

One of the quietest places Talon, Reza, and Jean could meet was the mews, where the great birds of prey were kept for hunting purposes. It was even better than the stables, as here there would be almost no intrusion of young stable boys or grooms. The three of them met just before supper. Once there, Talon told them about his adventure and how the princess had translated the letter for him. He told them what she'd said and what she feared, then what they had done to retain some form of proof.

There was a long silence when he had finished, as both Reza and Jean were stunned by the news.

At last Jean spoke. "Do you know, Talon, if this is true, there is most probably a plot to kill the master, and most of the people here will be Arash Khan's people now. *We* are outsiders, as well as Feza and the princess." He turned to Reza. "Don't you think this to be true, Reza?" He gave a wheezing cough as he finished.

"You did not seem to have had an enjoyable day," Talon said to Reza, who indeed lacked his usual buoyancy. "What do you think is going on?"

"I think Ahmad was annoyed that I came, and he got angry at Mehdi for bringing me. After what I have just heard I'm not surprised he's suspicious of me. I think that we're all in danger, Talon, but I don't know what we can do about it."

Jean said, "Reza, Talon, if there is no doubt in our minds that there is a plot to murder the master, we have to find a way to either send a message or take one ourselves. This will be almost impossible at this time. IEven if we could escape from this castle, they'd light the beacons to warn others up the valley that something was wrong, and from then on we would be hunted on all sides. We would never get out of the valley alive."

Reza added his own opinion. "If you think Ahmad is bad, Arash Khan, his father, is worse. I am very afraid of him." He shuddered. "If he thought for an instant that we suspect something, he would torture us all to death today."

Talon nodded. "Arash Khan's reputation follows him everywhere. He is a dangerous person to fall on the wrong side of.

Nevertheless, we have to do something. Our first duty is to the princess, Reza, as you well know, and this plot puts her in grave danger. We have to find a way to make her safe."

They all stopped talking as their ears picked up the distinct sound of someone walking their way. Talon pushed Reza behind him into the deeper shadows and sat down on the ground, motioning Jean to do the same as though they were engaged in a conversation. One of the men at arms came by, glanced at the two sitting and talking about the birds behind them, and walked on without another look.

When he had gone, Reza emerged from the deep shadow where he had crouched and put his hand on his friend's shoulder as he slipped by on his way out. He nodded to Jean and was gone.

"You two have become phantoms, and this place is full of devils," Jean said almost peevishly, as he looked across at Talon, who was looking down at the ground. "Talon, we should go to supper now. We cannot do anything tonight but think on it."

Talon sighed. "You are right. I am worried, though. I think Ahmad is so sure that their plot will work that he considers the princess his for the taking."

"That may be, but we may have to gather more information before we can be sure. I am hungry. Can we please eat now?"

"Yes, and when we have finished I shall bring you another blanket. I do not like the way you look."

"Don't worry about me, Talon," the priest said, but there was no conviction in his voice.

They got up and walked together to the kitchens, where soup and the enticing smell of roasting meat came to them. A large number of others were gathered in keen anticipation of this infrequent opportunity to eat deer meat.

* * * * *

Ahmad took his evening meal as usual in the company of his father in his father's quarters where there was a good fire and they could talk undisturbed.

Tonight Arash had a letter brought by one of the messengers who came and went like phantoms. This was from Damascus, telling him that the Vizier Nur Ed-Din was contemplating an invasion of Egypt and that he was calling it a *jihad*, a holy war, as the Shi'ites of Egypt were heretics, as were the Ismaili still there, although there were fewer now. Arash weighed the options out loud, one being that the Christians would try to stop the army, as they would not like the idea of having forces hostile to them on both sides of the Kingdom of Jerusalem. They had to make a treaty with one or the other. He surmised it would be with the Egyptians.

The conversation moved to their plan and its execution. Arash was not going to strike until the spring, he said, so he could move about freely. It was too late in the year to try to go to Syria, and he wanted to make sure that Alamut and Lamissar were his before he left. They would have to stay here for the three months it would take for the passes to reopen. This brought them to the two newcomers, the priest, and their association with the princess.

"I want the boy Talon. I have yet to complete my work on him," the Khan said. "He is to believe at all times that he is free to come and go as he pleases. He cannot go far, and in any case he is bound to his studies for the time being."

"When do you intend to send him to do his work?" Ahmad asked, sucking on a bone.

"In the spring, I shall take him with me. It is a little early to judge that I have him where I want him. I cannot just send him; I have to be there."

"I want the princess."

"Be patient, Ahmad, and do as I command. I do not want her to grow suspicious, or she may try to leave and could still do so. It would be difficult to recapture her in this country without causing a lot of trouble. She is liked by the peasants." His father spoke in a voice that brooked no argument.

Ahmad glowered, but he knew the sense of what his father said. Once the snows had come she would be trapped here, and then he could do as he wished. His father would want her killed at some point, but before then, he would have some fun with this high and mighty cousin of his.

"You can amuse yourself when the time comes," his father said, as though reading his thoughts. "I shall tell you when you can take her. After you're done, there will be an accident, perhaps while out hunting. What about the other boy? Is he trustworthy?"

"The other boy? Oh, yes, he is making friends with Mehdi at present. It seems that he had had a falling out with the Frankish boy. I think Mehdi can bring him round, Father."

Arash, a suspicious man by nature, looked hard at Ahmad across the food-strewn cover on the floor between them. His eyes told Ahmad that he had better be right.

"Will we dispose of the priest during the winter months too?" asked Ahmad.

"I do not think it will be necessary. I hear that he is very sick and may not last the winter," returned Arash, who seemed to know everything that was going on inside the castle.

They finished the meal, conversing in a desultory manner, Arash preoccupied with the news from Syria and Palestine and Ahmad wanting to get back to his quarters. Thoughts of what he was going to do to Rav'an made him want to act out his fantasies upon the girl waiting there. He left soon after, having said a very elaborate goodnight to his father. He, like everyone else in the castle, feared his father, having no love at all for the man; just fear. Thus it was always good to get away from him.

His father's parting words to him were, "Bring back that parchment that I gave you to read, as I want it back tomorrow. It should stay here. Have you even read it?"

Ahmad cringed. He could read, of course, but not well, having been a slow and dilatory student as a youth. His tutors had more or less given up on him at a young age and turned him over to the military arts group, who fared better with him.

"I have read enough to understand what is meant. I admire your cunning and skill at bringing Nur Ed-Din to your side."

Arash nodded. "Goodnight," he said dismissively.

As Ahmad left and hurried down the corridors to his own quarters, Arash motioned to the servant, who had been standing silent in the shadows throughout the conversation, to remove the debris of dinner, then he got u.

While he waited for the servant to clear the food and clean up, Arash moved to his work space and went through his correspondence. He was a meticulous man for detail and had an instinctive grasp of the art of gathering intelligence. The information that he gleaned from the world he lived in was copious and remarkable. His nephew, the Agha Khan, relied upon him for the most accurate and most current information, which formerly he, Arash, had supplied. Now, however, he was going to use this same information for his own ends.

There was much to be done beforehand. There was the whole

valley of the Alamut and the Shah Rud, the area of the Rudbar to bring over, which needed to be done before he went to Syria.

The southern regions were going to be harder to convince to come to him. They were more likely to try for independence. Isfahan and Shiraz both had solid enclaves of Ismaili representation with a healthy hatred for the local Seljuk Sultans. However, they might simply deny his right to become master. That would pose a problem, which he would have to deal with in due course.

He spent another hour at his work, composing letters that would be taken by messenger in the morning and each morning until the snows locked the great castle in for the winter. Later in the night, when his eyes grew tired due to the bad light of the oil lamps, he went into his bedroom and said softly, "Are you prepared, my young friend?" The form in the bed sat up and stared back at the dark shape in the door, rubbing sleep from his eyes. Arash was silhouetted by the oil lamps and appeared menacing to the young boy clutching the bedclothes to him.

"Don't be frightened," Arash cooed, as he disrobed. "I am looking forward to a night in heaven. You should be glad of my comfort."

* * * * *

The next day dawned overcast with a thin mist engulfing the castle. The day passed with rainy interludes that left the buildings dripping. People splashed through puddles in the muddy, unpaved yard in boots covered in mud. For the most part, the students huddled in the library around the fires, and servants sought out the kitchens for warmth. The sentries on the walls huddled deeper into their sheepskin capes and cursed the foul wet. They wished they were with their wives or concubines or some other company in their lean-to mud houses that were propped against the castle walls.

Talon and Jean braved the wet and found shelter near the mews again. The birds were miserable and huddled into their feathers on their stands with their eyes shut as though to keep the wet, dripping day at bay. Talon and Jean both had blankets over their shoulders as they squatted nearby. They had plenty to talk about. The letter was still uppermost in their minds, as was the possibility of escape.

Jean, as usual, was thinking forward and keeping the more impulsive Talon in check. His opening comment indicated how much thought he had given to the problem. "Talon, it is clear that we have to escape, or at least some of us must. That means at least you and the princess, as well as Reza."

"Don't forget you and Feza."

"I have been thinking about that, Talon. I'm not sure if that is even realistic."

Talon made an impatient gesture. "Father, there is no question that you have to come, too. They will kill you if you stay."

Jean ;looked pensively at Talon. "Let us leave that for the moment. What is more important is the manner and timing of the escape." Talon was going to speak, but Jean held up a hand. "Wait, I want to discuss an idea. When do you think that the snows will come?"

Talon thought about it. "I should think in about three weeks at most."

"I agree. Look to the peaks. There is already snow on them, and this is winter snow. I have never seen winter in these mountains, but I have been in the Alps, and this is very like that place. We are six weeks to Christmastide. I do not think it will be long."

"What are you thinking? *Please* explain."

Jean smiled. "Before the snows come there will be deep frosts to prepare the ground for the snow. Then when it snows, it will stay. This means that the passes will be closed during the first or the second big storm. Somehow, we have to pick the time when the passes are near to being closed. If we leave it too late, we are trapped and will be sure to die. To go too early will ensure capture as well. Our one chance, and a very slim one, is when the passes are about to be closed and to try to slip out before they can muster a hunting party to come after us."

Talon stared at Jean. For a long moment neither said anything, then he said, "You are remarkable. I do not know if this can work, as it is very farfetched, but it might work. I have to think about it with care. It is very dangerous. We do not know this country. How will we know when to move?"

"We have to keep asking people about the weather somehow, without making them suspicious." Jean shook his head. "Talon, I do not know, but somehow we have to be *right* when we make the decision. We must not run at the first snowfall. We have to be sure at the time that there is going to be a heavy snowstorm. It *must* be at the right time. We are very much in God's hands now," he ended, almost plaintively.

Talon put his hand out to his friend and touched him on the arm. "You are right. We have to keep our faith and watch for an opportunity. You know, I'd bet that there is a lot more information in the quarters of Arash Khan."

Jean made an exclamation of horror. "Talon, do not tempt fate too much! Surely you have enough to go to the Agha Khan with now?"

Talon nodded. "I hope we do. I would just like to have something more."

"My advice is to leave it alone for now. From what you told me of even the seal, they may suspect something, although I would have thought if it had been serious we would have heard by now."

*****

Events were to force their hand faster than they had imagined.

This time it was Feza who sought out the priest. He had just finished with some Latin lessons he was giving a small group of students and had started down the main stairs to the entrance to the keep, when he spotted Feza lurking in the shadows. He was about to greet her when she waved her hand at him, as though telling him not to acknowledge her openly, but to come over. He did so, and she whispered that the princess wanted to see him at once. He nodded, looked around furtively to ensure that no one else was listening, and then followed her back up the stairs to Rav'an's rooms.

Jean was not prepared for the shock of seeing Rav'an in the state he found her. Her eyes were puffy with lack of sleep and weeping, and her normally carefully groomed hair was adrift from its combs. Her eyes had a despairing, lost look that almost made him not recognize her as the self-assured young woman with whom he was familiar. Nonetheless, he was careful to bow deeply and stand in respectful silence, waiting to be addressed.

The princess came to stand in front of him. She looked more like a lost little girl in her huge woolen knitted boots and woolen cardigan that had sleeves much too long for her. It was clear to Jean that she was very agitated and wanted to tell him something, but she seemed unable to bring herself to begin.

Jean was an intelligent and sensitive man. He decided to offer comfort where it seemed to be needed, so he said, “My lady, what can I do for you? You seem to be very upset. Is there anything I can do to help?”

His words seemed to calm Rav’an enough for her to collect herself. “Thank you for coming, Priest, and I thank you for your words. I have to tell you something, but it is difficult.”

Anxious at both her condition and her words, Jean said, “Please tell me what it is that is worrying you so much, my lady.”

Rav’an took a deep breath. “You came to me with a rumor last week, Priest, and I told you that it was untrue. Indeed, it was, and for me it still is, but it would seem that Arash and Ahmad have different ideas. I am now more certain than ever that I am a prisoner here, and that Ahmad intends to take me for his woman.” She did not even say wife or concubine; she almost spat out the word.

Jean flinched. “Oh, my dear Lord,” he whispered. “Then it is true?” He had already guessed the fact but was still shocked. She nodded, her arms folded tight under her breasts, her eyes welling with tears as she struggled with her self-control. He looked away politely to allow her to recover. Then she told him of the clash with Ahmad on the stairs.

* * * * *

It had been just a matter of time before the princess and Ahmad should meet again, and this instance was in the keep, out of sight of others. She had been coming up the stairs to her quarters after seeing to her horses and did not have her hounds with her, when he came onto the landing above her and stopped there, looking down on her. He did not say anything, so she politely bade him good day and continued up the stairs. Ahmad muttered something. He had a strange expression on his face as she came up to him. She stopped, as he was barring the way. Rav’an decided that if he was going to act badly she was going to just walk past him.

As she brushed past him, his right arm went out and encircled her waist, restraining her. Rav’an could not push past him, so she stood still and turned to face him with a look of contempt. His face was now very close, and she was repulsed by the sour smell of wine on his breath.

"Why do you not spend more time with me, Cousin?" he said. "It is not polite to avoid me the way you have been."

"Cousin Ahmad, I have not been avoiding you. You go hunting and do not invite me. Well, I, too, have things I want to do, and they do not include you."

"What do you mean by that?"

"Cousin, I think you have the wrong idea about me," Rav'an said as she tried to extricate herself. "I am not one of your loose pillow companions. Will you please let me go?"

"Ah, no, indeed, you are not one of the 'pillow companions,'" Ahmad sneered, "but we could still enjoy the pillow, could we not, cousin?"

Her slap resounded in the narrow stairwell. "How dare you?" she cried. "Who do you think you are, Ahmad? When I tell my brother about your behavior, you will pay dearly."

He laughed. It was a nasty laugh that said much. "Your brother is a long way from Alamut, my pretty. My father is here right now, and he is in charge. You are as good as mine, anyway."

He dragged her to him and tried to bring his mouth down onto hers. She shook her head and he missed, bussing her on the cheek with his rough mustache. She began to struggle then, but he was a very strong man and held her easily and very hard. It hurt and brought tears to her eyes.

Enraged, she kicked him hard in the shin with her booted feet. He gave a gasp and his grip loosened. Needing no further chance, she twisted free and, dodging under his other arm, fled down the corridor to her rooms. He didn't follow, but cursed her as she ran.

Rav'an crashed through the doorway of her apartments and slammed the door. Leaning back against it, she tried to control herself. As her despair settled over her, she lost the battle for self-control and tears began to trickle down her cheeks. Then she stumbled to her sleeping room and collapsed onto the bed, sobbing.

Feza found her there an hour later and had to drag the story out of her bit by bit, her appalled expression growing more and more angry as Rav'an told her of the encounter and what she understood from it. She clucked and fussed about the red-eyed girl and then made some tea for her, forcing her to sip it, all the while rubbing her back and cooing softly to her.

"My lady, you have to get away from here. It is becoming impossible to live here with that man," Feza told her.

"I know, but how?" she sobbed. "How am I to escape when my uncle will not let me even leave the castle without Ahmad in charge? I am a prisoner here!" This last was said with a wail in her voice as she contemplated its full meaning.

* * * * *

Rav'an dashed some tears away and gave a crooked smile to Jean. "So you see, Priest, I am at the mercy of my uncle and cousin, who will never let me leave this place. I shall be watched, and there is no chance of being able to even send a message to my brother."

Tears streamed down her cheeks and she let fall her arms loose at her sides, as she stood in front of the burly priest, who took a small step to her and held out his arms.

Rav'an's self-control broke down at this point. She almost fell into his comforting hold. Jean held her as she laid her head on his chest and wept for several minutes.

Feza stood nearby, her wizened face wrinkled with worry, wringing her hands, trying to comfort her lady with gentle pats on her bowed back.

Jean waited for the sobs to subside, gently took the girl by the upper arms, and held her back so that he could speak to her. "My lady, do not despair, all is not yet lost. Remember your two protectors. You have friends here at Alamut who will do all they can to protect you and to ensure that this does not happen. We have been discussing the situation, Talon, Reza, and I. Let me explain."

She nodded and sniffled. Feza passed her a cloth with which she dried her eyes and blew her nose with an embarrassed snort. "I am sorry, Priest, I should not have done that."

"Please, my lady, call me Jean. I am not a priest here and that is my name. Under the circumstances, you have every reason to be as upset as you are, but as I said, I want to talk to you about what Talon and I have discussed. There is no doubt at all that you must leave this place, but let me explain what we have been thinking."

She motioned to a large cushion near the window. The shutters were closed but they still allowed some light into the room. He waited until she was seated and then sat down facing her.

"Feza, please, my love, bring us some tea," Rav'an said, with some of her old composure returning. "Now, Jean, tell me what you have talked about with Talon."

So he went over his reasoning about the weather and how there would be a very short window of opportunity for them to take advantage of. He voiced his concern that they could make a mistake, that it would mean disaster if they read the weather the wrong way.

Rav'an listened with interest, and when he was finished, she was thoughtful, saying nothing for a few minutes while she sipped her tea. Feza sat down nearby and watched while Jean also sipped tea and waited for Rav'an to speak.

"Jean, both Feza and I lived here for years when I was younger. We both know the weather in winter. I am afraid that if you asked questions someone will become suspicious, and then we are finished, as everything goes back to Arash. His mind is ahead of most peoples' thinking. He will come to the right conclusion all too quickly. On the other hand, Feza can talk about the weather to anyone without them becoming suspicious, even if I cannot do so any more.

Your reasoning is correct about the first storms. Here they are often very heavy, and a lot depends upon how hard the ground has become before the storm arrives. I would think we should begin to see the weather clear up soon and stop raining. After that, the frosts come every night until the snows arrive. Isn't that so, Feza?"

Feza nodded. "*Khanom* is right, Jean. If it is as it was a few years ago, we will see the first storm within three weeks. You were right about the passes, too; they are very high up the mountains. They will close for weeks after the first storm, perhaps for months if another storm comes soon after."

Rav'an was still looking at Feza. "We cannot go out of this valley past Lamissar. There is but one way we can go, and that is over the Chula pass to Ghazvin."

Feza nodded. "That is the only way, my lady, and even then you would have to be very careful of the watch towers near the top. If there are soldiers there, you will not be able to get past them."

They all sat in silence as they contemplated their narrow options in glum silence.

Rav'an was the first to stir. "Jean, I feel better for talking about it. I agree that it is the only plan we have. Will you talk to Talon and Reza for me?"

"Of course, my lady."

Rav'an held her hand up. "Please do not tell them everything, Jean, just that we should work on your plan and that I have to leave, I think my life depends upon it. It is too dangerous now to even think of staying."

He got to his feet and bowed very low. "It shall be as you ask, my princess," he said.

As he came to the door that Feza was about to open, Rav'an called from the door.

"Jean."

"Yes, my lady?"

"I would thank you for your kindness. May Allah protect you, for you are a good man."

He shook his head. "I am your servant, my lady. May God protect you in all things."

Jean hurried off, careful to ensure that he was not observed, although, as he said to himself, it would be unlikely for him to notice if he were. This place was populated by shadow-wraiths who would find him, a clumsy, heavy man, very easy to watch without detection.

He made his way to the kitchens; he was hungry. He wanted something in his stomach before he made contact with Talon. The princess' situation was becoming more and more fraught with danger as each day passed. And because of their association with her, all their lives were in danger as a result. There was no way out. They must follow a plan that would get them away from this predicament, or they would not survive the winter.

Talon and Reza were present when they met again near the mews. It was noticeably colder these days, so they were all dressed in waterproofed boots of horsehide and warm furs. Reza even had a blanket draped over his shoulders, because, as he said, this mountain weather was not to his liking, and his thin blood did not do well here.

Talon had scouted very carefully to ensure that there was no one about for the meeting before they settled down as though just wasting time. Their main concern was that someone would recognize Reza. If they did, it would be all over for him with Mehdi.

They were both eager to hear what the princess had told Jean. He concentrated on her resolve, leaving out the emotional parts, just delivering her announcement that she had to get out of the castle before winter and would need their help to do so.

They sat and mulled the situation over for an hour. They all agreed they would have to depend upon Rav'an and Feza's judgment as to the time to leave, and that worried the boys. Jean was less troubled by this, but as they talked, he began to feel there was a more ominous situation pending which concerned him.

He knew he would not be able to ride a horse at the pace demanded for the escape. His heart quailed at the thought of being out in the wilds, fleeing from a vengeful Ahmad. He also wondered what would happen to Feza. How would she manage? He didn't discuss this with the others as they were talking, but it preyed on his mind from then on.

Talon and Reza debated how they would be able to get out of the castle. When would be the best time, and how would they deal with the sentries who would not be asleep? What horses could they take, and how much food would they need? Now that they were presented with a plan, they were eager to attend to the details, knowing how important it was to be thorough and well prepared. There would be no second chances.

They separated after that, the boys to the kitchens, after which they were expected to go to their respective rooms for the night.

Jean bedded down in the area that was left for visiting vendors or men-at-arms, a cold couple of rooms that had a small fire that only just kept the moisture off the walls. He sat there on the threadbare *ghilim* on the floor, sipping tea, thinking of what was to come. He turned out the oil lamp and pulled his bedding over to be close to the fire. He prayed until late in the night for courage and guidance from his God, finally falling into a troubled sleep.

*****

As the days passed, the boys had no time to meet. They were still expected to continue their studies, for instance, about poisons and methods of applying them, important skills to be learned now that they were *fida'i*. Talon found it all very interesting, although not as much as the skills with sticks, knives, and all the other instruments of death that he had been taught to use both at Samiran and here at Alamut.

The training here was much more sophisticated. They were taught how to carry messages, how to approach a victim in the open, and the best places to strike for most effect. A great deal of careful mental training was used now as the more senior acolytes passed along their training to the younger members of the brotherhood.

The walls of Alamut were, to the uninitiated, unassailable. The boys were taught how to climb stone walls like spiders. There were accidents, as one or another either fell or was struck a wounding blow. Talon and Reza had both been at the top of their class in Samiran, and now that helped them to avoid being hurt here. They both realized, however, that there was an intangible sense of hostility toward them, most of it toward Talon, but now Reza, too, which made them both wonder how much influence he might have left with Mehdi. This honed their sense of survival even more.

The nights became colder and each morning glittered with frost. Soon, every day dawned bright and sunny with a biting cold wind from the north flowing over the tops of the mountains to chill the valleys. The ground became frozen hard and the few trees in the castle area were white with hoarfrost. The water in the buckets, if left overnight, was a block of solid ice in the morning. People went around muffled up in all the clothes they could find until the sun warmed the air enough to shed some of the outer garments. The sky remained clear blue, swept clean of clouds from horizon to horizon. At night, the stars, when not hidden by the cold mists of this time of year, were sharply defined and filled the sky with light as the moon waxed huge in the western sky.

The three of them watched the change taking place in the weather. Jean told the boys that Feza had informed him that when the wind blew straight from the north and grew very cold as it was now, the storms would not be far behind. They needed to prepare themselves.

Talon met Reza later in the day, and they, in turn, found time in the stables to talk.

"We have to prepare ourselves, according to Feza," Talon said to his friend.

Reza nodded somberly. "I agree. There is more and more talk of a journey the Khan will be taking to Syria in the spring. Ahmad is going with him, but I keep hearing unpleasant things. I do not think the princess will be traveling with them. I think we are right to be very worried about her safety, and that includes ours, Talon."

Talon nodded. "Then you and I must place our bows and sufficient arrows with spears and swords somewhere where we can get to them when we need them. It is very hard in this crowded place. There are people everywhere doing this or that, with the children being the worst, as they get into everything."

They discussed where they could hide the weapons. They finally settled on the small area that lay between the stables and the mews. No one went there, as it was a junk yard of bits of wood and old ropes. They would wrap the weapons in sackcloth to disguise them and protect them from the cold, and keep the strings of the bows with them to keep them from breaking in the freezing air.

That decided, they thought about food, where to steal it from, and how they could ensure that Jean and Feza would manage—neither of them was confident that either Feza or the priest could keep up the necessary pace. They had no such reservations regarding the princess, who had demonstrated often enough that she was a superb horsewoman.

"What are we to do about the sentries?" Reza asked. "They will be a big problem when the time comes."

"Maybe, but have you noticed that they are not anywhere as alert as the ones at Samiran?" Talon replied. Reza nodded. "So, I think they feel very secure here, that there is nothing to fear from outside, and they won't be expecting anything from the inside. What we have to do is avoid causing an alarm as we leave. We must have as much time as we can get to stay ahead of pursuit."

They continued to cast about for new ideas, but it was getting late; the sun now seemed to set in mid-afternoon. They got up and went off separately to the kitchens for supper and a warm fire.

Up in the higher reaches of the castle, Ahmad was having dinner with his father. This time they were discussing Talon. Arash was cautiously optimistic, as was his way. He told Ahmad that he felt the boy would remember nothing until the time came for him to perform. He, Arash, would be there to see Talon carry out his directives. Had not the Master himself ordered that the compulsion be imbedded deep within the boy, so when he was commanded he would act with devastating effect? All of his training had been for this moment, and what a moment it would be, Arash told his son.

Ahmad chortled with glee, his admiration for his father's skill and cunning outweighing his sense of prudence for the moment. He thought to ask his father yet again when he could make his move on Rav'an.

"Not yet," Arash replied sharply. "How many times must I say this? When the snows come you can have her, and not before; is that clear?"

Ahmad might have been a large, strong man, but he was no match for his father when it came to sheer will. He quailed and raised his hand in submission. "F-Father, I was just going to say that she has not come out of her quarters for days, so I never see her."

His father looked at him. "I shall go and see if she is ailing or something. Women get all sorts of problems. You will stay away from her until I am ready to serve her up to you. Then, my boy"—he grinned at his son—"you can have her, but she will not bear you sons, as we shall take another for that."

Ahmad leered back at his father, thinking, You, Father, are one of the most evil people I have ever known. Even I cannot trust you. If I do not get to quench my sword in that ripe young fruit, I shall want a reckoning with you. He did not say a word out loud, of course, and the rest of the meal passed amid desultory comment and the passing of news of the new war between the Egyptians and the Kingdom of Jerusalem.

* * * * *

The next day there was a knock on the door to the princess' apartments. Feza peered out and gave a start as she saw Arash Khan standing there.

"Where is the princess?" he demanded.

"*Gorban*, she is here. She is not well," Feza quavered back.

"I wish to speak with her," he commanded. Before Feza could say or do anything else, he pushed past her. "Get out of my way, you old crone," he grated and made for the bed chamber, leaving her to squawk.

"My lady is not ready to receive anyone, my Lord!"

"Indeed, she is not," Arash said dryly, as he stood at the door to Rav'an's bed chamber.

Rav'an was dressed in nothing but her shift of fine silk. She was sitting near the fireplace, combing her hair. As soon as she perceived Arash was at the door, she whirled around and reached for a robe. Arash stood watching her, admiring her young body as she hastily pulled the robe on. Her embarrassment and anger at being caught in such a manner heightened her obvious beauty. He had caught a glimpse of her full young breasts pushing against the thin silk of her shift as she stooped to pick up the robe. By Allah, he thought, I might even avail myself of this ripe young fruit before I hand her over to Ahmad and his cronies.

Rav'an was furious. "Uncle, why did you not give me more notice? It is wrong of you to come into a lady's room like this," she said, more loudly than she'd intended.

"My dear, Rav'an," he answered with oily tones, "I came because it is said that you are not well. Is that true?"

Rav'an regained her composure, keenly aware that she should be careful. "Yes, it is true, Uncle. I have not been feeling all that well. I think I am coming down with the grippe. I am cold all the time. I had forgotten how cold it is here in high Alamut."

He nodded thoughtfully, watching her. "You should still try to move about, my dear. Exercise is good for you. You should let Ahmad take you out for a ride soon. It will do you good."

Rav'an mustered up a smile. "Thank you for your concern, Uncle. I shall be happy to ride with Ahmad when I am feeling somewhat better. I fear it will snow soon, and I would like to ride at least once before it does so."

Even his keen senses did not get any clues from this. He smiled his kindest smile. "I agree it will snow soon. You must come to see me more often, Rav'an. There is much to read in the library and your education is still to go on. I shall see you again soon?"

She nodded politely and even curtseyed to him as he turned and left, but did not move again until she heard the door shut. She turned to Feza as she came back into the room, and said angrily, "I feel dirty every time I come close to that man. I would rather die than go out riding with Ahmad, and why should I go to the library where all his cronies are? To be stared at as they whisper about what he is going to do to me?"

Feza clucked and fussed. "I did not have time to warn you, my lady. He just barged past me. How I hate that man," she said venomously.

Rav'an nodded. "Feza, if I cannot escape, I shall kill myself. Oh, why did my brother send me here? Neither that lecherous toad, nor his monstrous son, will use me. I know he has young boys for sport. He didn't even try to hide his lecherous thoughts from me as he was standing there."

Feza looked frightened at that. "My lady, you must not talk like that. I know that our Protectors are busy, and Jean is thinking hard too. Remember that we still have a chance, and if it can be done they will do this for you."

Rav'an put an arm round the thin shoulders of her nurse. "I know they are doing all they can. I know, too, that they will die for me should it be necessary, but I don't want to be the cause of that. You are right, though, we must keep our courage up for the time when we need it most. I love you, my old friend." She hugged Feza hard. "We have to be able to meet when the time comes. I thought of these rooms, but we are too close to Ahmad's apartments down the corridor. Do you know of anywhere that's safe nearby?"

"I might. There are unused rooms below, on the same floor as the library. I could get a key for one and have a look inside."

"Please do that, Feza, my dear. I, in turn, shall find a way to keep food for when we need it. I think the snow is not far off now."

* * * * *

Three days later, the sky was leaden. Although it was still cold, it did not have that biting wind of before. There was moisture in the air, and the temperature even climbed a couple of degrees.

Rav'an and Feza looked out at the sky, and then at each other. "You must tell Jean to inform the boys to be prepared," Rav'an instructed her. "The storm is coming. Did you find a room, and is it safe?"

"It is safe, my lady. I do not think we will be disturbed there when we meet." She looked nervous. "My lady, can I speak?"

Rav'an turned, surprised. "Of course, Feza. Since when did you not speak when you wanted?" She smiled to take the sting out of the words.

Feza did not smile back. "My lady, I do not think I can go with you if it is to be at night and in a storm. I do not have the strength to do this thing, and I would surely slow you down."

Rav'an looked at her, appalled. "Feza, you *cannot* stay!" she cried in anguish. "Think what they might do to you!"

Feza looked at Rav'an, her wrinkled face calm. "I shall be in a different world by then, my lady."

Rav'an sat down suddenly, her face white as chalk. "Oh, Feza," she whispered. "Oh no, this cannot be! You *must* come with us."

Even as she said it, however, the sense of what her faithful old nurse had said came to her. She put a hand to her mouth. "Feza, I cannot leave without you, I cannot. You have been part of my life, all my life. What would I do without you?" Tears started in her eyes and there was a huge lump in her throat.

Feza faced her and said in her squeaky voice, "My dove, my dear, lovely princess. I have passed the best years of my life with you, but I am old and worn out now. I will not be able to survive a journey of the kind that you will have to face. Not even the boys will be able to protect me from the cold and exhaustion. I would better serve you by helping you to leave." She put an old, gnarled hand to the wet cheek of her child, as she considered Rav'an; they had been together since Rav'an came into the world. "You must let me do it this way, my dove. I must also tell you where to go in Ghazvin, or you will perish when you get there."

Rav'an nodded; she could not speak. She clasped the old, wrinkled hand to her cheek, then kissed it. "Oh, Feza, what have we come to?" she whispered brokenly.

Feza gave detailed and explicit instructions on how to get to her brother's house in Ghazvin. It would have adequate stabling and accommodation for them. She was sure of her brother. He was true Ismaili, had been living in Ghazvin for years now, and one of his occupations in life was to spy on the Seljuk rulers in Ghazvin and pass information back, when he could. After she finished, the two of them clung together for a long time. Rav'an could not let her nurse go. She felt that the bottom of her world was falling away, and she would soon be staring at the abyss.

I go, I depart, I leave this world of ours,
I journey beyond the furthest bounds of Chin,
And, journeying, ask Pilgrims about the Road,
"Is this the End? Or must I journey on?"

– Baba Tahir –

Chapter 15
The Escape

Five oddly assorted people sat on the floor around a low table in one of the chambers located in the second story of the castle. The room was lit by one guttering candle on the table in the center. Its flickering light cast huge shadows against the rough stone walls with barely enough light to allow each to make out the others' pale and haunted features. They were all muffled in furs and thick sheepskin coats to ward off the icy air.

A worn *ghilim* on the wood floor and some dark drapes on the walls did nothing to keep the cold from the stone walls from reaching the people huddled around the table. Their breaths made clouds as they whispered to one another.

The wind howled and banged the shutters outside in the darkness, its eerie wailing bringing to mind ghosts of lost souls searching for ways to get into the room. There was a constant spattering of small ice particles on the wood shutters. The chilling cold had penetrated the upper levels of the castle, and icy currents blew along the darkened corridors. There was the ominous promise of snow.

Rav'an darted an anxious look at Talon from under her hood. "We have to decide whether to leave tonight, but it is going to snow."

Talon nodded, as did Jean and Reza. "I know," Talon said. "But if we don't leave tonight, we will not get out of here until spring. I do not believe we would survive Ahmad's mercies until that time." He gave her the grimace of a smile. "Dear Father Jean, will you not come with us? I beg you to reconsider. They will not be kind to you. They will be sure that you had a hand in this and torture you!" His vehement whisper became a croak.

Jean laid his big, calloused hand on Talon's shoulder. "Who will delay them? Who will open and shut the gate? Besides, I would slow you down once we are on the road, and then we would all be captured for no gain. I must stay and pray that they do not suspect me."

Rav'an turned to the fifth person in the room. Small Feza was huddled into her dresses and furs, squatting on the floor with a blanket thrown over her shoulders. It was clear she was very cold, but that was not the only reason she was trembling.

"Feza, you must go to bed when we leave and stay there as though you know nothing," Rav'an said.

"I shall, my lady," the old maid croaked, "but I am so frightened." Tears welled into her eyes and coursed down her withered cheeks. "I shall pray to Allah that he protect you during this dreadful time," she whimpered.

Rav'an reached her arm over Feza's thin shoulders and hugged her. "My Feza, my dear friend, I would that we did not have to do this, but we know not what else we can do. Allah protect you, my old friend. I shall pray for you all the time we are gone."

The wind picked up outside as though to emphasize their lack of time. They all gathered themselves for the ordeal ahead.

"Reza and I must go to the stables," Talon said, getting up. He adjusted his sword and pulled his woolen sheepskin coat close. "We have work to do preparing the horses and binding their hooves, as well as making sure that no one is there to see us go."

Reza got up. He reached over to Jean and gripped his shoulder. "Goodbye, my old friend. May Allah and your God protect you, for you are a good man."

Talon looked into Rav'an's eyes. "My lady, will you see to Feza and then meet us at the gate in half an hour?"

She nodded, silent, her eyes full of tears.

Jean got up and put his hands on Talon's shoulders. "I shall go and make sure the guards are comfortable in their room. None should be out on the walls tonight, but I must make sure. Go with God. May he protect you always, all of you."

They embraced, Talon almost crushed by the huge arms that wrapped around his shoulders. He did not think they would ever meet again. His heart was so heavy that he wanted to weep. His emotions were close to the surface. He knew he must not cry, at all costs, so he gritted his teeth and whispered his response.

"You have been my father in so many ways. God protect you. I shall pray for you until we meet again."

They stood apart, and both could see in the dim light that the other's face was wet. Jean pushed him firmly to the door.

Talon opened the door very carefully, lifting the latch with both hands, and then slowly peered out. He listened attentively for any sound other than the wailing wind. Hearing none, he slipped out, followed closely by Reza. Jean pulled the door closed.

Once in the corridor, Talon and Reza were still in mortal danger. If caught, they would be hard pressed to explain why they were out of bounds and in the upper levels of the castle. They made haste to slip like shadows along the corridors and descend to the courtyard. They passed no one on the way. Everyone who could was near a large fire, out of the biting wind and cold, or in bed. Almost all activity in the castle had come to a stop this evening. Even the cooks were huddled in their kitchens near the fires, and the rest of the people in the castle had no interest in wandering around.

Reza opened the side door of the keep and slipped outside. Talon followed and pulled it close. Once outside, the wind tore their breath away. It ripped at their clothes as though it wanted to strip them naked. The biting cold very soon began to chill their fingers to the bone. The snow came at the two running boys in icy pellets, which stung the exposed parts of their faces.

Running across the courtyard to the stables that were placed against the west wall of the castle, the two boys came up hard against the wooden wall. There was a light powder of snow on the yard already, swirling into columns in the wind and making the courtyard treacherous to run across. Talon knew that they did not have much time to prepare and leave before the full force of the storm hit. He figured they needed to be at least half a day ahead before the pursuit began.

The doors to the stable were not locked, taking but a little effort to open. The wind in this corner was not as savage. Reza opened the door very cautiously and looked in. Warmth and the strong smell of horses greeted him. He could see no one there in the dim oil-lantern light. Reza had been sure that there might be, as it was a warm place for someone to take refuge on such a cold night.

Very slowly, they walked down the middle of the stable. The horses were not alarmed at their presence. They all knew the boys; both had spent a lot of time with them. For the most part, they continued to munch on their hay, some turning an eye on the boys as they came by. They gave the occasional snort as they blew out their nostrils at the dust in their hay, and the stamp of their feet on the hard earth was all the noise in the building as Talon and Reza approached the stalls where their own animals were stabled.

Talon was greeted with a quiet whicker from Jabbar, who left his feed to move over to the entrance to his stall and nuzzle. Talon grinned in spite of the tension inside him and rubbed the soft nose pushing against him.

"We have to be quiet, my friend," he whispered. "You have much work to do this night." He fished out a lump of *Ghant* he had stolen from the kitchens earlier and presented it to the nose in front of him. Jabbar delicately picked the small lump of sugar off his hand and crunched down on it.

Talon then moved along one stall to the mare, Kaleen, and whispered her name. She, too, came to him and enjoyed a small reward. Both horses stood looking at him expectantly. He hurried to uncover the bridles and saddles he had hidden earlier under three large and old rugs that Feza had given him.

"These will cover their backs in the cold," she had told him.

Reza was busy across the center aisle of the stables, whispering to his gelding and moving deliberately to saddle him up.

Talon fitted the bridle to each horse, eased the saddlecloths over the rugs, then the saddles onto their backs. He knew the horses would allow him to do this without much trouble, but he could not guarantee that they would not balk at the prospect of leaving the warmth of the stables.

He left the horses to go to the door to see if it were still safe, and just as he got to the door, he heard voices above the wind. He turned and ran back tiptoe to the stalls where his two horses were tethered and crouched down in the hay, out of sight of the center path. Reza saw his urgency and crouched down in the stall with his horse, watching and listening.

Talon's heart was beating wildly and his mouth had gone dry. To be discovered now would be a disaster. He pulled his sword forward in readiness for instant use and saw Reza do the same. For a long moment, they listened, and then the door crashed open and two people stomped in. It was Ali and a companion. They shut the door and then stood looking around at the horses. Their conversation was muted against the noise of the wind outside and the creaking building. Unless they walked down the aisle, they would not see in the gloom the three horses with their saddles on. They appeared to be making a last check of the animals before settling down for the evening in their quarters. After a low conversation and shuffling of feet, the two men seemed content to stay where they were.

Ali commented on the weather and then said more loudly, "I am going back to the fire and my woman. The horses are good for the night. Let's leave. Put out the lamp."

There was a blast of cold air as the door opened again, and then they were gone. The doors crashed shut, restoring darkness and an an eerie quiet to the stables.

For long minutes, Talon stayed where he was, peering across at Reza in the dark, almost lightheaded with relief. They both listened to the wind, straining to hear any other noises from the outside that might spell trouble.

At last, Talon moved and bound the animals' hooves with torn cloths that had been provided by Feza. It was not as easy in the darkness, but he was almost glad of it. This would muffle their hooves as they went cross the hard yard and provide some grip on the icy slope along the way down the mountain. He took his time, wrapping the cloths tight around the hooves and then tying them just below the joint. He was pressed by the realization that time was slipping away and that the others were about to take up their positions near the gates. The longer they stayed there waiting, the more chance there was of detection by some wandering sentry.

Eventually, he was done. Looking across at Reza, he nodded to indicate he was ready. Reza lifted a hand in acknowledgement. Talon led Jabbar out onto the center path between the stalls, and then did the same for the mare. Both horses were skittish. The howling of the wind around the building was disturbing them. With Reza following with his horse, they moved cautiously to the door.

Although Talon had bound them well, there was still a slight clomping sound as they made their way to the doors. He was wondering what he would do about opening the doors while holding both horses without making a lot of noise, when he heard a knock on the door. He reached forward and tapped back. The doors were eased opened from outside, and Talon saw Jean using all his strength to keep them from banging shut while he and Reza hurriedly led the horses out.

Jean battled the doors closed. Then they were outside in the biting, howling wind. They had to hang onto the three horses and try to calm them, as they were not happy at being taken out of their warm environment into this maddened, howling world of flying snowflakes and driving wind. They struggled across the yard, which was now almost completely dark, to the gates. The snow was beginning to fall in earnest now, laying down a thin carpet on the hard ground.

They came up to the solid mass of the great castle gates. Talon wondered if it were possible that their luck could hold before someone came out of one of the buildings set against the walls and spotted them. There were no alarms, however, as they neared the entrance to the castle. Instead, he recognized a black figure that slipped out from the shadows carrying a small sack and three long spears. Talon gave a sigh of relief when he saw Rav'an and moved as fast as the reluctant horses would allow him toward the oncoming figure.

Rav'an was bulky in the furs and cloak. Without greeting him, she thrust one of the spears into his hand and another to Reza, then took the mare's reins. Jean nodded to them and moved forward to the gates. There was a small postern gate that would just allow a horse through. He opened it while they held the horses. A gust of wind almost ripped it out of his hands. His thin hair streaming in the wind, he beckoned them furiously to go. Rav'an led the way, persuading her panicky mare to step through. Then she was lost in the darkness.

And at that moment, disaster struck. A figure hurried to them, carrying a spear. It was the sentry, who should have been there in the first place. He could not see them very well, but still he began to run to them, clearly concerned that something untoward was going on. The horses hampered both Reza and Talon while Jean held the door. Without any hesitation, Jean allowed the door to slam shut and walked right up to the oncoming man. They met a few yards from Talon.

To his utter surprise, the priest seized the man by the throat, chopping off a yell, and hung onto the man, forcing him to his knees with enormous strength. He continued to throttle the luckless sentry, who struggled hopelessly against Jean's huge strength. It took but a couple of moments before the man was unconscious, but to Talon, it seemed ages. Jean then picked the man up and dropped him in a corner. Running back to the boys, he glanced at them and re-opened the door. He gestured them to get through while he held the door. Talon hauled Jabbar along with him.

As he passed Jean, they exchanged looks. Talon reached out and touched his friend in passing, and then he, too, was outside. Reza hurried through. He, too, touched Jean in passing, mutely applauding his action. The door was forced shut against the wind. They were alone with the screaming gale and the daunting task of negotiating the dangerous path down the mountain in the dark.

They could not mount, as it would have been too dangerous. Talon took the lead. Rav'an kept to the middle with Reza in the rear as they searched for the path, a slightly lighter color in the dark. Then they started the treacherous downward journey.

The icy snow bit at their faces, and the wind tore at their clothing. The horses were slipping and sliding in spite of the wraps on their hooves. On several occasions, they had to stop in the lee of a rock face to hold and calm them. Then it was out into the wind again and another hundred yards of careful work, fear of the alarm sounding gripping their insides the whole time.

It was exhausting and terrifying for all of them. The horses were exposed to the wind and freezing cold, and had to trust their riders to know the way down the perilous path. Men who knew the worth of impregnability had built Alamut on the peak of a mountain. There was no real road to the gates for a purpose: to inhibit an army attempting to take the fortress. Now, as the fugitives descended the side of the mountain in the tearing gale, the dangers they faced at the very onset of their escape were brought home to them.

After what seemed to be hours later, they came to some level ground and paused. Talon glanced up at the looming shape of the castle in the dark above. No alarm yet, but he was keenly aware that should there be one any time soon, they were lost.

They were well protected by their furs and cloaks. Even so, the cold was penetrating; the wind seemed to cut right through all protection. It was clear to the three that their horses were cold as well, despite the extra covering they had placed on them.

The path was now less steep, and they could make better time, although they could not ride yet. After another few hundred yards, they came to the outskirts of the small hovels that housed the shepherds and their families at the base of the rock itself.

Stopping Jabbar and raising his arm, Talon signaled a halt. They listened intently for any sounds of activity that might represent danger, but heard nothing. No one was out in this weather, and as their horses' hooves were still muffled, they could move past the crude huts without disturbing anyone. Talon gave thanks that no one used common dogs as shepherds or watchdogs in this country.

Once past the huts and below their view, they stopped again, Rav'an mounted her mare and then he and Reza mounted their own horses. Down here the wind was far less violent, and they could make better progress along a wider track that led to the bottom of the valley far below. Small trees dotted along either side defined the path for them. Even so, they had to go at a walk, as there were still dangers. A carelessly placed hoof could throw both horse and rider over the steep sides to certain death.

All three of the riders watched the path with aching eyes to try to anticipate the bad patches and guide their horses around obstacles. The animals were more tractable now that they had riders on their backs and felt that they were being guided.

Hours later, not long after the middle of the night, they came to the bottom of the mountain and stopped. They heard the sound of rushing water ahead at the bank of the river. It was the Alamut Rud, a river that took the high mountain streams and carried their water down the steep valley to the Shah Rud and then the sea. The other side of the river seemed a long way off in the dark. Talon, Reza, and Rav'an knew that normally it would not be deeper than the height of the horse's knees, but this might have changed. They dismounted and removed the covers from their horse's hooves and threw them far out into the dark waters, which carried them away into the darkness.

Taking the lead, Talon urged Jabbar down the shallow, stony bank into the ice-cold water. His horse went unwillingly, but with the steady urging from Talon he splashed into the water, which surged around his legs. The force of the water was so great Talon had fears that it might sweep them off their feet. Jabbar moved solidly, but at about the halfway point the water was almost up to his chest and the current was tugging hard at his legs. Talon again wondered if they would have to swim when, with a lunge, Jabbar breasted the water and bounded for the flat, stony bank.

There he shook himself like a dog, and Talon leaned down to pat him and murmur praise. Talon turned and watched Rav'an bring the mare cross. The mare was shorter than the stallion by a hand, which made the crossing heavy work. Rav'an, at one point, lifted her feet out of the saddle and balanced on her rump with her legs up, looking comical as she crossed. The mare lunged through the water, nearly unseating her rider, as Rav'an still had her legs away from the saddle. However, she clutched the front of the saddle and the two made an undignified exit from the water. Talon grinned in the dark, and he caught the flash of teeth as Rav'an laughed silently at her near fall. Not for the first time, Talon regarded her with respect mingled with amusement.

Reza made it across in like manner. His gelding was responsive to his rider and trusted Reza to guide him well. The water was high, however, and there was a low curse as Reza's boots got soaked. Talon looked back at the river and then leaned out to Rav'an and Reza.

"I hope the river rises overnight, then we will have more time."

They nodded, then turned their horses west. Now they could hurry due west along a well-marked road in the narrow valley that would lead them to the pass on the southern ridge. This would take at least a day, and would be much harder if it snowed thickly. The stinging, icy snow pellets whipped into their faces by the horizontal wind did not settle on the path. If, however, it snowed much harder before they could cross over Chula Pass, they'd die on the side of the mountain, or worse, be captured. Chula Pass, if it could be called a pass, was just a nick in the side of the mountain range that faced south. It was still very high and would be clogged very soon once snow came down in large amounts. Talon prayed that the river behind them would rise and prevent any chance of pursuit.

They were halfway to the crossing where they'd take the upland road to Ghazvin when the first dull glow of dawn worked its way through the low clouds. The sun could not break through the dark-gray mass of clouds, but there was no mistaking the lightening in the eastern sky. The fugitives were all coated in a thin layer of ice that clung to their furred hats, thick sheepskin coats, and the accoutrements on the horses. They had trotted most of the way, so the horses were warm, but the ice on their manes and tails gave them a ghostly look in the pale light of the dawn.

They could still be in difficulty if there were others on the road, so they kept a sharp eye ahead. The wind had abated somewhat, but flurries of snow obscured the way forward and the horses were beginning to tire. The riders were numb with cold. Talon suggested that they walk for a while and give the horses a chance to regain their wind. Reza nodded, as did Rav'an, so they dismounted stiffly. They walked in silence, concentrating on the path ahead, fearful of pursuit, constantly looking back over their shoulders, then searching forward for any sign of people.

As dawn came up, they called a halt in a small grove of trees off the main track. The branches of the trees pointed stark and black into the gray sky. They ate sparingly of the food that Feza had snatched from the kitchen earlier that evening. The mutton strips, lumps of goat cheese, and the flat, unleavened bread called *lavash* were welcome, as was the sip of icy water they each drank from the skin Reza carried on his saddle. The three of them crouched in the lee of the trees, hunched over their food, holding tight onto the horses' reins. To lose one of them at this stage would be a disaster. The horses got nothing and stood forlornly with their backs to the wind, their tails, and manes blowing forward over their bodies.

Looking about, Talon could see only the desolate, frozen valley banked north and south by the sharp rise of the mountains. The peaks disappeared into the low clouds. They had crossed the river again. It had been much shallower, wider at this point farther down in the valley, and they had crossed without incident. Now they were on the north side of the river, in the foothills well above the bottom of the valley. It would descend again to bring them back to the river many miles farther down the valley. The mountains on either side of the steep valley were just vague shapes, shrouded in mist and clouds with even more snow promised for later in the day.

Reza leaned toward the other two. "We have perhaps five more hours before we have to climb the mountain to the pass. We should go faster now, and neither stop nor tarry at any of the villages we go through."

Rav'an nodded. "It is very cold, Reza. How will it be on the pass?"

"I don't know, *Khanom*," he said reluctantly. "It will be worse than this, and there will be much more snow. We have to go or we will die, for surely there will be pursuit."

As though to emphasize this point, they heard the distant, haunting call of a wolf to the north. Everyone cocked an ear at the sound and looked in that direction. The horses lifted their heads and looked hard, ears cocked in that direction, unhappy at the sound. Soon there came another howl, this one nearer. The riders looked at one another and, as one, mounted up.

There was enough light to see the way clearly now. They cantered along the rutted frozen path, steadily eating up the miles while trying to conserve their horses. The rode west, hour after hour. On occasion, they got off and walked the tired animals and, where they could, allowed them to drink in puddles of water they found along the way, breaking the ice first.

There were very few people on the road, and those were peasants who were hurrying to shelter on foot or with a donkey. No one greeted the fugitives, nor stopped them to ask what they were doing on the road, neither in the villages they passed through nor on the road. Talon was thankful for Alamut's sinister reputation. It helped for them to be thought of as its denizens and therefore to be left strictly alone.

At about midday the path started to descend toward the bottom of the valley. In the distance, they saw the wide, stony banks, then the river itself running down the middle. A much wider river this time, but they had no trouble crossing at the primitive ford. They watched the back trail for signs of pursuit with nervous glances while they paused to let the horses drink.

They now faced the steep climb up for thousands of feet along a very narrow trail. It would take them over Chula Pass and onto the high plateau and then on to Ghazvin, their final destination.

The snow that had blown in flurries all day under a gray and lowering sky now began to fall in a steady blanket of flakes that stayed on the frozen ground. They understood what this meant, so there was a renewed urgency as they guided the horses up the steep path. Reza took the lead and Talon the rear as they climbed. He watched behind them, praying that pursuit had not yet come close. Visibility was so poor that the chance of seeing a party on their trail was low.

Their horses, although tired, went at the steep path with a will. Strangely, the wind was dropping off, but the snow was getting heavier as they climbed. The path they followed was rutted, and iron hard, which made it treacherous. There was poor purchase for the horses' hooves. The only sounds now were the clink of iron from the horse's shoes on the stones and the creak of saddles. Talon hitched the sword on his waist in a fidget as his anxiety increased. This was where they could be taken if a fast moving party found them too low on the mountain.

He began to look around for some means of delaying any pursuit should this happen. For the moment nothing presented itself, so he had to be content with watching the road to the front, alert for any prospect, but he would often turn to stare into the gathering evening gloom back along the way they had come. Looking up the side of the mountain to the as yet invisible pass, he could see where the track led between two peaks and disappeared from view. As this was a new road for him—they had come from Samiran when last they rode the valley—he could not be sure what this meant. He hoped that it might provide both shelter from the thickening snowfall and concealment from anyone looking up from the valley bottom.

Horses and riders were covered with a light coating of snow that shed off in small falls whenever they turned or struggled with a patch of difficult pathway. There was no talking. Rav'an, Reza, and Talon were consumed with worry over their chances of escape and too afraid of communicating it to one another to want to talk. There were the occasional breathless encouragements to their horses when they stumbled, but that was all.

They continued up as fast as they could, finally to breast the first long slope and come to a space that allowed them to stop and move off the track. They were now about halfway up the mountainside. The horses were blowing and looked tired. Here they dismounted and stood facing each other. Steam rose off the horses. They rested with their heads down.

Talon handed Reza his reins, then turned to pace over to the edge of the track. From here he could look out over the valley, and had it been clear, he would have been able to see right across to the other mountainside about ten miles away. As it was, he felt that the clouds were level with him. He could only just see to the bottom of the mountain they were on, and even then not well. The snow was coming down in flurries, so he could see clearly just some of the time. He stamped his feet to keep warm and stared hard down toward where he thought the river should be. The snow flurry passed, and there! A flicker of movement! He thought for a moment his watering eyes had tricked him. Then he saw it again. He saw a faint, tiny mass that he could just make out as being several men on horseback galloping to the beginning of the track that they themselves were climbing.

He instinctively stepped back from the ledge, even though there was no chance that they would see him, and ran back to the other two. “They are behind us,” he cried. “We have to go on now as fast as we can.”

He caught Rav’an’s wide-eyed look of alarm as he snatched the reins from Reza. Immediately they were mounted and pushing the horses up the track. Talon began to see that the trail climbed for about a hundred yards more and again leveled off, disappearing into a cleft in the mountain.

He wondered if there might be a chance of holding their pursuers off at some point, but then discounted it as being impractical. There were many of them, and he and Reza could not hold them off long enough for Rav’an to escape.

By now, the snow was beginning to slow the animals down. There were drifts forming on old snowfalls that made for white patches of treacherous surface they floundered through. They had come to the old snow line, and there were banks of snow along the path on both sides. Although it was negotiable, it was becoming very narrow. They came up to the cleft in the side of the mountain, now completely out of the wind, passing through a narrow defile with less snow. Making better progress, they hastened though this toward the light at the other end. Any sound echoed now as they moved along the path. As they came up to the end of the defile, Talon looked up and saw, running parallel with them about eighty feet above, a lot of rocks in a wild jumble. This continued right up to the entrance of the defile that they were about to leave. There were thin saplings growing in clumps all over the steep hillside. If he could only dislodge some of the larger boulders he might be able to delay their pursuers enough for them to make it to the pass.

He called to Rav’an and Reza. “I am going to try something! Take the horses through!”

He tossed Jabbar’s reins to Rav’an and began to struggle up the steep slope to their right, using his spear as a staff to help him climb. Reza did the same and they both floundered up the steep slope.

Rav’an caught the reins, but exclaimed, “Talon, Reza, what you are doing? We have to keep going!” Neither answered, so Rav’an trotted several hundred yards along the narrow path, then turned around to watch.

Talon drew his sword and hacked at one of the large saplings that he came to on the way up the slope. It was about ten feet long, and once he had stripped its small branches, it provided him with another good pole for climbing with, despite its length. It was exhausting in the slippery snow, and they were both gasping before they had gone twenty feet, but they continued up. Talon made it to the first rocks, laboring for breath. His lungs ached, and his thighs and calves burned. Reza came up behind him, panting hard.

They were now about eighty feet above the track. On inspection, Talon saw that they might be able to dislodge some of the rocks but would need some kind of lever to get the larger ones to move. He quickly realized that if they climbed a higher, there was more chance of dislodging them from higher up.

"Come on, Reza, we have to go a little higher," he gasped.

Talon was hoping they could block the path and prevent the others from following on their horses. If they could just do that, they had a fighting chance of making Ghazvin and disappearing.

He stuck the pole tentatively under one of the larger rocks, which he saw could create a small landslide. It moved a tiny bit. The rock was about twice his weight and well settled into the side of the mountain. Feverishly, he dug the pole in deeper. By this time Reza was with him, and together they hauled down on the end. The rock slowly began to shift. Keeping up the pressure, Talon transferred all his weight to the end of the pole, and then he and Reza heaved for all they were worth.

They were rewarded by the rock sucking loose. It rolled slowly out of its nest and then started to tumble down the slope to crash into the pile of rocks twenty feet below. This, in turn, dislodged many more, and before long, there was a sizable landslide. With a roar, several dozen rocks tumbled down the mountain, taking saplings with them, to crash into the bed of the track. A cloud of disturbed snow exploded above the jumbled pile. For long minutes, neither could see the effect of what they had done.

Then Talon gave a whoop of joy. Reza jumped up and down yelling. The path was completely blocked with huge boulders, and from where they were standing it looked like a tangled mess of broken trees mixed with rocks, mud, and snow. It would be many hours, perhaps days, before anyone could clear the path to allow horses through. It was too steep for horses to climb the sides, which meant that if their pursuers still wanted to catch them it would have to be on foot.

The boys waved to Rav'an and received a wave in response. They leapt down the snow-clad slope in huge strides that were as rash as they were enjoyable. It was hard going, but Talon and Reza were exultant with their success and found more than enough energy to run most of the way down.

Although all he could see of her face were her eyes—her face was muffled from the cold—these were glowing, and she shouted something to him as he stumbled up to her.

"What?" he shouted.

"You are more cunning than a fox," she shouted back.

He ducked his head, grinned at Reza, who laughed back, and then they mounted their horses. Once again, they turned their faces up the mountain and pushed on.

Silence descended again and the snow continued to fall. Darkness came fast in these heights, but they hurried on, the track faintly illuminated by the snow, which was now up to the horse's knees and beginning to slow them down severely.

Several hours later, they came to the entrance to Chula Pass. Horses and riders were exhausted. They found what shelter they could from the snow in the lee of the cliff side above while they pondered their next move.

They could just see the large, conical tower that dominated the pass. There was no telling if there was anyone still in it, so Reza dismounted. He handed the reins to Talon and moved forward cautiously, sticking to the side of the mountain as he went to discover if there was anyone there.

He disappeared for several long minutes as they waited impatiently, and then reappeared near the tower, waving. There was no one, he shouted. The sentries had been withdrawn for the winter, and it was quite deserted. Moving forward on foot, they brought the horses into the meager shelter of the tower, out of the wind. However, it was clear that if they did not press on to better shelter they would perish of exposure. Crouching down, almost face-to-face, they ate the remainder of the food Rav'an had brought and stared without words at one another.

Rav'an was the first to speak, and then with difficulty, her face was so frozen. "We c-c-cannot stay h-h-here," she stammered, so cold her teeth chattered. "We have t-t-twenty more miles to g-g-g-go to Ghazvin. Then we are safe. Although you blocked the road, they c-c-can still climb over the rocks and c-c-c-come after us on foot. We have not made much better time with the horses."

Talon looked at Reza. They both nodded.

"I have been afraid of this, too," he said. "We should be able to make better time now that we have to go downhill. Will you be all right?" he asked Rav'an.

"I am, but I d-d-d-don't know about the m-m-mare. She is very tired and might not be able to g-g-g-go through so much snow."

Talon turned to look at the mare. She stood, feet apart, head down dejectedly. He thought he could see her shivering. Not a good sign.

"We must, my lady. We must somehow," Talon answered. "We're almost there. Try to hold her courage together. We will work with you to help. Reza shall break the path with his horse, then when his horse tires, I shall do the same with Jabbar for you."

He wanted to reach out to her to say, "Be brave, I am with you." He resisted the impulse as being impertinent. Instead, he stood up, his limbs stiff, gave her his hand, and helped her mount the mare. Reza stood as well and they looked at one another. Both knew this last part would be worse if the mare gave in.

Mounting Jabbar, Talon glanced back along the way they had come. He saw nothing to alarm him, then reined aside to let Reza lead the way down the mountain ahead of them. The road was wider on this side of the pass and they could see that, although faint, it was well marked, so they had no trouble following it.

But the snow was still falling, and the going became very hard in places where it had drifted. The horses stumbled and faltered, despite shouted encouragement from their riders.

The last few miles to the outskirts of Ghazvin were a nightmare. Rav'an's mare fell without warning, nose forward into the snow. Rav'an was caught by surprise and went over her head. The snow broke her fall and she sat up and wiped the snow off her face. Talon reined in Jabbar before they fell over the horse in front of them, to see a comical picture of Rav'an sitting up to her waist in the snow, covered from head to foot, her mouth open, her eyes wide with surprise. He could not stop himself laughing.

He shouted to Reza, stopped Jabbar, and dismounted. There was no question that the situation was serious. The mare was down, but for that short moment, he could not help himself. He just laughed.

Rav'an, after a moment of indignation and outrage at his rudeness, saw her situation and joined in. They faced each other, Talon clutching his knees and bending over her while she sat in the snow, both laughing hysterically. Reza was some way ahead, but turned his horse to come back to see what had happened, not having heard the fall. He smiled at this silliness, but then the reality of it hit them all. They stopped laughing almost as suddenly as they had started. Turning to the prone mare, they looked at her in dismay. She was on her side just panting, and it looked as though she were finished.

Rav'an fell on her knees next to the prone animal, whispering endearments,stroked her head and pulled her ears. Nothing seemed to work. She just lay there, panting and refusing to move. Only after Jabbar joined in the team persuasion and nudged her gently with his nose did she rouse herself to make the effort and struggle to her feet. Standing, shaking, and covered with snow, she consented to being led forward. Reza and Talon had already turned back to their respective horses, making ready to move off, when Talon looked back along their trail.

There, just two hundred paces back, were two black shapes moving swiftly toward them. Talon shouted and pointed. Reza let out a curse and grabbed his lance. Talon did the same. They mounted quickly and readied their lances. Then, without a word to each other, they forced their horses back along the trail toward the two figures. Talon faintly heard Rav'an calling that they should run, that they could leave them behind, but he shouted back that the men could track them and bring the others.

Talon concentrated on the one nearest him and went for him, his horse floundering forward in a clumsy charge. The black shape of a man came at him, screaming and brandishing a sword. He then stopped and calmly waited for Talon, his sword held at the ready in both hands. Talon's lance was knocked aside, but, he managed to boot his opponent in the shoulder as he went by so that man's sword hissed past him ineffectually. He forced Jabbar hard past the man, and then hurriedly dismounted. A knot formed in his stomach as he contemplated his options. There were really none. He had to go and fight. Muttering an oath, he hefted his spear and started to plod back to the oncoming man, holding the spear in front of him.

To Rav'an, the whole scene was unreal. She could not hear the men and could only watch from a hundred yards' distance as the four figures met and began their dance of death. She found that her heart was pounding and her mouth was dry.

She saw Reza have more luck with his first pass and strike his opponent. The man fell backward into the snow. Reza quickly dismounted and went back to finish his opponent off. His sword rose and fell. He stood up, turned to watch what was going on with Talon and his opponent, and then moved to help.

At first, not much seemed to happen, as they stood on guard facing each other. Rav'an could see Talon braced with his spear pointing at the other man's chest, who was facing him with his sword, on guard. They circled each other, shuffling in the snow, their dark figures ill defined to the watcher from afar. The momentum of their fight built up as they feinted and parried. All sound was muffled in an eerie silence. She heard the faintest sound of steel on steel as Talon blocked the sword slashes with the spear. The fight became very fast for a few minutes, then the swordsman seemed to charge Talon, who lunged, and the other was transformed from a charging man to one stopped in his tracks. The spear had gone right through him. His sword fell from nerveless fingers, and he dropped to the snow as though guided there by the spearman. With a quick movement, Talon stabbed again.

She heard the faint choking scream of the dying man, and then Talon was pulling the spear out. He stayed there for a few long moments, then took Jabbar and began plodding back to her. He joined up with Reza. They talked briefly, then they mounted up. At the point of weeping with relief, Rav'an forced herself to regain control and watched the two boys as they rode back to her.

As Talon approached, she could see his pinched white face. He was exhausted now, and it was clear to Rav'an that he was close to collapse.

"Who was it?" she demanded.

Talon replied through clenched teeth. "Mehdi. They have killed Jean. He laughed at me while he told me. I am glad I killed him."

Rav'an gasped and her hand went involuntarily to her mouth.

"Ah, Talon, I am so sorry," she whispered. His hunched shoulders stated clearly this was not the time to dwell on the subject. She turned to Reza and asked. "Who was the other one, Reza?"

His answer was just as tired, "One of Mehdi's friends, Gaspar. He had helped to kill the priest."

He took the reins in his left hand and turned his horse toward Ghazvin. His spear was wet with something dark. Rav'an followed with the exhausted mare. Talon took up the rear. She wished she could say something to help him with his grief, but it was not the time.

The wind was beginning to pick up again, which made visibility even worse, but they were within sight of the town. Rav'an gained heart now that they were close to their destination. In her newfound exuberance, she slapped her mare on her rump and was answered with a swish of her tail.

"Come on," she shouted, turning in the saddle. "We are there. We are there!"

Talon smiled at her. He lifted the spear and saluted her.

There was the usual collection of hovels on the outskirts of the town. No one was about, as it was late in the evening. They were startled at one place near the walls when the ground seemed to come alive, as a large pack of dogs came to its collective feet in total silence and stared at the passing horsemen. However, there was no barking, just an ominous silence as they were observed by the starving creatures.

They had been told that there were huge, un mended gaps in the walls of the town, and that they were not all guarded. This proved to be true on this cold, snowy night, so they got in without any trouble.

Rav'an had been given minute details of the location of Feza's brother's house, which would be a modest abode with a courtyard on the south side of the town. As they had come in from the north, they still had half mile to go, which meant crossing the town and perhaps being questioned. To pass anywhere near the sultan's palace, or the mosque in the center of the town, ran the risk of being stopped by troops and being questioned.

Very few lamps glowed in this part of town, and those people hurrying home on the streets paid them no attention.

Moving cautiously down the first large street, leading the horses, they soon realized that they were not likely to be accosted at this time of night and could move faster. The deep carpet of snow muffled any noise the horses made. Nonetheless, they did not want to bring any attention to themselves, nor to their future host by being too obvious in their approach to his house.

The snow was deep in places and the streets were slippery with filth in the center. No amount of cold and snow could quite cover up the stench of offal and excrement that covered their path.

They went in and out of side alleys, always heading south, until they came to within fifty yards of the location of the house. There was no light anywhere to see by, but they were reasonably sure that they were at the right place. Rav'an said that she should go to the gate, as they knew her through Feza. They would not know Reza, and Talon's accent would create suspicion and delay.

While she went to gain entrance, Reza and Talon stood in the darkest patch of the street with the horses. They stood between the horses to gain some warmth from them. They were wet through and frozen. Talon's inner clothes had been drenched with sweat from the long climb up the mountain, and then again during the fight. He could not stop himself from shivering, and his teeth were chattering. Reza seemed to be in the same condition. Talon realized that the mare was shivering as well, and he began to worry at the time it was taking Rav'an to get them entrance to the house. She had gone off and disappeared without a sound. He stamped his feet, nudged Reza, who looked as though he was about to fall asleep, and blew on his hands. He prayed that no one would come along the silent street and find them there. Seconds seemed like minutes as they whispered to one another, and Talon spoke gently to the mare and patted Jabbar to reassure him.

After what seemed hours, they saw two dark shapes coming toward them. Not sure as to who they were, Talon let go of the horses. Reza woke up in time to snatch the reins, while Talon made ready with his spear. A low whicker from the mare confirmed that it was Rav'an with another person who was taller, a man.

They came up quickly and hurriedly exchanged greetings. The man, Massoud, beckoned them to follow him as fast as they could go. Throwing caution aside, they ran with the horses to the walled enclosure to which he led. In a few seconds, they were passing through a small, arched gateway, and the wooden doors were closed behind them. There was an instant sense of relief. It was as though they were now safe from the outside world, even if it were an illusion. Massoud led them across a snow-shrouded garden with bushes on either side to some low buildings, then opened the door to a stable. He indicated that they could bed the horses down in the three tiny stalls, while he went to the far end to get some fodder.

The horses were glad to be out of the snow and into shelter at long last. Rav'an and the boys stripped them of their saddles and bridles and began to rub them down. Jabbar played his usual game of insisting that Talon give him a complete and vigorous face rub with the saddle blanket, from the underside of his jaw to the top of his head and either side of his ears. The horses were very tired but still very much able to function, there being no apparent lameness. They would be stiff and sore for a couple of days, but Talon hoped that would be all.

Reza and his gelding were having some kind of conversation in the corner, and the mare seemed to be recovering. Rav'an made much of her. Massoud came back with fodder and dumped it on the ground. They left the animals comfortable and warm in the shelter and eating a well-earned meal, to make their way to the owner's house set farther back in the courtyard.

They stamped the snow off their boots, shook the ice and snow off their coats and hats at the entrance to the low, flat-roofed house, and walked into the warmth of a parlor. There were two womenfolk in the room, who stood up from their seated position on the carpets to greet them. As soon as they saw Talon and Reza, they pulled their colorful cotton veils over their heads, leaving just their eyes exposed.

A few candles poorly lighted the room, but it was comfortable and, above all, warm. There was a small fire set against a wall, and that more than warmed the room. The three travelers eyed it longingly. The introductions were made and a brief explanation offered for their presence. The women hustled Rav'an off to another room. To the tired boys there was nothing so good as to be able to shed their coats of thick sheepskin and other outer clothing. Then their boots came off and they experienced the bliss of being able to sink down onto the carpet near the fire and drink a small cup of hot tea, which thawed out their frozen bodies.

Their host sat down with them and asked them about the journey. They replied in monosyllables. Both Talon's and Reza's words were slow and drugged with weariness. Talon was almost asleep when a bowl of wonderful smelling soup was thrust into his hands, a large plate of flat *nan* bread placed at his feet, and he was urged to eat.

This he did, as though he had not eaten for a week, dipping the bread into the soup and then stuffing it into his mouth as fast as he could. Rav'an came back in the middle of the meal and joined them. The women had provided her with some dry clothes and a warm woolen shawl over her shoulders. There was a lot more chatter when the two women came back, and the whole family joined in, demanding to hear all about their ordeal.

At last Rav'an protested, and told them all she'd give them the full story the next day, but for now could they please eat and then sleep, as they were exhausted. There was a quick, sympathetic response to this plea. Blankets were produced. The boys were encouraged to bed down in the room as soon as they had finished the meal, there being no spare bedrooms to in the house.

It was clear, however, that Rav'an would sleep in the room reserved for the women. Talon did not even hear them leave, just the touch of Rav'an's fingers on his wrist as she bade him goodnight. He crawled over to the blankets and fell on top of them, asleep before his head hit the pillow. Reza was already asleep, his half finished bowl of soup getting cold on the floor by his side.

But if in vain, down on the stubborn floor
Of Earth, and up to Heav'n's unopened Door,
You gaze Today, while You are You—how then
To-morrow, when You shall be You no more?

- Omar Khayyam -

Chapter 16
Death at Alamut

Alamut stirred awake that winter's dawn. The storm had continued unabated all night, and while the wind had decreased somewhat with the coming of the dawn, there were few good reasons for anyone to go out into the freezing, windblown day. The courtyard was covered with a foot of snow that had drifted against the walls, under stairs, and against doors. Huge icicles hung from the roof of the keep and the eves of the outbuildings. Small whirlwinds of light, powdered snow came alive for an instant in one place, subsided, and then reappeared again somewhere else. The whole world seemed locked into an icy silence.

The first up were the guards, as they knew that to be found not manning the walls would result in severe punishment, or worse. The captain chased three of them out into the snow with kicks and shouts of abuse. After arguing among themselves for a few minutes they split up, one to go to the gates and huddle in their lee. He had the best of it, as at least he would be out of the wind.

The other two luckless guards had to wade through the knee deep snow, climb the battlements, and stand square into the wind. One sentry was to watch the valley from the south battlements, while the other would stand on the north side and watch the path from above the gates.

The wind and snow had covered every sign of the departure during the night, so they had no suspicion of anything amiss. The only unexplained event was that one of their number had not reported the evening before. He was in trouble when he finally did report, that was guaranteed, growled the captain of the guard.

The womenfolk stoked fires that had been banked during the night, and people began to emerge from their lodgings. Few wanted to tarry, so they hurried about their business and got out of the cold as soon as possible.

No one stirred in the upper reaches of the castle. It was not Arash or Ahmad's habit to be up early, and on a day like this, there was even less inclination to do so.

The first indication that something was amiss came when Ali went with his boys to feed the horses. By this time, the sun was well up, even if it could not be seen. Ali hurried across the windswept courtyard, passed the midden heap, and opened the doors to the stables. Pushing his urchins before him, he forced the doors wide so that some light could penetrate the gloomy interior. With a sharp word to his boys, he went off to the feed bins to ladle the precious grain out for the animals. The boys would take hay to each animal and clean its stall.

It did not take long before one of them came to him and in a nervous squeak told him that three horses were missing. Jabbar, Kaleen, and the third horse that the boy Reza rode, belonging to the princess—all were all missing. Ali skeptically cuffed the boy but nonetheless sauntered over to their stalls. When he got there he stared in disbelief. It was true. They were missing. A hurried inspection of the area revealed that their saddles and bridles were missing too. By now near to panic, Ali hurried out of the stables and half ran over to the guardhouse to accost the captain of the guard and demand whether anyone had left early that morning for a ride.

"Some madman for sure," he exclaimed, shaking his head and wringing his hands. "Who would be insane enough to go out hunting on a day like this?" he wailed. "Why wasn't I notified?" and so on.

The guard captain went white at the news and insisted upon checking himself as to whether the horses were missing or not. Back they went across the yard, cursing the weather and each other as they contemplated the possible consequences of the situation.

True enough, the horses could not be found. They both came to the unwelcome conclusion that they had no choice but to inform Ahmad. They dared not go to Arash at this point. His rages were to be feared, and he needed no excuse to punish anyone for disturbing him. Ahmad was bad enough.

They headed across the yard again to bang on the main door to the castle keep. There was a long pause, so they thumped the door again. There was a shuffle from the other side, and one of the women who lived and worked in the keep lifted the latches and pulled open the locking bars. She peered out sleepily and demanded to know what they wanted. Without speaking, they barged past her and headed for the stairs. She squawked angrily and shouted after them, but they paid her no heed.

Stumbling up the wooden stairs, they came to the second floor, where a student who accosted them and blocked their way met them. As neither wanted to get into a tangle with one of the *fida'i*, they stopped and blurted out the news. He made them stop and tell it all again before he turned and beckoned them to follow him along the corridor. Halfway down, he turned right and knocked hard on the door in front of him. There was a muffled call and he entered, motioning Ali and the guard to stay where they were. There was a low conversation, and then he came out and beckoned them in.

Ahmad was standing in the middle of the room, his hair tousled and his nightclothes clutched around him. Although the chamber was well appointed, it was still cold, and he was obviously not in the mood to put up with any nonsense. He shouted at them to tell him what had happened. They stood at rigid attention, and the captain told him of the missing horses and equipment. Ahmad came awake very quickly then. He shouted questions at both of them. Gradually, some answers began to form in his mind. He called to Mehdi and the other *fida'i* to come in.

"Go and find Princess Rav'an," he snarled. "Find out if she is here or not. Those are her horses." Mehdi saluted and ran off with the other men. Ahmad turned like a panther upon the captain of the guard. "Whoever left did not fly away. Where were the guards? Why did they not tell you what was going on?" he hissed.

The captain quailed. "Your Excellency, the storm was so fierce no one could have left during the night, so it had to have been in the early hours of this morning. I shall flog him to death," he gabbled. His fear caused him to sweat, even in the cold room.

Ahmad stared at him balefully; his angry eyes and cruel mouth promised far, far worse if he decided the captain was guilty of negligence. "Get out of my sight," he bellowed.

They ran.

Ahmad decided that he would make sure of his suspicions before informing his father. He got dressed in a hurry, his temper not made any better by the bleating of the young woman in his bed, who made the mistake of thinking she could persuade him back under the covers. He shouted to his servant to bring the tea while he struggled into his boots. In his bones, he knew that something was terribly wrong, and that he was going to have to face his father sooner or later.

Mehdi came back, out of breath from his errand. “She is gone,” he panted. “But also there is something else.”

“Well, what is it? Do you want me to read your mind?” Ahmad shouted.

“It’s Feza, her servant,” Mehdi said uncomfortably.

“What about Feza, you stupid oaf?” Ahmad screamed, interrupting him.

“She is dead, Master,” Mehdi mumbled

Ahmad gaped. “Dead?” he spluttered. “How could she be dead?”

“I don’t know, *Gorban*. I went to find her before I called on my lady. It is usual to talk to Feza first,” he reminded Ahmad. No one went to see Rav’an before obtaining permission from Feza. It was one of the rules of the castle, and Mehdi would not dare to do otherwise, no matter what the emergency.

Ahmad decided to see for himself. “Take me there,” he snapped.

They hurried along the corridors to the women’s quarters. The door to Rav’an’s quarters was ajar. Ahmad stalked up to it and slammed it back on its hinges. There, on a low pallet in the anteroom of the suite of rooms, lay Feza, huddled in her blankets, even tinier than when alive, a small gnome of a person. Her small, dark eyes were wide open, staring at the ceiling from out of the myriad of wrinkles of her face. She lay half on her back, one thin arm hanging down onto the floor, the rest of her body covered by thin bed blankets.

Nearby were the two salukis. Both stood up abruptly when Ahmad stamped in, and backed growling toward the princess’ room. He drew his sword and advanced on them. They didn’t impede him; they just retreated and allowed him to move past. But they never took their eyes off him and it was very clear they resented his presence. He resolved to deal with them later. Ahmad barely glanced at Feza's corpse as he stalked past to go into the other rooms. He checked each of the two other rooms carefully and then walked out to the anteroom, his face pensive.

"She would not have gone alone," he told Mehdi, who had been hovering about in the anteroom, keeping his distance from Feza's corpse. "Go and find out who of her followers from Samiran are missing. Take Gaspar and Alum with you and find out. Hurry!"

Mehdi vanished.

Ahmad walked slowly around Rav'an's quarters. Her scent lingered in the rooms, on discarded clothing, in the air. He moved over to her bed and put his face close to her bedclothes. He sniffed her scent on the pillow. Everything bespoke of her, and his senses were giddy from it. This was the first time he had ever been in her quarters. It left him wanting her so much it ached. His fist closed with the need to have her in his grasp. She would not be free of him, not ever. Wherever she had gone, he would follow and take her for his. "And then, my proud princess, you shall beg me for the mercy I shall not give you!" He snarled

He came back to the present with a start. Mehdi was still not back with any news, so he went back to his quarters and made himself ready to talk to his father. He rehearsed his lines while he prepared for the chase he knew was to come. By the time Mehdi came back, he was dressed for the cold and ready to hear the news. Mehdi informed him that the only people not in the castle that morning, other than Rav'an, were the Frank, Talon, and his companion of Samiran, Reza. He, too, was missing.

Ahmad had heard enough. He made his way up to the tower where his father slept and knocked on the door to his quarters. A voice called and he entered, brushing past the servant his father employed to keep vigil while he slept. His father was up but had not yet completed his toilet. He was sitting near a glowing brazier, warming his hands. A tray with small cups of tea was on the low table nearby. Even though it was not as cold in the room, their breath still came out in streamers.

Arash's greeting was brusque. "What is it that you need to disturb me with on this hellish morning?" he demanded of his son.

Ahmad responded by giving his father a deep bow, then told him what had occurred, not forgetting the death of Feza and the absence of the three young fugitives.

His father's eyes gleamed. "The storm should have slowed them down if they left this morning. It is snowing, and they cannot have gone far. Send out a party and bring them back. We shall punish them."

Ahmad said, "I think there is more to this than we think at first. Why is Feza dead? Why did the guards not see them this morning when they left? I think they left some time during the night, in which case they are gone a long way, and we shall have to go swiftly to catch them before they disappear."

His father nodded. "If the captain of the guard did not know they were gone until this morning, then he is a dead man; but I have an idea. If they have escaped, then the priest will also know where they are going. The boy would never leave without telling him. Is he still here?"

Ahmad blinked. "I think so. Shall we bring him to you?"

"No, take him down to the cells below. I will ask him for answers there."

Ahmad grinned. "Yes, my father. Shall I bring the captain as well?"

"No, have him killed. Place his head on a pike over the gates. Let that be a lesson to all. I will tolerate no carelessness or disobedience to my will."

*****

Jean had spent the night on his knees praying for the safe deliverance of the three young people. He did not neglect to ask God for strength to take him through the ordeal he knew he was to face once their escape was discovered. He had seriously contemplated throwing himself off the battlements, but his creed forbade this act of self-destruction. All he could do was to await his fate in fear and trembling. He had finally fallen into an exhausted, troubled sleep, to be awakened by Mehdi and his man Gaspar. They stood over him and shook him, then dragged him up onto his feet. They all but carried him down the corridors of the castle to the area where the cisterns were located, and down to the dungeons. They shouted at him and cuffed him as they went, calling him names. He woke up properly along the way, his fear making him weak at the knees. He'd never thought of himself as a brave man, and now he was convinced that he would fail his young charges by confessing to anything these brutes asked of him. He did, however, bluster and whine that he knew not what they were talking about, and would they please stop hitting him?

Within minutes, they were down in the deepest regions of the castle. They came to a large, iron-studded door that Mehdi threw open. They forced him inside, where he found himself in a small, stone room with no windows. He was given a push from behind, and he stumbled against the far wall and fell down. Before he could turn and face his tormentors, the door crashed shut and he was in darkness. It was very cold, and before long he was shivering. His nightclothes did nothing to protect him from the icy cold of this rocky tomb. His fear settled into his stomach and he felt like retching.

He pulled his clothes around him, huddled in a corner of the cell and began to pray, which comforted him, despite his awful fear of what was to come. It calmed him enough for him to collect his thoughts.

He guessed that the escape had been discovered and that they were about to question him before they left to give chase. He hoped that the it would be quick and that they would spare him a long agony. He knew, though, that his captors would not be kind. He harbored a faint hope that they would believe him when he said that he had no knowledge of the escape and would perhaps have mercy on him, but he doubted it would be so. He continued to pray to his God for the deliverance of his three children. The darkness settled in, and there was a deathly silence.

He was jerked out of his dreamlike state when the door opened. Light shone in from two lanterns held high. There were several men in the corridor outside, looking in on him. He recognized his two earlier tormentors, and then his blood froze. Standing just in front of them was Ahmad. Just behind him was his father, Arash Khan.

Jean knew he was doomed.

Ahmad strode into the room without ceremony and slashed at Jean with a whip, striking him on his head and face savagely, shouting at him and demanding to know where the escapees were going to. North? West to Lamissar, where? Feebly trying to defend himself, the priest tried to cover his face and head with his arms. Ahmad continued to strike him, screaming abuse and repeating the question again and again. The pain and savagery of the attack left Jean crying and whimpering on the ground. He gasped out through bloody lips that he did not know what they were talking about, begging Ahmad to stop. He began to cough and felt a sharp pain in his chest grow. He spat blood onto the floor.

After a while, there was sharp command, and Ahmad was moved aside by a hand on his shoulder.

Arash stood over the priest. He smiled down on him. "Master Priest, do you not know that your young friend and the princess have left the castle? How can you expect me to believe that you would not know of this?"

Jean stared up at the cold eyes above the semblance of a smile, and his heart quailed. Nevertheless, he grasped his shredded courage and pretended he was confused and bewildered by the whole event and babbled, "Your Excellency, I swear that I do not know of this. They have left the castle?" He received another slash of the whip from Ahmad for his stupidity. "Your Excellency, I beg of you, I do not know of anything like this. I truly do not know."

The cruel eyes regarded him without expression. "How can I believe you?" Arash said quietly. "You were his closest friend in the world. He would not leave you without saying goodbye. You lie, Priest, and you shall be punished for it. Chain him to the wall."

Mehdi and Gaspar came forward quickly and, after placing their lanterns on the floor, heaved the priest to his feet and forced him back against the farthest wall. They hung him by his wrists l in chains hanging down from the ceiling. He could stand only on tiptoes.

"Now, Priest," Arash said in a quiet voice from the center of the room. "You have the chance of telling us where they are going now, and your death will be quick, or you can die painfully. I really do not care either way. Which is it to be?"

Jean hardly heard him. He thought that it was past dawn and the three children would have gained many miles by now. Every extra one he could gain would be a bonus. He croaked, "I beg you for mercy, your Excellency, but I do not know of what you are asking. I cannot tell what I do not know."

Arash stood back and motioned the two men forward. "Break his legs and then his arms, and then every other bone in his body, one by one. Start with his legs."

Jean did not see the first blow coming; it was skillfully applied from the side. The blow from the iron bar smashing into his shins was shocking. The pain was appalling. He gave a high-pitched scream that went on for seconds, and as the waves of pain continued, he screamed again and again.

The man standing in the middle of the room watched him without visible emotion, then walked forward and grasped his lower jaw in his hand, lifting his head until their eyes met.

"Tell me what I need to know and you will not suffer more pain," he repeated, his voice gentle.

Jean looked into the reptilian eyes and saw not a vestige of mercy. He shouted in French. "My God, protect me. Oh Lord, come to my aid!" He was hanging off the chains now, his broken leg useless and beginning to balloon at the break point.

Arash dropped Jean's face and, stepping back, motioned the man with the bar to go to work again. Again, Jean felt the incredible pain of the strike, followed by waves of white-hot agony that passed up his other leg. This time he fainted.

Jean came to when Mehdi threw the contents of a bucket of icy water over his head. His matted hair covered his swollen face. He began to babble with the agony of his injuries and a paralyzing fear. He vomited bile and wet himself with his terror. He somehow managed to hold his will in place, and still he would not answer the patient questions asked of him.

Arash shook his head. This priest was strong and brave, too, he reluctantly conceded. He, however, did not have the time to be patient. Each minute he was held up here gave the three escaped people more time to hide or run farther.

The beatings continued, as did the shrieks of agony following the ghastly sound of more breaking bones. Jean writhed in his chains constantly. His bowels voided, the stink filling the room.

At this point, Arash had enough enjoyment. He turned to Ahmad. "Break the rest of his bones and then throw him off the castle walls. Let the wolves enjoy what is left," he said. "Be quick about it. You have to ride after the princess and bring her back. Kill the boy. He is too much trouble. I will find another way to accomplish my plan."

Ahmad nodded. As Arash left, the grisly work continued. There was almost no sound now from the priest.

Jean gave himself up to his God. He no longer felt the hideous blows that were killing him. He saw instead a light ahead of him and knew a great calmness. His tormented mind told him that at last he was going to be admitted to heaven. As he died, he smiled up at the angels holding their hands out to greet him.

Ahmad and Mehdi stopped their savage task minutes after Jean had died. Lifting the dead man's head, Ahmad noticed with surprise the trace of a smile on the cracked and swollen lips.

"Take him out," he said. "Do as the master says. Although he was an infidel, he was brave. Give him to the wolves. Mehdi, be quick, we have to go this hour before we lose them in the passes."

Mehdi and Gaspar nodded. They were covered in blood and very relieved to have this revolting task over. They unfastened the dead man and dragged him out of the room and up the stairs. As they came to the courtyard, Mehdi started shouting instructions to the guards.

The priest was taken to the south battlements and his body tossed without ceremony over the wall. It tumbled hundreds of feet before it struck the side of the long slope below. It disappeared in a flurry of snow and then slid. It finally settled, head down, among some rocks.

Mehdi observed the scene from the battlements, then turned and hurried back to prepare for the chase.

*****

Ahmad and Arash, after some urgent discussion, decided that the best place for the fugitives to head for would be the Chula Pass. The fugitives had few other alternatives that would allow them to get free of the Shah Rud valley.

The party of horsemen left within the hour, walking their horses out of the gates upon which was placed the bloody head of the former captain of the guard on a spike, overlooking the path down the mountain. They moved with great caution down the treacherous slopes near the castle. Despite Ahmad's impatience they could not risk losing an animal in this dangerous area. They mounted farther down the slope and pushed down the mountain to the river.

Ahmad had to lead the way over the rushing water. It was high and came right up the shoulders of the horses. They lost a man here, but they didn't even stop for him as he was swept downstream, screaming for help. No one dared to delay Ahmad; that would be courting instant death.

They had a choice of going down the valley or back up it to the pass for Ghazvin. It did not take Ahmad long to decide to take the west road. He was confident that the three fugitives would try to get to Ghazvin, and then take the highway up to Tabriz when the weather eased off. Going down the valley would be easier for sure, but it would be a very long way to go round.

He, too, knew that it was a race against the weather, and that unless he could beat them to the pass they would escape. The metal-gray sky lowered over them and threatened heavy snow, and the wind brought stinging ice particles to hamper them and tear at their clothing.

Ahmad and his men flogged their horses unmercifully along the rutted road. They gave them no rest and this cost them, as the horses could not gallop the whole distance. One horse foundered after twenty miles. It just fell over and tossed its rider into the snow. They left him there with his fallen mount and raced on.

After several hours of punishing riding, even Ahmad had to come to terms with the fact that the horses could not keep up this pace. Unlike the three fugitives before him, he had not paced his horses to the distance, so he angrily gave the command to stop at about the halfway point to Chula Pass. Stamping about impatiently all the time the small party was stopped, he rewarded himself with imagining what he would do to them when they were his prisoners. The men were quiet in fear of drawing attention to themselves—with their leader in such a temper; it was not wise to do so.

There was almost no sound from the surrounding country, most of which was hidden under a blanket of snow, all life seemingly gone from its frozen waste. The men huddled into their furs, blowing on their hands through ice-layered mustaches, wishing they were near to a good fire instead of being out here in this frozen hell. The horses were nearly spent and stood near their riders, sweat covering their heaving flanks, clouds of vapor rising from their overheated bodies.

Abruptly, Ahmad gave the order to mount up again. He forced the pace to the base of the track that would lead up to Ghazvin Pass. It was snowing in heavy flurries by the time they came to the river at the base of the mountain. They splashed across as a group and then flogged the horses along the fugitives' tracks, which were now quite clear in the snow. The men began to sense that they were close, and they redoubled their efforts to close the distance.

As they climbed, they heard a deep rumble far ahead up the mountainside. The whole group stopped their heaving horses and listened, casting nervous glances at each other. Avalanches were common in these mountains and could sweep the lot of them over the side of the cliff should one strike. Nothing happened, however, so they continued.

The tracks were clear for all to follow, to the point where the leader Mehdi, looking ahead, imagined that he would see them just ahead at any time. As the party came to a cleft in the mountain, they found the going easier. However, as they came to the other end, Mehdi realized something was amiss. He reined in his horse and stared. The way forward was completely blocked. A jumbled mass of huge rocks and small trees was piled into the middle of the track. To the right there was a huge scar in the hillside, from which the avalanche had come down.

Ahmad rode up and the two of them stared. It was clear this had been the cause of the noise they had heard earlier. The sides were impossible for a horse to climb, and barely negotiable for a man. Ahmad and Mehdi stared at the blockage in silence for a few minutes, then Ahmad cursed and cursed. He raised his fist to the pile of rocks and screamed imprecations at the invisible fugitives, his anger radiating in all directions. Mehdi cringed away from the mighty rage that was consuming his unpredictable and dangerous leader.

Finally, Ahmad cooled down enough to take stock of the situation. It was clear that they could not take the horses through for many hours, by which time they would be running the risk of serious exposure out here on the mountainside. They could leave the horses and struggle through on foot, but that, too, meant the risk of dying out on the mountain. The snow was coming down very heavily, and one could lose one's way.

Ahmad told his men to dismount and try to clear the path, but it did not take long for him to realize that the landfall was far beyond the capability of his men. They lacked the most basic tools to clear the boulders and trees other than with their hands. They were freezing on this mountainside, and if they stayed much longer they risked death from the cold. He himself was beginning to feel the deadening numbness of the cold seeping into his limbs. After an hour of fruitless work, he told them to remount.

He explored his options one by one; there was little he could do. He felt the gall of defeat in his mouth and raged. He promised that he would one day be rewarded with their heads. There was nothing left with which to console himself. Then his eye settled on Mehdi. Mehdi cringed again. He knew what was coming.

"Mehdi, you and Gaspar will climb this hillside to the other side, and track them to their hiding place in Ghazvin." Ahmad, who had no compunction about sending his men to their deaths to achieve his objective, gave a grunt of satisfaction. Mehdi was a strong man and tenacious; he would succeed. The princess did not know yet of Ahmad's long arm, but she would learn.

He, Ahmad, would go back down the mountain and wait until the morning and then come back to clear the pass. He would have to make his way back to the castle to report to his father before too long, but he would make the effort to get past the obstruction first. They would have to hurry. This storm heralded winter's setting in, and the pass would soon be closed for weeks, if not months. He had to demonstrate to his father that he had done all he could to catch the fugitives.

Mehdi was visibly unhappy at the command but knew better than to argue. He tossed the reins of his horse to one of his companions, as did Gaspar, and they commenced to climb the steep slope.

Ahmad paused long enough to watch the bulky shapes of the two men climb the side of the mountain that would take them over the obstruction, then turned and led the remainder of his thankful men back down the mountain.

And not a drop that from our Cups we throw
On the parcht herbage but may steal below
To quench the fire of anguish in some Eye
There hidden – far beneath, and long ago.

– *Omar Khayyam* –

Chapter 17
Ghazvin

The three refugees woke up to a frozen world. Although the snow had stopped, it had done so a just few hours before dawn. Their tracks had been effectively covered, and they were safe for a while, at least.

When Talon and Reza woke, the house was already bustling forward into a new day. The sun that they had not seen for over three days now shone bright and warm through the sheets pulled over the windows. People were moving about, talking in low tones, and the smell of cooking pervaded the house.

Talon rolled slowly out of his blankets and looked across at Reza, who was still coming out of the deep, exhausted sleep brought on by the tension and labors of the day before. Talon felt stiff and tired and his heart ached with Jean's death. He felt the tears start as he thought of his friend's body out in the cold snow, not even given the privilege of a decent burial. He clenched his fists as he thought of his battle with Mehdi, and felt again the white-hot rage that had given him the strength to kill him for what he had told Talon.

He was there on his elbows, head down, trying to pull himself together, when the princess came into the room and saw him. She bade him a soft good morning but, receiving no reply, she came closer, and saw his hunched shoulders and drooping head.

She understood, and immediately she knelt on one knee and

touched his shoulder with a tentative hand.

"Talon," she whispered. "He was my friend, and I mourn him too. He was a very brave man."

Talon nodded, still not looking up. "He was all I had in the world when we first came here," he whispered into the blanket. "I shall miss him so."

Rav'an said gently. "Talon... you need to know something about Jean, the priest."

He turned his head to look up at her. His tear-streaked face looked very vulnerable. "What do you mean, Rav'an?"

There were tears in her eyes. "You know he was often coughing." Talon nodded. "Well," she went on, "Feza recognized it for what it was. She called it the cough of death, when the cough brings up blood and is painful to the lungs. I do not know what it is called by the physicians, but she said that few can live when it is as bad as it was with the priest."

Talon sat up, dashing away his tears with his hand. Still sitting, he said, "I knew he suffered, but I did not know of this. Why did you not tell me before?"

"Because when Feza went to see him and give him some medicine to help relieve the pain, she told him the truth, for which he said he was grateful, but that on no account were you to know." Rav'an said this softly, as though with regret that she had been forced to hold back on him.

Talon stared at the carpet. "He gave his life for us to get away. I am sure his soul is in heaven now. I have almost forgotten how to pray, but I shall."

Reza had woken now, and heard the end of the conversation.

"Talon," he said, sitting down by the two of them. "Your Jean is in paradise now. I, too, shall pray for him, as he was a very brave man. Although he was a mullah in your old faith, he was also a warrior at his death. He shall go to Paradise, I am sure."

This was a long speech for Reza. Talon smiled at his friend, and reached out to clasp him by the arm in a gesture of acceptance.

Rav'an stood up, her face a mask of grief, when Talon asked, "My lady, what of Feza? What will they do to her?"

Rav'an looked down at the two young men. "They will be able to do nothing to hurt her. She will have taken her own life during the night we left." She turned away abruptly, unable to hold back her own tears.

The two young men gaped at one another in horror. Talon jumped to his feet and, risking rebuke, reached for Rav'an in the only way he knew how to comfort her. He pulled her into his arms and held her close to him. She lay her head on his chest and wept for her faithful old nurse, whom she would never see again. Talon looked over her shoulder to a stunned Reza.

After a few long minutes, Rav'an collected herself enough to pull back. Although she would have been happy to remain encircled by Talon's strong arms, she knew, too, that it was not seemly. He released her and stood back. She smiled at him and Reza.

"Now I have only my 'protectors.' I don't even have my hounds," She sniffed as she dried her tears with her sleeve. "I am sure that my uncle will kill them. He will have no use for them, and Ahmad would kill them just to spite me if he could!" she began to sob again so that Talon had to hold her once more until she had collected herself.

Just then, Feza's brother came into the room with his wife, bearing breakfast trays. There was the usual tea, yogurt, boiled eggs and *nan,* as well as shreds of chicken in a soup of lentils. They greeted one another cordially, although he gave a sharp look at Rav'an. It was obvious she had been crying. He knew about the death of his sister; Rav'an had told him the night before. He and his wife had mourned her. Now he wanted to ensure that the three refugees escaped to avenge her and alert the master.

They all sat down to the first real meal the three had had since leaving Alamut. They wolfed the food down in virtual silence. It was after they had satisfied their hunger that the conversation began.

Massoud began to tell them something of their present situation. He had lived in Ghazvin for a long time, posing as a merchant, although his faith and loyalties were with the Ismaili camp.

The Seljuk Turks had controlled Ghazvin for many years. After their initial depredations, they had settled down to rebuild the town and make it into a significant seat of power for the sultan. There was a lot of work going on; the town walls had been pulled down and were now being rebuilt, although, as he dryly remarked, they were so full of openings that anyone could get in and out without difficulty, hence the ease with which the three of them had come in.

He told them about the Seljuks and the interaction with the Ghazvini people. It was an uneasy relationship, as the Seljuk rulers were Turkish and by nature nomadic, while the inhabitants of the cities were for the most part Persian, Kurds, and Lurs, and more settled as people. Many of the Ismaili faith lived here, although they kept silent about their faith and allegiance to the Agha Khan for fear of being killed if discovered.

There was a new mosque going up, and there were plans for a new and larger palace for the sultan when he migrated through the town from time to time. He, Massoud, as a *bazaari,* had many freedoms to come and go, as long as he carried the right passes. These he felt he could obtain for his three guests, but at a price.

Rav'an reached into her belt and produced the small bag of gold coins Talon had stolen before they left Alamut. Massoud smiled at that, and was even more amused when he heard how she'd gotten it. However, he refused it.

He thought that as soon as the weather eased and the roads opened, they should move on, but here he paused. "You do know that you cannot go north?"

All three looked at one another with surprise.

"What do you mean?" the princess demanded. "Why not?"

None of them had given the matter any thought, all of them thinking that naturally they would head north from Ghazvin to Tabriz.

Massoud looked at her. "My lady, you came over the passes when no one should have been able to, but you should also know that to go north is to trap yourselves. While you might make it to Samiran, you will be unable to go farther north until the spring. All of the roads are closed and impassible for at least three months. If you make it to Samiran you may find that you will be trapped there because of the blocked passes further north along the road to Tabriz. It's a sure thing that Arash Khan will send his first messengers, maybe even Ahmad, to Samiran to close that door. If he finds you, he'll have no difficulty taking you prisoner; he is the authority in these parts when the master is abroad."

"I am the master's sister. They will believe me, and protect me! I am sure of it." She didn't sound sure, however.

Massoud said in a conciliatory manner, "My lady, you run the real danger that there will be men in Samiran who might already be corrupted by the wiles of Arash Khan. Even if they aren't, they're not likely to risk a confrontation with the Khan if he decided to take you back to Alamut. Then all you risked would be for nothing, including the sacrifice of your friend and my sister."

Rav'an dropped her eyes at this rebuke. "What should we do? We for sure cannot wait here. They will come to Ghazvin at the first opportunity to sniff at our trail."

Massoud nodded. "You are right, my lady. You have to ride to Hamadan and wait there, and then make your way through the southern passes that lead to the Zagros. From there, you can strike across the Zagros Mountains when the weather eases and head south before heading west to Syria. It is a hard route and not for the fainthearted, but it can be done." He paused, looking round at his audience. "I see no other way that will bring you to the master any faster, nor any safer."

There was a long silence as the three of them digested the news.

Then Reza spoke up. "My lady, I think Massoud is right. I trust his judgment in this. We know ourselves that, from this time until spring, the north is not a possible route. I fear to go to Samiran, not because of the people there, for I think they would believe us, but because it's a trap that we cannot get out of if things go wrong. At least this way we have the freedom of movement and can run in almost any direction if danger threatens."

Talon nodded. "I cannot speak for the seasons like Massoud, but I agree with Reza. We have to be free to move if danger threatens. If we go to Samiran we will be trapped."

Rav'an gnawed at her lower lip. She seemed resigned to the general opinion. "But we should move away from Ghazvin soon anyway, should we not?"

Massoud relaxed and became more business-like. "Yes, my lady. I shall obtain a pass for you. It could take a few days and some gold, but without it, if the sultan's men stop you, they will take you prisoner. Once they realize who you are, then all is lost. Please be patient. Do not go out, except to the stables, as I do not trust all my neighbors."

Talon asked, "Where is Hamadan? And how far is it from here?"

Reza replied for them. "It is about three days from here, Talon. That is, in summer. We have to make sure the horses are in good condition before we go. I think I know the way. Do you, my lady?"

Rav'an shook her head. "Once, when I was very small, I went with my father's people, but I do not remember the way. I hope you do, Reza."

Reza smiled. "Do not fear, my lady, I shall find the way. We are coming closer to my people."

That settled it, and the party broke up, the boys to go out into the cold and see to the horses, while Rav'an stayed with Massoud to talk more of the situation she had left in Alamut. He was keen to understand what the implications might be for the Ghazvin Ismailis.

After the warmth of the house, the cold outside was biting. It took the boys' breath away as they stamped through the frozen snow, now about two feet deep. A million facets of the ice particles flashed and sparkled in the bright sunlight. Stalactites hung in long, pointed spears from the eaves of the low roof of the stable almost to the ground. Massoud had asked them to help him shovel the snow off his flat-roofed house later, an onerous task that he normally had to do alone, to which they willingly agreed. The trees and bushes in the garden were all blanketed, and every corner and ledge had a layer of snow dressing. A light but sharp wind bit deep into their warm clothing.

As before, they wore their sheepskin jerkins over thick woolen shirts, and thick woolen trousers over wool undergarments tucked into long, knee-length horsehide boots, though they had left their overcoats behind. Talon's fingers were numb by the time they had made it to the stables. He blew on them with his fingers in a vain attempt to warm them. They had to push hard to get the door to the stables open, then the smell of horses came to them, strong and warm, as they entered. The building was very low, as was common in this region. The very thick walls were of mud brick, the roof sloping in one direction and composed of crude, wood beams that fit any way that they could be placed. The floor was of dirt with layers of horse manure stamped down into a hard, insulated surface where now stood the three horses belonging to the fugitives, with one other horse and two donkeys in separate stalls.

The horses greeted the boys with whickers and stamping feet, indicating that they were hungry. Talon and Reza went up to their respective horses and fed them tidbits stolen from the breakfast meal. Talon managed to please both Jabbar and the mare, Kaleen, with sweet lumps of cake he had purloined for the purpose.

There was a loose stack of hay at the far end where Massoud

kept his horse, a poor specimen compared to the princess' beautiful steeds. His donkeys stood in another stall. They transported his wares when he traveled.

Talon and Reza went to work with a will to both feed and inspect the horses from top to bottom. Hooves, shoes, tendon, and muscles were checked and discussed by the two friends as they examined their means of transport. The horses were vital to their survival and both took their task very seriously.

Talon took the opportunity to ask Reza where they expected to stay each night during their three-day journey to Hamadan. Reza was at a loss. He said that they could stay at various towns along the way but didn't think they'd want to, as that would then give the pursuers a clear trail to follow. On the other hand, it would be foolish to spend the nights out in the freezing cold; a man could go to sleep in this and never wake up. They would have to discuss this with Rav'an and Massoud when they went back into the house. In the meantime, they had to make sure that they could leave at any time and that their weapons were ready for any eventuality.

In the house, Rav'an and Massoud had a long talk about events that she had both witnessed in Alamut and what she surmised was going to happen there.

He, in turn, told her about his real apprehension that the pursuers might have already come to Ghazvin and this very day be searching high and low for them. If it became known that he, Massoud, was here, and he didn't think that fact would lie dormant in Arash's mind for long, then every hour was vital.

Rav'an was horrified at the thought that he, too, was now in danger.

He shrugged and said that he was going to leave when they did and go east to Rayed, then south to Qom, where he had relatives and could set up his business without trouble. He had already told his wife to pack what they might need for the journey. He felt that it would not be forever, just until the present crisis passed and Arash was taken care of.

Rav'an felt a rush of affection for the old man. He seemed not to be fazed by the possibility of capture and certain death. Instead, he was making sure they were looked after. "I shall ensure that my brother knows of your help to me, Massoud."

He smiled. "You were the light of Feza's eye all your life, my lady, and I know she had a good life with you. What little I can do for you and the master, I shall."

Then they got busy. Massoud had to go out of the house and plow his way down the street to the bazaar, there to make contact with an official who was sympathetic to his cause and would appreciate the helping hand of money. On a day like this, Massoud told the princess, there was only a faint chance that anyone would be working at all. It might have to wait until the morrow. In any case, it would give him a chance to see if there had been any untoward developments during the night.

With Massoud gone and the boys still in the stables, Rav'an set to work helping the mistress pack up the simple home. Although he was a moderately wealthy merchant, Massoud kept his fortune in coin. Like all men of his kind, he preferred peaceful times that enabled trade and prosperity. Unfortunately, that had never been the case for him, so he lived carefully and kept money handy for all events.

So Rav'an helped the tearful women pack what they had for the two donkeys to carry, and they talked about Feza and her ways. It helped Rav'an to do so, as the pain of losing her was still acute.

Later she went outside into the frozen garden and to the stable to find out what was keeping the boys so long, and found them sitting in the pile of hay, talking while they cleaned the equipment. They jumped up at her approach and stood as she came in.

She looked them over. "It is warmer inside the house. How are the horses?"

Talon answered for them. "Well, my lady, even the mare seems to have recovered. They are stiff, but we brushed them and rubbed them, so they seem fine now. They will be ready."

She nodded, gave a faint smile, and then turned to go back into the house. Talon knew that she wanted nothing more than to be gone from Ghazvin. They were still too close to the Rudbar valleys, and it made her nervous.

The boys trooped after her and they all headed for the house's low doorway. Just as she reached for the door latch, a snowball thudded into the door right by her shoulder. Its explosion created a small cloud of icy dust that sprinkled her face. Rav'an whipped round and glared at the two boys, who were grinning guiltily. Reza even looked alarmed, as clearly they had overstepped their bounds.

Rav'an stooped quickly, scooped up a handful of snow, and flung it with all her might straight at Talon. It buzzed by his left ear so close he had to jerk his head out of the way.

After that, it was a free-for-all as the three-sided battle encompassed the whole of the walled garden. Reza was circumspect with regard to tossing snow at Rav'an, but not so at Talon, who before long was driven into a corner with two determined, but laughing, opponents firing stinging snowballs faster than he could respond.

It was Rav'an who decided the battle. She seized a huge lump of frozen snow and charged, the lump of snow held above her head with both hands, with the aim of dumping it on his head. Talon was laughing so hard he barely had time to dodge the lump as it came down on him. He seized the princess around the waist and they fell together into one of the nearby drifts. There was a squeal of hilarious indignation from Rav'an half buried in the snow under his weight. Then he was up, and with Reza was extricating her from the drift, both being very apologetic. Rav'an was laughing, however, having enjoyed the moment enormously.

They were all by now covered from head to toe with a thick dusting of snow and grinning at the sight of one another, a happy moment that they had all needed, a welcome respite from the tension, the fear and grief they all carried just below the surface. Not only that, it cemented them more closely than ever before. Rav'an, as always, set the mood. She dusted herself off, as did the others. She gave the boys a cheerful grin, then she led the way to the door a second time.

Massoud's wife and her sister had prepared a hot stew of vegetables, lentils, and bread. During the meal, the young people answered the shy questions about their origins, but for the most part the women stayed aside, as though they were servants.

At about mid-afternoon, Massoud came back to a household that was preparing for a journey. The weapons lined the wall near the door, the boys having painstakingly cleaned and burnished the spears and swords. The bows were freshly waxed to make them waterproof, while the strings had been re-greased with some lard from the cooking room and replaced in pockets.

Massoud had good news and no news. His discreet enquiries had led him to believe that none of the pursuers were yet in Ghazvin, although he didn't think that they would be long in coming if the present weather persisted. The snow was melting during the day and would freeze that night for sure. This would provide better footing for anyone intrepid enough to venture over the pass and then cross the wasteland to the town.

His other news was that he had a written pass, and it was a good one, although it had cost him a considerable sum of gold. He explained that he had arranged for two, one for himself and another for the princess. He had paid for both out of his money, as he felt that they would need all they had to get them along in their journey. He even offered to give Rav'an some more. She refused vehemently, telling Massoud that he had done enough already and would need all he had to survive the next few months, and to avoid being tied to their escape.

He nodded, smiling. "You are right, of course, *Khanom*, but I would not have it any other way. My loyalty is to your brother and hence to you. Feza was right to stay with you all those years. You are an unusual lady."

He reached forward and, seizing her hand before she could pull it away, he kissed its back, and then gently released it. Rav'an stood looking at him, her eyes glowing. She accepted his homage as her due, even as she fought to control her own emotions.

There was much to plan for. The first rule, Massoud told them, was that they should stay on the trail, no matter what. Second, they should stay in the towns each night; not to do so was to court death from the deadly cold or from marauding bands of bandits. If the bandits came across a small party of people at night, no matter what training the boys might have had, they would be outnumbered and killed. He didn't want to contemplate what would then happen to the princess. They all nodded somberly at his firm, blunt instructions.

He told them that they would be on the great high plains for most of the way and that the wind could come down from the north with such fury that it would be easy for them to be overwhelmed. They must protect the horses and themselves when it became too fierce by finding what shelter they could, or they would be frozen carcasses within a few hours. Massoud was direct and uncompromising as to the difficulty of their journey. He told them that as the moon was now full, they could travel some of the way at night but should try to get to each town early enough to avoid being caught out by the local curfew. The sultan's soldiers were unsympathetic to latecomers, who often had to huddle outside the walls through the night, waiting for the gates to open the next morning.

He gave an accurate description of each town, demanding that Reza wrack his brains for more information to share with the others so that if they were separated they could at least make it to the next town. They needed to know where to meet within each town if they got separated. They learned a lot that late afternoon and into the evening of the second night. They agreed they would slip away that same night, late, when the town was asleep, while Massoud and his women left the following morning to hide their tracks and also to get some way ahead of the pursuit which was sure to come. They could not afford to lose more time, tired though the horses might be.

After the instructions were over, the boys went out to feed the horses and give them a last look-over for the trip. Rav'an and Massoud continued to discuss what she should do once the party made it to Hamadan. He gave her a small dagger with runes carved on the blade. It was held in a sheath of rich leather with gold filigree. He told her it would open doors for her. He also gave her an address that she should go to as soon as they got to Hamadan. The people were Ismaili and, he thought, still faithful to her brother; but they would not be able to afford much protection, as the Ismaili were few in number there.

Nonetheless, this would be a safe refuge for a while at least. She thanked him and tucked the letter of passage and the dagger away within the folds of her blouse for safekeeping. He asked if she were armed, and she showed him her other dagger, a long, wicked-looking blade that had been made by Giv the blacksmith in Alamut.

He nodded, and said somberly, "If you are captured, my lady, you might have to use this on yourself."

She nodded. It was clear that the Turks could not be allowed to take her prisoner.

They all decided to get as much rest as possible. Night had fallen, and so after a meal, the party went to bed. Massoud would wake them about the middle of the night to prepare and get on their way.

Once again, Talon and Reza settled down in the main room while Massoud and his family retired. Rav'an went to the small room prepared for her alone.

In the still of the night Massoud entered the main room, holding a candle, and shook the two boys by their feet. He knew what their reaction would be, so he stood back as they came wide awake and reached for their weapons even as he touched them. He whispered that it was time and left the candle with them. As they were both almost dressed, it took but a minute for them to don all their outer clothing and their rabbit skin hats with pointed tops and huge flaps for the ears and neck. They pulled on their horsehide boots, picked up their weapons, and then went quietly out of the door to saddle up the horses.

They were still busy with this chore when the princess came into the stable with Massoud behind her. They carried bundles of food, some dried meat and soaked lentils that could be boiled, and some stale Barbari, as well as water to carry on the journey.

She was bundled into a large sheepskin jacket that came down to her knees, horsehide boots, and a huge rabbit-skin hat to hide her hair and leave just a small part of her face clear. Quietly, so that the neighbors would not hear anything, the three walked the horses out of the stable and across the garden. The horses made no noise, as the snow deadened the sound of their hooves. They could see their breath coming in huge steaming clouds. Massoud came to the doorway of the garden to see them off, after first checking the street for activity. The night was calm, lit by the full moon partly hidden by high clouds. They could see clearly, though, and this worried them, as they still had to get out of the town.

Massoud clasped hands with Talon and Reza. "Take care of her, and make sure you reach the master," he whispered. They nodded. Words were not necessary.

"Go with God," he added.

"God protect you," they whispered back.

He then seized Rav'an's hand and again kissed it. "Go with God, my Princess; may Allah protect you and lead you to safety."

She gripped his hand in reply, and they moved off in the direction he had indicated.

They walked the horses all the way to the edge of the town, keeping to the shadows and narrow streets as much as possible. They heard people talking when they came to the edge of town where the wall was being constructed and quickly moved deeper into the shadows of the street.

Talon handed his reins to Reza and went forward to discover what was going on. He peered into the street that crossed theirs and saw two sentries about fifty yards away near a brazier, keeping warm. Somehow they needed to walk the horses across the street without being detected, after which they'd be clear and could mount up.

He hurried back to the others and told them what he had seen. "I'll go on foot and show up farther down the street and create a distraction," he told them. "When they start to come after me, you should cross the road and wait for me in the fields across the ditch."

They nodded, and he disappeared down a dark alley.

Soon after, Reza and Rav'an heard a shout a long way down the other street. Peering around the corner, Reza could see the troopers near the fire, but not Talon. They heard the shout again and the two men at the brazier stood up, their attention drawn away down the street toward the shout. They were uncertain about what to do. All four heard another shout; this time it sounded drunken and abusive. The two soldiers muttered, picked up their spears, and then started to hurry in the direction of the noise.

As soon as they left the brazier, Reza and Rav'an quickly walked the horses across the way. Illuminated as the road was by the moon, if the soldiers had looked back the fleeing party would have been in full view; as it was, the soldiers' attention was fixed on a dancing, gesturing figure in the middle of the street.

Talon, who was pretending to be drunk, was shouting abuse at them as they came running toward him. Reza and Rav'an smothered laughter as they watched his antics. He allowed the soldiers to come within a hundred feet and then turned and ran into the deep shadows of an adjoining street. The soldiers came to the entrance to the street and stopped, peering into the darkness, but unable see him. They stood there for several minutes, undecided and angry, but in no hurry to enter the dark, narrow confines of the street with its potential danger. Cursing and waving their spears threateningly, they retreated to the fire. Neither noticed that horses had passed that way through the gap in the walls.

Talon came up to the others, breathing hard from his run. They grinned at him as he approached.

Rav'an said dryly, "That was a good performance, Talon. Have you ever been drunk before?"

"No, my lady," he replied. "But I saw a lot of drunks among the troops at my father's castle. They behave like that, so I thought it would do for the soldiers."

There was a collective chuckle as they mounted the restless horses and moved off at a walk. Soon the moonlight illuminated a well-trodden road, muddy and rutted, but nonetheless representing the main road for Hamadan.

The three of them pushed on all night, helped by the moonlight, which broke through the light cloud cover. It beamed down on the frozen wasteland, cold and remote. The going was not easy, and many times they had to walk the horses, as the road was so rutted as to be dangerous. In spite of this, they made good progress toward the first town of Takestan. They were still moving along the road when dawn came. The sky cleared and grew light in the east, then the sun came up over the horizon in a blaze of glory, lighting up a cold, harsh land, covered in a deep carpet of snow and ice. The few trees that they could see were bare of any foliage and stood gaunt and stark on the empty and vast Hamadan plain. It made them feel tiny and insignificant. They could see no other people on the road behind them, nor in front; no sign of life whatever. Each of them kept their thoughts to themselves, but they were the same: How long must we go without seeing other life? Were we foolish to attempt to try for Hamadan in this?

The hours passed and the sun rose higher in a cloudless blue sky. The glare of its reflection on the snow hurt their eyes. There was no wind, and for that they were grateful; nonetheless, the cold penetrated their coverings.

The wind began to rise after they'd eaten their meager rations and fed the horses some grain from the saddlebags. Reza, when asked, thought that the town Takestan was about fifteen miles farther on, and that if they hurried they could make it in good time before curfew. The wind grew more persistent, but as they were heading south by west it was behind them, so they didn't have to fight it.

At one point Talon looked back, as was his habit now, and saw, rising over the great mountains of the Alborz to the north, a bank of black clouds that extended from horizon to horizon. He called to the others and pointed. Reza and Rav'an, who had both been wrapped in their thoughts, looked startled, and the pace immediately picked up. No one wanted to be caught in more snow.

They came to the large, walled village of Takestan late that afternoon. There were no guards to stop them, which surprised them somewhat, but when they came to a dilapidated inn that they had been pointed to, they realized why. The soldiers were there taking advantage of the innkeeper's hospitality and keeping warm at a large fire.

The leader of the soldiers, although interested in the group of three, did not go beyond asking for their papers. None of them had taken their coats off, so the soldiers could not make out anything other than three heavily clad, booted travelers. Quite normal for this weather—the only thing not very normal was that they were traveling at all. But this did not occur to the leader of the troopers, as he was already half drunk.

Reza took the innkeeper aside and told him to provide food and drink in the one room they rented.

The horses taken care of, the three of them settled in the room. Both the boys lay their bedding on the floor and offered to sleep outside in the corridor, but Rav'an told them to stay in the room. She would sleep on the bed platform almost fully clothed. It was still very cold in the room, in any case.

The wind howled and rattled the shutters of the inn all night long. The cold crept into their beds and chilled them as they slept, and then, as they were so cold, they woke up and listened to the wind, wondering what the morrow would bring.

The next morning, a cold and tired group of travelers left the inn before the troopers could wake up and harass them. They had paid in small coin to a grateful innkeeper who, although curious, did not ask questions of them, and no one volunteered information. Reza managed to obtain some more food for the journey from him with a few more small coins.

They set off into the windy day, very different from the previous one. The sky was leaden with clouds scudding across the tops of the low hills. The wind was biting, so it was not long before they were all freezing cold. The one consolation was that it seemed too cold for snow yet. Their thick, woolen sheepskin coats protected the riders from the wind up to a point, but the temperature continued to drop. They were more and more often forced to dismount and clear the horses' hooves of ice that had accumulated in lumps that threatened to lame them.

The wind tore at their clothing and chilled any exposed flesh to the bone. Their faces were covered by both their huge furred hats and scarves wrapped round their lower faces, leaving only their eyes to see by.

Reza led the way with Rav'an in the middle and Talon at the rear. Reza was confident that he was on the right trail, but the light was diminishing to the point where the road was becoming indistinct. They pushed on, however, braving the miserable conditions, hoping that they were making better time than they in fact were. Late in the day when everyone, including the horses, was close to exhaustion, Reza spotted a grove of trees and what he thought might be a cluster of huts. He shouted to the others and pointed. They hurried to the object of his interest and came up to a group of four long, low huts almost buried in the drifts alongside the road. They were scattered among the trees and seemed deserted.

There was no sign of life anywhere, just the keening wind and the rattle of the frozen branches in the trees. There was a regular clinking sound of some metallic object that gave accent to the desolation of the place. The travelers didn't like the look of the deserted huts, but they knew without discussion that they could not push on for much longer, and there was no town in sight.

Talon leaned toward the other two from his saddle and spoke over the wind. "We have to seek shelter here, my lady. It has become too cold to continue."

She nodded and pointed to the nearest hut. "We have to take the horses in with us, or they will die in the cold."

The boys nodded. Talon dismounted stiffly, then taking his spear, he walked to the hut Rav'an had indicated. He paused at the doorway. Snow had piled high against the crude wooden door that was latched shut. He pushed at it gingerly with the point of his spear. It wouldn't budge, so he leaned against it and it fell inward on worn and cracked leather hinges that threatened to snap in the cold.

He peered warily into the darkness and then moved cautiously into the single room. It was quite empty, with a hard earthen floor strewn with old rushes. There was a broken bench on its side against the far wall, but no other furniture. To his right there was a fire hole, blackened with much use; a crude chimney of packed mud had been constructed above it to take the smoke away from the room. The thick mud walls and the dense thatch of the roof muted the sound of the wind. It would do for the night, he decided.

He went outside and called to the others, still mounted. His face and jaw were numb from the cold and he had difficulty speaking. "We can stay the night here; and we can get the horses into the room as well."

The others dismounted, and he led the way back to the doorway with Jabbar in tow. Jabbar had some trouble with the doorway, but once inside he seemed relieved to be out of the wind and calmed down. The other horses were the same. They hobbled the animals at the far end of the large room. It was not long before a flint had produced a small flame, and they had a fire going in the fire pit with pieces from the broken bench. They also found some frozen wood outside, against the wall. The riders settled down near the fire.

"How far do you think we are from the town, Reza?" Talon asked.

"I don't know," Reza replied, "but I think it must be at least thirty more miles. We would not have made it in this," he added.

Rav'an nodded. "We will have to sit it out here and hope it blows over. I am *so* cold." She shivered.

Talon made more room for her alongside him near the fire. They were no longer interested in the finer points of protocol. Survival was the more important priority, and if she were cold then she should be made warm.

Conversation was sparse, the cold and the keening wind outside made for a subdued trio that ate a light supper of cold meat and stale *nan*, then made ready for bed. Talon and Reza decided that one of them should stay awake all the time, as they were in country they didn't know. Talon elected to stay up for the first half of the night and let Reza get some sleep. The other two promptly went to sleep on their rolls and left him to wander about in the cramped, single room of the large hut.

He first went to the horses and made sure that they were not going to cause any trouble. They seemed contented enough. Although there was not much food, they were happy to be out of the bitter cold.

He listened to the wind as it played games with the trees. He could hear the snow battering the door and wondered when the weather would get warmer. He had never been so cold in his life. The winters at Samiran were cold, especially after the fierce hot temperatures of the summers, but he had never experienced anything like this. It was like a living thing. It crept into his bones and left him feeling weak and lethargic. It was tempting to just lie down and sleep. He fought the idea, unable to bear the thought that he might let his companions down. He realized that he would have to move around to stay awake, so during a lull in the wind, he eased the door open and slipped outside to check the night.

There was still a moon and the sky had been swept clean of clouds. Above him was the bright starlit sky in all its frozen glory.

It was almost as bright as day. He gazed up at the night sky in wonder. He had always been entranced by the myriad stars in the heavens. It was so clear that he could almost imagine the stars were tiny orbs of light suspended in the night for him to see by. He muttered a small prayer for Jean, and then made his way round the building to look down the road. Much to his relief, the wind was dying down and the swirling columns of frozen snow were less playful.

!@#$%He almost didn't hear it—the tiny jingle of a bit in a horse's mouth as it champed. Talon froze. He could not yet see where the sound had come from, other than that it seemed to have come from the road in the direction of Ghazvin, the one direction he did not want to hear from that night.

He eased slowly into the shadows thrown out onto the ground by the low bulk of the hut; he had to see what it was before he alerted the others.

Then he saw them, three horsemen coming over the rise of the road from Ghazvin. They were dressed for the cold, but it was clear to Talon that they were armed as well, all carrying lances.

As they crested the rise of the road that gave them a view of the cluster of huts nestled in the trees, they stopped, three black silhouettes, silent, menacing. They eyed the place for what seemed an eon. They were about three hundred yards away from Talon, so he doubted that they could see him in the shadows, but he remained motionless all the same. He checked his escape route and could see that if he needed to he could use the shadows to get to the hut's door.

The horsemen sat still. Their very stillness and silence was a sinister warning to him that all was not well. Normal travelers would be cautious, but these riders were checking the area very carefully indeed. Talon's heart sank. Could the men from Alamut have followed them so far so quickly? He could hardly believe it, and yet here were these three menacing figures watching the huts as though they expected someone to be there.

He decided to get back to the others. He would just have time if he moved now, as the three horsemen were now talking and pointing. They were getting ready to come closer to investigate. He slipped through the shadows like a ghost and within seconds was shaking the other two. In the dim light of the fire, he told them what he had seen.

"These are men of war. They are watching this place too hard for my liking. I think we're in trouble and may have to strike the first blow."

Neither of the others argued with him. Reza collected both bows and Rav'an picked up their spears. Each of them carried a sword and knife. The boys hurriedly strung their bows with the strings from their pockets, the fire was banked, and all three slipped out of the hut—to stay within it was to be trapped.

The horsemen were already much closer and well spaced out, as though they expected trouble, riding slowly, their lances held at the ready as they came.

Talon, Reza and Rav'an held a rapid council.

"We have bows," Talon whispered. "We have to take down at least two of them in the first shot and then deal with the other."

"We have to go out into the light to shoot. They will see us," Reza whispered.

"Yes, but we're both quick. We'll get one shot each; if we don't kill with the arrow then we have to use our spears as they can ride us down."

"If I hold the spears and two arrows will that help?" Rav'an whispered. They gave her an arrow each. The horsemen were now a hundred paces away.

"We have to go now," Talon whispered.

The two boys, holding an arrow knocked and string pulled taut, ran forward into the snow where they could get a good shot. The horsemen saw them straight away, and seeing what they were about to do immediately started to take evasive action. No raw recruits these. They spurred their animals in three different directions. The bows twanged and two arrows leapt forward. One arrow entered under the arm of the second horseman and penetrated deep into his chest. The force of the entry knocked him off his horse, dying as he fell.

The second arrow struck the lead rider's horse in the side just behind the front leg, Reza had quite deliberately aimed there once he saw the break coming, knowing that he could not hit the man.

The horse screamed and went down, tossing its rider, who landed on his shoulder and rolled into a snowdrift. The last rider had broken for the trees, but had changed his mind and decided to charge the three figures standing exposed in the snow. He yelled a war cry and turned his horse on its haunches in a cloud of snow. He lowered his lance, then, moving his small shield in front of his body, spurred his horse savagely into a charge. He was just seventy yards away when he started out.

Talon and Reza both snatched arrows from Rav'an, who then stepped back, lifting her spear to ready herself for the impact. Talon and Reza hurriedly notched their arrows and fired them, but the cold had done its work. Talon's string snapped and his arrow went off into the trees. Reza's numbed fingers could not get his arrow properly notched but he fired anyway, and his arrow struck the horse in the face. It tore out the left eye of the charging animal, which screamed with agony, threw up its head, and swerved, almost throwing the rider. He was nothing if not a very good rider, though. His aim had been thrown off, so he concentrated on getting his horse under control as he swept by the three of them, cursing, and shouting at the crazed animal.

Talon snatched his spear from Rav'an, who had stood braced to strike the rider as he went by, but had also had her aim thrown off.

Talon shouted at Reza to find the downed rider and finish him off; he'd deal with the rider still mounted. He shoved Rav'an back against the wall near the door so that she had at least that protection, then he hefted his spear. He would present a poor target for the rider if he came back, trying to charge with his horse.

Talon could see that Reza was heavily engaged with the other rider; he could hear the shouting and the clash of steel on steel. He prayed his friend could hold out until they could help him.

Talon's adversary gave up trying to calm his injured horse and dismounted. He was about fifty yards away. He hissed his sword out of its scabbard and waded through the snow to the boy and girl. The man approached Talon warily, his sword held high in front of him.

Talon drew his own sword, noticing with dismay that his opponent wore a chain-mail shirt, as well as his shield, which he had retained. Talon decided that he had to wear the man down; there was no other way. It did not look good, however. The man was older than he was and had the look of a veteran fighter.

The man grinned menacingly through blackened, broken teeth. He was in a hurry. He skipped a couple of paces as though testing the ground and then moved in very fast, swinging. His sword flashed down, then he whirled to the left and slashed at Talon's sword arm. If he had connected, Talon would have had his arm amputated at the elbow. Talon had to move very fast in his bulky clothing, in the syrupy, slippery, snow. He dodged and parried as much as he could while the man made a series of ferocious strikes. At one point Talon slipped, and the man's eyes gleamed as he tried to force Talon to the ground. Talon was able to parry the slashing sword with his own, but the jolt numbed his arm, it had come down so hard. There was a shower of sparks, and then Talon was back on his feet, retreating away from the hut. Both were panting, but it was clear the older man was gaining ground. He seemed to be enjoying the match now, which gave scant comfort to Talon, who had not felt any advantage at all thus far.

The man skipped forward once more, sword swinging, and Talon braced himself to parry and duck again. This time, however, the man gave a curious extra skip, and then arched his back as though he wanted to stare straight up into the sky. His sword arm fell back and his other hand tried to reach around to his back as though something bothered him. The look of surprise on his face was almost comical. Then, right in front of a stupefied Talon, he coughed up a gout of blood and fell forward, face down into the snow.

Talon stood paralyzed for a couple of seconds, staring down at his opponent. Then he looked up and saw Rav'an still holding Reza's bow. He had no time to compliment her, although his glance was admiring. He could hear the fight over by the trees was still going on, and if Reza's opponent was anything like his own, Reza was on his last legs. Indeed, as he turned to go to him, he saw Reza duck behind a slim tree and the other's sword hiss down in a wicked chop into the luckless tree with such force that the two opponents were almost buried in the snow that was shaken loose in a small avalanche. Neither seemed to notice, however; they just shook the snow off and continued their duel.

Although the fight was tiring both, it was clear to Talon that his friend was in trouble. He shouted encouragement and ran to them, snatching up a spear as he went. The man, who had up to this time been having it all his way, quickly realized that he was now fighting for his life. In a last desperate effort to end the fight, he redoubled his efforts to finish Reza off so that he could deal with the new threat. Reza ducked in and out of the trees, the maddened man following him, slashing left and right in wide arcs that downed some of the smaller saplings in his path. He realized too late that Reza had lured him to where Talon had been fighting, and that there were now three people facing him—Rav'an was holding a spear threateningly as well.

He stood in the middle of the trio, all pointing some weapon at him, his companion at his feet and very dead. He stopped moving, and very slowly lowered his sword.

Reza barked at him. “Do you surrender?”

The man seemed to think about it, then he nodded his head and grimaced as though to say: What have I gotten into? Then he dropped his sword in front of him.

Reza picked it up and then said loudly, “Turn around. You are our prisoner. If you try to escape, you will die.”

The man nodded and turned around. Talon looked at Rav’an, and asked her to see if there was cord in the hut. She nodded and ran into the darkened hut, returning soon after with some leather cord from their packs. He handed her his spear and, while she and Reza guarded the man, took off the man’s mailed gloves and tied his hands tightly behind him.

Now that they were safe, he turned the man around to face them all and then forced him to his knees in the snow. His fur hat had come off during the fall, so his long dirty hair fell across his dark face.

“Who are you and what do you want with us?” Talon asked, his voice harsh. The adrenaline of the battle was still high in his blood.

The man looked up at him. “We came this way because we were told that three criminals were on this road and were wanted back in Ghazvin.”

“Who sent you, you dog?” Reza shouted angrily. Moving forward, he seemed ready to strike the man.

“A man called Ahmad sent a messenger who offered us gold if we could capture the girl,” the prisoner responded, flinching.

The trio looked at one another.

“What do you mean, a ‘man called Ahmad’? Did you see him?” Rav’an asked.

He shook his head, his long greasy locks swirling about his dark face. “No. He sent a messenger, who knew where to find us. He told some of us to go north, and us three to come along this road. They have sent people along all the roads from Ghazvin.”

The three of them realized that they had just had a nasty brush with some mercenaries. These men lived by their skill with the sword and went to the highest bidder. The three of them had not reckoned with Arash Khan’s power. It was now clear that he could reach out a long, long way, and would do everything and anything to capture them... or just kill them.

Talon asked, "How much did they pay you?"

The man shook his head. "Not enough. And he kept half for payment on delivery."

Reza snorted. His relief at their victory was palpable. "We are *fida'i*. Did he tell you that?"

A look of alarm came over the man's face. Again, he shook his head, his eyes fearful now. He said nothing, but it was clear that he was frightened.

Talon was the first to collect himself. The night was now well advanced and they were all tired. The battle had been an unwelcome interlude, but they now needed rest before they fled the place.

He told Reza to search the man for weapons and anything else of value. They decided to take his chain mail as well. Untying the man, they stood over him as he struggled out of his chain-mail shirt. Then they retied him hand and foot, and Talon left Reza to guard him.

Rav'an ran off to capture the mercenaries' loose horse; Talon went over to the first man he had killed with his arrow. He, too, was dressed in chain mail, so Talon commenced the gruesome task of removing the shirt and weapons from the inert body. There was a lot of blood around, but he persisted, as he felt that they might need the armor one day. They had not been able to take armor when they left Alamut, but now they had the booty from the dead enemy.

When he had completed this, he went on to the second man. He pulled the arrow out of that body and cleaned it off in the snow. He was very impressed with what Rav'an had done and intended to talk about it with Reza as soon as they could find the time.

She, meanwhile, came back with the one horse that was of much use to them. The injured one she asked Talon to kill, as it was in agony. Reza was watching the prisoner and could not be spared to do the unpleasant task. Talon hated to do the deed, but he realized that there was no choice. He walked up to the animal that was standing near to some trees. Its head was down and it kept pawing at the ground in its pain. At his approach it tossed its head and turned to look at him with its one good eye. It started to back off as he came up to it.

He talked to it gently and held his hand out. It stared at him warily but let him come up and reach for the reins that hung loose to the ground. He held them, talking all the while to the nervous animal. He took the saddle and the full saddlebags off the horse. Then, slowly, he took out his knife. He stroked the neck of the animal, then felt for the strong pulse in the jugular. He placed the wide blade against the neck and then, with a muttered apology, he stabbed the animal straight into its neck. Before the startled horse could pull away, Talon had severed the large vein. The horse fell back onto its haunches, dragging Talon with it for a couple of yards, the flow of blood so strong it pulsed out in a jet that sprayed off to the left of the dying animal. It stopped and stood, legs apart, trembling.

Talon talked to it all the while, tears in his eyes. As he talked to the terrified animal, its remaining eye went dull, even as the weakened animal began to topple over. He followed it down and held its head as it died, remaining with it for a couple of minutes after it had ceased movement of any kind.

Dashing tears from his eyes, he collected himself and began to rummage in the saddlebags. The men had come well prepared for a long journey—that was certain. There was a lot of food that the young travelers could use. He found a small sack of gold in the bags, and extra clothing, although it was dirty and smelled bad. He discarded that and kept the rations and the gold. He went back to the others after a last parting look at the horse.

Rav'an had taken the saddlebags off the other horses, and they collected their booty in a pile. Now that the frantic activity of the fight was over, the cold reasserted itself. They began to feel it now as the reaction set in.

They got back into the hut and relit the fire. They led the new horse into the room and settled it down at the end where the others were standing. The horses inside were restless. They had heard the fighting and the noise, and their sharp noses could smell new blood. However, they calmed down when the three came in and talked to them.

It seemed unlikely that anyone else was going to come for at least the rest of the night. Leaving the protesting prisoner outside, they hauled all the chain mail suits, spare weapons, and saddlebags into the hut.

Rav'an was shaking with the after-effects of the fight as the tension began to leave her. Talon reached over and held her shoulder with his hand. "Reza," he said, "my lady saved my life, and I am indebted to her." He looked into the shadows of her eyes in the gloomy room as he said this.

Reza looked at them. "How?"

"She shot the man I was fighting with your bow," Talon said, grinning now.

Reza breathed out in awe. "My lady, you are indeed a warrior. You saved us both with your action. I thank you, too, from my heart." He clenched his fist and raised it high, his face glowing with a fierce expression of exultant satisfaction. "We are truly a band of warriors now! Each of us has wet his sword in the blood of our enemies."

For the first time since the journey began Rav'an smiled, looking straight at Talon, and Talon released his hand and smiled back into her eyes.

Then he asked, practically, "What are we going to do with the prisoner?"

There was silence. No one wanted to say what they all knew should be done.

Talon was the first to speak. "We took him prisoner, but we cannot take him with us. There is always the chance that he will escape, and then he will tell everyone where we are. But, I do not want to kill him. There has been enough blood for one night."

The other two looked at him. There were nods and then Rav'an said tentatively, "We could leave him here."

Reza said, "We don't leave him a horse, but we could leave some food and a knife to cut wood for the fire."

"That is settled then," Talon said with some satisfaction. Warriors they might be, but not bloodthirsty murderers. "I shall go and bring him in, or he will die out there."

He found the prisoner shivering near the door.

Dragging him into the warmth of the room, Talon stood over him and told him in his most aggressive tones to keep his mouth shut, and he might live. The man nodded meekly and tried to make himself comfortable on the cold floor. His arms and hands were still tied, and Talon took the added precaution of tying him by his leg to a chain-mail suit, so that any movement would wake his captors at once. Talon told him to get some sleep and tossed a blanket over him. Then, turning to the others, he nodded, and they all rolled into their sleeping blankets and went to sleep near a glowing fire.

Rav'an and the boys woke to another frozen day. The fire had almost gone out, so Reza quickly stoked it and then looked around for their prisoner. The man seemed to be asleep so he went over and cautiously nudged him with his foot. The man stirred and turned onto his back to look up at him. Reza pushed the man over onto his face in order to check his bonds. Satisfied that they were still tight, he rolled the man over.

"Stay there and don't move, or you die," he threatened fiercely. He joined the others, who were preparing the bags and rolls for the next part of the journey. Leaving a small bundle consisting of a blanket and some food near the fire, they loaded all the rest onto the horses. They rolled the chain mail into bundles and loaded the new horse with the extra equipment and spare weapons. They had already eaten a meager breakfast, so all that remained was to make the prisoner aware of his fate and to leave.

Rav'an went over to the man and stood over him. "If I were not the sister of the master himself, you would have been carved up for sport last night. You can count on your good fortune this time. However, if you cross my path again you will die."

He gazed up at her, real fear in his eyes. "*Khanom*, you cannot leave me like this, I shall die of cold before I can get free. Please do not leave me like this."

She looked at him contemptuously and walked off, ignoring his pleas. They walked the horses out into the frozen world. The bodies lay as they had left them, frozen bundles half covered with snow that had drifted during the remainder of the night.

As the other two led the horses out of the hut, Talon walked to their prisoner. The man cringed back into the corner of the wall. He was thinking Talon had come back to kill him, a thought reinforced when he saw a long knife, one that belonged to his erstwhile companion, in Talon's hand. He was about to shout with anger and fear, when the knife thudded into the ground at the far end of the room, away from the prisoner.

Without a word Talon left, shutting the door behind him and walked quickly out to the others who had already mounted. They turned south and moved off across the vast plain of frozen snow, following the faint track that indicated the way to Hamadan.

* * * * *

Four days later, three travel-stained riders with one packhorse arrived at the gates of Hamadan. They looked tired and haggard, their faces half hidden under the scarves and large furred hats. The whole party looked thin and worn with fatigue.

The horses' ribs were beginning to stand out, but a discerning man would have noticed that they were of very good stock. The soldiers at the gates were in a hurry and only glanced at the document produced by one of the riders, waving them on into the city, while they dealt with some large wagons that were stuck in the mud blocking the road.

If my Sweetheart is my heart, how shall I name her?
And if my heart is my Sweetheart , whence is she named?
The two are so intimately interwoven that
I can no longer distinguish one from the other.

— Baba Tahir —

Chapter 18
Hamadan

His daughter, tugging at his sleeve, awakened Ali Ferouz. He grunted and rolled over to stare fuzzily at the eight-year-old, who was tugging him awake.

"What is it, Borlour, my little one?" he asked somewhat querulously.

"Mama told me to wake you, Papa," she piped. "There are strangers in the street and they are standing at our door. Mama is frightened."

Ali scrambled off the mattress where he had been taking a late morning nap. It was cold, and he felt grumpy, but if his wife was worried perhaps he had better have a look and see what all the fuss was about.

He patted his daughter on the head, then padded along the corridor of his ground-floor house to the living room. He came awake in an instant when he saw his wife, however. She looked frightened, no mistaking that.

"What is it, wife?"

In reply, she pointed to the shuttered window that overlooked the street.

"There are some people at the door," she whispered. "They look dangerous and I am afraid."

He shook his head. "I shall go and talk to them," he said with more confidence than he felt.

He motioned her back into the living room and went to the door. Opening it, he was met by three figures dressed in sheepskin coats and fur hats that partially obscured their gaunt faces. They all carried weapons, large rolls of belongings, and looked to be very rough company. When he saw their eyes, he felt a chill. Their eyes were as cold as the snow at their feet.

"Who are you and what do you want?" he demanded, more aggressively than he meant. In answer, one of them pulled an object from his coat and showed it to him, concealed from anyone on the street to avoid any passersby seeing it. Ali's breath stopped, He gazed at the small, well-wrought dagger as though presented with a scorpion. Then he numbly motioned them into the house.

The tallest of the three, with strange eyes, moved past him and quickly glanced around the living room. He took in the modest furniture and carpets, as well as Ali's wife standing there petrified.

"*Khanom,*" he said with an accent. He was polite, but he then moved on into the corridor while the others came into the living room with an indignant Ali.

"What is he doing?" he asked the other two sharply.

The one who had produced the knife, now gone back into the folds of the coat, responded, "He is making sure that I am safe."

Ali turned and looked hard at the figure who had shown him the dagger, shocked that she had a woman's voice. She took off the large fur hat and shook out her luxuriant hair. He gaped, looking at a lovely girl who could not have been more than eighteen, but who carried herself with assurance and poise.

"Feza's brother, Massoud of Ghazvin, sent us. I am Rav'an, the sister of the master," she stated in a quiet voice.

Ali immediately knelt at her feet. "*Khanom* Princess, I did not know," he whispered. "If Massoud sent you and you carry the dagger, I am your servant before Allah, and in praise of the master. My name is Ali Ferouz, and I am your servant."

She nodded her face calm, accepting his homage. "We need a safe place to stay, Ali. Is this house safe?"

"This house is safe, *Khanom,* but it would not do for you to stay here, as I have inquisitive neighbors."

Just as that moment, the tall member of the group came back and stood next to the others. He whispered something to the young woman and her companion. They nodded in unison, and then he turned and looked at Ali.

If he had found the other two intimidating, Ali found this one's presence menacing. He gulped. "*Khanom*, we have a house that is only a short distance from here, with a large garden, set back off the street. It is much safer than this house. I shall take you there. Did you come with horses?" he asked, knowing the answer already. They could not have made it to Hamadan by any other means. They nodded.

"Then where did you put them, *Khanom*?" he addressed the princess with more confidence now.

"We found stables nearby. Why is that a problem?" she asked, concern in her voice.

"If we leave them there for too long, it will attract attention, *Khanom*. I suggest that in the morning you go there, as though you are about to leave Hamadan, and then walk them to the house where I am taking you. You can stable them there until you are ready to move on."

He was dying to ask to where that might be, but decided that it could be imprudent to ask just now. He had been in the company of Ismaili before, but this group was somehow different.

"We should go there now, *Khanom*, if it pleases you?" he said using an ingratiating tone.

She nodded, and they all waited in silence as he collected his coat, reassured his still worried-looking wife, and led the way out of the door onto the street. The princess smiled at the frightened woman in a vain attempt to reassure her, but to no avail. The daughter was now with her mother, clinging to her skirts, contemplating the strangers with awe and fright from wide eyes.

They trudged along a street of banked snow that was thawing in the sun. There was not a lot of traffic, and most of it was pedestrian, so the four people in their bulky coats drew no attention as they walked briskly up the muddy road.

Ali led them at a fast pace, as he wanted them out of sight as soon as possible. No one spoke, but passersby gave them a wide berth, as the three travelers were all armed with spears and swords, even if Ali was not.

He led them off to the right and then down a narrow alley to a long wall with a stout door halfway down its length. He fished out a large key and inserted it into the lock of the door, then pushed it open against the piled-up snow behind it. Motioning them into the garden, he shut the door in one quick motion and locked it. He turned and led the way across the virgin snow to a large, mud brick, single-story house at the far end.

Alert to any danger, Talon and Reza looked hard at the house and the adjoining outhouses, where they guessed they would stable the horses.

Ali opened the front door of the house with another key, showing them into the living chamber of the house. This room was larger than his private house, although it had a deserted air to it, as though it had not been used for a long time. There was a small pile of snow on the floor near one of the windows; the shutters had not been closed properly before the last snow. The three of them, glancing round, looked pleased.

"Is there water near by?" demanded the princess.

"*Khanom*, there will be water for drinking and for ablutions," Ali answered. "I will be sending round some womenfolk to help clean the place for you. One will remain who will attend to your personal needs, while the other will serve as the cook. Please make yourselves comfortable in the meantime. I shall leave the way I came and lock the door so that no one can come in uninvited," he said, trying to reassure them. Those suspicious looks came back.

"I shall only be as long as it takes to find the women and make proper arrangements for your comfort," he said hurriedly.

There was a nod from the princess, so he took his leave. They watched him all the way to the door.

* * * * *

When he had left, Reza turned to his companions. "Do you trust him, *Khanom*?"

"I'm not sure, Reza. But I have to believe Massoud when he says that Ali is as trustworthy as anyone, whatever that means."

"We should not let our guard down too much then," remarked Reza. He stretched. "I am glad we made it here, anyway. Perhaps we can rest for a couple of days before we have to move on."

The others agreed, and then without more ado, they set out to explore the house. There were plenty of food supplies in jars, oil for cooking, a place to cook, and even utensils, including a very large basin for which no one knew the use. There were four sleeping rooms with platforms for bedding, as the floor was far too cold to lie on.

The princess took the best for herself, leaving Talon and Reza to squabble good-naturedly over the others. They set about finding wood for a fire, as that was the most urgent thing to do. The house was very cold, and they could see their breath.

The boys went out and checked the outlying houses to see what they contained and returned with a good report on their condition and their potential use as stables. Horsemen had used this residence in the past.

The boys brought in wood, and soon there was a merry blaze going in the living room fireplace. There were carpets and *ghilims* spread in profusion around the floor so they could, for the first time since Ghazvin, take off their boots and luxuriate in the feel of a thick carpet under bare feet.

The princess wrinkled her nose at the boys and told them that at the first opportunity they should go to the baths and wash, that they stank like goats and looked worse. They laughed, a little shamefaced, and refrained from pointing out that she looked as scruffy as they did, but, although Talon could not understand it, she did not seem to smell.

Ali returned to find them grouped around the fire, waiting for him. He brought with him two women, who carried on their heads large bundles of food and bedding. They came into the main room, smiled nervously as they lowered their loads, and bowed to the princess, then without a word they went off to the kitchen to prepare food.

Ali also brought with him another man, who made respectful obeisance to the princess. Ali introduced him as his brother Karim, who lived a few streets away, and explained that Karim would look after them as gateman and guard while they were in the house. Ali also explained that his brother would take his place whenever he was unable to come.

At this point the princess sat straighter and told him, "We are here upon a secret mission for my brother, the Agha Khan. Under no circumstances are you to breathe a word of this to anyone, or I shall see to it that you and your entire family are punished." She left unsaid what that punishment would be, but it was clear to all in the very quiet room what that would be.

Ali and Karim nodded in mute acceptance of the ruling.

"Are you able to tell me anything that I might help you further, my lady?" Ali asked politely.

Rav'an looked at him, her eyes cool. "I have to go west as soon as the snows have thawed, perhaps as far as Dezful. We will need provisions and clothes for the journey. We are wearing all that we have and I wish to have new clothes."

Ali and Karim nodded. "When you are rested and have eaten, perhaps we can have one of the women take you to a place where you can buy cloth and my women can very quickly make you clothes." No matter how practical it might have sounded, he would not insult this beautiful girl by offering her his wife's clothing. "Do you have funds, *Khanom*? I have access to money." Rav'an was hard put not to let him see her interest in this piece of news. This was an unexpected surprise. With as cool a tone as she could muster she said, "I expect you to provide me with enough money to get me to Baghdad."

If Ali was surprised, he said nothing, just turning to his brother and saying, "Karim, can we obtain the gold by tomorrow or the day after, in several packets for the princess?"

Karim nodded and addressed the princess. "I have connections with several merchants who hold money for us, *Khanom*. I shall bring the gold as soon as I can."

The princess acknowledged the news without betraying any emotion, although inwardly she was excited. "There is no hurry, take your time," she said airily.

Her eyes shifted to her two companions to see what their reactions were. They were both pretending to search the ceiling for flies as though bored by the whole exchange, although Talon's lips twitched a tiny bit.

Business having been taken care of, Ali then got up and went off to see the women and how they were doing. Rav'an asked Karim where the local baths were. He told her that the nearest public baths were several streets away and that he would be glad to escort the men of her party there. He turned his gaze upon the two boys sitting cross-legged on the carpet opposite him.

"We can find clothing for you as well," he added. "We should dress you more as they do here in Hamadan, as you will stand out as you are."

The one with the green eyes and the long scar on the left side of his jaw stared at him. "Can we move about the town without being stopped?" he asked with an accent, but one that Karim could not place.

"Once you are dressed as the people here, you should be fine.

Do not carry spears, and I would recommend that you do not even carry swords in this town. Your knives will be sufficient, but keep them hidden. There are garrison troops here and they sometimes look for people. If they stop you, just say that you come from this area and that you are members of our family. You should not say too much," he said, looked hard at Talon. "*Khanom,* bathing facilities are limited for women in the public arena, but you can use the tub in the kitchen, and the women will see to your needs here in the house." He was embarrassed but wanted to make sure she was provided for.

Rav'an smiled a brilliant smile at him, whereupon he became her slave for life.

Ali and the women came back into the room, bearing food. There was rice in a large pan, wonderful, loose-grained white rice with a nutty flavor; there was mutton stew, vegetables, and dried eggplant soaked in sesame oil and fried. One of the women proudly displayed for their taste *Koofteh Berengi* as she called it, a delicious serving of large balls of rice, ground meat and onions, seasoned with herbs and nuts for them to enjoy. Lots of hot *nan* in a heaped platter came with the meal.

With no other word than a thank you, the whole party, excluding the two serving women, sat down on the carpets and ate. Both Ali and Karim refused to do more than eat a token amount, to show their good manners. Meanwhile, the boys and Rav'an ate as though they had not done so for over a week. They soon polished off the food. Ali nodded to one of the attending women, who produced a leather flask and poured some sweet wine to finish off the meal. The boys, being unused to wine, sipped theirs cautiously but with appreciation, while Rav'an, who knew the wine, complimented the man on his good taste. Ali and Karim joined in the wine tasting, and then the conversation moved to where they had just come from and how things were in Alamut.

But, because they had just come from Alamut, the three travelers were more interested in catching up on world affairs. Ali and Karim, living as they did in Hamadan, could provide plenty of local gossip and even some news of the wars in the west: Egypt, Syria, and Palestine. Neither person noticed Talon's keen interest. This was, in fact, the first real news of home he had heard since his capture.

Hamadan, Karim explained to the newcomers, was a very old city, and had formerly been called Ekbatan. It was ancient, going back to before Cyrus the Great. It was now a major seat of power for the Seljuks, who ruled the country. They constituted the rich and powerful in this city. There was an *atabeg*, or military governor, in charge of the city right now, but that could change. Ali explained that the Ismaili were no longer in any numbers here as they had been in the past, due to pitched battles with the Turks and others, battles the Ismaili had lost. The result was persecution, so they now went about disguised as locals and adhered to the Shi'a Muslim faith. This was not the Sunni faith that the Seljuk majority practiced; however, Shi'ites were not considered heretical enough to warrant persecution, as were the Ismailis. Karim advised them to go to the mosque and take part in prayers; if they happened to be caught out on the streets during prayer time, they should watch the washing rituals and take part, so that no one could point a finger at them any time. He would teach them, so that they would not be complete novices at the ritual.

They should expect to see women in veils, and some not, but on no circumstances were they to approach a woman in the street. That would get them into trouble and perhaps arrested, and then they would be lost. He looked at Rav'an, then advised her to use a light veil that would at least partially hide her features. They listened with full attention, knowing that this was good advice and that they would do well to heed it.

The boys were eager to go out, to get some new clothes from the bazaar and have a bath. The princess had made it clear that she wanted to be left alone to perform her own ablutions, and they were to take care of themselves at the public baths. They did not need to don the thick outer clothing that they had arrived in, but as they didn't have anything other than their heavy boots they were forced to leave with those. Some money changed hands, and they left Rav'an to her own devices with the other womenfolk. The boys tagged along with Karim, who was keen enough to take them. His curiosity was burning within him as to who they were and what they were doing in Hamadan; however, his brother had warned him that they looked to be dangerous, and that too many questions might provoke them, so he was very circumspect.

They came to the baths by way of muddy streets and narrow alleys. It was a combination of public baths, private booths, and even weight training, so it was called a *Zor Khane*. Men went there to relax in the hot baths and to get pummeled by a masseur, if they had the money, as well as to wrestle and weight train. These latter were sports and recreations that the Seljuks had brought with them when they came to Persia that were now quite commonplace, according to Karim.

The boys were ushered into the baths by people who knew Karim. Curious looks were directed at their rough clothing, but these turned respectful when confronted by one black pair and one green pair of dangerous eyes.

Karim told them to enjoy the baths, as he would be going off to get some clothes for them. He had a good idea now as to their sizes, so he left them at the *Zor Khane*. Reza was more at home in this environment than Talon, who had never had a bath before he came to Samiran, so this was again very new and embarrassing for him.

He stayed close to Reza as they went from the changing booths to the hot pools where the attendants were waiting. They were given bars of soft stuff that did not smell very nice, which Talon viewed with deep suspicion. Reza, however, seemed comfortable with it, saying it was just the same as the soap they had used in Samiran. So Talon copied his every move and soon they were luxuriating in the large tub big enough for four people while Reza, with much amusement, patronized his friend and showed him how to use the soap.

Talon could not remember a better feeling than this. It was wonderful to be able to soak away the aches and pains of the long ride from Ghazvin, and to feel the grime washing off. He looked down at his naked body in the water and realized that he had almost lost the tan from his long days of summer in Samiran and was turning a gray white. Reza was busy soaping his hair now and making the water froth with suds. He tossed the soap at Talon and showed him what he should do with it. Talon copied him, and at once got it in his eyes. The floundering and splashing that followed reduced Reza to helpless laughter. Talon was not amused and, reaching over, ducked his friend under the soapy water and then hurriedly stepped out of the bath.

Reza surfaced, spluttering and shouting revenge, until he opened his eyes and saw Talon standing outside of the tub grinning at him.

With much exuberance and many insults, they dried themselves. Wrapping the towels around their midriffs, they wandered into the large gymnastic area to watch the wrestlers and weight-trainers at work.

Talon thought the wrestling fascinating. The men wore leather breeches that were cut off below the knee. Some were covered in oil and were trying in a determined way for holds and trips. Most of the time, they seemed to stand leaning into one another, heads tucked into the other's shoulders as they tried to either push their opponent over, trip him, or pull him off his feet. They used their hands to slap and push, always looking for something to get hold of, most of the time without success because both bodies were heavily oiled. Friends and trainers stood around shouting advice to the two struggling combatants, who sweated and strained at one another. Occasionally it got very active, and then one or the other got thrown, or they fell over in a heap and the bout declared over. Then they would start all over again.

It was evident to Talon that it developed the upper torso. These were all very muscular men. He looked over to the weight-training area and could see other men heaving great clubs of wood onto their shoulders and performing a curious ritualistic dance, moving them around on their shoulders; others carried huge chains around with them. Off to the side of the small arena where all this was taking place, musicians played an accompaniment: one a reedy pipe, another tapped on a small drum with his fingers.

The boys were enraptured. They were in another world from the one they had escaped.

It was quite strange to be among so many other half-naked men in the first place. At the castle of Alamut, the serious business of training and indoctrination for the objective of killing had dominated their every waking hour. In the process it had taken times of simple enjoyment away from them, so that even this short sojourn into a new world awakened their curiosity and whetted their appetite for more.

Karim jolted them out of their reverie when he came up to them and murmured a greeting, then beckoned them back to the dressing rooms. He held bundles of clothes under each arm, which he held out to the two half-naked lads.

"Dress in these and we shall go," he commanded, and watched them as they stripped off their towels and began to dress. He rested an appreciative eye on their thin but lithe young bodies. Talon, he noticed, had some savage scars to go with the one along his jaw. He wondered what had been the cause, but refrained from asking.

Both Reza and Talon grew uncomfortable under Karim's scrutiny and hurriedly put on the rest of the clothes. Karim had provided calf-length boots of soft horsehide that fit reasonably well, although Talon found his a bit small. They also had loose turbans that they wound around their wet hair, leaving the one length to hang down their shoulder. Both looked just like any pair of youths who were part of the town population.

Tucking the bundles of their old clothes under their arms, they looked at their guide for directions. As Karim led the way out of the building, after having paid their costs, Reza nudged Talon, pointed at their guide, and smiled. Talon nodded and tucked the fact away for future reference. Reza had recognized the fact that Karim liked boys, too. He didn't resent the fact; it was just something to bear in mind.

Karim was a good guide. He took them to the center of the town where there was a milling crowd, even with the wind, melting snow, and mud. People were dressed in colorful clothes, the local dyes of yellow and ochre, along with multi-colored woven cloths of red and dark brown, interspersed with gray and white and blue. Horsemen rode along the main thoroughfares arrogantly demanding way. When this was not accorded as they thought fit, they, or their servants, would lay about the slow-movers with whips and curses. The traffic increased as Karim took them closer to the city's center *maidan*.

Men and women alike rode horses and took great pride in showing off to others. Talon and Reza were entranced by the parade of colorful silks and rich red and gold wools worn by the wealthier people. Men-at-arms, some in full armor, their chain mail clinking along with their weaponry, would ride by looking magnificent, showing off their Turcoman horses to all and sundry.

The noise was deafening to the two young men, who were quite unused to the bustle of a crowded city and its myriad occupations, all mixed together in a mass of humanity.

Karim explained to the two fascinated young men that Hamadan was the hub of commerce for the whole of the northern part of Persia. This was where merchants came in their great caravans from Isfahan in the southeast. They came from Kerman even farther south, or from Samarkand in the northeast, the gateway to the Chinese continent months and months away. Caravans came from Tabriz in the northwest, bringing the most exquisitely designed carpets and jars of olive oil from Anatolia and Constantinople.

Karim was proud of being a Hamadani and pointed out the

monuments that were becoming more numerous along the way. They saw in the distance a strange monument that Karim said was the tomb of Esther and Mordecai. Esther, he explained to the boys, was the Jewish wife of the great king, Xerxes; she was famous for saving her people. For their part, the boys were wide-eyed and agog at all the new sights and sounds they were being exposed to. Neither of them had ever been in a city the size of Hamadan. Their heads were swiveling to the left and the right as they took in things that neither of them had ever seen before.

Karim delighted in showing them the sights and kept them out of trouble with a hand on the elbow or a quick word, which helped them to get out of the way of a strutting warrior and his retainers. Both boys could not keep their eyes off the women who walked the streets or were carried in palanquins, nearly always escorted by their men folk, or by servants who glared at the boys when they caught them looking. It was hard not to. The veils the women wore were diaphanous, so it was easy to see the features behind them. Many gazed back at the two handsome young men, liking what they saw. Their clothes were a rich mixture of silks and furs that enhanced their figures and showed off the wealth of the lady or her husband. Their ornaments of gold and precious stones, emeralds and rubies, were ostentatiously displayed.

It was the first time the boys had seen women so made up. It was obvious that these women had had their eyes enhanced with makeup and their lips made more seductive with pomegranate juice, the resulting beauty visible behind the transparent veils.

Karim pointed out eating houses that were doing a roaring trade in this balmy afternoon. The smells of roasting chicken, goat meat, and succulent lamb on the charcoal fires along the side of the street were mouthwatering, in spite of the fact that they had eaten not long ago. Karim invited the boys to go into a teahouse with him, from where they could observe the pedestrians and the colorful parade.

Karim had noted the way the boys stared at the womenfolk with hunger, so it was with regret that he put aside hopes for their favors, but he was not surprised. He knew that the boys had become *fida'i*, which meant that they had seen paradise, and there were only women in paradise for these young men.

The bemused boys sat cross-legged on *ghilims* and carpets laid out on raised platforms, which gave a good view of the street outside, which bordered a small square with a monument to Baba Tahir Oryan, the great philosopher, poet, and writer. Both boys had heard of Baba Tahir. Ali pointed out that this particular *maidan* was a favorite place for wealthy young people to congregate on horses and litters. There were many plane trees along the avenues, which, while bare of leaves now, would in summer provide a welcome, shaded haven from the sun.

This was heady stuff for the boys, and the alert Karim, watching them, felt that he could begin to ask some questions. The atmosphere in the teahouse was relaxed, the patrons men, for the most part, although there were a few women with husbands or escorts present. Hookahs were being used at the back, and the acrid but not unpleasant smell of pipe smoke mingled with the aromatic scent of tea being prepared for guests.

Talon and Reza had never experienced this kind of indulgence before. They sat still, drinking the tea and nibbling the sweet little cakes brought to them by a serving man. They were absorbing as much of it as they could. Talon had decided that he would bring Rav'an here to show her what he was seeing. He wished that she were with them now and experienced a strange sense of something missing.

They parried the few but pointed questions that Karim asked. Both knew that to start talking would be dangerous, and like Rav'an, they had come to trust no one. Pretending ignorance of the princess' plans other than the direction they were to travel, they continued to watch the kaleidoscope of activity outside the teahouse. After a while, Karim stopped probing, frustrated, but not deterred.

It was getting late. "We should go," Karim said.

There were elaborate goodbyes to the servant who had been attending to their needs, whom Karim paid handsomely, and they set off for the house. Very soon, they had left the picturesque *maidan* with its parade of horsemen, for the narrow, dirty streets of the back world of the city. Talon was unfamiliar with beggars; he was astonished by how many there were. He had never seen one in the mountain world he had inhabited for the last four years. Here maimed and crippled beings in rags would push bowls of wood or leather at them, calling upon Allah to bless them for giving. Some clung to their clothing and had to be pushed away, while others shouted imprecations at them for not giving anything.

The streets became clogged with wagons that moved at a snail's pace, riders who swore and used their whips, and people who pushed and shoved without a word of apology. Talon was relieved when at last they came to the house. Just as they did, the call to prayers came from the nearby mosque. They looked a question at Karim, but he shook his head, let them in, and locked the door behind him. They plodded across the wet garden and were soon back in the warmth of a house with a good fire.

A young woman, who did not resemble at all the shapeless, bundled person they had become familiar with during the desperate ride from Alamut, greeted them. It was hard for Talon and Reza not to gape. Rav'an had been transformed. Her hair was loose and ran in a glossy river almost down to her waist. She was dressed in a pair of voluminous pantaloons of fine cotton and diaphanous silk that did little to hide her legs. Her fine ankles were bare, her small feet in slippers of delicate worked leather. Her blouse of rich, burnt-sienna with long silk sleeves, and the well-worked waistcoat of plain black wool with the large collar set off her oval face to perfection. She was even lightly made up.

She greeted them when they arrived, but as they settled in, she also admonished them for being out so long. Their story came out in a rush as both boys vied with each other to describe what they had seen.

Karim, after the polite greetings to the princess, went off to talk to the womenfolk and confirm that the house was running according to his requirements. Despite their wild and dangerous bearing, these were just two boys and a girl, he thought. I shall fear them not, if I help them. He and his brother were both consumed with curiosity as to what the three of them were doing here in Hamadan. His brother had said something interesting when he came to tell Karim about the visitors.

"They look hunted," he had said. "There is something going on here that they're not going to tell us. We have to be very careful."

It was getting dark outside. Karim, after ensuring that they had enough firewood for the night and morning, told the group that he and one of the women were about to leave and would be back in the morning to provide breakfast. The other woman, a girl barely out of her teens, would stay to look after their needs overnight. She would sleep in the room at the back of the house near the kitchen.

He assured them that they were safe in the house as long as they did not make too much noise and did not go out. There were many dangers, he said, that they might not be aware of, among them roving soldiers who would be drunk and therefore belligerent. There were also students who wandered the public square who could also be trouble for the unwary, as they too imbibed in the evenings and became unruly. Although there were many more during the summer months, people still roamed the streets, even on a cold night like this.

Rav'an and the boys professed to being too tired to want to wander the streets in any case. They bade him goodnight and settled down to an evening near the fire. Their journey across the frozen plateau to Hamadan had been a harrowing experience, which, as the young will, they began to recall in the light of their successes rather than the sheer bitter cold and the desperate times when they were unsure they would make it.

Conversation subsided as the three young people gazed into the embers of the fire, foremost in their minds the skirmish amomg the trees on the second night out from Ghazvin.

Talon broke the silence. "*Khanom* Rav'an, how long should we stay here in Hamadan?"

She looked up. "We have to rest, Talon. We are all very tired and the horses are hungry and weak from the journey."

"We should not stay longer than a week, *Khanom*."

At that moment the serving girl came in to ask if they would like some tea, as it was getting late and she wanted to bank down the fire in the kitchen. Rav'an nodded for all of them. The girl gazed at Reza as she bobbed her head. He was looking back with wide black eyes that followed her as she turned and walked off with a swing to her hips.

They tried to plan. It was obvious that they should quit Hamadan as soon as the horses were fit enough to do so. They would go two days west and south of the Zagros Mountains, which would be hard, but it would lead to the warmer climate where it never snowed. It would be cool beyond the mountains but not cold, and they could then make good progress onto the great plains of Mesopotamia with the two rivers, Tigris and Euphrates, still to be crossed.

None of them had ever been this way before, so they all viewed it with mixed feelings. Rav'an, as it would take her to her brother, and she would also see Palestine. Talon, because this was the way home, and deep inside him he wanted to honor Jean's wish that he get home somehow but also he was now bound to Rav'an in some way. Reza, because he was tied to the other two; they were all he had in the world. He worshipped the princess, not least because she accorded him respect and friendship, too. Talon was his brother; it was as simple as that.

The girl came back with the tiny cups on a tray. Kneeling, she poured the tea, her dark eyes moving to look at Reza under long lashes, a demure expression on her attractive, oval face. Reza took his cup from her fingers and they exchanged a look that was full of meaning.

Talon was not paying attention. His mind was concentrating on what they might run into on the next leg of their journey. Rav'an, however, did notice, and glanced at Talon to see if he had.

After the tea, Reza gave an exaggerated yawn and rose to bid them both good night. The others waved him goodnight, and Talon settled back to enjoy the first relaxed evening he could remember since Samiran.

"It seems so far off now, so long ago," he said.

Rav'an looked up. "What does, Talon?"

"Alamut, Samiran, the valleys."

He looked at her. Her hair was a tumble of long waves held by a comb at the back of her head so that her hair was drawn back, exposing her smooth features. He noticed the tired lines on her face, though, and realized that she was exhausted. He began to get up to bid her goodnight and give her the excuse to go to bed.

Instead, she looked surprised and said in a low tone, "Do not go yet, Talon. I want to stay here, but I don't want to be alone."

He subsided, grateful for the invitation. Then she moved so that she was closer to him. They were both lounging on the cushions in front of the fire on the soft rich wool of the sheepskins and carpets. The warmth of the fire was relaxing. There was a companionable silence for a few minutes. Talon found himself becoming very conscious of her presence. Although she wore no perfume, he was aware of the delicate scent of her skin. To him, it seemed as though she carried the hint of lavender mixed with other, sharper-spiced herbs. Her face glowed in the light of the fire and he noticed again the sprinkle of freckles on the top of her cheeks just under her eyes.

She looked across at him, into his eyes, and for a second he was so lost in their gray depths that he forgot to pay attention to what she was saying. She frowned, puzzled. "Talon, did you hear what I said?"

He collected his wits in a hurry. "I am sorry, Rav'an, I was thinking of our hosts," he lied. "What did you say?"

She noticed him blushing and smiled. "I said that I don't know the way across the Zagros and we might need a guide. And yes, I am a worried about them, too. We cannot trust anyone at all, can we?" She looked a little lost as she said this. Looking up at him, her eyes were wide and her lips a parted in a question.

He could have moved only an inch or two. She would have been in his arms and he could have kissed her full on the lips. He felt his heart begin to pound, and he lowered his eyes. With a real effort, he looked up again. "You are right, Rav'an, we cannot trust anyone, and I would be careful about these people, too. Reza thinks Karim likes boys," he said with a grin.

She laughed, her even teeth white against the full lips and light olive of her skin, and the tension was broken. "So he was with you in the bath?" she asked her eyes innocent.

"No," Talon exclaimed, then smiled at her. "But he was interested when we were changing. I am sure he was more interested in Reza, though."

She smiled at him under her lashes coquettishly. "Ah, Talon, does that mean you too would prefer girls to boys?"

"Rav'an," he exclaimed, pretending to be offended, "I have been initiated, so now I am *only* interested in girls." He sounded pompous to his own ears, but she knew he was teasing.

She wasn't going to let him off so easily, though. "Was it good? To be with a woman, I mean?"

Now he knew she was going too far, but he sensed something else too, a questioning. Then it hit him with a jolt. Rav'an had never been with a man. Here she was, a lovely girl right on the edge of womanhood, asking questions of him, knowing that he was familiar with lovemaking.

She seemed to realize that he was confused, and not wanting to lose him to the evening, she said, "I did not mean to embarrass you." She smiled at him then, her voice gentle. "You have become a man and I not yet a woman. I want to know, but not just yet. Will you hold me in your arms so that I can feel safe?"

He opened his arms without a word and she crept into them like a little child. He wrapped her in close to his chest, although he could hardly breathe for his surprise and joy. He swore that he would hold his own passions in check, but he also knew it would be very hard.

"Talon," she murmured into his chest, as though divining his thoughts. "I, too, have the wish to know these passions you have known. I long to reach them. I wish that I could this moment, but I am not ready yet. Will you be patient with me?"

He nodded. "I promise," he croaked.

For many long minutes, they sat together, warmed by their embrace, and watched the fire go down.

Then, reluctantly, she whispered, "Talon, I would that I could sleep in your arms all night, but it cannot be, so as I am tired, tired, tired, I shall go to bed."

She turned, and reaching up for his head, she placed her fingers along his scar. Without warning, she kissed him full on the lips. He felt her soft lips cover his and for a stunned moment, he did nothing. Then he tightened his hold on her.

Just as he did, she moved her head back and gazed into his eyes, her expression quizzical. "You would love me this minute, wouldn't you?"

He nodded and grinned ruefully. "Rav'an, you are so beautiful, I am hard put to behave."

The music of her laugh allowed them both to break free and gaze at one another. They both knew then that they had passed a point with each other that was momentous.

"Rav'an, I love you." Talon whispered as he helped her to her feet.

She came back into his arms then. "Talon, I have loved you for many years, since the day in the garden; do you remember?"

"Yes, my love, I do." He held her tight for a moment.

Then she was gone.

Talon went to bed that night; his blood racing and his heart so full he thought it would burst.

Not even the sounds that his keen ears caught coming from down the corridor mattered to him that night as he went to his room.

*****

There had been no snow, but the temperature had dropped during the night. There was a thin film of ice on the water containers in the kitchen and everything outside was aglitter in the sun. It gleamed off the stalactites and frozen snow that was still piled on any ledge that it could find.

Talon woke as though from a deep pit and stretched. He lay there listening to the call to prayers several streets away. His mind drifted back to the night before, and as he recalled the interchange with Rav'an, he was conscious of a deep feeling of contentment and excitement. He would have to be very careful, even with his friend Reza, he realized. She was, after all, the master's sister, and as such belonged not to him, Talon, but body and soul to the master to do with as he pleased.

Depressed by the direction his thoughts were taking, he rolled out of bed and padded in his loosened clothes to the living room, where he found the maid stoking the fire, and Reza sitting cross-legged drinking tea. Rav'an had not yet surfaced, it seemed. Reza grinned at him and gave a significant glance at the maid, who was obviously enjoying being in his company. Talon grinned back at his friend and then went off to relieve himself in the garden.

Rav'an had gone to sleep at once; even though the bed was so cold she almost got up and hurried down to Talon's room to creep into his bed. She woke up in the early hours of the morning and listened to the wind as it wailed in the eaves of the house. She remembered the evening before, and wondered at the way the two of them had come to this point in their relationship.

To love Talon now seemed to be so natural. He gave her a sense of security that she craved. More than that, he seemed to love her as much as she had grown to love him. She spent some time thinking of the endearing things he did or said that he seemed quite unconscious of: his grin when caught out or when embarrassed, his jokes when things seemed to be desperate. He could always find some stupid thing to say that threatened to reduce them all to hysterical laughter in the face of real danger.

She remonstrated with herself for being a silly girl with not a whit of common sense and forced herself to go back to sleep before she really did go and climb into bed with him. She hugged the thought to herself and fell asleep with a smile on her lips.

It was past sunrise when she woke again. There were birds in the garden singing and chirping to each other, despite the freezing conditions. She resolved to feed them, as it had been a long time since she had heard such music. She padded down to the living room along the cold tiles of the corridor and found Reza sipping tea, looking very smug. He must have tumbled the maid, she decided. He looked like a cat that had had all the cream. Nonetheless, he stood when she came in and was his usual deferential, polite self. She no longer felt that slight jealousy that had come over her last night when she observed him with the maid. She greeted him and asked where Talon was. As though in answer to her query, he came in from the garden, blowing into his hands. Karim came in, too, carrying some firewood.

They all said their *salaams* and the ritualistic good-mornings, and then began to plan the day. Karim told them that they had to retrieve their horses, and then they needed to go over their possessions and take inventory of their weapons and armor. The armor had remained packed since they'd won it in the fight against the mercenaries, and they, the boys, were curious as to how their prize would fit with what else they had.

Rav'an wanted to make a trip to the *maidan* that the boys had visited with Karim. Karim considered telling her that it would be wiser to stay in the house, but one look at Rav'an's determined jaw line told him to hold his peace. So he bowed and went off to the kitchen to get things ready for breakfast.

They ate breakfast together with Karim, who told Rav'an that Ali hoped to be able to come and visit that morning to discuss their next move. Rav'an nodded at that, and they continued to discuss the day ahead.

The sky was clear and blue as it can only be on the high plateau. It might have been cold during the night, but it now promised more thaw and a warm day, if one could keep out of the wind.

Talon and Reza went off to get the horses and bring them back to the house, while Rav'an prepared herself to meet Ali. He arrived at midmorning, and they sat down with Karim to drink tea and determine what her next steps might be. There was a lot of careful parrying from her to the equally careful questions on their part. However, she relied on the fact that they respected her position as the master's sister to not push for answers too hard.

They did look alike, she decided. Both slight, light-skinned, poor teeth, pointed features and balding under those turbans. Still, they were businesslike and seemed competent, so she relaxed and decided that there should be a conference with the boys when they came back.

They were circumspect and ready enough to provide information, such as they possessed, regarding the condition of the roads south over the Zagros. The news in that respect was not encouraging. The great storms that had ravaged the plateau had moved south and west along the ridge of the great Zagros mountain range. Travelers were straggling into Hamadan, talking about the desperate conditions that prevailed all along the route. The passes were blocked solid for at least another two weeks.

Ali noticed her alarmed expression. "There should be no problem with staying here, however," he said in an attempt to reassure her.

There were plenty of funds to support them in some style, so he didn't anticipate any difficulty there. Rav'an collected herself and agreed with him, trying hard to hide her concern. There was no possibility that they could stay that long. If the snows were thawing in the north, her Uncle Arash's hounds would be out on all the roads, looking, and it would not take them two weeks to reach Hamadan. She forced herself to listen to the respectful words of the two men, her mind in turmoil.

After what seemed like an interminable time discussing the few options they had while the weather settled in, Ali and Karim called it a day, and Ali left after making his obeisance to her. Karim left soon after to go to the market for food with one of the women, leaving Rav'an to think about the situation.

It looked like they were trapped, whatever they did. They could not go north, and they couldn't go west for two weeks, perhaps more, by which time Arash's killers would be here, and more than likely Ahmad would be with them. She was pacing the room like a caged animal when the boys came back with the horses. Glad to have a distraction, she put on a coat and boots and ran out to help them stable the animals. This took some time, as they had to clear space to accommodate all four horses. Finally it was done, but by this time, the boys had noticed Rav'an's preoccupation.

When they were back in the living room, Talon asked her, "Rav'an, what's bothering you?"

Her heart warmed to him. She motioned them toward the fire, and, looking in the kitchen where the young woman was busy, she whispered the bad news. Both the boys looked pensive at this revelation and the sudden obstacle to their plans.

Rav'an now looked so worried, with tears welling in her eyes, that Talon was hard put not to take her in his arms and comfort her. Instead, he tried to calm her fears.

"We have some time to think, perhaps a day or two; if the

weather gets better we will have to do something within one week or less. But I would like to get out of here and to a place where we can talk without Karim listening—or them." He indicated the kitchen with his chin.

Reza nodded. "Why don't we go to the teahouse where we were yesterday, *Khanom*? You would like it. There is so much noise no one could hear us talking."

The others looked at him. It made sense. They could not talk here privately, that was for sure, so after a quick, whispered conference, they decided to have a midday meal and then make their way to the *maidan* of Baba Tahir Oryan. The boys thought they could find it without too much trouble.

They managed to get through the midday meal, and then, when Karim said that he had to go home for a while, they blessed him in silence. Rav'an invited him to stay there as long as he felt the need, but he assured her he had to leave. The three companions made noises about going out to the horses for the maid's benefit and got themselves out of the house. They were in the street in seconds, looking either way, and then were off to the *maidan* and the teahouse.

*****

The boys and Rav'an, now veiled, found the teahouse after a couple of false leads that earned them the scorn of their princess and their own chagrin. But it was a cheerful group of two young men and a young woman who came at last to the square dedicated to Baba Tahir Oryan.

The teahouse was half full of people, young and old. There were students sitting cross-legged at low tables near the entrance, while at the back the older men sat and talked or smoked the hookahs and sipped strong black *khaffee* or tea from tiny cups.

The atmosphere, as with most teahouses, was congenial, and few people glanced at them as they took their places on a low platform that looked out onto the street. However, some of the students nearby could not help but stare at Rav'an, for no matter what she did to hide her looks, it was clear to anyone that she was an exceptional looking young woman. She, on the other hand, ignored the stares and pretended not to hear the whispered complements at the other platforms.

She and the boys ordered tea and some sweetmeats. Talon,

with a careful glance around, opened the conversation. They threw ideas onto the table and dissected them one by one. Nothing seemed to be right or safe. They grew more and more despondent as they considered the poor chance they had of getting out of Hamadan and going over the Zagros within a week. Despite the fact that they were all three still tired from their journey and the horses even more so, it was clear to them all that they could not, must not, tarry in Hamadan. A knot of panic continued to grow in each of them as they talked.

Rav'an, her irritation getting the better of her, said "We have gone from the trap of Samiran to that of Hamadan; there is no difference. Why did we listen to Massoud?" Talon and Reza looked at her.

"We had no choice, *Khanom*... you know that," Reza said. "But you are right. I do not know how we leave this city other than to go south."

Just as he spoke, Talon caught him by the sleeve and pointed to the open entrance of the teahouse. "Reza, Rav'an, I think I know that man!" he said excitedly.

They both stared out of the entrance in the direction he was pointing.

"Who are you pointing at, Talon?" Rav'an asked.

"That man there, with the yellow coat and expensive-looking boots, can't you two see him?" he asked impatiently. "Trouble is, I can't think where I have seen him before."

"Perhaps he was here yesterday when you two were here with Karim?" Rav'an tried. "Wait, I see him now... I know him, too! Isn't he...? Doesn't he belong to Doctor Farj'an, the physician? Is it possible?"

They looked at one another.

"Rav'an might be right," Talon said. "One way or another, I would like to know more about him." The others agreed, especially Rav'an, who knew the physician well and hoped that it might be true that this man was still in her brother's service. Throwing coins down among the tea bowls, the three hurried out into the crowded street.

It proved to be no trouble for them to follow the man. He was walking at a leisurely pace, pausing to look at shops and to sample food. He was obviously not in any hurry to go home. Just when they were wondering where he might be going, he picked up his pace and headed purposefully in one direction. It made it increasingly hard to stay well back and keep him in sight. There were horsemen about and others with carts sloshing their way along the muddy streets, forcing pedestrians to stick to the sides. And the three were hampered by vendors of every kind. Rav'an was enjoying it hugely, as this was the first time she had ever been in this kind of place. The smell of spices, dyed clothes, wet wool, cooking food, and the noise all combined into a heady mix of new and exciting experiences for the girl.

Talon and Reza, on the other hand, were more concerned with not losing their quarry, and not losing their princess at the same time, a difficult task. However, they eventually came out of the busy streets and into a quieter part of the city. This was quite unlike the area that they were staying in. The houses were set back off the tree-lined streets behind high walls and were of a richer quality than the trio had seen before. This man was either a wealthy man or still worked for one.

He moved more rapidly now, as though he didn't want to be late. The three had to fall back more, as there was little traffic in this area to hide them. What there was consisted of hawkers and servants on errands. They became conscious that they were more conspicuous here; not least because of the way they were dressed.

Abruptly, the man they were trailing turned into an entrance. They heard a door open and slam shut, and he was gone. They ran up to the wall and found the entrance to be a stout, well-made wood door. Immediately, Talon and Reza began to explore ways to gain entrance.

Rav'an stopped them. "It would not be a good thing if someone saw us at this time," she said sensibly. "We should come back in the night and find out what is behind this wall."

Talon agreed. "You're right, Rav'an. We should wait until dark, and then Reza and I can get in to explore. It is dangerous now."

Rav'an stared hard at him. "I meant that all three of us should come back, Talon," she stated in tones that brooked no argument.

He grinned. "As you command, *Khanom*," he said.

She grinned back at him. Reza held back a laugh.

"Why don't we go home now, then after supper we can come back here. Do you two think you could find your way back in the dark?" Rav'an asked sweetly.

The boys bridled. They scowled, and then they had the grace to look shamefaced.

"As long as you're there to guide us, *Khanom*," Reza said cheekily.

Talon snorted and Rav'an pretended to look threatening.

It was late afternoon by now, and the sun would set within two hours. They headed back to their house, noting the landmarks they would need to find this location in the dark.

They returned to the house to find the maid in a state of near panic. Karim had come back to find them gone and no explanation as to where they might be, so he had rushed off somewhere in hope of finding them. She told this to Reza through her tears.

Rav'an told her not to fuss and to start preparing supper, as they were tired and wanted to go to bed early. She gave a pointed look at Reza when she said this, as though to say, "You had better find some good reason for telling your pillow companion not tonight."

Reza's eyes told her he understood and he followed the maid into the kitchen, while Talon grinned at Rav'an over his friend's discomfort. She walked up to him, put one finger on his lips, and kissed him on the corner of his mouth. His look of bemusement was all the reward she needed for the time being, so with a smile of contentment and her head held high, she went off to her room.

Karim came in an hour later looking very harassed and jumped to lecturing the unrepentant trio on being out on the town without him to guide them. "There are gangs of students and soldiers all over this town, and with someone like you out there they would not hesitate to—"

"I know, Agha Karim. They would kill my escort and carry me off," Rav'an interrupted. "I am sorry we alarmed you. All we did was to go to the teahouse because I wanted to see the *maidan* of that Baba... something?"

"Tahir Oryan, *Khanom*," he finished for her. "*Khanom*, I was very worried about you. It's not often that we have guests of your stature here, and my brother and I are concerned for your safety. Please keep me informed as to where you want to go and I shall make sure I can escort you," he pleaded.

Rav'an gave him her most brilliant smile and responded, her tone contrite, "Indeed, Master Karim, I shall not forget your diligence and concern. When I meet my brother again I shall be sure to inform him of your kindness."

Karim simpered at that and, mollified, went off to berate the maid for not being quick enough with the evening meal.

They ate the meal with pleasure. The maid had had another bout of tears because of what Reza had told her, but somehow he had been able to reassure her that it was not for long, and she was back to her cheerful self. They enjoyed chicken kebabs with lime juice and dill sauce mixed into delicious yogurt, which was basted on as they cooked, a rare treat in wintertime. There was a bean stew to go with it. There was even some more of the sweet wine, but the trio, somewhat to Karim's puzzlement, did not imbibe that night, although the night before they had seemed to enjoy it very much.

He took his leave soon after, and this time both women left with him. The maid, as she left, gazed with undiluted adoration at Reza. Reza glanced at his two companions to see if they had noticed and was rewarded with elaborate disinterest.

Night came quickly. They gave Karim time to move out of the area, and then they moved fast to prepare for the expedition. They all wore warm trousers and light boots. They also wore the new, light leather jackets with lamb's wool on the inside, as well as a lighter head covering than their huge fur hats. All of them carried daggers, deeming it too dangerous to be caught with larger, more obvious weapons. The Seljuk soldiers' night patrols and the drunken gangs might see the weapons as provocation.

Talon looked at Rav'an thoughtfully. "Reza, I think the princess should have a turban."

Reza looked at Rav'an and then laughed. "Yes, my lady, we shall have to turn you into a boy for tonight."

Rav'an looked at them. "If you think it would be safer, but don't go painting a mustache on my face as well."

Talon laughed and Reza gigggled.

"Now, that sounds like a good idea, *Khanom*. No self-respecting man goes clean-shaven here, does he?" He looked at Talon inquiringly. Not waiting for a reply, Reza reached into the fire and picked up a small piece of charred wood.

"I agree with Talon, my lady," he said very formally, trying to keep the grin off his face as he advanced upon her.

Rav'an looked stubborn, backed up a little, about to dare them to come and get her, when she thought better of it. She submitted to having her glossy hair covered by a large, loosely bound turban and then to Reza's not-so-gentle ministrations as he marked a smudged black line across her upper lip.

She seethed at their poorly concealed amusement at her appearance, but they were now in a hurry to go, so she couldn't look at herself in any kind of bright metal to see what she looked like.

They scampered across the garden and peered out of the gate for the second time that day. It was quite dark and the streets were lit at long intervals by torches, and only those streets that could pay for it. Theirs did not, and as there was no moon this night, they were forced to get their night eyes adjusted to the dark and then set off. They had planned to walk the whole way, so that anyone who saw them would think they were students on their way home after an afternoon of lounging at some teahouse or other.

They arrived at the door without incident, although they nearly got lost during the journey across town and had more than one heated discussion as to the way. The street was not well lit, even though there were guttering torches in sconces along some of the walls, further indication that the resident was affluent.

Reza and Talon saw no difficulty with the wall, but they were concerned about how Rav'an would deal with the obstacles. They need not have worried. She was almost as fit as they were and demonstrated this by following them over the wall easily. They landed in an extensive garden and at once hid behind some large bushes while they took stock of the place.

The garden, full of large bushes and small trees, was a frontispiece for the impressive house. It was two stories high, made of wood, with a tiled roof. Only a very wealthy man could own such a place. There was a balcony along the length of the upper story, and a loggia ran all the way along the front of the house. It had numerous windows, most of which were shuttered against the cold night, but light could be seen in the ground floor and some of the upstairs rooms.

Now that they had made it into the grounds, they were at a loss as to what to do next. Talon was for getting closer to the house and finding out who lived there. The others agreed, but just as they were about to move forward, they noticed a bulky shadow moving in their direction from the side of the house. They stared at one another. They had not expected a sentry.

Talon faded into the bushes. Reza had already vanished,

leaving Rav'an crouching in the path. A hand came out and dragged her into the bushes' leafy darkness.

Talon held her close, his hand around her middle just below her breasts. In spite of the danger, she enjoyed the feeling very much. She could feel his breath on her neck as he lowered his breathing. The man came lumbering by; there was no doubt that he was a watchman, but he would have been no match for the two *fida'i* who now lurked in his beat.

He was overweight and wheezed as he walked by. Rav'an and Talon could almost smell him before he arrived, with the garlic and stew on his breath. Rav'an suppressed a giggle. She was very excited. This was proving to be a lot more fun than she had imagined. The man lumbered off, and they came out of the bushes, brushing themselves down. A soft snap of fingers and Reza was back with them.

Talon pointed at the house and made signs that it might be safer to climb onto the upper story than to linger down here in the garden. There might be others about, but up there on the balcony they could at least see danger if it threatened. The others nodded, so they scurried over to the dark shadows under the loggia at the front of the house. Talon looked up at the roof. It was not very high at all, but he was afraid the tiles might crack if they didn't take a lot of care. He whispered a warning to the others about this concern and then made a foothold for Reza.

Quick as a cat, Reza stepped into his hand and disappeared onto the tiled roof without a sound. He climbed with lithe movements over the exposed part, then over the balustrade and onto the walkway. He whispered that they should move to the right where there were very few tiles, as this was a doorway, and he could give a helping hand up. They skittered along the shadows to the point where he was now waiting.

Then it was Rav'an's turn. Talon gave her his hands to step into, and she jumped up, to be seized by the wrist by Reza above her. He hauled her onto the second story, and then it was Talon's turn. He negotiated the climb without difficulty and Reza gave him his arm, and then they were all three crouching on the verandah of the second story of the house.

They inspected the shutters to see if any were loose. They came to the third in the line, which was lit from inside. The light was streaming out of the slats in the shutters.

Risking detection from down in the garden, Talon lifted his

head to peer into the room through the slim gaps in the slats of the shutter. What he saw made him jerk back quickly and turn towards the others. They stared back with huge questions in their eyes.

"What is it?" Rav'an demanded in a whisper.

Talon pointed at the window. "It's the doctor—the physician," he whispered, his eyes wide.

Reza slid past, and he, too, looked. He sat down with them. "It's true, it is the doctor," he whispered.

Although they had been half expecting this, it still came as a surprise. It had to be coincidence, but to the three fugitives it was still cause for alarm.

Rav'an took the initiative. "I am going to talk to him."

Reza and Talon were silent, looking at her. She sensed a problem.

"You cannot just open the window and go in there," Talon whispered. "His first reaction to any noise outside will be to call the servants."

"What do you suggest we do, then?" she whispered back fiercely, her natural impatience getting the better of her.

Talon looked at Reza, then her. "We have to either wait until he leaves for a few minutes and slip in, or go in through another window."

Reza nodded. "Talon is right, *Khanom*," he whispered in her ear. "We don't know if the doctor is on our side. If he is, then we are fine. If not, it is better that we come upon him alone and by surprise, so that we can prevent him from calling for help."

She stared at him, a chill going down her spine. These two really were not about to let anything get in the way of her safety. The doctor's life meant nothing to them against hers.

As it happened, there was movement in the room, indicated to them by shadows crossing the light. Talon rose and looked inside. He watched for a moment or two and then hunkered back down to their level.

"We are lucky. He has just left the room. Now we have to move fast." He nodded to Reza, who moved silently to the shutters and slipped his knife in between them. There was a rasping sound and a metal catch slid open. He looked at the others, poised to follow him in.

Talon cast a penetrating look down into the shadows of the garden, and then brought his hand down in one sharp motion. Reza flung open the right-hand shutter, slid like a snake over the sill, and disappeared. Talon shoved Rav'an, and she leapt at the sill, emulating Reza, and fell in an untidy heap inside the room. Reza dragged her without ceremony out of the way, as Talon followed right on her heels, rolling lightly off to the side.

They pulled the shutter and snapped it shut, then sat listening for any sound that might spell alarm. There was nothing. Talon looked around and pointed to the drapes, then at Reza, who slid over to them and vanished behind the large tapestry hanging there.

Talon bent over Rav'an and whispered into her ear. "Hide with Reza."

She nodded and followed Reza to stand behind the large tapestry. Talon wedged himself into a dark shadow behind two large chests stacked one on top of the other in the far corner.

Then they waited for what seemed an eternity. The two boys lowered their breathing and settled in for the duration. Rav'an found it hard to stand like this for even a minute, but forced herself to do so, feeling that she would not be shamed by failing at this crucial time.

At last, after her legs had gone to sleep, they heard a footstep outside the door and heard the latch being lifted. The door opened, and in walked the physician who had treated Talon's wounds years before. Talon waited for the elderly man to shut the door and move well away from it before he showed himself.

When he did so, he lifted a finger to his lips in the universal sign of silence. The doctor stopped dead in his tracks. His eyes wide with surprise, he stared in silence at Talon, who stopped, opened both hands, and showed them to him.

Then Talon whispered, "Come out, Princess Rav'an, the doctor is here."

Both Reza and Rav'an came out from behind the drapes and moved to stand next to Talon, while the doctor, still silent, watched them, his bearded face tense with anger and fear. His left hand was on his chest as he stood, slightly stooped, in the middle of the room.

"Doctor, I am Rav'an," said the youngest of the hoodlums he was confronting. He looked hard at the young man. Then he noticed that the mustache was actually charcoal markings. The young man took off the turban and shook out his very long hair. The doctor realized with a shock that he was looking at a very attractive young woman dressed like a young man. The ridiculous crude mustache drawn on her upper lip was not flattering, but it was very clear who it was.

"Allah be praised, Rav'an, is that really you? What on earth are you doing here?" he managed to say, a tremor in his voice. "And who are these two ruffians with you?"

Rav'an laughed with relief. "I would like to introduce Talon and Reza, my protectors, Doctor. Do you not recognize Talon? It was you who saved his life when he was wounded by the lion."

He peered at Talon and then noticed the scar on his jaw. "No indeed, I would not have recognized you, young man, even with that scar. You are much changed from the time I saw you last. You seem to have grown into a good sized young man, however," he remarked. He looked at Reza. "Are you also one of the young bandits who grew up in Samiran?"

Reza nodded grinning. "I am Reza, *Gorban* Doctor, Talon and I have become brothers."

The old man nodded with some approval. Then he creased his brow and looked sharply at them. "But what are you doing here in Hamadan? It's a very long way from Samiran. Is something amiss?"

Rav'an nodded, her face grave. "Doctor, it's a very long story, but first I have to ask you—to whom do you owe your allegiance? Is it still to my brother?"

The doctor looked startled. "How could that ever be in doubt, my dear? Before God Himself, I stand loyal to the master. Do I have an accuser? Are you here to assassinate me?" he asked in an incredulous tone, glancing at the two boys. There was real apprehension in his eyes now.

Rav'an exhaled a large breath, and the other two visibly relaxed. "Doctor, we have a long story to tell you. Can you spare the time? It will take a while to explain our situation."

"Are you worried about the servants? Apart from my concubine, Fariba, who is asleep next door, the servants are at the other end of the house. My host is also in the other wing. Do not be concerned. They are loyal in all things to the master and to me. But to put your minds at rest, I shall not tell them anything you do not want me to." He stopped. "But I forget my manners." He smiled at them. "Please be seated, and we shall have some tea while you tell me what has passed and why you're here."

Farj'an waved them all to the rich, thick pile of the carpet. When they were seated, he went over to a small brazier where he had a pot of tea brewing and poured for them all. When he was seated, he said. "Now, my dear, you must begin."

Rav'an sighed. "I shall have to tell you everything, so that you can be the judge. We are in great danger, and so is my brother and now, perhaps, even you."

She began her tale, leaving nothing out, helped by Talon or Reza from time to time as she tried to recall every detail. An hour later, she finished with their discovery of his servant in the Maidan e Baba.

For a long time, the doctor sat sipping his cold tea in silence, staring at the floor, from time to time looking into the distance, tugging gently at his gray-and-white beard. None of the three wanted to break into his reverie, but they all wore anxious expressions.

Finally, he looked up at Rav'an. "My dear, I knew your father well, and although he had some strange ideas and we disagreed from time to time, I am still faithful to his memory. I have watched both you and your brother grow from children into adults. Your brother, Muhammad, has become a good leader and is wise beyond his years, as are you, it seems to me. I would not be at all surprised that he sent you to Alamut for precisely this reason. If so, he chose well."

He paused, sipped some tea. "How you escaped is a tribute to your courage and that of your protectors. I applaud you. It cannot have been easy to leave the priest and your servant behind to the tender mercies of Arash Khan and then make this journey in the middle of winter."

Rav'an made to speak.

He held up his hand. "With your permission, *Khanom* Rav'an, I would like to finish what I was going to say."

He smiled at her. "It is clear to me that you did the right thing in not going to Samiran. Massoud advised you well. However, in coming to Hamadan, you have almost trapped yourselves. If the weather continues like this, all the roads south of Ghazvin will be open long enough to allow Ahmad to follow your trail."

He had their full attention now. He looked around at their tense young faces, realizing just how young they really were, but also he did not discount the fact that they knew how to survive.

"You cannot stay here longer than, at most, a few more days, and even that might prove dangerous. The passes at the Zagros will stay shut now for at least a week, but I have an idea."

He glanced up at them. They had begun to fidget and look at one another, the worry beginning to be replaced by hope. "I have to go south to my home in Isfahan. I was going to leave in about a week, but we can move that forward. There's a large caravan just to the south of here in one of those new-fangled stopping places; I think it is called a *caravanserai*. It's about a day away. I want to join it for safety as we cross the corner of the Dasht-e-Kavir on our way south." He looked up at the boys, smiling. "The roads are dangerous, you know. A traveler could always do with a bodyguard as competent as I am beginning to think you two are. In addition, you'll be moving well off the path that Arash might think you took, so it's not likely that they will know where to follow. In a week, the trail will be cold, and they might, with luck, turn north to sniff for you there."

He looked at them, and saw surprise and hope mingled with concern in Rav'an's face.

"Doctor, how will we get a message to my brother?" she asked. "Going to Isfahan might save me, but my brother must be informed. I need to get a message to him to warn him that Arash is plotting something."

The doctor put his hand on her arm. "I think I can help there, too. My servant would deem it an honor to be able to take a message to the Khan. He is loyal unto death, even to the point where, although he is as my son, if the Agha Khan bade him kill me, he would not hesitate. He will need proof. That seal you mentioned will do nicely, as well as a letter from me and from you, Rav'an, explaining how you escaped and what you know."

Rav'an' eyes glowed. "Doctor, you are wonderful," she cried. "How can we ever thank you for what you're doing?"

"My dear," he said, smiling, "you are the master's sister, and I would serve him, but also you shall have to pay in kind," he added, a mischievous twinkle in his eye. "This old man and his retinue have to be protected during a long journey. Your 'protectors' are the answer to my prayers to Allah, the Almighty One."

They all laughed. Suddenly, the tension was gone, replaced by warm smiles and a new feeling of optimism. For the first time since leaving Alamut, the three fugitives felt that they had found an ally who could help, and whom they could trust implicitly.

"I should also warn you that the man Ali and his brother Karim are not unknown to me. They are part of the network of spies that Arash Khan has dotted about this country. What have you told them so far?"

He looked relieved when Rav'an told him that they had been very circumspect and had spun a tale of a mission for the master. The doctor nodded his approval. These ones learned fast, he thought to himself.

"You should not trust them with any information beyond what you've said already. Somehow, you must get out of that house within the next couple of days and meet me outside the city. I need to be able to send you a message when it is time to leave."

They discussed this and concluded that it would be far too dangerous to send a messenger to this house, as, if seen, it would send off alarms that would reach Ali and Karim.

"Why don't we use the teahouse?" Talon suggested. "You could send the same man we saw and he could slip us a message there. It's very crowded, so it would be easier," he finished, embarrassed at being so forward. The princess and the doctor had dominated the conversation so far.

Everyone thought this was a good idea, so they worked out a method of passing a message. They also set a rendezvous on the outskirts of the city where they would meet at the given time.

It was now very late. Doctor Farj'an estimated that it was almost the middle of the night. He told them to go back to their house and to prepare to leave at a moment's notice without giving any clues as to how and when. He also advised them to leave the way they had come in, as, although he trusted all his servants, he could not stop all tongues from wagging. Secrecy was an absolute necessity until they were out of the city and well on their way to Isfahan.

They bade him goodbye. The boys were very polite; but Rav'an impetuously hugged him, causing him to grumble about good manners among the young, although it was clear he was delighted with her.

She then had to rewind her turban and get a touch up on her now well-smudged mustache from the doctor. He doused the lamp and the three adventurers slipped out of the room, down the pillars, and across the garden without incident. Running down the street, their exuberance took over and Reza turned a cartwheel.

Talon walked on his hands for a couple of seconds before Rav'an pushed him over, and then they raced down the street to the cover of the darker streets, laughing silently together with relief and excitement.

They were walking happily along one narrow street, Talon in the middle, his arms over the shoulders of his less tall companions, when at the far end they saw several shadows walking toward them. Talon and Reza noticed them first, and Talon at once silenced Rav'an, who had been talking excitedly, with a tightening grip on her shoulder. He released his friends and whispered, "It might just be a few drunks going home, but be careful. Let's just try to walk past without getting into anything."

The others nodded, but hands strayed to knives all the same to make sure they could be drawn quickly.

Trying to appear casual, the three of them continued to walk toward the shadows that had become a group of four men. They were several years older than the trio. Worse, they were in their cups, but not staggering drunk. They noticed the three coming toward them and stopped to wait until the three silent people came up to them. If they had been less drunk, they would have been more alert to the way two of the three carried themselves, walking on the balls of their feet, light and lithe as cats.

As it was, the leader of the group of students, for that was what they were, let the three start to move past before he said in a loud voice, "What, no greeting? What are you that you should be so rude? The least should be, '*Salaam.*'"

The three muttered "*Salaam*" in unison and continued to walk past. But instead of letting them go, the leader of the students, who were now all looking at the three passers-by belligerently, seized Rav'an's shirt sleeve and tugged it.

She reacted by snatching her arm away and trying to push past.

Another of the students exclaimed, "What have we here? Some babies out for a walk? Hey, I'm talking to you," he said aggressively to Talon, who was walking with his head down. Talon continued to move forward, trying to look inconspicuous, as did Reza and Rav'an, who hurried two paces to keep up with them.

"Hey," the student shouted for the second time. "I am talking to you!" He turned to his companions. "They need to be taught some manners, for sure that taller one. I will do some teaching. Are you with me?"

In answer, the others laughed. There was the hiss of metal coming out of sheaths, and they began to follow the three companions, who had gone about ten paces beyond by now.

"They're looking for trouble," Talon whispered.

"We can't let them chase us all the way to the house," Reza said in a low voice.

"What do we do?" Rav'an had a note of desperation in her voice.

In answer, the two boys drew their knives.

"Stay behind us, Rav'an, and watch our backs. If they try to come behind us, call out and defend yourself. We will deal with them," Talon stated. His voice was cold and purposeful. She had never heard him talk like that before.

Reza and Talon went into a defensive position in front of the oncoming students. To the two boys, this was as natural as breathing. Killing with a knife was what they had been trained for—what they did. They were like two deadly cats with very long claws, waiting to strike. To the oncoming students the atmosphere was charged with something cold and menacing. The two young men to whom they wanted to "give a lesson" suddenly became crouching animals, lethal and menacing—no longer objects of amusement.

Although they could sense the change and should have immediately left, they had taken too much to drink, and were slow to realize that they were walking into a deadly trap. It was over within seconds. The students, shouting to give each other courage, came on at a rush. Reza was in and out like a snake and one was down, disemboweled, shrieking his life away as he tried to hold his guts in with both hands.

Talon blocked the swinging knife that was aimed at his chest with ease. He casually stepped inside the oncoming man's guard, and the next second he was holding the man upright with his knife in just below the man's sternum. As the horrified man gasped in agony, then choked his lifeblood out over his front, Talon pushed him back onto the man behind. As the third student tried to avoid the lifeless body coming at him, he was kicked hard in the knee and fell. His knife dropped out of his hands. He never got up. A body landed across his knees, and a knife went into his back straight to his heart.

Talon stood up quickly to take stock and find out where his companions were. Rav'an was just behind him, pale but resolute.

They exchanged looks, then Talon whirled to see what was happening with Reza and the last student. He need not have worried. The man had tried to run but was now dead, and Reza was just pulling his long knife out of his back.

The student who had been disemboweled had fallen to the ground, whimpering in agony, still holding his entrails that were falling about his bloodied hands. His tunic and trousers were covered in his own blood and urine. He looked up as Talon came to him. Talon knelt at his side and looked down into the dying man's sweating, gray face.

"You fools should not take on the *fida'i*," he hissed. The man's eyes widened and he began to cry. With one swift motion Talon cut the man's throat; the body jerked in his death spasm, heels drumming in the mud; then he was dead. Talon stood up and wiped his knife on the clothing of one of the other dead men.

"We must hurry now. The patrols will have heard his screams."

Without another glance at the bodies, the three of them ran off in the direction they had been going earlier. Just in time, as they heard shouts behind them, but no pursuit. They went on in silence and came to the door to their house within the hour.

Rav'an was shaking with the reaction from the fight; Talon, sensing this, took her hand and this calmed her as they slipped inside.

There was no one to greet them as they came into the cold building and settled before the fire. Reza began to stoke the embers into a few flames.

"I wish we had not met those students," Rav'an said, still shaken by the event.

"Why they couldn't have just let us go by defeats me. It was so stupid," Talon said savagely, anger and exasperation in his voice.

"You're right, Talon, but although their death is regrettable, they would have hounded us right back to this house," Reza said.

"I know, but taking life like that was so simple. It was like killing goats."

Rav'an, who had now recovered her poise, snorted. "Talon, Reza, you did what General Esphandiary told you to do... your duty. You protected me. Now I wish to hear no more of this. They deserved what they had coming and that's that." She washed her hands symbolically as though to say "enough."

They both looked at her: the one dark and slight, the other

taller and more muscular. Both had formed a respect for this determined young lady, and it just seemed to grow as they weathered one incident after another.

"We should be abed," Talon stated.

Reza nodded and bade the princess goodnight, leaving for his room. Talon waited for his door to shut, and then went into the kitchen to wash his hands, which were still covered with blood.

She followed him and put a hand on his shoulder.

"Talon, I respect what you are thinking. But you must let this go. You did what you had to do, and you protected me at the same time."

He nodded wordlessly, sloshing cold water over his wrists and hands. "I know, you're right, Rav'an. They were just stupid men and now they're dead. I won't brood over it."

She turned him to her; then, putting both hands on his face, she reached up and kissed him on the lips. His arms went round her waist and he pulled her hard into him. They kissed long and hard. When she pushed him away with a trembling hand and a small gasp, he almost seized her again.

Holding a hand firmly on his chest, she gazed up into his eyes. "Ah, Talon, you are my true warrior, my protector." Then she was gone.

He paused for a couple of long moments, savoring the kiss and wondering at the woman Rav'an had become. We have all grown up these last few months, he thought. Then he went to bed.

Lying awake that night, Rav'an relived the kiss and the embrace. After watching Talon kill the men in the street with such cold efficiency, and then the kiss that she had allowed herself, she wondered that she had not permitted it to go much further. She had wanted to couple right there in the kitchen, the urge had been so great. She had even felt his manhood grow hard against her. She lay awake long into the remainder of the night and slept only when the cock crowed and the mullah called from the tower of the mosque in the first hours of dawn.

What, without asking, hither hurried Whence?
And, without asking, Whither hurried hence,
Ah, contrite Heav'n endowed us with the Vine
To drug the memory of that insolence,

– Omar Khayyam –

Chapter 19
The Road to Isfahan

The call to prayers were shouted through cupped hands from the tops of the new-built mosque towers when the three woke to a very agitated Karim and Ali waiting for them in the living room. Ali was almost beside himself with worry and confronted the sleepy-eyed princess the moment she came into the room. The two boys were not far behind.

They arrived to hear Ali asking in a high, nervous voice, "*Salaam*, my lady. Did you and the boys go out into the town last night?"

Rav'an, who had been expecting something of this kind, was prepared. Stifling an elaborate yawn, she shook her head and then asked in a puzzled tone, "*Salaam*, Master Ali and Master Karim, how are you today? Why, what was going on in the town?" She looked across at Talon as he came into the room and asked him, "Talon, did you and Reza go off into the town last night?"

Talon, looking just as sleepy, shook his head. "No, my lady. Remember that we talked about it, but we were all too tired to even want to go for a walk. Reza and I went out to look at the horses, as you know, but we came back in because it was cold. We sat by the fire and then went to bed."

Rav'an turned and bestowed a sweet smile on Kemal and Ali. "You see, we are still exhausted from our journey. Now perhaps you will tell me what excitement we missed in the town?"

Looking somewhat mollified, Ali glanced at his brother, then said, "My lady, four men were murdered last night, most savagely, and the whole town is talking about it."

Rav'an and the boys had the grace to look shocked.

"They were not Ismaili, were they?" Reza asked with concern in his voice.

Ali looked at him. "No, they were students. The *atabeg* has promised a full investigation, but there was no one who saw the incident, as they were all killed." He looked at the three of them. "Some are saying it is the work of the Ismaili, though. It has all the marks of their trade." He sounded skeptical of their statements, but he did not pursue it.

Karim interjected on his brother's behalf. "Ali is worried that people will remember who are the Ismaili in this town and accuse us without proof."

"Who do you think it was? Was it just a brawl, or a settling of scores?" Asked Reza.

"Ali and I think that the students were killed by soldiers, but no one will tell the *atabeg* that," Karim said cynically.

Talon, looking puzzled, said, "In the first place we are three, and one of us a girl. How could we be involved in something like this? It's not in our interest to become involved in brawls in a town like Hamadan when we just want to move on."

Ali and Karim saw the sense of this and let the matter drop. However, Rav'an wanted to talk about just that—moving on. "I want to move on as fast as we are able to Baghdad. What news from the west?"

Karim answered, "The thaw is continuing, and there is some chance that the passes will open within four or five days, my lady. You must be patient, as there is nothing we can do at present to change that."

"I cannot wait four or five days in Hamadan," Rav'an stated, her tone imperious. "We could move out in a couple of days and wait nearer the passes in some village, could we not?"

"You could, *Khanom*, but why endure more discomfort when we are providing you with these quarters?" Ali replied, soothingly.

Now that the subject had been deflected from the incident in town, Rav'an suggested that at some time, perhaps in the afternoon, they could go to the *chai khane*. She felt that it was unfair to keep her in the house without showing her the part of the town that the boys had seen. She wanted Karim to take her there.

Although flattered by her wishes, neither Karim nor Ali was very keen. They said the town would be swarming with soldiers who, they said, would be stopping people and making themselves unpleasant; but they could go if the princess insisted. She did; so they sat down to breakfast and talk became general.

The verbal fencing began again as the two men tried to feel their way as to what they were really doing on the road to Baghdad. The three young people, in turn, were innocent and vague, which frustrated their hosts.

They broke up from breakfast late in the morning, and the boys went out to feed the horses. The day had brightened and was now sunny, which portended a continuation of the thaw. The boys looked at the sky and each other, then tramped through the slush to the stables to work on the horses.

The two men left the house, promising that Karim would come back for the mid-afternoon walk to the Maidan e Baba, leaving Rav'an alone with the womenfolk who, noticing that she didn't want to be disturbed, left her alone.

The next hour passed with the two boys engaged in the stables; the two women spent their time cleaning and cooking, while Rav'an took her ease in the sunlight, then returned indoors to rest. The boys had come in and seen her asleep on the cushions by the fire and left again quietly so as not to disturb her.

Talon was aware that she was very tired. They all were. The tension from the previous month, the escape, and the long, arduous journey to Hamadan had sapped her reserves. The fight had added to their sense of insecurity. He and Reza talked about it and decided that the best thing would be to let her rest as much as she could.

The boys came back a second time much later, stamping the snow off their boots, and bringing a draft of cold air into the warm room, waking Rav'an from her sleep. They passed the rest of the morning sitting and talking. Rav'an watched Reza beat Talon easily at Serratta, using some dried beans they had collected from the kitchen.

"It's a good thing that you have no money, my friend," Reza stated, laughing, on the third game. "You would be broke by now."

Talon gave a rueful smile, but Rav'an gave a hiss and then put her finger to her lips for silence, looking mysterious.

Then she produced the two bags of gold that chinked as she put them on the floor next to the speechless lads. Rav'an explained that she, Karim, and Ali had talked more about the finances of the ongoing journey, and Ali had handed over these two small but heavy bags of coins. They were at least financially independent now, and could, if they wanted, leave at any time. She had thanked the two men for their services and told Ali that she would be sure to notify her brother of their kind cooperation when she saw him next.

Reza grinned at her and Talon. "Now we can leave any time," he whispered.

Talon nodded and he peered into one of the bags. He had never seen so much gold in his life, so he hurriedly closed the neck and pushed the bag back at her with a grin on his face. "Now at last you are a *rich* princess," he whispered cheekily. She pretended to be about to slap him for his impertinence. He rolled back into Reza's arms and they all giggled happy that something had gone the right way for them.

Later, after a light lunch, Karim returned, and they all went off to the *maidan*. Ali was right; the streets were full of soldiers, both on horseback and on foot, moving around and stopping people. Most of time it was clear they didn't know what they were looking for, so they were just a nuisance. They bullied and shoved people, which was unpleasant.

A harassed sergeant and a couple of soldiers who wanted an excuse to ogle Rav'an stopped the small group once, though. They made a perfunctory search of the boys' coats, who had prudently left their weapons at the house on Karim's advice; so, finding nothing, the soldiers let them go.

Coming to the *maidan*, they found it as busy as ever, full of people wearing bright clothes, cloaks of blue wool, outer coats of warm brown camel hair and silks of reds and oranges and yellow underneath, either on horseback or in litters carried by struggling bearers, who slipped and slid in the mud and slush of the streets.

Vendors, taking advantage of the warm sunshine and the outgoing populace, were shouting their wares of fruit, cakes, and brightly patterned cloth from the Orient. Nuts, sweetmeats of all kinds, spices that left a sharp, pleasant smell in the air, and medicinal herbs in sacks were on display. Their attention was caught by the way merchants decorated their wares to attract passersby. The shops that sold pistachios were among the best, as the merchants would create intricate patterns of whorls and rings out of the big, delicious nuts. Karim was persuaded to buy some small sacks of pistachios, the three lingered over them so long.

They passed coppersmiths, who had young apprentices beating out intricate patterns with tiny hammers on brass and bronze work, working the surfaces with tiny hammers, tapping on needle-like pins. Beyond these, apprentice potters and their masters, clay up to their elbows despite the cold, created many varied shapes on their wheels.

Rav'an and the boys soaked it up, never tiring of the bustle and noise, the smells and the sights. To them it was a kaleidoscope of color, odor, and sound that both excited and enthralled them. Karim, on the other hand, found it too noisy and wanted only to settle into a cushion and smoke a pipe at the teahouse where he could watch his new charges and perhaps find out more about them.

They came to the crowded teahouse and found a small space between some students and a couple of older men, all smoking pipes. The students watched the group of young people come in, and then stared at the beautiful girl with them. The talk hushed for a few minutes, but she paid no attention, although there was a light flush on her neck that Talon noticed.

He felt proud to be with her on this occasion, as it was clear that wherever she went she was noticed. Both he and Reza were alert for trouble if some fool thought that he could make an advance on her. They need not have worried. The talk soon picked up, and, as might have been predicted, it was all about the killing of the four students. The conjecture in hushed tones was that a large gang of drunken soldiers had come upon them and overpowered them, killing them all to prevent anyone pointing fingers. Ironically, the incident had only added to the general dislike of the Seljuk garrison.

The three young people listened, saying nothing, while they watched the square with keen eyes for the doctor's servant. Karim, thinking they were just tired and bemused by the overpowering effect of the busy place and crowded teahouse, busied himself with asking for tea for them and a pipe for himself.

They sat there for about an hour, soaking up the atmosphere, talking quietly, and wondering if the servant would come. They were just about to call it a day when Reza spotted him coming across the *maidan*. The man moved towards the teahouse casually.

He wore much the same clothing as he had before, so they picked him out without difficulty when Reza nudged Rav'an with his knee.

With a smile and a look of apology, Reza came to his feet and said that he had a cramp that he wanted to ease, and he would be back. He got to his feet and moved off through the crowded room to the entranceway. Just outside, he ran into the servant and almost knocked him over. Standing there making abject apologies to a clearly angry man dressed in the fine clothes of a rich man's servant, Reza attempted to brush the man's waistcoat and was shaken off in irritation. They exchanged rough words, and while Reza looked shamed, the man stalked off. Reza came back into the teahouse looking contrite, muttering about people who were rude and unpleasant.

They all got up, and while Karim paid the hovering server, the three of them had a quick conference. Had the servant passed a message? Yes, but they would have to wait until they got back to read it, but the man had said that they should get ready.

Off they went, avoiding the crossroads that had soldiers milling about in them. On the way, Karim suggested that the boys might want to go to the bathhouse again. This sounded agreeable, so they decided that once they were back at the house they would again separate, and while the boys went off to the public baths, Rav'an would have the services of the women to perform her ablutions.

At the house there was no time for them to talk, so Reza slipped the letter to Rav'an, and the boys left with Karim leading the way.

As they went out Rav'an whispered to Talon, "Have a nice bath with Karim." She turned away before he could make a rude reply. The boys went off grinning at Karim's back.

Rav'an went to the kitchen, asked the women to prepare the tub for her to have a bath, and went off to her room to read the letter.

Afterwards she relaxed and enjoyed her bath with the help of the women, both of whom were young and attentive to her needs. The youngest, who had spent the night with Reza, intended to stay that night again, which did not bother Rav'an, but she lay the groundwork that ensured the girl would not be there the following night. She informed her that the occasional night was fine but not every night. The blushing maid nodded her head, reluctantly agreeing with Rav'an that to lock a man's passion one had to be spare about giving him one's favors. Rav'an was amused by this unlikely wisdom coming from her lips. All she wanted to do was to spend every night in Talon's arms from here to eternity, but as she could not, why should the maid enjoy Reza every night? Besides, they needed to be able to slip off without anyone at all noticing.

She was reclining among some comfortable cushions by the fire when the boys came back with Karim several hours later. It had been uneventful, except that both felt that Karim had come close to making propositions to Talon. Reza was merciless in his teasing, and the whole thing put out Talon. Although he laughed at the recollection, he was embarrassed.

Rav'an and the boys spent a pleasant evening over a mutton stew with eggplant, mushrooms, rice, and saffron. There was bread, with some nice red wine that Karim had conjured up. They had a treat of some sherbet to sip and *Baamieh,* a dish of flour, eggs, sugar, and rosewater. Then it was time for the servants to leave. Karim and the older woman left, leaving the younger behind to clean up the kitchen. It had been obvious all evening that she and Reza were planning to sleep together. They made sheep's eyes at one another during the meal whenever she came to serve them, and later he made a lame excuse to go to bed early.

Talon grinned at his friend as he left, leaving no doubt that he knew what was afoot, while Rav'an maintained a straight face and solemnly bade him goodnight.

When Reza had left, Talon asked what the message had said. Rav'an had been waiting to tell him. The doctor had informed them that they should be ready to leave the day after tomorrow, at dawn. They were to meet him and his entourage outside Hamadan, some ten miles to the east. He advised them to leave by the west or south gate, but definitely not to be seen leaving by the east gate. Their hosts would be expecting them to head south and west when they investigated their absence, and it would not do to give any indication of their real destination. He mentioned the killings and advised them to be very circumspect about what they said henceforth to Ali and Karim, as he thought suspicion could easily fall on them as *fida'i* skilled in the arts of knife-fighting. He looked forward to seeing them the day after the morrow, and warned them to make sure this letter was destroyed.

Rav'an had committed the letter to memory and then walked casually to the living room where she had placed the parchment in the fire and ensured that it was engulfed with flames before leaving.

They talked about the situation in low voices, working out what they had to do the following day. From the end of the corridor came a low cry as Reza and the maid coupled, oblivious of the noise they were making. Talon felt his face begin to get hot, but Rav'an's composure seemed firmly in place.

He was just beginning to feel that he should perhaps get up and bid her goodnight—if he stayed, he might make an unwelcome advance—when she sat forward and moved from where she had been sitting to come over to his side of the fire. She was on hands and knees when she kissed him—a long, slow kiss that sent his heart pounding. Then she lay alongside him on the soft carpet and invited him to embrace her as though it were the most natural thing in the world. He gazed down at her in frank admiration as she lay in his arms.

Her eyes were half closed and her mouth very inviting. He leaned over her and kissed her again. This time they kissed with passion. She locked her arms around his neck and pulled him down onto her, making a small mewling sound as he kissed her hard. She returned the kisses with fervor, then after long moments pulled away to gasp for breath, while he looked at her.

Her eyes blazed back at him as though to say, "Go as far as I allow." He nodded and then leaned over and kissed her neck. His kisses went down to the base of her neck and then onto the swell of her young breast. She held his head with her hands and he could hear her rapid breathing in his ear as he moved down. Moving the light material aside carefully with trembling fingers, he exposed her full, ivory breast, and then he placed his lips over the tight young nipple and sucked gently. Rav'an arched her back and gasped, her fingers tightening in his hair. Talon continued to kiss her around the area, and then he leaned down and kissed the other breast.

Again, she gasped. "Ah, Talon, ah... that's so good," she whispered into his ear.

Feeling bolder, his hand went down to her hip and stroked her there, moving slowly to her junction. Rav'an lightly but firmly pushed his hand away. She pulled his head to hers and placed her mouth on his, allowing his hand to move up to stroke her. At last, they broke free, breathing heavily and staring into each other's eyes.

"Do not be angry with me, Talon, if I cannot allow you

everything," she whispered to him, her eyes pleading with him.

Instead of answering, he leaned down and kissed her on her nose and then her eyelids.

She sighed with relief and embraced him hard. "I must go to bed," she said a tremor in he voice.

He nodded and grinned ruefully. "I, too, my love, or I shall go too far."

She gave a low, shaky laugh with him, and then her hand snaked out and placed itself gently on his groin. "I long for you, my love. Please be patient with me," she whispered as she held him for a moment. Then she was up and moving to her room with a look over her shoulder that turned his blood on fire.

Talon got up. He tried to shut his ears to the sounds still coming from the room at the end of the corridor and made his way to bed also.

"By all the *houris* in paradise, Reza, my friend, I hate you tonight," he muttered, smiling, but then consoled himself with the thought that Rav'an was a prize worth waiting for. How he envied his friend quenching his sword, though.

The next day passed without incident. The three of them made surreptitious preparations for their impending departure. They stayed in the house all day, the boys going out to work on the horses and to prepare the tack and baggage, as well as cleaning weaponry checking the chain armor they had taken from the mercenaries for a good fit and greasing bow strings.

Rav'an managed a brief moment to embrace Talon and received a hard embrace in return.

"I went to bed, trembling."

He stared at her. "I, too."

"I did not expect to feel the way I did, Talon," she whispered

He had just nodded, his blood racing. Could it be possible that they could ever be together? He went around for the rest of the day in a daze.

Karim and Ali had decided that their guests could be left alone for the most part, so they came and went on errands. They had both pretty much given up with their questions by now. Although they were still curious, they could not get past the closed-lipped trio.

Their preparations had been made by evening. The women

trooped out with Karim, the youngest giving Reza a heated look on the way out. The three were conscious of the excitement of another stage in their lives about to take place.

They all went to bed early and left it to Talon to wake them up in the morning before dawn. This he did by shaking Reza by the foot and standing back as his friend came out of his sleep, instantly awake. Then he strode to the room where Rav'an slept and moved cautiously into the dark room. He heard her steady breathing as he approached the bed and leaned over her. As he did so, her arm came up and she reached up with her lips to kiss him. The warmth of her and her light scent was a heady feeling in the dark. They embraced hard for a few seconds, and then with great reluctance she let him go.

It was cold and very dark, about four hours before dawn, so they had plenty of time to get ready. They had to complete packing their things, including the armor and weapons, and then lug the whole lot down to the stables to prepare the horses. They were afraid to light any lamps, so it was all done in the dark. As their eyes became accustomed to the gloom, they could make out each other and the horses. They saddled the four horses and then loaded the pack animal, securing as much as they could to its back, wanting to keep their weapons free and to stay light on their own horses in case of emergency.

At last, all was ready. They walked in silence across the frozen garden, Reza in the lead, the horse's hooves making loud crackling sounds, and then, with a sharp look about, they were onto the street. Navigating by using streets they knew, and what they thought they knew, of the stars, they headed south, coming to the gates just before dawn.

The guards were alert, but friendly. They understood why people left at this time of day, the early travellers were going to join some caravan on the outskirts of the city, or so they assumed. There was no trouble convincing them to open the gate for these travelers off to try their luck with the passes over the Zagros Mountains.

*****

Later that morning, Doctor Farj'an was informed by one of his servants, who had been riding out to the front of the small cavalcade, that they should beware, as there were some riders ahead. He had spotted them as the party came over a rise of the road leading to the *caravanserai* farther east. They looked well armed and menacing to the servant, who was quite disturbed by seeing them on the road. He looked at the doctor for advice and was surprised to hear him say, "Ah, yes, three you say, Abdul? I have been expecting them. Do not be afraid; they are friends."

Abdul Hakim looked past the doctor, whom he revered, to his co-servant Abbas, who nodded. It was fine if Abbas agreed with the doctor, he felt, as Abbas was the doctor's closest man.

The doctor's party slowly approached the shaggy-looking, well armed riders who sat still on their horses awaiting their arrival.

As they came closer, Farj'an turned to his servant Abbas.

"Inform all that these are members of the Ismaili, and that the girl is my niece. They are to be accorded all the respect and courtesies due my guests, and no one is to talk about them to anyone outside my entourage."

Abbas nodded. He already knew about the situation, and commended the doctor for not having said anything while in the house in Hamadan, where they were, in fact, guests of a friend. It would have traveled all the way round the city by now if he had. He went around to the men and womenfolk, laying down the law to all and sundry as they moved toward the riders.

When the party came up to the three, one of them rode down the small incline to greet the doctor.

"Honored Doctor, Farj'an," Rav'an said. "I am glad that you've arrived; we were beginning to think we made a mistake."

"I am glad to see you, Rav'an. I hope you are well?" the doctor asked politely, his tone almost a rebuke. He valued manners above all, and this young lady was about to lose ground in that regard.

Rav'an heard the gentle rebuke and hastened to say, "Honored Doctor, I hope I find you well. We are fine, and the day is good."

He nodded and smiled. "As is usual when leaving the house of a friend, whom I will not see for some time, the farewells were lengthy. Thus our departure was delayed, my dear," he said. "Now we have a full day before we make it to the *caravanserai*, so we should push on, and we can talk as we go."

Rav'an nodded eagerly. With a motion of her hand, the other two riders joined her, and they kept their horses to the slow and deliberate pace set by the baggage train belonging to the doctor. He had in attendance about twelve people, from donkey men to servants who doubled as bodyguards, and womenfolk who rode either donkeys or horses depending on their rank.

One and all, they were thankful that the three hard-looking young riders were on their side. Clearly, they were capable of helping out if trouble surfaced. These were very uncertain times in Persia, as there was no Seljuk Shah in charge of the country as a whole any more. The country was broken up into city-states and regions where overlords, *atabegs*, the military regents, ruled according to their whims. They preyed upon travelers as often as not, exacting a tithe for travel or just pillaging the weaker caravans.

Which was why, the doctor explained, they were heading for the safety of the new *caravanserai*, where they would join a large caravan heading for Isfahan within a day or so. Safety in numbers, he repeated. He had come north with a small caravan, and they had stopped from time to time with a *caravanserai*, deriving comfort from its protection. So although the noise and dust thrown up by the huge number of camels and other livestock was hard to endure, he had felt it was worth it.

He wasted no time in enquiring as to their involvement with the incident in Hamadan. Rav'an wanted to be truthful so did not deny their involvement. However, she went to great lengths to explain that neither Talon nor Reza had wanted trouble, but the students had pushed too hard, so they had had to defend her.

He nodded acceptance of their explanation. Although he did not approve of this kind of violence, in spite of himself he had been impressed when he heard what had happened. To kill four young men when these three were still in their teens was, to his mind, remarkable. He resolved he would not underrate them after their ordeal of the passes and then the scrapes they had survived. These three—he included Rav'an in his assessment—were a daunting trio. He was glad to have them traveling with him and on his side.

He broached the subject of the message they would have to send to the Agha Khan in Syria. The trouble was, they did not know the Master's plans, or even where he could be found; thus it was that the messenger would have to follow the most open route to intercept him if he should be on his way back to Persia. This meant that whomever they sent should go north via Samiran, and perhaps up as far as Tabriz, before heading south to Damascus. It was the longest route but the most probable one to intercept the Khan, he told Rav'an. He would send no lesser person than Abbas, whom he trusted with his life, and who could be guaranteed to carry the message to the Khan without interception.

When they arrived at the *caravanserai*, they should hand over the seal of Nur-Ed-Din, and then write the letters for Abbas, who would head back into Hamadan. From there, he would strike across country to Ghazvin with a larger party that he would join with some excuse. He would go north from Ghazvin. With luck, Arash's followers would still be cooped up in Alamut, although, he said, giving a worried look at the sky, it was unseasonably warm for this time of year.

The three young riders were, for the first time, able to ride at leisure with other people whom they could trust. As it was warmer today than before, they were able to take off some of their thick outer clothing and ride in relative comfort alongside the doctor, his trusted servant Abbas, and a striking woman introduced as Fariba.

The road was far better defined on the east side of Hamadan, being more traveled. To the south, they could see the short but high Alvant mountain range, brilliant white with snow from base to the peaks, that would keep pace with their path east for a good two days' ride. Their own path lay south after this, and then southeast in a rough line that meandered among the valleys and lower ranges of the eastern Zagros Mountains to Isfahan.

Once they joined the caravan, they would move even slower, as the camels would be laden with goods for the bazaar, from spice to silks that were now popular with the rich. They would be lucky if they made more than twenty miles in a day.

As they progressed, the snow became less and less thick until there were large, soft patches of open grassland emerging from the snow-clad countryside. On the road, though, here was mud in place of the snow and ice, which made the going more difficult for the smaller, burdened animals and their walking drovers.

That evening they arrived at the *caravanserai*. Before they saw it they heard the noise surrounding the cluster of walls and buildings that constituted the *caravanserai* itself. Breasting a rise in the road, they looked down on what they saw as chaos. There were several hundred camels, large flocks of goats, and fat-tailed sheep intermingled within the very large, grassy hollow that constituted the boundary of the *caravanserai*. Dozens of black, goat-hair tents, leather tents, and in some cases even crude huts, in all shapes and sizes, popped up between the squatting or standing camels. No attempt had been made to organize the assembly into some kind of order.

Men stood around in clusters, gesturing and arguing with one another, or sitting in the evening sun, smoking and warming themselves. Womenfolk were busy with the evening meals, while children ran around playing, getting underfoot, or guarding the animals. Over the whole was a haze of smoke from the hundreds of cooking fires. To make matters worse, there was a lot of mud.

The doctor's party headed for the *caravanserai* to make contact with the caravan's officials, who would accept them as a party or not, as the case may be. As he had sent a message forward several days earlier that he wanted to join, it was probable that the physician would be accorded welcome and respect, as doctors were in short supply anywhere. One with Farj'an's reputation and background at the Isfahan School of Medicine was surely a gem to be had for the long, tedious journey.

Their arrival was a cause of interest, as for the most part, the people in the caravan were herders and traders who knew one another. The doctor's entourage was composed of expensive-looking horses and fine clothing worn by his retainers. People clustered around discussing them, while children stared and chattered. It was slippery going along the rough path to the buildings, but they made it without incident. The doctor and Abbas led the way in with Rav'an, Talon, and Reza in tow, leaving the rest to watch the baggage and make sure that none of their possessions were stolen.

There were more camels and donkeys, grunting and braying inside the courtyard of the walled enclosure, while the shouting and waving of arms was, if anything, more pronounced. Abbas led the way over to a large cluster of men who were listening to an official-looking man standing on a pile of mud bricks. He was shouting that they would leave in the morning, or maybe not, as there were still people due to come.

"*Shyad, farda ya pas farda,*" he shouted. "Perhaps tomorrow or the day after tomorrow!"

Most of the men were merchants who wanted to get started, and they were shouting their frustration at yet another day of delay. Had they not been promised by the *rais* himself that they would be on the road a week ago? The man on the blocks, dressed in a long robe sporting a sheepskin jerkin and thick boots, parried the irritable, shouted questions for a while, then, looking up, he spied the doctor and Abbas with the three riders and waved. He jumped off his stand and pushed his way through the crowd to stand in front of the still-mounted newcomers.

"There you are," he shouted as though they were deaf. "I have been expecting you for these last couple of days!"

Abbas responded that they had made haste to come and they were now here. Where could they place their tents? Did they leave in the morning?

To which the man shouted back, "You can plant your tents inside the walls if you want. Who is the doctor? We leave tomorrow at dawn." He turned to the assembled crowd of men who had approached. "We have the last people for the caravan. Now will you leave me alone?" His boots and robes were splattered with mud and wet sand, as were the clothes of all the others. Their clothing ranged from heavy cotton robes with woolen caps and even scarves, the attire of merchants that did little to keep the wearers warm, to sheepskin-clad herders who knew all about how to dress for the cold.

Abbas, when he could attract the attention of the *rais*, who was named Al Tayyib, finally managed to introduce the doctor. Al Tayyib made a flourishing bow to the doctor and wished him welcome, asking at the same time if the doctor would mind treating the sick along the way. This was a courtesy request, as it was taken for granted that the doctor would provide this service in lieu of payment in full. They discussed the size of the party and where to put them for the night.

Once arrangements were made, the whole of the doctor's entourage came into the walled enclosure of the *caravanserai* and settled in. The tents went up with practiced efficiency on the only dry area left, and the women servants busied themselves with preparing the evening meal. There was no trouble bargaining for fresh goat's milk and cheese, as these were in plentiful supply. There was even bread to be had for a few small coins.

Rav'an was told firmly by the doctor that she would live in the tent reserved for his concubine and her servant. A bit resentful at being told what to do, Rav'an submitted with ill grace but handed off her mare to Talon; hauling her light pile of packed clothes off the packhorse, she stomped off to the tent in question, which had just been erected. The boys grinned at her retreating back.

Abbas came through the muddy area to the boys, who were still sitting on their horses watching the proceedings and beginning to wonder where they would sleep. He pointed to an area at the back of the doctor's tent where he himself would be sleeping that night.

"I shall be leaving in the morning, so you shall have my tent from then on," he said, his manner friendly. They thanked him profusely. Then the care of the horses took precedence over all else. They had to hobble them, as there was nowhere to tie them. Then they had to scrounge some fodder for the night.

When these tasks were completed, Abbas came to the tent and informed the boys that they were summoned to supper with the doctor. They came willingly, and upon entering the spacious area under the large tent, they found it warmed by a small brazier in the middle and illuminated by oil lamps, well furnished but not sumptuous. The doctor, although a wealthy man, was not prone to extravagance. He was seated cross-legged on a pile of carpets and *ghilims*, Rav'an alongside him, and she smiled at the boys as they came in.

Talon and Reza made deep bows to them both and then were invited to join the meal that was already laid out. Abbas and Fariba, the doctor's concubine, were the only other people in attendance. Her role seemed to be to ensure that the doctor was looked after and his every need met during the meal. She also helped Rav'an, while Abbas went out and brought in hot food from time to time.

The meal was simple, *doogh*, some thick *maast*, bread, some cooked and stirred eggs in bowls, strips of mutton that had been roasted over an open fire, some boiled lentils, and water from the water skins. The three fugitives were happy with this simple fare and shrugged when the doctor explained that this was to be their fare for the duration of the journey. He asked Abbas several times if there was sufficient tea for the journey. That worthy informed him solemnly that there was.

The doctor waited until the meal was over before he began to talk to the three travelers, so the meal passed in relative silence. Rav'an was the only one used to being served at all, so the two boys, feeling a bit uncomfortable, were forced to practice what few manners they had during the meal. It did not pass unnoticed by the doctor or his servants.

When the meal was over, they sat and sipped tea while the remains of the food were cleared. Abbas came back from giving some orders to the servants outside, and Fariba sat next to the doctor.

Farj'an cleared his throat and tugged at his beard before he started. He looked at Rav'an and then the boys.

"It is time to discuss more about the task we have for Abbas. My children, this is Fariba, who is my lady, and in whom I have the utmost trust. Likewise, you have already met Abbas, who is a son to me. That said, you can trust them as you trust me, and it is why they're here tonight." He paused to sip some tea and to cast a glance at both Fariba and Abbas. "Rav'an has given me the seal." He produced the object from his robes and held it up in the lamplight. "This will be perfect for our needs, as even I recognized it as belonging to Nur-Ed-Din," he said with satisfaction. "Abbas, you will leave us in the morning and go back to Hamadan, where you will find a large, safe group of travelers going to Ghazvin. Do not attempt to go alone. A man travels alone at his peril in this day."

Abbas nodded. "Master Doctor, I shall be careful," he said, his voice full of respect. "I go from Ghazvin north toward Tabriz. Before I get to Tabriz, I turn west and go to Miyandoāb that is near the great Lake Rezayeh. Then it is west and south to Damascus. I shall seek *Timsar* Esphandiary first, as he is the closest to the Khan, and tell him all while showing him the seal."

The doctor nodded. "You must guard the seal with you life, Abbas, my son. It is your passport to the Khan and the General."

Abbas nodded his agreement. "I shall be a merchant with special goods from Hamadan, and my name will be Abdul-Shahid, 'the servant of the witness.'"

Rav'an clapped her hands at that, and wished him well on his perilous journey. Talon and Reza did likewise. The instructions completed, Abbas rose, saying he had much to do before leaving in the morning.

The doctor gave him his hand, whereupon Abbas kissed it, saying, "My father, I shall honor this trust you have placed upon me. God's blessing be upon you."

Farj'an nodded, tears in his eyes. "Go with God, my son. May Allah protect you on your journey."

Abbas looked around the assembly, lifted his hand to his heart in salute to Fariba, Rav'an, and the boys, bowed, and left the tent.

The doctor had some other business to discuss with the people left in the tent. "I have thought much on this, so I want you to listen and consider what I have to say," he said firmly, his hand straying to his beard again. "Rav'an, my dear, we cannot have you as the sister of the Agha Khan while you are with me, neither on this journey, nor when we come to Isfahan. I would suggest that you become my niece, whose parents have died, and that Fariba is your aunt, while I am your uncle. That way we can deflect unwelcome questions."

Rav'an look surprised, but smiled at him. "I am of the same opinion, 'Uncle,'" she said with a laugh. Turning to Fariba she smiled. "I will make a difficult child for you, my 'aunt,' but I shall try to be worthy of you."

Fariba laughed. "Rav'an, I am more than content that we should be friends, but the honorable doctor is right, I think. We have to make Rav'an, the princess, disappear."

Rav'an nodded and looked at the boys, who were grinning. "What are you two monkeys laughing at?" she demanded, pretending to be annoyed. They hurriedly wiped the smirks off their faces, while she turned to the doctor. "I am to presume that these two will now be allotted duties, such as the care of camels and donkeys, Honorable Doctor?" she said sweetly, straight-faced.

Farj'an suppressed a smile. It was becoming clear to him that there was a strong bond between the three of them.

"If this is what you wish, my dear," he said, watching the dismay on the faces of the two boys with amusement. "I had thought that they might be more useful as part of the guard for the caravan. I had planned to talk to the *rais*, Al Tayyib, about it in the morning."

The boys looked less stricken. Fariba's lips twitched while Rav'an pretended to be doubtful. "I am not sure if they would be much use, Doctor. Do they have enough skill to be soldiers for the caravan?"

The boys glared at Rav'an, pretending to be mortally offended.

The doctor threw his hands into the air, pretending to be exasperated. "I shall have to overrule this," he said, chuckling. "They begin their duties tomorrow."

Both boys both directed smug looks at Rav'an, who poked her tongue out.

As it was getting late, and the doctor was looking tired, they broke up for the night and went to their respective tents.

Fariba, a fine-featured woman in her mid-thirties and still in possession of her good looks and figure, with luxurious black hair that was only just beginning to show the odd gray strand, stayed with Farj'an. They discussed the three additions to their entourage.

"They are like wild animals," she exclaimed.

He nodded. "They are exactly that, Fariba, my love. The two boys have been in the mountains all this time and have never, as far as I can tell, been exposed to even the environment of a city before Hamadan. You should know something else, Fariba," he said, touching her shoulder with his long fingers. "The boy Talon is a Frank."

She turned to face him, real surprise on her beautiful face. "I wondered where he was from," she said with interest.

He nodded. "I heard that he was captured when he was about thirteen, in Palestine. He was brought to Samiran and has spent his time there until becoming a *fida'i*, as did Reza, his companion."

She looked at him. "They both have a dangerous look about them. How did Talon get that long scar on his cheek?"

"He killed a lion when he was about fourteen." He smiled at her stunned look. "I know because I was called to the castle to help him recover. He has scars on his chest and leg to bear witness to that fact. People still talk about the deed at Samiran. Allah was kind to him that day. His companion during that fight died from his wounds."

He looked thoughtful again. She recognized his mannerism of stroking his beard as the prelude to another announcement.

"You're quite right about them both being wild. Even Rav'an is more like a mountain cat than a girl of her standing should be. I think we owe it to all of them to insist upon some education. We should consider how to do this so that they are not complete country bumpkins when we come to Isfahan."

She laughed. "I agree, although I think that you are going to have to insist on it. Learning to write well and deport oneself is boring to young ones who've had so much freedom. I shall think on it, too. Now, my lord, are you tired or would you like me to stay?"

He smiled back and pulled her into his arms. "I am tired, but I wish you to stay and warm my bed. Will you oblige an old man?"

She looked up at him, a clear love in her large hazel eyes. "My Lord, I am your servant in all things. I shall be happy to stay."

* * * * *

The caravan left the next day. The noise was deafening as the mass of animals and people woke and started to prepare for the first day. The merchants had been up since dawn, lashing down their loads onto complaining camels, heaping abuse on their groaning animals and waking the entire camp with their shouts.

It was impossible to sleep through that noise, so the remainder of the camp got out of bed grumpily and cooking fires were relit. There was much shouting and relaying of orders to and fro.

Prayers had to be observed. Fortunately, the three travelers now knew the routine and observed the prayers along with everyone else. The doctor was specific about this. Although he himself was an Ismaili, he went about in his travels as a Shi'ite and thus dispelled any suspicion as to his association with the Ismaili. His servants were instructed to do likewise, and the three newcomers were quick to follow the lead.

The animals had to be fed, and breakfast followed at a leisurely pace because it was clear that the bulk of the caravan would not get moving for a couple of hours at least. Then it was time to attend to the horses and donkeys. Tents came down with some fumbling. Rav'an and the two boys stayed out of the way while all this was going on, tending to their horses, and making sure they were ready for the departure. They watched in impatient disbelief as the caravan with much noise and loud protestations from the camels slowly lumbered to its collective feet, seeing the sun high in the sky before they set off.

The doctor and his entourage were placed in the center of the huge assemblage. The camels led by right of position, which, the doctor warned somewhat dourly, would be unpleasant when they came to the dryer areas of the route. The herds of sheep and goats and free camels came behind, bleating and groaning, small boys keeping them more or less on the track left by the advance guard.

They proceeded at what Talon and Reza considered to be a snail's pace for the rest of the day. Al Tayyib rode up on a small, wiry pony at one time and made sure the boys were aware that he expected them to be part of the caravan guard. He looked them over and nodded approval at what he saw. The boys had dressed in the chain mail they had taken off the mercenaries, with the shields hanging off their saddles. Both were rather proud of the fact that they were the only ones in the entire caravan who owned any armor at all. They looked capable enough, Tayyib thought; better than a lot of the other ruffians he had who aspired to be guards.

The doctor had told him that these two were from Tabriz and had escorted his niece south to meet him at Hamadan.

Al Tayyib was a perceptive man and had not swallowed the story entirely. He wondered who they really were, but the story would do for the moment. He had other things on his mind that day. As always, there were complications. People wanted this or that as a privilege. There were stragglers who hung back and idiots who wanted to rush on. Eventually, it all settled into a routine after about a week. Until then, he would be busy with all manner of issues to deal with.

Looking off to the north, the caravan *rais* noticed black clouds gathering on the horizon. There would be snow again soon, he reasoned. They needed to put miles between themselves and the plateau, or they would be stopped dead in their tracks.

The thaw had been good news for him, but farther back, the boys were glad to see the same clouds.

Reza looked at Talon. "I think it is snow again," he said with satisfaction. He turned to call to Rav'an, who was closer to the doctor and Fariba. He pointed north with his spear. They looked back and Rav'an waved happy acknowledgement.

That day, one of many to follow, was uneventful. They camped before dusk so that people could see to light fires and raise tents. The doctor had asked the boys to help with the work, which they did, although they were uncertain as to what to do at first, but the good-natured servants soon included them in their group as accepted members of the doctor's entourage. Reza and Talon enjoyed the newfound status of bodyguards and the respect it gained for them among the servants. Reza flirted with the womenfolk outrageously, much to everyone's amusement. It was not long before they adapted to the routine of assisting with the work of raising and lowering tents, attending to animals, which they liked, and making themselves useful.

The doctor played his part. Farj'an was a compassionate man who believed that as a physician, he owed it to God and his fellow man to practice where he could for the benefit of men. He had an ample supply of herbs and medicines in his baggage, so whenever the caravan stayed for more than a night he would allow people to come and visit him with their ailments. He prescribed castor oil for the constipated, extract of poppy for the sleepless.

He had in his chests caraway, cedar, peppermint, saffron, and wormwood, and many other herbs and ointments administered as poultices, infusions, lotions, and ointments to the sick, the lame, and sometimes the downright lazy. They all came as much to see him, and feel the better for doing so, as this man was famous. To the superstitious tribal people, he had medicinal powers that bordered upon the supernatural.

Rav'an often attended at these times and soon began to get to know the children and their mothers. They in turn repaid her care and interest in them by oft times inviting her to their tents.

She stayed with Fariba and the doctor most of the time, riding near him during the day, listening with eager attention to his discussions of events, and learning even as they rode. She thought both the doctor and Fariba very interesting people, with ideas and knowledge far beyond what her limited experiences in the mountains had taught her.

The two boys ranged farther afield on their well-bred horses. They were amazed at this new culture they had hitherto never imagined. Reza had glimpsed it as a young child but remembered very little of the world.

They learned that there was order to the seeming chaos. The people who minded the camels, horses, and other animals were concerned about two main things when traveling: access to water and fodder. Fully a third of the camels—their riders sitting on their heaving backs or walking alongside—either in the front with the merchants' beasts or trailing along with the sheep and goats, carried panniers full of fodder on on either side of their humps. If they didn't carry fodder, they carried huge bundles of wood for fires or leather water containers full of brackish water that was exchanged whenever they crossed a stream or river, which was not often. The huge, loose gaited beasts were still in their winter coats that looked tattered and moth-eaten as the hair fell out in clumps. They would keep these remnants of their coats until they came to warmer climes in a couple of weeks.

Talon had not had much experience with camels before, so he wanted to ride close to the leading animals and watch them as they walked the shambling walk that somehow seemed to eat the miles. Once he came in too close and a camel decided that it didn't like having Jabbar alongside, so it turned its sleepy eyes upon Talon and spat at him, its yellow teeth bared and its head ready to snake out and bite. Talon withdrew hurriedly on Jabbar, followed by the laughter of the drovers.

Grubby small boys and girls, dressed in the bright red and

yellow dyed skirts, coats, and head scarves of their tribe, would run alongside the animals that belonged to their families and carefully collect the dung, carrying it in bags slung over their shoulders. In the cold, dry air it dried fast and lost its rank smell and would then be used as fuel for the fires.

Rav'an was struck by how pretty the children were, pointing them out to Talon, who was surprised to note that many of them had eyes the color of the sky, they were so blue. Just like the people of his country, he told her. Others had eyes the same color as hers, rocky gray; while some had hazel-colored eyes; others, black eyes. The girls wore shawls of bright dyed reds and yellows, while the boys sported a kind of waistcoat just as bright over their dirty shirts and often filthy pantaloons.

These cheerful, barefoot children were always on the run during the day, chasing goats or sheep that had decided to take a break from the march and look for some food. Often as not, a goat could be found standing on its hind legs stretching its neck high into one of the few stunted trees along the way, trying to eat the sweeter bark at the top, or nibble buds, or even up in a tree, high amongst the thick branches, stealing leaves from even higher up.

Talon noticed that the boys carried slings with them and were terrific marksmen. They competed with each other, and it was not unusual for a boy of seven or eight to be able to strike a small stone off another at about twenty paces. He doubted that any birds would be able to survive this kind of accuracy, although in truth there were few birds in this vast, sparse grassland of few trees and almost no water.

They did sometimes see migrating birds still flying south, but most of the migrations had ceased for the winter. For the most part, the grassland was stony and bare, with rock formations that stood out in the bleak land. What there was in the way of trees were stunted and dry, poking through the snow patches in forlorn clumps. If anything, the land was almost poorer here than the mountain fastness he had become used to.

Those mounted men who did not have the responsibility of minding the camels were delegated to work for Al Tayyib. They were sent on ahead to scout for good grazing land or watering places the caravan could use, or to hunt, and to check that they were not riding into some kind of trouble.

It was not long before it became clear that Talon and Reza were the ones the rag-tag group of riders looked up to. Their skill with the bow was becoming legendary. For the most part, the men who were riding were tribal men who knew how to fight, but their skill with weapons was limited. It became a great sport during the long lulls in the caravan's movement, while they collected wood or water from some local source, for the boys to test their efficiency with the bows while on horseback.

They'd have a pole erected in a cleared space, and riders would gallop round the pole, shooting at a bunch of feathers high on the end of the pole. Invariably, it was Talon or Reza who struck the target. The two of them were natural horsemen and made it seem almost effortless. It always attracted a large crowd of children and men, who cheered at the spectacle.

Later, small boys with toy bows would pretend they were mounted, and gallop around, shooting slender sticks from makeshift bows at everything in sight, screaming and yelling as they went, until irate parents had enough. Then they would be cuffed and packed off to bed with or without supper, depending upon the offense committed by the exuberant child at the time.

It was easy to ride forward and explore, as it was very clear which direction the caravan was taking. Also, it gave the boys an excuse to leave the noise and smell behind for a time. Al Tayyib had quickly assessed the two as being useful scouts, so he sent them forward a couple of miles to check the paths and road. On their way, the two practiced their archery on targets ranging from the few trees to small animals they startled. Talon longed to have the two sleek salukis with him on these occasions, as they would have been invaluable for the kind of chase needed. He thought, too, that a falcon would prove useful in this environment. Still, they managed by dint of good marksmanship to bring in rabbits and once even some ground birds for the pots of the doctor and Al Tayyib.

Although Rav'an would join them on the odd occasion, it was not often now. She quite enjoyed her new role as the niece of the doctor and Fariba, though chafing a bit under the rule that she was expected to behave with decorum. The doctor was concerned that tongues would wag if she disappeared with the two young men for too long at any time. Farj'an and Fariba treated her with affection, and by subtle means continued her long-interrupted education.

Farj'an was a font of general information, having traveled extensively in his life. He was not averse to telling the seated group in the evening, when they were finished with dinner, all manner of stories about the places he had seen.

He'd fled Egypt some time after the persecutions began. The Nizirites had been part of the very strong Ismaili religious sect of Islam in Egypt until relatively recent times.

He laughed at the story that Talon and Reza volunteered about the first Ismaili leader, Hassan e Sabah, being the man in Ghazvin who had tricked the gullible people out of the castle of Alamut. He agreed that the wily old man had indeed tricked his way into Alamut, and having seized it by trickery, paid a sum of gold nevertheless, then held it against more than one attempt by the sultan's armies to dislodge him.

However, Farj'an pointed out, Hassan had not been fleeing the Shah of Persia. He had in fact been banished from Isfahan because his enemies had conspired to discredit him. Only his friend, Omar Khayyam, had been able to save him. Hassan had wreaked vengeance upon his enemies thereafter.

He, Farj'an, had been of the same faith and so had had to flee from Egypt along with many other Ismaili, his family wealth confiscated and his father killed. The divisions within the Shi'ite sect of Islam were more profound than most realized.

The Ismaili had gone from Egypt in three main groups. One to Yemin, another even farther east than Persia, while the group affiliated with Hassan e Sabbah had gone into the Alborz Mountains. Farj'an had been befriended by the Ismaili Khan in Persia but had wanted above all to become a physician. His new friend and sponsor, the Agha Khan, sent him to Isfahan, which was for that time the most prestigious city in the world for its understanding of medicine.

After many years, he had become a full-fledged doctor, traveling often at the behest of the Agha Khan but allowed, as often as not, to travel for his own interests. He owned a house in Isfahan, which he considered his real home, and because he had been on the road for a while now, he wanted to go back there and spend some time revisiting his colleagues at the college and resting up.

He told them about Egypt and the confused situation in that country regarding the power struggles. In spite of its great history, he told them it was a country fallen into decay and in need of new blood to rule it. The kingdom of Jerusalem he knew a great deal about, and it was not lost upon him that whenever he talked about the ebb and flow of that country's politics, Talon perked up and listened intently.

Being the wise man he was, he talked to Talon about the Jews and the Christians and their place in the countries. "You should know, Talon, that there are two main curses in this world. A man's tribe, and the color of his faith. Jews and Christians were once able to live with the Muslims without hindrance.

"However, they, too, are becoming victims of hate, as are my people. The divisions between all faiths, especially within the Muslim world, are becoming schisms and this will only become worse as men struggle for power rather than reconciliation."

He'd draw maps in the sand of the regions he was discussing and point out the larger cities, naming who was currently in possession of them. He painted a picture of continual change taking place, often violently, in all parts of their world.

Rav'an and the boys listened with rapt interest. His knowledge extended to the poets and the arts, to which Fariba would contribute. It was this love of art and skilled workmanship that had brought the two together.

Fariba was from Herat, in Afghanistan. She loved to talk about this beautiful city on the banks of a huge, slow-flowing river in one of the richest valleys of the whole country around. Men came from India and from Persia to work their crafts in that city, she told them with pride.

Rav'an had fallen into the manner of calling the doctor "uncle" and Fariba "aunt," so it was almost natural for the boys to do the same after some initial awkwardness. Neither of the two adults objected, so it soon became natural to have them referred to as such, even while the three were talking among themselves.

Together, as they were intelligent people, the doctor and Fariba encouraged the three young people to ask questions and to enquire as to the way of things. It was a heady experience for them, in particular for the boys, who were used to the rigorous, even ruthless codes, and the rote learning processes they had endured in Samiran and Alamut.

Under the doctor's careful tutelage, the two began to see the world in a very different light. None of this happened overnight, as sometimes they would fidget and become bored, so the clever doctor and Fariba would change the subject to one more interesting. But eventually, they would come back to the original subject and try again.

In this manner, the three young people learned about the full extent of the Ismaili sect and of its uneasy relationship with the other two Muslim faiths, Shi'a and the Sunni. They learned there were Ismaili enclaves in and around Isfahan and where to find them. They learned that the Seljuks, who were for the most part the rulers, however tenuous that hold might be, of the vast land of Persia, were dedicated to the destruction of the Ismaili people. And they learned that the Christians in Palestine were not their enemies, although there were difficulties there as well.

"Why do they call the Ismaili heretics, Doctor?" Reza asked one evening.

The doctor pulled on his beard and thought for a moment. "It's complicated, but I'll try to explain. It has been the practice of the Shi'ites to seek the guidance of their Imams. There have been many, many, schools of thought on the subject of spiritual interpretation. We Ismaili began in Kufa, the city of Ali ibn Abu Tlib, our first imam, that lies near to Najaf, another holy shrine for the Shi'ites. But the Ismaili school of thought grew to prominence in Egypt." He paused to see if the boys were paying attention, took a sip of tea, and continued.

"They were always more interested in purity and were seekers of the truth. Egypt has been ruled by the Fatimid Shi'ite dynasty—the Fatimids are named after Fatima, who was the daughter of the Islamic prophet from his first wife Khadija—for three hundred years. Over time, they became corrupt and venal. The Ismaili school clashed with the Fatimids. It is one of the reasons for so much disunity, as the schools often differ by just a small amount, but their followers think otherwise and fight over these things.

"The great Muhammad bin Ismā'il is for us the last and seventh imam. We await his return as the Mahdi, or *Qā'im*, otherwise known as 'the riser.' This among many other things distinguishes us from the Shi'ites and more particularly the Sunnis, who accuse us of being deviants and heretics. Thus it is that we are now few in number and disbursed across the world in small groups and persecuted by the Sunnis whenever they find us."

For the first time they learned about the Zoroastrians and their religion, their adherence to Ahura Mazda, the Sun God, and the influence of this religion over the ages in Persia and the Archimedean dynasties. The boys loved the stories of Kurush, or Cyrus the Great, and how he had started the Persian Empire from Persepolis in the region of Fars, south of Isfahan. It pleased them to learn that he came from Fars with his cavalry armies, among the first to conquer almost all the land between distant Afghanistan and Egypt.

The doctor described the hundreds of tribes in the country. He described the Lurs, whose land they would be moving through shortly, and of the fierce, intelligent Kurds, who lived farther west on the other side of the Zagros Mountains. He mentioned the Baktiari of that same region and the savage Baluchi to the distant south.

In the caravan there were many people of tribal stock, although these people were for the most part Ghashgai and were of Turkish origin, more nomadic than most, but fiercely loyal to the Seljuk regime. Hence, the need to be careful when talking to them.

The caravan turned a little more to the southeast. They had passed the southern tip of the Alvant Mountains long ago, those white peaks now formed their northern horizon.

Said one among them –"Surely not in vain,
My Substance from the common Earth was ta'en,
That He who subtly wrought me into Shape
Should stamp me back to shapeless Earth again?"

– Omar Khayyam –

Chapter 20
The Valley of Borujerd

Two weeks later, they left behind the last vestiges of the stony plateau and descended into richer grasslands. Al Tayyib informed the doctor that the city of Borujerd was their next stop. He came to the tent occasionally to pass the time with the doctor, whom he found congenial company. They would enjoy a game of chess together, while the boys looked to their lessons under Fariba's skillful tutelage.

The boys began to respect this stocky, solid man who guided the caravan. He had an onerous task, keeping the many groups of disparate people together in one formation and moving in the right direction. He was the law of the caravan, and they had often attended while he administered advice to complaining peoples. Within each group, a chieftain or leader had the right to administer justice of a harsher kind if one of its members was guilty of breaking one of the many taboos or rules.

His patient bullying and thoughtful attitude toward his wards was worthy of respect. He told the amused doctor and the others after one bad day that the merchants were the worst people to take anywhere, that if it were not for the fact that they paid him handsomely, he would abandon most of them as soon as they came close to a mountain range where he could lose them.

The caravan camped on the heights of the Kuh-i-Garri mountain passes overlooking the plain of Borujerd.

It might have been the fact that, over the weeks, the guards charged with keeping watch had grown complacent. There had been no trouble from any source for the whole period they had been on the road thus far, hence, no one expected it now. However, that evening, as everyone was settling down to the evening meal, the alarms sounded in the form of distant shouting and screaming on the side nearest the pass entrance.

The people in the doctor's tent heard the shouting, and without further ado, Talon, Reza, and Rav'an rushed out to try to make out what caused the disturbance. It was very hard in the gloom to make out what was going on, other than the direction from which the noise came.

The three rushed off to their horses, unhobbled them, hurriedly threw bridles and saddles on them, then, seizing their spears and bows, galloped off in that direction. They came upon a melee of people rushing about and shouting. Farther along, they heard screams and the clash of weapons as men struggled in the semi-darkness. Talon and Reza released their bows from their scabbards and strung them, and then pushed their horses forward against the throng. It was not easy, as panic had set in and there were people running toward them and camels everywhere, loose and bawling.

They cantered past Al Tayyib, shouting and gesturing, trying to marshal his men to counterattack the vague figures ahead. These figures were slashing and hacking at tent guys, baggage packs, and anyone careless enough to be in their way. They were so engrossed in their plundering that they didn't even notice Talon, Rav'an, and Reza coming upon them until two arrows found their mark and two riders toppled to the ground. The others of the bandit group—there were about twenty of them—looked up, startled, then two more went down. The whole group suddenly realized that they were up against dangerous elements they had not taken into account before. Those not on their horses ran off to try to mount them, while those already mounted milled about trying to decide whether to take on the three riders or not.

Their hesitation proved fatal for some. More arrows flew, and as they did, there came the banshee screams of the guardsmen, who, having found their courage now charged in a wild mob into the enemy's midst, Al Tayyib in the lead. Then it was a free-for-all. Rav'an stayed close to Talon and Reza, watching their backs as the two hurled themselves into the fray. It proved to be a short battle, as the men who came to plunder did not come to be killed. They evaporated from the scene, disappearing into the night as fast as their ponies could carry them, leaving their dead behind. The victors were jubilant and cheered, waving their mixed assortment of spears, axes, and clubs in the air, elated with their victory.

A wild-looking, exhilarated Al Tayyib came riding over to the group of three, reined in his excited mount, and exclaimed, "You won this battle for us! To you should go the praise. Thanks be to Allah you were here to make the difference. I thank you!" He reached across the distance between himself and Talon, grabbed his tunic, pulled him to him, and kissed him a great smacking kiss on the mouth. He then released the stunned Talon and did the same to Reza. He made an elaborate bow with a great flourish in the saddle to an apprehensive Rav'an, who laughed back at his beaming face.

The other men were gathering around now, all shouting and talking over each other in the excitement of what, to them, was a great victory. Reza looked at Talon and laughed at him. Talon laughed back and they both rode alongside Rav'an, putting their arms over each other's shoulders, laughing with the excited men.

Al Tayyib calmed down long enough to order that the dead and wounded be taken care of, sentries posted, and an estimate of the damage made. It was now getting quite dark, so there was not much anyone could do that night except hope that the bandits would not come back. The *rais* commented to Talon and Reza that he doubted very much they would, as they had had a nasty surprise. All the same, he insisted that men ride to the perimeter of the caravan and stand guard.

He made no such demands upon the three young warriors, who went back to the doctor's tent and told him their version of the scrap.

"By morning, this will have been a great battle against insuperable odds," was the doctor's dry analysis of the event. Nonetheless, he was pleased that they had acquitted themselves well. Fariba, on the other hand, was appalled that Rav'an had gone and joined the boys in the fight.

"How could you care so little for your safety, Rav'an, my dear?" she exclaimed, horrified at what they told her.

Rav'an laughed, shrugged, gave her a kiss and said happily, "Oh, Fariba, don't worry so much. I was with my protectors. I was perfectly safe."

To which the doctor responded, "Rav'an, my dear girl, you

might think it fine to go off fighting with these two ruffians," he smiled at the grinning young men, "but you have to realize that your personal safety is very important to us and your brother. Please do not be so reckless with your life."

Talon nodded, his face solemn. "The doctor is right, my lady, you should stay here in the tent next time."

Reza, looking serious, nodded agreement. "Yes, my lady, as a lady should."

He got no further. She attacked them both, beating them on their heads and shoulders with her large fur hat while they made feeble attempts to ward her off, falling about and pleading for mercy. Soon the doctor and Fariba were laughing. Rav'an was laughing, too, although she demanded, and got, abject apologies from the laughing boys for being so impertinent.

With order restored at the doctor's behest, they all settled down to complete the interrupted evening meal. There was much conjecture as to the nature of the attackers. Farj'an surmised that they were probably elements from the city of Borujerd at the base of the pass.

"We have to follow the length of the valley, so it is a fair bet that they came from there. I hope that they learned a good lesson tonight and will be more circumspect before they try it again."

That night, as he and Fariba were preparing for bed, she looked at him. "My lord, these young people are so wild. Are they all like this in the mountains of the Alborz?"

He nodded. "Yes, they are. It's a very harsh world these young people have come from, but I am confident that they can become more civilized over time, including that ferocious girl! Whoever marries her is in for an interesting time!"

They both chuckled over that. Rav'an was a constant surprise to them, not only as she had been this evening, but also because she seemed to be very intelligent and did equally as well with the poets as she seemed to do with arms.

*****

The next day, the caravan was delayed as the wounded came to the doctor, who dealt with the cuts and bruises. They were full of praise for the three young people who were part of his entourage.

Al Tayyib was with the boys when they came down the slopes

on the valley side of the pass the following evening. He pointed to the large river running through the rich valley grasslands as they reined in to look at the view.

"That is the Ab-i-Diz River," he said with satisfaction. "We are less than a month away from Isfahan now. We now have to be vigilant, as in this valley are the people who would like to take from us that which we have, and they do not." He looked significantly at the two. "You need to be very alert as we cross this valley. They will come and try to cut out portions of the caravan as we move along. They will watch for weak points."

"Who?" Reza asked. "Who are these people you talk of, *rais*?"

"They are Lurs, people who are the same as the bandits who attacked last night. We are somewhat safer with a large group, but they can still prey upon us. A smaller group they would just kill and take all." He shrugged. "I suppose it is part of what we must pay to cross this land, but I would like to pay less."

The boys looked at one another.

"Do you want us to chase them and fight them?" Talon asked, smiling at Al Tayyib. "We are just two; you should give us more men."

Al Tayyib nodded agreement, also smiling. "I shall call a meeting this night, and you shall have more men. I am putting you in charge," he said, pointing at Talon as he rode off, leaving the two boys looking at one another.

Reza grinned at his friend. "Now you're going to be a great leader, my friend," he teased.

Talon didn't answer. He was staring across the valley and along the route that he thought they might be taking. There were numerous places where the caravan could be attacked on either side.

Talon gave Reza a look, then said, "I think we would be foolish to stay as one large group, because we will not be able to guard against an attack that comes from the side we are not on. They will be able to come in and steal, perhaps kill, and leave before we can cross the middle."

Reza looked out onto the valley. He nodded thoughtfully. "You mean we should break into two groups, and patrol down each side of the caravan?"

Talon clapped him on the back. "And while I lead one group, you should lead the other. Then, if these bandits attack, the one on the side they come to can hold them off, while the others come at all speed to help."

"That is very good, Talon... you have been thinking again."

Reza ducked as the hand swiped at him. Laughing, they rode back to the encampment, where the doctor's entourage was setting up for the night. They told the doctor about the decision made by the *rais* for Talon to lead a group of men, then what they had decided to do instead.

He nodded his approval. "I think he has divined that you two are not quite what I said you were," he said reflectively. "All the same, I will feel a bit happier if you are out there doing something of the kind you described. I am sure the *rais* will approve."

They took their idea to the *rais*, who did not hesitate to agree. He had become quite impressed with the way these two behaved and now by how they thought. There were only about fifty men who could ride and carry weapons in the whole caravan, the remainder being merchants and drovers who could not be spared for this kind of thing; they were divided up into two groups and given Reza and Talon to lead them.

There was some grumbling from the older men as to why the two young men were given the leadership, but the *rais* shut them down by shouting that it was these two *thinking* warriors who had come up with the plan in the first place.

"Are there any among you great chieftains who can come up with a better idea? No? Then shut up and do as they tell you," he shouted at them.

The grumbling subsided, to be replaced by mocking from those who agreed with the *rais*.

The next day at dawn, the two patrols went out and waited for the caravan to get under way. Talon was concerned that even if they did have men on the alert, they could still not see ahead far enough. His experience with the ambush in Palestine came back to him—he thought that scouts would have prevented that incident and wanted to try his theory out. He singled out two of the best riders in his group and told them to move a couple of miles forward of his position and to keep that distance ahead. Their instructions were specific: They were to look for any sign of men with horses and weapons who might be watching or moving into position for an ambush. The two young men he had chosen rushed off eagerly, glad to be doing something special.

Talon then explained to the others that he felt that any attack would be most likely to come when the entire caravan was near a tightening in the trail or a wooded area. They should then be very vigilant when they came to any narrow passage in the folds of the valley. The men were beginning to respect this young man from the north, so they nodded agreement and spat earnestly into the ground as they discussed this information.

The caravan would bypass the city and move parallel with the river for most of the time until they began the climb to the passes at the other end of the valley. They were to keep their eyes peeled at all times and sound the alarm as soon as they saw anything untoward. Reza was issuing the same kind of instructions to his men. It had not escaped him that Talon had sent two scouts forward. He decided that was a good idea as well and picked two of his own to scout forward on his side of the caravan for the same reason.

Talon discussed the Lurs with his group of riders while they rode sentry. Although the Lurs were wealthy tribes, they still had a reputation for preying upon travelers. The group with Talon offered all sorts of tidbits of information gleaned from the many times they had come through this region. More often than not they had been forced to pay a tithe for moving through the area or had lost people and camels to this predatory people. They accepted this with a shrug, but they were excited about being able to do something about it now.

They gazed out at the town they were approaching. The palm trees and rich, fertile soil denoted a wealthy area. It was clear that, when in season, there were many fruit trees, fig trees, dates, pistachios, and an abundance of crops growing outside the walls of the town.

There were numerous water-lifting devices along the river that helped to irrigate the green fields. The caravan stayed well clear of the croplands, as they did not want to cause the townspeople to come out and seek retribution. Instead, they kept to the low foothills, where they found grazing for the goats and sheep along the way.

The people in the fields did not wave, but they did stop what they were doing and watch as the caravan moved slowly along the valley past the town. Talon could see people on the walls watching them, and wondered if the people who had been beaten off a couple of nights before were standing there watching as well.

He glanced back at the caravan and saw a lone rider come from the direction of the doctor's retinue. He knew before he could clearly see her that it was Rav'an. She galloped up the slopes to him and waved from some few hundred yards away. He waved back, happy to see her. They had not had much opportunity to be together during the past couple of weeks, so he welcomed her company, even if it included others.

The men with him were respectful of her, the more so as they had seen her in the fighting and that had impressed them all. So the two had a distance accorded to them to enable them to talk in private.

Rav'an cantered up, smiling and breathless from the short, fast ride. She was happy to be able to join him, and soon they were riding side-by-side, cheerfully discussing the town and its numerous orchards and fields. Because there were so many trees and winter plants about, they were enchanted by its emerald contrast to the brown hillsides they were used to. Rav'an pointed out various trees in the orchards, many of which Talon had never even heard of. She teased him about the fig trees, saying that the aroma of the fig, when ripening on the tree, was so powerful that it smoothed out wrinkles in old ladies' skin, and if a raging bull came near, he calmed down and became as placid as a lamb.

They were impressed by the size and laziness of the river with its many tributaries. Never having seen a river this large before, they remarked upon the ways men used it for their purposes. They noted the tools that brought water to the fields and the wheels that carried it even farther into long thin canals.

Talon pointed out the walls of the town and told Rav'an that they would be easy to scale to gain entry if the caravan decided that they needed to retaliate for the attack the other day. She looked at him, realizing that this man, for he was that now in her eyes, was maturing into a canny warrior.

They talked about the doctor and Fariba. Rav'an was convinced that both were good people, and Talon concurred. She enjoyed attending the doctor's regular medicine meetings with the tribesmen, where she got to know all manner of people, but also she was learning something about medicine as well. The wide range of herbal remedies that the doctor used was fascinating to her. She shared her interest with Talon, who, while he understood but little of what she alluded to, was receptive if for no other reason than she was so enthusiastic.

They managed to touch hands and get close to one another

during these times. However, other than that, they were forced to contain their ardor, as they didn't want to embarrass the doctor or themselves in front of the others.

She was not above teasing him, though. On this occasion, she looked straight into his eyes and told him without words just how much she wanted him. Talon's flushed face and neck reflected how well he understood her. Then, as usual, she would laugh, break the tension, and then they were off onto another subject, happy just to be together.

As Talon and his men were on the side farthest from the river, and the town was on the other side of the river, no one expected any surprises. Even so, when the caravan camped for the night, Al Tayyib placed mounted sentries well out from the caravan and changed them regularly through the night. Both Talon and Reza rode out and did their stint together on the side nearest the town.

There were no alarms, neither that night nor the next, by which time the town was a long way behind them. However, they were still not out of the valley, and Talon had an uncomfortable feeling that the town was not finished with them yet. He communicated his concerns to Reza, who nodded. He, too, was apprehensive about how they were to get through the pass without incident.

They talked this over as they rode together one night while on guard. At last, they came up with a basic plan. The next morning, they sought out Al Tayyib. Although busy with the usual duties involved with getting the caravan on the move, he gave them time. They squatted on the ground, and Talon used a stick to draw a crude map of the entrance to the pass. He and Reza both thought that if there were to be an attack, it would be in larger numbers than before and at, or in, the pass. Al Tayyib agreed. What did they have in mind?

There was no hiding the caravan, Talon told him, as it was large and noisy. They had to get through the pass; once through they would probably be safe. If they could get close to the pass and stop, they might be able to deceive the people watching them into thinking they could attack the caravan the next day as it entered the pass. Both he and Reza had been informed by their eager scouts that there were indeed people on horses watching the progress of the caravan from afar. Why would they bother watching unless they were up to something?

Al Tayyib agreed again, getting impatient. "Now, young lion, what is it that you have planned?"

"Would you be able to move the caravan at night, for one night? To get it over the pass?" Talon asked the surprised man.

The *Rais* reared back on his heels. "By Allah, that would be hard to do..." he said, his tone thoughtful. "But what good would that do us if they are aware of us doing it? You just told me that there are watchers."

"We know of four of them, and we can deal with them on the night we move out," Reza said.

Al Tayyib gave him a long, hard look. He stroked his mustache. "I shall have to talk to a lot of people to get agreement. Do you think it will work?"

"If you can get the caravan over the pass in the middle of the night, or early the next day, we can ensure that the city doesn't hear of it," Talon stated.

"I shall ask the mullah to call prayers for everyone tonight. I shall make a small *maidan*, and we can address the men of the caravan," said Al Tayyib, with more confidence. He got up, looking down at the two of them still squatting, looking back up at him. His expression was very curious, but he said nothing; he just nodded and walked off.

That evening, the call to prayers came from the mullah himself, who called people to the center of the encampment. Curious men came from their cooking fires to listen, as this was obviously not just a call to prayers. There they all lined up and prayed first, going through the time-honored rituals that so many drew comfort from in this very uncertain world.

When prayers were completed, Al Tayyib stood on a large pile of baggage and spoke to them all. He described Talon and Reza's plan, as they stood to the side while he spoke. Tayyib explained that everyone had to be alert to commands that would be transmitted in the dark by messengers. They must pretend to look as though they were settling in for the night when they got to the place near the pass whence they would depart during the night.

The two boys and their men would be hovering on the outside until it was quite dark, and then they would hunt down the enemy scouts. Al Tayyib did not give anyone the option of refusing to go. He made it clear that anyone left behind would be at the mercy of the people from the town, who might be rather frustrated, and not interested in listening to anyone who decided to lag back. The men who rode with Talon and Reza looked at one another, their excitement burning. There was a loud buzz of talk when the *rais* finished.

The merchants were a disagreeable bunch at best, but they saw the logic of doing as he said. Everyone was acutely aware they had come across the entire valley without being harassed except once, and this meant that they had to be attacked some time soon. If the plan worked then they might get out unscathed, whereas to stay and take it would do no one any good.

All the same, there was much discussion, as not even the chief of the tribal group wanted to agree without talking things over at great length. The discussion as to its merits raged on into the night. Everyone had to have his say about the matter. Later, much later, a tired, but contented *rais* of the caravan came to the doctor's tent and told the assembled party that there was agreement, and they would follow the plan.

One night later, they were camped on the slopes that led up to the passes. As a precaution, Talon and Reza had ridden up to the passes and checked to see that no band of men was waiting there to descend upon the caravan during that night. As they did so, they managed to find the locations of the watching spies.

The whole camp was tense that evening. The doctor's servants were not a warlike group, thus they were apprehensive about the impending move, but Reza managed to reassure them, as did Rav'an. She agreed to stay with the doctor's party, to lend it some backbone, as Reza unkindly put it, while the boys went out to deal with the scouts. They rode in two bands again. Reza would take the two nearest the passes, while Talon and his people would cut the path of the other two.

They rode their horses in silence in the general direction of where their two scouts were hidden. They were challenged with a quiet call by one of the young men who had been watching the outcrop since dusk. He whispered that no one had left, although he could not see the enemy in the bad light, so he didn't know if they were still there. A rocky outcrop made a perfect watch post. Talon's men surrounded the group of rocks and scrub trees in silence, then Talon and one of the tribesmen dismounted and, taking some rope, ascended.

Talon crept over the large rocks, listening intently for any presence. His keen ears caught a low cough, as though someone had tried to suppress it. He signaled to his companion to come forward and whispered into the man's ear to tell where he had heard the noise. They drew their knives and inched forward.

Far away, Talon heard the sounds of a camp that should have been going to bed but sounded now more as though it were getting up. Camels were groaning and there was some braying, cut off as people ran up to the luckless animals and stifled their noises. Then he heard a low voice, right below him. The spies were both there, trying to keep warm, and they were both wide-awake, listening, too. He heard one comment on the noise coming from the invisible camp. Talon touched the sleeve of the man beside him and pointed down. Then, crouching, they jumped down onto their victims' shoulders.

Although they had their knives out, Talon had told everyone that he wanted the men taken prisoners, alive, not dead. He felt that if they killed these men, they would have the townspeople on their trail for a long time. So when they landed on the two unsuspecting watchers, they dragged them to the ground, stuck knives under their chins, and warned them that any resistance meant death. The two men stared back with wide, terrified eyes, nodded mutely, and then allowed themselves to be tied up.

Leaving their feet free but their mouths gagged, Talon and his companion dragged and pushed their captives down to the waiting men. There were muffled congratulations, and then they were all riding hard back to the caravan with their captives bound to a horse each.

There they found everything in motion. The whole mass of people, camels, sheep, and goats was on the move. It was not silent, but it was a lot quieter than normal.

Talon had to wait for about twenty minutes before he spotted a group of riders approaching the caravan in the dark. It was Reza with his two prisoners. One of them was bleeding. A furious Reza told Talon that his man got too excited and started to use his knife. Reza had had to slap him hard on the face.

Talon nodded and told him about his success. Satisfied that there were no other watchers, they both went back to where the others were with the two bound prisoners. Talon then broke everyone up into two groups again, and while Reza went with one group to scout the passes to make sure they could get through, Talon took up the rear guard with his group to ensure no one came from behind. The mass of the caravan ambled forward over the pass, and, as dawn was breaking, moved steadily down into the shallow valley behind, continuing for another four hours until there were a good ten miles between them and the pass.

They settled down for the remainder of the day with guards posted and took their ease, most people getting some well-earned rest.

Talon and Reza went to find the prisoners, who had been put into the tender care of Al Tayyib's men. They found them still bound and very frightened, but otherwise unharmed. Talon had remonstrated with the men who wanted to kill them and dump them along the way. He and Reza had argued that to kill them would bring reprisals upon them, while releasing them, shamed but unhurt, would perhaps deter the townspeople from raiding passing caravans. After all, most of these merchants and travelers would need to use this route again in the future. It took time, but eventually people came round to the idea, which firmed into finality when Al Tayyib weighed in on the boys' side.

He ordered the men to saddle up and take the prisoners with them on horseback back to the pass, which they approached with caution, riding up to the narrow gateway to the valley beyond with care. They discovered that there was no one about, so they dismounted and took the prisoners off their horses.

Al Tayyib then addressed the prisoners. "We came in peace; all we wanted to do was to pass by your city, while all you wanted was to prey upon us. You are lucky to be alive. Now go back to your people and tell them that we could have gone into the city itself and murdered whom we pleased, but we did not. Be warned; allow caravans to pass unmolested from now on."

Reza was more direct. He whispered into the ear of one of the prisoner, who turned white.

The men of the caravan shouted abuse at the prisoners. "May you be visited by the fleas from a thousand camels that invade your private parts!" one yelled. "And may your arms be too short to scratch them!"

The remainder of the group howled as one. Shouting with laughter, they wheeled their ponies and galloped off, leaving the chagrined prisoners watching their departure.

Almost three weeks later, the caravan came to the low foothills that overlooked Isfahan. Talon, Rav'an, and Reza gazed on the magnificent city with awe. It was the largest and most beautiful place they had ever seen. Nothing the doctor or Fariba said could have prepared them for the sight of this exotic city. Its walls were white against the green of the orchards and plantations of trees surrounding the city itself.

"Isfahan is half the world, *Isfahan nis-e-jhan,*" the doctor had told them. "The people of this city are very proud of Isfahan and of themselves," he told them dryly. "When you go visiting this place or that, try to keep your mouths from gaping and try to look as though you have seen it all before. Do not shame me by behaving like complete country bumpkins," he said; his smile was kind, but there was a message there for them, too.

Sitting their horses on the rise overlooking the north side of the city, they had cause to gape. The city lay between the mountains that they had come along on the north and west, and a low range of mountains to the east. Beyond, eastward, lay the forbidding desert known as the Dasht-e Kavir, or Desert of Salt.

Al Tayyib rode up on his shaggy pony and joined them as they stared at the bustling gateway. They gazed at the busy roads nearby and the plentiful, well-watered fields across the plain. Farther off, they saw the huge, lazy river that fed the city, sails of small boats plying up and down its huge expanse.

"It is magnificent," he stated in a matter-of-fact way. "Are you going to stay here with your uncle for a time?"

Rav'an turned to him. "Indeed we are, *rais*, I can think of no place I would rather be."

He smiled at her. "We shall soon part. However, I wanted to thank you all for your help during the journey. You made a difference, and I am grateful, as indeed are the merchants, who got through without a single lost camel or bale of goods. Much gratitude you will receive from them, of course." He shot a shrewd look at the three of them. "You are all very young to know all that you seem to know about war. I know but one people who are like this. They are known as the Assassins."

They stared back, holding their breath.

"If you are ever in need of help, and I can provide it, you may find me at the bazaar by using the name Al Tayyib. May Allah be kind to you, my young friends." He smiled at them as he turned his horse and cantered back to the caravan that was moving slowly past them below.

They looked at one another, eyes wide with surprise.

"He is a good man," Reza stated finally, with feeling. "I shall remember him well."

Talon nodded and Rav'an said, "We could always do with friends like that. He knew. He could have denounced us, but he did not."

They, in turn, wheeled their horses and cantered down to join up with the doctor's entourage.

As the caravan came closer to the gates, they saw a vast area about a mile out from the city walls that seemed to be where the caravan would settle. There was a *caravanserai* built more or less like the one they had started from near Hamadan. It was here that the main party of the caravan would settle for the next month before starting on another journey. The tribal people would continue south to Shiraz, crossing the warm plains of Fars.

It was time for farewells. Friends had been made among the men of the tribe who had accompanied Talon and Reza upon their patrols. There was mutual respect on all sides, much shaking of hands and slapping of backs, and requests for one more cup of tea and to share one more bowl of *maast*. It was with a certain sadness that they bade their new-found friends goodbye, then joined the doctor as he bade farewell to many of his patients and merchant friends.

At last, the goodbyes were over. The doctor's group moved off to ride the last mile to the city walls and on to his house.

"I am looking forward to a hot bath," he exclaimed as they departed. "I've sent a servant forward to notify my house staff that we are here and expect to be greeted as returning heroes."

Fariba laughed, her white teeth shining. "Rav'an, you will love his house. It is like a palace, it is so beautiful."

They all rode forward, eager to conclude the journey. As they approached the gate, they came to a large open space among the palm trees that lined the road. There were men on horseback playing a game neither Talon nor Reza recognized. The players had a kind of stick with which they seemed to be beating at a ball, striking it in all directions. They galloped all over the place, kicking up lots of dust and shouting all the time.

The group had almost crossed the wide opening when one of the balls came whistling toward them. It bounced almost at Rav'an's mare's hooves. She calmed the startled mare and looked down at the small round object with interest.

Right behind it galloped a man on a splendid pony covered in sweat. He pulled the pony to a slithering halt close to her. He seemed intent upon hooking the ball and driving it back the way it had come.

Then he glanced up, stopped what he was about to do and stared. Rav'an was no longer wrapped in furs and woolen outer clothing. Instead, she was dressed in comfortable pantaloons of cotton, tucked into light horsehide boots, and wore a tight waistcoat of decorated fine wool over a wide, loose shirt that did nothing to hide her form. Her hair was loose and cascaded in a tumble down her back.

The young man on the horse collected himself and sidled his horse closer. Talon and Reza closed with him. He did not even glance at them.

"My lady," the young man said, "I am blinded by your beauty. From where have you come? I swear by the Prophet that I would have known if you resided in Isfahan."

Before Rav'an could respond, the doctor rode over and said sharply, although as ever he was polite, "Agha, I am the physician Farj'an Abdul-Ibn-Adnan, and this is my niece. I expect you to show her more courtesy."

The young man was instantly contrite. "Your Honor, Doctor, everyone knows who you are. I apologize for being so forward. Please forgive me." He continued to gaze at Rav'an. "I only ask that I might be able to come and visit you, sir, if you will permit it."

Farj'an pretended to consider this, all the while looking hard at the young man. The youthful man was dressed in very rich clothes and rode a magnificent animal.

"I wish to know *your* name." Farj'an's tone was peremptory, although he already knew.

"Honored Doctor, my lady, I am Dav'ud, son of Tawfig-e-Ubayy."

"I expect a formal request for an invitation from you after next week, young man," the doctor said stiffly.

Dav'ud smiled with delight, displaying even white teeth. He saluted with his stick and bowed to Rav'an with a brilliant smile. Then he galloped off to continue playing his curious game with his friends.

The three young people looked their question at the doctor, as did Fariba as she rode up. Farj'an nodded to the group of young men.

"You appear to have made a conquest, my dear," he said in his dry manner. "Those young men are noblemen, descendants of the

Old Persian families."

"What is it they are playing, Uncle?" Reza asked.

"It is called *Cho'gan* or *Pilao*. It is played a lot here in Isfahan, mostly by the nobles' sons."

"But you will see women play, too," Fariba commented.

Farj'an nodded. "It is a rough game, and people can get hurt. Some wild women join in on occasion. You three would like it; it's the perfect game for ruffians like you." His eyes twinkled. "We have other things to do just now. I am going home, and I want a bath."

He shook his horse's reins and headed for the enormous gate. Smiling at his straight, dignified back and the huge turban he sported for the occasion, the others followed him to their new home.

Wake , For the Sun behind yon Eastern Height
Has chased the Session of the Stars from Night;
And, to the field of Heav'n ascending strikes
The Sultan's Turret with a Shaft of Light.

– Omar Khayyam –

Chapter 21
Isfahan

It soon became apparent that the doctor was a well-known and influential man in Isfahan. As his entourage entered the city, even the guards greeted him with respect. Furthermore, he was greeted and saluted all along the way to his house by people of high and low rank. It also became apparent that he was a man of means, indeed quite rich, although not in an ostentatious way.

The streets grew wider and became attractive, tree-lined avenues. The houses were spaced farther apart and hidden behind walls as they neared the river. Soon it was clear that some of the houses were virtual palaces.

The doctor's entourage pulled up at one of the more modest of the large houses, placed square in the middle of a vast, walled enclosure. The grand looking house was a double-storied wood and mud-brick building set in the middle of a complex garden with fountains and pools dotted all about, through which meandered a wide path. There were high plane trees and even conifers mixed with palm trees in small clumps around the house to protect it from the summer sun. The trees gave the effect of a small forest to the surprised and delighted newcomers. The ochre tiles on the roof of the long logia that went round the outside of the house made it look old but comfortable. The gardens were well tended; indeed, gardeners came from the orchard to greet the doctor, along with other servants from the house.

It was a grand entrance for the doctor. His servants from the highest rank to the lowliest were lined up to welcome him home. Some waved palm fronds, while others waved colored scarves, giving the homecoming a festive atmosphere. The horses set to parading and high stepping with all the excitement. The young companions looked at one another with surprise. Fariba smiled at them and told them *sotto voce* that the servants were glad to see the master return after such a long absence. This was his real home, and they were all glad to see him again.

Rav'an nodded agreement, as did the other two. They were excited and thrilled to now be part of his inner group.

The doctor wasted no time in addressing his servants. He thanked them for the warm greeting and introduced the three newcomers. Rav'an was his niece once removed and would be his guest indefinitely. The two young men with her were her personal bodyguard and were to be accorded all the respect due to anyone in his own family. The servants murmured with curiosity, but as he did not go on to enlighten them more, they were left wondering about the newcomers. The servants were thanked and dismissed, and the family headed for the house.

In keeping with their new status, Talon and Reza took theirs and Rav'an's mounts round to the stables to make sure that they were well looked after. They need not have worried. There were three grooms and a yardman who made sure that the horses were well rubbed down and then placed in large, clean, roomy stalls.

After talking for a short while with the men in the yard in order to get to know them, the two young men carried their baggage along to the rear of the house. There they were met by other servants, who seized their bundles over their protests and led them upstairs to rooms in one of the long wings. They saw that the house was a hollow square with the main public rooms to the front, while the private chambers were to the rear of the house. In the center of the house was a tiled courtyard with a low-pressure fountain that allowed water to flow down a cascade of well-placed rocks and stones into the small pond below. The sound it made was muted but clear and called to mind a very small stream of water splashing down a hillside.

They were told that the wing where they were to sleep was for guests and that the other wing housed the doctor and his ladies. Talon wondered where Rav'an was and decided that she would have rooms in the other wing for propriety's sake. The servants placed their baggage on beds covered with fine material that impressed the two young men and asked politely if there was anything more they could do. Upon being dismissed by the two awkward young men, they informed them that dinner would be served in the main dining room at the front of the house.

The finery that greeted them at every turn awed the boys. Neither was used to sleeping on comfortable beds in a room all to themselves. Reza kept making excited grunts and yelps as he explored his room next door. Then he came bounding into Talon's room via the veranda that ran along the entire inside of the upper story to exclaim, "We have become princes! The doctor lives like a king! Have you ever seen anything like this before? It is wonderful."

Talon grinned at his friend's exuberance. Not even in his father's castle had he ever seen such fine fittings and furnishings. He was beginning to wonder if it were not all a dream, rather like the one they still remembered of their initiation. Still, there was Reza laughing, pacing about full of energy, pointing and exclaiming at the beautiful paintings and tapestries on the walls, the carpets on the polished wood floors, and the exquisite designs on the bed covers.

Finally, he threw himself onto Talon's bed and, spread-eagled on his back, he sighed. "Talon, I think we have died and are in heaven. I almost expect a woman to come in that door and take care of my needs."

He almost shouted this out. Just as he did there was a knock, and a woman appeared carrying towels and clothing. She was not young and her head was covered with a *hijab* of bright-colored material. They both whirled to look at her, too startled to speak. She murmured a greeting, asked them to excuse her for the intrusion. She asked them if they were ready for their baths. She had brought towels and a change of clothes for them.

Talon was the first to recover his senses. "Thank you, *Khanom*; it is good of you to come. Please leave the clothes and tell us where the baths for guests are," he said with exaggerated politeness. He prayed that she had not heard Reza.

The woman, who could have been their mother, explained where the baths were, handed the pile of clothing and towels to Talon, and left.

Talon looked at Reza and held his breath. They waited for the sound of her footsteps to disappear, and then they exploded with laughter.

"Reza, you donkey," Talon exclaimed, in between gasps for air.

"I swear by Allah, you will have us both in trouble with the crazy things you come out with."

Reza, who was doubled up on the bed, his face red from holding his breath choked back. "Well... I was close, anyway. But she was, I have to agree, more suited for your tastes."

He didn't get any further. Talon jumped on him, and they had a wrestling match there and then, finally falling off the bed into a tangle of sheets and bedding covers, panting for breath and still laughing. They got up and went off to have their baths, the first in many weeks; and even more to their liking, they were waited upon hand and foot.

For Rav'an, it was much the same experience. She later told Talon at one of their morning meetings in the garden about what she'd done. Although she had been exposed to a somewhat more luxurious life in the past than the boys, she was awed by what she saw here in the doctor's house. Fariba went with her to her rooms, which were situated in the women's section. There Fariba showed her the large rooms and living area that were for the exclusive use of the womenfolk of the house.

It delighted Fariba to be able to show off the fine furniture, ornate vases, some of the new glass that was now popular, and other artifacts of fine workmanship that decorated the household. It did not escape her that Rav'an was impressed. Fariba had grown to like this striking young woman, who was now more or less her ward, so she resolved to spoil her.

"We shall first have our baths and then dress as women in Isfahan should," she stated. She took Rav'an by the hand to show her where she would sleep. Rav'an gasped at the fine décor and the wonderful materials used to cover the bed. The simple elegance impressed her.

"It is beautiful, Fariba. I feel like a mere peasant from the mountains," she said in doleful tones. "We have nothing so fine in Alamut, not even in Samiran."

Fariba gave her a fond look. "Rav'an, my dear, there is one thing the mountains have produced that is rare enough here in Isfahan, and that is your beauty. I intend that you should partake of and enjoy all that Isfahan can provide. We will dress you as a princess should be dressed, even if we cannot tell people about you. Then I shall spoil you until you cry for mercy."

Rav'an laughed, her wide smile replacing her normally serious demeanor. Fariba realized that she had not seen this child laugh very often, so it warmed her, as did the impulsive hug that Rav'an gave her.

"Fariba, my dear 'aunt,' you have already done that. I am so very happy we are at last here. I have been worried for so long, I am not sure if I know how to enjoy myself anymore. The thought of being a lady again and sleeping in a real bed is sheer heaven."

Fariba smiled back at her. "My dear, you must tell me about it some time when you are ready to. In the meantime, this is your home. Be at peace here, and rest as well. Now we should take our bath and prepare for the evening meal."

The women servants came to assist the two ladies with their clothes, and then they bathed together in a large tiled tub in the room adjoining the living quarters. This was a luxury for Rav'an; to have the water almost on call, as it were, was quite outside her normal experience. Nor had she expected to be washed by a servant. Fariba soaked in the large bath, watching with an amused smile the bemused expression on Rav'an's face as she was ministered to by the willing servants who helped wash her luxurious hair and then used perfumed oils on her body as she stood naked on the exquisite tiled floor.

Later, in Fariba's bedroom, she found herself being helped to dress in silk and light cotton materials with rich silver and gold threads woven into its fabric. The voluminous pantaloons were of finest cotton, the slippers complimented her delicate feet, while the blouse she wore over a light silk slip set off her throat and breasts to perfection. Over this, the maids placed a sleeveless coat of fine wool that came down below her knees. It was a light tan color with intricately woven patterns down its length. There was even gold filigree woven along its borders.

Her hair was dried and then coifed into the ringlets and curls of the current style. Another servant, who clucked at the sight of her nails, manicured her fingers and toes, making complimentary remarks all the while about her well formed feet and ankles. The transformation was extraordinary. Fariba and the girls who had worked on Rav'an stared at the wonderful creation that pirouetted before their delighted gaze.

"You are so beautiful, my Rav'an, no one will recognize you. I cannot wait for the time when the others see you." Fariba clapped her hands with delight and then commanded her servants to bring tea and sweet cakes to celebrate with. While the servants hastened off, she bade Rav'an sit on a cushion while she talked to her.

"Now, Rav'an, you should know that the moment the young nobles get to know you are here, and hear about your beauty, you will be beset with suitors. We have to be careful about who we meet, as there will be spies here in Isfahan, too. The doctor has allowed Dav'ud to come next week, which I did not think wise of him, but he might have his own reasons. He may have in mind *taqiyah*, which means to hide our true being. You will have to wear a veil whenever you travel into the city, whether on horseback or just walking. It is also very important that you are escorted everywhere you go, my dear. It is unthinkable for a young woman, especially one such as you, to go unescorted anywhere outside a house."

"That should not be a problem, Fariba. I have my two protectors. Talon and Reza will escort me everywhere I want to go."

Fariba nodded. "I agree. I would also suggest that if Dav'ud asks you to attend some spectacle with him, that the boys go with you as well."

"Do you think he will do this?" Rav'an asked curiously.

"Oh, yes, indeed I do. I do not intend, however, that he should think it will be easy to do so. Unless..." She looked at Rav'an out of the corner of her eye. "You decide that you might want to."

Rav'an laughed. "Aunt Fariba," she said, pretending to sound indignant, "how can you suppose that I might? I don't even know the man."

Fariba laughed, too. "We have to see what the doctor has to say about it all. However, you should be prepared to receive visitors, my dear."

The servants came back with trays of hot, light tea and small cakes of crushed almonds mixed with honey and sprinkled with sesame seeds. Rav'an pronounced them delicious.

*****

The boys and the doctor were seated cross-legged on the expensive Tabrizi carpets at a low polished table inlaid with ivory and brass filigree. They were discussing his plans for them while in Isfahan, when the doctor suddenly stopped talking and stared past them at the entrance with a very surprised look on his face.

The boys both turned and gaped, quite forgetting their manners. They sat and stared at the beautiful apparitions that appeared, gliding towards them. It was Rav'an, alongside an amused, equally well-dressed Fariba. There was a cough from the doctor and they scrambled to their feet to stand with looks of utter astonishment on their faces. Then they bowed low.

Fariba was the first to speak. "My dear doctor, boys, your mouths are open. Please shut them. Do you not recall seeing Rav'an before?"

Rav'an gave a shy smile as she came up to them. She was beginning to realize what an effect she had on men.

Fariba held her hand, asked her to turn in front of the men, and then laughed. "Is she not now a real princess?"

The doctor smiled at them both. "I shall have to say it for all three of us, as the other two are still catching flies. Rav'an, you are exquisite. Fariba, you have transformed her. I am delighted to see your handiwork. And you, too, my dear, are exquisite as ever. Come and be seated, and we shall talk, then eat supper."

He clapped his hands for the servants. Rav'an was placed opposite Talon, who sat down after her. He could not take his eyes off her, while Reza looked stunned. The doctor gave orders for some more wine and sherbet to be brought to them.

Rav'an gazed back at Talon, straight into his eyes, and smiled. He thought his world had stopped for a moment. Then he had to look down to regain his equilibrium. He was afraid his expression would give too much away. He had always known she was a good-looking girl, but here in front of him was a beauty he could hardly fathom. He had to force himself to concentrate on what the doctor was saying.

Farj'an was saying that he was going to be visiting his colleagues in the college of medicine in the following weeks. He hoped that sometimes they would accompany him, but there were also several things that he wanted from the three of them.

"You are all three accomplished in the arts of war; that has been demonstrated to me, and others," he said in his dry manner. "But there is more to being a person than simply that. I wish that you would all continue your education here in Isfahan, and I will arrange for tutors to come and instruct you in the arts, history, the languages, and more." He smiled at the barely hidden dismay on the faces of all three.

"My children, if you are to survive in this world, it is important that you know more than you do. Endure the tutors and you might even enjoy it. You will have much free time to see the city. Indeed,

I wish for you to do so, but we should be careful, even here in Isfahan. There are Ismaili in the region who know me and who will be curious. You are not entirely out of danger, Rav'an, my dear."

He paused, sipping his wine from a small silver goblet. "Rav'an, you have also to understand that there will be young men who will want to come and meet you. I am sure that Fariba has explained to you that you cannot go into the city without an escort. I would recommend that the boys, at least one, always accompany you whenever you do go out. Please defer to Fariba for advice in all things."

Rav'an nodded. "Indeed, I shall, Uncle; she is taking good care of me." She grinned at the boys, her mischievous nature reasserting itself. "I am sure I shall have no difficulty with an escort, either."

The boys smiled back, uncertain as to what she might be referring.

Farj'an tugged his beard, smiling. "No, I suppose not." He glanced over at Fariba, who was looking at Talon speculatively. "We must always be careful with your visitors as well. The young man Dav'ud will try to come next week. I could deny him, but he will persist, so it might be better to let him come in controlled circumstances. We shall practice a form of *taqiyah* and conceal ourselves in their midst."

The servants came back and served everyone wine and tasty pieces of dried, spicy meat with goat's cheese mixed with herbs on biscuits. They feasted on smoked olives in oil with garlic and herbs. Small quail eggs were provided, along with eggplant cooked crisp in sesame oil.

There was *badhinjan buran*, as Fariba explained it, pureed eggplant with yogurt and spices. The main course was called *bastaniya* and was composed of spiced chicken and lamb with pears, peaches, and almonds. This was followed by a desert of honeyed dates stuffed with almonds and scented with rosewater that Fariba told them was called *rutab mu'assal.*

Rav'an was enthusiastic about the foods, most of which she had only heard about and some she knew not at all. The remote fastness of the mountains did not cater to the imagination when it came to exotic recipes. Fariba delighted in explaining the foods and the combinations to her, proud to show off the rich culinary heritage of the city of Isfahan. As for the boys, they ate what came in front of them with appreciative expressions on their faces.

The group relaxed and conversation became general as they all settled into the atmosphere of the comfortable house the doctor possessed. Fariba excused herself. While she was away, the servants brought a dark liquid called *khaffee*, which the doctor explained, came as beans from the dark continent of Africa by way of Omani trading vessels. It was crushed and then boiled in water until it became a thick syrupy liquid and was served in tiny cups. Fariba come back a little later with a *tar* in her hand. The doctor sighed and settled back into his cushions. His water pipe glowed and he smiled at her.

"I am happy that you decided to sing for us, my dear. Now you shall impress these children."

She smiled at him fondly, and began to play the long, twelve-stringed instrument with delicate fingers. She played with skill in a practiced manner that indicted she had done this many times. Rav'an and the boys did as the doctor did, settling into the cushions and listening raptly.

Fariba was an accomplished singer, too, having been in the court at Herat in Afghanistan when a very young woman. Her music varied as she carried her audience with her in songs of happiness and then legend, followed by a lullaby. These were the songs of ancient Persia, which had come about long before the heavy hand of Islam came with the Arabs.

They told of heroes and heroines, of tragedy and happiness, free of inhibition and pure in their innocence. When she began to sing a lullaby, Talon sat up abruptly. He looked startled but then settled down into the cushions again to listen.

As the haunting notes of the song, combined with the notes of the *tar*, rose to the ceiling, Talon's memory recalled the time when he was stricken with fever. It seemed like another world where he'd been wounded by that lion. He'd heard the song then; he didn't know who'd sung it. He experienced a wrench as his mind went back to that time and the days he'd spent with Jean the priest. Once again, he mourned his old friend and mentor.

That night Talon dreamed that Rav'an came to him and they made love. He woke to find that he had spilled his seed. He lay in the bed trying to recall the images of the dream, and it was a long time before sleep finally came to him.

The next day and many thereafter, the young trio were guided by both the doctor and Fariba's gentle but firm hand as they learned the customs and expected behavior for living in their very new world. A routine developed that suited them, with variations in the afternoons, when there were visitors to the house or they themselves went out to see the city. There was a constant stream of visitors to see the doctor, and much of his time was spent at the academy of medicine, where he practiced his work and met with colleagues.

He also sent the boys on errands, by which they contrived to go together with Rav'an about the city; they explored Isfahan in this manner. Talon had never been in a city of any kind other than the brief sojourn in Hamadan. For him, Isfahan and its proud people represented a world that he soon came to love. He was often the center of discussion because of his physical contrast with the local people. He now stood several inches taller than average and was filling out, becoming a handsome young man.

Women gazed at him from under their *chadors*, while men of lesser stature envied him. Most everyone answered his questions for directions or even provided him with an explanation of his whereabouts.

He admired the long bridge that crossed the wide, sluggish river, not yet in spate from the spring thaws. Farj'an told him that Roman prisoners had originally constructed it. The three of them spent some time on the bridge looking into the water and at the boats on the river. It was novel. It was fascinating.

Portions of Isfahan was still under construction. The Seljuk Sultans had great ambitions to build, using the new and more versatile method of kiln baked mud bricks. There were people who thought it dangerous to place too many of these bricks one upon the other, but in fact it seemed that one could build very high and quite safe buildings by this new-fangled method. The conservatives hinted darkly that they would all see how good it was when there was an earthquake. Never having been in one, Talon could only speculate as to what they might be talking about. Reza had told him a long time ago about how his parents died in one, so he decided that he was not eager to experience it.

They'd been in the house now for almost two weeks. Previously, almost every day they'd gone to a new place, looking over their shoulders most of that time. Now they were a long way from perceived danger, and some of their former wariness was gone.

Talon loved the comfort of their surroundings, from the easy access to bathing facilities, to being able to enjoy the garden and the excellent food.

Even the tutors that the doctor had engaged were interesting, although they were somewhat pompous and condescending to the two rough young men. He had been introduced to the tutors as Talon from Anatolia, hence his looks and accent. Reza came from Tabriz, as far as they were concerned, which deflected any further curiosity. The two young men woke early, when the mullahs called the faithful to prayers from their minarets. The sound was echoed and repeated as first one and then another would take up the call. Soon, the whole city seemed to be calling the faithful to prayers. The servants who were already up would be kneeling, facing Mecca. The boys slipped into the same practice without difficulty and would follow the ritual washing of the face then hands and arms, taking care that they did it without mistake, then they'd join the servants as they prayed.

Following prayers, they'd go into the gardens and spar with one another to keep their fighting skills honed. The garden provided a large private area within which to practice. They could even practice their archery. There was an orchard in one corner of the garden with a long, clear path, right down between the pear trees and cherry trees, ideal for shooting arrows down its length.

Rav'an, not to be left out, would join them at archery as often as she could and became proficient with the small bow. The other servants treated them as though they were related to the doctor, left them alone, and accorded them all the respect due to members of his family. The house servants had learned from the servants who came with the doctor from Hamadan that the two young men were not to be trifled with.

Rav'an came as much to ensure that she saw Talon as to practice. In spite of the wondrous things to which she was being exposed, he still represented her anchor, and there were few other opportunities to be alone together. They would often sit near the larger pond in the early mornings after practice and watch the huge carp move sluggishly in the dark water beneath the lily pads. The garden was also waking up. There would be birdcalls from the doves and the ducks. Rav'an loved the cry of the two peacocks that roamed the garden as though it belonged to them. The male was forever showing off his magnificent plumage to his mate, much to the amusement of the girl, who used to tease the boys about this common male attribute.

Sometimes Reza would stay, and the three would talk about their impressions of Isfahan or some visitor or other who had been to see the doctor. This was the time when the three of them opened up to each other and become closer as friends. Finally, Reza would go off to clean up before breakfast, while Talon and Rav'an often lingered, finding some excuse to do so. It was stolen time for them both. Neither wanted to make it known that there was anything going on between them, unsure as they were about what the reaction might be.

Nonetheless, there were intense moments. It happened as they were conversing in low tones, Reza having just left. Rav'an leaned over to Talon to wipe beads of sweat off his forehead. Her arm was extended, causing her breast to stretch the thin fabric of her blouse. He was entranced by the clear outline of her small, perfectly shaped breast and the darker nipple pushing forward. Talon could not restrain himself. He reached and cupped her gently in his hand. In an instant, her hand went behind his head, and they sought each other's lips like starving people. The embrace was passionate, and they kissed hungrily for a long moment. At last, Rav'an drew away, gasping. They were both disheveled by now.

She gave a shaky laugh. "Ah, Talon, I am so hungry for you. I cannot wait much longer," she whispered, leaning her forehead against his shoulder.

He nodded. "I, too, my love. By God, I too."

Her eyes glowed. "Do you love me, my protector?"

He fell to his knee. "Forever and forever," he said in solemn tones. They smiled into each other's eyes.

She touched his lips with her fingers, gently and with regret. He held her hand and then released her to stand up and lift her up with him. They parted, with Rav'an running off to greet Fariba and commence the day's activities.

Talon walked pensively towards the house. He reflected on their growing need for one another. He was without doubt deeply in love with this beautiful creature. Hitherto, he had not thought much beyond the next day. During their escape, and even before then, he had been busy. Their meetings, although intense, had been occasional, more of an adventure in risk and excitement.

Now, however, he wondered how he could be without her for a day or even an hour. He wondered if it showed. Reza never said anything, but Talon knew he was observant. Neither the doctor nor Fariba had even hinted that they knew about the relationship. He was full of doubt as to where their future lay.

He was a trained *fida'i* for the Assassin sect. His complete loyalty lay with her brother, the Agha Khan, the master, who, when they were free of Arash, could then command him to go on a mission and ultimately to his death. He knew, too, that he would be bound to obey.

What then of Rav'an? Was she to be given to some old, lecherous sultan, vizier, or caliph to seal a pact that was advantageous to the master? He actually growled to himself in frustration at the thought of one of these people with his hands on her. He would not allow it to happen. But how? There was a deep, hopeless feeling in the pit of his stomach at the thought.

As he came to the entrance of his room deep in thought, scowling to himself, Reza, full of excitement, came out of his room and told Talon that he had heard the young man Dav'ud was going to pay a visit that day. Talon groaned.

Dav'ud did indeed come to visit in the late morning, as was fitting. He rode up to the house gates and was allowed entrance by one of the servants acting as the guard for the day. This was an event to be conducted along very formal lines. In Persia, although a young lady had far more freedom than her counterparts in the Arabian south, there were still very strict codes of conduct that had to be adhered to. All this Talon learned from Rav'an, who had in turn been instructed by Fariba.

Talon was just angry that some noble youth could come to the house with the sole purpose of making eyes at the girl whose heart, he believed, belonged to him. Reza, ever quick to notice his friend's moods, mentioned that Talon seemed put out. Thinking that it might be a simple protective instinct for their princess, he clapped Talon on the shoulder and told him not to worry, as they would still be with her when and if she went out on the town with the young nobleman.

They whiled the time away with the horses, as Talon was proving fidgety, and the only place Reza knew where his friend would settle down was with the horses. They concentrated on grooming the animals, which had lost their thick winter coats and were beginning to fill out from their former quite thin appearance.

Jabbar liked being groomed, especially by Talon, who enjoyed it just as much. Talon finished brushing the horse's long, silky tail, and then stroked his long, glossy flanks with a light piece of fine cotton. The coat shone to his approval, then Jabbar nudged his master with a soft nose, looking for some sweet thing. Pretending to be impatient with him, Talon told him to behave, but, as usual, he reached into his pockets and pulled out a small honey cake. Jabbar slurped up the cake and the crumbs from his hand with his large tongue and inquisitive nose, leaving it wet and sticky.

He rebuked the animal for his bad manners and wiped his hands absently on the cloth. He was still thinking about his last encounter with Rav'an, wondering how he could change what he perceived to be their ordained fate. He was content with the fact that he saw more of Rav'an than ever before, although that often left him frustrated. He became aware that Reza was talking to him and called out.

"Reza, I did not hear you. Repeat what you said?"

"I said, for the deaf people here," Reza called back, "remember the game we saw Dav'ud playing when we came to the city? Didn't the doctor call it *Cho'gan*? I would like to learn that game. Why don't we ask him if we can take part?"

Talon was silent. It seemed a good idea; he was ready for some excitement too. "We should go into the house and play chess, perhaps, and wait for Dav'ud to begin to leave. Then we can talk to him without being intruders," he said.

He knew all to well that he had ulterior reasons for saying this, but he was also intrigued with the game of *Cho'gan*.

They finished with the horses and made their way to the inside courtyard where they would be able to play near to the fountain and also be able to keep an eye open for the departing visitor.

The game of chess, from the doctor's point of view, was one that challenged the intellect, and the two young men enjoyed it immensely. It tested them and made both of them consider moves with great care before they rushed in, which they had done at the beginning. The doctor could still beat either of them, or sometimes, both at the same time. In his quiet, subtle way, he offered lessons as they played, pointing out that chess was something like real life, either on the battlefield or in a palace full of intriguing nobles. Talon liked that, and made a point of studying the game. It amused him that the doctor also said that many of the religious leaders of the day condemned the game as being wicked. But he said that the Mullahs usually disliked anything that could not be associated with some law or other in the Quoran, throwing his hands into the air in exasperation at the pettiness of mankind yet again.

Talon and Reza were well into the game when they heard the

unmistakable sounds of impending departure. They made their way to the main entrance, where they hoped to be able to intercept the young noble. He came out accompanied by Fariba and a manservant. Rav'an was walking demurely behind them. Both women were veiled, even though they were in their own house. They were talking in low voices, but it was clear that Dav'ud was happy with the proceedings.

He looked up as he came to the young men, who bowed and wished him good health. He returned the pleasantry, and Fariba graciously introduced him to Talon and Reza, briefly explaining their presence in the house. Dav'ud appraised the two. He saw two young men of about his age, but they looked tough. The taller one had a long scar along his jaw that made him look dangerous. He sensed that these two could look after themselves. However, Reza spoke politely enough, saying that he had seen *Cho'gan* being played. Was there any chance they could learn?

Dav'ud's response was quick: He would like to take them all to watch a game. Turning to Fariba, he all but begged, "*Khanom*, would you and my lady, Rav'an, do me the great honor of being my guests at a game tomorrow? I could then show you all the game?"

Fariba looked stern. "Young man, you have but just met us."

"I know, *Khanom*," Dav'ud replied, with a disarming smile, "but *Cho'gan*, or *Pilao*, as some call it, is a king's game, and you will love to watch. And as it is late winter now, spring just around the corner, the days are cool and the afternoons warm but not hot, so our timing is perfect!" His eyes pleaded with her for a yes.

He turned to Rav'an. "My lady Rav'an, I am sure you are a good rider; this is a game that demands the skill of a warrior in battle and the keenest eye for the ball. It is wonderful to watch and play."

His enthusiasm was infectious. Fariba relented enough to say sternly, "I must ask the doctor. If he gives permission, then we shall see. You shall have your answer tomorrow morning."

Dav'ud smiled a brilliant smile that showed off his white teeth beneath his well-groomed mustache and bowed deeply to her, and then to Rav'an. "I shall send a servant for your answer in the morning. Until then, ladies, may Allah protect you."

With a short bow to the two young men, he walked out the doors to the waiting servants. He sprang into the saddle and cantered off down the garden road, horse, and rider looking very elegant as they passed through the gates. His small retinue of personal guards was waiting for him outside.

As he went out, he turned his horse, looking back at the watching people at the door as though he wanted to catch a final glimpse of Rav'an as he left, raised his hand and was gone.

Fariba directed the three of them to come and share a sherbet with her in the cool of the inner courtyard, where they discussed the visit. Rather Rav'an and Fariba did for the boys' benefit. It was clear that Fariba approved of the young man. Dav'ud was a nobleman's son. His family came from Old Persian stock that could go back over two hundred years. Somehow, they had managed to do well even under the Seljuk sultans' rules. He was very polite and observed all the protocols. Fariba could find no fault with his manners.

It went without saying he was besotted with Rav'an. She herself had little to say. Indeed, she did like the young man for all the reasons Fariba had stated, but that was as far as it went. The last thing she wanted to appear to Talon was enthusiastic about Dav'ud. She was sure of where her feelings lay in that respect.

They enjoyed the evening warmth while the two boys finished off the game of chess. It was Reza's turn to win, as Talon played in a distracted manner, which did not escape Rav'an's—nor an observant Fariba's—notice.

To soothe their collective minds, Fariba called for her *tar* and played for them. They were all entranced by the beautiful notes she drew from the stringed instrument, and listened intently to the songs she'd learned as a courtesan. As the notes filled the courtyard, the house went silent as even the servants quieted their background murmur. Indeed, the house itself seemed to be listening.

When the doctor came back to the house, Fariba waited until they were alone in his rooms that night before broaching the subject of the *Cho'gan* game for the next afternoon.

He hesitated, but then agreed. Farj'an was concerned that a girl as attractive as Rav'an might be recognized if they went out into the public forum too often. But then, he reasoned with Fariba, there was not much likelihood that there would be anyone at all who would make the connection. His other concern was that Dav'ud would become too eager and propose. Fariba laughed at that, but then pointed out that a courtship, if that was what was coming, would take many months, and by then the issue of the master would be resolved and Rav'an could go home.

Fariba had trouble understanding why anyone would want to go back to the cold, savage mountain fastness that Rav'an had come from, but supposed that was what would happen sooner or later. She did not mention to the doctor, as they went to bed, that she suspected that Talon also was smitten with the girl, promising herself that she would have to keep an eye on this situation and see where it went.

The next morning, when the three came together, Talon was subdued and distant. Reza was too busy practicing to notice, but Rav'an, ever sensitive to Talon and his moods, noticed at once. The tension got worse when Talon drew on his bow and it broke. The string twanged and the arrow went off into a palm tree and he got a blow on his jaw from his own right fist. He cursed quietly and rubbed his jaw, looking down at the broken bow.

Rav'an skipped over to him and asked, concerned, if he were all right, to which he replied, somewhat brusquely, "I'm all right; the bow must have gotten wet at some point on the road. Where will I now find another bow?" he complained.

"We will find one in Isfahan," she said soothingly. "There are bow-makers here, I am sure of it. We will ask the servants."

He nodded without looking at her. Reza joined them and they discussed the bow, looking it over. It had not been new, but it had been a good one all the same. Talon didn't tarry in the garden that morning. He went off directly with Reza to clean up for breakfast.

Rav'an was hurt, and she made her way to her rooms and the morning ritual bath with Fariba in a somber mood. She was sure the reason for Talon's surliness was because of Dav'ud's visit and decided to ask Fariba to cancel the visit for the afternoon to the *Cho'gan* games.

However, when she got to the rooms, Fariba told her in a pleased tone that the doctor had given his permission. The messenger had come and gone to say that they would be waiting for Dav'ud to come and collect them all that afternoon. She also looked forward to the games, and indeed, the doctor would accompany them as well. It would be nice to have an outing with this kind man, whose work kept him away most of the day.

Rav'an decided not to ask for a cancellation. She determined to catch Talon alone and demand an explanation for his unkind treatment.

Indeed, Talon was asking himself the same question. He was a surprised at how he had behaved, but his doubts had come home to him the night before and left him sleepless. How was he to match up to someone like Dav'ud, who was of the nobility, wealthy, and more than able to bring to Rav'an all the things a beautiful woman could need? The fact that the man had come to the doctor's own house to meet her meant that he was serious.

To Talon's tortured mind, it meant the beginning of the end. It would not be long before that stuck-up prig was negotiating with the doctor for the princess' hand. He knew he was becoming very jealous, and berated himself for this. It didn't stop the thought of killing Dav'ud from crossing his mind all the same. But then he argued against it because that would then hurt Rav'an, and so it went round and round until the early hours. He'd slept very little before Reza kicked his feet to wake him, cheerfully telling him to stop dreaming and come and practice.

After breakfast, which he ate in silence while the others talked about the impending games, he stayed away from the house, working on the horses and oiling the leather of the bridles until it was time to get ready to go to the games.

* * * * *

High above the valley of Alamut, a party of horsemen led by Ahmad Khan left the great castle and cautiously wended their way down the steep, icy track to the valley bottom. Ahmad was in a foul mood. He was to find a way out of the snowbound Shah Rud and get to Samiran as fast as possible. His father had told him that he was to intercept the escaped trio at all costs, to detain them at Samiran, and to wait for him to follow and deal with them.

As he rode through the frozen wastes of the Shah Rud valley on his way first to Lamissar, then on to the head of the long Shah Rud, his thoughts were bitter as he contemplated the harm the princess and her cursed two bodyguards had inflicted upon him.

He had come back to the castle of Alamut after two days of fruitless attempts to get over Chula Pass. All their efforts to clear the landslide had proved worthless. Then, to make matters worse, it had begun to snow again, which had left him with no choice but to send men once again over the mound to get to Ghazvin on foot. They carried gold and were to discover what direction the refugees had taken, even if it meant paying mercenaries to do their work for them; when he did get over the passes he would follow them with a large body of men.

He told them to find mercenaries and promise them the gold as payment. They were to kill the boys but spare the princess at any cost. He had heard nothing, and finally he had to get back to Alamut to report to his father, something he dreaded. His father, in the kind of rages he was capable of, could easily order his own son killed. Fortunately, although Arash had been in a towering rage that had cowed Ahmad to the point of babbling, he had not taken his life.

Instead, the seething Arash had told him to prepare to go to Samiran, and this time to get there despite the snow and the weather, or else he *would* kill him with his own hands.

Ahmad had stumbled out of his father's rooms a frightened man. He had rushed down the stairs and told his men to prepare to move within a day. The tired, frightened men had grumbled under their breath, but none dared to argue with Ahmad. In the mood he was in, he would have killed them on the spot.

So Ahmad left with twelve men and some spare horses on a cold, clear day that promised eventually to warm up. He looked up at the sky and prayed that it would not snow again before he made it out of the valley. He was going to take his chances at the far western end, where the princess' party had first come into the valley. On the way, he would pick up the captain and his men and so add to his force in case he had the misfortune to run into some marauding men from the sultan's army. It was so cold they were more likely to be huddled in their houses with a bright, warm fire and a woman to keep them warm in bed, he thought resentfully. He wished he was doing the same instead of risking his life out on the frozen waste of this forbidding land.

A week later he and the remnants of his party arrived at the gates of Samiran, demanding entrance from a surprised guard. They had encountered raging rivers and downed bridges because of the warm snap, as well as waist-deep snow when the weather changed. Several were missing from the group of men that had set out from Alamut. As they rode into the castle *maidan*, they presented a sorry sight. Their horses were worn out, the men exhausted and ragged.

Ahmad wasted no time in taking control of the castle by right of being the son of Arash Khan. The castellan reluctantly deferred to him from then on, wondering why it seemed to be so important that Ahmad have full control. Ahmad issued orders that the roads were to be watched for three people: one a girl, the other two the foreigner Talon and his companion, Reza, both of whom had been trained at Samiran.

There was a buzz of surprise at this news, as almost everyone knew both the boys. What could they have done to bring the wrath of Arash Khan down upon them like this? Nevertheless, much more attention was paid to anyone at all who now came through the castle and the nearby town. Travelers still moved around the country, even in winter, so although it was very difficult, some few intrepid groups of travelers struggled from town to town along the main highway. Most often, they sought shelter in the town of Samiran, or if they were a larger group, they stopped at the castle to pay their dues.

Ahmad and his men questioned the residents of both the castle and the town as to whether the three fugitives had been through the area on their way north. It was hardly reassuring to hear that the road to Ghazvin had been open on occasion and that travelers had indeed passed through. However, most of them had stayed, as the roads north were still blocked most of the way to Tabriz. Ahmad and his men bullied and harried people, to the point where they became thoroughly unpopular with both the townspeople and the residents of the castle. People began to avoid them, taking care to go in another direction if they saw any of the newcomers coming.

Talon and Reza had been popular young men while in Samiran, in particular with the women, who asked themselves what the two boys could possibly have done. Not just that, who was the mysterious woman with them? Had they not escorted the princess to Alamut? Where was she in all this? The gossip and whispering grew as the bullying went on.

Having satisfied himself that the three fugitives had not slipped through his fingers, Ahmad sent the captain and his men north to wait in Tabriz while he settled down in Samiran, much to the unhappiness of the local people.

The Ball no Question makes of Ayes and Noes,
But Right or Left as strikes the Player goes;
And He that toss'd you down into the Field,
He knows about it all—HE knows—HE knows

– Omar Khayyam –

Chapter 22
Cho'gan

The doctor's party was met by Dav'ud, elegantly dressed and with a modest escort of men-at-arms and servants. The ladies were dressed in fine riding clothes and rich, soft, leather boots for riding. The doctor looked very distinguished in his fine town robes and enormous turban, while the boys wore their best clothes for the occasion.

The doctor was greeted very respectfully by Dav'ud, as was Fariba. Then he bowed politely to a well-veiled Rav'an and acknowledged the boys with a smile and a nod. Salutations done, they all moved off toward the center of the city. It was quiet in the tree-lined avenue down which they rode, but already there were other parties heading for the same place.

Greetings were called and acknowledged between parties as they met. Riders mingled and then moved off again, heading for the great square in the center of the city known as the *maidan*. There were other veiled women riding elegant ponies that day, moving without hindrance among the men, greeting each other with elaborate phrases and polite conversation.

Everyone knew Dav'ud, so he played host and introduced people to one another as they went. There were lingering glances bestowed upon Talon by ladies who were with other parties. He stood out, not least because he was a strong-looking young man, but the scar lent a dangerous air to him. His eyes were commented upon in whispers, some of which came to Fariba's keen ears, who smiled inside. She herself was quite taken with the quiet young Frank, liking his manners and thoughtful approach to things.

Dav'ud explained that they were heading for the great *maidan* of Isfahan, where the vizier held the tournaments for the *Cho'gan* games. Today there were several games to be played in a knockout set, leading to a final game a month away. He said that it would be instructive to see the games now, so that they would have a better appreciation when the final game was held. He gave a brief explanation of the rules to them as they rode. *Cho'gan*, he told them, was a game for warriors and developed their tactical skill.

"If they care to learn it," the doctor commented.

Dav'ud smiled at that, then continued. It was a fast game that required the best of horsemen to compete. To be recognized as a good *Cho'gan* player was considered a prerequisite for high rank in an army and brought much adulation, as the people of Isfahan worshipped the champions and their teams. There was a lot of rivalry.

There were two teams of four horsemen to each side. Open goals were set up at each end of the *maidan*, and the riders carried mallets, or sticks of whippy cane with a wooden head, with which to hit the ball. The purpose of the game was to put a small round ball made from willow root, about the size of a man's fist, between the goalposts belonging to the other side as many times as possible before the referees on the sidelines blew trumpets to signal the end of the game. That moment was determined by the whim of the judges and their enthusiasm for that particular game at the time. Although, he said, the games usually lasted for about a half hour of frantic activity.

If a pony went down or was injured, the game stopped for the rider to change mounts; otherwise, it only stopped when someone scored a goal, and the riders went back to the middle for a "throw in" from the grand pavilion overlooking the playing field. A man would hurl the ball into the midst of the assembled riders, after which it was a free-for-all. He grinned at the boys when he said this, as though it excited him just to think about it. They smiled.

They heard the noise from the great *maidan* before they came to it. There were already crowds of people on foot; the common man of Isfahan was an avid follower of *Cho'gan* and each had his favorite team. Everyone was trying to get a look at the middle of the field, where there were many riders strutting their ponies. The men were dressed in the height of fashion, wearing no armor, just as though they were about to go on an elaborate parade instead of taking part in a simulated battle.

It was a huge space of cleared ground, smoothed over so that it was almost flat. Talon estimated that it must be two hundred paces long by one hundred wide, bordered on all sides by the milling crowd. There was an enormous mosque of great beauty, which was still under construction at one end, set well back from the field itself. Even in its unfinished state, the mosque dominated the *maidan*.

Dav'ud's family had a pavilion of their own on the same side of the grounds as the grand pavilion. They were given space to make their way through the eager, gawking, noisy crowd to the pavilion, where there were already people seated or standing. As they made their way, the people in other pavilions greeted Dav'ud and commented on the newcomers. It did not escape many people's notice that, despite the veils they wore, there were two very beautiful women in Dav'ud's entourage.

Just as they dismounted and handed their horses off to waiting servants, a trumpet sounded and the crowd hushed expectantly. A man in herald's clothing, wearing an impressive turban with a huge feather in it, stood on the edge of a platform by the grand pavilion and shouted out names. Men whose names he called saluted with their sticks or shouted back acknowledgement and made their way to the center of the field, where they sat bestride their ponies. Those not called left the field to the eight men on ponies in the middle.

Dav'ud made introductions while they seated themselves on cushions placed on large carpets upon a platform. Thus, they could be seated but still have a good view of the entire *maidan* at the same time. The game was about to start, Dav'ud whispered to them. Talon and Reza sat at the back, while Rav'an, the doctor, and Fariba were seated to the front. Dav'ud stood nearby in attendance, his eyes often looking over at Rav'an.

Talon hated him, but he had to admit the man was good company and had treated him and Reza with respect. He resolved to concentrate on the game.

The herald who had done the announcing now stood at the very edge of the grand pavilion with a small white ball in his hand. It gleamed with polish and oil as he held it to the sun. Then, in a swift motion, he hurled the ball straight into the middle of the group of men on horseback. To the confused eyes of the newcomers, what followed seemed like nothing less than a savage fight with sticks by men on horseback. The sticks went up and down, slashing and hacking in the melee of ponies and riders. The dust began to rise, but then, after a few frantic seconds, the ball hurtled out from among the tangled group of ponies, a rider in hot pursuit.

The lead rider rode right up to the fast-bouncing ball and swung his stick in a huge arc, leaning into the strike. To Talon's amazement, he struck the ball with a loud click as the mallet connected with the ball, and it soared into the air, flying scores of yards before landing and bouncing along the ground straight to the goalposts. The crowd roared its approval. The rider galloped furiously after the ball, followed by all the other riders now trying to catch him. One of the closest was leaning out over his galloping pony with his stick held out in front of him. As they caught up with the front rider, the one behind tried to hook his stick as he, in turn, tried to hit the bouncing ball again. The sticks touched, and he missed the ball. Cursing, both riders rode over the ball in a cloud of dust, trying to stop and turn their already sweating animals.

Meanwhile, others from the group descended upon the ball, fighting each other for a good shot at it. Elbows and sticks were used with wild abandon on each other as they battled. Five riders swung at the ball and missed, and there were more shouted curses, flying hooves, and ponies down on their haunches as riders brutally forced them to stop and turn.

The last of the riders came up to the ball, steadying his horse as he did so. He struck the ball deliberately from the front, driving it behind him with considerable force. The ball went into the air again in the opposite direction. The game now pirouetted on that point as the whole group, shouting and yelling, charged after the flying ball to the thunder of hooves on the hard ground.

Once again, the eight riders raced down onto the bouncing ball, slashing and striking at its elusive shape. It was struck again in the same direction, and this time it flew to within twenty yards of the opposite goalposts. The crowd screamed and yelled with excitement as they saw a point coming. The riders closed as a bunch on the slowing ball and swept over it in a cloud of dust and galloping shapes. Incredibly, every player missed the ball. There were howls of laughter and derision as the crowd berated their respective teams for letting the opportunity go by. Insults as to their pedigree and their ability to play the game were shouted with noisy abandon.

Then once again a lone rider came out of the thick of the struggling group and rode down upon the stationary ball half-buried in the dust. He galloped straight up to it and tapped it out of the depression it was in, knocking it forward. The crowd screamed at him that he was going in the wrong direction. To Talon and Reza, who had not a clue as to which direction he should have been going in, it was very confusing. The rider knew what he was doing, though. As the ball rolled free he rode over it, and then, with his mallet across his body, he leaned well out over the moving ball and struck it back-handed. Once again, there was a loud click and the ball lifted high into the air, flying well over the goalposts and landing deep among the now ecstatic crowd. There was an approving roar from all around the *maidan*.

The trumpet sounded, and the riders trotted or cantered back to the center of the *maidan*. There were back slaps and much leaning over to kiss the hero of the moment on the cheeks by the team to which he belonged. As they came to the middle, the riders paused to wait while a servant on the side of the pavilion where the goal had been scored placed a red flag.

Once again, the man in the grand pavilion stood straight and held a ball over his head, and again he threw the ball into the players' midst. This sequence was repeated several times, with both sides gaining goals, until the game stood at two all.

Talon and Reza were riveted. This was entirely new to them, but both being excellent horsemen, this was a game they could appreciate and imagine taking part in. Neither saw Fariba nudge Rav'an and both smile as they looked at the two concentrating on nothing else but the game. Rav'an, too, was caught up in the excitement of the moment and was enjoying herself. She smiled at the two boys as she thought of them.

Dav'ud, thinking she smiled at him, blushed and gave her a joyful smile. He could hardly believe his luck. Rav'an was one among thousands, he thought. He could not wait to brag to his friends about her. He decided to talk to her two young companions and ask them what they thought of the game so far. He turned and moved towards them.

"Do you like the game?" he enquired pleasantly.

They both nodded vigorously.

"It is a game for warriors, just as you said," Reza said, his enthusiasm bubbling over. "I would love to learn how to play, and I know Talon would, too." He turned to his friend and tapped him on his arm. "Wouldn't you, Talon?"

Talon nodded. "Yes, it's a fast game that requires good horsemanship and a good eye."

Dav'ud thought he saw a way to get to know these people better, thus ensuring that he could see more of Rav'an. "If you're interested, I could teach you. We practice in that place where we first met. Would you like to come tomorrow?"

Their enthusiastic looks told him all he needed to know.

"Then come in the morning, a few hours after dawn when it's cool. I'll be there, and we can start."

"Thank you, Dav'ud," Reza said, speaking for both of them. Talon nodded his thanks. He was not yet ready to be friends with his competition.

The game had started again. This time, Dav'ud explained the way it was going. These two teams, he said, were not the best they would see. They should watch how the men clustered together and how many passes there were. Talon wanted to know what he meant. Dav'ud explained that if a team could open the game up, they could pass to each other and move the ball down the field very quickly and score more goals, and so win. That made sense to Talon and Reza, who resolved to listen to this friendly young man who had entered their lives.

He pointed out good shots and how the better riders, who leaned well over the ball and moved their arm in a long sweeping motion, achieved them. If the mallet hit the ball just right, he told them, it could travel a very long way in the air. "But"—he smiled at them—"notice that the best shots are not the ones that the rider swings hard at. The best shots are the ones that seem to be effortless."

That got their attention. But by this time the game was over, three goals to two, and the men and their lathered ponies were walking off the field.

"How do the ponies manage to keep going?" Reza asked.

"Have you not noticed that from time to time a rider leaves the field and remounts a fresh pony? Although the game does not stop, they're allowed to leave for a change of mount at any time. But remember that when you leave the field," he said, "you leave your team one man short. It's important in a tight game to remount when a goal has been scored or if it went out of play. A few seconds can make the difference between scoring a goal or not."

During the interval, as the dusty ground was being splashed with water by men with goatskins and leather buckets, Dav'ud introduced his guests to an older couple, who were his uncle and aunt. The uncle had played in his youth and never lost his love for the game. He encouraged Dav'ud to teach the young ones, as he called them, to play, telling them it was an experience only matched by actual battle. Both Reza and Talon were ready to believe him.

There was a young woman among the guests who was introduced as Jasmine, Dav'ud's cousin twice removed, who lived with his family. His father and mother, Dav'ud explained, were caught up in some important work on the estates to the south, and were out of town for a month or two. Jasmine had eyes only for Talon from the moment she laid eyes on him. Talon, quite unaware of this, continued talking to Dav'ud about the game, asking many questions, as did Reza.

At last Dav'ud laughed. "My friends, enough! I am overwhelmed by your questions, all of which I shall try to answer tomorrow when we meet. The next game will please you more, as they're both good teams, one of which I will have to beat in the near future with my own team. Watch them carefully and you'll see how good they are." He excused himself, turned to the doctor, and asked him what he thought of the game.

"It's perfectly suited to these two ruffians of mine," the doctor responded with a smile in their direction. "And it's kind of you to offer to teach them, Dav'ud. For my part, it is quite interesting up to a point, but not my type of entertainment, if you know what I mean."

Dav'ud laughed. "I understand, Agha Doctor. One thing I can say is that it sometimes gives the physicians work to do."

Farj'an nodded. "Yes, I am a bit surprised we have not seen an accident as of yet. Perhaps the crowd will not be disappointed. The afternoon is still young," he added wryly.

Fariba tapped him lightly on the forearm with her fan. "My dear, you are too cynical for words. It is indeed a dangerous game, but it can be wonderful to watch. Dav'ud is right. The last game was more of a riot than a game. Let's see what the next one can produce."

Dav'ud's uncle, listening to her, laughed. "My lady, you're quite right, Let's hope we see some skill in the next game, or we'll have to go out there and show them how."

They all laughed at this, then turned to watch the new teams line up. They were not disappointed. After the initial melee of the throw in, both the teams demonstrated their skill at teamwork as well as at hitting the ball. To the delight of the crowd, who knew a good game when they saw one, the two teams kept the ball moving up and down the field at bewildering speed, with hits that, on many occasions, carried it aloft for scores of yards at a time. Players came together when there was good reason, otherwise they spread out as much as they could and relied upon the two men who played defense to hit the ball well and far, sending it up to the two forward players.

There was far less pushing and roughhousing between players. Instead, a small tap against an opponent's stick would suffice to hamper his strike. A player might even steal the ball back at the same time by tapping it to a point where he could hit it a long distance to his friends.

The game took on a new aspect to the fascinated Talon. He was awed by the horsemanship on display. These men were truly part of their mounts. He began to see where tactics could make a difference, and his appreciation grew.

The two teams were not evenly matched and it soon became clear who was going to win. The team with the side that could pass just that much better soon began to show its heels to the others. The more talented players gave the spectators a grand display of hitting the ball. Some could take the ball almost the length of the field, hitting the ball on the near side of their pony all the way, elbowing off their opponents on the other side. Others could hit the ball from under a galloping pony's neck, while others could hit it elegantly under the tail. All of it provided fascinating entertainment to Talon and Reza. The game was faster and hence more dangerous, which could have been why there was a collision.

A player lofted the ball along the sidelines very near to the pavilion, and one player came galloping along the line after it. Suddenly, a player came out of nowhere and tried to cut in front of him. The two ponies came together in a violent collision and went down in a tangle of legs and bodies. There was a scream, both riders were thrown forward, and one of them was crushed under a pony that somersaulted onto its back and onto the player.

There was a collective gasp from the crowd. The rider who had cut in managed to wriggle and duck his way out from among the flailing hooves but the other lay very still. Finally, the ponies struggled to their feet, caught by other riders, who then dismounted and came over to the prone rider, who was face down in the dust, his turban spilled, his rich clothes torn and dirtied.

Farj'an was on his feet, as were all the others.

Dav'ud hastened to the doctor's side. "Can you help, honored Doctor? I am sure he is hurt."

"Perhaps," Farj'an replied; his tone was non-committal, but he moved to go to the riders. As the doctor came over, one of them tried to turn the downed rider onto his back, but stopped as the man on the ground screamed in agony. Farj'an hurried then. He waved the riders away, and Dav'ud hastily explained who he was. There were nods from the disheveled riders and they made room for him.

Farj'an knelt by the side of the man on the ground and placed a hand on his shoulder. He asked him questions that were answered between gasps of pain. Farj'an stood up and spoke to Dav'ud. "I think his back is broken. We must have a table or board that we can place him on, and then I recommend that he be taken to the academy of medicine," he said firmly. "If we do not, he will be paralyzed and perhaps die. We might not be able to do much for him as it is."

Dav'ud bowed agreement and spoke in turn to the other riders. He then shouted instructions to his servants, and within minutes, the injured man was carried off the field. Farj'an went with the escort that Dav'ud pulled together from among his and the injured man's retinues. Farj'an told the others to stay and asked Dav'ud to escort them home when the time came. Dav'ud responded that he would be honored to.

There now remained the question as to whether the game could continue. There was a lot of shouting at the man who had caused the incident, who shouted back, and his team defending his actions vehemently. The team players who had lost the man clearly felt that the game should stop there and they be declared the winners. They had been ahead in any case.

The other team stated that the game time was not over and they wanted to continue until the trumpet sounded, by which time they hoped to be able to gain ground and pull off a win. Dav'ud, being known by all the players, joined in the discussion. At last, they appealed to the man who threw the ball into play, offering to abide by his decision. He responded that there were still nearly ten minutes of play left, but the injured man's team should be allowed a substitute. The opposite team looked disconcerted by this. The crowd was becoming restless and made it clear that they wanted the game to continue. They began to shout advice, and a gradual murmur of discontent began to swell.

Then one of the players leaned down and asked Dav'ud a question. He stood looking up, said nothing for a moment, and then nodded his head. That settled the discussion, as he walked back to the pavilion, shouting to his servants for his pony, while the players moved to the center of the field.

Dav'ud came up to the group, smiling. "They asked me to play for the rest of the game for them. I have agreed."

Fariba clapped her hands in approval and then so did Rav'an. Even Talon and Reza nodded their approval. This young host was more and more to their liking.

Without further ado, Dav'ud leapt onto his pony, seized one of the proffered mallets from his syce, and galloped onto the middle of the field to the rousing cheers and claps of an appreciative crowd. He was well known on the field and would make a difference in the game. The other team seemed to be put out at his joining the team but could do nothing about it.

Once again, the ball was hurled into the group of players, and the scrimmage began. The ball was knocked out of the pack, followed closely by a player on Dav'ud's team, with him close behind. The two remaining players stayed just behind, making it as difficult as possible for the opposing team players to give chase. They screamed into their faces, whacked them with their sticks, and tangled their mallets into their bridles, making an impossible situation for the angry players. Tempers flared and kicks and blows were exchanged.

Meanwhile, the lead player had lofted the ball high into the air and then followed it at a gallop. Before the ball could even hit the ground, he rose in his stirrups and hit the ball again, knocking it forward again many yards. There were respectful "Ahhs" from the crowd. The two riders were now within sixty yards of the goalposts and the ball had landed, bouncing wildly onward. Behind Dav'ud came vengeful players who had escaped the confusion, trying desperately to catch up. The lead player raced up to the ball, took a mighty swipe at it, and missed. He galloped right past it, trying to stop his pony and turn all at the same time.

Dav'ud, galloping at a slower, more deliberate pace, glanced behind him to see where his pursuers were, then concentrated on the ball, which had stopped rolling. He guided his pony right alongside the ball; leaning over, his arm went back, the mallet held high, and he took what seemed to be a lazy swing at the ball. His mallet caught the ball just below center and lifted it in a high arc well over the top of the goalposts but right down the center.

The crowd howled its approval, and the group on the pavilion cheered with uninhibited pleasure to see their man score so well, laughing and talking all at once.

Dav'ud's team members lavished praise upon him as they cantered back to the center of the field. Time was running out, but now they were virtually unassailable. The game continued for another few minutes and then the trumpet blew, and it was over.

The crowd cheered as the players, sweating and disheveled, paraded their ponies back to their lines. Dav'ud came up on his lathered pony, grinning with pleasure and happiness, to be greeted as a hero. He was sweaty and dusty and had a streak of blood on his chin, but clearly very happy to have been able to demonstrate his prowess to the group. He glanced at Rav'an, who was smiling approval, and grinned back at her.

Talon and Reza, although less effusive, made it clear that they were impressed and told him so. Fariba and the older people in the pavilion clapped and heaped lavish praise upon him.

The boys talked about the game and the tactics all the way back to the doctor's residence. Dav'ud managed to maneuver his pony next to a quiet Rav'an, who gave him a somewhat pensive smile as he came up. He happily talked about the game and then the city, asking her questions as to where she had come from, to which she replied in monosyllables. A happy, tired group came home that evening. Dav'ud bid them goodbye as he turned his pony and escort for his own home.

Later that night the doctor came back, tired and dispirited. He told them that his colleagues agreed with him that the man's back was broken and that it was possible the young man would never walk again. Over a supper of grilled chicken covered with pomegranate sauce, rice, and stewed fruit, he told them what they'd done for the fellow at the academy. He seemed distracted, though, and when the meal was nearly over and they were munching on honey cakes and sipping strong coffee in tiny cups, he started tugging at his beard.

Fariba, who knew the signs, touched him. "Farj'an, my dear,

you have something you wish to say?"

He nodded. "You all saw what happened today. While it is not that common, you have now seen what can happen. So while I know you want to go and play *Cho'gan,* you must be very careful, as it would not do to have any of you injured in that manner." He looked sharply at Rav'an. Before she could say anything, he held his hand up. "You must never forget who you are, my dear. If you are injured, the master will hold me responsible. So, while I know you will want to play, I will only permit you to do so in the light practice games." He turned to the boys. "I heard Dav'ud offer to teach you two, but I am not a fool. I know that Rav'an will want to go with you and play. Please assure me that my instructions are followed." He said the last in a manner that brooked no dissent.

They all nodded meek acceptance. Talon, who had his eyes down, missed the glance. Rav'an had wanted to share a moment. She looked puzzled; for some reason he was not being responsive.

Then the doctor had something else to say. "I also must remind all of you that to declare oneself Ismaili is almost certain death here in Isfahan. They despise us, fear us, and hate our kind. Do not talk about any of this with Dav'ud, even if he is a nice fellow. It is his kind, the nobility, who hate us the most, as we threaten their existence. You will not like his reaction if you do." He smiled to take the sting out of his words, but they all knew how serious he was.

Talon felt he should ask the question. "Why, then, are we meeting with him, Doctor?"

Farj'an looked at him. "Because in this manner, we become less visible," he told them all.

They all discussed the plans to ride to the practice grounds the next day. The boys would act as Rav'an's escort. Neither Fariba nor the doctor would accompany them. The boys left for bed with stern admonishments from both Fariba and Farj'an to protect Rav'an.

The boys went off to talk late into the night about the game they'd just watched. Talon, his former somber mood gone, contributed his share to the excited chatter. Both felt that it was something they would love to master. Being excellent horsemen, it was a challenge that seemed like enormous fun. Neither gave a second thought to the man who had broken his back.

Rav'an went to bed in a pensive mood. She thought she knew why Talon had been distant and was annoyed that he should be jealous, as she divined. Didn't the silly boy know her better than that? Dav'ud was a nice young man with impeccable manners and could play *Cho'gan* well, being a fit and excellent horseman, all good attributes for a man of his rank. But he was not the one for her. Why didn't Talon understand this? she asked herself, resolving to have it out with him as soon as she could. She missed his wide, happy smile when they were together. She had not caught him looking at her all day, and that bothered her. Going to bed that night, she felt an ache in the pit of her stomach that kept her awake for hours.

* * * * *

The next morning they were all up, and the party headed out to the practice fields. Talon had recovered his good mood, so he and Reza talked all the way about the game the day before and what they expected to do that morning. Rav'an was a little tired, so she was not as talkative as the other two, although she made a big effort not to let them sense her low spirits.

They came out of the gates of the city and rode the short distance to the practice area, to find that already there were many riders galloping about, striking balls in all directions. Dav'ud came cantering up on his fine pony, smiling with pleasure at seeing Rav'an with the boys. He didn't fail to notice that she was dressed as they were, in clothes fit for the practice session. She looked divine to his admiring eyes. He knew his friends were watching, but he had forbade them to come up until he had spent some time with the trio and they were more used to the place. However, behind him came another rider whom they recognized as Jasmine, who waved and called a greeting. Dav'ud glanced over his shoulder at her and smiled apologetically to his three guests.

"Jasmine is a good rider," he explained. "She likes to come to the practices with us."

Jasmine cantered up and bade them all a breathless good morning, her eyes going straight to Talon. He smiled back uncertainly. She was a pretty thing. Slim and fit, looking somewhere between nineteen and twenty-two, he judged, wondering where her husband was.

The exchange didn't escape Rav'an's watchful eyes, who then and there decided that she would make sure that Jasmine was kept at a distance... which proved harder than she had imagined.

Dav'ud took them all in hand and had his servants pass them mallets, then he began to show them the rudiments of the hitting moves. He demonstrated the forward hitting from the right side, or off side, first, and told them to find a space and practice this one, as it was the most common strike.

Then he turned his attention to Rav'an and proceeded to work with her, leaving the boys to practice on their own, except that Jasmine was there to help them. For the boys, it was fun to try to strike the ball from a pony. Jasmine was a good hitter with a good eye. Although the boys were not used to *Cho'gan*, they, too, had a good eye, so once they understood the method she explained and demonstrated again and again, they began to get the hang of it.

To have a woman with them other than Rav'an was novel, especially one as attentive as she was. Riding close to Talon so that their knees touched on one occasion, she pretended that there was nothing to it, but it left Talon feeling hot. He could smell her fresh scent, which was quite different from Rav'an's familiar scent, but no less alluring to his already already fired senses.

Reza made matters worse by sidling his pony up to him at one time, winking, then whispering, "That one is very interested in you, brother."

Talon glared at him, his face going red, and nudged him with his elbow. They horsed around for a couple of seconds and then Jasmine was back, offering to show them the backhand.

Rav'an was cut off from the other two by this time, as a very attentive Dav'ud proceeded to show her how to hold the mallet and make the swing. He took her hands and put them in place, careful at all times not to be improper. It would have been enjoyable for her if it had not been for the fact that she was constantly looking for Talon and checking the whereabouts of Jasmine. She kept trying to maneuver herself and Dav'ud into the same area as the others, but that didn't work since the balls, when hit, would go in all directions and they would have to follow.

After an hour, she had had enough and asked Dav'ud if they could go into the shade of some palms and rest while she thought about the moves. He, not sensing anything out of kilter, agreed willingly and took them to the standing pony lines and a group of his friends. Rav'an was an instant hit with all of the young men. They could not help but admire her figure. Honed by the hard journey, she was firm and trim, unlike many of the softer women of Isfahan.

She *was* striking. Her poise, natural beauty, and quiet confidence were an aphrodisiac to these energetic, cheerful young men of rank. They plied her with questions after the introductions, all of which she was careful to answer vaguely. Deflecting as much as she could, she entranced them with her warm laugh and smiling eyes. They were respectful, treating her as though she were one of them. The group grew and diminished as riders came and went, people joining out of curiosity and others leaving to practice more.

Talon and Reza had seen the group and were somewhat torn between continuing to practice and their duty. Talon, while he could not say he didn't enjoy Jasmine's ever-close attentions, was not at all happy with the group of adoring young men surrounding Rav'an, who, it seemed to him, was enjoying their company far too much. He stopped his pony and, with a word to Reza, started toward the group of laughing people. Jasmine came alongside him

"Where are you going, Talon? Have you had enough?"

He smiled at her politely. "I think we should join the others, *Khanom*."

"Talon, please do not call me *Khanom*. It is Jasmine," she admonished him with a laugh, looking archly at him from under her lashes.

He mumbled an apology, and they rode over to the group under the palms. A happy Dav'ud, greeted them and made introductions all around.

Rav'an turned to Talon. "Talon, I mentioned that you were looking for a new bow, and that we did not know where to go for a new one. Hussein here knows a bowyer in the city who makes the best there are. He has offered to take us there."

Talon nodded politely to the man she indicated. Hussein was a dark, wiry man who was dressed very well and mounted on a superb pony.

"The man makes bows along the lines of the northern people. They are larger bows than our own Persian ones, but you might prefer that?" he asked.

"Hussein is one of my team members," Dav'ud said. "Reza, Talon, you should see his nearside shots. Are you a good bowman?" he asked Talon politely.

Rav'an snorted. "He and Reza are the best," she declared confidently.

Reza laughed and made a depreciating gesture, clearly

embarrassed.

Dav'ud laughed, too. "I see you two have an admirer. Talon, why don't we find you a good bow, then one day we can have a competition?"

Talon grinned at him. "I would like that." He glanced at Rav'an, thanking her with his eyes for championing him. She smiled back at him enigmatically.

The convivial party broke up eventually to head back into the town. Jasmine came with them to the gates of the doctor's house. When they said their goodbyes, she had eyes only for Talon.

* * * * *

The three went through the garden to the stables at the back of the house and dismounted. Talon was about to go with Reza to their quarters, when Rav'an motioned him to stay. Reza glanced at her, but she said, "I need to ask Talon something, Reza. Please, do not wait."

He nodded and left.

Rav'an turned to Talon. "Come with me," she said firmly.

He followed meekly as she led the way into the front gardens and to their favorite bower.

There she turned to face him. "What's the matter with you?" she demanded, still standing.

He stood looking at her. "Nothing," he said, his tone cool.

She stamped her foot. "Nothing? You've been cold to me all day, and you make fool's eyes at Jasmine because of *nothing*?"

He had the grace to look down, mumbling something about Jasmine being a good-looking woman. Rav'an came up close to him so that he could pick up her scent. He longed to take her in his arms, but he just stood there.

"Talon, do you not understand where my heart is?" she demanded almost angrily.

He turned away, his back to her. "Really?" he asked. "I am just a slave of your brother, Rav'an. He is my master. Let's not forget that fact," he ground out between clenched teeth. "For all our 'love,' in the end you are the princess. I cannot compete with these rich nobles. Your brother will decide my fate... and yours, too." He choked at that, standing rigid in his frustration and rising anger, his hands clenched into fists at his sides.

There was silence for a long moment.

Then she touched his shoulder. "Talon, look at me," she whispered, tugging his reluctant form around so he was facing her. He was looking down, his features locked into a stubborn expression of shame and anger.

"Talon... do you still not understand, after all we've been through?" she said in a low voice. "Please look at me," she pleaded.

He lifted his eyes to hers; she gazed into his hopeless face with her eyes full of tears. "Dav'ud is a very nice young man, and yes, he plays good *Cho'gan*, and yes, his manners are very good, much better than yours"—she smiled through her tears at him—"but it's you to whom I have given my heart, Talon, no one else. Do you really think I would give it away to someone else after all we've been through together? You're my protector and my love. Nothing will change that. Not Dav'ud and not my brother."

Some light came back to his eyes, but he shook his head in a hopeless gesture. "How can we defy the master, Rav'an? How can you resist him if he should decide to use you by marrying you to some fat vizier? Or for that matter, how can I defy him should he command me to go to my death?"

She moved into his arms. "Do you love me, Talon?"

His arms tightened around her. "How can you doubt that? I love you more than life itself," he murmured fiercely.

"Then I have hope that we will find a way, my love," she murmured into his shoulder. Pushing herself back, she said, "Now you must kiss me, and make me forget that witch Jasmine—and you must forget her, too."

He laughed then and pulled her to him, a huge relief within him. They kissed with passion for long moments. She pulled him down onto the bench, and there was no more talking for a long time.

Finally, she sat up, tidied her blouse and touched her messed-up hair. She gently touched him on the lips with the tips of her fingers. "My Talon, we must pretend while here in Isfahan; can you bear it? I shall never shame you, I promise. You can talk to Jasmine, but do not allow her to take your heart, do you hear? Or I shall cut it out," she growled.

Talon grinned. "If you will bring me here from time to time, I shall have no difficulty with that, my lady."

She gazed at him. "Be patient, my warrior. I shall give myself to you and no one else."

He reached for her and kissed her very lightly on the corner of her lips, a long, feather-light kiss. When they pulled away, she was looking at him with huge eyes.

"Are you still my protector and my love forever?" she whispered. He went down on his knee and gave the response she wanted to hear. Holding her hands in his, he said with feeling, "Forever and forever."

They went from the bower without holding hands, although they wished that they could, both happier than they had been all morning.

Reza was waiting for him when he came back to his room.

"Is the princess upset with you for some reason, Talon?" he asked his friend, a tone of concern in his voice.

Talon clapped him on the back. "She told me that women of Jasmine's rank are too far up the scale for the likes of us, and I was not to get too excited about the woman," he said lightly.

Reza snorted. "And who is the princess to say that?" he answered indignantly. "I have not had a woman since Hamadan, and I am ready to go to the bazaar. Even you look enticing sometimes. It's horrible."

Talon choked. "You toad, Reza! You come near me and I'll skin you." He laughed. "Why don't you ask the gardeners or the man in charge of the stables... what's his name?"

"Butrus. Yes, I could. Would you be interested if I can find out where to go?" He looked eagerly at his friend.

Talon didn't want to disappoint his friend, so he nodded in a non-committal manner. Why not, he thought. It might give him some release from all the pent-up emotions. The thought of getting a woman excited him, but he was acutely aware that neither of them had any experience in the matter of acquiring one. They would have to see what happened.

"Then we should go out tomorrow night," Reza said. "We have to find out where to go and how much it will cost."

He babbled happily on about what he was going to do and what kind of woman he wanted. Talon told him to go and get ready for classes, as they were late, and the doctor would not take kindly to their missing out on their education.

The rest of the day passed uneventfully. He had time to reflect on what Rav'an had said, but it didn't solve the issue he felt that they would face when they were once again reunited with the master. No other woman appealed to him. Not Jasmine, not a whore, no one. He wondered about that as they went down to dinner.

He looked forward to the evenings, as that was the time when the doctor might challenge one or both to a game of chess, or Fariba and Rav'an would sing. The first time he heard Rav'an sing he'd been enraptured. Never, when he was a boy, had he hear his mother sing, although sometimes the maids in the courtyard would, but none with so clear and pure a voice as Rav'an's. Fariba commented that she, too, was impressed and told Rav'an that with some instruction she could impress kings with her singing. This was greeted with a toss of her luxurious hair as Rav'an dismissed such people. She looked over to Talon and he read a message in her eyes.

That night they played chess as he had hoped, or rather the doctor played a match with Reza while he, Talon, offered useless advice to his friend while the doctor was trouncing him. Then the ladies did sing, and again Fariba sang the haunting lullaby. He asked Rav'an about it and told her of his dream during the time he had been wounded. She responded that the only person she could think of who might have sung it would have been Alaleh, who, with Feza, had been looking after him at the time.

Then she stopped Fariba and made Talon tell the story of his fight with the lion. When he finished, he looked down self-consciously while Fariba, full of praise for his courage, smiled.

"Truly, you are brave, Talon. One day some lucky woman will have you as her husband and will know she is safe."

He dared not look at Rav'an then, although he suspected that she was smiling at him with mischief in her eyes.

Reza clapped him on the shoulder. "We are brothers, Talon and I. We are *fida'i*. We cannot marry, *Khanom*. It is our fate to go to paradise while young."

Farj'an interjected then. "That depends upon how Allah decides it, Reza. I hope that the both of you live to be old men. Now it is late, and I have to be at the academy in the morning."

This prompted enquiries as to the condition of the young man who had been injured during the game of *Cho'gan*. Farj'an replied that he was going to live, but for the moment was heavily sedated with opium, and he would never walk again, thanks to the accident. He looked sternly at them all as though to remind them that the instructions he had given earlier should be heeded.

That night as she lay in his arms, Fariba asked Farj'an. "Is it true that the boys are *fida'i* and slaves of the master, as you call him, my love?"

He nodded with regret. "It is true, although I wish it were not. One day he may command them one or both of them to go somewhere and take the life of a political enemy, losing theirs in the process, as that is the way of it."

She shuddered. "It is such a cold thing to do. They are but young men, and both intelligent. Do you not like them?" she asked sitting up and looking at him.

He nodded again. "Fariba, my love, these children are ours for a short time only. I feel that Allah has been kind to both of us in allowing us to know them, and perhaps guide them. However, when the master calls they will leave us, and although I might see them again, you will not. They are not of the world of Isfahan."

"Why then, my love, do you lavish education upon them and treat them like sons, and Rav'an like a daughter?"

He smiled at her fondly. "You have me there. I've thought on it too, and thought to ask the master if I could keep them as my guards. These are unsafe times, and these two are very skilled at what they do. I don't know if he will permit me to o so or not. That will be very much in the hands of Allah. Rav'an, however, will have to stay with him until he finds a husband suitable to her rank and position. She will be useful to him if he can conclude a treaty with some sultan or other."

This was not something that was strange to Fariba. This was the way of life, and she herself had come to the doctor as a servant, a concubine. It was because he loved her that Farj'an, who had once been married but had lost his wife long ago, had elevated her to the position of virtual wife in all respects save name. That would come with time, she knew, although she would not ask it. This would have to come from the doctor when he was ready, to make her his wife in all things.

She nestled into his shoulder again. "I feel like we've been blessed to have Rav'an with us. To me she's like a daughter, and I'll miss her sorely when the time comes for them to leave us. May Allah protect them," she murmured to Farj'an, who was already half asleep.

And if the Cup you drink, the Lip you press.
End in what All begins and ends in __Yes;
Imagine, then, you are what heretofore
You were – hereafter you shall not be less.

– Omar Khayyam –

Chapter 23
The Bow

The next day a small party, with Dav'ud and Hussein in attendance, wended its way through the bazaar, where the bowyer was located.

The sights and smells of the bazaar assailed their senses as they progressed ever deeper into the labyrinth of small streets. The spices displayed in heaps on the ground in small dark recesses, on *ghilims*, or in rolled open sacks, were tantalizing, and the precious cloths and silks were an attraction to the two young ladies. Rav'an and Jasmine would have tarried, but they were urged to move on. Hussein guided his party through the crowded streets unerringly, waving off the urchins who begged for alms and ignoring the beggars in the gutters as they went by.

Eventually, they came to a very quiet area where the tunnel they had been following opened out into an uncovered street. Not far off was a doorway almost hidden by a wisteria vine, which Hussein went up to and banged on with his fist. A grille high in the door opened and a face peered down at them. Hussein gave his name, and with a screeching of bolts, the door opened.

They all crowded in with Hussein leading and talking to the burly man on the other side. The man bowed and led them down a dark corridor into the sunlight where there was a small fountain, low, leafy trees, and stone benches arrayed in a semi-circle around it. Polite, silent servants served them all sherbet, and the party was left to itself for a few minutes.

Jasmine had been hovering very close all the way along the route, which Talon had not found unpleasant at all, but he was resolved not to hurt Rav'an by appearing too attentive.On the other hand, Dav'ud had been very protective of Rav'an, treating her as though she were a weak and helpless female. If he only knew, Talon thought; this girl has killed a man and could do so again should she need to. He was smiling at the thought when Reza nudged him and winked, looking at Jasmine. Talon glared back, going red.

A heavy set man had appeared from the house, dressed in long, comfortable robes, with an impressive turban on his head. He walked up to the two young noblemen and bowed, but not in a subservient manner. They stood up and exchanged greetings with him, then Hussein turned to his four companions and introduced the man as Shah'ab, a northerner famous for his bows.

Shah'ab appraised Talon carefully, as Hussein had already indicated that Talon wanted to buy a bow.

They went through all the elaborate greetings. He bowed very low to the ladies, who pretended to simper behind their *chadors*, and then they got down to business.

He clapped his hands and several of his workmen came out of the building, carrying bows of various sizes and types. Talon's interest quickened. A servant carried a small target to the far end of the yard, about fifty paces away.

Shah'ab came up to Talon, measured his right arm with a measuring stick, and then called something out to his men. One of them ran into the house and returned with another bow. Shah'ab presented it to Talon and, looking keenly at him, watched as he handled it.

Talon was impressed. This was a larger bow than his previous one, and very solid. It was composed of laminated horn on both the arches, cunningly blended into the polished wood of the hand stock; its center looked very strong and fit his hand comfortably, even being somewhat large. He knew it would be very expensive.

Shah'ab then presented him with an arrow and invited him to use the bow on the small butt down at the end of the garden.

Talon was a little embarrassed with everyone looking at him expectantly. He felt self-conscious, but shrugged it off and lifted the bow with his left arm and notched the arrow. He loosed the arrow with a "twang" from the string and it sped down to the target, striking it just a finger high and left of center. The arrow had almost no trajectory at all, he noticed. It was a superb bow.

There were murmurs of approval from his companions; even Shah'ab grunted appreciation.

They commenced the long and careful process of negotiating for the right price. *Chai* and sweet cakes were offered to the group while the discussions continued.

There was also no doubt that they would leave with the bow; however, Shah'ab would have been very offended if they had just agreed to his price and walked off.

Finally they concluded the deal, gold exchanged hands, and everyone rose to make the exchanges required for parting. Lengthy and protracted though they were, it was instructive to Talon how the young nobles treated Shah'ab with respect and did not condescend to him.

He decided to ask a question. Did Shah'ab know a man named Al Tayyib?

"Yes, I know him," Shah'ab said, his voice guarded.

"Please give him our greetings," Rav'an stated. "Where can he be found?"

"In the bazaar, *Khanom*. Al Tayyib is well known, and can be found if one asks for him by name," came the again guarded reply. "Do you wish that I send a message to him to come here?"

"No, although I thank you," Talon said. "We simply wish him well."

* * * * *

Later that night Reza came into his room, and throwing himself on Talon's bed, he asked, "Talon, are you and Jasmine becoming serious?"

Talon looked at him sharply. "No. Why do you ask?"

"Because my friend, take it from an experienced man. She wants you."

Talon pretended to look around the room. "Who said that, I wonder?" he asked the room at large.

Reza grinned. "Me, I say so, Talon. Are you blind?"

"Nonsense," Talon exclaimed on the defensive now.

"No, not nonsense, my friend. What's the matter with you? She is beautiful, a widow, and ripe for the taking. Have you lost your love of women? What did they give you when they showed you paradise? "

Talon snorted with laughter. "You seem to think of only one thing, Reza!"

Reza snorted back with derision at his friend's naïveté. "It is plain to me that she likes you a lot and is willing to let you come closer, much closer!"

Talon gave his friend an affectionate slap on the shoulder. "Reza, I swear that I got the real woman, while you got the goat or some other creature that left you with just one thought in your head. You can only think of women and how to bed them these days."

Reza held his crotch with both hands and laughed. "No, but I did get a glimpse of heaven on earth while in Hamadan and I intend to enjoy earth as much as I can before they send me to paradise."

He was so comical in this position that Talon had to sit down and laugh helplessly with him. It was time to go to classes, so they tidied up and left, arms over shoulders.

"Don't forget, Talon, that tonight we go to the bazaar to find women. Do you remember what they look like without clothes?"

Talon punched him on the arm

*****

That night Talon went with Reza on foot to the bazaar. He did it more because it was an adventure than because he wanted to do what Reza wanted, plus he wanted to make sure his friend came home in one piece.

They had no difficulty in finding the bazaar's main entrance. They slipped along the shadows to what they both remembered as having been a promising-looking place they had seen on their way into the bazaar with Dav'ud and Hussein.

It was a wall that had windows with grilles opening onto the street, and there they had seen several well-dressed men talking to women on the other side. A man had been in charge of operations, opening the door upon the presentation of money. The payee had slipped in as though he were embarrassed to be seen.

They came up to the wall to find that it was dark and closed. Disappointed, they stood looking at it, toying with the idea that they might gain entrance some other way, when they were called to in a low voice from the shadows.

Turning quickly, they reached for their knives as they stared into the darkness. An urchin who looked vaguely familiar came out of the dark and stood in front of them. He gave a start as he did so.

"You are Talon of the bow," he said in a surprised manner. Looking hard at Reza he nodded. "And you are Reza of the knife."

They stared back at him in dumb silence. He was somewhat older than they had thought at first, perhaps fourteen years.

"Who are you?" they both asked at the same time.

"I am Yousef, nephew to Al Tayyib," the boy said. "I was waiting for one of my friends to come along the street. What are you doing here?" He looked at the wall and then snickered. "Are you after women?" he asked with a smirk.

Reza took a step toward him. The boy shrank back.

Talon placed a hand on Reza's arm. "We wanted to meet with Al Tayyib, Yousef. That is why we came. This place was the one location we recognized from our last visit. Can you take us to him?"

Yousef looked at them with shrewd eyes. "I can... " he said with a crafty look on his face. Reza tossed him a small coin. "I can," he said with more assertion.

Once he was with them, he explained that he had been one of the boys who tended the goats and camels at the back of the caravan. It was clear to the two young men that he was in awe of them. Just now, he explained, he was like all the rest of the *bazaari*, earning a living from day to day and trying to make ends meet in order to survive.

Talon and Reza began to see more signs of life as they followed Yousef, and soon came into a well-lit series of streets deep in the bazaar, far from the entrance, where people moved about preparing food and drinks. The smell of chicken kebabs with roasting vegetables cooking on charcoal fires came from all sides, making their mouths water.

The streets got noisier, and soon they were in the midst of a crowded community of men, women, and children taking their ease at various *chai khanes* and food stalls. It was well lit and busy. Most of the people were either merchants or men who worked at the bazaar.

The incredible noise that they had encountered formerly was

replaced by the clatter of pots, the hiss of cooking meat, and the chatter of people taking their ease after a long day of work. There was a haze of smoke in the air as men stoked their fires or smoked pipes, the rank smell of *hashish* noticeable over it all.

Yousef continued to talk, ignoring the sounds and bustle all around. He led them straight to a *chai khane* that seemed to be just a hole in the wall, until they came up to it and saw that it was well lit by many oil lamps and went back into the depths of the building. There were many people sitting on piled carpets, smoking or drinking tea. Talon and Reza looked at one another. They had not known this kind of underworld existed.

There came a shout from within and they turned to stare across the crowded, smoke-filled space. They saw someone waving at them from the back of the room. It was Al Tayyib, clearly delighted to see them. He waved and gestured for them to come in and join him.

Yousef led the way past the curious people sitting all around and the servants, who skillfully avoided others as they carried brass trays of tea and small cakes around the room to guests.

Al Tayyib greeted the two young men as though they were long-lost cousins. He rose and kissed them on both cheeks, embracing them and shouting welcomes to them. Yousef settled down close by, watching everyone and saying nothing.

"These are the two young men who saved our caravan from the Luristani bandits," he shouted to his companions. "Look at them! Have you ever seen such a pair of cut-throats in your lives?" He laughed his great laugh, made them sit next to him, and introduced the other guests.

One was a spice merchant who had been on the caravan. He smiled at the boys and nodded his head. "You got us here without any losses. I am thankful to you both. If ever you need me, come and see me. I owe you *taroff*," he said.

The others were *bazaari* associated with Al Tayyib. He told Talon and Reza that he was busy negotiating for a caravan to go all the way to Dezful on the other side of the country, across the Zagros. These men were helping put it together. He ordered more *chai*, and they all settled on comfortable cushions.

Talon noted that no one asked them what they were doing here in the bazaar. He guessed that the question would come up later when they had all relaxed. He cast about desperately for a suitable reply when it did come up. He knew it would be a lame one and hoped that the silver-tongued Reza would be able to produce a good reason.

There was a familiar smell in the air that he tested with his nose. He remembered with a growing feeling in his groin just what it had been—the prelude to their glimpse of heaven, the smoke that had transferred him from a bare room to the luxury of the paradise he had woken up in, and the woman who had serviced him. He woke from his reverie with a start.

Reza was talking to Al Tayyib. "This caravan, is it going to Baghdad after Dezful?" he asked innocently.

Al Tayyib contemplated him through foggy eyes. He was smoking the strange stuff that Talon remembered.

"It goes south from Dezful; however, there are other caravans that go west," he answered very slowly. "Is that why you came here? To ask me that?"

Reza smiled at him. "Al Tayyib, we have been in Isfahan for more than a month now. Do you not think it would have been rude not to come and visit you?"

"They were standing in front of the house of women," Yousef put in.

There was a startled silence, and then Al Tayyib started to shake with laughter. "Reza, you almost had me convinced," he shouted.

The two young men were red with embarrassment. Reza wished he had slit Yousef's throat earlier, while Talon was mortified.

Wiping tears of laughter from his eyes, Al Tayyib groaned with mirth. "I might have known. You two horny young goats can't do anything with that beautiful niece of the doctor's, so you came here to fuck Isfahani whores." He had another fit of giggles and had to dry his eyes on his sleeve.

The other men smirked with equal amusement, although none of them seemed shocked.

Talon put on a good face and gave a helpless smile. "Reza is so desperate he is looking at the horses these days, Al Tayyib," he said, spreading his hands.

Reza grinned shamelessly at the assembled company.

There was more helpless laughter from Al Tayyib and his companions. Talon and Reza relaxed and joined in the laughter. No one was shocked or offended, it seemed.

"Why didn't you say so at first?" Al Tayyib asked, wiping his eyes.

"Because we *are* pleased to see you, Agha, although we did come here to find out if there were women, too," Reza answered.

"Well, now, we'll have to see what we can do about that as well," Al Tayyib said.

The boys both protested that it was not necessary anymore, Talon most vehemently. It was no use. Al Tayyib was determined to ensure that they were not disappointed. He turned to Yousef. "You can earn the coin you lost for leaving the wall by taking them to the house of Benjamin As'ad. Take them there and ask for the best young maidens he has for these two heroes of ours."

Yousef scrambled to his feet. "Uncle, they paid me to bring them to you, so I have some money this night."

Talon took the boy by the arm. "You shall have more from us, too, if you will guide us out of this warren when we are finished."

Al Tayyib laughed again. "You're right, Talon. You have to be able to go home, too. Yousef will help."

An embarrassed pair of young men bade their new acquaintances goodnight and, feeling rather helpless, were led off by a smirking Yousef while Al Tayyib's booming laughter followed them down the street. "Don't be strangers, and bring that beautiful girl with you next time," he bellowed.

They hastened to catch up with the all-but-running Yousef. He brought them to another darkened entrance and banged on the heavy wooden door. A grille snapped open and a surly voice asked them what they wanted. Yousef piped up that they were from Al Tayyib and were to be given entrance.

After much grumbling, the door opened and they were admitted. They followed Yousef straight into a small courtyard that had potted plants arrayed around the walls. It had a nice atmosphere to it, with benches in between the plants that gave the feeling of privacy.

Yousef told the two to wait while he went with the guard into the house at the other end of the yard. Talon was by now feeling very uncomfortable, while Reza was beginning to pace nervously about; it was clear, though, that he was looking forward to the encounter to come. Talon, on the other hand, was wondering what on earth he would say to Rav'an when it came out that they had been in the bazaar. He knew without doubt that she would find out some way or another, and then he was a dead man, he thought morosely.

After some time a plump lady came out of the entrance across the small yard and greeted them politely. She had obviously been asleep, but she maintained her dignity, and neither of the boys felt like being smart with her. She enquired as to their preferences, which Reza gave willingly. Young, beautiful, and slim, which, thought Talon sourly, just about covered anyone at all. She turned to him with an enquiring look on her face. He nodded as though to say, "I'll take the same." She gestured them to come with her. Yousef was told to stay out in the yard, which he did with ill grace; he was becoming very curious about what was to come.

Talon and Reza followed the woman along a passage and then into a poorly lit room where she stopped. Indicating alcoves that went off from the room, she pointed to one for Reza and then another for Talon. To their surprise, she did not ask for money at all.

Talon climbed onto the platform that was the alcove and found it lit by one oil lamp. It was really a large bed on the floor with a low table nearby and the lamp. The curtains hid it from the main room. He sat cross-legged in the middle of the bed, waiting.

He heard the first girl come into the larger room and whisper a few words, then the rustle of her entrance to the alcove where Reza was waiting. There was a low murmur of conversation, then a brief silence, followed by rustling and giggles. Soon after, there was a movement, and the curtain to his alcove was drawn apart.

A very young and pretty girl moved with fluid grace onto the bed, drawing the curtain closed as she did so. Talon looked at her. She was partially dressed in diaphanous pantaloons that were tied with a silk thread at the hips, exposing her slim waist. Her breasts were covered, but only just. There was a fine gold thread around her ankle that drew his eye. Her long black hair, although not as fine as Rav'an's, was still attractive, with a clean sheen to it that he found alluring. His senses were aroused as she came over the bed to him, a question in her large black eyes.

There were now sounds coming from the other alcove that could not be ignored that added to the sexual mood, little cries and noises that both he and the girl were acutely aware of. She slid alongside him and then slowly started to take off the long scarf that hid her breasts.

He put out a hand and stopped her. Then he put his finger to his lips and whispered to her, "I will not insult you, as you are very beautiful, and I would love you, as you can see."

She giggled quietly and placed her hand on his erection through his pants, but she looked worried as well. "You do not like me?" she asked, looking afraid.

He shook his head. "It is not that; you can see that I want you, but I am promised to another."

She smiled at that as though she approved. Leaning into him, she kissed him and whispered, "Then why are you here?"

"For my friend, who is not promised to anyone," he responded, his heart beating loud in his chest. He wanted to make love to her so much his body ached with desire.

She whispered to him, "Then you are a good man. Will you tell me your name?" She stroked the scar on his jaw.

"Talon," he whispered back.

She pulled him down to her. "Lie with me for a while, Talon. If you want me, you may have me, as I think you are a good man. I am called Esther and I am from Meshad. I dare not go out until it looks as though we have finished, or I shall be beaten. Can we lie together while we wait for them to finish?"

He gathered her up and lay with her in his arms, her clean-hair scent in his nostrils as they listened and smiled together at the noisy couple next door.

When it was time to leave, he gave her a silver piece, and enjoyed seeing her eyes grow large. Again, he put his fingers to his lips and kissed her on the forehead.

But she seized his head between her hands and kissed him on the lips. "*Khoda Hafez*, God protect you," she whispered, her tone regretful. "I would have liked to feel you in me. She is a lucky woman you are promised to."

Yousef woke to find them standing over him. He yawned and stood up, rubbing his eyes, then he led them all the way back to the main entrance of the bazaar. There they gave him a silver coin for his trouble, which made him very happy, and they headed home, arriving in the early hours of the morning.

Talon went to bed thinking about Esther in his arms, longing for it to be Rav'an. He went to sleep dreaming of women who came up to him but always slipped through his fingers, calling his name all the while.

I am the ocean poured into a jug,
I am the point essential to the letter;
In every thousand one greater man stands out,
I am the greater man of this mine Age!
– Baba Tahir –

Chapter 24
Attack

If anyone noticed how sleepy the two young men were the next day, no one remarked on it. Talon decided that he would only answer for that night if Rav'an brought it up. He spent a pleasant hour with her the next morning, but as they had to go to *Cho'gan* practice, they were unable to linger, as they might have wished.

Reza, although tired, was very happy and made it clear to Talon that he was going back to the house in the bazaar in a week. Talon groaned, as he didn't think he could refrain from taking the girl called Esther next time. It had been an exquisite ordeal the last time.

That evening after dinner the doctor added to their list of concerns. They had gathered in the main dining room and the servants had cleared the food away. He was resting against cushions, smoking his water pipe, while Reza and Talon were playing chess. Fariba was preparing the *tar* with Rav'an at her side, when he looked up and asked, "How long have we been back in Isfahan?"

Everyone stopped what they were doing and looked at him.

Fariba answered for all of them. "Almost six weeks, Doctor. Why do you ask?"

He tugged at his beard. "Because I would have thought that by now we would have heard something. We spent almost six weeks on the road to here from Hamadan, it is true, and then another six here in Isfahan. Three full months, when I know that a messenger can travel from Hamadan to Isfahan within three weeks if escorted and traveling at speed. It is almost *No Ruz* and we have heard nothing."

"Perhaps the winter was more severe than we imagined it would be, Uncle," Reza suggested politely.

The doctor nodded, but he didn't quite seem comfortable with that. "It is possible, Reza; as you say, the winters in the north are always unpredictable. I am just a little uneasy." He shook his head. "Don't pay any attention to me; I am an old man with a change of weather in my bones."

Rav'an came over to him and kneeled in front of him. "To me you are more than that, Uncle. You have been my family, our family, and I, for one, have been very happy here. It is a beautiful world you have made, and I would love to stay."

Talon and Reza nodded. They, too, were entranced with Isfahan. Never in their wildest dreams had they imagined that they could be in such a place, and they all but worshipped the doctor for having provided it.

Fariba said to the doctor in a matter-of-fact way, "My dear, you are probably right, there is a change of weather coming, and you might be feeling low because of it. Let me play for you some music to cheer us all up."

She played for them for more than an hour and then had to stop because she complained her fingers were sore. They applauded her enthusiastically; her music was something they were all in love with.

That night, before going to bed, Rav'an came to Fariba's bedroom to talk for a while together.

"Why do you think he was concerned about the time we have been here?" Rav'an asked as she helped Fariba undo and comb her luxurious hair.

"The doctor is sometimes like that, my dear. He has some kind of timekeeper inside that tells him when something should happen. He is always right. I expect we shall have a messenger here soon." She turned to Rav'an and took her hand. "Then we'll have to say goodbye, my dearest Rav'an. I shall be so unhappy when you have to leave." She had tears in her eyes already.

Rav'an answered quickly, "My Fariba, please, don't be so sad. I am sure we'll be able to stay for some time more. I want to so much, and I know the boys do as well." She embraced Fariba, who kissed her and returned the embrace.

*****

The morning dawned like any other for the people at the house of Farj'an the physician, except that it was overcast and threatening rain, which prompted the doctor to mention that fact at breakfast.

"I may have mentioned it last night," he said with a smug twinkle in his eye, "but these old bones never make a mistake when the weather is changing."

They all smiled at his good humor.

Fariba tapped him on the knee. "My dear, you should stay home today. It's cooler than normal, and if it rains you will get wet, and then your aching will come back.

The others were undecided as to what they could do if it rained, but if their host stayed, they could play chess and hear some of his stories, which always provided good entertainment.

He shook his head. "I have to go to the academy for a report on the condition of one of my patients," he said with regret.

Talon put his hand up. "I can go if it is just a report, Uncle. I would rather go than see you get wet, if it should rain."

Farj'an looked at him. "It is just a report, my boy, that's true. Would you do this for me?"

Fariba smiled. "Of course, he will. Thank you, Talon. You can give him exact instructions, my dear, and he can go directly and come home straight away."

So it was decided, and while the doctor wrote a note to his colleague Haddad, Talon and the other two finished breakfast and discussed the up-coming Cho'gan match. They were all excited, as they hoped that Dav'ud's team would take the championship. They admired his skill with the ball and thought that he and his team would do well.

Reza could not resist the opportunity of teasing Talon about Jasmine, and Rav'an, joined in, enjoying teasing her "Protector".

Just at the time when it looked as though Talon was going to jump on Reza and dish out some punishment to his laughing friend, the doctor came back into the room and gave him the note. Getting to his feet, Talon said, "Thank you for coming when you did, Uncle, I was just about to take care of these two, which would not have been pretty."

There was a squawk of laughter from the other two as they fell over on their sides in simulated pain at this sally. The doctor smiled fondly at them all.

Fariba came in then and said to the remaining two, "Do not think you have escaped with doing nothing while Talon is running an errand, my children. You are going to help me with preparations for *No Ruz*. You know how important it is for us to start the New Year in the correct manner. I have all the servants cleaning this house from top to bottom and I expect all of you to join in and help with the preparations. I don't know what barbaric practices you had in the mountains, but here we shall perform it the right way." She was pretending to sound stern, but fooled no one.

Rav'an jumped to her feet, sending a significant glance at Talon. "No stopping off to see Jasmine, Talon. Come straight back."

He glowered at her, pretending anger. The others laughed. Everyone knew that Jasmine was set on Talon.

Rav'an then hauled a reluctant Reza to his feet. "Come along, Reza, you will not be allowed to do nothing today. You shall be my helper." With a feigned look of pain, Reza got up, and bade Talon hasten back.

Talon strode off, smiling at the thought of Reza running around at the princess' bidding, who rarely exerted her right to command them.

He mounted Jabbar, allowing him to pop a couple of times to get the springs out of his system, then scolded him in good humor before settling him into a canter along the tree-lined avenues. There were new leaves starting on the trees, lending a light-green shade to the streets that was delightful to ride through. They went at a good pace onto the main streets until he crossed the great bridge. The water was now quite high, as the spring thaws were commencing; water would fill the river bank to bank within a couple more weeks, testing the strength of the old bridge and its Roman design. Cantering along the road, he looked around at the town that he now felt part of. He liked Isfahan very much and hoped that they could stay for much longer.

Then he spent some time at the academy gates awaiting entry before he was allowed in. He was impressed with the efficiency of the hospital, for that is what it was. Many people came to the gates each day to be treated by novices and their physician mentors.

He had gained entry because he used Farj'an's name and held up the note that requested the physician Haddad allow him an audience. Once within the extensive compound, a harassed member of the hospital staff, who obviously had other duties on his mind, led him to the area where the physicians congregated. There, with a deep bow, he presented the note to one of the men and asked for the physician Haddad. The man received it with a mild thank you. Another man with a very long beard and an impressive turban read the note and then shook his head, but motioning Talon to stay, he got up and left.

It was some time before anyone came for him, and the delay allowed Talon to observe the coming and goings of the people at the hospital. He could see people on beds in the arched walkways that formed a large square all around. The building possessed a second floor where he could see a great deal of activity. For the most part, the patients on the beds seemed to be asleep. Even with the cloudy, threatening sky, there was an atmosphere of calm and peace.

Some of them had relatives or friends with them, who sat about on the flagstones or on the grass nearby, talking in low tones. Pigeons competed with sparrows, flying overhead in large numbers, knowing crumbs would be left behind by the careless visitors. The physicians of Isfahan thought that the chances of recovery for a patient were enhanced with the ever-present birds chirping in the orange trees, the cool weather, and open-air dormitories.

Orderlies seemed to be going in all directions at once, yet there was an aura of calm around the group of old men with beards who were seated nearby. He assumed that they were all doctors and was awed being in their presence. Here were men who knew so much, great men who were Farj'an's colleagues, while he, Talon, knew so little. He shrank into himself at the thought and decided to watch and observe to add to his little store of knowledge.

It seemed to be hours before he was called by an orderly, who guided him along one of the open passageways clogged with beds and patients. They went up stairs and along another long passageway before coming to a doorway. The orderly knocked and they were bade entry. Talon saw the physician Haddad sitting with a note in his hand.

"You are the messenger the doctor sent me?" he asked.

Talon nodded politely.

"Why he decided to stay at home today I am not sure. I am here, and so are many of his colleagues."

"It is going to rain today, *Gorban* Doctor, and he decided to stay at home because of his rheumatism."

"Yes, I suppose so. Anyway, here is the report he wanted. I have written it all down. Off you go, young man." He waved Talon away after giving him the sealed note.

Talon bowed low, murmuring, "May Allah protect you, *Gorban*," and let himself out. He went quickly down the stairs and out to the courtyard. There he tossed a brass coin at the boy who'd held and watered Jabbar through the wait, then leaped catlike into the saddle. He headed back to the house happy to be free of the hospital and its concerns.

Talon came to the same entrance he had left earlier that morning, and it was only when he had gone through the gate that he realized something was wrong.

Dreadfully wrong.

The silence screamed a warning at him. No birds, no voices, not even the normal stamp of horses' hooves was to be heard, just the faint sound of flies. The hair on the back of his neck rose, and his whole body stiffened with alarm.

As he came through the entrance to the stables he found the head groom, Butrus, face down in a pool of blood on the stable yard cobbles. Flies were already buzzing about his wounds and the puddle of blood congealing around his body. Over nearer the stables he could see a foot sticking out one the doors, which his mind registered as belonging to one of the boys.

He senses flared as he cast a quick look around to ensure that no one was going to attack him and then dismounted, leaving Jabbar where he was, snorting at the smell of blood and backing away. Talon drew his knife and ran silently to the house. He came to the door, listened, and then slipped into the gloom of the doorway.

He nearly tripped over another body just inside. It was the woman who looked after their laundry. With barely a glance at her and a rising panic in his stomach, he regained his wits and quickly and lightly ran to the main courtyard.

He could hear his heart pounding.

There were other servants lying where they had fallen. It looked as if most of them had died trying to put up some kind of a fight, but had been overwhelmed and had died of sword thrusts and knife wounds. There was a lot of blood spattered on the columns and the tiled floor, its smell rank in his nostrils. He dared not call out yet. He could not be sure if there were attackers waiting for him.

There was no doubt at all in his racing mind as to who it had been. Ahmad or Arash had found them. Something had gone terribly wrong, and the messenger had been caught. He searched desperately with his eyes for any signs of Rav'an or Reza, Fariba or the doctor. None of them were in sight. He slipped silently through the dining area, finding the body of another of the menservants with his throat cut, arms flung wide, staring at the ceiling, a look of total surprise on his bloody face. Talon did not pause. With a leaden feeling, he forced his legs to carry him up the stairs to Farj'an and Fariba's rooms.

There he found them. The doctor was lying across the opening to his study, a bloody bundle of rags. They had made very sure of him before moving on. Talon's agonized gaze went from the body of his beloved mentor to the still form on the polished floor in the other room. His face was a cold, frozen mask, his insides in a turmoil, he wanted to vomit but forced himself to move the last couple of yards to where Fariba lay in pool of blood. As he kneeled over her, praying for the first time in a long time, he thought he saw a tiny movement. Yes, there it was again. She had moved.

He kneeled closer to her, trying to find out where she had been stabbed. He lifted her limp body, which elicited a whisper of pain from her bloodless lips. He found the entry wound just below and to the left of her right breast; it was still bleeding. He sought to staunch the bleeding with a torn cotton cloth from the bed sheets, desperately trying to remember what the doctor had taught them about this kind of care while they were on the caravan.

Fariba opened her eyes and gazed blindly about. Her breathing was shallow and it looked very painful for her to move.

He whispered, "Fariba, it is Talon. They are gone. Can you tell me what happened? Where is Rav'an?"

Her eyes focused on him, then her left hand fluttered as she lay it on his arm. "Ah, Talon. They came and took her."

"Who?" he almost shouted, although he knew.

"A man called Ahmad came with his evil men and took her

after he killed Farj'an." Tears burst from her eyes and ran down the sides of her head.

Talon picked her up and put her gently on the bed. She weighed nothing, he thought. He decided that he had to do something about her wound or she would surely die. He looked about for water and found it in one of the pitchers near the bed.

Soaking a clean cloth, he tore her blouse open and exposed her right side. The wound had gone in just below the breast between the ribs. Knowing nothing of wounds of this kind, he guessed that it had gone deep, as it still welled blood, but not in a spurt, so he hoped that it might not have cut anything vital. He cleaned the wound with gentle careful fingers, containing his panic and impatience as he did so. He could not leave her now, even though he wanted to charge off, find Ahmad, and kill him this minute.

He concentrated on her wound, binding it tight around her chest with a long strip of clean cotton he tore from the bed sheets. Then he made her comfortable. He could do nothing but watch her mourn her keeper and lover. At last, she slept or fainted, he was not sure which, but he made sure she was covered by the warm blankets he had found for her.

He went back with heavy steps to the doctor's body and carried it into another bedroom, lying it with tender care straight out on its back on the bed. He closed the half open eyes of the man he had come to love. He kissed the cold cheek and then allowed himself to weep bitter tears as he began to realize how utterly his world in Isfahan had been destroyed.

He said a prayer over Farj'an body, consigning him to Allah's care. Talon asked that he be received with honor and kindness for all the good things he had done on this earth. He felt that Jean might approve of his action. He hoped indeed that they might meet somewhere and play chess together. His heart felt as though it would break open within his chest, it hurt so much.

Finally, he went back to see how Fariba was doing. She was asleep, so he left a lit oil lamp beside her. He made his way to his room to get his sword so he could be better armed if anyone came back for him, as he was sure they would. He was just moving out of his room to the front of the house when he heard shouts and froze in place to listen, waiting to see who it might be. There was a clatter of horse's hooves outside and then the rattle of bits and metal, and men shouting. Talon sped down to the ground floor, his sword drawn, ready to fight to the death the interlopers, whoever they might be.

He almost ran into Dav'ud, who was striding into the main hallway with his sword drawn. Both men stopped and stared at one another. In the brief silence that followed their meeting, other men crowded in behind Dav'ud.

"Talon," Dav'ud all but shouted, "what has happened? Where is Rav'an? Who did this? By God, we must have revenge for this outrage!" His good-natured features were creased with anger and concern.

"I should ask you the same question, Dav'ud. How did you know to come here?"

"One of the servants fled from here, and came to our house. He knew we were friends of yours."

Talon lowered his sword. "Come with me," he said tersely. "No... tell the others to either stay here or to check to see if anyone is alive on the grounds."

They fanned out and began to check out the house. They were all armed and went prepared for any trouble.

Turning on his heel, Talon left the room, Dav'ud in tow. Talon wordlessly took him up the stairs to the doctor's quarters. Here, just before they went in, he put a finger to his lips indicating silence, and led the way into Fariba's room.

A light rain was falling, so it was gloomy in the room. The light of the oil lamp was the only cheerful thing there. She was as pale as death and very still. For a horrible moment, Talon thought she had gone, but as he moved swiftly to her bedside, she opened her eyes.

He bent close and said in a low gentle voice, "Aunt Fariba, I have Dav'ud with me; he has brought his men with him. You are now safe."

She gave a weak smile. "Ah, my Talon, no one is safe from those people."

Talon turned to a shocked Dav'ud. "You can see she is very hurt. They wounded her on her right side with a knife. I don't know how deep is the wound, but we have to get her to the academy, to Doctor Haddad, who might be able to save her. I met him today. He is a friend of Farj'an's."

Dav'ud looked at Fariba and then Talon. "What about the doctor? Can he not help?"

Talon beckoned and took him to the other room where Farj'an

lay.

"Here lies the doctor, my friend. They murdered him along with all the others. We are lucky Fariba was not killed, although I think she wishes that she had been."

Dav'ud gave a gasp of anguish. "Who has done this to them? Talon, do you know? Who is it? And where have they taken Rav'an, or is she...?" He left the question in the air.

Talon looked at him with equal anguish. "I don't know, Dav'ud. But I know who it was and I also know this: They will try to come back to finish me off as well, then they will kill her and Reza, if he's still alive."

His anguish was so evident that Dav'ud collected himself. "We must see to it that they cannot come back. That's first. Second, as you said, we have to help Fariba. I shall order my people to take her to the academy at once. Can she be moved?"

"I don't know, but if she stays here she's still in mortal danger, and not even God can protect her. We have no choice but to move her."

Dav'ud nodded. "I shall see to it. Then, my friend, I want an explanation. You know a lot more than you've told me as yet."

Talon nodded. "I shall tell you what you need to hear," he said quietly.

Dav'ud was as good as his word. He rushed downstairs and gave orders to his men, who did not need to be told the urgency. They came to take Fariba downstairs to a palanquin that they found in the stable area, rarely used by the doctor, as he rode most of the time. They carried her with gentle hands down the stairs and settled her comfortably in the heaped cushions. Talon and Dav'ud were in attendance all the time. She weakly asked Talon to come with her, but he said no. He had to hurry and find Rav'an and Reza, and time was at a premium.

She understood and reached for his hand. "Talon, please, come back to me alive," she pleaded.

Tears coursing down his face, he swore he would and gripped her hand before waving the men on. They left with a heavy guard in attendance. There were more men coming in as they left, men who worked for Dav'ud's father who would be loyal to the son and do his bidding.

They gathered the servants' bodies, hunted through the gardens for others, and found the gardeners dead behind some bushes.

There was no sign of Rav'an or of Reza.

Talon nodded. This was what he had expected. It would be a long, slow death for Reza and something almost as bad for Rav'an. He cursed himself for having not been there to defend her and the doctor. At least he would have died in the attempt instead of being here alive and wondering where in all of Isfahan they might be.

Dav'ud came over to him after talking to his men. "Talon, tell me all you know of this terrible thing. What happened?" he demanded, his voice stern.

Talon walked to the fountain where he had known such happiness and sat down on the edge of the pond. He felt tired. Dav'ud followed and stood facing him. Talon looked up and asked, "What do you know of the Nizirin Ismaili from the Alborz?"

His new friend blanched. "They are accursed; they are murderers and killers without conscience. A profanity on this earth, all men fear and curse them. Please don't tell me that it is they who did this?"

Talon nodded. "I need your word before God that you will tell no man what I am about to tell you."

Dav'ud looked at him. "Why do I have to swear before God?"

"Because if you don't, then I shall do this alone, and you will never know more," Talon said resignedly, but it was clear that he meant it.

Dav'ud shuffled his feet looking down. "I have not known you for long, but I've found you to be honest and trustworthy. I swear before God that I shall say nothing of what you tell me to anyone, may He strike me down if I lie."

So Talon told him everything, who he and Reza were, who Rav'an was. That wet afternoon he described to Dav'ud how they had escaped with the news of the Agha Khan's betrayal by his own uncle, Arash, and how the son named Ahmad must have found out somehow; perhaps he had caught Farj'an's messenger, Abbas. By whatever means, Ahmad was here in Isfahan and had wreaked his first vengeance on the doctor. It was only a matter of time before he killed the other two in some gruesome manner.

"The man is cruel as few men are, and Reza will suffer much agony before he leaves this world."

"What of Rav'an?" Dav'ud whispered, horrified by the tale that he had just heard, staring at Talon with new eyes, almost as though he were a complete stranger.

Talon opened his hands. "Before God, I don't know, other than I know he lusted after her. He will either kill her or take her as a prisoner to the north."

Dav'ud banged one fist into the other. "We can't allow this to happen, Talon. We simply can't!"

Talon looked at him his eyes hopeless. "But I don't know where in Isfahan he could be. It's a large city and it's unimaginable that anyone followed these people. How can we find them?"

There was silence for a while as both wrestled with the horrifying thought that they were quite helpless to do anything for their friends. Talon felt like weeping like a child and imagined that Dav'ud was in the same state.

He stopped his banging of the side of the pond with his fist for a second. Looking up at Dav'ud, he said slowly. "There is one person who might be able to help... it is a very faint possibility, but just maybe..."

Dav'ud shook him excitedly. "Who, Talon? Who?"

"A man I know in the bazaar. Dav'ud, it's just a chance, that's all, but we must hurry."

They rushed out of the courtyard. Dav'ud told his men to be vigilant and capture anyone they found on the grounds and hold them until they came back. They took two men with them, and while they mounted up, Talon retrieved a very nervous Jabbar, and then they all galloped off to the bazaar.

* * * * *

Al Tayyib was walking to his favorite *chai khane* when Yousef came running up to him. He bent down to hear what the breathless young boy whispered to him. Looking very concerned, he almost ran to the *chai khane.*

There he found Talon with someone he had not met before. Talon looked like death; pale and so tense he was trembling, while the other, who was introduced as Dav'ud, was not in much better shape. Hastily gesturing them both to sit, Al Tayyib clapped his hands for *chai* and then without further ado asked Talon, "What brings you to me? It is not for the usual reason, I can tell." His attempt at humor went unnoticed.

Talon looked at him with anguished eyes. "Al Tayyib, I am here in the hope that you can help me. The doctor is slain, Fariba is near death with a terrible wound, and Rav'an and Reza are prisoners."

Al Tayyib gasped. "What did you say? The doctor's dead and the others are prisoners? What in God's good name are you talking about?"

Dav'ud nudged Talon. "Perhaps if you told him what you told me he will understand better, Talon."

Talon nodded and launched into his tale once more, although he kept it short. Al Tayyib nodded. The pieces fit with what he had supposed. Although Talon left a lot out, he could guess what had transpired and how this tragedy had occurred. It was not the first time Al Tayyib had run into the Assassins.

When Talon lapsed into silence, he spoke. "Now you want me to help you find out where these people might be, Talon?"

Talon and Dav'ud nodded together.

"It will take time, but I will do this because of the good doctor, and because you and your two friends helped me. But I can't promise that we will succeed—only that we shall try. With the help of Allah, we shall succeed."

Talon nodded. He reached over and gripped Al Tayyib's arm hard, his emotions clear on his face.

The older man patted his hand reassuringly. "We must pray to God that he assists us in this endeavor," he said his voice gruff. "Be of good heart, my young friends. Where can I find you? It will take longer than an hour."

Talon told him where the doctor's house was. He told Al Tayyib to make sure the messenger was clear with his response to the guards, as they would be jumpy.

They parted then, and while Al Tayyib sent Yousef off on an errand to collect his people together, the two young men made their way back to the doctor's house. It was now late afternoon and it was still raining when they left the bazaar. To Talon's feverish mind, it was as though the heavens themselves were mourning Farj'an.

More of Dav'ud's father's men had arrived while they'd been gone. They now had about twenty men, defenses were out in the garden in force; and, in spite of the light rain, the men were very much on the alert. If the son of their master was so obviously concerned, then they were, too.

Not long after they arrived back at the house, Hussein came to them with some of his friends. Word was out that there had been a tragedy at the doctor's house and that Dav'ud was there. Talon welcomed Hussein and his friends and told them that all they could do for the time being was to stay on the alert, as there could be another attack, but otherwise they would have to wait for news from Al Tayyib and his people. Hussein's dark features creased with anger at what he heard. Talon knew he could rely upon this man.

Dav'ud talked in low tones to Hussein, but as he had given his word he could not tell him everything, just that Talon thought that Rav'an had been kidnapped for ransom, but they were not sure who at this time. That seemed good enough for Hussein, who then went off with his friends to find a place to wait.

It was a somber group that ate the hastily prepared food on the carpet of the living room that evening. Talon ached as he listened to the drip of rain off the roof. He could not remember being so numb, not even when he was first captured those long years ago.

Dav'ud did not try to cheer him up. He, too, was numb with shock. The beautiful girl he had fallen for was a princess in a society that all men loathed and shunned? How could this be? She was so full of light. How could she belong to this kind of people, who lived dark, murderous lives away from the light of God? He believed Talon, though, every word. It was clear to him that Talon was devastated by the catastrophe that had overtaken them. Dav'ud felt a chill as he recalled the look in Talon's eyes when he talked about the man named Ahmad. Dav'ud didn't think Talon would show any mercy when and if they met. He hoped that they would. The man deserved no mercy.

Talon paced about, too agitated to sit. The waiting was driving him mad with worry as his wild imaginings took hold, going from what they might be doing to Reza at this very minute, to the unspeakable things Ahmad had in mind for Rav'an. How he hated that man. He wished only one thing, and it was that God would grant him the right to kill him.

The object of his loathing was, at that moment, walking up the stairs to the second floor. For Ahmad it had begun in Samiran. His mind went back to the moment when he had been granted his wish for revenge.

He had stamped his way down into the dungeon at Samiran. It

was dank and cold and there was a nasty smell to the place. The torchlight flickered and guttered in the hands of one of his men, casting huge shadows along the rough-hewn walls as they walked by. He had wrinkled his nose as he came to the door of the cell where he was been shown. The smell of urine and feces was strong.

The wreckage of what had once been a man lay on a large wooden table in the center of the cell; it was clear, even in the dim light of the oil lamps that sat on shelves cut into the walls, that he did not have much longer to live. The two men in the room were spattered with blood and bone.

"What has he told you?"

"He was going north to find the Master, and inform him that his sister is in Isfahan, *Gorban*," one of the men answered.

"What else?"

"The doctor Farj'an sent him, and he is looking after the princess in Isfahan."

Ahmad had stepped close to the recumbent wreck of a man. Seizing his bloodied hair, he twisted it, forcing the dying man to stare through swollen eyes up at him.

"Did you really think to defy Arash Khan?" he had asked incredulously. "How long ago did they leave for Isfahan?" he rasped at the torturer, looking down at the man on the table.

"He told us that it was two months ago."

Ahmad let the victim's head fall with a thump back on the table. "Get rid of him," he told the men. "Bury him outside the walls somewhere or leave him to the wolves. We have what we need."

He'd walked out of the room, leaving the grisly work to be finished by his two men. His hand closed upon the wax seal in his pocket. So this is what Rav'an had discovered and why she had fled the castle. He was elated. His father would be very pleased to hear the news. They had them now, he thought.

"Rav'an, my pretty, you will be mine after all," he had exulted. "I shall make you watch your two 'protectors' die slowly as I skin them alive. I shall force you to watch the *ferengi* die shrieking for his God," he gloated.

The next day he had sent a messenger on a good horse off to Alamut with the news. Ahmad was going to take the party of *fida'i* from Alamut and a couple of *rafiqi* he had with him from Samiran and race to Isfahan. The captain was to come back to Samiran and take charge of the castle. The castilian could not be trusted. It would be up to his father, Arash, he had reflected, as to whether he came to Samiran or met him at Ghazvin, or even Isfahan. He, Ahmad, was going to go to Isfahan and deal with the doctor Farj'an and the three fugitives. It would take at least a month before he got there, so every day counted.

They had arrived in Hamadan to be told that the fugitives had left long before. The two bewildered men, Ali and Karim, assured Ahmad that they must have left for Baghdad. Ahmad had slapped them both hard across their faces and scornfully told them that the group was with the doctor Farj'an in Isfahan. He almost killed them then and there but decided that he would leave them for his father to deal with when the time came.

Ahmad and his men had stayed at the same house as the fugitives before them, but just long enough for the two terrified men of Hamadan to obtain the best horses they could buy with their depleted funds. Then it was off to ride hard all the way south along the rough roads, through the passes along the ridges of the eastern Zagros, to Isfahan.

Many nights later, Ahmad and his men had arrived at Isfahan. They were stopped at the gates but had no difficulty in paying the sentries a bribe to let them in. Making their way swiftly through the silent streets of the city, the group of men, a mix of *rafiqi* and *fida'i,* came to a house set well back from the street within its own walled space.

Located in a modest residential area, but some distance from that of the doctor, this house had a garden that no one looked after, and the house was run down, although it boasted two stories and was of mud-dried brick construction in the old style. The walls were very thick. The top story was more of an open balcony with rooms and a corridor behind them to accommodate an indoor staircase, and a flat roof to top it off.

Ahmad and his men had slipped into the garden and stabled their exhausted horses in the rude stables to the back of the large building. The caretaker who lived there lighted the oil lamps. Then the men had crowded into the main room. They were all unkempt and haggard from their long, hard ride from Samiran.

Ahmad had commandeered the top floor for his operations center and placed guards round the garden and at the entrance. He went to sleep, confident that neither he nor his men had been detected coming into the city. On the morrow, he would find the doctor's house, and very soon, he had promised himself, he would have his cousin Rav'an here in this room all to himself.

His men had searched for and finally found the doctor's residence after two frustrating days. Ahmad had placed his men to watch and keep him informed as to the activity going on there.

His men had told him that each day the group of three would ride out from the residence and go out of the city to play *Cho'gan* with other people on a large space provided for that purpose. They would always come back about midmorning, sometimes with others from the field, and then rarely went out again, except on occasion one or other of the two boys, Reza or Talon, would go off on some errand or other. The men had taken care not to be seen. They knew that the boys were *fida'i* and if any one of them showed himself, and would be alerted.

Ahmad had thought about ambushing the group on their way back to the house, but decided that he would only have one chance to catch everyone. As he wanted to punish the doctor, too, he had decided that he would attack the house when the young people came back from practicing *Cho'gan*. It would not be very hard to gain entry. There were no sentries on the gate, other than a servant who would easily be overcome. His men would swarm over the people in the house and kill anyone who got in the way.

He wanted to kill the doctor as much as to take the others prisoner. He considered the doctor a traitor to the Ismaili, and in particular to his father, and would make sure he died for this.

After three days of waiting, he had sent a man back to Samiran, telling his father that he, Ahmad, would be taking the boys and Rav'an prisoner and would join him in Samiran when he had finished with them. Ahmad did not intend to bring anyone back with him, nor did he think his father intended that he should.

* * * * *

After Reza had been knocked unconscious, he'd been trussed up, then hauled like a sack of vegetables to Ahmad's quarters. There on the ground floor, he was dumped onto a large bench, retied and hoisted so that he was hung off a hook by his bound wrists, his feet just touching the ground.

Reza was awakened by a dash of cold water thrown at his face. Shaking his head to clear the pain from the blow and the water in his hair that now hung down over his face, he glared at Ahmad. "You filth!" he shouted. "Why have you killed the doctor and his people? What harm have they ever done to you?"

By way of response, Ahmad strode up to him and slapped him very hard across the face. Reza's head whipped round at the impact, and then he hung there in his bonds, a trickle of blood dripping from his mouth.

"You are going to regret that I left you alive, you traitor," Ahmad grated, barely controlling his temper. He punched Reza as hard as he could in the ribs. Reza gasped and jerked in his chains. He felt ribs break under the impact. Now it was hard for him to breathe. He was frightened. He knew that they would make it very bad for him, but he was determined not to show them any fear. He grit his teeth and spat some blood out. Whether intentionally or not, the gob of spit landed on Ahmad's boot.

Ahmad completely lost control. He kicked and punched the hanging figure until he was exhausted. Not finished yet, he seized an earthenware pitcher from the side of the room and hurled it at Reza. It smashed against the almost unconscious man's lower right leg. All the people in the room heard the bone break, and the victim's scream of agony confirmed it. For some reason, this stopped Ahmad.

He stood there staring at Reza's writhing figure, breathing heavily. There was silence in the room as the other men watched. These were hard men who were loyal to Ahmad, but even they were frightened by his rages. Still glowering at Reza, Ahmad spat at him and left the room.

"I shall come back when I have finished with the girl," he snapped at the men. "Keep him awake for me."

Stamping out of the room, he headed upstairs to where he had had his men place Rav'an. He entered the room to find her sitting on the floor, her hands tied to the legs of a truckle bed. She was disheveled both from the fight in the doctor's house and from her struggles against her bonds.

She glared up at him from a tear-streaked face.

"You have no right to hold me prisoner, Ahmad. When my brother hears of this, you will be a dead man."

Ahmad came over to the bed and then sat on the carpet a safe distance from the girl. He rubbed his knuckles. "I doubt that you will be telling him anything after I have finished with you," he said with dangerous calm.

Rav'an felt a chill go down her spine. She had heard the scream and knew it had been Reza. She had wept for him as she had wept for the doctor and Fariba, both of whom she had seen struck down. Reza had fought like a tiger to protect her, wounding and killing several. But they had overwhelmed him, and then knocked him out right in front of her. Now they were torturing him, just as Ahmad had done with the luckless man in the village near the main pass to Shah Rud. Ahmad observed her while she tried to still a shudder as she imagined what they were going to do to Reza.

Ahmad looked at her, elated with his success. The operation had gone almost exactly according to plan. His men had swarmed over the garden walls and dealt with the servants so quickly that Reza barely had time to get the doctor upstairs with the women before they were in the house and all over them. The only fly in this particular ointment was that the boy Talon was missing when they had attacked.

Ahmad resolved to punish the man who had been on watch for not mentioning this to him at the time of the attack. Now they would have to find him and kill him. That was a pity, as he would have been useful, and his father had wanted him alive, if possible.

Now, however, he, Ahmad, was here in the room with the girl. What a beauty she was. She looked even better when she was angry and frightened. If she were not frightened now, she soon would be, he promised himself.

He wanted to show her how helpless she was, so he smiled and drew out of his sash the remnants of the wax seal he had kept and showed it to her. He was not disappointed in her reaction. Her eyes widened with shock and surprise even as she tried to appear disinterested. He knew she had recognized it. "I also have the letters from you and the good doctor written to the master. Would you like to know how I obtained them?"

She looked at him with loathing. "I imagine you butchered the poor soul as you usually do," she said between her teeth.

He smiled and nodded, saying conversationally, "Yes, you're right. He tried hard to deny everything, but it did not take too long to wring information from him. My father has taught me well. I imagine it will be as easy with Reza. He's just a boy."

"He is more of a man than you shall ever be," Rav'an snapped.

"Well, cousin, that's something you're going to find out before we're done." Ahmad leered at her.

She turned her head away from him in disgust. In truth, it was to hide how terrified she was, not wanting him to read in her eyes what he wanted to see.

"I really don't know who to start with," he said contemplatively. "Should I deal with the boy or should I start on you?" He giggled to himself. "So many choices, my dear cousin. You have caused me so much trouble I think I shall reserve you for last. I intend to make it a long night."

He sat forward and then quickly slid down so that before she could react, he was sitting on her legs, pinning them. Then he leaned over her, his breath on her face. Rav'an turned away from him in a vain attempt to avoid the kiss he planted on her mouth. He forced her face round with a strong hand on her lower jaw and stared into her eyes.

"You might as well enjoy this night, my dear cousin, as it will be the last time a man knows you the way I shall. After that, you will be dead, and it will not matter any more."

His hand stayed on her jaw, holding it rigid, while the other went to her blouse and tore it to the waist. Her breasts were bared and his hungry eyes roamed over her chest and neck.

Rav'an gave an enraged whimper of frustration at not being able to strike him. He shifted his hand from her face, closed it around her breast, and squeezed hard. Her cry of pain made him laugh with gratification.

Taking his time, he stood up and grinned down on her. Rav'an's head hung down as she fought the wave of pain, her hair over her face. He stooped and grabbed her hair and pulled at it until she was staring him in the face.

"You might have once been a princess, my pretty, but tonight you will be my whore. Please me, and Reza will die a quick death. Do not, and I shall skin him from feet to head while he lives." He let her head fall. "Think on what I have said," he told her as he turned to go. She said nothing. He gave her one last look and then left to get some food. All the excitement had made him hungry. He wanted to be fed and to have some wine before he began the evening's entertainment.

Rav'an choked back the sobs that she knew she could not control much longer. It had been all she could do not to beg for Reza's life and her own. Ahmad terrified her, and now all he promised them was a horrifying death.

"Oh, Talon, where were you when I needed you? Where are you now? Allah please protect him, even if you will not protect me or Reza," she whispered out loud.

Struggling against her bonds, she decided that she must somehow get out of there, find a weapon, and try to escape. But her bonds were tight, and the blood in her wrists was almost cut off. She was terribly thirsty; no one had offered any kind of relief. Tears trickled down her bruised face as she thought of the doctor and Fariba. Her world had come crashing down upon them, too, destroying them and all their servants, and she blamed herself for having been responsible for their deaths.

* * * * *

Talon was at that moment riding hard with Dav'ud and his men through the streets of Isfahan behind Al Tayyib, who led the way on his pony. The messenger had come early in the evening to find Talon, and had been accosted by a hostile group of men before he could convince them that Al Tayyib had sent him.

Talon at once rode with Dav'ud to the bazaar, where a cautiously optimistic Al Tayyib informed them that the beggars of the city had noticed that a house they knew to be usually unoccupied was now full of activity. A large party of men had come in almost a week ago, and some of the beggars had noticed them coming back in the rain earlier that day with two people who might have been prisoners.

Talon was convinced it was the Ismaili. "We must go and find out who they are. It's vital I see for myself."

Al Tayyib nodded. "I shall take you there myself," he said.

They came to within a couple of streets of the house in question and dismounted. Talon had brought his bow with him. This he now carried with his sword and his knife. Dav'ud was armed with his sword, as were many of his men, who also had spears. This was a very determined party of men, who wanted to have all the benefits of surprise. Talon had argued with Dav'ud and Al Tayyib, who had simply wanted to charge the place.

He pointed out that the people they were up against would be happy to die if that were ordained, but they would also make sure that the girl and Reza did, too. He told them that if they could gain a rapid entrance, he would make it his mission to reach Rav'an, who would probably be held in the living area or bedrooms. Reza would be in the basement if there was one, or else in one of the lower-floor rooms.

They came to the house just as darkness descended. The light rain gave them some cover, as even at this place the sentries would seek shelter. Talon hoped that the people inside the compound would have no idea that they might be a target for retribution that night. He told his newfound companions to wait for him while he had a good look around the walls and checked out the house.

Dav'ud wanted to come with him, but he shook his head. "No, my friend, this is what I have been trained for. Wait for me. When it's time, help me get in, and then you can help me kill them."

Dav'ud nodded and then grinned. In spite of his concern for Rav'an, he was excited at the impending fight.

Talon seemed to disappear from view; one moment there, then gone. Even Al Tayyib was impressed, looking at Dav'ud and Hussein, then opening his hands and shrugging. They looked at one another, unsettled by their newly acquired knowledge of Talon. A comradeship was being formed by the circumstances, nonetheless.

Talon slid noiselessly into the shadows of the wall and the trees nearby. He effortlessly climbed one of the taller plane trees, then, sitting in a fork of the tree, he gained a good view of the garden and the house.

He saw that, as Al Tayyib's men had described, there was a second story and even an outside staircase leading up to the verandah in the front. There was one light on the top floor, while all the windows were lit downstairs. Most windows were shuttered, but light still spilled out onto the ground outside. He noted that the sentries, who should have been on watch, were hiding in the shadows and under cover to avoid the chill of the rain.

He resolved to take out at least three of them before the assault on the house started, as that would reduce the odds. But he still didn't know for certain how many men there were, estimating the number at fifteen or more, from what he had heard. He almost jumped down into the compound then and there, as he could hardly restrain his impatience, but knew that would be one of the last things he ever did.

Instead, he climbed down making no noise and scouted the whole area to see if there was any kind of alternative entrance to the one in front. There was a back door of solid old wood that looked interesting. He cautiously climbed onto the top of the six-foot wall and peered over. There was an overgrown pathway leading to the sheds at the back of the house, which was in darkness from this vantage.

He heard a slight noise and he froze. A man had left the shadows near the sheds and was coming toward the door. Talon moved back and off the lip of the wall, holding onto the top, desperately hoping the man had not heard him. The man came up to the door and checked to see if it was still shut, then strode back. Talon moved back onto to his perch to watch where he stopped, noting it carefully.

He climbed down and made his silent way back to the group of men huddled in the next street. He appeared as silently as he had gone and gave them all a start.

"Where did you come from?" Dav'ud demanded when he realized that Talon was again among them.

Talon wasted no time. "I think it's them," he said quietly. "They are nervous and have guards all around. Who else would be placing sentries like that? There's a back door that I want to get into. Once I am inside, I will signal you, and you must attack the front and get to the house very quickly. Can you do that?"

Dav'ud looked at Al Tayyib, who nodded. "How many men do you need with you?"

"Just you and two men, if you want to bring them," Talon said. "Agha Tayyib, Hussein, can you and your men take the front gate and assault the front of the house? I don't know if any of these people have bows. It could be dangerous."

Al Tayyib grinned in the dark. "Hussein and his men want to have a fight, and so do my men and I."

"When I call, you must break through the front entrance and get into the ground floor as fast as possible, because they will kill Reza once they know they are under attack," Talon said urgently. "I and Dav'ud will go for the top floor, as I think that's where Rav'an is. I am only guessing, though."

Al Tayyib placed a large hand on his shoulder. "You get into the place and find out for sure. We can adapt once we know more. Allah will point the way, my young warrior," he said reassuringly.

With a muttered "Go with God" from all sides, Talon led the way back to the old door with Dav'ud. Once again, he scaled the wall and helped Dav'ud up next to him. They crouched on the wide top surface, watching the shadows. The other two men waited below. Talon watched carefully to see if there was any movement by the guard. He detected a movement in the darkness where the sentry was standing, and then made out the whole shape of the man. He was barely visible, fifty yards away.

Talon nudged Dav'ud and moved his bow forward. Then he stood up carefully on the wide mud wall. Dav'ud reached out and held onto his ankle. Very slowly, Talon knocked an arrow and drew with care. He was invisible against the black background of the trees. There was a *twang!* The figure in the shadows clutched his throat and fell forward without making any noise. Talon jumped noiselessly down on the garden side of the wall, then opened the gate very slowly to ensure no noise.

Dav'ud climbed down and the other two men came inside. Taking the lead, Talon went ahead by about ten paces, just enough to ensure that those behind did not make too much noise, but so they could still see him. He could hear horses nearby in the sheds behind the house. He fervently hoped that there were no men with them.

Just before they got to the house, a door opened at the back and lamplight blazed out just in front of him. He dived into some long grass and prayed that his companions were out of sight. The door shut, but a man was coming toward him. He lay very still, wondering what the man was doing. He soon knew. The man stopped just on the track and began to urinate into the long grass. His stream landed right next to Talon's right hand, which he dared not move for fear of making a sound. The fellow was full and took his time, at last finishing and then turning to go.

He got no farther than two paces. Talon came up behind him, seized his face with his left hand, jerked his head back, and flashed his knife across the man's throat. There was a struggle and gurgle, blood sprayed, and then the man went limp in his arms. Talon dragged the inert body into the long grass next to where he had been and waved in Dav'ud's direction; he rose with his two men and came forward. They were all looking at Talon with new respect.

"We have to move fast now; they might miss him," Talon whispered. "I'll make the call, then we head for the stairs."

He gave a call that sounded very much like that of an owl to anyone listening, and then he called again. They waited for a couple of minutes and then heard the gratifying sound of shouting at the front gate.

Ahmad was just finishing his dinner with his men. One of them had gone out the back of the house to relieve himself when they heard noise outside near the front of the property. They all looked to Ahmad for guidance. He didn't hesitate. He seized his sword and ran out of the room, heading for the upstairs rooms. Several men grabbed bows and ran to take up positions on the verandah. As they piled out of the front door, they could see figures running toward them, brandishing weapons and shouting.

Talon could see the heads of two bowmen as they ran up the outside stairs, notching arrows as they went. From the cover of the stair wall, they both loosed arrows off into the crowd of men chasing them. Then they turned and ran up the stairs to gain a better vantage point. One of them stopped as he came level with the top floor as Talon loosed an arrow straight at him. He fell back with a shriek, clutching at the arrow sticking out of his head.

The other was as fast as a striking snake. He stood up and loosed an arrow at the four men crouching with Talon. Talon had only just managed to notch another arrow when one sped by him, and he heard a choking cry behind him. He loosed his arrow immediately at a fast-moving man behind and below him and had the satisfaction of seeing it strike him in the chest. Turning, Talon didn't even think, he crashed through the latticework of the shutters to the room that had the lamp glowing in it. As he did so, he heard a scream, and knew it was from Rav'an. He landed on the floor and rolled, coming to his feet in a dimly lit room to see Ahmad leaning over someone sitting on the floor.

He knew then that he had to move swiftly, or it was all over for Rav'an. Launching himself, he struck Ahmad high on the shoulder and drove him off the screaming Rav'an. They both fell in a tangle, but Talon was on his feet in a flash and backing off, trying to get space from Ahmad.

Ahmad fell away with a curse, rolled to his feet, and came up several yards away, a sword in his hand. He crouched like a cat, grinning savagely, ready to strike. There was a wild madness in his eyes.

"So you have come to be killed, young Frank, the Lion Killer," he sneered. Then he snickered. "You have saved me the trouble of coming to find you. Or did you come for the princess? She will go with you to hell."

Talon slid his sword and dagger out of their scabbards and went into a crouch, facing Ahmad. "I have come to send you to hell, you rapist pig," he taunted.

The two men who had come with Talon and Dav'ud forced their way into the room, looking undecided. The shouting and screaming continued below with the clash and scrape of swords as men fought for their lives downstairs.

Never taking his eyes from Ahmad, Talon waved the two men to the bed, indicating that he wanted them to get to Rav'an before Ahmad managed to. He placed himself in front of her, not daring to look at her. He was confronting a man who was an expert swordsman and very strong. Ahmad came at him with his slim, curved blade flickering in the dim light of the lamp. Their shadows played grotesquely against the wall as they feinted and struck.

Talon quickly realized that he had to keep moving to avoid Ahmad's thrusting, ever-probing blade. This was not a man thrashing at him in the hope of intimidating him, but an accomplished killer who had fought and slain many times before. Although Talon had a low opinion of Ahmad's intellect, he had a high respect for his fighting prowess.

Talon kept his own blade high and used his wrist as much as he could to parry and counterstrike. Several times he took advantage of the furniture and attacked around it, but Ahmad did the same, demolishing the furniture with a slash of his sword or kicking it aside, driving him back.

Ahmad began to taunt his smaller adversary. "You are, after all, just a boy, *ferengi*; you should have run when you had the chance."

His blade flickered out and the tip slashed across Talon's left shoulder before he could parry. He felt the burn of the cut and then the blood dripping down his arm as they danced back and forth across the room.

Ahmad laughed, a wild laugh that chilled. "I might not leave this place, but I can assure you that neither you nor Cousin Rav'an will either," he shouted and stabbed again and again at Talon's face.

Behind him, Talon could hear the men releasing Rav'an and moving her out of harm's way. He felt his anger become cold and focused—now he would be able to deal with his man any way he could.

The intricate movements of sword and dagger were bewildering to the watchers. It was clear that Ahmad had the advantage of size and weight, and that he was a superb swordsman. Talon, however, was a little more practiced in the two-weapon technique than Ahmad.

Attacking hard, he came up against Ahmad and forced him to lock swords. They stared into each other's eyes for the briefest of moments. Then, before Ahmad could react, Talon flicked his left hand down and out to knick Ahmad's wrist. As Ahmad's hand involuntarily jerked back a few inches, he continued the motion, curling his hand around the outside of the wounded wrist then back inside again to plunge his wide-bladed dagger deep into Ahmad's midriff. He held it there briefly, and then began slowly lifting it, tearing the man's insides apart. As he glared into the eyes of the man he hated, he saw surprise and rage, then despair and agony on his opponent's face.

The strength of the mortally wounded man's sword against his eased, and Ahmad staggered back. His sword dropped as he clutched his middle with his left hand, a large, red stain forming on his shirt. Talon didn't wait. He leapt forward and plunged his own sword deep into Ahmad's chest. With a groan of agony, Ahmad fell to his knees, his strength falling away from him. His eyes searched upward to find Talon's, but then a great gout of blood poured from his mouth, his eyes glazed over, and he fell face down on the floor.

Talon was panting and giddy with the exertion. He knew he had been very lucky. This man would have killed him if they had fought much longer. Shakily, he turned to look for Rav'an and saw her kneeling, holding the rags of her shirt together while the two men, also kneeling, tried to reassure her.

She was weeping and clutching her torn blouse to herself. Talon dropped his sword and knelt in front of her. She looked at him through her tears, said his name, and then fell into his arms. He tried to calm her wracking sobs as she huddled and shook in his arms. Stroking her back and hair, he looked at the other two men, who looked stunned and very unhappy.

Still holding Rav'an tight in his embrace, he asked them what was wrong. They both pointed outside. Gently easing Rav'an away, he asked, "What's the matter, and where is Dav'ud?"

Their looks told him all he had to know. With a low groan, he placed Rav'an in the arms of one of the shaken men and leapt out the window. There on the verandah, very still and on his back, was Dav'ud. He was dead. His eyes were still open, staring up at the rain, his clothes now soaked. The blood from the wound in his chest formed a large stain on the front of his tunic. He had taken the arrow from the *fida'i.*

Talon moaned in anguish and cradled his new friend in his arms for a couple of minutes, unable to think clearly. His senses were nonetheless alert to the activity below. He realized that the noise had stopped and that men were now collecting in the front of the house. Reza! He had to find Reza. He lay Dav'ud down gently on the sodden floor and stood up. With a quick command to the two men in the room to bring Rav'an downstairs, he made his way down the outside stairs past the dead bowmen and round to the front.

There he met Al Tayyib. They looked at one another, both covered with other men's blood, Al Tayyib still holding his gory sword.

Talon burst out, "Reza, Al Tayyib! Where is Reza?"

Al Tayyib held up his left hand. "Alive," he said carefully.

Talon yipped with relief, his hands going to his face as he staggered with the sheer relief of knowing.

Al Tayyib wiped his sword on a rag. "Listen, Talon. He is very badly hurt."

"Where is he? Al Tayyib, where is he?" Talon reached for the older man to grip his arm. "Please tell me he will live."

"I think he may live. He is in there," Al Tayyib said slowly and pointed inside.

Gripping Al Tayyib's arm in gratitude, Talon hastened into the candle-lit room at the front of the house. What he saw there staggered his already badly mauled senses.

His friend lay on a table, the only thing they could put him on. Talon was shocked at his condition. Reza's bloody face was swollen to the point of being almost unrecognizable, black and blue, one eye closed shut with a severe cut above it. The men around him pointed at his leg, which lay at an unnatural angle on the table. It was obviously broken below the knee. Someone had fashioned a crude splint for it.

Reza was semi conscious; when Talon knelt by the low table and said his name, he opened his good eye and tried to smile. He winced at the pain of doing so, but his hand came out and gripped Talon's firmly.

"I knew you would come," he whispered. "You were almost too late; they were ready to surrender to me. Is the princess safe?"

Talon loved his friend more that moment than ever before. He gave a broken laugh through his tears and croaked, “She is safe and so are you, my brother. Ahmad is dead. We got them all, I think.”

Reza gripped his hand again in approval. “Well done.” Then he said, with despair in his voice, “I tried to protect the doctor, Talon, but they were too many. They killed him, the dogs killed him.” Tears swelled in his good eye and leaked down the side of his face.

Talon, too, wept. He gripped his friend’s hand hard. “We have to take care of you and Rav’an. I must see to it, Reza. We shall talk later. There will be time to talk later. Rest now, my brother.”

Reza nodded, too exhausted to talk further.

Talon stood up to find Rav’an standing nearby, a blanket over her shoulders, also crying. He touched her and drew her to Reza.

“Stay with him, my lady. I have to see to other things.” She nodded and he left to find Hussein. He found him bent over Dav’ud’s body. It had been brought down from the verandah and his men were gathered around it. The arrow had been removed and a cloth placed over his face. Men were weeping openly at the death of this popular young man.

Talon went over to Al Tayyib. “How many men did we kill?” he asked bluntly.

Al Tayyib looked about him. “Fifteen. We have collected the bodies. Do you want to see them?” Talon nodded. He was sure that he would recognize most of the men they had fought. The sect was too close a community for this not to be. His main concern was to be sure no one got away. He didn’t think so, as it was unlike the Ismaili to run in the face of death.

He stared down at the faces of the dead men. Most of their features were calm, as though they had been resigned to it once they knew the hopelessness of their fight. Others looked surprised, like the two he had killed. Most had many wounds and had died like men. Killing was their trade, and they knew how to leave the right way, he reflected. He considered how fortunate he had been to have found friends like Al Tayyib, Dav’ud, and Hussein to help him escape the fate of these men.

He did indeed recognize most of them, having seen them and even spoken to them at Alamut. There were *rafiqi* from Samiran as well, he noted with surprise, which meant that indeed it would have been suicide to have gone there. He was glad that Jemal, his former instructor, was not one of them.

He turned back to where Al Tayyib and his men were preparing to move the wounded out. Through his tears for Dav'ud, Hussein offered an escort to take the three companions home to the house of the doctor. Talon accepted willingly.

They had lost men, too. Ten men had gone down, including Dav'ud, and many more were wounded. It had been an expensive fight. Talon, Hussein, and Al Tayyib stood together and organized the removal of the wounded and their own dead. They would be taken care of at the house of Dav'ud, where his father was waiting for word of the operation. "He will be devastated," said Hussein hoarsely. He was not looking forward to having to bring it.

Talon asked Al Tayyib what they should do with the bodies of the of men who had come with Ahmad.

"Leave them, they are carrion now," Al Tayyib said.

The news would get to the vizier's office soon enough and then soldiers would be swarming all over the place within a day. They needed to leave as soon as they could so that no one of consequence could place them here. He urged Talon to leave with his friends just as soon as a litter was prepared for Reza. Talon agreed.

When they came back to Farj'an's house, there were a few men still on guard who wanted to hear all about the fight they had missed. Their escort spent time telling and embellishing the battle. There were cries of grief for Dav'ud.

Talon concentrated on making sure that Reza was taken upstairs and placed on the bed in his room. Once he was made as comfortable as possible, Talon turned to Rav'an and found another blanket for her. Placing this over her shoulders, he sat her down near the sleeping man and asked her to stay there.

He got help to bring another bed for Rav'an into the room, and told the men to keep watch. He helped the exhausted girl to sit and then lie on the bed. She was looking up at him as she fell back. She had a nasty bruise on her jaw, but otherwise seemed unharmed. He knew, however, that she was shocked and exhausted, so he knelt at her side and commanded her to sleep. Rav'an held onto him as though she would never let him go.

"Talon, my warrior, you came for us. Allah has blessed me to have you as my champion," she whispered, pulling him close.

He smiled into her hair. "You cannot get away from me quite so easily, my princess," he growled through his tears.

He lay her back and pulled the blanket over her now fully dressed form. Then, leaning over, her he kissed her gently on the forehead.

"Sleep, my love, sleep if you can. I will be here, and I shall guard you all night."

She whispered something, but he could not hear it. Rav'an slept, secure in the knowledge that she was safe. But both she and Reza had nightmares, and he held them both and calmed them throughout the night.

Strange, is it not? That of the myriads who
Before us pass'd the door of Darkness through
Not one returns to tell us of the Road,
Which to discover we must travel too.
– Omar Khayyam –

Chapter 25
The Mourning

The next day dawned bright and clear with a fresh breeze, the clouds scudding by, high in the sky. A sun climbed into the heavens, trying to dry the wet world of Isfahan.

A bleary-eyed Talon left Reza and Rav'an sleeping while he went downstairs to take stock of the household. He could see that there had been some damage done, but not wholesale destruction. He even surprised a single men servant, who had survived the attack, cleaning up. The man turned with a terrified look before he realized who it was, and then begged for instructions as to what he should do.

Talon, who was rapidly finding out that he had to make decisions, and a lot of them, gave him the task of rounding up others who might have survived and bringing them to him.

Talon went to pay his respects to Farj'an, whose corpse was still where he had left it.

He knew that they should wash the corpse and prepare it for burial but had no idea how to start. He resolved to call upon Al Tayyib for help yet again. He was contemplating his mentor when he heard the sound of softly approaching footsteps. Turning sharply, his knife out, he saw a disheveled Rav'an approaching. She looked hollow-eyed and exhausted but determined.

Coming up to him, she kissed him in greeting; then, holding his hand, she looked down at Farj'an's body. "If I could ask Allah for one favor that he would grant, it would be to give this good man back his life," she said quietly. "His life was not completed. He had more to give. I shall remember him with love all the rest of my life."

Talon squeezed her hand. "At least he is at peace. I prayed for him last night," he said in a low tone. "How do you feel?"

She shook her head. "I am all right, especially now that Ahmad is dead. Do you think anyone else will come for us now?"

He shook his head. "I don't know, Rav'an. It's possible... but unlikely. I think we dealt with them all last night."

"Then we must bury the doctor with honor. We have to take Reza to the hospital. His leg is broken and he says his ribs are too. God knows what else is hurt. Ahmad tortured him."

"I know," Talon said, putting his arm round her shoulders. "We also have to see how Fariba is doing at the hospital."

She nodded and leaned against him, looking at the still figure on the bed. "Ahmad destroyed our world and theirs. I hope he burns in hell for eternity."

"It will be as Allah wills it."

The servants, who were trickling into the house, interrupted them. A good half of them had died the day before; the ones who came back did so only because they loved the doctor and Fariba.

They were nonetheless terrified. There was much wailing and tearing of clothing and hair as they realized how thoroughly their world had been overturned . It took a lot of persuasion for Talon and Rav'an to convince them that the menace had been dealt with, that they could come back and should help clean the house.

Talon pointed to the men in the garden who were guarding the house and told the frightened people that they were safe. These same men had killed the murderers who had come the day before, he assured them. He then put them to work, cleaning the blood away and clearing up the damage.

He sent a messenger to Al Tayyib, asking him to come see him. Then he and Rav'an went up to see Reza. Reza was in pain, but in good spirits. He was very thirsty, so they gave him some cold tea. Talon brought him up to date, explaining that Fariba had survived but was dangerously hurt and was at the hospital, where they intended to take him as soon as they could.

Reza's face was black and blue from the beating, but he assured them that he could see both of them with both eyes, squinting comically at them while he did so.

Talon wondered if Reza could ever be serious, as he smiled at his friend's display of nonchalance. Reza could not move his leg and found breathing difficult, but he was not spitting blood, so Rav'an, who had assumed the role of nurse, told Talon that she thought his lungs were probably all right. She was more worried about his leg.

Talon left them to go to the kitchen and get some food. Servants there treated him with respect and informed him that, as the doctor was deceased, they would take their orders from him. The story of his deeds the night before had come to their ears. They were in awe of his prowess as a warrior and had no problem accepting his orders.

He organized some food for the two upstairs, seized some bread and meat, then went out to the garden to wait for Al Tayyib, who arrived about an hour later, grumbling good-naturedly that he was an old man and did not need to be rousted out of his bed so early. Talon grinned, greeting him with exaggerated respect, bowing and wishing him all of God's good blessings. Al Tayyib laughed and clapped him on the shoulder, forgetting that it was the one that had been slashed. He saw Talon wince and immediately became serious.

"Were you wounded, Young Lion?" he asked with concern in his voice.

Talon explained the light wound away and then shrugged it off. He needed advice. Al Tayyib immediately understood what was needed and said that he would arrange for the body of the doctor to be washed and prepared for burial. He knew people everywhere, it seemed. Talon insisted that some gold be paid to these people, to which Al Tayyib agreed, as funerals could be expensive.

Then they talked about moving Reza. Again, this was easy to manage, so Talon asked Al Tayyib to come upstairs to meet the other two. He agreed willingly, and they crowded into the room where Rav'an sat near to the recumbent Reza. They both called joyous greetings to Al Tayyib. Reza croaked his pleasure at seeing the man, and he received a grateful kiss on his bearded cheek from Rav'an, which made him go red as a beetroot.

Talon told them that he'd had to inform Al Tayyib as to what was really going on when he called upon him for help. Rav'an and Reza looked a little nervous, but the older man quieted their concerns.

"Listen," he said, "you three helped me with my caravan, and because of it I am held in high esteem. People now want to come with me on caravans. I am about to leave for Dezful within a couple of weeks. I am inundated with requests by merchants, who feel they'll be safe with me. I could do no less when you were in trouble. I do not care a fig for what your former lives were. Besides, we all respected and liked the doctor, may Allah cherish his soul."

There was a silence after that, as they all thought about what the future could now mean. Talon broke it by saying, "We must eat and then get Reza to the hospital."

That said, they set about taking Reza on a litter to the hospital, where Talon searched for the physician Haddad. He found him in his rooms and was welcomed somewhat warily.

"I have heard the dreadful news of my friend's untimely death, young man. I will want a full accounting of it."

Talon nodded, but then asked about Fariba. The doctor rose and led the way to where she was being tended. On the way, Talon explained about Reza, and the doctor agreed to examine him. They stopped by Reza, who was lying on the litter placed on the damp grass among the orange trees, waiting patiently. The examination was brief but thorough. Reza would have to stay here and they would have to operate on him, said the doctor. He beckoned to one of his orderlies. It was apparent that Reza was in considerable pain, so he ordered a potion of opium to be administered to relax him and allow him to sleep.

Leaving Reza in the hands of another orderly, he led the way to Fariba. She was, by virtue of her position as the distinguished doctor's concubine, in a sparely furnished room of her own, a light, clean, quiet, and airy room with large windows.

She was asleep, but when they filed in, she awoke, staring round bewildered. Haddad explained that she was still drugged and might seem sleepy. She was dressed in a cotton shift, and they could see the heavy bandages around her chest through the material. She was very pale and looked a lot older than she had the day before.

Seeing Talon, she smiled wanly at him in welcome and lifted her hand for him to hold.

He moved forward and very gently took her hand in both of his. "Aunt Fariba, I have brought you a visitor," he said, his voice husky with emotion. He released her hand to stand back and show her Rav'an, whose eyes were wet with tears.

Fariba gave a low cry of delight as Rav'an came forward and kissed her on the cheek, both of them now weeping. Rav'an crouched by the low bed and held Fariba's hand. They talked through their tears about the attack and how Talon and Al Tayyib had rescued her and Reza.

Both men were embarrassed and shifted uncomfortably at the praise, but Al Tayyib was pleased. Doctor Haddad was listening, and he turned to Talon.

"It is clear to me that there is something of a mystery here, young man. As I said, I want a full explanation later. In the meantime, you should know that your aunt is still in very critical condition and must remain here until we are sure she is not going to relapse. We have much to thank Allah for, as it was touch and go yesterday. The boy outside will also have to stay, for we will have to set his leg if he is to ever walk again."

Talon gave a short bow. "Thank you, Honored Doctor. I do not know how I shall repay you for what you are doing for my friend and my aunt," he said politely.

The doctor shrugged. "We shall think of something, I am sure," he said, gruffly but kindly. "Now this lady needs rest and peace. You should all leave."

Rav'an stood up and, still looking down at Fariba, asked, "May we at least visit each day, *Gorban* Doctor?"

"You have to come and see me before you do, but I think so, yes."

They thanked him and filed out, after bidding the tired Fariba goodbye. They bade a groggy Reza goodbye, too. He grinned weakly and lifted a hand in farewell, and then they headed back to the house. There, with Al Tayyib as company, the three had an impromptu conference.

Al Tayyib had a concern that he wanted to get out onto the table right away. "Talon, are you sure that no one got away?"

Talon looked at both of them. "I am reasonably sure, but only because the Ismaili will not flee from a fight of this kind. They all stayed to be with their leader and died." He nodded. "I am sure."

They then talked about the funeral arrangements for the doctor. It was to be as private as possible, but, Rav'an warned them, there would be many people at the graveside; he'd been a well-liked and respected man. Al Tayyib had arranged for people to come to the house and remove him for the washing and dressing. He was to be buried on the morrow, as by Islamic custom he should be interred as soon as possible.

They agreed, also, that the place of burial would be in the main Isfahan burial field outside the city. As neither Reza nor Fariba could come, Rav'an agreed to represent the female side and Talon the male side. These arrangements concluded, they parted, as Al Tayyib had business to deal with at home. He promised to return to the house on the morrow, midmorning, to attend the funeral.

When they were alone, both Rav'an and Talon looked at one another. It was noontide, so they decided to eat. Going to find the servants, Talon noticed how quiet the house had become. He mentioned this to Rav'an, who said, "The house is in mourning."

He nodded his bleak agreement. Their world would never again be as it had been. They had to find a way forward somehow without Farj'an's stabilizing force. He missed him dreadfully and wondered what Fariba would do now. They talked about this as they went through the silent house, greeting the rare servant who had stayed to clean up. The place was almost back to its former state, except that there were still large stains on the wood and some carpets had been removed. Otherwise, it was hard to tell that a terrible massacre had occurred here the day before. Rav'an and Talon ate a silent midday meal in the living room, both thinking of the future.

Talon voiced what was on both their minds. "If we stay here, we cannot warn your brother, and somehow Arash will find out what has happened, we can be sure of that. His spies are everywhere. One of us should go and inform the master; I think it has to be me."

She regarded him from her clear gray eyes. Her full lips set in a determined line.

"Talon, where you go, I go." She raised her hand as he began to protest. "No, hear me, my love. I will not stay here and let you go all that way without me. It's not a subject I wish to discuss. After what happened, I will not."

He held up his hand in surrender. "Reza will not be able to ride for a long time, and there is Fariba, who has lost her whole world. What will she do?" he asked as though Rav'an might know the answer.

"We do not have to leave tomorrow, Talon, but I agree we do have to leave within two weeks. We cannot leave later than that. It will take us at least two months to reach Damascus."

He nodded somber agreement. "I hate to leave Reza here."

Rav'an gave a sharp laugh. "I somehow don't think he will stay here if we leave. He'll find a way to sit on a horse, no matter what."

Talon grinned. "I agree. He won't stay. He is dedicated to you."

Rav'an didn't say it, but she was quite sure that Reza was as dedicated to his friend as he was to his promise to the general to protect her.

"We could ask Al Tayyib if he would take us with his caravan, at least as far as Dezful," Rav'an suggested, who'd learned that their new friend was going that way.

"He has all but asked me to do so," Talon replied, with a smile. "I think we could do this, and if Reza is with us we will not be hurrying. It will give his leg a chance to heal. I pray Allah it will heal," he said doubtfully. "That pig Ahmad smashed it."

For the rest of the day, they helped the servants set the house in order. They decided that Talon would sleep in the doctor's room and Rav'an would be within calling distance in the rooms she had shared with Fariba.

The servant Abol, who had managed the kitchens and the preparation of food before, came in and bowed respectfully to Rav'an and Talon.

"*Khanom*, Agha, we have collected many of the former servants that survived the disaster. A few have not come back from their homes yet. We need instructions as to what to do for the future." He was almost wringing his hands with worry.

Rav'an stood up and went over to him.

"Abol, I understand your worries and those of the other servants. I can assure you that the terror is over, and we must now look forward. Although the doctor is dead, Fariba is not, and we are still here. You must tell the others not to worry. I shall talk to them all."

Late that afternoon Rav'an gave a gold coin to each of the seven servants left and told them that she expected them to remain loyal to the doctor's memory and to look after the house for Fariba, who would be coming home soon. They were surprised and very grateful for the unexpected gift and for the news about Fariba.

A gold coin was more than they were paid in three months. Smiles and bows of gratitude followed her out of the kitchen.

Talon did not think it was so much the money, however useful that might be for them. He had watched with keen interest as this lovely young woman enslaved the servants, one at a time, men, and women, with her charm and personality. He did not think they would abandon her, in spite of the horror of the preceding day, not after this performance.

Because he was smiling as they left, she looked at him sharply. "What is it, Talon, did I say something funny?"

He put an arm around her waist, an act of familiarity she enjoyed. "No, my love, on the contrary... I am beginning to realize that there is one person I know who needs neither spear nor sword to enslave people."

She chuckled at that and skipped with him for a couple of paces.

That evening, it was very quiet in the large house. The servants had either gone home or were at the back of the house in their quarters, Rav'an having dismissed them all for the night. She and Talon ate dinner prepared for them by the willing Abol and his assistants.

After the simple meal, Rav'an put her beaker of wine aside and looked at Talon. "It is late, my love. We should go to bed."

He looked at her and smiled. "I shall follow you up, my lady. I have to check that the sentries provided by Hussein are awake, then I shall go to bed."

She nodded as though agreeing with him. "Do not be too long," she said enigmatically. She stood up from the carpet with him and then leaned toward him. She gave him a long, lingering kiss, full of promise. "Do not be long," she said again, and the look she gave him set his blood on fire.

He went out into the damp evening by the back entrance and stood in the shadows, listening and looking to see if there might be anything at all to alert him to a dangerous presence. There was nothing, so he went around the walls and gardens, enjoying tapping a man here on the shoulder and startling others there by just appearing under their noses. Their surprise was always unfeigned and nervous.

He terrified these people, he could tell, but he also made them aware of the importance of staying alert. He told each of them they would have died if he had so wished and left them straining at every shadow and noise for the rest of the night. They were so jumpy they could not sleep now, he told himself and smiled.

Making his way up to the family quarters, he saw lamplight coming from the rooms where Rav'an was staying. He made his way to the door and knocked. There was no answer, so he opened the door and called her name softly.

There came a splash from the rooms beyond the bedroom and she called his name. He made his way to the entrance to that room and stopped, his eyes wide. It was well lit by candles and oil lamps, the light bathing the walls of the room with golden glow. But he had eyes only for the figure in the large half-sunken tiled bath. Rav'an was in the bath, seated in the steaming water that just covered her breasts. Her hair was piled up above her head in a coiled bun with a large piece of bamboo stick holding it in place.

She smiled at him. "Come and join me, Talon, it is very warm here. I asked the servants to prepare the water before we ate." She beckoned him playfully with her finger.

He stood rooted to the spot for a couple of seconds, then he moved slowly to her, taking off his head cloth and then his other clothes. He felt embarrassed, because she continued to look at him, but her eyes told him that she was not only curious, but hungry, too. When he was completely naked, he stepped into the bath and allowed the very warm water to flow over his tired body.

She moved over to him, disturbing the water. "It is time for us, Talon," she murmured as she came up. Then she began to wash his arms and neck. Rav'an washed him carefully, examining him as she went. She discovered the wound on his shoulder from the fight the previous night and sighed at the length of it. Then she came to the wounds the lion had inflicted, running her forefinger along each one of the wide scars as though paying homage to them.

"If you had died of these I would have missed my glimpse of paradise," she whispered.

Even though he was relaxing with the utter contentment of being treated so by this girl he loved, this still gave him a jolt in his groin. He felt himself begin to grow. He was, at the same time, admiring her figure. Her small, full breasts were so close he wanted to lean over, fondle, and kiss them. With great restraint, he resisted the move, as he didn't want to interrupt what she was doing to him. He admired the tight muscles of her flat stomach. The water hid the rest of her. Her hand came down and moved the soapy cloth over his own tight stomach, then turned him around and washed his back. She leaned over him, letting him feel the tips of her breasts on his back and pushing her self onto his buttocks.

Her arms went around his waist and held him while, for a moment, she leaned her head on his shoulder, kissing his neck.

He turned slowly to her, his manhood proud, and held her tightly. He was stiff against her. She pushed her hips against him, gently nudging him, smiling coyly up at him. Her hands went down and cupped him. He thought he would explode then and there, but they were now kissing. He moved his lips on hers and felt her tongue touch his tentatively as they used to. They played with each other, enjoying the slipperiness and the erotic suggestiveness. He moved his hands from her back and cupped one breast, noticing that it looked bruised. She froze for just an instant then leaned back as though to say, my trust is in you, take me.

He leaned over her, holding her with one arm while he kissed her nipple and licked it around. He felt it harden under his tongue and heard her sigh. Her eyes were closed and her lips slightly parted as he kissed her breasts one at a time, bringing the nipples to a hard tightness that he found enormously erotic to his already inflamed senses.

"Talon, take me to bed," she whispered, her tone urgent.

He lifted her in his arms and stepped out of the bath carefully, carrying her cradled in his arms to the bed next door, her arms round his neck, her head buried in his shoulder.

Placing her gently on the bed, he leaned over her again, and they kissed for a long moment. She lay back as he climbed onto the bed and kneeled over her.

Looking up at him, she murmured. "I love you, my warrior. You are truly my protector. Love me now."

He nodded and bent to kiss her breasts again, sucking gently on her tight nipples. Once again, she groaned with pleasure. His hands kneaded her body, exploring, as he kissed her along her arms and then down her ribs. Then he moved down to her ribcage, kissing her in the central hollow where her ribs met, and moved onto her stomach, then her belly, his hands moving gently over her taut skin, delighting in the silken feel of her. He stopped just as he came to the fine curls of her pubis and looked up.

Her eyes were shut and her lips slightly parted, but her hand pushed his head firmly downward. Needing no further encouragement, he kissed her in the hollow of her stomach and then on the rise of her pubis, caressing her outer thighs and the rise of her hips. His tongue came to her female core. Her scent set his blood racing again as he very gently moved her thighs apart. She complied as though in a dream, and then he could taste her. As his tongue met the sensitive area, she arched her back, her head going to the side, her hands grasping his hair, uttering a low cry. He continued his probing, and felt her tremble, and then her pubis moved against his lips.

She cried out then. "Ah, Talon, now please take me. Oh, take me, my love." Drawing him up over her, he felt himself slip into her wet entrance. Just inside, there was a brief resistance, and then he was suddenly deep inside her. Rav'an gave a long groan of utter pleasure as he did so. Then her arms were around him and her lips were seeking his. They lay like this for long seconds, both feeling the wonder of their coupling, kissing deeply, losing themselves in each other. He lifted himself over her enough to look down at her face, her eyes were huge and almost glazed with the sensations she was experiencing for the first time.

"Oh, my love, I had not imagined the... the pleasure... I..." Her words trailed off.

He nodded and smiled deep into her eyes. He thought, I, too, have not really glimpsed paradise until this moment, my princess.

He began to move very slowly in her, then she joined him, and they began the timeless dance of lovers, locked into each other, looking into each other's eyes as they moved. It was all Talon could do to hold himself back, but he need not have worried. Rav'an was racing toward her climax, and as it built up, she became lost in the orgasm that swept over her. It carried her on the crest of a wave that shook her all over and made her scream once, and thrash in his arms, bringing him to his own climax on a huge wave of his own. They rode the climax together until spent, collapsing into one another's arms to lie panting and inert for long minutes.

Talon felt he must be crushing Rav'an and began to move to lift off her, but she held him close to her, "Stay for a while, my warrior, I still want you inside me."

He gave a muffled laugh. "But I may not be able to stay much longer, my princess." His manhood had shrunk and slipped out of her. She gave a disappointed "Oh," and then allowed him to lift himself off her.

He lay to her side and recovered his breathing. In truth, he was shaken at the power of their coupling. Rav'an turned her lovely naked body to him and stared into his eyes with her huge gray ones.

"Talon, truly I have glimpsed paradise with you. Was it like this for you when you were in Alamut?"

He shook his head.

Rav'an looked puzzled, on the edge of being hurt.

He sat up and took her head in both hands either side of her face. "This is better than that, by a thousand times, my princess," he told her, and kissed her long and gently on the edge of her mouth.

Rav'an pushed at him and gave a delighted laugh. He loved to see and hear her laugh. He had heard it so seldom. "Then Allah has been kind to us both today, my lover and warrior."

Slowly they became immersed in each other again, and their eyes locked once more in the unmistakable invitation from her to the growing need for her in his eyes. They made love again, he slipping easily into her welcoming embrace. This time she came more than once with him moving in her, crying out and sometimes even screaming with the exquisite pleasure of losing complete control while in his arms, finally to come to the shattering explosion that would leave them exhausted and spent, to fall asleep in one another's arms for the rest of the night.

Talon came wide-awake in the dark. The lamps had gone out and there was the predawn chill in the air. He could not think of what might have woken him. He felt rather than saw Rav'an asleep next to him, feeling her warmth and the scent of her in his nostrils. But his ears told him that there was something else. He lay rigid, listening with straining ears to the room and beyond.

There, did he hear the slightest scrape of something? Like cloth on wood or something just as light? It came from the other room. The hair on the back of his head lifted and he felt a cold sense of dread. There was someone coming to complete Ahmad's work.

He cursed himself for leaving his clothing and thus his knife in the bathroom. He doubted if he could possibly retrieve it before it was too late. His eyes were accustomed to the dark by now as he frantically cast about for a weapon of some kind. He noticed a bronze water jug with a pointed spout just by the end of the bed. As there was nothing else, he decided to put his faith in this.

He slipped out of the bed silently and grasped it firmly. Just as he did so, the door began to open. He had not locked it, but every other door had been. Talon was not surprised; he could have done the same. He moved very quietly out of sight of the opening, keeping the door between him and whoever was making the entrance. The figure slipped in without a sound. It made directly for the bed, and Talon could see a long, slim knife held high as the man approached the bed on the side where he had been.

Talon knew he did not have the luxury of time, so he screamed as loudly as he could and charged the man who had his back to him. The scream was enough to freeze the man for a split second, long enough for Talon to cross the few yards to him. Even so, the figure whipped around like a snake striking, but not fast enough.

Talon took a swipe at his head and felt a satisfying crunch as the metal made contact. The man let out a yell of pain, his turban fell off, and he slipped to his knees, Talon lifted the jug and beat the man as hard as he could on the head again, knocking him face down onto the floor. As though from a distance, Talon heard a scream from Rav'an behind him. But he was too intent upon his victim.

The knife had fallen out of his opponent's nerveless hands, to be retrieved by a lightning fast Talon, who lifted it high and brought it down hard onto the exposed back of the now prostrate man. He struck true. The knife went through the ribs and into the man's heart. There was a choked cry, a brief convulsion, and then it was all over. Talon was panting as he stood up.

Rav'an called in the dark, "Talon, what is happening?"

Her voice was on the edge of panic. He hastened to light an oil lamp and held it high. There on the floor, in a growing pool of blood, lay the last of the Assassins who had been at the house the night of the battle. He was dressed in a pair of dirty white pantaloons, a wide, dirty cotton shirt, and his turban had a red stripe running through its length. Talon thought he might know the dead man from Samiran. He was younger than Talon and looked like one of the boys in the group that had come behind his.

His first act was to go to Rav'an and hold her trembling in his arms, quite unconscious of their nakedness, trying to reassure her that the danger was past. She looked down at the body and asked him as though pleading,

"He is dead?"

He nodded.

"How many more must you fight before they are finished?" she asked in a hoarse whisper.

He held her away and in the light of the oil lamp told her that while he might have been wrong about the number of people left, he felt very sure now. If there had been others, they would have come all at once to make absolutely sure. This must be the last one from the group with Ahmad.

Rav'an nodded, but it took a while to bring her trembling under control. The awakening had been like having a nightmare, and to find that it had been real made it even more horrifying. Talon comforted her, impressed with her determination to gain control of herself. He told her to get back into the bed, and then he put on his pants. He dragged the dead man out of the room and wrapped him in a sheet before carrying the body downstairs. He knew it would be pointless to yell at the sentries. One of them would be dead in any case, so he left the body in the small courtyard, still wrapped, and went back upstairs, checking and locking doors and bolting all the possible entries to the rooms he could find. He had done so earlier in the night but was not surprised to find one of the shutter latches open.

He spent the rest of the night holding Rav'an close. Astonishingly, she slept in his arms, and he listened to her slow breathing, marveling at her ability to do so. He could not sleep at all and listened intently to every creak and groan the house made for the remainder of that night.

He watched the dawn come creeping into the room through the closed shutters and knew that it would rain again that day. He eased out of bed, turning to look at Rav'an while he donned his clothes. He knew he was now bound to her in every way, but the nagging worry as to what would happen to them when they finally found her brother returned to haunt him.

He left the room quietly and went downstairs. The body was still where he had left it, so he heaved it in its sheet over his shoulder and went out the front door to leave it on the pathway near the entrance of the garden. He went round looking for sentries then. He found three of the original five huddled together in a tense group near the stables. So much for their protection, he thought wryly.

Their greeting was fearful as he came up, all talking at once, protesting and waving their hands in the air. He raised his hand to quiet them.

"The Assassin who came is now dead; where are the other two of you?" They didn't know, so he ordered them out into the gardens again, and it was not long before they found both of the other sentries dead, their throats cut.

The three remaining men were now even more terrified, but Talon would not let them go until they had seen the dead Assassin. He told them to collect the bodies and get them out of sight of the servants before any showed up. He said that it was unlikely that anyone else would come to disturb them now and produced a small amount of silver to get their attention. They were glad that someone was taking charge, so they did his bidding, collecting the bodies into a cart to take them away for a quick burial somewhere. Talon didn't care.

He went back to the house to get the other servants up and moving. They had a funeral of their own to deal with, and he was not sure when they would have to leave. He wanted to visit Reza and Fariba beforehand, if possible.

He woke Rav'an with some hot *chai*, and almost jumped back into the bed when he saw her stretch naked on the bed.

She knew what she was doing to him and smiled wickedly. "Do you think there is time for us this morning, my love?"

He smiled ruefully at her. "We should not be seen by anyone in this state, my princess—at least not yet. We don't know what the reaction will be."

Rav'an set her mouth. "My love, I want to shout it all over the city. I never want to sleep again without you near me, and I want to be able to love you as a wife should, clear in conscience and before God. But I know what you mean. We have to decide how we intend to go forward. It will be difficult."

He agreed. "It will, but know one thing, as you love me so do I love you. Forever, and forever."

She laughed, clapping her hands with delight. "Kiss me," she commanded.

So he did, only pulling away reluctantly when they both heard the movement of the servants downstairs. One of the women would be coming upstairs soon to wake her and offer hot water for bathing. Talon quickly checked to see that there was no longer any blood on the floor and left the room.

The morning passed in a flurry of things that had to be done. The doctor's body had been washed, dressed, and brought back to the house by mid-morning. Talon and Rav'an paid their last respects to the doctor. His features were now calm, as though he had found peace. They gazed at him for long moments. Then the attendants took over and the body was wrapped in sheets and bound, then with great ceremony then they laid Farj'an in the casket.

Rav'an and Talon escorted the body to the graveyard. The mourners who turned out for the funeral could be counted in the hundreds. The procession started at Farj'an's house and went the length of the street. Many of his medical colleagues and students were there to pay their respects; he had been a persuasive teacher and well respected by all in the medical world.

He also had a following of patients who were there to pay their respects. The murders of doctor and many of his servants had shocked Isfahan. It led to much speculation, as did the presence of the beautiful young woman who attended the funeral and the watchful-looking young man who never left her side.

Al Tayyib had hired professional mourners. The women tore at their hair and wailed, while the men, clad only in pants and barefoot, followed, beating themselves with rods, drawing blood along the way. Others of the mourners carried garlands of flowers, fruit, and other food. The wailing was taken up by members of the crowd, who came close to the entourage, pressing in upon Talon and Rav'an, who was heavily veiled. He began to worry about the possibility of danger, but as there was not much he could do, he simply came very close to Rav'an and prevented her from being pushed about.

There was no headstone as yet at the graveyard, only two small plaque-like stones, one laid at his head and one at his feet, that would be engraved at a later date. To Talon it seemed almost perfunctory, but he knew nothing of the protocol, so he was silent. As he went through the ritual motions with the others, he remembered the good times he'd had with the man whom he had begun to think of as his father. In too short a period, he had lost two such men. He felt a sense of being adrift.

As though sensing his thoughts, Rav'an squeezed his arm. He guessed that she was feeling the same way. Their eyes met and held for a long moment. Others eulogized the doctor, calling on God to see to it that this good man was admitted to paradise without delay. Al Tayyib was there to help and to walk with them back to the horses and then ride to the hospital with them.

"A small bird told me that one of them got away," he said casually as he rode beside Talon.

"No, he didn't. I dealt with him last night," came the laconic reply.

Al Tayyib nodded. "Do you intend to stay in Isfahan and keep it on its toes forever, or might you be leaving some time soon?" he asked innocently.

Talon gave a short laugh. "Rav'an, he has divined our intent already," he said louder for Rav'an's benefit. "We can hide nothing from him."

Al Tayyib barked a laugh. "Some things, my children, but not all."

Rav'an looked at him. "We were going to ask if we could come with you to Dezful, Agha Tayyib. We would pay our way, of course."

He smiled at her. "Of that I am sure, my lady, and in more than coin if I know this young warrior. I was hoping that you might be interested. To tell you the truth, the facts of this incident will be hard to keep secret for very long. I do not know what you have told Hussein, or what you said to Dav'ud, but sooner or later someone will put all the pieces together, and then the vizier and his people will get interested. Worse still, the Ismaili who live nearby probably know enough to be dangerous to you as well. After that, things will become very difficult, very quickly."

"When do you plan to leave, Al Tayyib?" Talon asked politely.

"Within a couple of weeks, *In Shah'Allah*. I have almost the complement of people I can handle. Your addition will be most welcome, Talon. Of course, you too, my lady."

"We hoped that we might be able to take Reza with us. In spite of his leg, it will be hard to stop him coming, I think," Rav'an said. "We want to hear from the doctor Haddad today about his condition. Would you like to come with us to the hospital?"

They asked how Dav'ud's funeral had gone as they walked the horses to the hospital. Hussein had previously told them that it would be a good idea for them not to be at the funeral, as Dav'ud's father was terribly upset and would undoubtedly lash out if they had come.

Al Tayyib had been there and described the large family group that had been present. There'd been many expressions of anger at the funeral, and people of some influence promised to get to the bottom of the cause. What was the reason for the battle, and who was the mysterious woman he had rescued, where was she, etc.

He winked at them then and told them that was why he had asked how long they intended to stay. "I would not continue to stay at the doctor's house if you can avoid it. I have a house that is in another area of Isfahan. It's not as grand as that one, but you'll be safe there."

They looked at one another. He could be right; it might be prudent to simply disappear from view and avoid the many awkward questions that were bound to come. Talon thanked him feelingly and told him they would give it serious consideration, but they had to spend at least one more night at the doctor's home to make sure that the house was not left without someone in charge. Al Tayyib said that he could make sure of this for Fariba's sake. For some reason, he seemed quite taken with her.

They arrived at the hospital and were speedily lead to talk with Doctor Haddad, who smiled and told them to follow him to the room where Fariba was convalescing.

They were surprised to see her sitting up in bed. Although pale and tired, she looked a sight better. She greeted them with a happy smile.

Fariba demanded to know how the funeral had gone, and the condition of the house. They told her in detail about the funeral and she shed tears again, but then they moved on to the house, about which she questioned them closely. They reassured her that it was being well looked after by the remaining servants and that she should not be concerned but to just concentrate on getting better. They spent some time with her, answering questions as to how they had managed to deal with Ahmad, at which she pronounced satisfaction again.

Finally, the doctor came bustling in and told them all to leave. Talon noted the fond smile he gave his patient as he said that she needed rest above all, but they could come back the next day. When asked if she had everything she needed, she motioned to the doctor and told them that all she needed was being provided by Haddad and that he was looking after her very well indeed.

They left soon after and made their way to see Reza, who was resting out on the long, airy, covered walkway along with several other patients. He was delighted to see them and tried to raise himself in deference to his princess, who immediately pushed him down, gently. His face was still very bruised, and he showed them his bandaged chest, which to Talon looked very raw and sore.

But he looked a lot less pale and was definitely more cheerful.

His leg was firmly splinted and held rigid in a wooden brace. Haddad told them that the bones would set, but it would be at least a month, maybe two, before he could walk.

Rav'an and Talon exchanged a worried look. They didn't share their concern with Reza, nor did Al Tayyib say anything, but he, too, frowned. Instead, Rav'an told Reza in a whisper about the last of the Assassins who had come in the night. They spent some time with him, and then Haddad motioned to Talon and Rav'an to come with him, as he had something he needed to talk about. He also invited Al Tayyib, as he could see that he was clearly one of their close friends.

They went up to his office where he called for tea. He looked pensive, then seemed to make a decision.

"I do not know if you are aware of the situation regarding the doctor's estate?" he asked them. They looked blank, so he pressed on. "He has willed most of it to his concubine Fariba, and some to the hospital. That part I was responsible for, as he confided in me to a considerable length. I am not altogether aware of some of the more mysterious comings and goings of his, but for the most part I know about the disposition of his estate. You, young lady, are, as far as I am aware, the only living relative he had left. Did you know of this?"

Rav'an stared at him, a look of complete surprise on her face.

Talon was slow to react, so Al Tayyib came to the rescue. "Indeed, she is, Doctor. She is his niece several times removed, is that not so, my lady?"

Rav'an nodded mutely, sending a look of gratitude to him.

"Then there is some difficulty that we have to deal with," Haddad stated and, it seemed, regretfully. "As you are the only relation and Fariba only a concubine, and not his wife, it falls upon me to make some changes to the will."

"What do you mean? What changes to the will?" Rav'an had found her tongue.

"I need to change the remainder of the estate to your name and strike her off," he said in a calm tone. It was clear, however, that he was not happy with the idea.

Rav'an said hurriedly, "Wait... Doctor." Her mind was racing. "That will not be necessary. I am the inheritor of large estates in the north. You have no need to change the will. As it now stands, will the house and other things go to Fariba?"

The doctor nodded, looking curious. "Yes. The doctor has looked after his lady very well indeed. She would not want for anything in life again to keep her comfortable."

"How can I ensure that the will stays as it is, Doctor?" Rav'an asked, sounding suspicious.

"There is only the need for an attachment to the will, stating that you renounce all claims to the estate," the doctor said, looking puzzled but a lot happier. "We have to have witnesses, of course."

He looked up. Al Tayyib and Talon both volunteered at the same time, and the doctor greeted their action with unfeigned relief. *Chai* came, and they settled down to wait for the document to be drawn up. The doctor explained that a small bribe would ensure that the full legality of the document would be taken care of by the vizier's office in the center of town.

They left, having signed the papers, and told Haddad that they would be back the next day.

On their way back, they had much to discuss. Al Tayyib had to leave them and attend to business, as he put it, but he reminded them that his house, although small, was theirs if they decided to use it. He gave them instructions as to how to get there in case they had to leave the doctor's house in a hurry. Before he left, he looked at Rav'an. "My lady, Allah has blessed you with a kind heart. I know something of the Ismaili, of which I know you are one. You are not as they are."

She blushed at that. "Fariba should not be left on the street, Agha Tayyib. She is too good a person for that, and the doctor would not have wanted it that way," she stated, looking hard at him, lifting her chin.

He nodded. "I think the physician Haddad would like it to be the way you left it, too, my lady. He likes her, it is clear. I hope it is for herself."

"I do, too," Rav'an said. "Do you fear otherwise?"

"No," he said thoughtfully. "But I am a man of the world, and it is not a good world on the whole that Allah placed us upon. There is greed and deceit all over."

Talon said, "I agree with you, Al Tayyib. I shall be having a word with the good doctor to ensure that all goes well."

Al Tayyib roared with laughter at that. "I think he would be persuaded, my young warrior. You can put fear into even very brave men."

They laughed with him and bade him goodbye, then went home.

On the way, Rav'an nudged him. "Do you intend to threaten the doctor, Talon?"

"No, my lady, just to leave him with the thought that if we should ever come back to Isfahan, and not find Fariba in charge of her own estates, then his life would be forfeit."

She chuckled. "I think Al Tayyib was right. You can frighten people."

The two of them spent the rest of the day talking about the need to stay out of sight. There were already some messages that had been left for them. One of them was from Jasmine, who had come during the late morning. Rav'an lifted an eyebrow at that one and commented that Jasmine had better stay away, or she might have something to say to the woman. Talon was amused but refrained from saying anything. He was rapidly concluding that they would just have to disappear, or things would get difficult in more ways than one.

They decided to move out without letting anyone know when or where they had gone. However, the problem remained as to how they could ensure that the house remained in the care of the servants until Fariba had recovered. Rav'an decided she'd talk to each one and make sure that the servants understood that if they worked at the house and kept it in good condition, as though the master were only absent and would return, they would have a future.

This done, Talon followed up quietly with Abol, telling him that he hoped the man would stay and make sure Rav'an's orders were followed. He, Talon, would like that. Abol got the message, and some gold helped sweeten the request. He was told that if he had anything of importance to impart to the lady Rav'an, he should send a message to the Agha Tayyib.

That night they made love again in the same bedroom. Neither gave a thought for the morrow as they explored each other's bodies. Talon was awestruck by the beautiful girl who shared his bed. Rav'an was eager to make love, as though she wanted to make up for the lost time, and Talon was quite happy to do so. Their loving lasted until late in the night, when they fell asleep in one another's arms.

Early the next day they left the house with their horses and their travel things. They took with them the armor and weapons that they had brought from Hamadan, and Reza's horse as well as a pack animal. They left as silently as only they knew how, even with horses.

*****

When they told Reza that they were preparing to leave, there was a look of panic in his eyes.

"When?" he asked.

"Within two weeks," Talon said. "Do you wish to come with us?"

Reza's reply left Talon in no doubt as to what he wanted to do.

Talon smiled and nodded, then went to see Haddad.

The doctor rose when he came in, and motioned him into an ornate chair. He seemed pleased to see him. Talon had come to the hospital with Rav'an, but she was now with Fariba, explaining what they planned. After the usual greetings and a cup of tea, Talon came to the point.

"Doctor, we have to leave this city, and we want to take Reza with us. I need to know your opinion if this will be possible."

Haddad looked back at him and stroked his beard. The action was so like Farj'an that Talon smiled.

Haddad considered his reply. "I am of the understanding that you have to leave. That being the case, you should take the young man with you, but he must put no weight on that leg for another two weeks, at least. Have you the means to take care of him?"

Talon thought. "He is a good rider, Doctor. If we keep the wood splints on his leg, could he ride?"

"It will be painful, but he might. He should not ride too hard nor land on the leg when he dismounts," said the doctor.

Talon agreed with that, so he thanked Haddad, went back to Reza, and told him that they would take him with them, provided he were very careful. Reza was overjoyed at the news, although Talon suspected, doctor or not, he would have come, no matter the pain.

Talon then went to see Fariba and found both her and Rav'an in tears. Rav'an had broken the news to Fariba, who was desolated.

"I have lost the light of my life and now you abandon me," she accused Talon as he came in.

He dropped to one knee and took her hand in his. "Aunt Fariba, I am sure that Rav'an has explained why we must leave. We still have a duty to inform the master, her brother, as to the treachery of his uncle. And we should get out of Isfahan for a while until the noise of the battle has died down. Al Tayyib made it clear to us that we should not be caught by the vizier's men."

Fariba agreed, although she was still deeply saddened. She looked much better now, so Talon took the chance of talking to her about her inheritance. She stopped him with her hand. "My dears, I thank you for your care of me, and you in particular, Rav'an. Doctor Haddad came to see me and told me everything. He was very impressed with you both, especially you, Rav'an, for making the sacrifice on my behalf." She smiled. "He said that if I wished it, he would assist me with the administration of my estates. I think he likes me."

Rav'an snorted. "I am sure he does, now that you are a wealthy woman, Aunt Fariba."

Fariba frowned thoughtfully. "No, it's not that, my dear. He and Farj'an were very close friends, although he didn't visit much socially. They were students together. He is devastated by what happened and asked me to tell him everything I know. I only told him what I felt he should know, and I think he has accepted that. He, too, is quite wealthy, you must remember. I trust him."

They parted once again, promising to come as often as they could before they left.

Talon and Rav'an stayed in the compound of Al Tayyib's house for the next week. There were no servants, so they made do with what there was, enjoying the uninterrupted time spent together. Both knew that it would end when they brought Reza back, and although Rav'an wanted to tell him of their changed relationship, Talon was not sure.

"He made an oath to the General, my love. I take that seriously, and so does he. I am unsure of what he will think of our being lovers. Rav'an laughed. "Well, how was the General or my brother to know that I would fall in love with you? How do you change the seasons?"

They left it at that for the time being, but it remained in the air. They visited the hospital stealthily, as they did not want to be recognized by anyone. They saw only Yousef, who kept them abreast of events. There had been a lot of consternation at their disappearance. Hussein had come to the doctor's house and questioned the servants closely, and Jasmine had come more than once.

Yousef leered at Talon as he said this, and got an amused cuff to the back of the head from him and a wagged finger from Rav'an. He seemed to enjoy visiting them and asked many questions of Talon about his bow and other weapons.

"I shall grow up one day and become a warrior and a bowman," he told them.

Talon took him into the garden and showed him how to hold a sword and toss a spear, which made Talon his hero for life.

Finally, Yousef brought the message they had been dreading. It was time to leave. They had another day, and then they should meet Al Tayyib and his caravan outside the city on the west side where he was camped. Yousef was very excited at the prospect of another adventure.

They hurriedly went to the hospital to collect Reza and to say a tearful goodbye to Fariba, who was well on the way to recovery, but Rav'an noted some new gray strands in the rich color of her hair. The tragedy had left its mark on the beautiful woman.

Fariba took Talon's hands in hers. "I wish you a safe journey to wherever you are going, Talon. I give you both my blessings. Be happy together. If God wills it, then I shall see you both again in my house, and we can stay together for a while."

She was crying now, so Rav'an, who was crying, too, knelt by her bedside and tenderly embraced her.

"My Fariba, God has been kind to me to allow me to know you. I will pray that Allah spreads his kind protection over you for all time."

Talon looked at the lady he had come to love. She looked so forlorn and small. Doctor Haddad came in just then and began to cluck around her, fussing and comforting her more like an attentive old rooster than a doctor. Then he left her to come outside with them, telling Fariba he would be back.

He looked directly at Talon. "You do not have to say anything, young man. I've loved her since I met her, but Farj'an was faster than I to ask for her. I do not intend to allow anything to hurt her again."

Talon looked at him hard, then he took the doctor's hand in a tight grip.

"Thank you, Doctor. She is a very important person to us. We want to come back one day to find you both happy and in good health."

Haddad nodded and harrumphed. "Go with God, all of you. I know not where that might be, but you will always be welcome in my house," he said gruffly.

He gave them some opium liquid for Reza, admonishing them to use it sparingly and only when he was in real pain.

They collected an ecstatic Reza, who was hobbling about on crutches, and gingerly placed him on his horse. His one leg was hanging down useless for the time being, but he still insisted upon being allowed to ride on his own. So they made their way back to the house, watching for anyone who might know them.

When they arrived, they took great care to ease the now pale Reza off his horse. Then Talon picked his friend up, and despite his loud protests, carried him into the house, where he laid him down on a mattress in the living room near the fireplace.

That evening they told him what they were about to do. Talon assured Reza he had his armor and weapons to hand. In fact, he gave him his knife and sword to hold onto.

They had a simple meal together, enjoying each other's company again. Despite their sadness at leaving Isfahan, their city of sunlight and shattered dreams, they were excited to be together again and to be moving toward their ultimate destination.

Rav'an told Reza to take a small dose of the opium drink, as he looked a little pale, and to sleep in the spare room. He complied without demur, and after they had made sure he was comfortable—he was half asleep already—they went back to the living room.

Rav'an took Talon by the hand and led him to their shared room, where they made love with a silent passion that took their breath away and left them both clinging to one another, panting. They did not know when they might be able to do so again, so there was an edge of poignancy as they made love.

* * * * *

The next morning, Al Tayyib looked up from a discussion with his helpers and some of the merchants who were pestering him, to cock an ear at Yousef, who was telling him something and pointing. The large man looked up and beamed as three riders with one horse trailing on a lead came into the encampment. "At last," he said, "now we can leave. My army is here."

Comest thou thyself? I will cover thee with caresses,
Comest thou not? For thine absence will I surely grieve.
Be thy sorrows what they may, lay them upon my heart,
And I will either die of them, or be consumed by them,
Or bear them bravely.

– Baba Tahir –

Chapter 26
The Master in Banyas

Late in the summer, a party of three horsemen with one baggage horse approached the city of Damascus. They had just parted from a larger group of horsemen whom they had joined a week before. Unknown to the Turks and Kurds they had ridden with, the three riders were of the Ismaili and had been on the road for almost six weeks.

Talon, Reza, and Rav'an wore the traditional dress of the Seljuk men-at-arms that could be found all over this region. Like their counterparts, they wore the travel-stained clothes and light chain mail of the light cavalry. Each wore a cotton cloth wound around their faces, leaving only their eyes visible, while the rest was covered to protect them, ostensibly, from the sun and dust. Their once new horsehide boots were now cracked and scuffed, their outer clothes very ragged. Had they not been armed to the teeth, they could almost have been mistaken for ragged Bedouin who had lost their way and come too far north. At night they had kept to themselves, although Reza had from time to time mixed with the men who were going to Damascus as reinforcements.

The wars with the Egyptians and the Christian kingdoms, not to mention deaths from disease and plague, were depleting the sultans' armies, and Nur-Ed-Din was no exception. He had called upon men from Baghdad, and even farther afield, to come to fight for the glory of God and help drive the infidel into the sea.

Those who had known them at Samiran would have noticed a subtle change in the three, a maturity to their behavior that had not been there before. Their former impulsiveness and carefree youthful attitude had been replaced by a watchful wariness, which belied their youthful features. These three were now experienced, seasoned travelers. They had become so close as a unit that a few words sufficed for each to know exactly what the other was thinking.

Talon had become the natural leader. Despite his faint accent, he dealt with strangers for the group up front, but he would defer to his friends in any situation that demanded council. He was, however, the one who thought on his feet and had demonstrated this often enough for his two companions to respect his ability to lead. Men instinctively respected this tall young man when he came up to them.

There had been quarrels on the way, small, often trivial arguments that could have gone too far. Talon had developed the ability to bring the tense atmosphere back to where it belonged on such occasions by applying humor and good sense. Fortunately, those occasions had been rare.

His two companions were also changed. Rav'an was aware of her part in the cohesion of the group and treated this with care. Her innate intelligence allowed her to know how far to take each of her men, each in his own way. Thus, she managed to avoid the natural jealousies that could well have developed. It was clear to her companions that they were her family, and her status as the princess was less a part of the formula.

Reza had changed perhaps the least. He was the same carefree young man in search of adventure, but like the other two, the journey and its hazards had matured him enough to make him someone people were respectful to, should he walk into their midst. He walked with a slight limp, the legacy of the incident in Isfahan, but it had not impaired his ability to ride. He and Talon practiced incessantly at weapons, so his agility was as good as ever.

The reason the three were at Damascus was because Rav'an knew that there they would at least obtain information from the hidden Ismaili as to where the master would be. It was one of the quirks of the situation in Syria that Ismaili still existed in Damascus, invisible to the soldiers of Nur-Ed-Din, and from here, they could keep an eye on the sultan's activities.

Slipping into the city was not hard. They came in with a loud group of men, young and old, from Baghdad, men who were keeping their spirits up by pretending to be old soldiers instead of raw recruits. Bidding their newfound acquaintances goodbye, the three quietly disappeared with their horses in the direction of the house of the Assassins that Rav'an knew vaguely about. She recalled overhearing a conversation her brother and the General had had once, describing the house.

To Talon's discomfort, it turned out to be very like the one in which he had passed a terrible night as a prisoner with Jean, those many years ago.

Guardians, who were of the fida'i but dressed like the locals, challenged them at the heavy gate. They wore Arab dress with the long, flowing robes of a people who were not about to ride to war. Even so, they were easily recognizable to Reza and Talon by their watchful eyes and demeanor.

Rav'an demanded entrance, and when they had received it, several men quietly surrounded them. They were asked in Farsi who they were and why they were here. Rav'an threw off her veil and then her head cloth to display herself to the surprised people. She then demanded to see the master.

The consternation was gratifying to see as some among the *fida'i* and *rafiqi* who were in charge recognized that she was indeed the Princess Rav'an.

The leader of the *rafiqi* came forward and with a deep bow, said, "*Khanom*, I regret that the master is not here. He is in Banyas Castle. However, General Esphandiary is here. We will tell him you have arrived."

He waved his hand and one of the younger men rushed off to pass the news. The leader signaled again, and other young men came and held their horses while they dismounted. There was nothing overt about it, but to Talon and Reza, it was clear that they were being carefully watched. Any untoward movement on their part would be viewed as dangerous. Keeping their hands off their weapons, they accompanied the man and Rav'an as he led the way into the cool of the main building. They walked up some wide, polished stone steps. Rav'an led, while Talon and Reza followed. They were ushered into a very ornate anteroom and told respectfully to wait.

The man, who called himself Zahedi and was a *rafiq,* disappeared into the room behind the heavy drapes. There was the murmur of voices and then swift footsteps coming back to the small group.

General Esphandiary came through the curtain, flinging it aside as he did so to stand and stare in complete surprise at the three of them. He was dressed as they remembered him, in his light riding armor, but he wore on his head the dress turban of high rank. He carried his sword on his belt, and there was one hand resting upon its hilt when he appeared.

Then, as recognition dawned, he collected himself and bowed respectfully to Rav'an. "My lady, it gives me deep pleasure to see you. Allah be praised, we had begun to be very concerned as to your safety."

Rav'an drew herself up to her full height and looked the General in the eye. "I need to speak to you in absolute privacy, General, and it has to be now."

His eyes widened. "We can talk in my quarters, my lady."

"There must be no one else there at all, General. It is strictly private."

He looked at the two young men with her. They had changed, he could see. There was something about them, watchful, dangerous even. Rav'an glanced back at them.

"Talon and Reza can stand guard while we talk, General. I have had reason to trust them with my life."

He nodded. "Then please come this way, my lady."

Rav'an glanced at the other two, nodded to them, and then followed the General to the back rooms.

Talon looked at Reza, and together they stared at Zahedi, who now stood at the doorway, staring back. They all stood watching one another while the murmur of voices rose and fell behind the curtain. There were sharp questions from the General from time to time followed by Rav'an's more melodious voice as she answered.

Then there was a pause. The curtain was jerked aside again, and the General motioned all three of the men back into the room. He looked at Talon and Reza and then said to Rav'an, "This is Zahedi, who is my own bodyguard. He is my man. I trust him with my life. Zahedi, is the Arash Khan with the master as we speak?"

"Yes, *Timsar*. I know they are still at Banyas Castle. You will remember they wanted to see for themselves the disposition of the Christians around Tiberius."

"Who among his retainers did Arash Khan take with him?"

"The few men he brought with him from Persia, my lord."

"Are there any of his retainers here in Damascus remaining?"

"There are four, three *fida'i* and one *rafiqi,"* Zahedi replied.

"Arrest them at once, and hold them in the dungeons," the General ordered. "You must do this quickly or they will escape. If they saw or heard that the princess is here, they will try to get away. Hurry, man, hurry!"

Zahedi bowed and ran out of the room.

The General said, "My lady, I forget my manners. We shall have tea and you shall tell me more of your adventures." He appraised the young men. They stood respectfully, as befitted students, but he could see they had become men since their time in Samiran. He nodded his approval. "It is clear from what the princess has said that you two are responsible for saving her life more than once."

They gave him uncertain nods.

"I am happy that you did your duty so well. I would consider it prudent if you continued to do so," he added with a thin smile. "You are not out of danger yet, *Khanom.*"

He clapped his hands and bade them be seated on the leather cushions laid about on the luxurious carpet. Tea was served with sweet, sugared dates and figs on a fine fret-worked table with brass inlaid patterns in its polished surface.

He asked them many questions during the time they waited for Zahedi to come back and report. His respect for the young men and Rav'an grew as the story unfolded. He nodded when she surmised that the master had sent them to Alamut to spy for him, though he guessed the master had not known the extent of the treachery, nor the danger he was placing his sister in. He was impressed that they'd managed to escape the way they had. He expressed no regret over Jean and Feza's deaths. This was a hardened warrior of his times, who expected casualties and did not dwell upon them.

Zahedi came back breathless. He bowed to them all, then made his report. They had managed to detain three of the men, he told them, but one was seen escaping. They were giving chase, but the man was on a fast horse and would be well on his way by now.

The General smacked his fist into his hand. "Then we must make all haste to get to Banyas either at the same time or, if possible, before him. Make sure that the others do not escape,

Zahedi," he growled.

Zahedi all but groveled. "I shall personally make sure, *Gorban*," he whispered.

Although tired, the three travelers agreed that having come this far, they should follow as fast as they could to prevent Arash from doing something before they could warn the master. The General and his men slipped by twos and threes out of Damascus. They reassembled in a large stand of palms alongside a canal, well out of sight of anyone on the walls. When they were all together, the General set a fast pace south to Banyas, where they hoped the Master was still in residence.

It felt strange to Talon to be riding south to his former home in this manner. Then he had been a hostage with no future. Now he was a respected member of the very group of people who had captured him.

* * * * *

Talon was apprehensive, uncertain about the future of their endeavor. He could not be sure of what might happen to either himself or Rav'an once they had concluded their mission. He was confident that the General could persuade the master that his uncle was plotting against him. That would result in summary justice, he knew that, but he couldn't see into the future beyond that point, and his heart ached with the thought that he and Rav'an might be parted.

Without thinking, the three of them rode abreast, with Rav'an in the middle as it had always been. They talked of what they expected to see and what might happen when they got to Banyas. Reza and Talon wanted to go in and kill Arash Khan and get it over with. Rav'an told them that they would have to let the General do the talking and keep alert for whatever might happen.

"We have to protect my brother and keep Arash away from him. I do not know what his plan is, but it must be to kill the master."

They arrived late that evening at the massive fortified castle of Banyas, which had become an Assassin stronghold because of its strategic placement almost on the edge of the Christian Kingdom of Jerusalem, yet still within easy reach of Damascus.

As the large party of men lead by the General came up to the gates, the men on the walls called down to them and were answered by Mahmud Esphandiary himself. He shouted his name but no other, bidding the three with him to keep themselves ready but inconspicuous, their faces covered.

The gates swung open with a crash and the whole party rode into the main courtyard. There were men about who studied the party suspiciously, while others greeted them.

"I think the traitor has made it here," the General told them under his breath. "Be ready for trouble," he growled to his men as they dismounted. "I wish to see the master," he called out in a loud voice.

The *rafiq* who greeted him said respectfully, "*Gorban Timsar*. The Master is with Arash Khan and is not to be disturbed."

"I am to see him this instant," the General thundered. "Do not try to prevent me!"

He glowered around at the men in the yard, his hand on his sword. His own men closed in around him, along with Rav'an, Talon, and Reza. Talon had his bow at the ready while Reza had his hand on his sword, as did Rav'an.

The man who had spoken stared at the menacing force in front of him with a puzzled expression, then shrugged. He indicated that he would lead the party himself. The General told his men to guard the entrance, while he followed the man with Rav'an and her two companions.

As they walked, the General asked the *rafiq* if he had come to the castle with Arash Khan. The man shook his head in the negative; he seemed confused and puzzled by the urgency of the General's visit.

Then Esphandiary remembered that the man was among the *rafiqi* who were the master's immediate bodyguard. Esphandiary quietly told him to gather all the men he could trust who had not come with Arash Khan to Banyas. He was to place reliable guards on the gate to prevent anyone leaving, and then he was to arrest Arash's men, after which he was to come back to the master's suite. The man nodded his acceptance of the orders, even as he looked shocked. He brought the party through the large entranceway to master's private quarters.

The General and his three wards entered. There were arches to the left and right that led off to rooms, but in front of them, down at the end of the wide passage, was a small garden and a pond, where the Agha Khan was standing. Just beyond him, standing on the path facing him, was Arash Khan.

Rav'an took a sharp intake of breath when she saw him. Talon and Reza looked at Arash as though they were seeing a snake about to strike. The two men had been conversing, but the interruption made them both look up sharply from their discussion.

The master was about to say something when Esphandiary yelled, "My master, forgive the intrusion, but there is treachery here in this garden!"

Mohammed Khan straightened and demanded, "What do you mean, General? Are you accusing someone?"

Esphandiary pointed at Arash Khan, who was clearly shocked at the sight of the three young people now removing their head scarves. He had believed them dead. Nonetheless, his recovery was quick and confident. "What nonsense is this?" he asked. "Who accuses me? And of what?" his tone was authoritative and intended to intimidate.

He seemed calm enough; his dress was, as usual, ornate and expensive, that of a man at his leisure, but his expression was tight.

"I do," Rav'an said, in a clear voice. "You have been in correspondence with Nur-Ed-Din, you intend to kill my brother, and I can prove it."

Arash turned to his nephew as though for support. "Master, I do not understand. I have spies with Nur-Ed-Din and keep aware of his movements and even his thoughts. This is my duty."

The master looked askance at Rav'an. "Sister, please explain what you mean," he demanded, his surprise at her sudden appearance quite evident.

Rav'an reached into her belt pouch and pulled out a piece of cloth, which she unwrapped and displayed as being the broken seal from Nur-Ed-Din.

"Oh my brother, this man," she indicated Talon, "took this from a letter to Ahmad from Nur-Ed-Din; it was an agreement to work with Arash once Arash was the *new* master."

"If that is not enough, Master, he sent his son Ahmad to kill these three when they fled Alamut for Isfahan with the doctor Farj'an," the General added.

Arash bared his teeth. "They fled Alamut because the boy here killed the priest," he hissed.

Talon took a step toward him. "You are a lair," he choked. "It was you who killed Jean, may you be damned for doing so. He was a man of God," he shouted.

Rav'an grasped his sleeve to hold him. "Wait, Talon. It is true, my brother. He is plotting with Nur-Ed-Din to take your place," she said in a clear voice that carried round the courtyard

The master whirled to his uncle. "What is this, Uncle? You are dealing with Nur-Ed-Din? What has he promised you that I could not give you?"

Arash snarled then. "All the power you possess, my nephew, and more!" Then Arash did something odd. He stared straight at Talon and spoke in low, sibilant tones.

"You have to protect me, you have to kill the one I point out; it is your duty to die for the master." He pointed at Mohammed Khan, continuing to talk to Talon, ignoring the others in his intensity, his eyes boring into Talon's.

Arash had hypnotized Talon while he was in Alamut under the influence of the drugs of his initiation. Arash now expected to awake Talon to the deeply buried orders.

Talon was drawn into the man's eyes, and the words came from deep in his mind. His command was to kill whoever his master pointed to. Without a word he dropped his bow with a clatter to the stone tiles and his hand went to his knife. He moved as in a dream. He heard Rav'an call his name from far away, but all he could hear was that insistent voice, telling him where to go. Then his knife was up and he was ready to plunge it into his victim's chest.

There was a scream and he looked down. Rav'an was standing in front of him with her hands on his chest. His knife was poised over her. There was a terrified look in her eyes as though she could not believe that this was happening. Talon felt something snap in his head as he regained control over his mind. The spell had been broken by the one person who could break it—Rav'an.

He stood there, bewildered, with Reza's hands gripping his arm and Rav'an right in front of him. Behind her was the master with a shocked look on his face.

"Talon, what happened? What is going on?" she asked of him, her voice breaking, holding his head between her hands as she looked up at him.

Talon shook his head to clear the cobwebs and turned to where Arash Khan had stood, but the man who had caused him so much pain was not there. Arash was moving quickly to get out of reach. He knew that he had lost the battle; now all he wanted to do was escape.

He was already thirty paces away, relying upon the shock of the others to slow them. Reza gave a shout, as did the General, and both started after the shadow that was receding into the gloom of the archways ahead. Talon, in one swift move, retrieved his bow, snatched an arrow out of the quiver by his right thigh, notched it, pulled, aimed, and released. The bow gave a sharp twang, and the arrow sped to its mark, transfixing Arash Khan. Its force carried it almost completely through his body and flung the man forward to sprawl onto the marble tiles near the colonnade he was trying to escape behind. He died without a sound.

There was a long silence as Reza went to investigate. He then came back to report, "He is dead, Master," he said. There was a long silence.

Mohammed sighed. "He had everything, but he wanted even more, the fool." He turned to his sister. "When I sent you to Alamut, I thought it was just to watch him and report to me in the spring. You did more, much more, my sister. Allah has protected you from this dog, and you have protected me from him as well. I am in your debt."

Rav'an spoke then. "My brother, it was these two men who protected us both." She pointed to Talon and Reza. "Talon and Reza saved my life multiple times, including from Ahmad when he was about to rape and kill me."

The master looked at the General as though to ask, "Is this so?"

Mahmud Esphandiary looked back at him and nodded. "The princess told me the whole story in Damascus, my lord. I believe her."

There were faint shouts and the clash of steel outside. They all looked at one another, then down the length of the hall to the main entrance.

The General spoke again. "Now we have further confirmation of the plot. We have to make sure that Arash's followers are taken into custody, my Lord."

The master nodded and indicated that the General should go about his duties as he saw fit. Esphandiary left in a hurry with the two young men right behind him. In the silence that followed, the master and his sister looked at one another. They could hear Esphandiary shouting as he took charge of the castle and dealt with the fight in the courtyard.

Talon had his bow with him. Reza and the General, swords drawn, headed for the entrance to the courtyard. They saw immediately what was happening in the darkening evening as they appeared on the steps. Arash's followers were fighting for their lives. They knew a horrible fate lay ahead if they were captured alive, so they fought like tigers and were acquitting themselves well. Too well. Already there were more dead and wounded belonging to the master's men than of their ranks. No quarter was being asked nor given by these masters of death.

The men who had been standing at the doorway were fighting at the head of the stairs; some were down, either dead or wounded.

Talon wasted no time. He asked the General to stay behind himself and Reza and drew his bow to shoot man after man off the battlements. Then he targeted the others down in the yard. From his commanding position on the steps, he had a very good view of the whole battle area. Reza acted as the General's bodyguard and to prevent anyone from getting by to get to the master. The next few minutes were chaotic as Arash's followers ran in all directions, trying to get away from Talon's deadly arrows and still inflict damage upon their adversaries.

Their courage was born of desperation, and five of them made a last, furious race straight at the General and the two men on the steps. Talon had run out of arrows by now, so he drew his sword and joined ranks with the General and Reza to fight them off. It was very close, as the desperate men, knowing they were about to die, attacked fanatically. Caring not about wounds, they pressed forward, striking furiously at the three men, who were forced to give ground.

Blood flowed from wounds, making the stone surface slippery. More than once Talon, the General, or Reza slipped on the bloody steps, to be pulled back up by one of the others. They stood shoulder to shoulder, preventing anyone from getting near the entrance to the passage.

Then, almost as suddenly as it started, the men in front of Talon and Reza were down and being finished off by a counterattack from behind as the General's men rallied and came to finish them off.

General Esphandiary turned to the two young men at his side and nodded approval. "You have become true warriors. I thank you," he panted.

They both knew they could not have received higher praise.

*****

In the garden, with the faint sounds of the battle outside still audible, the master turned to his sister. "I think you have grown up, my little sister." He bade her be seated next to him on the low wall of the pond then, ignoring the noises coming from outside, and said, "I wish to hear with my own ears all that you have to tell me. Those two young men are very faithful to you, I can see. Do you remember that the taller is from the Franks of this land?"

Rav'an nodded. "I do recall that, my brother." She feigned disinterest, and then she went over their odyssey in some detail, leaving out the parts that she would never tell him. It took time, but he listened patiently as though he needed to hear of her trials.

As they talked, they began to regain some of the old familiarity of siblings, but it was becoming more and more clear to the master that his sister was no longer the eager, innocent young girl of the previous year. Talking to him now was a confident, poised young woman who'd had to grow up in a hurry. The difference was remarkable. He studied her as she spoke and saw how beautiful she had become and how well informed she seemed to be, but there was also a quiet reserve about her that was unfamiliar.

When Rav'an finished, they were silent for some time. The sounds of battle had stopped. Evening had set in and the garden was cloaked in darkness. Servants came in noiselessly and lit oil lamps in the entrance near the door. The lamps illuminated the small garden where they were seated, but there were dark shadows beyond. In the quiet, Mohammed sipped his tea and contemplated her fine features in the dim light provided by the lamps.

At last he said, "What should be the reward for the young men who have kept you alive for me?" he asked with a small smile on his lips.

Rav'an had been waiting for this question. She pretended to consider it with care. "My brother, the Frank, Talon, although faithful to you, should be allowed his freedom. You should let him go back to his people."

He looked very surprised. "He is a *fida'i* now, is he not? As such, he's still useful to me. Why should I let him go?"

"Because he saved your life as well as mine, and this is the least we can do for him."

He didn't answer. Her request did not sit well with him, but he was deeply in her debt. He decided that his sister had earned the right to ask him for whatever favor, and if she wanted it that way, then he could do this for her.

"What of Reza, the other boy? Are your going to ask me to give him his freedom as well?" he asked a trace of sarcasm in his voice.

Rav'an looked at him and then dared to take his hand. "Why not ask him what he wishes? What could be more fair?"

He laughed, the small tension broken. "I agree. It will be as you wish it to be. I shall talk to them tonight, as we leave in the morning for Allepo Castle to visit Rashid Ed Din, who will be in control of Syria while I am in Persia. I have unfinished business to discuss with him before we depart for Persia. Then I shall escort you home, my dear Rav'an," he said fondly. "Allah be praised that you're safe after all you've been through." He left her.

She watched him leave, then sat on the edge of the pond and felt that her heart would break. The tears came later when she realized the fullness of what she had asked of her brother. In giving freedom to Talon, she had lost the one person in the world who mattered to her most. Rav'an felt that her world had closed in on her. She found it difficult to breathe. She put her hand on her stomach and felt it with a shaking hand. Her body had told her true, but she could see only darkness ahead.

* * * * *

The master's summoned Talon to his presence that evening. With him was the General, who looked very grim. After prostrating himself in front of the master, Talon was told to stand.

The Agha Khan wasted no time. "You have proved to be a good warrior and I owe you my life, at least that is what my sister tells me. To me it seemed as though you were ready to kill me. However, you also saved my sister's life, fulfilling the duty placed upon you by Timsar Esphandiary.

"I am thus granting her wish that you be given your freedom. If I had my way you would stay as a *fida'i*." The import of his words was clear. "You are to leave as soon as possible, as I do not wish to have you in the castle by tomorrow."

Talon ventured to ask one question, although his mind was reeling. "May I bid my companion goodbye, *Gorban* Agha Khan?"

The master hesitated, then nodded abruptly. Talon bowed very low and backed out of the chamber, his mind in turmoil. Could it be possible that Rav'an had done this? In doing so she had as good as told him to leave her life. She would still be a prisoner and a pawn of her brother. He felt bile rise in his throat at the thought of this. He must find a way to talk to her.

He wondered if she would still be in the garden, so he found his way back there, emerging near the pillar where he had killed Arash. As he silently approached the pillar, he could see the dark patch of dried blood where the body had lain. He moved very cautiously to look at the place where they had all stood earlier, and his heart leapt. He saw a figure sitting on the edge of the pool. It was Rav'an and it looked as though she was bent over in pain.

He looked around to see if there was anyone about, even in the shadows, as he must not be seen with her. He came up to her noiselessly, realizing as he did that she was crying, and touched her on the shoulder. Rav'an whirled around, and seeing him standing there, threw herself into his arms, ignoring the danger of doing so. He held her as tight to himself as he was able as she wept into his chest.

"Ah, Talon, my love, you are lost to me now. You are free."

Talon pushed her down to sit and then crouched at her feet, looking up at her. "My love, you did this for a reason. I shall not leave you, you know that," he said urgently.

Rav'an nodded and smiled through her tears. "Place your hand here, my love." she whispered. She took his hand and placed it on her belly. He felt the smooth fabric and the warmth of her taut stomach underneath.

He looked puzzled for a moment, and then it dawned on him. Talon stared at her with wide eyes. "You are... you are...?" He never finished.

Rav'an gave a tremulous smile coupled with fear. "I am with child, my love. When my brother finds out, I shall be put to death, but you shall have your freedom. At least I could do this for you."

He reared back, anger suffusing his face in the dark. "No! Rav'an, no! That shall never happen!" He jumped up and began pacing. He thought for a moment. "Will Reza come with you and me?"

Rav'an thought about that for a moment. "I think so, but you must reach him before my brother does, as he wants to keep him."

Talon seized her cold hand in his. "You must not lose faith, Rav'an. I will come for you. Do not forget this. Keep this in your heart. Never lose faith, and do not tell anyone about this other thing. I am leaving tonight, but know this, I shall not be far away."

She gripped his hand with her two ice cold ones and looked into his face. "I trust you Talon. You... You give me hope. I will wait. God be with you, my love." The last was whispered.

He came close, and oblivious of the danger, he kissed her quickly on the lips, then disappeared the way he had come. To Rav'an it was as though he had never been there, except for the feel of his lips still on hers. She touched her fingers to them, a new confidence rising within her. She bowed her head, not daring to think of the consequences if he failed.

Talon wasted no time in finding Reza. He pulled him into a dark corner of the castle and told him what had transpired. The shock on his friend's face reassured him that he could still trust Reza, so he began to speak.

"Reza, they expect you to stay with them now that Rav'an is safe. I, of course, have to leave tonight, but I shall be near at hand. I think the master is leaving for Allepo in the morning. It will take several days and nights to get there. I want you to be with her in her tent or near it at night. Will you do this for her and me, my brother?"

Reza stared at him aghast, and then held him with both hands by the shoulders. "What you're proposing to do is very dangerous, my brother. You are quite mad, and so is the princess. If they catch you they will kill you, and her, and perhaps me, too."

"They will kill her soon anyway," Talon answered bitterly. "She is with child."

Reza gave a short gasp. "Then she must escape," he said his voice hoarse. "The master will have no use for her now. Talon, where do you think we will go? There is nowhere he cannot find us."

Talon came close to Reza. "There is only one choice for us, my friend, and that is the Kingdom of the Franks. Do not forget that I am one, and I think I still have family in Palestine. It's been over four years since I last saw them, but if we can make the sanctuary of my father's castle, we will be safe. It's no more than half a day's ride from here, if I am not mistaken."

Reza looked doubtful but he gripped his friend's arm. "I am with you, Talon. We've seen much together, and to stay here will mean a short life at best. Besides," Reza was now smiling, "I have a hunger to see other parts of the world now, and you're just mad enough to take me there. I'll make sure I am near or in her tent during the night. But when you leave here, can you take two horses?"

Talon sighed with relief. "Reza, never did a man have a more trusted friend. I think I can take two horses as long as the General doesn't see me go."

"Then go and prepare to leave. I'll place the horse with all our baggage near the main gate and hand it to you as you leave. If few know you are ordered to leave, then they will not know that you cannot take the extra horse with you."

Talon nodded and the two parted, Talon to go to the stables and Reza to go to the kitchens and beg some food for Talon to take with him, as none of them had eaten since dawn that day. Then he went to check on the baggage horse's whereabouts. In fact, their horses were near to one another, the baggage horse still not unloaded, so instead of coming with him to the gate Reza handed the lead to Talon, who rode out of the gates as though he were on a mission. The gates were slammed shut after him, and he was alone out in the desert.

He had studied the lay of the land from habit when they came, so he was somewhat familiar with the country even in the dark. All the same, he found it hard to find a place a couple of miles away that would give him a clear view of the road while allowing him to remain hidden.

Back in the castle, Reza sought out Rav'an. She was now situated in chambers suited to her rank. He gave a light knock on the door, and when she called he answered with his name. She came quickly to open it, and as he slipped in he noticed that her eyes were red. It was clear that she had been crying.

He said softly, "*Khanom*, be of good heart. Talon has talked to me. He has left the castle with two horses."

Although that was all he said, he saw its immediate effect upon her. He saw hope rise in her eyes and wished he had the nerve to comfort her. But the habit of obedience was strong, so he just smiled at her. She smiled back tearfully.

Reza then said formally, "*Khanom*, no one has discharged me from my duties as yet, so I wish to remain your bodyguard, as long as you so wish it."

Rav'an nodded vigorously. "Yes, Reza," she said. "It is as I wish it to be."

They smiled at one another conspiratorially. At that moment, there was another knock on the door, and when Rav'an asked who it was, there came the unmistakable voice of the Master. Reza looked alarmed, but Rav'an motioned him to stand by the wall and went to open the door. The master seemed surprised to see Reza, but Rav'an spoke up quickly.

"My brother, Reza has asked that he continue to be my bodyguard now that the Frank has gone. I would wish it to be so, if you consent?"

The master looked over at Reza as though about to ask him a question and then nodded. "I will reward you for your courage and help in protecting the princess at some later date," he said. "In the meantime, it is good. You may become her official bodyguard." He turned back to his sister. "My sister, you look as though you have been crying. What is the matter?"

Rav'an gave a tremulous smile to her brother. "I am so relieved that at last my journey is over, and that you are safe, my brother. I was just telling Reza here that I am glad the Frank is gone, as he was a rough fellow."

He nodded in understanding. "They are that. I had hopes for this one, though. Never mind, it is as Allah wills it. I came to tell you that we will be leaving early in the morning to make as much progress toward Allepo as we can. I do not wish to go into Damascus on the way there, so we'll pass tomorrow night in tents. Don't worry, with a guard you'll be safe," he said reassuringly.

He left soon after. Reza, thinking he should observe the proprieties, left soon after to find a place to sleep. Neither he nor Rav'an said anything to one another, but their thoughts were outside the castle with Talon, wondering where he might be. Rav'an spent an almost sleepless night thinking of how she might escape.

Oh, if the World were but to re-create
That we might catch ere closed the Book of Fate,
And make the Writer on a fairer leaf
Inscribe our name, or quite obliterate.

– Omar Khayyam –

Chapter 27
The Return

The subject of their concern was passing an uncomfortable night with the two horses in a gully where he was out of sight of the road, but where, in the morning, he would be able to see the castle in the distance. He blessed Reza for the stale *nan* bread and cheese he had purloined from the kitchen earlier. He was a low on water, but he could conserve that, as he was now used to the desert. He decided that he could last for at least another night if the need arose. He did not intend to wait two nights before he made his escape with Rav'an, however.

Nonetheless, it was a night of worry and turmoil as he considered his options. The escape would have been hard enough against a normal group of people, but to try to rescue her from men like the *rafiqi*, men of considerable skill at stealth and evasion themselves, was very dangerous indeed. He could not let Rav'an be taken away, however, and so he had no choices left. He prayed to both God and Allah, hoping they were one and the same. He knew Jean was watching over him, so he felt better when he finished.

He also knew that what he was about to do was rash and dangerous, even insane; but the thought of losing Rav'an made him sick to his stomach. Inexperienced he might be, he told himself, but determined and well trained he was. That had to count for something. He settled in for a long night, staring up at the stars above and trying to remember the constellations that he had learned from both Jean and Al Tayyib.

He thought about his parents, wondering what it would be like to see them again. He had left a boy but was now a man, and very different. His world was one that they could never comprehend, and theirs was now almost as alien to him. He still had memories of the place where he had grown up, but his life for the past few years had pushed most of those memories into the background.

* * * * *

The next morning dawned cool and clear. Talon woke with the first light in the sky. He stood and stared to the east, just standing there, and then almost without thinking, he knelt, prostrated himself, and began the ritual prayers that he had learned while in Isfahan and before. He prayed for the doctor, and for Jean, and then for Fariba's health and safety. Then he addressed God.

"I only ask that Rav'an and Reza can come with me tonight to safety, as for them to stay is not safe. They do not deserve death."

He unhobbled the horses and re-saddled them. After that, it was time to wait and see what became of his friends. He did not have to wait long. Just as the sun rose over the low hills to the east, he saw a group of horsemen exit the gates. As it was too far to see who it was, he climbed the low rise of the hollow and peered over the edge to get a glimpse as they passed.

The party of horsemen came at a canter along the road, so it wasn't long before they rode by. He breathed a sigh of relief. Rav'an and Reza were among them. He counted about twenty people in the group, including the master and the General. He regretted that he had not been able to know Esphandiary better. The man was a legend to Talon, but now their lives were forever barred to one another.

He waited until they were a good distance down the road, smiling as he saw Reza looking around to see if he could spot him. Checking to see that there was no one else on the road, he let the group move on until they were out of sight, and then went onto the road himself. The party in front moved at a leisurely pace, so he had no trouble keeping up. He followed their route all day, careful to stay out of sight. This proved very difficult to do with the additional burden of the pack animal, so he resolved to leave it when he felt that it was safe to do so.

They came to several villages along the route. The road took them in a northwesterly direction. Allepo was a long way north of Damascus, so for the most part the roads would head toward the coastal valleys and then travel along these to the various cities on the seaboard. Each time he approached a village, Talon was very concerned that there might be people from the party ahead who had dallied and he would stumble over them.

It was while entering one of the villages that disaster struck. Jabbar went lame. It was not sudden, but as they came into the village and stopped by the well, it became clear to Talon, that Jabbar was not going to take him much farther. The sense of desperation grew as he studied Jabbar's off hind hoof and found that it was both cracked and bruised from some injury that he supposed Jabbar had incurred the day before. That had been a hard ride, but he could have sworn that Jabbar was fine that morning.

As usual, the villagers were distant, keeping out of sight of this well-armed, lone, Saracen rider. It might have been his concentration on the injury, and the fact that the trees grouped around the center of the village muffled the approach of the horsemen, but Talon was taken unawares.

They were in the village and almost upon him before he could do much more than reach for his bow. Suddenly, the small square was filled with men on huge horses who advanced on him from all sides. One, indeed, seemed ready to attack him with his lance, as it was lowered and the man was hunched behind his shield, his horse picking up speed. The thunder of the huge animal's hooves and the shouts woke Talon up to his situation in a hurry. He let go of his horses and dodged behind the low wall of the well, putting it between himself and the charging man.

He barely had time to note that these were not from the Assassin group he had been following. In fact, they all seemed to be dressed in the same manner, with chain mail hauberks, steel helmets and large shields. Emblazoned upon their left breast was a cross in red material that stood out from the dirty white of their over-tunics.

With a wild shout of his own, Talon yelled at the man coming at him with all the force in his lungs. "I am French! Do not attack!" He snatched off his head cloth and waved it, then shouted again, "I am French, do not kill me!"

The man coming for him hauled his huge horse to stop scant yards in front of Talon. His lance was only a foot or two away from

Talon's chest.

Men in chain armor surrounded talon. Another knight rode up and, towering over him, asked in a loud voice, "If you are French, then why are you dressed like a sand rat?"

"My name is Talon... Talon de Gilles, son of Hughes de Gilles." He looked up at the helmeted face, partially obscured by a bushy beard. The eyes were hard and wary. They showed recognition at the name, however, and there were others among the men who muttered with surprise.

"What are you saying, Saracen? Where did you learn to speak French?"

"I was taken in an ambush south of Banyas five years ago. I am Talon, the son of Sir Hughes from Montfort Castle, I swear it."

The man stared at him, then nodded to two of his companions to dismount. "We shall see about that. In the meantime, you are our prisoner. I am taking you back to our base at Montfort to find out if this is true."

Talon tried desperately to think of something that would set him free to follow Rav'an. He got no further than to open his mouth to ask the man if he knew his uncle, when the two men closed on him. He realized that they were going to bind him. With a speed borne of desperation, he twisted free and shouted at the man above him on the horse. "You must let me free! It is vital that I travel north, *now*. I beg of you let me be free!"

The men drew their swords and closed on him. There was but one way out and that was to kill one and then try to evade the others. He realized that his options were hopeless that way. He opened his hands and allowed them to bind him with his hands to the front.

"My horse is lame, but he can still walk," he said between gritted teeth. "At least lead him back with us to wherever we are going."

The leader of the knights nodded grudgingly, and the packhorse's light load was transferred to Jabbar, while Talon was placed none too gently on the back of the pack animal. While this was going on, the troop was watering its horses at the well. He noticed that most of the men had long, unkempt beards, which gave them a fierce aspect. They regarded him with hard eyes that had seen a hundred fights. To them, although he could speak their language, he was the enemy unless he could prove otherwise. Until then, he was a prisoner.

There was a sharp command, and the whole party moved off with Talon in between the two ranks of riders, his horse being led so that he could not even control the animal. Jabbar limped along behind on another lead rope.

His mind was numb. What could he say or do that would persuade these uncompromising men that first, he was who he said he was, and then to let him go? The leader of the twelve men turned in his saddle and addressed him.

"If indeed you are Talon de Gilles, where have you been? I heard that de Gilles lost a son to the Saracen. Why are you here dressed like this, and why are you going north instead of south?"

"I was taken to Persia as a boy and kept there by the people there. I have escaped. It's a very long tale, Sir... Who are you?"

"I am Sir Velliers of Aix and we are Knights of the Temple. How did you escape?"

"I was let go by the master for saving his life."

There were looks of incredulity from the men around him, then some laughter.

"The master? The master of whom?" Sir Velliers asked.

The Agha Khan, the Ismaili master; the master of the Assassins."

"Hmm. So in gratitude for this he let you go? They are not noted for their kindness to others. That does not explain why you were going north though, does it?"

"No, sir, I was following him because I wanted to set his sister free," Talon said, already beginning to feel that his words were somewhat lacking in conviction.

By now there were open grins of disbelief and amusement from those around him. He felt his anger and frustration rising at their skepticism and inability to understand him. All the while he was being taken farther away from Rav'an and Reza, his friends, his family. He threw a desperate look behind him.

Sir Velliers was speaking again. "I know of Sir Hughes. We are in possession of the castle of Montfort now. It is a Templar stronghold. We will be going there, and it is there that we can find out if what you have been saying is true."

"How are my father and my mother, sir?" asked Talon

"In truth, I cannot say, but I assume they were well when they left the castle two years ago. They have gone to France to take over some estates left to them after the pest wreaked havoc there." Talon slumped in the saddle, hopeless, and for the first time fearful. These men would neither listen to him nor let him go until they had taken him all the way back to Montfort. By then it would be too late to do anything for Rav'an. His opportunity to escape was becoming slimmer.

He could not afford to lose more time, as once they had escaped, they had had one day to find and gain refuge. Should she move farther north, they had no chance of doing that. She would either be in Aleppo or on her way back to Persia and certain death, once her pregnancy was discovered. He hunched over as though in pain, with an overwhelming sense of defeat gnawing at him.

Then his anger began to smolder. They had not taken his knife, and he could still try to escape. He looked around for some avenue that would allow him the slim margin, which was all he needed.

As they came to the crest of a low hill and Banyas' stark form loomed up, he decided to try to make a break. He jammed his heels into the pack animal's sides and let out a yell. The animal leapt forward, wrenching the reins from the man holding her. Talon slammed his heels into her again and headed for a gap in the ranks. There were surprised shouts and curses from the men all around as they reacted.

He almost made it. The mare was head and shoulders past one of the surprised knights when that individual slammed his shield backhanded into Talon's path as he rode past. The force of the blow knocked him over the animal's rump, and he tumbled to the ground in an unconscious heap.

He woke up to the slap of a heavy leather glove on his face. His head ached and he could not breathe through his nose. There was a lot of blood on his tunic. The man slapping him stopped, and as he focused groggily on the face suspended above him, he heard Sir Velliers say, "Well, you didn't break his neck, although he's lucky you didn't, Mark you, Talon, if that's your name. That was stupid and now we will have to tie you up even tighter. If you try to escape again you will finish the journey over someone's pommel. Do you understand?"

Talon glared at him but said nothing. They hauled him to his feet and placed him with rough hands back on the captured mare. Once again the troop proceeded on its way with a wary eye on Banyas Castle as they passed it by.

The rest of the journey to Montfort was a painful blur for

Talon. His broken nose hurt, he had a huge lump on his forehead, and one eye was closed. He was physically sick from the headache that threatened to make his head explode. The utter helplessness at not being able to do anything for Rav'an threatened to overwhelm him. Her face kept coming into his mind to torture him with his failure.

The troop rode up the broad gates of the castle just as the sun began to set, a red orb in the western horizon. When the men entered the yard, he saw that the place seemed to be much the same as he remembered it, and at the moment was a hive of activity; this was a well-manned outpost.

As soon as the knights had dismounted, two of them were designated by Sir Velliers to take Talon and march him up the stone stairs of the keep to a large wood door set in the wall. Talon was weak with his pain and groggy from his massive headache, but he was alert enough to realize that he could not escape, so he went with them docilely enough. Sir Velliers pushed the door open after a perfunctory knock and entered, motioning Talon and his guards in after him to the room once occupied by Sir Hughes and Talon's mother.

Talon realized that it had changed in one important respect: Gone were the items of comfort that his mother had placed here and there: the curtains, the small tapestry on one wall, carpets, and other feminine comforts had vanished, to be replaced by a stark, monastic atmosphere.

Seated at a large wood table in a large, high-backed chair with papers all around and some on the stone floor was a large man with the standard beard and partially shaven pate. He was dressed, as were all the knights, in a chain-mail hauberk and leggings with heavy leather boots, spurred as though he were about to ride. He wore the uniform: a light, dirty-white overshirt with the red cross sewn onto the left shoulder.

Attending him was another man, dressed in different attire. Talon guessed from his memory that he was a clerk or some servant who knew numbers. Sir Velliers addressed the seated man. "Sir Guerin, I have a visitor for you."

The burly man who had glanced up at the opening of the door sat back in his chair and smiled. "Ah, Sir Velliers, Where have you been? I expected you some time ago."

"A small altercation with this young man. He claims to be Talon de Gilles, son of Sir Hughes."

Guerin's surprise was evident. "You may go, Antoine; we shall deal with these tiresome papers later, or even tomorrow."

The servant bowed and left, casting a curious glance Talon's way as he went.

Sir Velliers walked up to Sir Guerin, motioning Talon and his guards over.

"Be seated," Guerin commanded Talon.

Talon sat on the edge of the wood bench indicated. His guards left the room at a nod from Sir Velliers.

"Now, Velliers, what's this all about?" Guerin asked. "Are you now rescuing the enemy? By my troth, he looks as sinister a Saracen as ever I've seen."

Sir Velliers laughed. "I have yet to have a good explanation as to why he was traveling in the opposite direction to this castle that he professes to call home." He glanced again at Talon.

Sir Guerin seemed to sudenly register what had been said earlier.

"Wait a moment. What did you say? The son of Sir Hughes?" He stared at Sir Velliers. "He looks like a Saracen bandit, how can he be?" He glared at Talon. "Young man, you had better be telling the truth. I know Sir Hughes. He has no son that I know of."

"Do you not remember the disappearance of the boy during an ambush about five years ago?" Velliers asked.

"I do, indeed. It was a sorry matter for everyone. Weren't you involved in trying to discover what had happened?"

"I was not. Sir Guy was involved, but five years is a long time, and who knows? This might be a ploy of some kind. Why don't we send for Sir Guy and for Phillip?"

"Good idea," agreed Sir Guerin. "Except that both men are right now down south in or around Ascalon, and I don't know when they will return." Guerin turned to Talon. "Then you must stay here until they return to provide proof that indeed you are the son of Sir Hughes."

Despite his massive headache and his painful face, Talon made another desperate attempt to make them understand. "Sirs, I beg of you, please let me go. I am truly the son of Sir Hughes, but I was going north to rescue some friends who are captives of the Assassins. I beg you to allow me my freedom to do this. Then I swear I shall return with them here."

Guerin hesitated, but Velliers was having none of this. "You tried to escape before and we had to stop you, you young villain. I think he will just run off and get up to some mischief as soon as he's free. We should keep him under lock and key until Sir Guy or Phillip comes and identifies him. Which I doubt they will," he added skeptically. It was becoming clear that he didn't like Talon and was not prepared to believe him in anything.

Guerin nodded. "You will stay here until we have proof that you are who you say you are. Lock him up, Sir Velliers."

Talon heard the words with disbelief. It triggered frustration and rage with these two men, who were going to ensure that Rav'an died. He shouted, "You stupid people, I am Talon the son of Sir Hughes, you must let me go free. They will kill her, they will kill her!"

He leapt to his feet and made for the door, his still-bound hands in front of him. In two quick strides, Velliers was on him and buffeted him a mighty blow on the side of his head. Talon went down and Velliers kicked him. He curled into a ball, trying to protect himself from the worst of the kicks.

A loud command from Sir Guerin stopped Velliers. "Enough, sir. What are you doing? Leave him alone and get the guards to take him to a cell where he can cool off."

Two knights who came at Sir Guerin's call hauled Talon to his feet and dragged him unceremoniously down the stairs, then he was thrown into a small cell. The door slammed shut and he was in darkness.

His ribs ached and his nose had begun to bleed again. The pain was fierce, but he barely felt it as he contemplated his situation. It was bleak indeed, but he knew it paled compared to what he imagined would happen to Rav'an. He got to his feet and staggered over to the pallet and fell on it, rolling onto his back. He tried to staunch the bleeding with his sleeve while he lay there.

In his anguish he felt hot tears running down his cheeks. It took an enormous effort of will to stop himself from wailing with the awful pain that welled up in his chest at the thought of what he had lost.

* * * * *

Almost three weeks later a tired and dusty Sir Guy de Veres, accompanied by his assistant knight, Sir Phillip de Gilles, rode into the gates of Montfort. Sir Guy was in possession of a brief letter from Sir Guerin. It stated that they had a Saracen prisoner who kept saying he was the son of Sir Hughes. Could he come with Phillip and verify this?

Sir Guy had not needed more than that. He'd called Phillip over and told him about the letter. Phillip had hurriedly packed his meager belongings and they'd set off from Ascalon in the very south of the Kingdom of Jerusalem to go to Montfort north of lake Tiberius.

They were greeted by Sir Velliers, who told them that Sir Guerin had been away for the past two weeks at Acre. He would not be back for a few more days as far as he understood. After the horses were taken, the men were led up to the keep and given wine.

"Where is the boy?" Sir Guy asked.

"We have had to keep him in a cell, Sir Guy. He is like a wild animal. He has tried to escape at least three times, and in doing so, he has injured knights and men alike. He is extremely dangerous," Sir Velliers stated, looking uncomfortable. "He claims to be the son of Sir Hughes de Gilles, Phillip, but once you see him you will know at once that he is a common Saracen, perhaps even one of those Assassins who wants to ingratiate himself, then commit mischief."

"Where did you capture him?" Sir Guy asked.

"North of Banyas castle, from where he had just come. It was luck, as his horse had gone lame. He claimed to be going north to rescue some friends. He keeps shouting about how they will kill 'her' if he cannot save 'her'. If indeed he had escaped, as he claims he had, why go north when he should have known Montfort was south? He is a lying sand pig, that's all there is to it," he finished with an air of satisfaction.

Sir Guy sipped his wine, reflecting upon what he was hearing. He did not like Sir Villiers' manner but decided to ignore the man's attitude for the time being.

"Bring him here; we want to see him."

Sir Velliers hesitated, but Sir Guy was the senior man in the castle now, so it would do him no good to argue. He said, however, "This is a very dangerous man. I cannot take responsibility for what he will do once he is here."

"Bring him here," Sir Guy said sharply.

Two men dragged Talon into the room. He had chains on his wrists and ankles that had rubbed the skin raw. To Sir Guy he looked filthy, his torn clothes spattered with dried blood and other filth. He was barefoot, his hair long and lank. His face was swollen still from the last beating, and his nose looked as though it had been broken.

Talon was pulled to a stop; he stood defiant, glaring at his captors, his spirit unbroken, but it was clear that his captors had not been kind to him during his captivity.

Sir Guy walked up to him and stood a few feet away. "I am told that you claim to be Talon, the son of Sir Hughes de Gilles?" he said.

Talon glared at him from behind his filthy hair. He nodded. "Yes I am, and you are another of these stupid bastards who won't believe me," he snarled.

Sir Guy's lips twitched. "We are here to find out if that's true or not," he replied, his tone level. "Do you know this man?" He indicated Phillip just behind him.

Talon looked past him to where Sir Phillip de Gilles stood looking at him curiously without a trace of recognition.

Talon recognized him at once, still as bulky and strong as ever. Although five years of fighting and hard living had left their mark, it was without doubt his uncle. "Yes. Uncle Phillip, do you not remember me? It is I, Talon."

Phillip gave a start on hearing Talon's voice. He saw a young man in ragged, bloody Saracen clothes, torn pantaloons and a large, loose shirt. He was barefoot but still stood proud. The young man had a mustache and a light beard of fine, light-brown hair, all of which were filthy. There was a gash on his forehead and there was dried blood around his nostrils and a long scar along his jaw line. One eye was half closed and bruised, but Phillip also saw that the good eye was green. In front of him was a tall, lithe young man who looked more like a Saracen soldier than the Talon he remembered, and yet...?

He stared hard. "I do not recognize this man who stands in front of me," he said slowly, "but there is something about him..."

"Ask him some questions about his childhood here at Montfort; he does appear to know you, Phillip," said Sir Guy, now very interested in what was going on.

"Tell me the name of your mother, may God bless and preserve her," Phillip demanded.

"Marguerite."

"What did your father give you for the last Christmas you were here?"

"A sword. I took it on my journey when we were ambushed," Talon said quietly. "I can also tell you what you gave me, uncle. It was the mare that I rode on our last journey together when we were ambushed. She was killed when I was captured."

Phillip went pale under his tan. He rubbed his long beard and then his shaved pate. "Dear God, is it really you, Talon? It has been so long... we... we gave you up for lost many years ago. Although the truth be said, Sir Guy here did tell us that you would not be killed. Marguerite did not believe it, and it broke her heart. It is your eyes, my lad, they give you away. God be praised, you are Talon, our long lost boy. Come here."

He had tears in his eyes as he engulfed the young man in his massive arms and gave Talon a bear hug, nearly crushing him. Talon winced at the pressure on his bruises.

"Uncle, there is so much to tell. I have traveled very far, and I was going north to free my friends when the knights captured me. They will not believe me, no matter what I have told them." He glared at Sir Velliers when he said this, which was not lost on Sir Guy.

"Sir Velliers, I would assume the chains are of no further need. I want them off the boy at once!" Guy said.

Sir Phillip glared at Velliers as well. "I doubt that he merited this kind of treatment either, sir. You had better make it fast."

The armorer was summoned, then and there, and struck the chains off Talon as they watched. He nodded at Phillip and Sir Guy when they were finished but then turned to Sir Velliers.

"You refused to believe me, even when I swore before God that I was telling the truth. As a result, you may have condemned someone I love to death. For that I will not, and cannot forgive you. If you and I meet outside this castle alone, I shall kill you."

Sir Velliers grew red with rage at this.

Sir Guy stepped between them.

"I think enough damage has been done for the moment, gentlemen. Talon, we have to ask your forgiveness for being so slow to come to your help. Now, however, we are here, and I, for one, want to hear all about your adventures." He looked at

Velliers. "I think we have proved without doubt that he is who he said he is. From this day forth, he is under my protection. Do we understand one another?

"First we will provide him with good clothes and clean him up. Then we will talk about what comes next. We shall drink to the event, and then we must decide what to do with you," Sir Guy said to Talon, then went over to the table and poured wine for them all. He handed over a leather beaker to each of the men in the room and they all drank a toast. It took all the control Talon had to taste and then swallow the dreadful brew, what these now more friendly people called wine.

"What are you talking about regarding rescuing your friends?" This question came from Sir Guy.

"I traveled with them from Persia all the way here to Banyas Castle, where we saved the Agha Khan's life. For that I was granted my freedom, but that also meant I had to be thrown out of the castle. I was following the master's main party on its way to Aleppo to try to rescue my friends when Velliers stopped me."

Sir Guy looked at him. "What was this about the Khan's sister that you mentioned earlier?"

Talon hesitated. "We were together, sir, almost betrothed, and I would have brought her here to be my wife." He said this with such obvious anguish in his voice that the three knights stared at him.

Sir Guy looked hard at Talon. "It is obvious that you have been through a long ordeal. It's also clear that you need to clean up that face of yours and get some rest. We can talk after that and decide what to do with you once we know more." He turned to his companions. "Phillip, take your nephew to one of the other cells and help him get some attention for that gash, then find him some clothes so that he can look more at home here. Let him rest and we'll talk with him in the morning."

Phillip nodded. He put a huge arm around Talon's shoulders and led him off to find a place other than his prison cell, and some food.

Sir Guy rounded on Sir Velliers. "I am unimpressed with your hospitality to the young man, Sir Velliers. You seem to have made an unnecessary enemy from what I can see."

Velliers laughed; there was contempt in his voice. "He is but a youth. I can cut him in two if he is stupid enough to try his luck with me."

Sir Guy shrugged. "This young pup was about to kidnap the sister of the Assassins' king, all by himself. That makes him either mad or very skilled. I would not underrate him, if I were you." Sir Guy was a perceptive man.

"I think that it might indeed have been a tragedy you captured Talon when you did. I need to find out more about this interesting young man. Think of what he can tell us of the world he has lived in for those years. There are few, if any, among us who have seen what he has."

Talon suffered his uncle's kind and rough ministrations. Phillip told him, while cleaning his face, about his parents and how the news of Talon's capture had almost broken his mother's heart. They had not needed much persuasion to leave the castle of Montfort and return to France, where land and an estate was waiting for Sir Hughes. Most of his wife's family were dead from the plague. Phillip urged Talon to think about sailing for France and seeing them.

All the while he listened to his uncle, Talon searched for ways to reach Rav'an and at least let her know what had happened. He ached with the thought that he might not be able to tell her that he had been unable to stop the events that had taken place, to let her know that he would still try, although he knew deep in his heart that his chances of reaching them were minimal once they got to Aleppo. He'd be killed on the spot if he were discovered there. He had lost his horse and had few resources that would enable him to go to her.

He followed what his uncle was saying without paying much attention, then something Phillip said made him look up. "What was that, Uncle?" he asked.

"I said that we have intelligence provided by the Assassins here in Palestine."

Talon sat up. "Then we might know where the master is at any time?"

Phillip looked confused. "I suppose so. Sir Guy speaks their language and has a good knowledge of these people."

Talon got up. "I have to ask him to find out what has happened to Rav'an," he said, as he limped off. Phillip looked after him, then shrugged and got up to follow.

Sir Guy did indeed have ways of finding out things, but it all took time. During the wait, which Talon endured only because Sir Guy asked him to stay at the castle and not run off on a wild chase, he curbed his impatience and his ever-present anguish.

He concentrated on getting fit again, forcing himself to eat the food that he had become quite unused to. He longed for the fare that had become so familiar in Persia. He practiced his sword play in private, and went through all the exercises that he knew to keep himself supple and quick. The enforced inactivity of the prison had slowed him and he was determined to regain his former speed.

His bruises gradually went away and his nose healed—although it was now somewhat crooked—as did the cuts and chaffed limbs. He was able to wash away the filth and get into clean clothes. Sir Guy made sure that he was given back his weapons and the possessions that had been in the packs on the horses. He was even given the gold back that had been found among the packs.

He kept away from Sir Velliers, who did the same. It was clear to Talon that the knight did not like him, but he didn't care. He felt numb; the loss of Rav'an and his friend Reza left him feeling terribly alone. Not even the welcome that Phillip provided could reach him. That kind bear of a man finally left him to his own devices.

Not so Sir Guy, who had an enquiring and inquisitive mind. He demanded to know everything that had happened to Talon, from the day he had been kidnapped to the day he'd killed Arash. In a way, it was good for Talon to tell him, but it was still painful because the ache of the loss would not ease.

News eventually arrived of a sort that Sir Guy shared with him. The Agha Khan had gone to Persia, having been at Aleppo. That was all. That evening Talon spent longer than usual on the wall, staring eastward.

People learned to leave the strange young man alone, and if someone needed him, others would always point to the eastern battlements where he would be standing long, long hours, staring northeast. Talon said little to anyone those days. He felt wounded, and there was a sickness in him that he did not think could heal. Many were the nights when he would wake in the dark, feeling her presence, and call her name. The silence of the night would greet him and he would fall back onto the pallet, his face wet from the tears.

Anger burned deep inside him at his failure to rescue Rav'an, and this could have been why things came to a head with Velliers. Sir Guy had left to go to Acre for two days, leaving Phillip and Talon in the castle. Talon was already thinking of saddling Jabbar and disappearing, when Velliers, still smarting from Talon's threat, took advantage of Sir Guy's absence to provoke an argument with him.

Talon was in the main yard looking at his horses. He was thinking of how he could leave without being detected and catch up with Rav'an when Velliers walked in his direction.

"Hey, you, Sand Rat, do you still feel brave enough to try your luck with me?"

Talon stood up. He was feeling fit now and had regained his former speed. "Is it sticks or swords you want?"

People nearby had heard the exchange and were curious about what was going on. It was no secret that there was bad blood between the strange young man, Talon, and Sir Velliers. Everyone knew that Velliers had beaten Talon when he was defenseless and a prisoner. The boy had been wild, but not all thought that he merited the treatment meted out by Velliers.

"Are you afraid of steel?" the knight mocked him.

Talon's eyes glinted. "Then we can use sticks and knives. Are you brave enough to fight me with both?" His tone was equally mocking.

"So be it. Prepare yourself, Sand Pig."

Within minutes, they were both armed with a short, thick staff and a dagger. They circled each other. A crowd of onlookers gathered quickly, watching and murmuring. There was tension in the air as people sized up the young man in light cotton clothes against the heavier knight, who was now clad only in his shirt and kilt. Both were barefoot. The crowd felt the undercurrents as they watched the lithe young man close with the knight. There was something menacing about his every move that was eerie, but they also sensed he didn't seem to care about the outcome.

Talon drew a deep breath. He was relaxed, as though he were about to release something in himself. He really did not care at that moment whether he lived or died.

The two fighters closed and the sticks began to click and clash as they wielded them against one another. Velliers feinted and attacked, only to find no one there to strike, and often as not a quick parry followed by a sharp blow to his elbow, head, or leg each time. He began to realize that his opponent was better at this than he was, and much, much faster. He had been taunting the boy to get him to make a mistake, but the calm, almost detached figure in front of him refused to be drawn.

Before long it was clear to everyone that Velliers was feeling the strain. His breath came in gasps, and he was slow to react as blow after blow fell on his head, back, and knees. Talon was not even breathing heavily.

The anger, however, was still there, right under the surface, white hot. He wanted to beat the man to a pulp for what he had done to him, so he continued to hit Velliers every time the man left an opening. The crowd grew amused at the treatment he was dealing out and applauded him openly.

Talon wanted Velliers to get so angry he'd go for the knife that he still had in his waistband. Finally, Velliers did lose control. He was sweating heavily in the hot morning sun, and his shaven pate was red and bleeding from blows that Talon had dealt out. He closed with Talon, and as he did, he dropped his stick and drew his knife. Talon had been waiting for this, and lured Velliers in close. Velliers never knew how it happened, but he never struck his own blow. Instead, he felt a white-hot pain in his right side, just below his ribs. He tried to pull away, but Talon held him close, his eyes boring into those of his enemy.

Talon let Velliers drop to the ground in front of him. He stared with utter indifference at the dying man for a few moments, then turned and walked off.

There was a commotion in the crowd. Knights rushed forward to pick Velliers up and carry him away to his pallet, where they tried to stem the flow of blood. He died in his bed with a long, drawn out groan.

It was fortunate for Talon that Sir Guy came back that evening. He found the castle in an uproar. The people of the castle were enraged. The man Talon had killed was one of their own, and the provocation didn't matter. It was only because of Phillip's strong intervention that they hadn't hanged him. As it was, he was once again chained in a cell. There were those with Phillip who said that Velliers provoked the fight, but others, who disliked the silent young stranger, thought he should, at the very least, be locked up and then put on trial.

Exasperated, Sir Guy solved the problem by putting the

chained Talon on one of his horses and with Phillip and a small escort, took him straight to Acre. He had come to like the remote young man who had so much to impart. Now he would have to get him out of the country for a while. He found it hard to reach him, and this frustrated him, as he wanted to use his talents. Instead, they had to put him on a ship to get him out of the way until the dust had settled.

Talon begged him not to do this, asking that he be allowed to leave, that he would come back once he had rescued his friends, but Sir Guy was having none of it. He was not sure himself if he would see Talon again if he let him go off into the desert. Instead, he told Phillip to take him back to France and at least show him to his parents. Phillip agreed, although he was not sure if he could control this wild young man who called him uncle.

Thus it was that two days later, Talon stood on the quayside of the harbor of the great city of Acre. He had never been in a port city before, and almost against his will, he was fascinated by the noise, the pungent smells, and endless activity. The port nestled hard up against the looming, white shape of the city walls. The harbor, the city's lifeline, was well protected. The screaming of the gulls as they swooped and dipped over the dirty waters of the inner harbor, and the creaking of rigging and wood hulls all bestowed an atmosphere of calm, in spite of the activity around the many ships unloading and loading along the quay.

Talon was enjoying some isolation as he waited on the quayside for the ship to sail. He was still chained. Sir Guy had told Phillip to release him only when the ship was at sea. They were waiting for the ship to finish loading the goods and merchandise for the journey to the port of Famagusta on the island of Cyprus. The horses had already been lifted into the well of the boat without mishap, although to the watching young man it looked a risky business. Sir Guy assured him that the people on these ships knew all about transporting horses. How else did he think most of them got to Palestine?

Sir Guy had proved to be an entertaining man, albeit shrewd and knowledgeable. He had interrogated Talon for hours about his former life until the young man was groggy from all the questioning.

Then he had discussed his future. He, Sir Guy, felt that Talon could be of use to him some time in the future and had asked him if he'd be interested in working for the Templar Society. He need not be a knight, but he could help Sir Guy with his intelligence gathering. If he wanted to be a knight, he could enlist when he got to a Templar stronghold in France. One way or another, he should stay away for about a year, by which time the incident with Velliers would have all been forgotten.

Talon had agreed in principle to the idea, not being sure of what the future held for him. He was ready to agree to almost anything that would provide him with some kind of anchor while he rode out the uncharted seas of his future. Sir Guy had left it at that and given Phillip a parchment to hand off to the Templar commander he would meet in France. This, he told him, would allow the two of them to live frugally and be enough to provide transport for them on the next part of their journey.

He, Phillip, had decided that his future now lay with the Templar order as a partial penance, but he was not cut out to be a man in charge of others, he told Talon. The life suited him, with its simple demands and austere way of life. He said that as far as he knew, his parents were still alive in France and that the two of them would be going there together to see them.

Talon thought about that on the deck of the heaving ship as he stared at the receding coastline. Then his thoughts winged many hundreds of miles eastward to his friend Jean, for whom he had said a prayer and lit a candle in the gloomy chapel of his father's old castle. There he had gone on his knees and wept for the man who had helped him through his late boyhood and given him the strength to survive. His thoughts moved on to Isfahan where he had been happier than at any time before in his life. He had prayed for another man who had given him the ability to think for himself, a gift beyond measure, and for the wonderful woman who still lived there, who sung such a haunting lullaby.

He sent his mind to the soaring peaks of the Alborz to where he thought Rav'an might be, and prayed that she could feel a tiny waft of hope from him to keep faith and trust him. He said a prayer for Reza and hoped that his brother would understand somehow.

As the deep sea swell moved under the ship, the young man swore an oath that he would return.

The End

Acknowledgments

This book could not have been written without the dedicated help of my wife, Danielle, who thrilled to the research. To my friends I offer my heartfelt thanks for their enthusiastic encouragement: JC and Carleen. Don, Gail, and Michael, Will and Emma. And then Robin and Jackie and Terri Windling, who gave me the will to finish.

Finally, I would like to thank my editor, Dorrie O'Brien, for her patience and encouragement in helping me complete the story. Also Chris Paige for her determination to do the final work and ensure presentability.

RECOMMENDED READING

Rubaiyat of Omar Khayyam;
Persian Miniatures - LiberPress
Dungeon Fire and Sword: The Knights Templars - John Robinson
The Castles of the Assassins - Peter Willey
The Assassins - Bernard Lewis
The Legendary Cuisine of Persia - Margaret Shaida
The Valleys of the Assassins - Freya Stark
A Fool of God [Poems of Baba Tahir] - E. Heron Allen
A Short History of the Ismailis - Farhad Daftary

About the Author

—

James Boschert

James Boschert grew up in the then colony of Malaya in the early fifties. He learned first hand about terrorism while there as the Communist insurgency was in full swing. His school was burnt down and the family, while traveling, narrowly survived an ambush, saved by a Gurkha patrol, which drove off the insurgents.

He went on to join the British army serving in remote places like Borneo and Oman. Later he spent five years in Iran before the revolution, where he played polo with the Iranian Army and developed a passion for the remote Assassin castles found in the high mountains to the north.

Escaping Iran during the revolution, he went on to become an engineer and now lives in Arizona on a small ranch with his family and animals.

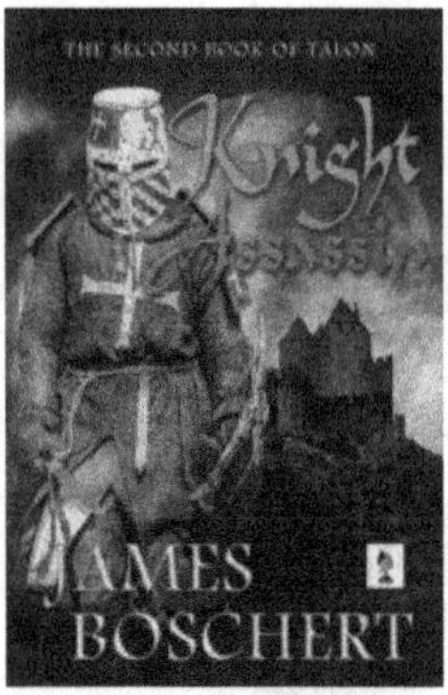

Knight Assassin

The....second book of Talon

by

James Boschert

A joyous homecoming turns into a nightmare as a Talon must do the one thing that he didn't want to - become an assassin again.

Talon, a young Frank, returns to France to be reunited with his family who lost him to the Assassins of Alamut when he was just a boy. But when he arrives, he finds a sinister threat hanging like a pall over the joyous reunion. A ruthless man is challenging his father's inheritance, aided by powerful churchmen who also stand to profit by his father's fall. When Talon's young brother is taken hostage, Talon has no recourse but to take the fight to his enemies.

All is not warfare, however; Talon's uncle Philip, a Templar knight, brings him to the court of Carcassonne, where Queen Eleanor has introduced ideals of romance and chivalry. And there Talon is pressed into the service of a lion-hearted prince of Britain named Richard.

Knight assassin is a story of treachery, greed, love and heroism set in the Middle Ages.

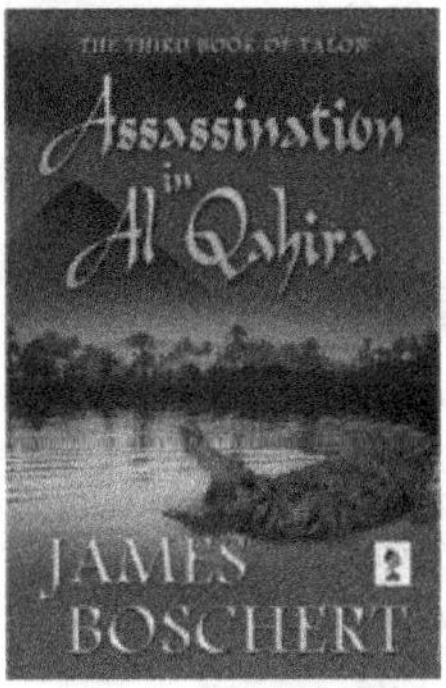

Assassination in Al Qahira

James Boschert

Talon, a young Knight of the Order of Templars is finally returning to the Holy Land to search for his lost friend, but Fate as other plans for him.

He and his companions find themselves shipwrecked on Egypt's shore. In that hostile land they face the constant threat of imprisonment, slavery and execution.

When Talon thwarts an attempted murder, he finds out that a good deed can lead to even greater danger. Soon Talon becomes a pawn in a political game within a society that is seething with old enmities, intrigues and treachery at the highest levels. To save the lives of two children and a beautiful widow he is now oath-sworn to protect he must call upon all of his skills as an assassin.

A page turner that you will not be able to put down. It grips you from the very beginning

Review:

I was completely unfamiliar with this period and found it fascinating once I got started. I have gone on to read all of the books in the series (that have been written) and find them exciting, interesting, very well crafted, informative and difficult to put down.

So thank you James Boschert for writing such an amazing book. I am extremely glad I found it and extremely glad you have such a passion for the period and such creative flare.

I highly recommend this book and the rest in the series.

From a reviewer on Amazon

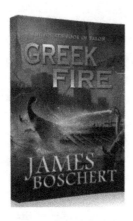

A Falcon Flies

by

James Boschert

Talon has returned to Acre, the Crusader port, a rich man after more than a year in Byzantium. But riches bring enemies, and Talon's past is about to catch up with him: accusations of witchcraft have followed him from Languedoc. Everything is changed, however, when Talon travels to a small fort with Sir Guy de Veres, his Templar mentor, and learns stunning news about Rav'an.

Before he can act, the kingdom of Baldwin IV is threatened by none other than the Sultan of Egypt, Salah Ed Din, who is bringing a vast army through Sinai to retake Jerusalem from the Christians. Talon must take part in the ferocious battle at Montgisard before he can set out to rejoin Rav'an and honor his promise made six years ago.

The 'Assassins of Rashid Ed Din, the 'Old Man of the Mountain', have targeted Talon for death for obstructed their plans once too often. He is forced to take a circuitous route through the loneliest reaches of the southern deserts on his way to Persia to avoid them, but even so he faces betrayal, imprisonment, and the threat of execution.

His sole objective is to find Rav'an, but she is not where he had expected her to be.

CPSIA information can be obtained
at www.ICGtesting.com
Printed in the USA
LVHW021201160720
660845LV00005B/186

9 781942 756125